T0359193

Bestselling Authors

COLLECTION *2024*

LYNNE
GRAHAM

MAUREEN
CHILD

BRENDA
HARLEN

KATE
HARDY

MILLS & BOON

BESTSELLING AUTHORS COLLECTION 2024 © 2024 by Harlequin Books S.A.

CINDERELLA'S DESERT BABY BOMBSHELL
© 2021 by Lynne Graham
Australian Copyright 2021
New Zealand Copyright 2021

First Published 2021
Second Australian Paperback Edition 2024
ISBN 978 1 038 91978 6

JET SET CONFESSIONS
© 2020 by Maureen Child
Australian Copyright 2020
New Zealand Copyright 2020

First Published 2020
Second Australian Paperback Edition 2024
ISBN 978 1 038 91978 6

THE RANCHER'S PROMISE
© 2021 by Brenda Harlen
Australian Copyright 2021
New Zealand Copyright 2021

First Published 2021
Second Australian Paperback Edition 2024
ISBN 978 1 038 91978 6

SECOND CHANCE WITH HER GUARDED GP
© 2021 by Pamela Brooks
Australian Copyright 2021
New Zealand Copyright 2021

First Published 2021
Second Australian Paperback Edition 2024
ISBN 978 1 038 91978 6

Except for use in any review, the reproduction or utilisation of this work in whole or in part in any form by any electronic, mechanical or other means, now known or hereafter invented, including xerography, photocopying and recording, or in any information storage or retrieval system, is forbidden without the permission of the publisher.

This book is sold subject to the condition that it shall not, by way of trade or otherwise, be lent, resold, hired out or otherwise circulated without the prior consent of the publisher in any form of binding or cover other than that in which it is published and without a similar condition including this condition being imposed on the subsequent purchaser.

All rights reserved including the right of reproduction in whole or in part in any form. This edition is published in arrangement with Harlequin Books S.A. Cover art used by arrangement with Harlequin Books S.A. All rights reserved.

This is a work of fiction. Names, characters, places, and incidents are either the product of the author's imagination or are used fictitiously, and any resemblance to actual persons, living or dead, business establishments, events, or locales is entirely coincidental.

Published by
Mills & Boon
An imprint of Harlequin Enterprises (Australia) Pty Limited
(ABN 47 001 180 918), a subsidiary of HarperCollins
Publishers Australia Pty Limited (ABN 36 009 913 517)
Level 19, 201 Elizabeth Street
SYDNEY NSW 2000
AUSTRALIA

MIX
Paper | Supporting responsible forestry
FSC
www.fsc.org   FSC® C001695

® and ™ (apart from those relating to FSC®) are trademarks of Harlequin Enterprises (Australia) Pty Limited or its corporate affiliates. Trademarks indicated with ® are registered in Australia, New Zealand and in other countries. Contact admin_legal@Harlequin.ca for details.

Printed and bound in Australia by McPherson's Printing Group

CONTENTS

Cinderella's Desert Baby Bombshell

Lynne Graham

MODERN

Power and passion

Books by Lynne Graham

Harlequin Modern

Indian Prince's Hidden Son
The Greek's Convenient Cinderella
The Ring the Spaniard Gave Her

Cinderella Brides for Billionaires

Cinderella's Royal Secret
The Italian in Need of an Heir

Innocent Christmas Brides

A Baby on the Greek's Doorstep
Christmas Babies for the Italian

Passion in Paradise

The Innocent's Forgotten Wedding

Visit the Author Profile page
at millsandboon.com.au for more titles.

Lynne Graham was born in Northern Ireland and has been a keen romance reader since her teens. She is very happily married to an understanding husband who has learned to cook since she started to write! Her five children keep her on her toes. She has a very large dog who knocks everything over, a very small terrier who barks a lot and two cats. When time allows, Lynne is a keen gardener.

CHAPTER ONE

THE HEIR TO the throne of the Middle Eastern kingdom of Alharia, Prince Saif Basara, frowned as his father's chief adviser, Dalil Khouri, knocked and entered his office with a charged air of importance and the solemn bearing of a man about to deliver vital information.

In recent years Saif had heard every possible story relating to his father's eccentric dictates and views. He was thirty years old, his difficult parent's successor, and the courtiers of his father's inner circle were now routinely playing a double game—nodding with false humility at his father's medieval dictums and then coming to Saif to complain and lament.

The Emir of Alharia was eighty-five years old and horrendously out of step with the modern world.

Of course, Saif's father, Feroz, had come to the throne in a very different age, a feudal ruler in an unstable era when a troubled country was overwhelmingly grateful to have a safe and steady monarch. Oil had then been discovered. Subsequently, the coffers of Alharia had overflowed and for decades everyone had been happy with that largesse. Unhappily for Feroz, the desire for democratic government had eventually blossomed in his people, as well as the wish to modify cultural rules with an easier and more contemporary way of life. He, however, remained rigidly opposed to change of any kind.

'You are to be married!' Dalil announced with so much throbbing drama that Saif very nearly laughed until he registered that the older man was deadly serious.

Married? Saif stiffened in surprise, well aware that only his father's misogyny had allowed him to remain single for longer than most sons in his position. After four failed marriages in succession, Feroz had become deeply distrustful of women. His final wife, Saif's mother, had inflicted the deepest wound of all. An Arabian princess of irreproachable lineage, she had, nonetheless, abandoned both infant son and elderly husband to run away with another man. That she had then married that man and become joint ruler of another small country and thereafter *thrived* in tabloid newspaper photographs enraptured with her beauty had definitely been salt rubbed in an open wound.

'Married to a very *bad* choice of a woman,' Dalil completed with regret, mopping his perspiring brow with an immaculate linen handkerchief. 'The Emir has turned his back on all the many respectable possibilities both in Alharia and amongst our neighbours' families and has picked a foreigner.'

'A foreigner,' Saif repeated in wonderment. 'How is that possible?'

'This woman is the granddaughter of your father's late English friend, Rodney Hamilton.'

As a young man, the Emir had undergone a few months of military training at Sandhurst in England, where he had formed an unbreakable friendship with a British army officer. For years, the two men had exchanged letters and at least once there had been a visit. Saif dimly recalled a whiny, weepy little girl with blond pigtails appearing in his nursery. His future bride? Was that even possible?

Dalil dug out the mobile phone he kept carefully hidden from the Emir, to whom mobile phones were an abomination.

He flicked through photos and handed it to Saif, saying, 'At least she is a beauty.'

Saif noted that his father's adviser took it for granted that he would accept an arranged marriage with a stranger, and he swallowed hard, shocked by the apparent belief that he was required to make that sacrifice. He stared down unimpressed at a laughing, slender blonde in an evening gown. She looked frivolous and wholly unsuited to the life that he led. 'What do you know about her?' he prompted.

'Tatiana Hamilton is a socialite, an extravagant party girl… not at all the kind of wife you would wish for, but in time…' Dalil hesitated to avoid referring to the reality that the Emir's failing health would not conserve the ruler for ever. 'Obviously, you would divorce her.'

'It is possible that I will refuse this proposition,' Saif confessed tautly.

'You *can't*…it could kill your father to go into one of his rages now!' Dalil protested in consternation. 'Forgive me for speaking so bluntly, but you do not want that on your conscience.'

Saif breathed in slow and deep as he faced the truth that he was trapped. He banked down his anger with the ease of long practice, for he had grown up in a world in which personal choice about anything was a rare gift. He had been raised to be a dutiful son and, now that his parent was weak and ailing, it was a huge challenge to break that conditioning. It didn't help that he also understood that it would be very painful for his traditional parent to be confronted by a defiant son. Arranged marriages might have been out of fashion for decades in Alharia but, at heart, the Emir was a caring father and Saif was not cruel. He was also very conscious that he was indebted to his father for the loving care he had practised in an effort to ensure that his son was less damaged by his mother's abandonment.

Consequently, he would wed a stranger, he acknowledged, bitterness darkening his stunning green eyes.

'Why would a spoilt English socialite want to marry me and

come out here?' he demanded of the older man in sudden incomprehension. 'For a title? Surely not?'

A look of distaste stamped Dalil's wrinkled face. 'For the money, Your Royal Highness. For the lavish dowry your father is prepared to pay her family,' he replied in a tone of repugnance. 'They will be greatly enriched by this marriage and that is why you will wish to divorce her as soon as possible.'

Saif was aghast at that statement. It gave him the worst possible impression of his future bride and filled him with revulsion. He knew that he would find it very hard to pretend any kind of acceptance of such an unprincipled woman...

'George has just asked me to marry him!' Ana carolled, practically dancing out of the bathroom where she had been talking on the phone to her ex-boyfriend. 'Isn't that typical of a man? It took me to come to Alharia and be on the very brink of marrying another man to get George to the point!'

'Well, it's a bit foolish, him asking you this late in the day,' Tati opined with innate practicality as she studied her beautiful and lively cousin with sympathetic blue eyes. 'I mean, we're here in the *royal* palace and you're committed now. The preparations for the wedding are starting in less than an hour.'

'Oh, I'm not going through with this stupid wedding now—not if George wants me to marry him instead!' Ana declared with sunny conviction. 'George has already booked me on a flight home. He's planning to pick me up at the airport and whisk me away for a beach wedding somewhere.'

'But your parents...the money.'

'Why should I have to marry some rich foreign royal because my father's in debt to his eyeballs?' Ana interrupted with unconcealed resentment.

Tati winced at that piece of plain speaking. 'Well, I didn't think you should have to either, but you did *agree* to do it and if you back out now, it'll plunge us all into a nightmare. Your father will go spare!'

'Yes, but that's where *you* are going to *help* me play for time and ensure that I can get back out of this wretched country!' her cousin told her without hesitation.

'Me? How can I help?' Tati argued in bewilderment, because she was the most powerless member of the Hamilton family, the proverbial poor relation often treated as little more than a servant by Ana's parents.

'Because *you* can go through these silly bridal preparations pretending to be me, so that nobody will know that the bride has scarpered until it's too late. I mean, in a place as backward as this, they might try to *stop* me leaving at the airport if they find out beforehand! I bet it's a serious crime to jilt the heir to the throne at the altar!' Ana exclaimed with a melodramatic roll of her big brown eyes. 'But, luckily, no member of the groom's family has even seen me yet and Mum's certainly not going to be getting involved with these Alharian wedding rituals, so the parents won't find out either until the very last minute, by which time I'll be safely airborne!'

Tati dragged in a ragged breath as her cousin completed that confident little speech. 'Are you sure this isn't an attack of cold feet?' she pressed.

'You know I'm in love with George and I have been...*for ever*!' her cousin stressed with strong feeling. 'Didn't you hear me, Tati? George has finally proposed and I'm going home to him!'

Tati resisted the urge to remind her cousin how many other men she had been wildly in love with in recent years. Ana's affections were unreliable and only a month earlier she had claimed to be excitedly looking forward to her wedding in Al-haria. Back then, Ana had been as delighted as her parents at the prospect of no longer being short of cash, but of course, that angle would no longer matter to her, Tati conceded ruefully, because George Davis-Appleton was a wealthy man.

'I can understand that you want to do that.' Tati sighed. 'But

I don't think I want to get involved in the fallout. Your parents will be furious with me.'

'Oh, don't be such a wet blanket, Tati! You're *still* family,' Ana declared, impervious as always to her cousin's low standing in that sacrosanct circle. 'Mum and Dad will get over their disappointment and they'll just have to ask the bank for a loan instead.'

'Your father said that he'd been refused a loan,' Tati reminded her gently.

'Oh, if only Granny Milly was still alive...she would have helped!' Ana lamented. 'But it's not my problem...it's Dad's.'

Tati said nothing, only reflecting that their late and much-missed Russian grandmother had had little time for her son Rupert's extravagant lifestyle. Milly Tatiana Hamilton, after whom both girls had been named, had controlled the only real money in her family for many years. Tati had been surprised at her uncle getting into debt again because she had assumed that he had inherited a sizeable amount after his mother's death.

'Sadly, she's gone.' Tati sighed heavily.

She did not, of course, point out that she had a vested interest in her aunt and uncle remaining financially afloat because she felt that that would be utterly unfair to Ana. She could hardly expect her cousin to go through with a marriage that would be abhorrent to her simply for Tati's benefit. In any case, Ana appeared to have no idea that her father paid for his sister Mariana's care in her nursing home. Tati's mother, Mariana, had lived there since her daughter was a teenager, having contracted early onset dementia.

'So, will you do it?' the beautiful blonde demanded expectantly.

Tati flinched because she knew that she shouldn't risk angering her aunt and uncle lest they withdraw their financial support from her mother, but at the same time, she was as close to Ana as a sister. Ana was only two years older than Tati's almost twenty-two years. The pair of them had grown up on the same country estate and had attended the same schools. Regardless of how different in personality the two women were, Tati loved her cousin. Selfish and spoilt Ana might occasionally be, but Tati was accustomed to looking after Ana as though she were a young and vulnerable sister because Ana was not the sharpest tool in the box.

The whole 'marrying a foreign prince sight unseen to gain a fat dowry' scenario had never struck sensible Tati as anything but ludicrous. Naturally, her cousin should have had the sense to refuse to marry Prince Saif from the start because Ana was not the self-sacrificing type. But at first, Ana had seen herself as a heroine coming to the aid of her family. Furthermore, the tantalising prospect of increased wealth and status had soothed an ego crushed by George's refusal to commit to a future with her. Sadly, now that reality had set in, Ana was ready to run for the hills.

For a split second, Tati felt rather sorry for the bridegroom, whoever he might be, for he had no presence whatsoever on social media. Alharia seemed to be decades behind in the technology stakes—decades behind in most things, if she was honest, Tati had reflected after their drive through the desert wastes to the remote palace, which was an ancient fortress with mainly Victorian furnishings.

'All that money and no idea how to spend it or what to spend it on,' her aunt Elizabeth had bemoaned in envious anguish, soon after their arrival. And it was true: the Basara royal family might be oil billionaires, but there was little visible sign of that tremendous wealth.

Ana had met someone who had sworn blind that Prince Saif was 'absolutely gorgeous' but, as even Ana had said, how much faith could she place in that when people tended to be more generous when it came to describing rich, titled young men? Even if the poor chap were as ugly as sin, most would find something positive to say about him.

Tati knew all about that approach and the accompanying unkind comparisons, having grown up labelled a plain Jane beside her much prettier and thinner cousin. Of course, Tati was the family 'mistake' being illegitimate, something which might not matter to others, but which had seriously mattered to the uptight Hamilton family and had embarrassed them.

Both girls were blonde, but Tati had blue eyes and Ana had brown and Ana was a tall, slim beauty while Tati rejoiced rather more simply in good skin, a mane of healthy hair and curves. Well, she had never exactly *rejoiced* in her body, she conceded ruefully, particularly not after her only serious boyfriend had taken one look at her cousin and had fallen in love with her to the extent that he had made an embarrassing nuisance of himself, even though Ana had not had the smallest interest in him.

'Have you even thought of how you're going to get back to the airport?' Tati asked her cousin when she returned to the bedroom they were sharing.

'Already sorted,' Ana said smugly. 'You don't need the lingo to get by here. I flashed the cash, pointed to a car and it's downstairs waiting for me already.'

'Oh...' Tati whispered in shock as she watched her cousin scooping up her belongings and cramming them back into the suitcase she had refused to allow the maid to unpack. 'You're definitely doing this, then?'

'Of course, I am.'

'Don't you think it would be better to face the music and tell your parents that you're leaving?' Tati pressed hopefully.

'Are you joking?' Ana exclaimed. 'Have you any idea of the fuss they would make and how bad they would make me feel?'

Tati nodded in silence because, of course, she knew.

'Well, I'm not putting myself through that for anybody!' Ana asserted. 'Now, you be careful. Don't let them realise that you're not the bride for a few hours...that's all I'm asking you to do, no big deal, Tati! Come on, give me a hug and wish me well with George!'

Tati rose stiffly and hugged her, because she knew how headstrong Ana was and that nothing short of a nuclear bomb would alter her plans once she had made her mind up. 'Be happy, Ana,' she urged with damp eyes and a sense of dread she couldn't shake.

Tati hated it when people got angry and started shouting and she knew that the moment her aunt and uncle realised that their daughter had departed there would be a huge scene and furious raised voices. They would blame *her* for not telling them in advance. At the same time, though, she understood her cousin's fears. Ana's parents were so set on the marriage taking place that they were quite capable of following her to the airport and trying to force her to return to the palace. How could she subject Ana to that situation when she no longer wanted to marry the wretched man? After all, nobody should be forced to marry anyone they didn't want to marry.

Ana departed with the utmost casualness, a gormless servant even carting her luggage for her without a clue that he was assisting the Prince's bride to stage a vanishing act. Tati sat on the edge of a seat in the corner of the bedroom, panicking at the very thought of allowing people to credit that she was her cousin and the bride-to-be. She supposed that that meant she was a coward and she felt ashamed of herself for being so weak. Deception of any kind was usually a complete no-no for Tati, whose birth father had gone to prison for financial fraud. Her mother, Mariana, ashamed of the character of the man who had fathered her daughter, had raised her to be honest and decent in all situations. And what was she doing now?

While Tati was struggling with her loyalty to her cousin, her anxiety about her mother's continuing care and her troubled conscience, someone knocked on the door and entered, a brightly smiling young woman, who greeted her warmly in English. 'Tatiana? I am the Prince's cousin, Daliya. I am a student in England, and I have been asked to act as your interpreter.'

'Everyone calls me Tati,' Tati told her apprehensively, thinking how silly it was that she didn't even have to lie about her name because she and her cousin were both officially Tatiana Hamilton, thanks to her rebellious mother's obstinacy. Tati's mother and uncle had never got along as siblings. When Mariana's brother, Rupert, had named his child after his mother, his sister had seen no reason why he should claim that privilege and she should not. Of course, back then, her mother could never have foreseen that she would end up living back at her birthplace and that there would be two little girls rejoicing in the same name.

'I am sure you are wondering about the importance my people put on the bridal preparations,' Daliya assumed. 'Let me explain. This is not typical of weddings in Alharia because it is no longer fashionable. But you are different because this is a *royal* wedding. All the women who will attend you here today consider this a great honour. Most of them are from the older generation and this is how they demonstrate their respect, loyalty and love for the Basara family and the throne.'

'I shall feel privileged,' Tati squeezed out between clenched teeth, the guilt of being an impostor on such a solemn occasion cutting her deep. The pretty brunette's explanation had made her want to die of shame where she sat. The very least she could do was be polite and respectful...until the dreadful moment when people realised that she was *not* the right Tatiana Hamilton. Inwardly she was already recoiling in horror from the thought of that dramatic unveiling.

'All the same, I'm sure the unfamiliar will feel strange, and it may possibly intrude on your privacy to accept these diverse customs,' Daliya suggested, her intelligent brown eyes locked to Tati's face. 'You are very pale. Are you feeling all right? Is it the heat?'

'Oh, it's just nerves!' Tati exclaimed shakily as the other woman showed her out of the room and down a corridor. 'I'm very robust in the health stakes.'

Daliya laughed. 'The elderly women obsessed with your fertility will be delighted to hear that.'

'My f-fertility?' Tati stammered helplessly in her incomprehension.

'Of course. Some day you will be a queen and the natural hope is that you will provide the next generation to the throne.' Daliya frowned in surprise as Tati stumbled in receipt of that explanation.

For a split second, Tati had almost divulged the truth that she was not the right Tatiana, because it seemed so wrong to deceive people at such an important event. But they were already entering a very large room crammed with older women, some of whom wore the traditional dress but most of whom sported western fashion like her young companion.

Aware of being the centre of attention and ill accustomed to that sensation, Tati flushed just the way she used to do at school when the bullies had christened her 'Tatty Tato,' mocking her for her shabby second-hand uniforms and worn shoes. Her uncle's generosity in paying her school fees had not extended to such extras, and why should it have? she reflected, scolding herself for that moment of ingratitude. Tati had adored her loving mother growing up, but sometimes she had been embarrassed by her parent as well. Mariana Hamilton had never stood on her own feet and had never done anything other than casual work when it suited her. Relying on other people to pay her bills had come naturally to Tati's mother and that had made Tati both proud and independent. Or as proud and independent as one could be when forced to live in her uncle and aunt's country house and be at the family's beck and call while working for barely minimum wage.

All those thoughts teemed in Tati's busy brain while she calculated how many hours she would need to play the bridal role to allow Ana to make her getaway, and that introspection got her through the hideous public bathing rite she endured. Herbs and oils were stirred through a steaming bath and then she was wrapped in a modesty sheet, just as if she were entering a medieval convent, and settled into the water to have her hair washed.

Keeping up an air of good cheer was hard. Daliya lightened the experience with explanations of the superstitions that had formed such rituals and cracking the occasional discreet joke.

'You are a very good sport,' Daliya whispered in quiet approbation. 'It is a good quality for a member of the royal family. I think all the women were afraid that you would refuse their attentions.'

Tati contrived to smile despite her discomfiture because she knew for a fact that nobody would have got to roll Ana in a sheet and steep her in a hot herbal bath that smelled like stewed weeds. Ana would have flatly refused any such ritual, too attached to her own regimented beauty routine and too afraid that her hair would be ruined. Unfamiliar with such routines, Tati had told herself that she was having a treat, a rather exotic treat admittedly but pretty much a treat for a young woman who generally washed, cut and styled her own hair. What little she earned only kept her in clothes and small gifts for her mother when she was able to visit her.

'You are very brave,' Daliya told her as her hair was being combed out.

'Why do you say that?'

'You are marrying a man you have never seen, never spoken to…or have you and the Prince met up in secret?' she prompted with unconcealed curiosity.

'No, we haven't. Isn't that the custom here? The sight-unseen thing?' Tati queried.

Daliya laughed out loud. 'Not in Alharia now for generations. We meet, we date. It is all very discreet, of course. Only the Emir follows old cultural traditions, but with the Prince you need have no fear of disappointment. Had His Royal Highness desired to marry any sooner, he would have been snatched up by any number of women.'

'Yes, I believe he's quite a catch,' Tati remarked politely.

'Saif is of a thoughtful, serious nature,' Daliya murmured quietly. 'He is very much admired in our country.'

Tati had to bite her tongue on the flood of curious questions that she wanted to fire at the brunette. It was none of her business. Even the Hamiltons knew next to nothing about the Crown Prince, for none of them had cared about the details. That the marriage should take place and the dowry be given had pretty much encompassed the extent of her relatives' interest and that awareness shamed Tati, because everything that her present companions took so seriously had been treated with scornful indifference by Ana and her parents.

At that point, Daliya contrived to persuade their chattering companions that the waxing technician could take Tati into the giant bathroom with its waiting treatment couch alone. Tati had never been so grateful for that small piece of mercy in the proceedings. Discovering that she was only an hour and a bit into the lengthy bridal preparations, she heaved a heavy sigh, knowing that her cousin needed longer to make good her escape from Alharia. She felt worse than ever about her deception.

After the waxing, the preparations moved on to a massage with scented oils. Her nails were painted and then henna patterns were drawn on her hands. Mentally exhausted, Tati drifted off into sleep and when she was wakened gently by Daliya, she sat up and was immediately served with a cold drink and a tasty little snack while all the women hummed some song around her. Her watch had disappeared, and she had no idea what time it was. Daliya was now telling her that she had to leave for a little while but would be back with her soon.

That announcement plunged Tati into an even deeper dilemma. She had originally planned to share her true status and the reality that the bride had fled with the chatty brunette, but she was painfully aware that Daliya had been very kind to her. As the only English speaker she might well receive considerable blame for not having registered the fact that the bride was not who she was supposed to be. After all, everybody was likely to get very worked up once the truth emerged. Tempers would be fraught, angry accusations would be made. Uneasily, Tati decided to wait for a less personal, more *official* messenger before confessing that she was a complete fraud in the bride stakes.

A long silk chemise garment was displayed for her benefit and it was evidently time for her to get dressed. She would be making her big reveal very soon, Tati acknowledged, sick at the prospect, her tummy hollowing out. But she had to be clothed to do anything, she reflected wretchedly, and she stood in silence while she was engulfed like an Egyptian mummy in layers of tunics and petticoats and her hair was combed out and a cosmetic technician every bit as slick as the type Ana used at home arrived to do her work. By the time Daliya reappeared beaming, Tati was ready to nibble her nails down to the quick, only she couldn't because they too had been embellished and she didn't want to offend anyone. And even that thought struck her as ridiculous, considering how offended everyone would be when the awful truth came out.

'It's time,' Daliya informed her cheerfully.

Tati feared she might throw up, so knotted were her insides by that stage, and the brunette's reappearance didn't help because she honestly didn't want to involve Daliya in her disaster. And it would *be* a disaster, she thought wretchedly. However, her aunt and uncle were the proper people to be told first that their daughter had fled. As they were to be witnesses to what Ana had described with a sniff of disappointment as a very *private* ceremony, she was sure to see Ana's parents very soon in the flesh.

A posse of chattering women walked her through the palace, down stone staircases, across inner courtyards, through endless halls and corridors until finally they reached a set of giant ornate double doors set with silver and glittering gems and guarded by two large men in traditional dress brandishing weapons.

'We must leave you here…but we will see you soon,' Daliya smilingly told her, exchanging a brief word with the guards that had them springing into action and throwing wide the double doors…

CHAPTER TWO

ONLY A SMALL number of people awaited the bride's arrival in
the ancient splendour of that giant painted and gilded room,
which was surrounded by elaborate carved archways and pil-
lars. A regal elderly man was stationed by the side of another,
taller figure shadowed by the archway below which he stood.
Another pair of older men hovered beside a table, and across
the room stood Rupert and Elizabeth Hamilton, Tati's uncle and
aunt, glaringly out of place in their fashionable Western attire.

Rupert Hamilton frowned the instant he saw Tati and he
strode forward. 'You're not supposed to be here for the ceremony. Where's Ana?'

Tati's mouth ran very dry. 'Gone,' she croaked.

'Gone?' the older man thundered. 'How can my daughter be
gone? Gone where?'

Saif watched with keen eyes from the sidelines and wondered what was happening. Seemingly the bride had arrived,
but her father was angry and that word, *gone*, was remarkably explanatory in such circumstances. Who on earth was
the woman who had arrived in her place dressed as his bride?
Saif almost laughed out loud with relief and amusement at the
confirmation that the Basara family's bad luck with wives was
continuing into his generation. Beside him, he could feel his

father bristling with impatience, and he translated that single word for his benefit. 'The bride is gone,' he murmured in their own language. 'This is a different woman.'

'Gone to catch a flight back home. She'll be airborne by now,' Tati explained in a rush. 'She didn't want to go through with this.'

'You bitch! You helped her to run away!' her aunt Elizabeth shrilled at her in a tempestuous bout of annoyance, stalking across the room and lifting her hand as though to slap Tati.

'No...there will be no violence in the Emir's presence,' another voice intervened—male, accented, dark and deep in pitch.

Tati looked up in shock at the very tall young man who, for all his height and build, had approached so quietly and quickly that she hadn't heard him. He had caught her aunt's hand before it could connect with Tati's face, and he dropped the older woman's wrist again with a chilling air of disdain at such behaviour. And Tati's first thought was foolishly that Ana would be raging if she ever saw a photo of the bridegroom she had abandoned, because there were few women who appreciated a handsome man more than her cousin.

The big, well-built man towering over them, sheathed in an embroidered traditional tunic and trousers in opulent shades of brown silk worn with boots, was absolutely gorgeous. He had unruly black hair, eyes that were a startlingly unexpected and piercing green and lashes long enough to trip over, set deep below slashing ebony brows. He had skin the colour of creamy coffee whipped with cinnamon and stretched taut over spectacular bone structure, with a straight nose, a strong jawline and a wide sensual mouth. He was so good-looking that Tati's tongue was glued to the roof of her mouth and she simply stared at him as if he had suddenly materialised in front of her like an alien dropped from a spaceship.

'Be quiet, Elizabeth!' Rupert Hamilton snapped to silence his wife's ranting accusations. 'How long has it been since Ana left the palace?'

'It was hours ago,' Tati confirmed reluctantly.

The elderly man at the front of the room erupted into an angry speech in his own language. Saif shot a highly amused glance down at the bride who was not a bride. A sense of regained freedom and strong relief was now powering through him. She was tiny and she had huge blue eyes and a mass of wheat-blond hair that almost reached her waist...if she had a waist. The women had put so much clothing on the fake bride that she closely resembled a small moving mound of cloth. It was possible that she was rather round in shape but equally possible that she was built like a twig...and it didn't matter either way to him now, did it?

'And who are you?' he prompted with what he felt was excusable curiosity.

'Ana's cousin, Tati.'

'Which is a diminutive of?'

'Tatiana.'

'The same as the bride who is...*gone*?' Black lashes swooped down low over his glittering gaze and his mouth quirked. 'Is there a shortage of names in your family?' he enquired with complete insouciance, apparently untouched by the angry outbursts emanating from everyone else in the room.

A determined hand closed over her elbow, pulling her away from the silk-clad Prince. 'I want a word with you,' her uncle told her angrily. 'Here you are clearly *desperate* to take your cousin's place! That's why you helped her, isn't it? The temptation was too much for you. The thought of the clothes, the jewels and the holidays you'd be able to enjoy...the rich lifestyle that you've always dreamt of having and now, with Ana out of the way, it can *all* be yours!'

'Keep your voice down,' Tati pleaded with the older man because the Prince was only a few feet away from them.

She was absolutely horrified by her uncle's accusation that she had deliberately schemed to step into her cousin's shoes, that unspoken but deeply wounding suggestion that she must always have been envious of Ana and her superior financial prospects. 'Of course, I'm not trying to take Ana's place. Right now, you're upset—'

Dalil Khouri was endeavouring to explain to the enraged Emir that although a bride had arrived, she was not the chosen bride, she was a substitute even if she was another grandchild of the Emir's late friend. 'Well, then, let the ceremony proceed!' the old man commanded impatiently.

Saif, repelled by the brutal condemnation he had heard the uncle aim at his niece, made an attempt to reason with his exasperated parent, but his father could not move beyond the perceived affront of his precious only son and heir being jilted by his bride. The Emir could not accept that outrage. He felt it too deeply, chiming in as it did to his own unhappy past experiences with the opposite sex. 'I will not have my son left without a bride when the entire country knows he is to be wedded today,' he told his adviser with barely leashed anger. 'That is an insult we cannot accept. The other girl will do.'

Saif's brows shot up and he encountered a pleading look from Dalil, which almost made him roll his eyes. *'The other girl will do?'* Why not go out onto the street in Tijar, their capital city, and grab the first single woman they saw? Was he expected to marry *any* available woman? The volatile temperament that Saif usually kept restrained was suddenly flaring with raw, angry disbelief. What kind of insanity was his father proposing now? If the bride had run off, goodbye and good riddance was Saif's response, as he was no keener on the marriage taking place than evidently she had been. But, tragically, his father was reacting with very real wrath to what he saw as a loss of face and an insult to the throne of Alharia.

Dalil aimed a powerless glance of regret in Saif's direction and crossed the room to speak to the Englishman. Saif twisted to attempt to reason with his father and then registered that the Emir was tottering and swaying where he stood. With a shout for assistance, he supported the frighteningly pale older man, and a guard came running with a chair.

'I am fine... I am good,' the Emir ground out between gritted teeth.

'Allow me to call Dr Abaza,' Saif urged.

'Unnecessary!' the Emir barked.

Dalil returned. 'It is your wish that the ceremony proceeds?' he prompted his ruler, while Saif thought in disgust of the mercenary young woman he was to be cursed with.

'Why else am I here?' the Emir demanded on a fresh burst of annoyance.

On the other side of the room Rupert Hamilton was cornering his niece. 'The Emir simply wants his son married off.'

'Why? What's wrong with him?' Tati questioned with a grimace.

'Well, you should be happy that all that needs to be altered on the paperwork is your birthdate,' her uncle told her, as though what he had suggested were a perfectly reasonable change. 'You will be marrying him in Ana's place.'

Tati stared up at the older man in disbelief. '*I'm* not willing to marry him!' she snapped half under her breath for emphasis.

Rupert Hamilton gave her an offensive smile. 'So you say,' he said, clearly unconvinced.

'I didn't seek this development,' Tati argued in a low, desperate undertone.

Her uncle shrugged. 'Then think of this as a long-overdue repayment for my family's generosity towards you and your idle, feckless mother,' he told her thinly. 'You owe us, Tati. You haven't put a bite of food in your mouth since you were born that hasn't come from this family. Now your mother's draining our resources like a leech...all these years in that overpriced nursing home—'

'She can't help that!' Tati exclaimed chokily, shaken at being confronted by his heartless resentment that her poor mother had not yet seen fit to die of the disease that had already robbed her of memory, physical health and enjoyment of life.

'If you want her to stay on there, you *will* marry the Prince,' her uncle told her callously. 'And if you don't marry him, she can go on welfare benefits and move to some council place where she'll be a damn sight less comfortable!'

'That's a horrible threat to make,' Tati whispered shakily. 'You can't still hate her that much. She's a frail shell of the woman she once was.'

'You made your choice. For whatever reasons, you *helped* Ana skip out on us…now *you* can pay the price!' her uncle slammed back at her bitterly.

For a split second, Tati lingered there, frozen to the spot as she stared into space. But she knew she didn't have a choice. The mother who had loved and appreciated her throughout her childhood deserved to be contented for what remained of her life. Dementia patients found any sort of change in their routines distressing and if Mariana Hamilton were moved to another home, she would very probably decline at an even faster rate. Tati neither liked nor respected her uncle, but she was willing to concede that perhaps he needed the dowry he was to receive from the marriage to help maintain her mother in her current home. He had called her mother a leech and apparently regarded his niece in the same light. That hurt, when she had spent the past six years industriously cleaning, cooking and fulfilling her relatives' every request to the best of her ability in repayment for her mother's care. Her work had begun while she was still at school and had eaten up every free hour, becoming a full-time job once she had completed sixth form.

'I'll do it,' she breathed stiffly. 'I don't have any other option.'

'Good.' Squaring his shoulders, her uncle walked over to the table and nodded at the older man. 'Well, let's get this over and done with.'

Barely able to credit that she was in such a position, Tati followed the older man across the room. The Prince approached the table but kept his distance, which suited her fine because she was already wondering what was amiss with him that his father could be so eager to marry him off that even a last-minute change of bride didn't dim his enthusiasm. Maybe he was a lecher and marriage was aimed at making him appear more respectable.

Good grief, he couldn't be expecting a *real* marriage, could he? Real as in sex and children? Ana had never actually discussed much relating to the marriage with Tati because in recent years Ana had spent most of her time in the family apartment in London. And when her cousin had come home to the country she'd often brought friends with her and Tati had not liked to intrude. Ana had once remarked that Tati couldn't clean and cook and then expect to socialise with her cousin's guests because that would be too awkward. Tati breathed in deep and slow to counter the pain of rejection that that recollection reawakened. Well, she guessed it would be quite a while before she had to cook and clean for her relatives again…if ever. And all of a sudden, her biggest apprehension assailed her, and she put out a hand and yanked at the Prince's sleeve to grab his attention.

'I have to be able to fly home regularly to visit my mother,' she told him apprehensively. 'Will that be allowed?'

I may be buying you, but I don't want to own you or be stuck with you round the clock, Saif almost replied before he thought better of being that frank.

'Of course,' he confirmed flatly, his attention on his seated father, who had regained his colour and his temper now that everyone was doing what *he* wanted them to do. Just as quickly Saif despised himself for even having that ungenerous thought.

Yet never had Saif more resented the reality that his father's state of health controlled him and deprived him of the options he should have had. His fierce love for his ailing parent warred against that resentment. Had he not had the fear of the Emir succumbing to a second heart attack after his first small attack some months earlier, Saif believed that he would have refused to marry a stranger. As it was, he dared not object. And what the hell was a sophisticated English socialite likely to find to do with herself in Alharia?

Why had his father selected such an unsuitable wife for him? Saif lifted his chin in wonderment at that question while the marriage celebrant droned on. He would organise tutors for his bride, Saif decided, ensure that she studied their language, culture and history. If she wanted to be his wife so badly, if she was *this* determined to be rich and titled, then she would have to learn to fit in and not expect others to accommodate her. If he were to be cursed with a wife he could neither like nor respect, he would not allow her to also be an embarrassment to him.

'Sign your name,' he urged as he scrawled his own name on the marriage contract and handed his bride the pen.

Her palm perspiring, Tati scrawled her signature in the indicated spot. 'Is that it? I mean, when will the ceremony take place?'

'It's done,' Saif told her grimly. 'Excuse me.'

That was it? That was them *married*? Without even touching or indeed speaking? Tati was shaken and taken aback by his immediate departure.

'Are you happy now that it is done?' the Prince asked his father.

'Very,' the Emir confirmed with a nod of approval. 'And I hope that soon you will be happy as well.'

'May I ask why you wanted this for me?'

His elderly father regarded him with a frown. 'So that you will not be alone, my son. I am unwell. When I am gone, who will you have? I could not stand to think of you being alone.'

Saif swallowed the sudden unexpected thickness clogging his throat, stunned by that simple explanation and the strong affection it conveyed, acknowledging that he had misjudged his father's intentions. 'But why...an Englishwoman?'

'I had no good fortune with the wives I married and yet they were all supposedly wonderful local matches. Like to like didn't work for me and I sought a different experience for you. It is my hope that your lively and sociable bride will make you relax. You are a very serious young man and I thought she might help you have some fun.'

'Fun,' Saif almost whispered, barely crediting that such a word could have fallen from his strait-laced father's lips.

'And provide you with company. Like you and unlike me she is westernised and sophisticated and you should have more in common.'

Saif was now ready to groan out loud. His father believed that he was westernised and sophisticated because he had spent five years abroad studying business and working while the Emir had only spent a matter of months out of Alharia and had never gone travelling again. Saif, however, had spent more time working to gain the necessary experience than in clubs or bars.

Tati went through the hours that followed in a daze. Men and women were segregated in the celebrations, but Daliya was very keen to assure her that that was the habit only in the Emir's household and that no such segregation was practised by the Prince or anyone else in Alharia. 'The Emir is as old as my great-grandfather,' Daliya told her in a polite excuse for what she clearly saw as an embarrassing practice.

In the all-women gathering where she was very much the centre of attention, Tati watched her aunt, Elizabeth Hamilton, partake of drinks and snacks and ignore her niece. Tati's rarely stirred temper began to spark at that point. She had learned the hard way to be hugely tolerant of other people's rude behaviour, but being studiously ignored by her aunt when her marrying Prince Saif had won her relatives a large amount of money left a bitter taste in her mouth.

She thought of all the humble pie she had eaten at Elizabeth's hands over the years and simmered in silence, too accustomed to restraint to surrender to the anger building inside her, the resentment that, *once again*, she was the fall guy even though she had not enjoyed even one day of the expensive life-style her aunt, uncle and cousin took for granted with their de-signer clothes and glamorous social lives. She and her mother had always scraped along, living cheap, never living well and never ever enjoying the choices and outings that the better off took for granted.

'It's time for you to leave,' Daliya whispered quietly. 'You have scarcely eaten, Your Highness.'

Your Highness, Tati thought in disbelief as she was escorted from the room and down all the endless corridors and up the staircases and across the halls to a totally different giant bed-room, where the maid who had unpacked her luggage in the room she was sharing with Ana already awaited her. Daliya and the maid together assisted her in removing the tunics and petticoats until at last she was down to the final layer, the sort of lingerie layer, she called it, and she finally felt as though she could breathe freely again.

'Where am I going now?' she enquired of Daliya.

'To Paris,' the brunette informed her with a beaming, envi-ous smile. 'On your honeymoon trip.'

Oh, joy, Tati reflected, the angry resentment stirring afresh as she rustled through her slender wardrobe to extract cloth-ing of her own in which to travel and tugged out a pair of leg-gings and a loose top, neither of which, she could see, satisfied Daliya, who, after asking permission with an anxious look, resorted to fumbling through Tati's case herself in search of something fancier.

'I don't have many clothes,' Tati muttered, mortified for the first time ever by that admission. Of course, she had a dress she had packed in case she got the chance to go to the wedding reception, she recalled wryly, but that slinky, glittery gown, which had originally belonged to Ana, wouldn't be remotely suitable for travelling.

'It is fine, Your Highness. It is more sensible to travel in com-fortable garments,' Daliya assured her kindly.

Just as Tati was about to change, a knock sounded briefly on the door and it opened without further ado, framing Prince Saif—all flashing green eyes and what Tati inwardly labelled 'temperament and volatile with it'—who stalked into the room. He instantly dominated his surroundings and her pair of companions muttered breathless apologies for their presence and immediately took themselves off.

My husband, Tati conceded in shock. *The stranger I have married...*

'Now here we are at last with no more barriers between us,' Prince Saif pointed out curtly.

All his bride wore was a silk shift. She *had* a waist, a tiny one, and curves, distinctly sexy curves, Saif noted unwillingly, for he was determined to see no saving grace in the wife who had been forced on him, although he could not help admiring that long wheaten-blond hair that rippled down her spine like a sheet of rumpled satin. Nor could a thin silk slip hide the firm thrust of pouting breasts and prominent nipples or the luscious shape of her highly feminine bottom. Involuntarily Saif hardened and he clenched his teeth against the throb of arousal, a natural response for a man whose sex life was, by virtue of necessity, non-existent in Alharia. Only when Saif travelled could he indulge his sensual appetites and that amount of restraint did not come naturally to a young, healthy man, he allowed wryly.

Any reasonably attractive woman would turn him on at present, he assured himself, but, at the same time, Tatiana *was* his wife and that made quite a difference, he registered, wondering why that aspect had not occurred to him from the first. Yes, he could definitely do with a wife in that department. And what was more, the substitute was infinitely more to his taste than the original bride put forward. Unlike her cousin, Tati wasn't artificially enhanced to pout like a pufferfish on social media. Her lips had a naturally full pink pucker. She had a handful of freckles scattered across the bridge of her undeniably snub nose, but her face was still remarkably pretty, shaped like a heart with big blue eyes the colour of pansies.

Tati gazed back at him, heart starting to hammer inside her chest, breathing suddenly a challenge. 'Why are you staring at me?' she asked tightly.

'Why do you think? How many gold diggers do you think I meet and marry in the space of the same day?' Saif enquired with a lethal chill in his dark drawl, his shrewd green eyes glittering with sheer antipathy. 'And I am disgusted to find myself married to a woman willing to sell herself for money!'

Utterly unprepared for that attack coming out of nowhere at her, Tati whirled away from him, stabbed to the heart by his scorn. Of course, she hadn't thought beyond meeting her uncle's demands to ensure her mother's needs were met. Ridiculous as it was, she had rushed in where angels feared in too much of a hurry to consider what she was actually doing in marrying Prince Saif of Alharia for the wealth that would protect Mariana Hamilton's continuing care. But even as her shoulders drooped, they as quickly shot up again, roused by the fiercest anger she had ever felt.

'How dare you try to stand in judgement over me?' Tati launched back at him angrily. 'I did not sell myself for money and I am *not* a gold digger.'

Grudgingly amused by the way she straightened herself and stretched, as if she could magically gain a few inches of more imposing height just by trying, Saif regarded her coldly. 'From where I'm standing—'

'Yes, standing with your mighty dose of sexist prejudice on show!' Tati condemned wrathfully. 'You don't know what you're talking about because you don't know anything about me.'

'As you know nothing about me. You married me for cold, hard cash…or was it the title?'

'Why the heck would I *want* to be a princess? I wasn't one of those little girls who dressed up as one as a kid! And for that matter, if you're so darned fastidious and critical, why did you agree to marry a total stranger?'

'That is my private business,' Saif parried with a regal reserve that was infuriatingly intimidating.

A furious flush lit Tati's cheeks at that refusal to explain his motivation. 'Well, then, my reasons are my private business too!' she snapped back at him. 'I don't have to explain myself to you and I'm not going to even try. I'm quite happy for you to think of me as a gold digger, but I'm not selling myself or my body for cash! Be assured that there will be two blue moons in the sky and pigs flying before I get into a bed with you!'

Saif was outraged. He had never been exposed to such insolence before and her attitude came as a shock. Somehow, he had expected her to be ashamed when he confronted her, *not* defiant. 'If the marriage is not consummated, it is not a marriage and will be annulled,' he pointed out for no good reason other than the pride that would not allow her to believe that when it came to sex she could have any form of control over him.

'Is that some kind of a threat?' Tati yelled at him, barely recognising herself in the grip of the anger roaring through her slight body. She had simply been pushed around too much for one day. She was fed up with being forced to do what she didn't want to do, first by Ana refusing to face her own parents and then being bullied and threatened by her uncle. Now it seemed that the Prince, her *husband*, was trying to do the same thing. And she wasn't having it! In fact, she was absolutely done with people ordering her around and never saying thank you, taking her loyalty and gratitude for granted, acting as though they were the better person while they blackmailed and intimidated her!

Saif stilled, a very tall dark man who towered over her like a building. 'It is not. I do not threaten women. I simply voiced facts.'

'Right… OK.' Tati hovered, fighting to compose herself again when she had the most extraordinary desire to cry and shout and yell like an hysterical woman at the end of her tether.

And that wasn't her, had never been her, she reminded herself. She had always been the calm, practical one compared to Ana, who flung a tantrum when she didn't get her own way and sulked for days. But for Tati, it had been a truly horrible long strain of a day and it was not done yet, and she did not feel that just then she had the necessary resources to cope with Saif's antagonism on top of everything else.

'I hate you,' she told him truthfully, because no guy that good-looking, who had *chosen* to marry her, had the right to tell her that she disgusted him. He was gorgeous to look at, but he had no manners, no decency and no sense of justice. If she were to blame for marrying him, he was equally to blame for marrying her. 'You're just one more person trying to blame *me* for *your* bad decisions!'

CHAPTER THREE

THE BRIDE AND the groom dined at opposite ends of the cabin.

A private jet, Tati acknowledged, covertly admiring the pale sleek leather and gleaming wood fitments in the cabin while telling herself firmly that she was not impressed. There were a lot of stewards on board as well. The level of contemporary luxury on the jet was not even remotely akin to the Victorian grandeur of the palace. A bundle of glossy fashion magazines was brought to her. She was waited on hand and foot and the meal that duly arrived was amazing. Only then did she appreciate that she was starving because she had barely eaten all day.

That terrible looming apprehension that had killed her appetite had drifted away, but the anger still lingered. Her face burned afresh at the recollection of being labelled a shameless gold digger. But wasn't that kind of woman what Prince Saif of Alharia deserved in a wife? After all, he had agreed to marry without demonstrating the smallest personal interest in his bride. He had not bothered to engineer a meeting or even a phone call with her cousin before the wedding! So, if he was displeased with the calibre of wife he had acquired, it was all his own fault! Still fizzing with resentment, Tati shot a glance down to the far end of the cabin where her husband was working on a laptop, once again showing off his indifference to the woman he had married. She wasn't one bit sorry that she had told him she hated him!

But my goodness, he was, as her mother would have said, 'easy on the eye.' Black hair tumbled across his brow, framing his hard, masculine profile. Those ridiculously long ebony lashes were a visible slash of darkness even at a distance and the curve of his shapely mouth was as obvious as the dark stubble beginning to shadow his jawline. Annoyingly, he kept on snatching at her attention. And she didn't know why he interfered with her concentration. Well, that was a lie, she acknowledged ruefully. A guy that gorgeous was kind of hard to ignore, especially if you had just married him, even though there was absolutely no way it would ever be a *real* marriage.

By the time the jet landed, Tati was smothering yawns. She was too incredibly weary to do more than disembark from the plane and climb into the limousine awaiting them without comment. The Prince was silent as well, probably busy brooding over the sheer indignity of being married off to a money-grubbing foreigner, she thought nastily. She had assumed they would be staying in a hotel, so it was a surprise when the limousine purred to a halt outside what appeared to be a rather large three-storey house in an affluent tree-lined street.

A little man in a smart jacket ushered them into a big opulent hall with a chandelier hanging overhead that was so spectacular she suspected it was antique Venetian glass. And she only knew that because her aunt Elizabeth had once had one made to look as though it were an antique and had regularly passed it off as such to impress her guests. Saif addressed the man in fluent French.

'Would you like a meal? A snack?' he then enquired politely of her.

'No, thanks. I just want to sleep for about a week.' Her face flamed as she belatedly realised that it was their wedding night and she stiffened, averting her attention from him in haste, although she didn't think he had any expectations whatsoever in that field. The look the Prince had given her when she had earlier told him she wasn't going to have sex with him should have frozen her to death where she stood. He had been outraged, but at least he hadn't argued. There was a bright side to everything, wasn't there?

'We will have to share a bed tonight,' Saif informed her in an undertone. 'We were expected to remain in Alharia until tomorrow. This place will not be fully staffed until then and only one bedroom has been prepared. Marcel is already apologising in advance for any deficiencies we may notice.'

The concept of having to share a bed with the Prince almost made Tati groan out loud. But she was too tired to fight with him. She didn't think he would make any kind of move on her. She was quite sure that she could have located linen and made up a bed for herself, but she was in a strange house, wary of treading on domestic toes and too drained to make a fuss. 'I'm too exhausted to care.'

It went without saying that she was not accustomed to such luxurious accommodation. Her aunt and uncle's home, Fosters Manor, was a pretty Edwardian country house but, as such houses went, it was not that large and it was definitely shabby. When her grandmother had still been alive, it had been beautifully kept, but maintenance standards had slipped once her uncle took over and dismissed most of the staff.

'It has been a long day,' Saif gritted, relieved she hadn't thrown a tantrum over the bed situation. He wasn't in the mood to deal with that.

Yet after the way he had confronted her with his opinion of her, it was little wonder that she had lost her temper with him, he conceded grudgingly. He had been insanely tactless when he had told her the truth of what he thought of her. It would have been more logical to swallow his ire because he was trapped in their marriage until such time as he was able to divorce her. On the other hand, he *could* take the annulment route, he reasoned thoughtfully. But that would upset his father, who would feel responsible for the whole mess because he had insisted that the wedding go ahead with the substitute bride.

He wondered if the little blonde beside him and the cousin who had taken flight had planned exactly this denouement. Clearly, her uncle had suspected her of that duplicity. Who would know her nature better than her own flesh and blood? Furthermore, anyone with the smallest knowledge of his father's character would have guessed that he would do virtually anything sooner than accept his son and heir being jilted. The Emir loathed scandal and he was very proud and touchy about any issue that might inflict a public loss of face on the throne. It seemed rather too neat that the original bride had vanished at the eleventh hour and her stand-in had appeared in her place, dressed as a traditional Alharian bride. He needed answers, Saif acknowledged, because now that she was his wife, he wanted to know precisely who and what he was dealing with. How calculating was she? How greedy? Could he make her less of a problem simply by throwing money at her? It was a distasteful idea but one he was willing to follow through on if it granted him peace.

Marcel cast open a door at the top of the stairs into a superb bedroom suite. Saif was reluctantly amused by the opulent appointments, thinking fondly that his half-brother, Angelino Diamandis, certainly knew how to live in luxury. Having worked hard to put any personal issues with his deserting mother behind him, he had gained sufficient distance from that betrayal to seek out his younger half-brother. A smile illuminated his lean dark features, softening his set jawline. If he was honest he occasionally envied his brother, Angel, for his freedom and independence, but he was not prepared to lose his father and step up to the throne to attain that same lack of constraint.

Barely able to credit how a single smile could light the Prince up to reveal ten times the charisma he had so far shown her, Tati got all flustered and heard herself ask, almost as if it were normal to speak to him civilly, 'Does this house belong to you?'

'No, it belongs to my—' Saif hesitated and swallowed what he had almost revealed, because he couldn't trust her with that information lest it reach the wrong ears. 'It belongs to a relative of mine. He offered it to me because he was unable to attend the wedding.' Well, at least *not* in his official capacity, Saif adjusted with a winning smile of satisfaction, for he had contrived to spend almost an hour with his brother that same afternoon. 'I prefer this to the anonymity of a hotel.'

'It's a fabulous place…from what little I've seen,' Tati adjusted awkwardly, moving past him to scoop up her toiletries bag and nightwear from the case that a maid had already begun to unpack, just as another had embarked on Saif's luggage. *Two* maids and yet supposedly the household was understaffed this evening?

As she bent down Saif stared, focused hungrily on her curvy bottom and the bounce of her full breasts as she straightened again, blond hair flaring like polished silk round her heart-shaped face, big blue eyes skittering off him at speed. She wouldn't meet his eyes. He didn't like that. It made him wonder what she was thinking, what she could be planning. The more he considered the manner in which she had immediately stepped into her cousin's shoes, the more suspicious he became of her every move. He winced at the current of lust still trying to pull him in a dangerous direction. Possibly an annulment would be the path to take if he could sell the idea to his father without shocking him too much. In the interim, he definitely needed to keep his hands off his bride.

Through an open door Tati could see a bathroom and she hastened into the sanctuary it offered. She didn't really need a bath but she ran one just the same, determined to make the most of her time alone. She took off the make-up, cleaned her teeth before finally lying back in hot, scented water and striving to relax. But how the heck could she relax with *him* out there? Ana would have charmed him out of the trees by now, she reflected ruefully. Men adored her cousin for her looks, her smiles and her flirtatious ways. Tati had never had that light, fluffy, girly vibe. She was sensible, practical, blunt. Life had made her that way, forcing her to be responsible. She loved her mother, but she had also learned very young that *she* had to look after her only parent, rather than the other way round.

Having a man in her life had been the least of her ambitions. Mariana had had a whole raft of unsuitable boyfriends, among them drunks, abusers and cheats. After Tati's first serious boyfriend, Dave, had ditched her to chase Ana instead, Tati had decided that men drummed up way too much drama in a woman's life. Once or twice, she had wished that she had got a little more experience out of the relationship and had tried out sex with Dave, because sometimes still being a virgin at her age made her feel out of step with the world she lived in. But the attraction had just never been strong enough for her to experiment with Dave and once he had succumbed to her cousin's allure, she had been relieved that she had held back.

An hour later, Tati emerged, flushed and soaked clean from the bathroom. Saif, casually clad in jeans and a black shirt, twisted round from his laptop to glance at her. His bride wore nothing suggestive, nothing even slightly sexy, so evidently seduction did not feature in her current plan. Saif strove to feel suitably relieved by that reassuring reality while wondering how the hell pink and white shorts with little bunnies on them and a plain white vest top could offer such dynamite appeal. It was all about shape, he reasoned abstractedly, a mathematical arrangement of feminine proportions in the exact combination that most appealed to the average male.

Evidently he was very much an average male, he decided, attention lingering on the smooth upper slopes of the soft firm breasts showing above the top, the shadow of the valley between, her tiny waist and the pleasing swell of the pert derriere that the clingy shorts enhanced. A pulse kicked up in his groin and he swung back to his work with a curse brimming on his lips.

'What are you working at?' she asked to break the taut silence, her face still flaming from his lengthy appraisal.

'I'm checking figures. I manage Alharia's investments,' Saif murmured tautly.

What had that long look of his been about, for goodness' sake? Tati supposed that she should have worn a dressing gown, but she hadn't packed one. Her inclusion in the trip to Alharia had been very much a last-minute thing, an added expense loudly objected to by Ana's parents. Ana, however, had said she could not go through with the wedding without Tati's support and that had got Tati on the flight, her case packed in a rush and not even full. She had left behind several items which she should have brought.

'Is the bathroom free now?' Saif enquired without turning round again.

Momentarily, Tati froze, mortified by her thoughtlessness: she was a bathroom hog. 'I'm sorry, I should've thought that you might want—'

'There must be a dozen such facilities in this property. Had I needed to do so, I could easily have found another.'

In silence, Tati nodded. 'Goodnight,' she said in a muffled tone and dived below the duvet.

Strange little creature, Saif decided, glancing at the bed, seeing her curled up in one small corner, only a tousled mop of blond hair showing above the duvet. If he hadn't known what he did know about her he might've thought that she was shy. He smothered a laugh at that ridiculous idea, shut down the accounts he had been working on and started to undress.

Tati peered out from under her hair and watched the jeans hit the polished floor in a heap. So, he was untidy as well as obnoxious, she thought without surprise, as he left them lying there and the shirt drifted down to join the jeans. He stretched in a fluid movement and for an instant she saw him standing there, naked but for a pair of boxers, every muscle flexing and pulling taut...and he had an awful lot of muscles enhanced by coffee-coloured skin that resembled oiled silk. Tati stared, remembering the ghastly charity calendar of half-naked men her mother had once put up on the wall. Mariana had accused her daughter of being a prude when Tati had said it embarrassed her.

But it *had* been an embarrassment to have that hanging in the kitchen, particularly after Ana had seen it and had told everybody at school. Tati had had to live through a barrage of sniggering 'dirty girl' abuse for weeks afterwards. Compared with Ana and her mother, she *was* a prude because, from what she had seen of their experiences, a more adventurous approach to men and sex more often led to hurt and disappointment than happiness.

Now watching Saif stretch and muscles ripple across his hard, corrugated abdomen and down the length of his smooth brown back, Tati reminded herself that it was just a body, truly a more blessed body than most men rejoiced in but simply a body, an arrangement of bones, flesh and muscle that every single living person had. Only that very grounded outlook did not explain why she was still staring and why she had a hot, tight, clenched sensation tugging at the junction of her thighs. She had stared because he was beautiful, and she hadn't realised that a man could be beautiful that way. *Really, Tati*, she mocked her excuse. All that Adam and Eve stuff in the Bible hadn't tipped her off about that essential attraction? Cheeks hot enough to fry eggs on, she rolled over and buried her face in the cool pillows, trying not to listen to the distant sound of water running in the shower.

Saif was unaccustomed to sharing a bed and his bride's every movement disturbed him, reminded him of her existence and pushed rudely past his wall of reserve. He couldn't ignore her, he couldn't forget the allure of those eyes with the velvety appeal of a flower, her pale slender thighs or her surprisingly full breasts. That failure to maintain his usual mental discipline only made him even angrier with her. As he lay awake, he came up with a plan as to how to keep her occupied and marvelled at its simplicity. He could send her out day after day...

Tati wakened in the early hours because she felt cold. As she flipped over, she discovered the reason: the duvet had been stolen. That fast, she remembered that she was sharing a bed and she dug two hands into the bedding and yanked her side of it back with violent determination. Saif sat up with a jerk and flashed on the light.

'I was cold,' Tati announced in a snappish tone of defence and she hunched under the section of duvet she had reclaimed, turning her back on him.

Saif thought with satisfaction of the bride-free day ahead of him and lay back down. Even hunched in the bedding, she contrived to look unbearably alluring. How could she make him want her so much? Were a few sexless weeks sufficient to make him desperate? He lay there thinking of the many sensual ways he could have raised his bride's temperature without recourse to warmer bedding. Just considering those pursuits, indeed leafing through them with the intensity of an innate sensualist, left Saif as hard as a rock and it was dawn when he finally gave up trying to rest and rose to start work again.

The maid bringing her breakfast wakened Tati. She sat up while the curtains were being opened and registered that she was alone in the bed and expected to eat there. Pushing her hair off her brow, she accepted the tray, setting it down again once the maid had gone and scrambling into the bathroom to freshen up before she ate.

While she was enjoying her cup of tea and a buttery, flaky, delicious croissant, the Prince strode in. Saif emanated pure sophistication and sleek good looks in his perfectly tailored dark business suit. Involuntarily, her mouth ran dry, her tummy fluttering, responses she struggled to suppress. Expensive fabric outlined and enhanced his wide shoulders, his narrow hips and long, strong legs. He was very well built...as she had cause to know after ogling him while he undressed the night before, she reminded herself irritably. He was also infuriatingly calm and in control while she still felt as though her life had lurched off track without warning and fallen into a very large, very deep pothole.

As she sat there, Tati was extremely tense, her fingers locked tight to her china cup. It had occurred to her for the first time that she had overlooked one very obvious point of dissension between them. Saif had expected to marry her glamorous, sexy cousin and had instead ended up with her dull, plain and unsexy substitute. Of course, he was disappointed; of course, he was angry. No man would choose Tati in place of Ana, she reflected painfully. 'I'll sort out another bedroom for me to use tonight,' she proffered stiffly, meaning it as an olive branch of sorts in the aftermath of the duvet tussle.

In the sunlight slanting through the windows, the brilliant green eyes locked to her were as jewelled and intense as polished emeralds. All of a sudden, a bizarre level of annoyance was gripping Saif. Evidently it was one thing for him to want to be rid of her, but another thing entirely when she appeared to return the compliment. 'That will not be necessary,' he began before he could question the far from sensible reaction steering him off course.

Tati tilted her chin. 'It's necessary,' she pointed out. 'I don't think either of us could have got much sleep last night.'

Saif discovered that he did not like being told what was necessary by *her*. It set his even white teeth on edge and brought out a self-destructive edge of pique he had not known until that instant that he possessed. 'We will *continue* to share the same room.'

'But why on earth would we?' Tati exclaimed with incredulity.

'You wanted this marriage... *Live with it!*' Saif spelt out without apology or, indeed, further explanation. Even had he tried to do so, he could not have explained the gut instinct that was driving him because he did not know what had roused it or even what it meant.

'You know…' Tati began, her chest heaving with a sudden dragged-in breath, furious that he appeared to be taking out his disappointment that Ana wasn't his bride on her…as though it were *her* fault. Did he think that? And shouldn't she know by now what he was thinking? The lack of communication between them was only adding to their problems. 'Sometimes, you make me want to hit you!'

'I noticed the streak of violence in your family when your aunt attempted to slap you. Make no attempt to assault me. There is no reason in the world why we should descend to such a degrading level,' the Prince asserted.

His mind was wandering again, questioning how she could utter such a threat while still looking so fresh and tempting. It was first thing in the morning as well and her hair was tousled and she had utilised not a scrap of cosmetic enhancement that he could see. Indeed, in harsh daylight her porcelain skin had an amazingly luminous quality that confounded his every expectation. She might be a substitute; she might be everything he despised in the wife he had not wanted in the first place, but one truth was inescapable: she was much more of a beauty than he had initially been prepared to acknowledge.

'You don't even have a sense of humour, do you?' Tati gasped, staring accusingly at him.

'I have made arrangements for your entertainment today,' Saif informed her smoothly, refusing to react in any way to the charge of a lack of humour. Certainly, he found nothing about their current situation worthy of amusement.

'How very kind of you,' Tati muttered tautly, wondering what was coming next.

'I have hired a team of personal shoppers to give you a tour of the best retail outlets in Paris,' the Prince completed.

Send the little woman out shopping, Tati thought furiously. He simply wanted her out of his hair. And what did you do with a gold digger when you wanted peace? Throw money at her! And when you had more money than a gold mine, throwing money was the easy option. Tati clamped her teeth together hard on a sarcastic response. She recalled her Granny Milly telling her that you caught more flies with honey than vinegar. But sheer rage rippled through her in a heady wave that left her almost light-headed because she wasn't some greedy tramp the Prince could tempt, control and ultimately debase with cold, hard cash!

'How wonderful,' Tati told him with a serene smile. 'I shall feel as though all my Christmases have come at once. Do I have a budget?'

Saif interpreted the glitter in her big blue eyes as pure avarice. 'No budget,' he retorted with a flashing smile of reassurance.

He was giving her a free ticket to spend, spend, spend and she would be sure not to disappoint him. After all, if ever a guy deserved to have his worst expectations met, it was Saif, and she would *enjoy* playing the gold-digging bride, she told herself fiercely. If anything, he would learn to know better than to send her out shopping in one of the most expensive cities in the world without a budget.

She put on her jeans. Her brain could still not quite encompass the reality that the Prince was now *her* husband instead of her cousin's. He didn't even act as a husband would, did he? Well, like a very reluctant one, she decided ruefully. Possibly he hadn't wanted to get married either.

My goodness, maybe that could even explain why he had been married off in the first place...was it possible that the Prince was gay? And that he had been married off to conceal the fact? But if that were true, why, given the opportunity, wouldn't he have wanted to claim a bedroom of his own?

Tati frowned and conceded that Saif was a mass of confusing contradictions. He insisted they *had* to share a bedroom. For the sake of appearances? Did he want their marriage to look normal even if it wasn't? Out of pride or out of necessity? If he was gay and if it was impossible for his father to accept him as such, their crazy marriage made sense. Of course, understanding didn't make her like Saif any better for the way he had accused her of being a gold digger.

In fact, she hated him for that. Tati had spent her entire life being pushed around and put down by those who had more power than she had. Her own relatives had done that to her and, even before her mother had succumbed to dementia, Mariana had urged her daughter not to 'rock the boat' by defending her. Sadly, swallowing her pride and turning the other cheek had never improved matters in the slightest for Tati. In fact, that attitude, both at school and at home, had only made the bullying worse. And she wasn't prepared to settle for that again, for being abused when she hadn't done anything wrong, for being insulted simply because she was poor and had fewer options than other people. Her head came up, her chin lifting. No. No way was His Royal Highness the Crown Prince of Alharia about to get away with doing her down as well!

Thirty minutes later, Tati stepped into a long cream limousine containing three very ornamental and chatty women. At first glance, she could see that she was a surprise, a disappointment, in that she wasn't as decorative as they had expected and, as it was normal for her to want to please people and she fully intended to spend, spend, spend as directed by her bridegroom, she said, 'I need a whole new wardrobe!'

And the smiles broke out, betraying the visible relief that she was likely to be a keen buyer. Presumably, her companions worked on commission and why shouldn't they profit from her pressing need for clothes? Starting with nightwear and lingerie, she required everything. It was one thing to be proud and independent, another thing entirely to be the most poorly or inappropriately dressed person in the room. And she had no plans to start washing and drying her knickers in the nearest bathroom any time soon. In fact, she had to suppress a giggle as she attempted to picture the Prince's reaction. She doubted that he had ever been exposed to that kind of common touch.

The first stop on their trip was the Avenue Montaigne, a tree-lined thoroughfare packed with high-end fashion outlets. Aside from the uneasy acknowledgement that her cousin, Ana, would have truly revelled in such an opportunity, Tati concentrated on the practicalities of buying as much as she possibly could without ever consulting a price tag lest it send her into shock. She strayed from one designer boutique to the next with her companions, having by then established her preferences, working hard to locate the casual and formal items she specified. They moved on to the Boulevard Saint Germain, where she found chic dresses aplenty and the shoes and bags to team with them. She eventually succumbed to the temptation of putting on a new outfit. They visited a trendy rooftop café, where she enjoyed the spectacular views of the city and drank champagne. Of lunch there was no sign and only a handful of nuts came her way.

Mid-afternoon, she was professionally made up and equipped with enough cosmetics to provide a makeover for half a city block. Perfume specially mixed for her came next and she loved the perfume as much as the professional jargon of the scent world, which talked of hints of jasmine and spice, redolent of hotter climes. She allowed herself to be talked into buying a new phone and a new watch as well.

The guilt of enjoying herself while being wildly extravagant soon engulfed her in a tide. She had spent, spent, *spent* to hit back at Saif for his condemnation of her when in truth he knew nothing about her and evidently didn't care to find out anything about her either. But only on the drive back to the house, while her companions were cheerfully breaking out the champagne again to celebrate a successful day of shopping, did she ask herself how meeting every one of Saif's worst expectations of her character could benefit her in any way. She refused the champagne because she wasn't in the mood to rejoice.

What had she done? Why had she let her raging resentment at her position and his attitude take over and drive her? Why had she set out to prove that she was every bit as greedy as he had assumed she was?

A severe attack of the guilts gripped Tati as she watched a procession of staff march through the echoing hall to deliver the boxes and bags of her accumulated shopping upstairs to the bedroom. There they would proceed to unpack and organise her many, many purchases before storing them in the empty drawers and closets. She flopped down on an opulent couch in the drawing room, her face burning with mortification as she pictured the sweater she had bought in *four* different colours. The cringe factor was huge because in all her life she had never made an extravagant purchase before.

When would she contrive to wear a sweater in a desert kingdom? Presumably, she would wear the winter garments when she went home to visit her mother, she reasoned weakly. As for the fancy dresses, the high heels and all the elegant separates, where was she planning to wear them? Observation currently suggested that the Prince she had married would be in no hurry to take her anywhere, particularly now that she had shown what he would no doubt deem to be her true colours. And yet she had *needed* clothes, she thought wretchedly, for not only had she packed very little to fly out to Alharia for what she had assumed would be a very short stay, but she also had nothing much worthy of packing back home. The kind of casual wear she had worn to run her aunt and uncle's household wouldn't pass muster in her current role.

But neither of those facts excused her extravagance. She could have gone to a chain store to cover her requirements and only bought the necessities, she conceded unhappily. Instead she had shopped and spent recklessly in some of the most exclusive designer shops in the world.

Marcel brought her tea and tiny dainty macarons on a silver tray. She glanced up when she heard a step in the hall and saw Saif still in the doorway. He had shed his jacket and tie and his sculpted jawline was shadowed with stubble. His gorgeous green eyes clashed with hers and she felt hot all over as if she had been exposed to a flame. She went pink and shifted uneasily on her seat, her mouth running very dry.

Saif was trying very hard not to gape at the blonde beauty on the opulent sofa. Like a fine jewel once displayed in an unworthy setting, she had been reset and polished up to perfection since their last meeting. A dark off-the-shoulder top clung to her like a second skin, lovingly hugging pert full breasts and skin that looked incredibly perfect and smooth. A short skirt in some kind of toning print exposed slender knees and shapely calves leading down to small feet shod in strappy heels. Off the scale arousal inflamed Saif as fast as a shot of adrenalin in his veins. An uncomfortable throb set up an ache at his groin.

Tati gazed back at him, dismay and a leaping hormonal response that unnerved her darting through her tense body. She found it utterly impossible to look away from Saif. His raw desirability was that intense from his tousled black hair to the rich green deep-set eyes fringed with ebony lashes that magnetised her.

'We have to talk,' she told him awkwardly. 'We have to sort stuff out.'

His half-brother, Angelino, the consummate playboy, had once told Saif that the minute a woman mentioned the need to talk, a sensible man should go straight into avoidance mode. Saif collided warily with huge blue-pansy-coloured eyes and parted his lips to shut her down.

'Please,' Tati added in near desperation. 'Because right now, everything's going crazy and wrong.'

'Is it?'

He did not know why he questioned that statement when he should have agreed because the arousal afflicting him was both crazy and wrong. He *had* to remain detached and in control. Nothing good could come from giving in to his baser instincts;

nothing good could come from him backing down when confronted with her feminine wiles. And those flowery eyes of hers were shimmering with what might have been tears, her full lower lip quivering. The sight stabbed him to the heart, and he strode forward, a forceful, instantaneous urge to fix whatever was wrong powering him.

'Tatiana,' he began, determined to continue the conversation in private where they could be neither overheard nor seen. It was second nature for Saif to consider appearances, raised as he had been in a palace swarming with staff where keeping secrets was an almost impossible challenge.

'Nobody calls me that,' she told him in a wobbly voice.

'Except me. I will not call you Tatty like your relatives. It is an insult and I don't know why you've allowed it.' Without another word, Saif bent down and scooped her off the couch as if she were no heavier than a doll.

'What are you doing?' she exclaimed in stark disconcertion.

'Taking you upstairs where we may be assured of discretion,' the Prince countered, striding out across the hall with complete cool as if carrying a woman around were an everyday occurrence for him.

'Why on earth would we need discretion?' Tati queried nervously. 'You can put me down now.'

'You were becoming distressed... *Crying!*' Saif pointed out with a raw edge to his dark, deep drawl.

'I wasn't crying!' Tati protested, highly offended by the charge. 'I don't cry. You could torture me and I wouldn't cry! Just sometimes my eyes flood when I'm upset—it's a nervous thing but I don't start crying, for goodness' sake! I'm not a little girl!'

'No, definitely *not* a little girl except in height,' Saif quipped, pushing through the bedroom door to set her down on the big bed. 'Now tell me, why are you upset?'

'Because I let you *goad* me into behaving badly today and

I'm furious with myself and with you!' Tati told him roundly. 'I went out today and spent a fortune on clothing because—'

'I urged you to…how is that bad behaviour?' Saif prompted, his gaze locked to the beautiful eyes angrily fixed to him, his fingers rising to brush back the silky blond hair rippling across her cheekbone. The long strands fell over his wrist, pale wheaten gold against his skin.

That light touch that seemed perilously close to a caress made Tati shiver while her skin broke out in goosebumps of awareness. 'You don't understand…'

'The only thing I understand right now is that I want you,' Saif breathed in the driven tone of harsh sincerity, his beautiful jewelled eyes smouldering as she looked up at him.

'Me? You want…*me*?' Tati almost whispered in disbelief and wonderment.

'Why wouldn't I want you?' Saif turned the question back on her in equal surprise. 'You are a remarkable beauty.'

That was a heady compliment for a woman who had never been called beautiful in her entire life, who had always been in the shadows, either unnoticed or passed over or summarily dismissed as being unimportant. Tati stared at him in astonishment and she was so blasted grateful for that tribute that she stretched up and kissed his cheek in reward.

As her breasts momentarily pressed into his chest and the intoxicating scent of her engulfed him, the soft invitation of her lips on his skin burned through Saif's self-discipline like a fiery brand and destroyed it. Without any hesitation, he closed her slight body into the circle of his arms and brought his mouth crashing down on hers with a hunger he couldn't even attempt to control.

Oh, wow, Tati thought abstractedly, *wasn't expecting this, wasn't expecting to feel* this…

CHAPTER FOUR

AND THIS WAS the amazing sign that Tati had always been waiting and hoping to feel in a man's arms: electrified, exhilarated, physically aware of her own body to the nth degree. Only until that moment she had honestly believed that that kind of reaction was simply a myth, something that some women chose to exaggerate, which didn't truly exist. But with that single kiss Saif had knocked Tati right out of her complacent assumptions, knocked her sideways and upside down and just at that moment, regardless of whether it made sense or not, her stupid body was humming as fiercely as an engine getting revved up at the starting line.

'So...er...you're not gay,' Tati commented weakly as he released her mouth and dragged in a shuddering breath. 'Obviously.'

Saif gazed down at her in complete astonishment. 'Why would you think I was gay?'

'Your father marrying you off like that, not caring that I was a substitute for the bride that he had chosen,' Tati pointed out breathlessly. 'It seemed like he didn't care who you married as long as a marriage took place.'

'It *was* like that. All of Alharia knew that it was my wedding day. My father viewed the bride's disappearance as an absolute humiliation and an outrage against the throne itself. He could not accept that shame. As long as a wedding took place and he could cover up what really happened, he was appeased,' Saif explained, a lingering frown drawing his sleek dark brows together.

'I didn't appreciate how far-reaching the effects of Ana running away would be,' Tati admitted. 'I didn't understand that it would be such a crime and an embarrassment in your father's eyes either... I was stupidly naïve.'

'Kiss me again,' Saif husked, his attention locked to the full pink lower lip she was worrying at with the edge of her small blunt teeth.

'I'm not sure that we should.'

'Nothing that tastes as good as your mouth could be wrong,' Saif told her.

'Quite the poet when you want to be,' Tati whispered, barely breathing as she looked into those stunning green eyes of his and felt the flutter of butterflies in her tummy and the wicked heat of anticipation. A 'what the heck?' sensation that felt unfamiliar but somehow very, very right was assailing her. Other people took risks all the time, but she never did and the acknowledgement rankled.

'We are married.'

She wasn't thinking about that, all she was thinking about was how he made her *feel* and that felt wildly self-indulgent, something she never allowed herself to be. But what were a few kisses? No harm in that, no lasting damage, she reasoned with determination. Why did she always stress herself out by trying to second-guess stuff? Why did she take life so seriously and always behave as though the roof were likely to fall on her if she deviated from her set path of rectitude? In a resentful surge of denying that fretful and serious habit of generally looking on the downside of life, she tipped her head back and said tautly, 'So we are...'

Saif tasted her soft pink mouth, which had all the allure of a ripe peach, and then he yielded even more to the hunger storming through his tall, powerful frame, nudging her back against the pillows, a lean hand gliding up from a slender knee to skate along the stretch of her thigh.

Tati gasped, her hips rising, her thighs clenching on the sudden ache stabbing at the heart of her. It was terrifyingly intense. 'You make me want you… I don't know how!' she exclaimed helplessly, every nerve ending in her body on the alert.

Saif smiled down at her, green eyes aglow with energy below well-defined brows. 'You know how…you're not that innocent.'

But she was, she *was*, she conceded uneasily, because absolutely everything felt so novel and fresh and exciting for her. And why wouldn't it when she had never felt that way before? He shifted over her, one long, strong leg sliding between hers, and her breath snarled in her throat, her tummy fluttering with an incandescent mix of nerves and craving that left her lightheaded. He kissed her again, parting her lips, delving between, his tongue flicking across the roof of her mouth, making delicious little quivers circulate through her lower body.

The weight of him against her, the clean, musky, all-male scent of him engulfing her, the way he plucked at her lower lip and teased it with the edge of his teeth. It all drove her a little crazy, igniting an insane impatience that made her fingers spread and dig into his shirt-clad back, needing to touch the skin below the cotton, clawing it up to finally learn that he was every bit as hot in temperature as his kisses promised. She squirmed up into the sheltering heat of him and he pressed his lips to the slender column of her throat, discovering yet another place that was extraordinarily sensitive, tracing it down to the valley between her breasts.

Saif pulled her top over her head and cast it aside. His big hands spread to cup the full swell of her breasts cupped in lace-edged silk. His thumbs found her prominent nipples, stroked, and an arrow of heat speared down into her groin, making her hips rise. The bra melted away and she barely noticed because the feel of his hands on her naked skin sent literal shivers of response through her. He lowered his head over the pouting mounds and employed his mouth on the straining peaks, and she discovered a new sensual torment that utterly overwhelmed her as his tongue lashed the swollen buds and set up a chain reaction inside her that increased the ache tugging between her thighs.

He brushed away her last garment and her whole body rose as he finally touched her *there* where she had the most powerfully indecent craving to be touched. A light forefinger scored across the most sensitive spot of all and her spine arched, a gasp parting her lips. Her hand travelled up from his shoulder into his ruffled black hair and rifled through the silky strands to draw him back down to her again.

He nuzzled her parted lips, plucked at the full lower one with the edge of his teeth, teasing and rousing while he traced the damp, silky flesh between her thighs. She moaned and shifted her hips, the fiery pulse beating at her core rising in intensity in concert with her heartbeat. As he circled the most tender spot, the sizzling desire thrumming through her took an exponential leap and her fingers dug into his scalp as she fought for control. She wanted more, she *needed* more, she wanted him inside her to sate the tormenting hollow ache. She didn't recognise herself in the blind hold of that overwhelming craving.

Indeed she was at the agonising height of anticipation when Saif suddenly stopped dead and stared down at her with green eyes glittering with frustration. 'I don't have contraception here.'

'I'm on the pill...it doesn't matter!' Tati gasped.

'I have not been with anyone since a recent health check.'

Unaccustomed to such sensible conversations even while accepting that they were necessary, Tati could feel the heat of embarrassment burning her already flushed cheeks. 'I haven't been with anyone either,' she hastened to assure him.

Relief flooded his expressive gaze. 'I wasn't expecting this... *us*,' he admitted tautly, rearranging her under him, unzipping his trousers.

The instant she felt the satin-smooth touch of him against her entrance she tipped her legs back, hungry for the experience. He pushed into her slowly and she tensed at that strange sensation, closing her eyes tight and gritting her teeth momentarily when the sting and burn of his invasion broke through the barrier of her virginity. It hurt but not as much as she had feared it might. In fact, if there was such a thing, it was a *good* hurt, she reasoned abstractedly, her ability to concentrate still utterly controlled by that overriding hunger for the fulfilment that only he could give her.

Pleasure skated along her nerve endings as he bent her further back and drove deeper into her needy depths. Excitement climbed as he picked up his pace and her heart began to thump inside her, her breath catching in her throat. The whole of her being was caught up in the tightening bands of tension in her pelvis that merely pushed the craving higher and then the storm of gathering excitement coalesced in one bright, blinding instant. Like fireworks flaring inside her, it was electrifying. The excitement pushed her over the edge in an explosion of incredible pleasure that engulfed her in a sweet after-tide of blissful release. She tumbled back into the pillows, winded and drained but feeling light as a feather.

Saif achieved completion with a shuddering groan of relief and quickly pulled away from her, afraid of crushing her tiny body beneath his weight. He flung himself back and whispered, 'I've never had sex without a condom before. That was…unexpectedly…much more exciting than I ever dreamt…but you… you were *amazing*,' he stressed, locking brilliant green eyes to her burning face with sensual appreciation.

Tati's light-as-a-feather sensation was fast fading and the regrets were kicking in even faster. 'How did this happen?' she whispered shakily. 'We don't even like each other—'

'Speak for yourself. I like you very much indeed at this moment,' Saif countered with dancing eyes of amusement.

Tati was remarkably disgruntled by that light-hearted comment. There he lay, confident, calm and absolutely in control, while she felt as if she were falling to pieces inside herself. She couldn't believe that she had had sex with him, didn't want to accept that she had urged him on like a shameless hussy. A strand of nagging anxiety pierced her.

'Did you...er...withdraw?' she mumbled in mortification, ashamed that she hadn't noticed, hadn't thought to suggest, hadn't acted on a single intelligent thought.

'Why would I have done that when you are protected by contraception?' Saif enquired.

Tati said nothing but she paled. She had left her contraceptive pills behind in the rush of packing for Alharia and could only wonder how effective those pills would be when she had already missed a couple of doses. She had never had to worry about anything like that before because she was only taking the pills in the first place to ease a difficult menstrual cycle.

Saif sat up. 'I need a shower... I'll use the one next door.' He sprang out of bed, stark naked and unselfconscious. 'We could share it...it's a big shower.'

'I don't think so,' she said flatly, downright incredulous at the suggestion that they could share a shower.

He didn't need to be self-conscious with his lean, athletic physique, she thought ruefully, but, personally speaking, she would not be getting out of bed in front of him without sucking her tummy in to the best of her ability. As she watched, he flipped through drawers and brought out fresh clothing to pull on trousers and a fresh shirt and stride out of the room.

How on earth could she have been stupid enough to have sex with him? How the heck had that happened? She hadn't been her usual self, she reasoned ruefully—she had been angry, guilty and upset about the situation she was in and ashamed of her extravagance. But then *somehow* curiosity and desire had combined to blow all common sense out of the water, she reflected unhappily as she darted out of bed and raced into the dressing room to extract fresh underwear before speeding into the bathroom.

Where would she be if she fell pregnant? She had just had unprotected sex and she knew the risks. Her parents hadn't conceived her by choice. She had been an accident, conceived at a party with a man with whom her mother had had only a casual relationship. In every way, never mind her birth father's eventual arrest for fraud, Tati had been a mistake even if her mother had made the best of her arrival and had always assured her daughter that she had no regrets whatsoever.

As he stripped again next door, Saif was thinking that he would buy his bride something special as a mark of his appreciation. She deserved a handsome gift for not holding against him the cruel accusations he had made. He had been harsh and much less generous but that *had* to change, he acknowledged ruefully, because Tatiana was his wife and, for as long as they were together, she had a right to both his respect and his care. Just as he was about to switch the water on, he noticed the streak of blood on his thigh and he stopped dead with a frown.

When Tati emerged from the bathroom, she was fully dressed and unprepared to find that Saif was waiting for her. His impact stole the breath from her lungs. Black hair still damp from the shower, his lean dark features unnervingly grave, he was strikingly handsome. Tailored black trousers outlined his long powerful thighs and his plain white shirt was open at his throat. He was the very definition of casual, elegant sophistication.

'Is there something wrong?' she prompted, striving to appear more composed than she indeed felt.

'Before I showered, I noticed that there was blood on me... I must know—did I hurt you?'

Tati's face flamed crimson because she was utterly unprepared for that question. 'A little, but it's par for the course, isn't it...the first time, I mean?' she completed awkwardly, trying to pass it off casually, wishing he simply hadn't noticed anything amiss.

Saif froze in astonishment. 'You *were* a virgin?'

'Yes. Let's not make a fuss about it,' Tati urged tightly.

'It is not something I can ignore... I am guilty of having made assumptions about you, assumptions that clearly have no basis in fact,' Saif breathed tautly, far less comfortable after she had made that confirmation.

Tati breathed in deep and slow, but it still didn't suppress the rage hurtling up through her. 'So, because I was greedy, I also had to have been... What do we call it? Around the block a few times?' she paraphrased with a grimace.

'At twenty-four most young women have some sexual experience,' Saif countered, standing his ground on that score.

'But I'm not twenty-four. I'm twenty-one... Within a few weeks of my next birthday, but not quite there yet,' Tati filled in thinly, her spine rigid as she moved to the door. 'Perhaps you should find out a little more about me before you start judging.'

'I am not judging you,' Saif countered with measured cool.

'You've been judging me from the moment you met me, and it stops here and now,' Tati told him, lifting her chin in challenge, her accusing blue eyes bright as sapphires. 'Clearly you weren't any keener on this marriage than I was, but I'm done taking all the blame for it! I've been pushed around and used by my cousin and then by my uncle and aunt but I'm *not* going to accept being pushed around and used by you as well!'

With that ringing assurance, Tati stalked out of the room, her short skirt flipping round her slender knees, her breasts taut and firm and highly noticeable from the rigid angle of her spine. Challenged to drag his attention from her, Saif swore under his breath, rebelling at the temptation to follow her and argue. He didn't do arguments with women. He didn't do drama. He didn't believe that he had ever pushed around or *used* any woman. He had been force-fed his father's deep suspicions of the opposite sex from an early age and had done his utmost to combat that biased mindset with his intelligence.

Yet he had never wanted to fall in love and run the risk of

giving up control of his emotions to a woman and trusting her. The rejection dealt by the mother who had deserted him had cut him deep down inside. He had learned to live with that reality, though, by burying his sensitivity on that issue.

And life experience had made him more cynical. He had been used by women, used for sex, for money, chased and feted by those in search of status and a title. Once or twice when he was younger and more naïve, he had been hurt. As a result, he was *not* prejudiced, he was *wary*, he reflected grimly.

CHAPTER FIVE

As Tati reached the foot of the sweeping staircase without any idea of where she was going, she was intercepted by Marcel and shown across the hall into a dining room with a table already beautifully set for a meal. She took a seat with alacrity because she was more than ready to eat. She had been hungry even before she got into bed with her prince, she thought wildly, although she had done nothing there worthy of the excuse of having worked up an appetite. That belated reflection birthed a host of insecurities. She had lain there like a statue, she thought in dismay, as much of a partner as a blow-up doll. The slow-burning heat of mortification crept up through her like a living flame and it was not eased by Saif's sudden entrance into the dining room.

'I forgot about dinner,' he said almost apologetically.

'I didn't get lunch either,' she hastened to admit.

'Why not?' Saif queried, his startlingly light eyes bright against his olive skin.

'Nobody else seemed to be interested in eating.' Tati shrugged, still fascinated by those eyes of his.

Saif frowned as Marcel arrived with little plates. 'It was for you to say that you wished to eat,' he told her gently. 'You were the client. You were in charge.'

Stiffening at that veiled criticism, Tati looked down at her plate and shook out her napkin. 'I usually go with the majority vote and endeavour to fit in.'

As Tati shifted awkwardly in her seat, in the silence the dulled ache at the heart of her almost made her wince, and recalling exactly how she had acquired that intimate ache made her flush to the roots of her hair. In haste she began to eat, struggling to suppress the overwhelming memory of his lean, powerful body sliding over and inside hers, the heart-thumping excitement that had gripped her and the sheer unvarnished pleasure of it.

As Marcel arrived with the main course, she glanced up, desperate to distract herself from such thoughts. 'Your green eyes... So unexpected, so unusual,' she heard herself remark gauchely, inwardly cringing from the surprise that lit up those extraordinary eyes of his.

'I inherited them from my mother,' Saif proffered, amused by her embarrassment and how little she was able to hide it from him. 'I don't know where she got them from or if anyone else in her family shares them because I have no contact with her family.'

'Why's that?' Tati pressed, unable to stifle her interest.

'You really don't know anything about me, do you?' Saif registered. 'My mother ran off with another man six months after my birth, deserting me and my father. Her family took offence when my father spoke his opinion too freely of her behaviour.'

'My goodness, that was tough for both of you. What was it like growing up, torn between two parents? I presume they divorced?'

'Yes, there was a divorce. I have no memory of her, though, and I was never torn between them. She never asked to see me. She wiped her first marriage out of her life as though it had never happened.'

Tati grimaced. 'That was very sad for you.'

'Not really,' Saif countered, his jawline stiffening as he made that claim. 'I had three very much older half-sisters, who devoted themselves to my care in her place.'

'How much older?'

'They were born of my father's first marriage and are in their sixties now. I was spoiled as the long-awaited son and heir,' Saif told her quietly. 'I have much to be grateful for.'

He had dealt with his troubled background with such calm and logic that she was slightly envious, conscious that she had more often been mortified by her own. She dealt him a wry glance. 'You notice that we're talking about everything but the elephant in the room.'

'I didn't want to give you indigestion by mentioning our marriage,' Saif delivered straight-faced.

Tati stared at him, entrapped by those striking eyes as green as emeralds in his lean dark face, and then her defences crumbled as she spluttered and then laughed out loud, grabbing up her water glass to drink and ease her throat. 'So, you *do* have a sense of humour.'

'Yesterday was trying for *both* of us,' he pointed out as he pushed away his plate and leant back fluidly in his chair to give her his full attention.

'Why did you agree to go ahead with the marriage?'

'My father has a serious heart condition. I didn't want to risk refusing to marry you and stressing his temper,' Saif admitted grimly. 'He needs to remain calm, which is often a struggle for him.'

Tati was disconcerted by that admission. It had not occurred to her that he might have an excuse as good as her own for letting the ceremony proceed. That knocked her right off the moral high ground she had been unconsciously hugging like a blanket while silently blaming him for being willing to marry her.

He hadn't had a choice either.

'You must've been disappointed that I wasn't my cousin, Ana,' she said uncomfortably.

'Why would I have been? She was a stranger too.'

'Yes, but she's much prettier than I am and she's sophisticated and lively. I'm none of those things. Ana's one of the beautiful people... I'm a nobody.'

'How a *nobody*?' Saif framed, his nostrils flaring with distaste. 'She is your cousin. I assume you have led similar lives.'

Tati breathed in fast and deep as Marcel arrived with a mouth-watering selection of desserts. 'Not for me, thank you,' she said in creditable French.

'Saif,' she said quietly once Marcel had departed. 'You married the poor relation, not the family princess. I'm illegitimate and my birth father, whom I never met, was imprisoned for fraud. He's dead now.'

'Why are you telling me this?' he demanded.

'You need to know who I am. I grew up in a cottage on my uncle's estate. My mother and I were never welcome there because my uncle didn't get on with my mother and viewed the two of us as freeloaders. I received the same education at the same schools as my cousin but only because my grandmother insisted. This is only my second trip abroad...'

Saif was watching her closely. 'I'm listening...' he told her.

'When I was about fifteen my mother began getting forgetful and confused. Eventually she was diagnosed with early-onset dementia. She was only forty years old.' Tati looked reflective, her eyes darkening with sadness. 'I looked after Mum for as long as I could but eventually she had to go into a nursing home. She's been there for almost six years and it costs a fortune. My uncle pays for her care—'

'Which is why you married me,' Saif assumed, slashing ebony brows drawing together in a frown. 'So that you could take care of her yourself.'

'I didn't receive that dowry for marrying you or whatever it's called,' Tati told him immediately. 'My uncle got that. He has debts to settle. That was why Ana was originally willing to marry you, because she has never worked and she's reliant on an income from her father.'

'So, what changed?' Saif pressed.

'Out of the blue, her ex got back in touch and asked her to marry him on the phone while she was here. That's why she ran back to England at the very last minute, leaving me to face the music... She asked me to pretend I was her to give her enough time to leave Alharia. She was afraid her parents would try to prevent her going. I really didn't enjoy deceiving your relatives into believing I was the bride, but I didn't truthfully expect any lasting harm to come from my pretence. I certainly *didn't* realise that I would end up married to you instead!'

'Then why did you agree?' Saif asked bluntly.

'Uncle Rupert threatened to stop paying my mother's nursing home bills. I couldn't let that happen,' Tati murmured heavily. 'She's happy and settled where she is—well, as happy as she can be anywhere now.'

'Will you excuse me for a moment?' Saif asked tautly as he stood up and left the room.

Out in the hall he pulled out his phone and contacted the private investigation agency he often used in business. He wanted information and he wanted it fast. He needed to know everything there was to know about the woman he had married. Ignorance in such a case was inexcusable and had already got him into trouble. The last-minute exchange of brides had plunged him into a situation in which he was not in control and he refused to allow that state of affairs to continue.

Alone in the dining room, Tati felt like dropping her head into her hands and screaming out loud. Why had she told him all that personal stuff? What was the point? She might even be giving him information about herself that he could use as another weapon against her. Saif was not a man she could trust. She cringed at the recollection of what she had said about herself, as if she was apologising for who and what she was, as if she was openly admitting that she was something less than he was just because she hadn't been born into either wealth or status.

Her pride flared at that lowering image and it shamed her,

even more than he had already shamed her with that outrageous shopping trip. She had fallen head first into that nasty trap, she conceded painfully.

As Saif strolled back into the room, dark head high, green eyes glinting with assurance, Tati's small hands flexed into claws, that family trait of violence he had accused her of harbouring leaping through her instantaneously. 'You sent me out shopping so that you could snigger behind my back when I met all your worst expectations!' she condemned furiously. 'And I was mad enough at you to allow you to goad me into behaving badly!'

'I don't know what you're talking about,' Saif countered with unblemished cool. 'I do not snigger.'

Pansy-blue eyes now as hard as diamond cutters, Tati tossed her head back, soft, full mouth rigid. 'I'm done with talking to you. I'm done with telling you the truth and letting you judge me for what I can't help or change. You set me up to get me out of your hair and to make a fool of myself and I played right into your hands!' she condemned.

'I didn't set you up when I sent you shopping,' Saif retorted crisply. 'I arranged the outing to entertain you.'

'Like hell you did!' Tati raged back at him.

'And if you played right into my hands, surely that is your own fault?' Saif drawled smoothly.

'Oh, you...*you*...!' The exclamation was framed between gritted teeth. Tati's hands knotted into fists because she wanted to swear at him and she didn't swear, not with the memory of her Granny Milly telling her that only people with a weak grasp of language needed to use curse words. 'I've never been in shops that exclusive in my life. I've never owned clothing such as I'm wearing now. I went shopping to punish you.'

'Why would you have wanted to punish me?' he enquired in wonderment.

'I thought you deserved to have a spendthrift wife after labelling me a gold digger! I know it doesn't sound like much of a punishment right now but at the time…*at the time*…it made sense to me,' she confided in an angry challenge that dared him to employ logic against her. 'But then I got tempted by all those beautiful fabrics and designs and how I looked in them. I started to actually enjoy myself…and I'll never *ever* forgive you for that, for tempting me into wasting all that money.'

'I arranged for you to go out shopping and I would not describe the outfit you are currently wearing as a waste on any level,' Saif asserted softly. 'You look amazing in it.'

'And do you seriously think that *your* opinion makes any difference to the way I feel?' Tati flung back at him furiously. 'Well, it doesn't! I hardly brought any clothes with me to Alharia. Why would I have? As far as I knew I was only staying for forty-eight hours and I certainly didn't factor in marrying you and being swept off to Paris!'

'In other words, you *needed* to go shopping,' Saif interpreted with an unshakeable calm that simply sent her temperature rocketing again because it was infuriating that the more she freaked out, the calmer he became. 'I don't understand why you're so upset.'

'Because I could have bought ordinary cheap clothes and proved to you that I'm *not* a greedy gold digger!' Tati yelled back at him.

'You're my wife and entitled to a decent wardrobe. I wouldn't want you swanning round in what you describe as "cheap" clothes,' Saif pointed out with distaste.

'For heaven's sake, I'm not your wife!' Tati fired back at him in vehement disagreement.

'From the instant you shared that bed with me, and an annulment became an impossibility, you also became my wife in law *and* in my eyes,' Saif informed her with fierce conviction. 'You were a virgin. While you urged me not to make a fuss about that fact, it did make a difference on my terms. Perhaps that is old-fashioned of me, but you do now feel very much like my wife and all this nonsense about how much you spend on the clothes you needed is pointless now.'

'I'm not your wife,' Tati argued in a low, tight voice. 'If you wanted an annulment to end this marriage then you didn't want a wife and we could still apply for an annulment. We could *lie*.'

Her prince threw his handsome dark head back and surveyed her with narrowed, glittering green eyes. 'I do not tell lies of that nature and, now that the marriage has been consummated, neither will you. For the moment, we will make the best of our situation until such time as our circumstances change and we are free to go our separate ways. In the meantime, you are entitled to a very healthy allowance as my wife and I will take over the cost of your mother's nursing care, so let us have no more foolish talk about how you shouldn't spend *my* money.'

'I would lie to get an annulment,' Tati told him stubbornly. 'I don't normally tell lies but in this instance I would be prepared to lie... Just putting that out there for you to consider.'

'I have considered it and I reject it,' Saif stated curtly. 'I—'

'No, there's no need for another moral lecture,' Tati hastened to assure him. 'I do know the difference between right and wrong but I *also* know that neither of us *freely* agreed to marry the other.'

'And yet you gave your virginity to me.'

Tati's face burned red as fire. 'I didn't give you anything... Well, I did, but not the way you make it sound! I was attracted to you and we had sex. Let's leave it there.'

'But where *does* that leave us exactly?' Saif demanded impatiently.

Tati winced at his persistence. 'You can't put a label on everything.'

'I need to know where I stand with you,' Saif breathed with driving emphasis. 'You have to put *some* kind of label on us.'

'Friends...hopefully eventually,' Tati suggested weakly. 'Maybe friends with benefits. Wouldn't that be the best description?'

In the tense silence that gradually stretched, a slow-burning smile slowly wiped the raw tension from Saif's expressive mouth and his vaguely confrontational stance eased. His extraordinary eyes clung to her blushing face. 'Yes. I could work with that,' he murmured in a husky tone of acceptance. 'Yes, I could definitely work within those parameters.'

'I'm really sleepy,' Tati mumbled, putting a hand to her mouth as if to politely screen a yawn, a potent mix of embarrassment and confusion assailing her. 'May we call a halt to the post-mortem for now?'

'It's been a long day,' Saif agreed, deciding to look into whether or not that phrase 'friends with benefits' encompassed what he thought it did.

Naturally, he had heard the expression before. He knew there was a movie by that name but he had never watched it and had never entertained the concept of attempting so spontaneous and casual a relationship with any woman. Although he was close to some of his female cousins, he was mindful of his position and there was no one in whom he confided. He had only once had a female friend. He had been a student at the time and his supposed female friend had suddenly announced that she was in love with him and everything had become horribly awkward from that point on. His sole sexual outlet was occasional one-night stands and that kind of informal never led to a misunderstanding.

At the same time, he marvelled at his bride's audacity in making such a suggestion. He had always assumed that there was truth in that old chestnut that women generally wanted more than sex and friendship from a man, but obviously there were exceptions to every rule. Possibly his own outlook was a little out of date, he thought uneasily, wondering darkly if his father's rigidly traditional attitudes could have coloured his views more than he was willing to admit. Even so, if he and his bride had no choice but to remain together for the present, why shouldn't they make the best of it in and out of the bedroom?

Bearing in mind his distrust of committed relationships, formed by his inability to forget how easily his mother had walked away from him and his father, he suspected that being friends with benefits might be an excellent recipe for temporary intimacy.

Tati sped back upstairs as if she were being chased because she was reeling in shock from what she had accidentally said to Saif, and the manner in which he had received what had undoubtedly struck him as an *invitation*. Her face burned afresh as she got ready for bed, every movement reminding her of what had occurred earlier because the ache of her first sexual experience still lingered with tingling awareness. And, strangely, so did the hot curling sensation she experienced deep down inside whenever she thought about it.

Not strange, she adjusted, simply normal. There was nothing weird about sexual chemistry and Saif had buckets of sex appeal. Even moving across the room, all loose-limbed grace and earthy masculinity, he entrapped her gaze and when she collided with those startling green eyes of his she felt light-headed. So, no mystery there about what had led to her downfall, she told herself plainly. She had never been affected like that by a man before, certainly not to the extent that he interfered with her brain and her wits and smashed through her every defence.

She even *said* the wrong things around Saif, she acknowledged unhappily. She had been desperate to hide how deeply affected she had been by their intimacy, desperate to keep up an impenetrable front. After all, Saif had taken the sex in his stride without betraying any emotional reaction whatsoever. She had wanted it to look as though she took such steps with equally bold panache, so she had seized on the chance the friends idea offered with alacrity and had added in that ghastly *benefits* tag to coolly attempt to dismiss the reality that they had already got far more familiar than mere friendship allowed. She had been referring to the past, *not* to the potential future. Was it any wonder that he had seemingly got the wrong message? And was she planning to disabuse him of the idea that she was willing to continue their relationship as a friend with benefits?

Her head beginning to ache with her ever-circling thoughts and a growing sense of panic that she had let her life get so out of control when she was normally a very calm and organised person, Tati slid into bed, convinced that she had not a prayer of sleeping. And yet moments later, odd as it seemed to her the following morning, sheer emotional and physical exhaustion sent her crashing straight into a deep sleep.

Saif went to bed in a totally distracted manner far from his usual style. His wife, that much-maligned bride of his, had without warning become a *real* wife. It might be a casual bond, it might not be destined to last for very long, but he was much inclined to believe, even though he had yet to receive concrete facts in an investigation file, that Tatiana was telling him the truth about herself.

Saif was a shrewd observer and he trusted his own instincts. His assumptions about her had been laid down from Dalil Khouri's first reference to her as a fortune hunter, an adventuress, a gold-digging socialite with expensive tastes, who could find no wealthier husband than a Middle Eastern prince from an oil-rich country like Alharia. That might well be true of the woman he *should* have married, the one they called Ana. She was the daughter of the grasping uncle and aunt. He had himself witnessed their threatening behaviour towards their niece with their raised hands, angry voices and devious looks, he conceded grimly. Now he believed that those original allegations were *not* true of the woman he had actually married.

The very beautiful, sensual woman he had married, Saif repeated inwardly as he glanced at her, sound asleep on the pillow beside his, long wheaten hair tumbled across the linen, soft pink mouth relaxed, porcelain skin flushed. He had stayed up late watching *that* film. It had struck him as fashionable and he didn't do, or certainly never before had done, 'fashionable.' But the creeping, unpleasant suspicion that he could be as much of a dyed-in-the-wool traditionalist as his father, unable to adapt to the modern world or to a modern woman, had cut through him like a knife and hammered his pride.

So, although it went against his *every* instinct, Saif was determined to do the 'friends with benefits' thing even though the movie had already demonstrated the pitfalls. After all, he would not be emotionally vulnerable, would he? He did not have the habit of attachment, he reasoned with resolve, he had never been in a proper relationship and had always kept his distance from that level of involvement. He would not be guilty of attaching feelings to sex. He knew all about sex. They would be friends, *sexual* friends. A pulse beat at his groin stirred at the mere thought of repeating that encounter with her.

Even so, he would exercise caution, he told himself fiercely, scrutinising her delicate profile and feathery eyelashes, noting the tiny group of freckles scattered across her nose, the gentle curve of her pink lips. He wanted to see her smile for a change. And why not? She was his wife, deserving of respect and consideration, regardless of how casual and temporary their alliance was. He might not be cutting-edge trendy, as she appeared to be, but he believed that with the exercise of a little imagination and research, he knew how to treat a woman well...

CHAPTER SIX

TATI STUMBLED AS she walked away from the giant Ferris wheel on the Place de la Concorde. Her head was still spinning from the experience and the fabulous views of Paris. Saif's hand shot out to steady her and she glanced up at him with a huge grin. 'My goodness…that was amazing!' she exclaimed.

Saif gazed down into her glowing face and the bright blue eyes lit up with enjoyment and he bent his head and crushed her mouth hungrily under his. That hunger speared through Tati like a flame striking touchpaper. Her knees wobbled and her hands closed into his sleeves to keep her upright. The urgent plunge of his tongue formed a pool of liquid heat in her pelvis and she gasped.

Saif jerked his head up, momentarily disconcerted to discover that he was in a public place, his bodyguards all politely looking away and probably astonished by his behaviour. In the crush of tourists and cameras flashing, he clenched his jaw hard. A very faint darkening scored his high cheekbones as he closed a hand over his wife's and walked her in the direction of the picnic lunch awaiting them on the Champ de Mars. He felt vaguely as though she had intoxicated him.

'The Louvre was exhausting.' Tati sighed as she sank down on the rugs already laid across the springy grass for their comfort. She imagined that going sightseeing with Saif was very different from the usual tourist trek. They didn't queue, they didn't wait anywhere for anything and everything that they required was instantly provided. Her elegant black sundress pooled around her feet and she tugged off her high heels to curl bare pink toes into the grass beyond the rug.

'We did only do the highlights tour. I spent months working in Paris and I went to the Louvre several times,' Saif imparted with amusement, watching the way the sunshine bathed her luxuriant mane of hair in gold. He wanted to touch her again and the temptation entertained him because it was a novelty.

Usually, one taste of a woman was sufficient for him and he would move on. Sex, however, was a great leveller, Saif allowed cynically and, clearly, he hadn't enjoyed enough of it for too long because around Tatiana he was on the constant edge of arousal and it was a challenge to resist her appeal. Yet, only a few yards away, young lovers were lying in the grass kissing passionately with their bodies entwined and their mouths mashed together. The Crown Prince of Alharia, however, had always known that he was not able to practise that kind of freedom and he told himself that he was too disciplined to give way to so juvenile a display. Yet he had kissed her in the street, utterly forgetting where he was, *who* he was.

'I'm not really into art. Mum was,' Tati confided. 'She could look at a picture and make those highbrow comments the way people do, but then she went to art college and originally planned to train as an art historian.'

Dainty little bites of food were set out on a low table in front of them along with china plates and wine glasses in an elaborate spread.

In terms of an outside space, it was a picnic, but not quite the kind of picnic Tati had naïvely envisaged when Saif had first mentioned it. The Prince, she was starting to realise, didn't truly know what informal or casual was. He was far too accustomed to top-flight silent service. Marcel had arrived laden down with hampers and his spry companion, who was an Alharian, had served them, moving forward on his knees with a bent head as though even to meet the eyes of the Emir's heir would be a familiarity too far. A lot of people were watching the display but Saif seemed no more aware of that scrutiny than of the presence of the plain-clothes police hovering beyond the ring of their personal protection team, keeping a watchful eye over a foreign royal. But then why would he be aware? she asked herself ruefully. Presumably, this was Saif's world as it always was, surrounded by security and hemmed in by tradition and formality.

'Why didn't *you* go to college?' Saif asked softly.

'Further education wasn't an option for me after Granny died. Uncle Rupert was covering the cost of the nursing home and I was already living below their roof because, when Mum went into care, my uncle needed to rent out the cottage we had been using to set against the bills and I was too young to live alone,' Tati explained wryly. 'I felt obligated to help around the house because they couldn't afford full-time staff and I was able to plug the gaps.'

'Your relatives should not have allowed you to make such a sacrifice,' Saif opined, impressed by the sacrifices she had made on her mother's behalf. When he had been younger, he had been much more curious about his absent mother, particularly after her death. He might even have initially sought out his brother to find out more about the woman who had brought him into the world and then walked away. Angel had told him all he needed to know about his absent parent, had satisfied that empty space inside him.

'She's my mother and she was a loving one. It was my duty to do what I could to pay my uncle back,' Tati contradicted gently. 'If I'd gone to college I would have built up thousands of pounds in student loans and it would have been years before I was in a position to make a decent financial contribution. I'm only twenty-one. I've still got loads of time to study and focus on a career.'

'That was a mature decision,' Saif acknowledged, wryly recalling the party girl he had assumed he was marrying while conceding that, undeniably, her cousin made a far more appropriate wife for a man in his position.

Tati nibbled at the delicious finger food on the plates and quaffed her wine.

'We have one personal topic which we haven't yet but *must* touch on,' Saif murmured in a low voice, and he topped up her wine glass, impervious to the shocked appraisal of the server hovering only yards away, keen to jump at the smallest sign of either of them having any need for attention.

Smooth brow furrowing, Tati glanced at him, thinking how incredibly good-looking he was with sunshine gleaming off his black hair and olive skin, lighting his eyes to a sea-glass green shade. 'And what is that?' she prompted abstractedly.

'Yesterday I was negligent in my care of you. As the experienced partner, all the blame on that score is mine. But that recklessness must not be repeated. In our position, the potential consequences would bring complications we would not want to deal with,' Saif framed in a taut undertone of warning.

It took a rather long moment for Tati to grasp what he was talking about. *'Negligent in my care of you...consequences... complications...mustn't be repeated...'* And then the penny of comprehension dropped with a resounding thump and her tummy curdled in dismay. He was referring to their lack of contraceptive common sense the day before. What else could he be talking about? He hadn't used birth control and she had reassured him, it only occurring to her later that her contraception was scarcely reliable when she had already been off it for a couple of days because she had left her strip of pills behind in England. Losing the rosy colour in her cheeks, she paled and swallowed down her misgivings before sipping her wine while studiously not looking in *his* direction.

There was no point worrying him ahead of time when really...what were the chances that she would conceive the very *first* time she had sex? She gritted her teeth, anxiety flashing through her as she reminded herself that she was not a naïve teenager, thinking that that should be sufficient to keep her safe. There was a chance, *of course*, there was when, even with precautions, no form of contraception was foolproof.

'We need to be responsible,' she said, proud of the steadiness of her voice until it occurred to her that, once again, she was throwing up a green light for further such intimacy.

And she shouldn't be doing that, of course, she shouldn't be. Even though she had *enjoyed* the experience? Her cheeks hot, she argued with herself inside her head. If they were careful going forward, there was no reason why she shouldn't be intimate with Saif again. She was an adult woman capable of making that choice on her own behalf. There was nothing morally wrong about having a sexual relationship, she reminded herself irritably, as long as the same consequences that had derailed her mother's life did not assail her.

Sadly, unplanned pregnancies sometimes extracted the highest price from the female partner, she reflected ruefully, because a man might have to contribute to his child's maintenance, but that did not necessarily mean that he took on any share of the childcare or indeed had any further interest in the child involved.

Her father had been of that ilk, indifferent from the day that her mother had informed him of her pregnancy. Even after his release from prison, he had pleaded poverty when pursued by the law for child support payments. She had never met her reluctant father in the flesh. As a teenager she had once written to him asking for a meeting but, even though the courts had verified her paternity, he had only responded with the denial that she was his child. That had hurt, that had blown a giant hole in her secret hope that he was curious about her as well.

'Yes,' Saif agreed, relieved, it seemed, by her attitude, which only made her feel even guiltier for not being fully honest with him from the outset and just admitting that there was a risk, admittedly, she *hoped*, a very slight risk that conception was a possibility.

Only telling the truth would make her sound like such an idiot, she conceded ruefully. She had told him it was safe. She had told him she was on contraception, only to recognise when it was too late that the pill method only worked if taken on a consistent schedule.

'We're attending a party tonight,' Saif murmured, disconcerting her with the ease with which he flipped the topic of conversation. 'You should enjoy it. I believe it's usually quite a spectacle.'

'Fancy, then,' Tati assumed, mentally flipping through her new wardrobe and realising with some embarrassment that she had bought so much that she couldn't remember all of the outfits without the garments being physically in front of her. That was not a problem that she had ever thought she would live to have, she acknowledged ruefully.

'Very,' Saif confirmed lazily, watching her with eyes that were sea-glass bright green seduction in the sunlight, his gaze enhanced by dense black spiky lashes. He wasn't touching her, he didn't *need* to touch her, she acknowledged in wonderment, he just had to look at her a certain way and that certain way was, without a doubt, incredibly sexy and potent.

Heat rose at the heart of her, butterflies fluttering in her tummy. Dragging her gaze from his, she sipped at her wine, reminding herself afresh that she was an adult woman, able to make her own choices…and right now, she thought, dizzy in the grip of that sensual intoxication, her choice was *him*.

Ana had always told Tati that she was very naïve about men. Her cousin prided herself on being as ruthless as any male in taking what she wanted from a man and then moving on, regardless of how the man felt about it. Ana often left broken hearts in her wake. Tati not only didn't *want* to leave broken hearts behind her, but also didn't think she would ever possess the power her cousin seemed to have over the opposite sex.

* * *

No, she couldn't compare herself to Ana, Tati acknowledged back at the magnificent house while she browsed through her wide selection of gowns. She was not and would never be a heartbreaker, but she rather suspected that Saif fell into that category. He emanated that cool, sophisticated air of unavailability that her cousin found so attractive in a man, so it was rather ironic that he had ended up married to Tati instead. Tati, unrefined, clumsy...and so angry from the moment he had met her.

Tati had never argued and fought with anyone the way she had with Saif. And where had all that rage come from? She supposed it had built up over the years below her uncle and aunt's roof where she had been consistently bullied and reminded of her lowly place in life on a daily basis. The smallest request for a wage that would at least fund her bus trips to visit her mother and little gifts for the older woman had been viewed as an offence of ingratitude. That she was a 'charity' child dependent on the goodwill of others for survival had been brought home to her hard and often and that label had ground her pride into the dust. Her mother's troubled past, her care bills and even the family embarrassment caused by Tati's illegitimate birth had often been used as a stick to beat Tati with and keep her down. Her uncle would not have dared be so offensive had her mother been around still possessed of her cutting tongue.

At the same time, her grandmother had had no idea what went on in her own house and Tati had shielded the frail old lady from the ugly truth. Even so, her Granny Milly had once taken the trouble to assure Tati that her mother would *always* be looked after, and Tati had prayed that sufficient money would be laid aside in the old lady's will to cover the nursing home costs. Unhappily, though, her late grandmother had forgotten that promise and had remembered neither her daughter Mariana nor Tati in her last will and testament.

That oversight had hurt, Tati conceded ruefully, because she had been deeply attached to her grandmother. In addition, the soothing knowledge that her mother's care was secure would not only have meant the world to Tati, but would also have released her from her virtual servitude in her uncle's home. But she had long since forgiven the old lady, who had been quite ill and confused towards the end of her life.

Shaking her head clear of those disturbing recollections of the past, Tati tugged a silvery-grey evening gown out of one of the closets. The delicate lace overlay was cobweb fine and it shimmered below the lights. She had fallen in love with the elegant dress at first sight, thinking comically that it was a princess dress for a grown-up, it not occurring to her that she was, technically speaking anyway, now a princess, thanks to her marriage to a prince. The modest neckline and long sleeves might not be eye-catching, but the gown had a quiet, stylish elegance that appealed to her.

As she emerged fully clad from the bathroom, her make-up applied in a few subtle touches, Saif stilled halfway out of his shirt. Tati paused as well, reluctantly enthralled by the expanse of muscular bronzed chest on view. He was beautifully built from his broad shoulders to his narrow waist and long, powerful thighs. For a split second she remembered the weight of him over her and she was suddenly so short of breath she almost choked, her cheeks flaming as she coughed and croaked, 'Sorry, wasn't expecting to see you!'

'That dress is spectacular on you,' Saif breathed appreciatively, because that particular shade of grey enhanced the deep blue of her eyes and lent a glow to her porcelain skin while the tailoring of the dress sleekly outlined the feminine curves of her lush figure.

'Seriously?' Tati queried, her head lifting high again.

'Seriously,' he confirmed, strolling across the room to indicate the gift boxes on the highly polished dressing table. 'These are for you.'

'Presents? It's not my birthday yet,' Tati told him, lifting a gift box with the certainty that such packaging could only contain jewellery and uncomfortable at the prospect.

'As my wife, you need to wear jewels. It's expected,' Saif said smoothly.

Tati dealt him a suspicious glance before opening the boxes to reveal a diamond necklace and earrings. 'These are...spectacular,' she whispered truthfully, a fingertip reverently stroking the rainbow fire of a single gleaming gem. 'But I *shouldn't*—'

'No. These are family jewels that my father once gave to my mother. My mother left everything behind when she left Alharia and it would please my father very much to know that his gifts are being worn again.'

'Is your mother still alive?' Tati asked gently, detaching the necklace from the box, feeling the cool of the beautiful gems against her skin as her reluctance to wear the diamonds melted away.

'No, she passed away about three years ago in a helicopter crash with her husband,' Saif explained.

'Did you ever meet her again after she left your father? Or even see her?' she prompted, intrigued by his seemingly calm attitude to his abandonment as a child.

'I was devastated when I heard of her death,' Saif heard himself admit, disconcerting himself almost as much as he surprised Tati with that declaration. 'While she was alive I could toy with the idea of looking her up and getting to know her—should she have been interested—but once she was gone, that possibility was gone for ever.'

'I know what you mean,' Tati murmured wryly. 'I wrote to my father when I was a teenager asking him to meet me and, even though it had been proven in court that I was his daughter, he wrote back telling me that he wasn't my father and didn't wish to hear from me again. It hurt a lot. My mother had tried to warn me that he wasn't interested, but I was too stubborn to listen.'

'My father told me that he didn't think that my mother had

many maternal genes. Some women don't, I believe, and presumably fathers can suffer from the same flaw. Let me help,' he murmured, crossing the room to remove the necklace from her fingers and settle it round her throat, his fingertips brushing the nape of her neck as he clasped it, sending a faint quiver of awareness through her.

Awesomely conscious of his proximity and the familiar scent of his cologne, Tati struggled to behave normally as she donned the earrings and finally turned to let him see her.

'Perfect,' Saif pronounced.

'I'll wait downstairs for you,' Tati told him breathlessly, not sure that she could withstand the desire to watch him while he undressed, and mortified by the temptation. It was as though Saif had cast some weird kind of sex spell over her, she conceded shamefacedly as Marcel offered her a drink in the grand main salon.

It was normal, healthy lust, Tati supposed of her fixation and her growing obsession with Saif's extraordinary eyes, Saif's hands, what he could do with them, how it felt when he touched her...

Enough of this nonsense, she mentally screamed at herself. She was behaving with all the maturity of a schoolgirl with a first crush. None of it was any big deal, she told herself bracingly, deciding that she was only so bemused and off balance because she was a decidedly late starter when it came to the opposite sex. All over again, she wished she had acquired some of her cousin's glossy cool and confidence. But, marooned on a country estate without money and with few social outlets, Tati had not enjoyed her cousin's opportunities to meet men and date. In reality, Tati thought with regret, she probably *was* as naïve as an adolescent.

When she climbed into the limo with Saif she was, momentarily, tempted to pinch herself before accepting that the designer gown, the incredibly handsome man by her side and the opulent mode of travel could figure in *her* new lifestyle. It was even more ironic to know that her uncle and aunt would now be furious that *she* was the one benefiting from the marriage rather than their daughter. They had needed her to marry the Prince to gain access to that dowry, but it would still outrage them that their niece was now living in luxury. And for the first time, Tati acknowledged that she was grateful to have escaped her relatives' demands, relieved to know that in many ways she was finally free and that her mother's residence in her care home was secure. She would eventually be able to look towards her own future, unfettered by the limits imposed on her by others.

'You're very quiet this evening,' Saif remarked as they crossed the pavement to the large illuminated mansion with its classic gardens that were equally well-lit to show off glimpses of women in elaborate dresses and men in dinner jackets, their necks craned as they watched the glorious fireworks shooting and sparkling across the night sky in a rainbow of colour and illumination.

'Gosh, these people know how to party,' Tati commented, hugely impressed by her surroundings as they stepped into a brilliantly lit hall and a crush of little groups of chattering people. And everybody, literally *everybody*, looked as though they might be a celebrity of some kind. In such company, neither her gown nor her magnificent diamonds could ever look like overkill. 'Are the hosts close friends of yours?'

'No. I owe this invitation to the relative whose house we are using,' Saif admitted. 'But I have no doubt that I will see familiar faces here.'

'Yes. I suppose you get to meet a lot of people.'

'Because the Emir doesn't travel. I take care of Alharia's diplomatic interests in his place. It entails attending formal receptions and dinners. You'll be accompanying me to some of them,' he declared, startling her.

'*Me?*' Tati stressed in a low mutter of disconcertion as he curved a guiding hand to her taut spine.

'The joys of marrying a crown prince,' Saif murmured teasingly, his breath fanning her cheekbone. 'Some of that kind of socialising is boring but, equally, sometimes it's fascinating.'

'I should've realised that there would be...er...duties to carry out in this role.' Tati sighed. 'It all happened so fast, though... One minute Ana was running for the airport and the next we were married.'

In the midst of that speech, Saif was hailed by two men, who addressed him in another language. It wasn't French and it wasn't English, and she was introduced and served with a drink of champagne by a passing waiter before they moved on into a room. 'Could we go out and see the fireworks?' she pressed once they were alone again.

Saif glanced down at her in surprise, for in his experience women in their finery avoided the outdoors like the plague. The unhidden eagerness brimming in her upturned gaze, however, made him laugh and for a moment she seemed much younger than her years. 'Why do you want to see them?'

'Mum was so terrified of fireworks that I never got to see them properly as a child. When she was young she witnessed a dreadful accident, which injured a friend at a firework event, and it put her off them for life,' she explained. 'Every Bonfire Night, we sat indoors with the curtains closed and then, the next day, Ana would tell me how much fun she had had at whichever party she had been invited to and I would feel madly jealous.'

Saif's expressive lips quirked. 'Naturally.'

They stood on the paved terrace watching the display until a low murmur of a comment made Tati turn her head. A very tall brunette in a startlingly see-through dress was stalking towards them. For a split second, Tati was guilty of staring, taken aback by a woman revealing that much flesh in public, showing off her bare breasts and her nipple rings below the thin white chiffon gown. Truly, however, Tati was forced to admit, the woman had a *superb* body. In haste she turned her head away from the conspicuous beauty, only to stiffen in astonishment when the woman appeared in front of them and greeted Saif with the kind of familiarity that no woman wanted to see her male companion receive in her presence.

'Saif!' she carolled, followed by a voluble gush of French as she walked her long, manicured fingertips up over his chest in a very inviting gesture.

'Juliette,' Saif murmured with rather more restraint. 'May I introduce you to my wife, Tatiana?'

'Your *wife*?' Juliette gasped in consternation while walking her fingers down over his flat muscular stomach in unmistakable invitation.

Tati couldn't stop herself. In a knee-jerk reaction, she reached out and pushed the brunette's hand away from Saif. 'His wife, sorry,' she said with a smile that she was sure was unconvincing.

A split second later, Juliette having languorously taken the hint and strolled away, Tati was shattered by her own possessive and wholly inappropriate reaction to another woman touching the man she had married. Saif didn't belong to her in the usual sense of married people. They weren't in love either. She had come up with the label of friends with benefits but even that wasn't a fair tag for them, because people in that kind of relationship were generally those who had had a reasonably long and close friendship before intimacy developed and she and Saif didn't fit into that category either. The intense colour of mortification swept her cheeks and she felt as though she were burning alive inside her own skin.

'I'm sorry… She was annoying me,' she said uncomfortably.

'It was unseemly for her to touch me in that way,' Saif murmured, appraising her with gleaming green eyes fringed by black lashes. 'There is no need for an apology.'

But regardless of what he said, Tati felt very differently. She had shocked herself with that little show of possessive behaviour. After all, she wasn't entitled to be that territorial with Saif. She should not be experiencing any prompting to react as though she were jealous of another woman touching him. Of course, she wasn't jealous or possessive of him, she told herself fiercely.

'And it was sexy,' Saif murmured in a husky undertone, gazing down at her with potent green eyes of appreciation. 'Very, very sexy.'

Stunned, Tati looked back at him in wonderment and then she couldn't help herself—she laughed, and all her discomfiture was washed away as though it had never been. Evidently, Saif took a very different view of her attitude, but as the evening wore on she continued to marvel at the way she had behaved. Clearly, she *was* possessive of Saif. Was that simply because she had gone to bed with him?

Brow furrowing, she attempted, during all the chatter, the dancing and the eating that comprised the lively party atmosphere, to pin down what she was feeling about the man she had married. It was surprisingly difficult. She had travelled at speed from raging resentment and frustration over her powerlessness to grudging acceptance that Saif had had little more choice than she had in their marriage. And somewhere along the line she had begun lusting after him, *liking* him, appreciating his calm, measured approach to life. It certainly didn't mean that she was developing any kind of mental attachment to him, she assured herself confidently.

She wasn't so naïve that she would confuse lust and love, was she? Admittedly, she was enthralled by the fluid movement of his hips against hers on the dance floor, the pulsing ache building between her thighs and the provocative awareness that she was having the *same* physical effect on him. Unlike her, he couldn't hide his response. She was insanely conscious of his arousal. And that sheer reciprocity thrilled Tati because it made her feel powerful and seductive for the first time in her life, no longer a weak pawn in someone else's game, but an equal. She was finally making her own choices and doing what pleased her, rather than someone else.

'So, you and Juliette?' Tati whispered as she stretched up to Saif. 'Do share...'

Saif tensed, wondering why on earth she would ask such an

awkward question before reminding himself that women were often morbidly curious about a man's past. His three older sisters had taught him that, always prying where their interest was least welcome.

'Was she your girlfriend?' Tati prompted.

'No. It was a casual connection.' Saif shrugged in emphasis, hoping that her curiosity concluded there, long brown fingers skimming soothingly down the side of her face. 'I can't keep my hands off you,' he breathed with a sudden raw edge to his dark, deep drawl that sent a responsive shiver of delight down her taut spine.

'It's mutual,' she whispered.

Even so, she was still assailed by a sudden perverse attack of guilt and discomfiture because, try as she might to be a bolder version of her old self, being bold still felt sinful and brazen. She would have to work harder on that outlook, she told herself firmly, because being quiet, accepting and the person others preferred her to be had only served to deprive her of her freedom and her choices in life. Wanting Saif, allowing herself to succumb to that sizzling chemistry that went way beyond anything she had ever experienced, was probably the most daring thing she had ever done. And one of the best things about Saif, Tati reflected happily, was that he hadn't known her as she used to be and, with him, she could be entirely her true self.

He curved an arm round her in the limousine on the drive back to the house. She was gloriously aware of the strength of his lean, powerful frame up against her and the subtle musky, fragrant scent of him that close. Her heart was pounding in her chest when he stopped on the landing halfway up the fabulous staircase of the town house and hauled her up against him to kiss her with all the fierce hunger she craved. The lancing touch of his tongue inside her mouth set her on fire and a choked moan escaped low in her throat.

Her whole body was surging with wild anticipation and, lifting her, he cannoned into the bedroom, pushing her back against the wall and pinning her there afresh to crush her lips hungrily beneath his again. Her heart was thumping, her pulses thrumming because that rocketing passion of his took her over and thrilled her to death. It was the exact match of her own, a wild, seething need that drove out every other logical thought, leaving only the wanting behind.

Saif turned her round to run down the zip on her dress, pushing it off her shoulders, stroking it down her arms until it dropped round her feet. Kicking off her shoes, heartbeat accelerating, she stepped out of the dress. His lips traced the line of her shoulder and every nerve ending in her body leapt to attention as she pressed back into the heat of him, breathless and boneless with need.

'I like the lingerie,' Saif husked with appreciation as he carefully lifted her and lowered her down onto the well-sprung bed. 'But I think I'll like you even better out of it.'

Flushed and wide-eyed, her eyes very blue in her face, Tati watched Saif shed his tailored dinner jacket and bow tie, standing over her while he unbuttoned his dress shirt, smouldering emerald-green eyes locked to the silvery-grey cobweb-fine bra and panties she sported and the firm, soft curves they enhanced. 'Your eyes are so unusual,' she whispered, and then wanted to cringe at herself for saying it just at that moment.

'As I said, my only inheritance from my mother,' Saif muttered, his shirt fluttering to the floor, exposing an impressive bronzed torso composed of chiselled abs and a flat, taut stomach and the intriguing little furrow of black hair that ran down below his waistband. 'But I didn't like being different as a child when everyone else's eyes were dark. You occasionally see blue eyes in the desert tribes but never this shade.'

Something clenched almost painfully in Tati's stomach as she looked up at him. He came down on the bed beside her, naked and aroused and, oh, so sexy to her riveted gaze. 'I *like* your eyes,' she framed unevenly, her chest lifting as she dragged in a sustaining breath.

His expert mouth toyed with hers while he released her bra and explored the pouting swells and hard tips eager for his attention. He trailed his lips down to tease those rosy, sensitive crowns and her hips rose and she gasped, her entire body shimmying on an edge of gathering anticipation, desire twisting sharp as a knife inside her, tensing every muscle. He skimmed away the panties, parted her thighs and she trembled, feeling shy, tempted to say no but too aroused to have that discipline.

And then he employed his tongue on her and exquisite sensation flooded her. He dipped a finger into her tight channel and her spine arched, the craving climbing again. Melting heat liquefied her pelvis, excitement gripping her taut, and before she could even work out what was happening to her, she became a creature only capable of response, so worked up to a peak that she could only moan and gasp while her body moved in a compulsive rhythm. When she reached a climax it was fast and furious, ripping through her quivering length in an explosion of raw heat and ecstasy, leaving her flopping back against the pillows, limp as a noodle.

Saif dug into the cabinet beside the bed and donned protection. 'We will take no further risks,' he murmured with a slanting, charismatic smile.

Relief filled Tati because she had been thinking that perhaps she ought to go out and look for an English-speaking doctor and ask for replacement pills. But wouldn't Saif's precautions be sufficient until she went back to England to see her mother and reclaimed her possessions from her uncle's home? Convinced that she no longer needed to worry on that score, Tati wrapped her arms round him as he came down to her again. Her body was still pulsing with the aftermath of satiation and highly sensitive.

'I've been thinking about this moment all day and all evening,' Saif groaned, startling green eyes alight with desire.

'*All* day?'

'Yes.'

'Then why did we wait this long?' she whispered as he shifted against her tender core, sliding into her in a sure rocking motion that sent her heart rate flying.

'You tell me,' Saif urged thickly, awash with surprise at the sheer mutuality of sex with Tatiana.

With a twist of his lean hips he pushed deep and fast into the tight, damp welcome awaiting him and he listened with satisfaction to his bride moan with a pleasure that only echoed his own.

His hard, insistent rhythm enthralled her in the wild ride that followed. Excitement roared higher for her with his every thrust. She moved against him, lost in the experience as her excitement rose higher and higher, the need tugging at her every sense pushing her to a frenzied peak where only mindless sensation controlled her. When the glorious wave of excitement tipped her over the edge, she cried out in writhing delight before the last of her energy drained away, leaving her limp and winded.

Saif thrust away the bedding and fell back from her. 'I'm hot...'

Tati grinned and rolled closer, a possessive hand smoothing down over his heaving chest. 'Yes, *very* hot.'

Saif sat up and pulled her to him. 'And you're joining me in the shower.'

'Why? I'm not fit for anything else right now,' she protested, shy about getting out of bed naked in front of him and knowing how silly that was after what they had shared.

'I'm not ready to let go of you yet,' Saif told her truthfully, his fertile imagination already arranging her in erotic positions round the marble bathroom and seeing possibilities everywhere. *Cool off*, his brain told him, *step back, regain control*, because he suddenly felt as though he were in dangerous territory, a territory without rules or boundaries and not his style at all.

That uneasy feeling, that sense of wrong, stabbed at him because Saif liked everything laid out neat and tidy, nothing left to chance. And yet here he was with a wife who wasn't a genuine wife, a lover who wasn't a simple lover and a friend who wasn't a real friend. Where was he supposed to go next? What was his end goal?

And even though Tati knew in her heart of hearts that she shouldn't go there, she was too curious to silence the question brimming on her lips. 'And when will you be ready?'

Having switched on the shower, Saif swung back to her, startlingly handsome with his black hair tousled, his green eyes very shrewd, sharp and bright, his strong jawline defined by black stubble. 'Ready for what?' he queried.

'Ready to let me go?' she almost whispered in daring clarification, sliding past him to take refuge behind the tiled shower wall where he could no longer see her.

Saif froze. 'You're asking how soon we can decently go for a divorce without unduly surprising anyone?' he murmured flatly, unprepared for that sudden far-reaching question and wishing she hadn't asked before he had even had the time to decide on the wisest approach to their predicament. 'Possibly six months...a year? I don't really know yet. We *should* make it look as though we've given the marriage a fair chance before throwing in the cards.'

Six months to a year, Tati mused, thinking what a very short space of time that was. A mere blink and their relationship would be over, done and dusted, ready for the archives. Her tummy hollowed out and sank while she busied herself washing her hair, her movements slowing as she became aware of the little muscles she had strained and the ache between her thighs, the inescapable reminders of their intimacy. Friends with benefits, she reminded herself doggedly, but that tag no longer enjoyed the same exhilarating ring of daring that it had first seemed to have. Indeed, all of a sudden that style of thinking seemed a little sad and immature, she acknowledged ruefully. Saif was making it very clear that what they currently had was a casual fling with an ending scripted in advance.

An ending written and decided at the same instant they had married, she reminded herself. There was nothing personal about his decision, she reasoned, determined not to take umbrage. Saif could never have planned to stay married long-term to the bride his father had picked for him and she could hardly blame him for that, could she? Saif was way too sophisticated to settle for an arranged marriage with a stranger. And when the stranger was also an unsuitable foreigner, a divorce was a fairly predictable conclusion.

Of course, *she* wanted a divorce as well, Tati assured herself. Naturally, she wanted to reclaim her own life again. Yet it was a challenge for Tati to consider a future that she had never been free to consider before. And *would* she be free?

After all, for how long would her marriage to Saif ensure that her uncle would continue paying her mother's expenses? Now that he had got the money he wanted, it was difficult to have faith in the older man's word. Perhaps her mother *would* eventually have to be moved to a cheaper care facility, Tati reasoned unhappily. Beggars couldn't be choosers. There were worse options, she reminded herself impatiently. Whatever happened, she would handle it and she would help her mother to handle it too. Although, had Saif meant it when he had said that from now on *he* would handle her mother's care bills? But, for how long would he be prepared to do that? Would there be a divorce settlement that covered that need?

Tomorrow, she decided, she would phone the nursing home to check on the older woman. She would also ring her mother's cousin, Pauline, who lived only yards from the care facility and who, as Mariana's only other visitor, always had a more personal take on Mariana's condition. She would discuss the possibility of a move with Pauline.

How could she possibly accept *more* money from Saif? Neither she nor her mother were his responsibilities. They could not acknowledge on the one hand that theirs was not a real marriage and then behave as though it were when it came to money. She had to grow up and stop looking to other people to support her, Tati told herself in exasperation. Saif didn't owe her anything!

CHAPTER SEVEN

ALMOST THREE WEEKS into their stay, the bridal couple were viewing the catacombs beneath Paris.

Saif was uncomfortable with his surroundings. He had done all the tourist stuff without complaint for his wife's benefit. He had taken her for a cruise on the Seine and they had climbed the Eiffel Tower at night when it was an illuminated beacon of golden light across the city. He had even dutifully snacked on macarons at the famous Ladurée, while treacherously thinking that they could not match similar Alharian delicacies. But the catacombs were proving a step too far for him because he felt claustrophobic below the low ceilings, and the skulls and remains of six million souls stacked up to make artistic patterns in the walls did not improve his mood. Tatiana might enjoy the morbid atmosphere, but it spooked him.

Tati sidled up behind Saif, forcing his bodyguards to back away, and stretched up to cover his eyes with her hands. 'I'm a zombie… *Run!*' she whispered in the creepiest voice she could contrive.

Saif whirled round and gazed down into her lovely smiling face as she giggled, eyes dancing with mischief. It was one of those occasions when she made him feel twice her age, yet it was also one of those times he cherished because she brightened his days like sunshine while simultaneously turning the darker hours into sensual experiences of indescribable pleasure. He valued a bride, blessed with such advantages, obviously he valued her greatly.

That wasn't something he thought about much, though, because she had been with him round the clock since their marriage. He did know, however, that he wasn't looking forward to her departure the following day for a trip back to England to see her mother. She had refused the offer of his company, saying it was unnecessary. He should have been relieved by that breezy dismissal because he had a duty to return to Alharia and see his own parent, not to mention needing to deal with at least a dozen tasks he had been unable to tackle from a distance. For the first time he was acknowledging how much he missed his father and how lucky he had been in the older man's reliable care. Yet Tati's regular references to her mother and her deep attachment to her often made him wonder what he had missed out on.

As a further complication for Saif, there were the worrying irregularities uncovered by the investigation agency he had initially hired to provide him with a background check on his bride. As yet he had no idea what those anomalies meant, and he didn't want to upset Tatiana with concerns that might yet prove to be groundless. He wished to handle that matter in person, rather than allow a member of his staff to deal with such a confidential matter, but if the agency's suspicions *were* true, there *would* be criminal charges brought, he thought with angry disgust.

'Sometimes…you are way too serious,' Tati scolded softly, a fingertip gently tracing the firm sculpted line of his full lower lip.

'But I have you to remind me of the lighter side of life,' Saif countered, closing an arm round her to move her on. 'Let's get out of here…we're eating out tonight.'

'It's sort of our last night,' Tati muttered abstractedly, small fingers toying with the magnificent emerald that hung on a chain round her slender neck as they emerged back into the sunshine, the light momentarily blinding her.

Saif had somehow contrived to talk her out of returning to England the week before and she wasn't quite sure how he had done it, because she did miss that regular connection with her mother, slender though it was. It was true that her mother didn't look for her if she was absent. Indeed, Mariana had to be introduced to her daughter at every visit because she no longer recognised her. The time for producing the family photo albums and reminding Mariana was long past because it only confused and upset the older woman now to be confronted with faces and events she had forgotten. So, Tati was accustomed to a mother who greeted her each time as a stranger. And every time, it broke her heart a little more.

For dinner, she picked a dress from her array of choices that she had been saving for a special occasion. It was a cerise-pink print with slender straps and that whole summery vibe somehow encapsulated the holiday spirit of freedom that she had revelled in since her arrival in Paris. Saif, she thought ruefully, really knew how to show a woman a good time. Although he spent several hours a day working, he had devoted more time to ensuring that she enjoyed herself. And whether they had been admiring the gorgeous cathedral of Sainte-Chapelle or wandering hand in hand around Saint-Germain-des-Prés, where she had explored intriguing little shops full of wonders or sat outside cafés watching the world go by, Saif had made a praiseworthy and highly successful effort to entertain her. She had gathered a handful of little gifts that would make her mother's eyes sparkle but she felt guilty as hell for not returning sooner to England.

She had worried too when she hadn't heard anything more from Ana and her texts had failed to receive a response. She was beginning to suspect that the beach wedding that her cousin had been so excited about hadn't happened because Ana documented the big moments in her life with photos and she would definitely have sent at least one photo. Sadly, Tati was reluctant to contact her uncle and aunt to check on Ana's well-being because of the way they had behaved at the wedding in Alharia. She would be staying in a hotel near the care home because she wasn't sure that her relatives would even be willing to offer her hospitality.

'I'll have to pack up and collect my stuff from my uncle's house while I'm in England,' she sighed over dinner in a sophisticated bistro in possession of several Michelin stars that evening.

'No, that would be unwise. You should *avoid* visiting Fosters Manor,' Saif startled her by intoning with a harsh edge of warning to his dark drawl.

'Why on earth would you say that?'

Saif studied her. She was pretty as a picture in her dress, blond hair gleaming below the low lights, soft blue eyes politely enquiring, so naturally lively that she exuded a positive glow of vibrance, but she was also so trusting that she would be innately vulnerable to anyone wishing her ill.

As Saif looked, a stab of lust pulsed in his groin and he almost winced at his own predictability. *That* was beginning to bother him and make him think that the absence of his bride for a week would do him good. He couldn't afford to want Tatiana too much or too often, nor could he allow himself to depend on her for anything when she was only passing through his life. It was the first time he had ever had a longer, more intimate relationship with a woman and he told himself that it was excellent practice for the future when he would surely find a more lasting partner. Unhappily, however, Tatiana, with all her little individual quirks and inherent sensuality, didn't feel like a practice run for *any* other woman. Even so, he knew that he didn't have Tatiana to keep and he acted accordingly.

'Why did you say that?' Tati pressed again, her smooth brow furrowing.

'Your uncle and aunt are hostile towards you, and I don't trust them,' Saif told her truthfully.

'You think they might murder me and bury me below the floorboards?' Tati teased.

'Safety concerns are not a joke, Tatiana,' Saif sliced back, pushing away his serving of Baba au Rhum with a frown as his appetite died. 'If you *do* choose to visit your relatives, keep your bodyguards with you at all times. But there is no need for you to visit their home merely to collect your possessions. That can be arranged for you.'

'I don't want my aunt Elizabeth going through my belongings,' Tati said with distaste. 'And that's what would happen if I don't go myself. Are you serious about bodyguards accompanying me to England?'

'Of course. You are my wife, the Crown Princess of Alharia, and as such require security measures,' Saif parried without hesitation. 'It's not as though you wear a label saying that you are not my "real" wife, as you are so fond of telling me…or as though anyone wishing me harm would even believe that.'

Tati reddened and shifted uncomfortably in her chair. That was a comment she had regularly made as much for her own benefit as his, because there had been several occasions of late when she had felt that they had crossed boundaries that she had not foreseen at the outset of their agreement. For a start, Saif could not be dissuaded from buying her gifts, not least the huge emerald currently nestling above her breasts.

He seemed to be the sort of guy who liked to buy things for women, and time and time again he had surprised her. She had a gorgeous silk scarf that had cost the earth, designer shoes that looked as though they had been sprinkled with stardust and a diamond bracelet that was blinding in daylight. On her twenty-second birthday, he had engulfed her in gifts and treats and that lavish desire to spoil her rotten had touched her to the heart. There had been a whole host of presents from flowers to

little trinkets she had admired. He was ridiculously generous
and totally out of touch with what being friends with benefits
should encompass—that being, in her view, a much looser and
more casual connection.

Only she could hardly criticise Saif when she had been
shamelessly, wantonly hogging his attention whenever she got
the opportunity. There was nothing casual about her behaviour,
she allowed guiltily. They had had sex on his office desk the
day before because she was turning into a stage five clinger
who found it hard to keep her distance when he was working
for several hours.

'Will you promise me that you will be careful of your security while you are away from me?' Saif pressed gravely. 'Even
though you think that my concern is unnecessary.'

Tati nodded hurriedly, disconcerted by his reading her so
accurately, something he often did and which she found un-
nerving. The sea-glass brilliance of his eyes made warmth pool
in her pelvis, sent her pulse racing, made it difficult for her to
catch her breath.

'You haven't eaten much this evening,' Saif commented.

'I probably ate too much all day,' Tati quipped, reluctant to
explain the very slight sense of nausea that had afflicted her
when the scent of meat assailed her nostrils. She wasn't actually sick and didn't think that she was falling ill, but her usual
enthusiasm for food had recently dwindled. Possibly it was the
result of eating too many rich, elaborate meals, she reflected
ruefully, thinking how easily she had become accustomed to
being thoroughly spoiled on the gastronomic front. Now she
was clearly getting fussy, craving salad when there were barely
any cold options on offer.

An hour later, she walked into the dressing room off their
bedroom to check the case she had already partially packed.

'The staff could have taken care of this,' Saif told her from the doorway, moving forward to glance down into the case with a frown. 'You don't seem to be taking very much.'

'At most I'll be away a week and I won't be going any place where I need to dress up,' Tati proffered.

A week. A kind of relief engulfed Saif. A week was no time for a man accustomed to living without a woman although it was astonishing, he acknowledged, how quickly he had become used to her presence and how rarely she irritated him. He was reserved, a loner, and had always suspected that marriage would be a challenge for him, but Tatiana was accepting rather than demanding and took him as he was. He ran an appreciative fingertip over the porcelain pale expanse of her back, caressing the soft silky skin.

'Need some help getting out of this?' Saif husked, tugging on the strap of the dress.

Tati stifled a grin. 'Go ahead...'

The zip went down, and the dress floated to her feet. She stepped unhurriedly out of her heels, superaware of the fine turquoise silk bra and panties she wore and the intensity of Saif's appraisal. When she glanced up, his stunning green eyes glittered like emeralds and butterflies took flight in her tummy, her body's programmed response to that appreciation as natural as her need to breathe.

Lifting her out of the folds of cloth on the floor, he pinned her slight body to his, a large masculine hand splayed across her bottom to hold her close. His tailored trousers could not hide the hard heat of his erection, and as she felt the raw promise of him against her stomach, fierce desire flashed through her like a storm warning. Her arms snapped round his neck as his mouth came crashing down on hers with a ravaging, smouldering hunger that matched her own.

Somewhere in the background a vaguely familiar snatch of music was playing, and her brain strove to rise to alert status again. There was a reason why she should know that sound, only it didn't seem important with her fingers raking through

Saif's silky black hair while her heart was racing and her body was pulsing with insane arousal. He was tumbling her down on the bed with scant ceremony when she realised that that sound was her mobile phone ringing and that there were very good reasons why she always leapt to answer it on the rare occasion that it rang. Consternation gripping her, Tati broke free of that kiss and rolled over, almost falling off the bed in her haste to reach her clutch bag and the phone within it.

Half-naked, she sat on the floor clutching the silent phone and checked the call that she had missed. It was from her mother's nursing home as she had feared. Within the space of a minute she was ringing back, identifying herself, listening with an anxious expression to what the manager was telling her and asking apprehensive questions, all beneath Saif's frowning gaze. Assuring the older woman that she would be returning to England as soon as she could arrange it, she sat silent, tears prickling her eyes and stinging them before slowly overflowing to drip down her cheeks.

'I should have gone back last week. I should have known better. If anything happens to Mum, I'll never forgive myself for neglecting her,' she whispered brokenly.

'You haven't neglected her. Even the most dutiful daughter is entitled to a holiday.' Saif crouched down in front of her. 'What's happened?'

'Mum has a chest infection…she's had a few of them but they think she'll have to go into hospital this time,' Tati muttered wretchedly. 'I should've visited her last week, Saif.'

'That wouldn't have prevented her illness,' Saif pointed out shrewdly. 'You will want to return to England as soon as possible. I will make the arrangements.'

While he engaged in phone calls, Tati stayed on the floor, rocking slightly in self-comforting mode as she thought with a shudder about how horribly selfish she had been. She had always placed her mother's needs first…until *Saif* came into her life. And then everything in her world had changed. Saif had turned her world inside out and upside down. Emotions had come surging in a colourful explosion: anger, excitement, attraction, a shocking awakening to all the feelings she had no reason to feel before. And, unforgivably, she had stopped putting her mother first because Saif had turned her head and made her as irresponsible as a teenager.

'I will come with you,' Saif informed her gravely.

'No...no, that's not necessary,' Tati said sharply, reluctant to expose her fragile mother to a stranger, even though she knew that Saif would be kind and respectful. But that protective instinct was hard to combat and, what was more, she didn't want the temptation of Saif being with her in England when she needed to focus solely on her mother.

'I think it is necessary when you will need my support,' Saif overruled.

'If I hadn't been forced to stay abroad, I would never have been away from her for so long,' Tati argued, knowing she was making a veiled and unjust accusation but wanting to punish him as much as she wanted to punish herself. 'Mum's had these infections before. I don't want anyone with me. She gets upset if she sees a strange face, particularly male ones. I don't need you.'

Tati watched his lean, darkly handsome face freeze in receipt of that ungenerous response and her conscience smote her. She didn't need him, couldn't afford to need him, had to persuade herself that she didn't *need* Saif in any corner of her world. Why was it that only at the moment she realised that she *did* crave his support she grasped why it would be even more foolish to rely on him?

Because they weren't a *real* couple or a *real* husband and wife where such troubles as family illness were shared. They were friends with benefits at most, casual lovers at the least and in that type of relationship people didn't get involved in the commitment of deeper problems. And she couldn't afford to forget that because very soon, perhaps sooner than she even believed, she and Saif would be separating, their intimacy at an end. That was what her future held and wanting anything more was nonsensical and unrealistic...

CHAPTER EIGHT

'GO ON,' URGED PAULINE, Mariana Hamilton's cousin, as Tati hovered at the foot of the hospital bed, torn by indecision. 'Your mum's sleeping peacefully. This is the time to go and take care of other things.'

Tati thanked the older woman warmly. In recent days, she had been very grateful for Pauline's unflagging support and affection for her parent. Her mother's chest infection had exacerbated, and she was still in hospital and upsettingly weak. The medical staff seemed to doubt that her mother *could* recover, which had made Tati afraid to abandon her vigil because she didn't want her mother to slip away without her. Lack of sleep had drained her complexion and etched shadows below her eyes.

She had phoned her uncle to update him on her mother's condition but his lack of interest in his sister's state of health had been unhidden. She had explained that she would be calling to collect her possessions and had asked after Ana, relieved but a little surprised to learn that her cousin was currently back at home. If that was true, why on earth hadn't Ana responded to her texts? Tati suppressed her disquiet, which was, after all, only one of several worries haunting her and giving her sleepless nights.

Having initially assured Saif that she would only be away a

week, she had now been absent for almost three. He had suggested that he join her, had offered his assistance, had, in short, done everything a committed partner could be expected to do in such circumstances, but Tati had held him at arm's length. After all, their marriage was only temporary, and he had no obligation towards her mother. But at heart, Tati had a far stronger and more personal reason for avoiding Saif: the pregnancy test awaiting her in her hotel bathroom. If her worst fears were proved to have a solid basis in fact, she didn't know what she would do or even how she would face telling him.

Was sheer cowardice the reason that the test had sat unopened for a week? She was ashamed of her lack of backbone but at the same time she was dealing with the awful awareness that her mother's life was slowly and inexorably draining away. For the moment that was sufficient to cope with.

As she settled into the limousine that Saif had insisted she utilise, she nervously fingered the emerald on the chain that hung beneath her silk shirt. It had become something of a talisman through the dark days of stress and loneliness. She missed him *so* much. Her breath caught in her throat as she stifled an angry sob because she was so furious with herself for failing to keep her emotions under control.

When had she begun caring about Saif, needing him, wanting him around? Those feelings had crept up on her without her noticing in Paris and, now she was deprived of him, those longings and the sense of loss inflicted by his absence had only grown stronger.

She had been in England for only a couple of days when she'd registered that her period was very late. At first, she had blamed that on stress. Eventually, she had acknowledged that the smell of certain foods made her tummy roll and that the coffee she usually enjoyed now tasted bitter. Her breasts were tender and bouts of nausea troubled her at odd times of the day. The fear that she could be pregnant had made her very anxious, but it had still taken time for her to muster the courage to buy a pregnancy test. She would do the test once she got back to the hotel, she told herself ruefully. No more putting it off!

Pulling up outside her uncle and aunt's home, Fosters Manor, Tati was enormously conscious that she was making a swanky arrival in a limo accompanied by a carload of diligent security men. As she climbed out, she straightened the light jacket she wore teamed with neat-fitting cigarette pants, a silk top and high heels. Yes, her life and her appearance had certainly changed, she reflected ruefully, heading for the front entrance rather than the rear one that she had once used.

'You can wait for me in the car,' she told the men standing behind her. 'I'll be an hour at most.'

Not one of them moved an inch into retreat, she noted without surprise. They all became uniformly deaf when her requests contravened Saif's instructions, which seemed to encompass keeping her in physical view at all times. Her aunt answered the doorbell wearing a sour expression.

'It won't take me long to pack up,' she assured the older woman quietly.

'It's been done for you,' Elizabeth Hamilton asserted, indicating the dustbin bags messily littering a corner of the dusty hall.

'Oh, thanks,' Tati said stiffly, forcing a fake polite smile and advancing on the collection, leafing through the pile for the only items of value in her care. 'Mum's jewellery box doesn't seem to be here. It's probably still sitting on the dressing table,' she remarked.

Elizabeth's face froze. 'What would you want with that old thing?'

'I want it because it's Mum's. I'll go and fetch it,' Tati said decisively, directing her companions towards the pathetic collection of bags and asking them to put them in the car.

As she started upstairs, her aunt said thinly, 'That box contained some of Granny Milly's pieces.'

'Yes, and they belong to my mother,' Tati retorted crisply. 'They were given to her by *her* mother.'

'I think you and my sister have done well enough out of this family,' Rupert Hamilton informed her from a doorway, his big bluff form spread in an aggressive stance. 'The jewellery should stay with us where it belongs.'

'No,' Tati argued, lifting her chin. 'Any dues my mother or I owed were paid in full in Alharia.'

'Call off your watchdogs!' her uncle instructed with a scowl as two of her protection team followed her upstairs.

Ignoring him, Tati continued up another two flights to her small bedroom. It wasn't quite in the attic, but it was close enough and in bygone days it *had* been a maid's room. It was a relief to see her mother's jewellery box on the dressing table but when she opened it, she found that it contained only the inexpensive costume pieces. A pearl pendant and earrings and a rather distinctive diamond swan brooch were missing. She tucked the box under her arm, wondering what to do next, reluctant to stage a showdown with her relatives that there would be no coming back from, wondering what Saif would advise because he had a cool head.

'Well, well, well, you're looking...*different*.' Ana selected the word with a sneering curl of her lip as she leant against the landing wall. 'Very fancy.'

'Ana!' Tati responded in cheerful relief at seeing her cousin again. 'Why haven't you called me or answered my texts? Did you change your number?'

'Why would I call you when you stole my bridegroom?' Ana asked with wide eyes, shattering Tati with that absurd question.

'What happened with George?' Tati asked gently.

Ana contorted her lovely face into a grimace. 'He only proposed to stop me marrying someone else. He wasn't willing to set a wedding date once I was home again.'

'I'm so sorry,' Tati said truthfully.

'Oh, I'm sure you're not... How could you be?' Ana demanded thinly, her voice a rising crescendo of complaint. 'My departure worked out *very* well for you. You married a billionaire and now travel around in a flippin' limousine with body-guards! You robbed me of what should have been mine!'

Mindful of the presence of the protection team, Tati winced. 'Let's talk downstairs in private,' she suggested.

'I don't want to talk about it,' Ana told her stridently. 'I want you to step aside, agree to a divorce and give me back the future you stole from me!'

Tati frowned at that preposterous suggestion. Ana talked as if Saif had no will of his own and as though Tati had entered the marriage freely, which she had not. 'It's not that simple, Ana,' she responded quietly.

'It can be as simple as you're willing to make it. I mean, the Prince would be getting a far superior bride in me. I'm a beauty, classy and educated, the perfect fit for a royal role, which you are not!' her cousin proclaimed as she stomped down the stairs in Tati's wake. 'And I saw a picture of him in the papers.'

Tati faltered. 'A picture?'

'Yes…a photo of you with *him* in Paris,' Ana told her bitterly. 'He's wasted on you. He's absolutely gorgeous! I'd never have walked away had I seen him first!'

'That's…unfortunate,' Tati remarked, although she was terribly tempted to laugh out loud. If George had gone ahead and kept his promise to marry her cousin, Ana would have abandoned all thought of Saif, but because George had disappointed her Ana was looking back with regret to what might have been.

'It's more than unfortunate, Tati!' Ana almost spat at her in her resentment. 'It's wrong and unforgivable that you, a member of my own family, should have taken this opportunity from me!'

'Ana…' Tati's voice was reduced to a discreet whisper. 'I married him in your place because your father threatened to stop paying for my mother's care home. Let's please stick to the facts.'

It amazed Tati how calm and unintimidated she now felt in the face of her relatives' animosity. She rather suspected that

Saif's attention and support had contributed to the stronger backbone she had developed.

Her cousin gave her a stubborn, stony appraisal and went on downstairs ahead of her. Tati reached the hall with relief, eager to be gone. The box tucked below her arm, however, slid out of her precarious hold and fell on the rug. In that instant as she stooped down to retrieve it, the emerald round her neck swung out from beneath her shirt into view and glittered in the light.

'Good grief!' Ana exclaimed, reaching forward and almost strangling Tati in her eagerness as she yanked her closer to get a better look at the jewel. 'Is that real? A real emerald *that* size? And there're diamonds all around it!'

Tati's fingers closed over the chain to stop it biting into her neck. 'That's enough, Ana…'

One of her bodyguards stepped forward. 'Let the Princess go before you hurt her,' he told Ana curtly.

Disconcerted, Ana dropped the emerald and took a step back. 'I *feel* like hurting her!' she snapped back in a sudden burst of spite.

'You don't mean that,' Tati said gently, but she was taken aback when her cousin slanted her a look of open resentment.

Sadly, she knew and understood Ana well enough to comprehend her feelings. Ana envied what she saw as Tati's good fortune and believed that Tati had moved up in the world at her expense. She took no heed of the reality that Tati had not wanted to marry Saif in her cousin's place. She chose to forget that she had not been willing to marry Saif sight unseen and had opted to turn her back on the marriage. All she saw now was how handsome Saif was, and the designer garments and the valuable, opulent emerald that Tati wore that had ignited Ana's avaricious streak. Ana felt cheated even though she had chosen to walk away.

Unexpected and unwelcome tears stung Tati's eyes as she climbed back into the limousine to be driven back to the hotel. She had always been very fond of her cousin and until now she had had a much warmer relationship with Ana than she had ever had with her uncle and aunt. Rupert Hamilton and his wife had looked at their niece as though they hated her too and she couldn't understand why.

Did she remind her uncle so strongly of her mother? What had she ever done to them to deserve such treatment? Hadn't she done them a favour by marrying Saif when their daughter ran away? Hadn't that been what they wanted her to do? And now that her mother was so ill, couldn't her brother have some compassion and forgive and forget the petty resentments he had cherished throughout his life?

As for her mother's missing jewellery, what was she planning to do about that? It had to be returned. Those were family keepsakes she valued. She would have to phone her uncle and speak to him once tempers had hopefully settled.

Entering the luxury suite that had been put at her disposal, thanks to Saif, who saw no reason why his wife should sleep in one single room when she could have a giant lounge and two bedrooms all to herself, she went into the bathroom to freshen up and the first thing she saw was that wretched pregnancy test. Gritting her teeth, she picked it up, wondering why she was hesitating when she had to find out one way or another. After all, she might be worrying about nothing!

Ten minutes later she sat staring at the result, her tummy flipping at the confirmation she had received. She had told Saif she was on the pill and, whether she liked it or not, that had been a lie when she had accidentally left her contraceptive supply behind in England. After the test she had planned to acquire a fresh prescription with which to return to Alharia, but that precaution would be wasted when she had already conceived.

For an instant her despondency lifted and a sense of wonder filled her while she allowed herself to imagine a little boy or girl, who would be a mix of her genes and the genes of the man she loved. And she *did* love him, she thought ruefully. There was little point telling herself that it was an infatuation that would soon dissipate when she had fallen head over heels for Saif in Paris. Sizzling chemistry had first knocked her off her safe, sensible perch and scrambled her wits, but the connection had turned into a much deeper attachment on her side. They had shared a magical few weeks, and all her common sense had melted away in the face of Saif's charismatic appeal. But there would be nothing magical about his reaction to the latest development, she reflected unhappily. Saif had warned her that a pregnancy would be an undesirable consequence, a *complication*. She shivered at the memory as she changed to return to the hospital.

And how would he feel about having a child with a woman who wasn't a permanent part of his life? With his own history of maternal abandonment, might it not make his reaction even more emotive?

That evening, her mother passed away without ever regaining consciousness. Tati had fully believed that she was prepared, but when it happened shock flooded her. As she left the hospital again, Pauline gave her a consoling hug before heading for the exit that lay closest to her home. When Tati turned away again in search of the limousine, she saw Saif striding towards her across the car park. Her steps quickened. Her gut reaction was to run to him. She had never been more grateful in her life to see anyone. She was at her lowest ebb and Saif had arrived. Without even thinking about it, she flung herself at him.

'You should've let me join you sooner,' Saif scolded, holding her fast, so strong, so reliable, so reassuring.

A stifled sob rattling in her throat, she allowed him to tuck her into the car drawing up. 'I didn't ask you to come and yet here you are.'

'I've been keeping in touch with the hospital, following the situation. I'm so sorry, Tatiana,' he breathed, his deep dark drawl hoarse with sympathy. 'I would have flown over last week, but you were insistent on doing this alone.'

'I've always done stuff like this alone…apart from Pauline, and she only moved here after her husband died, and began visiting Mum a couple of years ago,' she muttered shakily. 'I'm so tired, you wouldn't believe how tired I am.'

'It's anxiety and exhaustion. And you have been skipping meals, which won't have helped,' Saif remarked with disapproval.

'Sometimes I haven't been hungry… How do you know that?' And then comprehension set in. 'The protection team… my goodness, they're like a little flock of spies, aren't they?'

'It is their job to look after your well-being in my absence. I also believe you visited your aunt and uncle today and that there was an unpleasant scene,' Saif breathed in a driven undertone. 'I did ask you to stay away from them.'

'Later, Saif,' she sighed, her face buried in a broad shoulder as he kept his arm round her and she drank in the warm familiar scent of him. 'We can talk about it later.'

Afterwards, Tati barely remembered returning to the hotel. She did recall having a meal set in front of her and Saif encouraging her to eat. She had the vaguest recollection of her determination to have a bath and although she recalled getting into the warm scented water, she did not recall getting out of it again. She wakened alone in the bed and, in reliving the day's sad events, suddenly felt a fierce need for Saif's presence. She slid out of bed and padded out to the lounge where he was working on his laptop while watching the business news.

'Sorry, I just collapsed, didn't I?' She sighed. 'Now I have arrangements to make.'

'Those arrangements are being dealt with by my staff. The care home manager permitted me access to your mother's wishes with regard to her interment. I believe she wrote her instructions before she even entered the home,' Saif told her, striving not to stare at her in the fine cotton top and shorts he had put her in after he had lifted her fast asleep out of the bath.

Days of watching her mother's slow decline had marked her,

bringing a new fragility to her delicately boned face and shadowing her eyes but in no way detracting from her luminous beauty. He shifted where he stood, uncomfortably aroused. He had pretty much stayed in that condition since he'd found her asleep in the bath and, in the circumstances of her grief, he was anything but proud of his susceptibility.

The weeks without her had been long and empty. For the first time, small foolish things had annoyed him: stodgy courtiers, petty squabbles, long boring meetings. Usually he took such issues in his stride as part and parcel of his life as his father's representative, but recently his temper had taken on a hair-trigger sensitivity and he had had to watch his tongue. His father's adviser, Dalil Khouri, had infuriated Saif by drawing the Emir's attention to a photograph in the newspapers of that stupid kiss in Paris, using it as ammunition in his eagerness to show Tatiana to be an unsuitable wife, who lacked the formality and restraint Dalil believed a royal wife should have. Of course, Dalil had only been trying to do Saif a favour by encouraging his father's disapproval in the belief that it would enable Saif to request a divorce sooner. It had been unexpectedly funny, however, when the Emir startled them all by chuckling and telling his son that he had hoped he would have fun in Paris and, by the looks of it, he *had*.

Tatiana was grieving for her lost parent in a way he himself had never had the chance to do, for how could he have grieved for a woman he had never met, a woman who had walked away while he was still a babe in arms? For that reason he was keen to give his wife all the support he could during so testing a time.

'Thanks,' Tati said in a wobbly voice. 'You know, I thought I was prepared for this.'

Saif set down the laptop and rose fluidly upright, very tall and dark and breathtakingly handsome in the open-necked black shirt and jeans he now wore. Her heart skipped a beat, her mouth ran dry as she thought of what she was hiding from him and instinct almost made her hand slide protectively across her still-flat stomach. She resisted the urge while wondering if she ought to be afraid.

How big a complication would her pregnancy prove to be? Would he ask her to consider a termination? Although he had no hope of persuading her into that choice, she conceded ruefully. She wanted her child even if it hadn't been planned, even if that was an inconvenient preference. But at the same time, she also wanted her child to have a father, because she hadn't had one of her own and knew how much that could hurt.

She would tell him about the baby once they had returned to Alharia, she decided, when life had calmed again, when she had recovered from the first vicious onslaught of loss and felt more able to cope with the stress.

'Tell me about your visit to your relatives,' Saif prompted.

Tati winced. 'Actually, I wanted your advice about something,' she admitted, and she told him about her mother's jewellery. 'She was given the pearls on her eighteenth birthday and the diamond brooch on her twenty-first and I want them back because they have great sentimental worth and Mum loved them.'

'Leave the matter with me. I will handle it,' Saif assured her.

Tati breathed in deep. 'I didn't...er...want to get a solicitor or anything involved,' she warned him. 'When all is said and done, they are still my family.'

'Even when a family member assaults you?'

Tati paled. 'It *wasn't* an assault! The emerald simply attracted Ana's attention and she wanted a closer look at it.'

'If you say so,' Saif sliced in, even white teeth flashing against his bronzed skin, his spectacular green eyes unimpressed by that plea and cool as ice. 'But I say that you are not safe in that house and that you will not be returning there unless I am with you.'

And she thought that that protective instinct of his was one very good reason why she had fallen in love with him. After all, nobody had ever tried to protect Tati before. When she had been oversensitive as a child her mother had simply talked to her about the need to grow a tougher skin. At school she had been bullied and the bullying had been even worse in her uncle's house. Saif, however, stepped right in to help and protect on instinct. And that drew her, of course, it did, particularly when she was feeling vulnerable and raw. Yet she was equally aware that normally she cherished the concept of independence and was keen to make her own decisions, options that her mother's illness had long denied her.

Saif extended a hand to her and drew her down on a sofa beside him. 'Now share your happiest memories with your mother with me...it will help you to keep them alive and turn your thoughts in a better direction. I have no memories whatsoever of my mother, so make the most of what you have left.'

Tears burned and brimmed in her eyes and she blinked them away, digging deep for self-discipline before speaking.

In the early hours, she climbed into bed, lighter of heart and having talked herself hoarse. Saif emerged from the en-suite bathroom still towelling himself dry, black hair ruffled, green eyes very bright against his bronzed skin. Her gaze strayed down the long length of his body, grazing wide shoulders, corrugated abs, a taut, flat stomach, and turbulent warmth tugged at the heart of her, shocking her with its urgency. She lay down and closed her eyes.

'My life felt dull without you around,' Saif breathed in a driven undertone.

Heartened by that admission, Tati slid her hand across the divide between them and closed it over his. 'You can't expect ordinary routine to live up to three sunny weeks in Paris,' she teased.

'It's not a matter of comparisons. You're not always going to be a part of my life and I must adjust to that,' Saif pronounced very seriously.

For a split second it was as though he had plunged a knife

into her heart with that reminder and then her natural spirit rallied. 'But I'm here right now,' she pointed out daringly.

'Yes, you are,' Saif conceded huskily as he tugged her closer. 'And nobody has the ability to foretell the future.'

'That's right,' she agreed, frustrated when he made no further move.

'You must be tired.'

'Not since I slept the evening away,' Tati told him, leaning over him and then slowly, gently bringing her lips down to his, because there was a great driving need in her to reconnect again and to make the most of every moment left with him.

Saif lifted a hand and framed her flushed face. 'I assumed touching you would be inappropriate. I didn't want to get it wrong.'

'I want to forget the last three weeks,' she confessed. 'I don't want to think.'

He circled her lips with his and hauled her down to him without any further ceremony, tasting her soft lips with a scorchingly hungry kiss. While he kissed her, he dealt with removing her pyjamas with ruthless expertise. He rolled her under him, parting her legs and sliding his lean hips between her thighs. Her entire body stimulated, she quivered, momentarily mindless with desire, her fingers curling convulsively into his smooth back as he drove into her in one masterful stroke. Jolt after jolt of pure pleasure coursed through her as the excitement mounted. All the tension that had held her taut was now locked in her pelvis and when the exhilaration peaked and she almost passed out from the intensity of her climax, she held fast to him in the aftermath, lost in the blissful wash of relaxation.

'I almost forgot to use a condom.' Saif laughed as he rolled back, carrying her with him. 'You get me so worked up I can still be careless.'

And that was the instant that she should have spoken up. She recognised it as the moment immediately and froze, the truth of her condition clawing at her conscience, but her lips remained stubbornly sealed. Her confession might well lead to an angry confrontation and more distress and worry and right then she couldn't face it.

Reality reminded her that she had entered an intimate relationship in which conception was forbidden from the outset. She had acted without due consideration or concern because the risk of pregnancy had not crossed her mind. Saif might joke that she made him careless, but *she* was the one who had been thoughtless and had chosen not to speak up at the time her oversight occurred. She had conserved her pride rather than lose face and she had simply hoped for the best.

And the price of that silence had now truly come home to roost and there would be no escaping the fallout. Saif would hate that she hadn't warned him. He would hate how long it had taken for her to come clean and own up. He would hate the whole situation and maybe by the end of it he would hate her as well...

CHAPTER NINE

TATI STUDIED SAIF over breakfast in the sun-dappled court-yard, around which their wing of the old palace was built. Her surroundings were beautiful, and she was very much at peace there. Colourful mosaic tiles covered the ground around the softly playing fountain that kept the air fresh and cool. Palm trees and mature shrubs provided shade from the hot sun above while a riot of exotic flowers tumbled round the edges of the dining area.

Saif was checking the business news on a tablet, black hair flopping over his brow, lustrous black lashes shading his spectacular eyes.

'I need to talk to you this evening,' she mustered the courage to announce, because if she mentioned that necessity in advance she couldn't then weaken and back out of it again.

'What about?' Saif sent her an enquiring glance from glittering light green eyes that riveted her where she sat and sent entire flocks of butterflies fluttering inside her.

'Just something important that we need to discuss,' Tati extended uneasily.

Saif did not like to be kept in suspense. 'What's wrong with right now?'

Like the answer to a prayer, Dalil Khouri appeared in the

doorway opposite, bowing his head deferentially as he greeted them and addressed Saif. Saif rose with a determined smile to greet the older man. His unfailing courtesy in the face of the constant demands on his time never failed to impress Tati. He was very tolerant. She hoped he brought that tolerance to the fore when she admitted that she was carrying his baby. But she needed the rest of the day to work out the right words with which to frame that admission and that was why Dalil's interruption had been timely.

Tati had learned that the royal palace was always a frantically busy place. Everyone had a role and a schedule, even her. She was currently attending language classes every morning while also enjoying the benefits of a tutor employed to give her a crash course on Alharia's history and culture.

'You cannot be left so ignorant of our country that you will be embarrassed,' Saif had told her. 'People ask questions at the events we attend. I hope you won't object to being effectively sent back to school.'

And she had merely chuckled and shaken her head while wondering what the point of such lessons was intended to be when she wasn't likely to be Saif's wife for longer than a year at most. But at a dinner she had attended with him at an embassy earlier that week, she had been grateful for the ability to join in on a discussion relating to Alharia's current dealings with one of its neighbours.

Only two weeks had passed since her mother's funeral. Her uncle and aunt had not put in an appearance, which had very much shocked Saif's sense of propriety. That evening while she was packing, Saif had gone out for a couple of hours and when he had reappeared he had handed her two worn jewellery boxes that were familiar to her. In wonder she had studied the pearl set and the swan brooch that had belonged to her late mother and she had looked at Saif and asked, 'How on earth did you manage to get hold of them?'

'I simply told your uncle that your mother's possessions

should be returned to you. He apologised and blamed your aunt for taking the items. He said she was like a magpie with jewels. I believe that your relatives were so used to taking advantage of your good nature that they assumed they could get away with their behaviour... Now they know different,' he had completed with satisfaction.

'Thank you... Thank you so much,' Tati had told him, relieved that he had understood how precious her mother's former possessions now were to her.

Back then, on the brink of a return to Alharia, it hadn't occurred to her that she might struggle to find the optimum moment in which to tell Saif that she was pregnant. Unfortunately, work had engulfed him in long working hours when they had first come back, and he had been very much preoccupied. They were only ever reliably alone in bed, but she had shrunk from destroying those brief moments of trust and relaxation with a shock announcement. Only now, after almost two weeks of procrastination, was it finally dawning on her that there *was* no right moment for such a revelation. As if the timing were likely to influence his attitude!

Thoroughly exasperated by her apprehensions, Tati thrust away her plate impatiently and leapt up, stepping away from her chair. Her head swam sickly and she tried to grab the stone table as everything swam out of focus, but the darkness rushed in on her and she folded down onto the ground in a heap.

She surfaced groggily to discover that she was lying on her bed with an older man gazing down at her. 'I'm Dr Abaza, Your Highness, the Emir's personal physician. May I have your permission to examine you?'

'Is that necessary?'

'It's necessary,' Saif asserted, stepping forward out of the shadows to make her aware of his presence. 'I would prefer you to have an examination. You passed out. It's possible that you have caught an illness.'

Registering the gravity stamped on his lean, dark features,

Tati subsided, quietly responding to the doctor's polite questions and realising too late the direction in which those questions were travelling. Bearing in mind that she was on the very
brink of telling Saif the truth, she could not lie, and as she answered she could not work up the courage to look at him. Dr
Abaza completed a brief physical examination and smiled at
her. 'I will carry out a test later to be sure, but I am almost certain that you are pregnant. Certain distinct signs characterise a
first pregnancy. Low blood pressure most probably caused you
to faint. It is a common issue in the first trimester but, naturally, you must guard against it lest you injure yourself in a fall.'

The silence seemed to stretch into every corner of the room
and back again and Tati could hardly bring herself to draw
breath. She heard Saif thank the doctor. Ice trickled through
her veins as he closed the door again.

'How long have you known?' The simplicity of that first
question startled Tati.

'I... I—'

'When the doctor told you, it was obvious that you were
not surprised. You were already aware of your condition,' Saif
conjectured with disturbing discernment. 'For how long have
you known?'

'Well, I suspected weeks ago but I sort of...sort of chose to
ignore my suspicions.'

'You *ignored*?' Saif emphasised in open disbelief.

'I didn't think it was very likely and I was coping with
Mum's illness. I didn't do a test until just before you arrived in
England,' she recited breathlessly as she dug in her elbows and
sat up.

'But that was over two weeks ago!' Saif exclaimed.

'I was planning to tell you this evening.'

'You should have told me the instant you had grounds for
concern,' Saif grated, striding away from her only to swing
back, green eyes iridescently bright with anger in his lean
bronzed face. 'You have been less than honest with me.'

In receipt of that condemnation, Tati lost colour and slid her legs off the side of the bed. At least he hadn't outright labelled her a liar, she thought ruefully. But she also wondered if his own mother's desertion had made him so wary of women and pregnancy that he expected the very worst of her.

Saif made a commanding staying motion with one hand. 'Don't stand up until you're quite sure that you're not dizzy.'

'Telling you sooner than this that I was pregnant wouldn't have changed anything.' Tati argued her case tautly, still perched on the side of the bed.

'Regrettably, nothing you have yet shared tells me *how* this happened,' Saif framed grimly. 'I believed we had taken every possible precaution.'

'I know that I told you it was safe that first night in Paris. I *was* on the pill, but then I had to pack in a hurry to fly to Al-haria for the wedding and I forgot to bring the pills with me. So, I wasn't *lying* when I said there wasn't a risk... I just hadn't thought the situation through properly,' she explained uncomfortably. 'It was only afterwards that I realised I'd left the pills behind in England and that I'd already been off them a couple of days before we...er...got together...and that that was dangerous. It was a genuine oversight, but just then it didn't seem like much of a risk.'

'How did unprotected sex fail to strike you as a risk?' Saif shot at her with raw incredulity.

Tati reddened at his tone and then she shrugged. 'It was only the once and I assumed I would still be semi-protected by the pills I had already taken that month. You were very careful after that, so I thought we would be all right. I didn't see any reason to worry you when there was probably going to be nothing to worry about.'

'You should have told me. I had a right to know,' Saif breathed in a driven undertone as he paced in front of the doors that led out to a balcony.

'Yes, but the only option at that point would have been me

taking a morning-after pill and I didn't feel comfortable with that option,' Tati admitted bluntly.

'I would not have suggested that, but I dislike the fact that you chose to keep me in the dark when I am *equally* affected by this development!' Saif shot back at her crushingly.

It was a fair point and she didn't argue. 'Well, at least you know now,' she pointed out, feeling forced into the role of Job's comforter.

'I should think that half the palace is now aware of Dr Abaza's diagnosis!' Saif retorted drily. 'He will have reported straight back to my father and I would imagine others will have overheard sufficient to comprehend.'

'For goodness' sake…' Tati groaned in embarrassment.

'Why? It's not as though it is something that you could keep a secret for much longer.' Saif subjected her to a long intense appraisal. 'You're carrying my child. That is very big news in Alharia so we could not hope to keep it to ourselves. I very much doubt that you currently appreciate how much this development will impact our situation, which is naturally why I tried to ensure that it didn't occur.'

Tati stood up and lifted her head high, rumpled blond hair rippling round her shoulders, blue eyes mutinous. 'Oh, do stop talking in that deadly tone, as though it's the end of the world. It's a baby…and I love babies! I mean, we didn't plan this, and I know you like to plan stuff in advance, but how much difference can one little baby make to our *situation*, as you call it?'

Saif dealt her a bleak appraisal. 'A huge difference. I would never have chosen to conceive a child in a marriage that is not intended to last. I *know* what that situation is like from my own childhood. It is unfair to our child and will likely affect his or her emotional well-being and sense of security.'

'Don't talk to me as though I'm stupid, Saif,' Tati countered angrily, her eyes flaring with temper. 'Neither of us planned this. Both of us tried to be careful. Yes, I agree it's *not* perfect, but neither of us had perfect when it came to parents and *we* survived!'

'It's clear to me that you have still not thought through the ramifications of this development and the effect it will have on *your* freedom,' Saif grated, raking lean brown fingers through his black hair in a gesture of unconcealed frustration. 'My mother didn't want this sort of life in Alharia and she walked away from it. How will you be any different? The main point I would make is that although you grew up without a father and I grew up without a mother, neither of us was torn between two opposing households and cultures.'

'Parents do successfully work together to raise children after a divorce,' Tati protested. 'We're not enemies. We're both rational, reasonable people.'

'If you give birth to a boy he will be an heir to the Alharian throne and he will have to spend the majority of his time in *this* country, which will naturally have an influence on where you choose to live,' Saif spelt out.

'Why would he have to spend the majority of his time here?' Tati demanded with a frown.

'How else could he prepare for his future role? He must grow up amongst our people, with the language and the culture. His education and future training would be of the utmost importance and could not be achieved if his main home were to be in another country. And if you have a girl, she may well be the next ruler because I have every intention of changing the constitution when I ascend the throne. It is what our people want and expect in these days of equality,' Saif completed, his darkly handsome features troubled and taut. 'I would not want to see my child, girl or boy, only occasionally or for visits. That would bother me.'

Tati was tense. 'It would bother me as well. So, you're saying that to share a child I would have to make a home for myself in Alharia.'

'Yes. Becoming parents will make a clean break impossible,'

Saif delivered heavily. 'I appreciate how much that would detract from your independence.'

Tati was almost paralysed by the pain of hearing Saif refer to the option of 'a clean break.' In that scenario, after a divorce he would never have had to see her again and obviously that would have been his preference. Yet the same concept devastated her even as she finally grasped the obvious truth that the birth of a child would entangle their lives for a long time and that, self-evidently by his tone, was not what Saif wanted. He didn't *want* to share a child with an ex who lived elsewhere. How could she hold such honesty against him? But why did he have to be such a pessimist about the future? Why couldn't he make the best of things as she was striving to do?

'Your attitude annoys me,' Tati told him honestly. 'I tend to believe that the mixing of two cultures and lifestyles is more likely to enrich our child.'

'In an ideal world,' Saif slotted in grimly. 'But we don't live in one. If this *were* an ideal world, I would be able to openly acknowledge to my father that I have a close relationship with my half-brother, Angelino Diamandis.'

'You have a brother?' Tati exclaimed in complete surprise, disconcerted by that sudden revelation from a man who could, at the very least, be described as reticent.

'He is two years younger than I, born from my mother's second marriage. I sought him out years ago, but I think initially I wanted to meet him to see what he had that I didn't because my mother stuck around to raise him,' he pointed out curtly, the darkening of his bright eyes the proof of how emotive that topic was for him. 'Instead I discovered that my half-brother had enjoyed little more mothering than I had and I was surprised at the depth of the bond that developed between us. That relationship, however, had to remain a secret because I did not want to upset my father. He was devastated by my mother's desertion and the wound never really healed because after her second marriage she was rarely out of the newspapers. She was a great beauty and she revelled in publicity,' Saif explained ruefully. 'Children born across the divide of divorce are often placed in difficult positions out of loyalty to their respective parents. Step-families are created and other children follow. The experience may strengthen some, but it injures others.'

'That relative of yours who owns the house in Paris. Is that your brother?' Tati prompted with sudden comprehension.

'Yes, that house belongs to Angel. He also attended my wedding incognito and I got to spend some time with him before he had to leave again,' Saif told her. 'I value my relationship with my younger brother although it shames me to keep it a secret from my father. However, I cannot mention my mother or her second family to him without causing him great distress, which I obviously don't want to do when his health is poor.'

'He must really have loved her to still be so sensitive... Or is he just bitter?' Tati questioned with open curiosity.

'No, she was truly the love of my father's life, but the marriage was always destined to fail,' Saif opined fatalistically. 'She was too young and worldly, and he was too old and traditional. When you consider the very public social whirl she embarked on after deserting her husband and son in Alharia and her complete lack of regret for what she had done, you realise that they were ill-suited from the start. Whatever else he may be, my father is a most compassionate man. Had she given him the opportunity he would have given her a divorce and there would not have been a huge scandal. But the Emir was not the only one to suffer her loss... I did as well and spent many years wondering why she couldn't have stayed for my benefit.'

'That's very sad,' Tati acknowledged reflectively. 'But not really relevant to us. I'm not planning on deserting anyone, least of all my child, nor am I the sort of person attracted to the idea of publicity.'

'Who can tell what you will be enjoying in a few years' time?' Saif said with sardonic bite, his sheer cynicism infuriating her.

'You are such a pessimist!' Tati exclaimed. 'Do you always expect the very worst of people?'

'I'm a realist, not a pessimist. I would be foolish to ignore the truth that you will be a young and very wealthy divorcee and that inevitably you will remarry, have other children and change from the woman you are now,' Saif breathed, untouched by her criticism.

'I bet that, right now, you are really, *really* regretting that you consummated our marriage!' Tati accused tempestuously.

'My only regret is that I wanted you so much that I went along with that "friends with benefits" idea even though I *knew* from the outset that it was absolute madness!' Saif flung back at her in a raw-edged tone of self-loathing.

Tati froze as though she had been slapped and lost colour. It was clear that Saif could not get onboard with her conviction that they should make the best of her pregnancy. He hadn't planned the conception; he hadn't agreed to it and he seemed unlikely to move on from that position. But it was even worse to be confronted with the truth that he now regretted their relationship in its entirety.

'Madness,' she repeated through taut, dry lips with distaste, feeling totally rejected.

'What else could it be in our circumstances? This relationship of ours is insane and you know it!' Saif condemned harshly. 'Once we had both acknowledged that we didn't want to be married, we should have abstained from sex.'

Tati reddened. 'You weren't a great fan of abstinence either,' she reminded him accusingly.

'I am not solely blaming you,' Saif countered grittily. 'I was also tempted, and I gave way to that temptation, but it is exactly that self-indulgence that has landed us both into this predicament. A divorce is out of the question for the foreseeable future.'

'But why?' Tati prompted in stark disconcertion at that statement.

'It is far too soon for us to separate and I refuse to seek

a divorce from a pregnant wife. I should be with you during your pregnancy, offering whatever support I can. I feel equally strongly that for the first crucial years of our child's life we should remain together, trying to be the best parents we can be for our child's benefit,' Saif explained heavily. 'It would be selfish to only consider our own wants and needs. I wouldn't ever want our child to know the pain of not being wanted by a parent.'

His outlook made Tati feel wretched and like the most selfish woman in the world. She stood up to move towards the door, saying, 'I have a language lesson in ten minutes, and I don't want to miss it. We can talk later, and it might help a lot if you could come up with something positive rather than *negative*.'

Saif swore under his breath as she left the room. So fierce was his frustration that he was tempted to punch the wall, but bruises and a loss of temper would not change anything, he reflected with grim resignation. His wife was planning to leave him just as his mother had left his father and her son. Saif, however, was determined not to lose either of them. There was also a very real risk of his losing his child because Tatiana was, he surmised, a great deal more maternal than his mother had been.

In a different scenario he would have been overjoyed at the news that he was to become a father and he was angry at being deprived of that natural response, but it was, sadly, an issue clouded by his own experiences. Being abandoned by his mother soon after birth had hurt and changed his attitude to childbirth and parenthood because he already knew that he could never leave his child as his mother had done.

Yet how could he celebrate the birth of a child in a marriage that was a fake? A marriage that had been deemed over before it even properly began? Tatiana had never given him a fair chance, not one single chance. She had not budged an iota in her attitude since their first day together. She expected and wanted a divorce as her recompense for agreeing to a marriage that she had been blackmailed into accepting. And during the weeks they had been together she had frequently alluded to the prospect of that divorce and was obviously perfectly content with that outcome. And, even more revealing, she had refused Saif's support when her own mother was dying. She had in every possible way treated Saif as though he was superfluous, merely a casual sexual partner in a fling without a future. What she had never done, he thought painfully, was treat him like a friend.

And how much could he blame her for her attitude when he had become her first lover? Tatiana had had a difficult life with little liberty, even less money and few choices, he reminded himself. Furthermore, although she had yet to find it out, she had been ruthlessly used, abused and defrauded by relatives who should have cherished her, most especially after her mother fell ill. Saif frowned, wondering if he should tell her the truth about her grandmother's will and her uncle's wicked greed, but he had withheld what he knew on the basis that the police were in charge of the investigation now and the truth would come out soon enough when arrests were made. Saif had no desire to be the person who broke that bad news and hurt her.

Naturally, that revelation would adversely affect Tatiana because she remained blindly, ridiculously attached to those relatives of hers. From her teenaged years she had depended on them, and they had been all she had once her grandmother died and her mother sank into dementia. She had even excused their greed to Saif by explaining that her uncle had always been hopeless with money and had married an ambitious woman with grand expectations. How would she feel when she appreciated that they had lied and cheated to deprive her of her inheritance and had been busy ever since overspending *her* money as fast as they could?

When that grievous knowledge was unveiled, his bride would be even keener to enjoy the freedom she had never had. The freedom *he* didn't *want* her to have, Saif reflected bitterly. Was it any wonder that he was such a cynic?

* * *

Tati struggled through the language lesson with tears burning the backs of her eyes while she fought to relocate some seed of concentration. She struggled to dwell on the positives rather than the negatives of her plight. Saif wanted their baby and was already anxiously considering the potential effect of a divorce on their child. Why didn't he thread her into that problem and realise that if he *stayed* married to her, he wouldn't have to worry about their child's security? Obviously because he didn't *want* to stay married to her, Tati reflected miserably. Why was she set on beating her head up against a brick wall?

And what would it be like to continue living with Saif for another four or five years? Wouldn't that simply make the whole process of breaking up more agonising? It would drag it out and place her under heavier stress. She would always be waiting for the moment when he decided they had stayed together long enough and were in a position to separate. How could a future like that appeal to her?

It would freeze her life and prevent her from moving on. How could she truly move on if she were to be forced to live in Alharia for her son or daughter's sake? The prospect of standing on the sidelines watching Saif with other women, having to share her child with those same women, made her shudder. No, that wouldn't work for her. He would have to come up with a better, more bearable solution. When her mother was ill, she had accepted that being bullied, being forced into a position she didn't want, was a situation she could not escape. But life had changed for her and she herself had changed, she reflected ruefully. Ironically, Saif had made her realise that she was much stronger than she had ever appreciated. With regard to future arrangements between them for their child, she was prepared to be reasonable, but she wasn't a martyr. She would get over him at some stage, but how was she to achieve that if she was still forced to live with him?

* * *

Saif spent an hour that afternoon listening to his father wax lyrical about the joys of fatherhood. Thinking of the disappointments the older man had suffered in the wife department convinced Saif that Tatiana had been right to denounce his pessimistic outlook. Somehow, it would all work out, if they both made an effort, if he controlled the urge to lock her up and throw away the key, not because he was a controlling creep, but because, try as he might, he kept on thinking of the way his mother had just abandoned ship and run for greener pastures. Might not Tatiana also choose to bolt if he put too much pressure on her? She was pregnant and she couldn't be feeling well when she was fainting, he reasoned worriedly.

A man famed for his cool, logical approach to problems, he wondered how it was that in a moment of crisis he had said and done everything wrong. He had *told* Tatiana that they would have to stay married for years longer. He had *told* her that she would have to live in Alharia. How could he have been that clumsy, domineering and stupid? And he hadn't *once* mentioned how excited he was about the baby they had conceived.

It was at that point in his ruminations that Dalil Khouri joined Saif to announce that his wife's cousin, Ana Hamilton, had arrived at the airport and intended to visit them. It was normal for an alert to be sent to the palace when a prospective guest arrived, but Saif frowned at that news, questioning why the woman had chosen to fly to Alharia when only months earlier she had run away as fast as she could sooner than marry him. Was it possible that Ana's parents had already been arrested? Could their daughter be here to plead their case? What else could she be doing in Alharia?

Saif appreciated that it was his task to tell his wife what he had learned several weeks earlier because he could not let her meet with her cousin while still in ignorance of his recent discoveries.

'Have her brought to the palace,' he told Dalil. 'But drive her around for a while—take her to see some tourist sight, or something... I don't want my wife to be taken by surprise or upset and I need some time to prepare her for her cousin's arrival.'

'Of course,' Dalil agreed earnestly. 'The Princess must be protected at all costs from anyone who might seek to take advantage of her.'

Tati was enjoying mint tea and a savoury snack in the courtyard when Saif strode down the stairs into the courtyard to join her. He was breathtakingly handsome in an Italian wool-and-silk-mix suit that was exquisitely tailored to his lean, powerful frame. Her wide blue gaze clung to him and then pulled free of him again, her soft mouth tightening as she told herself off for being so susceptible. *That* kind of nonsense, that mooning over him like a silly sentimental schoolgirl, couldn't continue.

'First of all, I bought these for you in Paris, but after your mother fell ill there didn't seem to be a right time to give them to you,' Saif intoned, setting a jewellery box down on the table. 'This seems the appropriate moment to express my happiness about the child you are carrying and present you with this small gift to mark a special occasion.'

'You must've had to dig deep to find that happiness,' Tati opined tartly.

'You took me by surprise, but once the news sank in, I was thrilled,' Saif asserted defiantly in the face of her dubious look. 'Everything changed for me when you told me that you were pregnant. When my mother walked away from me when I was a baby, it made the whole topic very emotional for me. I tried not to dwell on her abandonment. I suppressed the sadness that that awareness inflicted because I believed that that is what a man must do to be a man...'

'Oh, Saif,' she whispered, her body stiffening as she fought the pressing need to go to him, to comfort him, to soothe the hurt he had felt that he had to deny as an adult man. But that was no longer her role, she reasoned. Furthermore, it was becoming ever more clear to her as he talked that Saif was not driven by love to wish to remain married to her for their child's sake but by fear for their child's hurt in the future. She couldn't fault him for that, she decided heavily, but that he should only want to be with her to be a father for their baby pierced her deeply.

Brushing off those emotional responses, Tati flipped open the box on a superb pair of emerald earrings in the same design as the magnificent pendant she wore. 'Wow,' she whispered without being prompted because it was yet another exciting gift that no sane woman could fail to appreciate. 'They're beautiful—'

'Perhaps you could wear them for dinner tonight,' Saif proposed. 'We have a surprise guest joining us.'

'Oh…and who would that be?' Tati gazed at him enquiringly as she twirled the emerald earrings in the sunlight. She put them on with the kind of defiance that denied that there was anything special about the occasion while reminding herself that she ought at least to enjoy the frills while she still could.

'Your cousin, Ana, is about to arrive here,' Saif imparted. 'Of course, you may be grateful for the company of a female friend at the moment.'

Utterly taken aback by the idea of Ana visiting Alharia, Tati stiffened, wondering if it was crazy to suspect that her cousin might be turning up to give Saif a belated opportunity to see what he had missed out on on his wedding day. When Ana got an idea into her head, it was hard to shift, although even Tati was a touch disconcerted by her cousin's lack of embarrassment at visiting the home of the same man she had refused to marry only weeks earlier. 'Why would I be grateful?'

Saif breathed in deep. 'Because of the discovery you have recently made and the complications—'

'I'm not going to share any of that with Ana!' Tati protested. 'That's *our* business and much too private.'

'I think that is for the best, but before she arrives there is information about your family which I have to share with you,' Saif proffered heavily.

Tati became tense, noting the grave expression he wore. 'What information and about whom?'

'Your uncle and aunt. I'm afraid I genuinely do not know if your cousin was aware of what's been going on for the past few years.'

'Going on?' Tati interrupted. 'What do you mean by "going on"?'

'Three years ago, after your grandmother died, your uncle and her solicitor worked together to deprive you of your inheritance. Your grandmother not only set up a trust to cover the cost of your late mother's care, but she also left the Fosters Manor estate to you.'

'That's impossible,' Tati broke in afresh. 'I wasn't left anything! My uncle told me that.'

Saif ignored the interruption. 'You were to inherit the estate when you reached twenty-one, but you were supposed to enjoy the income from it immediately. In effect your uncle was disinherited in your favour. Your uncle had made continual financial demands on your grandparents during their lifetime and your grandmother apparently believed that he had had his fair share before her death. Unfortunately, she appointed both your uncle and the solicitor, Roger Sallow, as executors of the will. The solicitor was corrupt. Your uncle bribed Sallow to remain silent and at the official reading Sallow read an invalid will that had been written years earlier. Your uncle has since made regular very large payments to the solicitor. The size of those payments probably explains his continuing financial troubles because Sallow became increasingly greedy.'

'I can't believe this...' Tati massaged her pounding forehead with her fingers. 'Granny Milly actually chose to leave it all to *me*?' she exclaimed in disbelief. 'How did you find all this out?'

'The day I married you, I asked a private investigation agency to do a report on you,' Saif revealed tautly. 'At that stage, I knew nothing about you and I wanted the facts. The investigator met with an old friend of your grandmother's who had witnessed the will without actually seeing the contents and she chose to share her concerns with him.'

Tati frowned. 'Her concerns?'

'She knew what your grandmother had originally planned and was very surprised when she saw that nothing changed at the manor after her friend's death, but she didn't come forward because she decided that it was none of her business and she didn't wish to offend anyone. She could, of course, have *asked* to see the will, which was on public record, but she didn't know that,' Saif recounted wryly. 'Basically, she is an elderly woman who didn't want to risk getting involved in what she suspected could be a crime.'

Tati parted bloodless lips. 'A crime?'

'You have been defrauded of your rightful inheritance and that is a crime,' Saif pointed out grimly. 'The investigation agency consulted me as soon as they uncovered the irregularities and I told them to find the evidence and put the whole matter in the hands of the police.'

If possible, Tati turned even paler. *'The police?'* she whispered in horror.

'Fraud has been committed, Tatiana,' Saif asserted grimly. 'How else may such wickedness be handled?'

Tati lifted her aching head high and looked back at him with icy blue eyes of condemnation. 'I don't know, Saif. You would need to tell me because, even though this concerns me, *I* wasn't consulted.'

'I imagine the police will seek some sort of statement from you, but they have all the evidence they require for a prosecution.'

Tati nodded, in so much shock that she was barely able to absorb what she had been told. She couldn't quite credit her hearing. She had never liked her uncle, but that he could act so basely and deliberately defraud her, while still treating her like a despised poor relation who was a burden, took her breath away. As for the trust that Saif had mentioned, the trust set up to care for her poor mother's needs, the knowledge that that information had been withheld filled her with nauseated rage on her late parent's behalf. She had been controlled and threatened with lies when all along her uncle had had little choice but to keep on paying those care home bills because stopping payment could have drawn dangerous attention to him.

'*When* did you find all this out?' Tati prompted sickly.

'The first week we were married…well, I didn't know the whole story then, but I was informed that there was every sign that your uncle had committed fraud and that he was being blackmailed by the solicitor for his misdeeds.' Saif studied her anxiously because she was very pale even if she was handling the whole business more quietly than he had somehow expected. 'I didn't want to make allegations against your relatives without adequate proof, which is why I remained silent about my suspicions.'

'And why are you finally telling me now?' Tati enquired stiffly, a glint in her unusually bright gaze, resentment and bitterness and anger all flaring at once inside her.

'Only because your cousin is about to arrive and, if the police have made a move against her father, she could be visiting with a plea that you intervene…although, to be frank, I doubt that you have the power now that the police are involved and have the evidence of his crime.'

'I gather you think that Ana must know about this!' Tati commented stiffly.

'I imagine she does,' Saif said very drily.

'I doubt that very much. Ana is spoiled, selfish and materialistic but she's never been dishonest or cruel. There's no way *she's* involved!' Tati told him with firm emphasis.

'Since you are so fond of her, I can only hope that you are correct.'

'No, my belief is that Ana is visiting to subject you to a charm offensive,' Tati mused, grimacing a little at having to voice that opinion because it mortified her.

'*Me?* A charm offensive?' Saif repeated blankly. 'What are you saying?'

'The man Ana ran away from you to marry let her down and now she has regrets about not marrying you.'

'A little late in the day,' Saif remarked as dry as the desert sand.

'As far as Ana's concerned, I'm only a substitute for her and not a very good one at that,' Tati explained as she rose from her seat. 'You're rich, generous and good-looking. She's probably hoping you'll be willing to consider a swap.'

'A *swap*?' Saif sliced back at her in sheer disbelief.

Tati gave him a long, considering appraisal, ticking all the mental boxes he occupied in her head. It was no wonder she had fallen for him like a ton of bricks when he was gorgeous and capable of immense charm when he wished to utilise it. 'Ana isn't particularly intelligent. But, you know, you would still have done much better with her than with me,' she told him ruefully. 'I doubt that my cousin would ever have become accidentally pregnant.'

'I *am* pleased about our baby,' Saif countered fiercely, displeased by the sarcastic tone of words that hinted that her cousin was welcome to him.

Tati flung up her head, blond strands rippling back from her troubled face, her eyes full of newly learned cynicism. 'So you say...'

CHAPTER TEN

ANA LOOKED STUNNING, her golden hair a silken swathe, her brown eyes beautifully made up, her silky short dress showing off long shapely legs. Initially full of peevish complaints about the 'old boring ruin of a castle' she had been dragged to view by some palace official, she soon switched to a playful smile when she realised that she was being rude. She then embraced Tati without hesitation and pouted in disappointment when Saif excused himself to make a phone call.

'Good grief,' she muttered as the door closed behind Tati's husband. 'Saif's even better looking in the flesh! Those cheekbones, that amazing physique!'

'How's everybody at home?' Tati enquired rather stiffly.

Ana sighed. 'Much the same as usual. Mum's nagging Dad about this autumn cruise she fancies and Dad's saying he doesn't want to miss the start of the shooting season. I'm so sorry I was rude when you came to the manor. Everything just got on top—George, the change in your fortunes…and I missed you.'

'I missed you too.' Warmed by that little speech, Tati searched her cousin's face and was fully satisfied that the blonde had no clue that legal problems could be hovering over her family. *She* herself was still struggling to accept the situation that Saif had outlined. She was outraged that he had kept her out of his enquiries and that only Ana's unexpected arrival had persuaded him to come clean about what was *her* business, rather than his. At heart too she was still reeling in shock at what she had learned while trying not to dwell on what was likely to happen in her marriage in the short term.

Saif didn't love her, and if he wanted her to stay married to him longer it was only because he was keen to protect their child. There was nothing she could do to change that, but she could still act on her own behalf and...walk away. More and more that was what she wanted to do, and she kept on suppressing that thought, reminding herself that her child deserved a father, but still the prospect of escape pulled and tugged seductively at her. Saif had sent her crashing from the heights of happiness down into the depths of despair. If she couldn't have Saif fully and for ever, she didn't want him, and she certainly didn't want some empty, pretend relationship dragging on for years with him, because the pain of that would kill her by degrees.

'*Oh...my...goodness!*' Ana exclaimed with emphasis, leaning closer to Tati to brush a fingertip against a dangling emerald earring gleaming like a rainbow in a shaft of sunlight. 'Now you have earrings worth a fortune as well!'

'Saif's very generous.'

'Then hand him over,' Ana urged cheerfully, as if she were asking to borrow something quite inconsequential. 'He's the serious type, isn't he? He needs someone more exciting like me in his life. You could go back to England and I could—'

Tati's stomach hollowed out. 'I'm pregnant, Ana. It wouldn't be quite that simple.'

'You mean...' Ana stared at her in open astonishment. 'You mean *you* actually *slept* with him? And you've conceived?' Ana shook her head slowly and took a moment to regroup. 'Well, good on you because I don't want kids until I'm well into my thirties.'

Tati wore an impassive expression. 'I think you'll have to see how Saif feels about that.'

Ana laughed. 'Of course, he'll want me...men always do!' she carolled with enviable confidence. 'I could see that he was working hard not to look at me when I arrived, trying to hide his interest, and now I understand why. Obviously, if you're pregnant, he feels he can hardly jump ship.'

Tati wondered if it was true that Saif had been trying to hide his interest. Ana was beautiful, lively and sexy. Of course, he would have noticed, particularly when Tati was pale and quiet because she was barely speaking to him and their relationship was at an all-time low. 'But doesn't it bother you that he's been intimate with me?' she pressed, striving to turn her cousin's thoughts in a more appropriate direction. 'Doesn't that put you off?'

'Oh, not at all. Men aren't that fussy when it comes to a willing woman,' Ana said knowledgeably just as her phone began playing a favourite tune.

Tati knew instantly what the call was about because Ana was no dissembler. Her eyes flew wide and she said sharply, 'You can't be serious! The *police*? I don't believe you!'

While she was talking and becoming more and more distressed, Tati got up and left the room to trek downstairs to Saif's office.

'Ana's just found out that her parents have been arrested... and *no*, she didn't know anything about it. I want to fly back to England with her.'

Brilliant green eyes locked to her flushed face. 'That would be unwise.'

'I don't care whether it's wise or not,' Tati responded truthfully. 'This is a family matter. You interfered and let me find out the hard way, but it's not your decision or your business... it's *mine*.'

'I was trying to protect you. I didn't want to risk telling you anything false. I don't deal in unsubstantiated stories,' Saif intoned with cool dignity. 'Becoming involved in the fallout from your uncle's actions at this stage could be very challenging for you. You would be in a very awkward position as his victim.'

'I'm not a coward. I can deal with unpleasant things,' Tati told him, lifting her head high.

'If you go to England, I will be accompanying you. We'll fly out in the morning,' Saif announced.

'Even if I don't *want* you to?' Tati snapped angrily.

Saif breathed in deep and slow, his green eyes glittering as bright as the earrings she wore. 'Even then.'

'Well…' Tati stomped back to the door in a temper. 'I'll just ignore you. I'll pretend you're not there getting into business that has nothing to do with you!'

'Everything that relates to you involves me because we're a couple.'

'I wouldn't use that word about us,' Tati said in fierce denial, leaving his office to return to her cousin.

'The police have let them both out on bail and have confiscated their passports like they're *criminals*!' Ana wailed at her incredulously. 'Dad's being charged with fraud and Mum's being charged as an accessory. How on earth could Granny have done this to us? I mean, Dad was the eldest child, everything *should've* gone to him. It's not surprising he went a little crazy and did wrong.'

'Actually, my mother was the eldest by eighteen months,' Tati chipped in gently as she rubbed her sobbing cousin's spine in a soothing motion.

'But the will that they pretended was still current left the estate to Dad. So, Granny must have changed her mind.' And then Ana sobbed. 'Oh, hell, Tati, how could Dad lie and do such a thing to you when you're part of our family as well? I never dreamt he could sink so low!'

'I think his hatred for my mother…and in her absence, *me*… overwhelmed his judgement. But I shouldn't be discussing this with you, Ana. I'm too close to it. Talk to your friends,' she urged.

'I can't tell *them* about this! When this gets out into the papers everybody will think I'm as guilty as my parents are of robbing you blind!' Ana sobbed. 'Oh, Tati, can't you please stop this happening?'

But as Tati discovered, late the following day when she was interviewed by the police in England and had answered their questions, the prosecution had nothing to do with her. Crimes had been committed and the solicitor was in even more severe trouble than her uncle and was suspected of having suggested the substitution of the outdated will to Rupert Hamilton in the first place. His dealings with his other clients were now under careful scrutiny.

When the official business was complete, Tati felt drained and she climbed into the limo that came to collect her and focused on Saif's lean, darkly handsome features wearily. 'Well, you were right, there's nothing I can do.'

'But why would you *want* to do anything to help your persecutors?' Saif demanded in driven disbelief.

'Not because I forgive them, because I don't,' she said quietly. 'I had a hellish time after Granny passed worrying about my mother's security in the care home. I could never forgive them for that or for treating me like dirt. But I pity Ana because she loves them and she's ashamed and mortified and she had no idea what had been done.'

'Then compensate her in some way if you wish to be generous. You seem to forget that you have become a very wealthy woman with considerable sums at your disposal. What your uncle deprived you of was a mere tithe of what you are now worth,' Saif informed her.

Tati fixed dismayed eyes to him. 'How am I wealthy? You may be, I'm not!'

'When we married, I settled funds on you that would make you wealthy by most people's standards...if not mine,' Saif told her coolly.

Tati clasped her hands together tightly. 'I don't want your money. I'm not being rude or ungrateful, but it's not right for me to be taking money from you when we were never truly married in the first place.'

Saif expelled his breath in a sudden hiss and clamped his even white teeth down on a swear word. *'Truly?'* he derided. 'We had the ceremony. We have shared a bed, made love and conceived a child. How is all that *not* a marriage?'

'The intent was missing. You didn't want to marry me,' Tati reminded him stubbornly.

'Is it enough to say that I would have that intent now and would marry you again, given the chance?' Saif shot at her in a raw undertone.

Tati paled and studied her linked hands, reckoning that he was only saying that because she was pregnant and had to be placated. 'No, it's not. Let's stick to our agreement for the moment.'

'Which agreement? The "friends with benefits" idea seems to have died a death,' Saif breathed curtly. 'The agreement to part within months is impossible as matters stand.'

Tati bowed her head. 'I'm not in the mood to talk about it right now,' she told him shakily, feeling terrifyingly close to a bout of overwrought tears.

She was acting like a shrew and an indecisive one at that, Tati mused guiltily, and yet he had been endlessly kind and supportive. Despite her discouragement, he had escorted her to England and had sent a lawyer to the police station with her when she'd turned down his company. She loved him so much and, even when she was angry with him, that love burned like a torch inside her and made her want to do silly stuff like grab him and hug him just for being there when her life was tough. Nobody prior to Saif had ever stood up for her before. He was so loyal, so caring that he made her love him more than ever, but that only made her feel worse and more of a burden to him.

'Your uncle contacted me this afternoon to request a meeting. He and your aunt have moved out of the manor.'

Tati dealt him a startled look. 'They…they *have*?'

'An obvious first move. It's your house where they treated you like a servant,' Saif pronounced with distaste. 'He will now wish to impress you with his repentance.'

Tati couldn't even picture a repentant version of her pompous relative. 'What did you say?'

'I said it was your decision as to whether or not you would see him,' Saif murmured grimly.

Tati could tell by the hard slant of his wide sensual mouth what *his* decision would have been, but she appreciated that, for once, he hadn't interfered. 'I'll see him at the hotel this evening if it suits.'

For the first time she was asking herself why she had got so very angry with Saif. She had deeply resented the admission that he had known about her uncle's crime before she had, even though she would never ever have found out the truth on her own behalf. She had spent her adult life being pushed around by people with power over her or her mother and she had often been browbeaten into doing what she didn't want to do. Saif had decided that he knew better than her even though the wrongdoers were her relatives, and she knew them best. But there was one crucial difference with Saif, she acknowledged now that she had calmed and taken a step back from shock and anger: Saif did what he did from an engrained need to protect her, not from a desire to belittle or control her, and that made a huge difference.

Tati slanted a glance at his lean, bronzed face, recognising the hard tension bracketing his mouth. 'I'm sorry I've been so unreasonable about all this,' she told him before she could lose her nerve. 'It's such a nasty, sordid business.'

'And I don't want you dealing with this right now,' Saif slotted in honestly, his stunning green eyes enhanced by his dense black lashes.

'It's almost over,' she pointed out. 'And I want to go and see the manor again tomorrow.'

'Why?'

'I spent a lot of my time there when my grandmother was still alive. It was a place of happy memories until Mum fell ill,' she admitted stiffly. 'I refuse to let my last few unhappy years there when my uncle was in charge spoil that for me.'

Saif was prepared to admit that Tatiana had a backbone of steel under that fragile exterior of hers, a quiet dignity, which had very much impressed the lawyer who had been at the police interview with her. He had phoned Saif the instant he'd emerged from it, full of praise for the calm, intelligent manner in which Tatiana had dealt with the situation. But Saif was much less fond of that reference to the house that was hers here in England and her attachment to it. He said nothing, however, convinced that he would strike a wrong note if he commented. He had never been in an equal relationship with a woman before, he reflected with a frown. Perhaps that was why he had erred and dictated rather than discussed.

Her uncle Rupert arrived at eight that evening at their hotel. Tati saw him alone, hardening her heart while he recited his woes and excuses, not to mention his embittered recriminations against the grandmother she had loved. It was always someone else's fault, never his when anything went wrong in Rupert Hamilton's life. When she told him of her decision his mask of discomfiture slipped for a second, and his hatred showed. He argued with her until she lost patience because she could not have cared less what happened to her uncle and aunt or where they went, but their daughter, Ana, was a different issue. If she could protect her cousin she would, and she would not apologise for it. The older man left in a very bad mood.

'I almost intervened when I heard him raise his voice,' Saif confided as he strode out of the room next door.

'I'm not scared of him and he no longer has any influence with me,' Tati admitted tightly, very pale, her blue eyes shadowed. 'But it was very unpleasant. He was shocked at what I had to tell him. Even after what he did, he still thought he could talk me into giving him the Fosters Manor estate, but I refused him and told him that when the time came I will be signing the London apartment over to Ana, so that she will still have a home. If she chooses to have her parents live with her there that's their business, not mine. I will warn her that her father is likely to try to persuade her to put the apartment in his name and that she must not agree to that. I can do no more. I understand that my uncle is likely to get a prison sentence of short duration as he has no previous record and that my aunt is likely to get community work. So, that's it now, all done and dusted.'

'You're exhausted,' Saif pronounced, bending down and scooping her bodily out of her chair before she could even guess what he was planning to do.

'I don't know why,' she sighed as he carried her through to the bedroom and settled her down on the bed.

'You're pregnant and the stress hasn't helped. Dr Abaza said that you would probably be unusually tired these first weeks.'

Tati got ready for bed, wondering if Saif would be joining her, because there was another bedroom available. She was thinking that it was far too early for him to even be thinking of sleeping and recalling that the night before he had not come to bed at all when her own eyes drifted shut.

In the morning, she felt strong enough to deal with just about anything. Even leaving Saif? She studied him over breakfast, a clenching low down in her belly as she collided with those spectacular eyes of his, hunger flaming through her in warning. Heat built in her cheeks and flushed through her entire body and she pressed her thighs together, thinking that Saif still mesmerised her. Swearing off him, taking a step back, was horrendously difficult when every natural impulse drew her back to him.

'You're coming down to the manor with me?' she queried in surprise. 'I thought you had work to do.'

'The work is always there. If I didn't ignore it sometimes I would never have any free time at all,' Saif asserted with a flashing smile that was nonetheless distinctly tense to her gaze.

He couldn't actually have guessed what she was thinking about doing...could he? For goodness' sake, Tati scolded herself, he's not telepathic! And yet she couldn't escape the sneaking suspicion that somehow he knew, somehow he had worked out already that she had decided she could not continue their marriage on the basis he had suggested. It might be the sensible, kindest approach for their unborn child, but she was only human and neither a saint nor a martyr and, if he pushed her, she would just tell him the truth so that he fully understood her position.

Tati dressed with care for the visit, donning a pretty polka-dot sundress that matched the summer sky. As she had already discovered to her consternation, pregnancy changes had kicked into her body a lot sooner than she had expected and quite a few items no longer fitted comfortably. Her breasts had swelled while her waist seemed to be vanishing. Luckily, a looser dress hid the fact.

Saif watched his wife's shuttered face begin to light up as they turned into the driveway of the old house. She was happy coming back here, happy that she was going to leave him. He straightened his wide shoulders and breathed in deep as they approached the front door, and she began to dig in her bag for the keys her uncle had handed over.

'Use the doorbell. When I realised you were coming here, I had cleaners and a housekeeper hired to greet you,' Saif divulged stiffly.

'Good grief, why would you do that?' Tati exclaimed, discomfiture claiming her afresh.

'You will not be a servant in your own home,' Saif breathed thinly.

'I'm pregnant, not disabled!' Tati protested. 'I'm not like Ana. I'm very self-sufficient. I can cook, clean, do *anything.*'

'But you will not...today anyway,' Saif completed flatly.

A pleasant older woman welcomed them into the wainscoted hall. It shone with cleanliness and the scent of beeswax polish was in the air. Tati smiled, recalling it that way from her childhood. Wandering into the pretty but faded drawing room, she went straight to the piano to study the photos there, picking up one of her grandparents when they had still been hale and hearty. She wasn't remotely surprised that, while there were a few gaps where her uncle and aunt had removed their own pieces of furniture, they had left behind all the family photos.

Two little blonde girls were in the background of the picture, giggling, and beside them stood a tall, elegant blonde with a bright smile. 'Ana and me,' she told Saif. 'And that's my mother with us.'

Her eyes throbbed and her throat ached as she thought back to those days at the manor before her uncle took over.

'I won't let you leave me!' Saif breathed with startling abruptness into the silence.

In consternation, Tati spun round to look at him, her face as red as fire because he *had* guessed what she was planning. 'You make it sound so emotional when it's not,' she muttered uncomfortably. 'I don't know how you guessed that I was thinking of living here and of not returning to Alharia with you.'

Saif lifted his strong jaw, green eyes glittering. 'I know you and I won't let you do it.'

Regret softened her blue eyes. 'I'm afraid I don't see how you can stop me.'

'I'd kidnap you,' Saif announced, disconcerting her so completely that she simply stared at him with a dropped jaw. 'Maybe after the baby was born. I wouldn't want you harmed by the exercise…obviously.'

But there was nothing remotely obvious in that threat that Tati could understand. She adored him but there was no denying that he was a conventional guy, occasionally even rather strait-laced. Remarkably handsome and sexy and full of charisma, but not the sort who broke rules. Hadn't she watched him freeze before her very eyes when Ana had tried to flirt with him? He had been appalled and he hadn't known how to handle it without being rude. So, for Saif to talk about kidnapping her with apparent seriousness shocked her beyond bearing.

'You wouldn't do anything like that,' she told him gently. 'It just wouldn't be your style.'

'If I am forced to live without you, I can make it my style,' Saif assured her with perfect gravity.

Tati sighed with regret. 'Look, you said a lot of true, logical things when we talked. Yes, it would be better for our child if we stayed together for the first years, but I just can't face a future where I'd be living a lie.'

'I will do whatever it takes to keep you…even if I have to change myself. I will change for you,' Saif swore with sincerity.

Her eyes stung with tears. 'You don't need to change. It's *me* who has the problem. I broke our rules: I fell in love with you…and I want much *more* from you than a fake marriage, and that's unfair to you.'

'You…you love me?' Saif almost whispered, staring at her fixedly as if that were the biggest shock he had ever had.

'I wouldn't have told you if you hadn't been talking that… er…weird way,' she muttered in mortification.

'Weird?' Saif's mouth quirked. 'As in being willing to consider kidnapping you? Doesn't it occur to you that while you were falling in love I might have been too?'

Her blue eyes widened, and she shifted infinitesimally closer to his tall, muscular frame. 'Might you have been?'

'First time I've ever been in love. First and last time,' Saif intoned hoarsely, curving a not-quite-steady hand to the curve of her cheekbone. 'I want you in my life for ever and ever like the stupid fairy tales.'

'Fairy tales are not stupid,' Tati told him tenderly, happiness surging up through her in an ungovernable flood. 'How come I'm your first love? There *must* have been someone else at some stage.'

'Maybe I was a late developer,' Saif quipped. 'I was always very careful not to spend too much time with any woman because I feared falling for someone I couldn't have. I knew that eventually my father would expect me to marry a woman of his choice.'

That caution was so much in his nature that she almost laughed. She turned her head to see the new housekeeper in the doorway offering them coffee. 'That would be lovely but... perhaps, later,' she suggested. 'I want to show my husband round the house first.'

'I suppose we should take a look at the outside first,' Saif remarked levelly.

'No, we're heading for the nearest bedroom,' Tati whispered, amused by his innocence. 'I'm about to jump your bones like a wild, wanton woman.'

'With you, wild and wanton works very well for me,' Saif murmured with a sudden laugh of appreciation. 'I'm more relaxed with you than I have ever been with a woman. I suppose we'll be stuck with visits from your ghastly cousin, Ana, for ever.'

'No, she won't be flirting with you the next time we see her. You withstood her attractions and that hurts her ego and turns her off. Next time, she'll be telling me that she doesn't know how I stand you being so quiet... She doesn't realise that you were only quiet because she embarrassed you,' Tati commented cheerfully.

'I wasn't embarrassed,' Saif contradicted. 'I just don't like women who are all over me like a rash.'

'Like me?' Tati teased, stretching up on tiptoe to kiss him, her hands roaming across his chest beneath his jacket as she pressed into his lean, strong length in an act of deliberate provocation.

'You're the sole exception,' Saif husked as she linked her fingers with his and urged him towards the stairs. 'Would you really have stayed here and left me?'

'If you hadn't said you loved me, I think...yes,' she muttered guiltily. 'I would have been so unhappy believing that you were only tolerating me until you felt it was time for us to split up.'

'I tolerate you with pleasure...that doesn't sound quite right,' Saif husked on the landing as he bent over her, nibbling a caressing trail down the slope of her neck. 'We need a bed.'

'I'm not sure there'll be one made up.'

'I ordered a new bed for the main bedroom and said we would be staying the night.'

Tati gazed up at him, impressed to death by that level of preparation. 'How did you know we'd be here for the night?'

'You've been so distant since we had that discussion at the palace that I knew I was in trouble,' Saif confided. 'I was determined to persuade you to stay with me...*somehow*. But I didn't know how I was going to do it, only that I would need a good few hours to have a chance of accomplishing it.'

'You're so modest,' Tati muttered, tugging him into the main bedroom, relieved to see that, aside from the new bed and bedding, it looked much as it had in her grandparents' day. Thankfully, her uncle and aunt had removed every shred of their presence. 'I can't believe we are here in this house together and that you love me.'

'Believe,' he urged fiercely as he flipped off her shoes and unzipped her dress, lifting her to arrange her on the bed like a precious sacrifice. 'I love you so much. You have no idea how it felt to think that I was losing you for ever...and all because I said the wrong things.'

'It took you a while to realise how you felt,' Tati told him forgivingly, stroking a fingertip across one high cheekbone.

'No, it didn't. I started suspecting way back when I kissed you in the street after we got off that Ferris wheel in the Place de la Concorde. I've never done anything like that in my adult life, but I couldn't resist you when you smiled. I knew then that I'd never felt that way in my life...it was *so* powerful,' he admitted. 'But I refused to examine my emotions because it didn't fit in with our plans and I was afraid that you would walk away the way my mother once walked away from me.'

Tati groaned and wrapped her arms round him tightly, touched to the heart. 'I'm not walking away. I'm never going anywhere. Gosh, you were a pushover. It took me much longer because I was working hard at trying not to get attached to you. Trouble is…' she sighed blissfully, sitting up helpfully to make the removal of her bra easier '…you're an attachable guy.'

Saif chuckled. 'You just made up a word. What does it mean?'

Her fingertip traced the sensual line of his lower lip. 'It means that there's a whole lot of stuff I like about you…like how protective you are. I've never had that before and at first I confused that protectiveness with you trying to boss me around, and I'd suffered way too much of that kind of treatment here.'

'You start shouting when I try to boss you around,' Saif pointed out with unholy amusement gleaming in his stunning eyes. 'I like your feistiness and your lack of guile and greed and also…your generosity. I still want to lock your uncle and aunt up and starve and torture them for the way they mistreated you, but I admire and respect your compassion.'

'They're already losing everything they value…the house, the money, the lifestyle, their reputations. That's enough of a punishment, but I will have to watch out that they don't take advantage of Ana.'

Saif winced. 'That will be a lifelong challenge.'

'But I can do it,' she told him gently while pushing him flat and unbuttoning his shirt, spreading appreciative hands over his bronzed hair-roughened skin and lingering with a boldness she had never dared to utilise with him before. 'I'm feeling much more confident since I met you…'

Saif gave her a wicked grin. 'I am more than willing to lie back and think only of the greatness of Alharia for your benefit, *aziz*.'

'I can't believe it only took you a couple of days to start falling in love with me,' she told him happily.

'You're a class act,' Saif husked, winding long fingers into her rumpled blond hair, the warmth and tenderness in his gaze like a sublime caress on her skin. 'An act no other woman will ever match.'

'I think you're pretty special too,' she whispered against the marauding mouth circling hers with unhidden hunger, and then they both forgot to talk and got entirely carried away into their own little world of mutual satisfaction and happiness.

EPILOGUE

Five years later

SAIF GLANCED ACROSS the room to where his wife was seated beside his father. It was the Emir's birthday. He was ninety years old and just months earlier had stepped down from the throne to allow his son to become Regent. Freed from the stress of ruling, the older man had become much more relaxed, in a way his son had never expected to see.

Their children—Amir, who was four, and the toddler twins, Farah and Milly—were playing at the Emir's feet, absorbed in the latest toys he had presented them with. For the first time ever, Saif reflected fondly, his father was enjoying a peaceful family atmosphere and he owed that blessing to Tatiana.

His father adored his daughter-in-law. He was fond of telling people that his own life would have been very different had he had the good fortune to meet a Tatiana. As to his pride in having married his son off to the grandchild of his old friend, that went without saying. But the knowledge that his father was happy and at peace and delighted in his grandchildren made Saif's duties a lot easier.

The Emir had not changed personality overnight, but he had become less authoritarian and more willing to listen to other points of view. On the other side of the room his three older sisters, engaged in their endless embroidery and crochet, were chattering to Tatiana, smiling and laughing, patting the slight swell of her stomach affectionately.

Thanks to his rashness, their fourth child was due in a handful of months, Saif mused ruefully. Strange how he had never had a reckless bone in his body until Tatiana came along, but then he had also never been happier. When Tatiana had learned that she was carrying twins the last time, they had decided that three children were enough, and then Tatiana's amazing fertility had collided with his desire to have sex in their private pool and the result was before them. He smiled abstractedly as he watched his beautiful wife weaving her magic with his family. The pool encounter had been spectacularly worthwhile.

As Tati's mobile phone buzzed she excused herself and walked through an open archway out to a terrace to take her call. The Emir had not noticed the phone ringing and she was relieved. While the old man was a lot less grumpy than he had once been, he still held on to many of what his son deemed to be 'medieval prejudices.'

'George wants a baby,' Ana proclaimed in a tragic voice.

'Well, you knew it was on the cards,' Tati reminded her cousin, who had been married for four years. George had finally proposed and stuck to his word after Ana began seeing another man. A banker, George Davis-Appleton was a clever character, more than equal to the task of keeping his avaricious in-laws at bay, and that had meant that Tati could finally relax and know her cousin was safe from exploitation.

'You love my kids...why shouldn't you love your own child?' Tati asked cheerfully.

'It's not that, Tati.' Ana sighed. 'But when you have a baby you have to grow up and I'm not ready for that yet.'

'But George is, so you have to consider him as well. Look, it's the Emir's birthday party here, so I can't talk for long,' Tati warned her cousin, soothing Ana's fears about motherhood aging her overnight.

Rupert and Elizabeth Hamilton had both received prison sentences after the crooked solicitor had declared that her aunt had been present at his meetings with his client. Within eighteen months, however, both of them had been released and they had moved in with their daughter. With Ana married, they still lived there, and Tati hadn't seen her uncle since their last meeting at the hotel, a situation that she was quite content with.

Saif and Tati regularly stayed at the manor when they were in England and spent every Christmas there. Her mother's cousin, Pauline, had moved in as a sort of caretaker for the property when it was empty. Tati's life had changed radically but very much for the better, she conceded cheerfully, because she was fiercely content and happy with Saif and their family.

She glanced up and saw her husband watching her from the archway.

'Hi,' she murmured softly, blue eyes locking to him, brimming with love and appreciation. Tall, dark and devastatingly handsome, he still rocked her where she stood every time she looked at him.

He closed his arms round her slowly. 'You look tired.'

'It was exhausting trying to explain Father Christmas to your father…because there isn't really an explanation and he doesn't like fanciful stuff.'

'It's what you call an own goal, *aziz*. You persuaded him to join us in England for Christmas this year. He wants to be prepared for some weird old man in a red suit trying to squeeze himself down a chimney…' Saif laughed softly.

Tati mock-punched a broad shoulder. 'Don't you dare tell Amir that version. He's already very excited about Christmas.'

'Relax. It's still summer,' Saif reminded her, bending his dark glossy head to steal a kiss from her soft pink lips and a little flame ignited low in her pelvis, provoking a moan deep in her throat.

His mouth circled and teased hers and she squirmed against him, helpless in the grip of that hunger as he backed her up against the wall edging the terrace, ultimately dragging his lips from hers with a groan. 'We can't leave until my father retires for the night,' he reminded her hoarsely.

Tati chuckled and bumped her brow in reproach against his shoulder before stepping back from him. 'You're like oil on a bonfire for me... I'm not complaining,' she murmured with reddening cheeks as she smiled up at him with adoring eyes that he cherished. 'I love you so much.'

Their little private moment was invaded by clattering feet and noisy voices. Amir pelted out with his two-year-old sisters hard in his wake, shouting at him to wait for them. He was tall and black-haired like Saif with the same wonderful green eyes. Farah and Milly were an identical mix of blond-haired blue-eyed little girls with pale golden skin and as lively as Amir was steady like his father.

Saif hoisted up his daughters in his strong arms and walked back indoors. Amir's hand slid into his mother's and he yawned. 'I was trying to tell Grandpa about Father Christmas, but he got all mixed up,' he complained.

As Saif's keen gaze encountered Tati's, he was smiling, warmth and tenderness a vibrant presence in that appraisal, and happiness that was as solid as gold shimmered through her. She had everything she had ever wanted in life.

* * * * *

Jet Set Confessions
Maureen Child

DESIRE

Scandalous world of the elite.

Maureen Child writes for the Harlequin Desire line and can't imagine a better job. A seven-time finalist for the prestigious Romance Writers of America RITA® Award, Maureen is the author of more than one hundred romance novels. Her books regularly appear on bestseller lists and have won several awards, including a Prism Award, a National Readers' Choice Award, a Colorado Romance Writers Award of Excellence and a Golden Quill Award. She is a native Californian but has recently moved to the mountains of Utah.

Books by Maureen Child

Harlequin Desire

The Tycoon's Secret Child
A Texas-Sized Secret
Little Secrets: His Unexpected Heir
Rich Rancher's Redemption
Billionaire's Bargain
Tempt Me in Vegas
Bombshell for the Boss
Red Hot Rancher
Jet Set Confessions

Visit her Author Profile page at
millsandboon.com.au,
or maureenchild.com, for more titles.

You can also find Maureen Child on Facebook,
along with other Harlequin Desire authors,
at Facebook.com/harlequindesireauthors!

Dear Reader,

Hi! It's new book time again! And I think you'll really enjoy *Jet Set Confessions*.

In this book, you'll meet Luke Barrett and Fiona Jordan. Luke is the heir to the Barrett Toys and Tech Corporation, but he's frustrated by his grandfather's refusal to take the company into the future. He finally goes out on his own and his grandfather Jamison is desperate to get him back.

Jamison hires Fiona, who has her own company, ICANFIXIT. Fiona can find anything for anyone and now has the job of convincing Luke to rejoin the family business.

Sparks fly between them, but their relationship was founded on the lies Fiona had to tell Luke. When the truth finally comes out, will they be able to get past the mistrust?

I had a great time with these two, and I'm hoping you enjoy them as much as I did!

Visit me on Facebook and let me know what you think!

Until next time, happy reading!

Maureen Child

To my mom, Sallye Carberry,
who opened up the world of books to me.
Mom, you taught me to love reading and so much
more. Thank you. I love you.

CHAPTER ONE

"YOU'VE COMPLETELY LOST your mind." Luke Barrett stared across the room at his grandfather. "You said you wanted me to come over to really *talk*. This isn't talking, Pop. This is nuts."

Jamison Barrett stood up from behind his desk, and Luke took just a moment to admire the fact that, at eighty, the old man still stood military-straight. Fit and strong, Jamison was a man to be reckoned with—as he always had been. His steel-gray hair was expertly cut, and he wore a tailored navy-blue pin-striped suit with a power red tie. The look he gave his grandson promised a battle.

"You should know better than to tell an old man he's crazy," he said. "We're sensitive about that sort of thing."

Luke shook his head. His grandfather had always been stubborn—Luke was used to that. But a few months ago, the old man had dropped a bomb and, clearly, he hadn't changed his mind about it.

"I don't know what else to call this," Luke argued, feeling as frustrated as he had when Pop first brought this up. "When the president of a company suddenly makes a U-turn and wants to cut off its most profitable arm, I think that qualifies as nuts."

Jamison came around the corner of his desk, probably hoping to put this little meeting on a friendlier footing. "I don't have any intention of pulling out of the tech world. I only want to dial it back—"

"Yes," Luke interrupted. "In favor of wooden rocking horses, bicycles and skateboards."

"We're a toy company first," Jamison reminded him. "We have been for more than a hundred damn years."

"And then we *grew* into Barrett Toys and Tech," Luke pointed out.

"Grew in the wrong direction," his grandfather snapped.

"Disagree." Luke blew out a breath and tried to rein in the exasperation nearly choking him. He had always trusted Pop's judgment. But in this, he was willing to fight the older man because, damn it, the path to the future wasn't through the past.

"I've got studies to back me up."

"And I've got profit and loss statements to prove you're wrong."

"Yeah, we're making plenty of money, but is that all we want?"

Luke's jaw dropped. "Since that is sort of the whole point of being in business, I'm going to say *yes*."

Jamison shook his head in clear disappointment. "You used to have a broader vision."

"And you used to listen to me." Irritated, Luke shoved both hands into his slacks pockets and gave a quick glance around his grandfather's office.

It was familiar and warm and pretty much fit the old man to a T. Jamison's desk was a hand-carved mahogany behemoth that dominated the huge room. If there was ever a tidal wave that swept this far inland, Pop could float on that thing for days.

On the cream-colored walls were framed posters of their most popular toys over the years, and family photos dotted the shelves that were also lined with leather-bound books that had actually been read. It was a prestigious Victorian office that seemed at war with the present times.

But then, so was Jamison.

"I don't want to argue with you about this again, Pop," Luke said, trying to keep the impatience he was feeling out of his tone.

He owed this proud old man everything. Jamison and his wife, Loretta, had raised Luke and his cousin Cole after the boys' parents were killed in a small plane crash. Luke had been ten and Cole twelve when they went to live with their grandparents as broken, grief-stricken kids. But Jamison and Loretta had picked up the pieces in spite of their own grief at losing both of their sons and daughters-in-law in one horrific accident. They had given their grandsons love and protection and the feeling that their world hadn't ended.

Luke and Cole had grown up working at Barrett Toys, knowing that one day they would be in charge. The company was more than a hundred years old and had always stayed current by leaping into the future—taking chances. When Luke was in college and convinced his grandfather that tech toys were going to be the next big thing, Jamison hadn't hesitated.

He'd gathered up the finest tech designers he could find, and the Barrett toy company got even bigger, even more successful. Now they were on the cutting edge. Counted as one of the biggest toy and tech companies in the world. For the last few years, Luke had been running the tech division, and Cole worked on the more traditional outlet.

Okay yes, Cole wasn't happy that Luke was the heir apparent, especially since he was two years older than Luke, but the cousins had worked that out. Mostly.

Now, though, none of them knew where they stood. All because Jamison Barrett had gotten a bug up his—

"I'm not talking about an argument, Luke," Jamison said, clearly irritated. "I'm talking about what I see every time I walk out of this office. Hell, Luke, if you weren't glued to your phone like the rest of humanity, you'd see it, too."

As irritated as his grandfather, Luke bit back his temper.

He'd heard this argument over and over during the last couple of months. "Not this again."

"Yes, *this*. This is about the kids, Luke. As attached to their phones and screens and tablets and games as you are to your email." Jamison threw both hands high. "Used to be, children were running amok outside with their friends, getting into trouble, climbing trees, swimming." He glared at Luke. "Hell, you and Cole were in constant motion when you were kids. Making you stay inside and read was looked at like torture!"

All true, he thought, but he only said, "Times change."

Jamison scowled. "Not always for the better. Kids today, all their friends are online, and they wear headsets so they can talk to each other without actually having to see each other. Instead of getting outside, they build 'virtual' tree houses. They have carefully written adventures via game boxes."

"Hell, most kids probably don't even know *how* to ride a bike anymore."

Luke shook his head. "Bikes aren't going to teach them how to navigate what's becoming a completely digital world."

"Right. A digital world." Jamison nodded sharply. "Who's going to fix your cars, or air conditioners, or the damn toilet when it breaks? You going to pee digitally, too? It's going to get mighty hot in your house if you're only using virtual air-conditioning."

"This is ridiculous," Luke muttered, amazed that he had allowed himself to get sucked into Jamison's fixation. He had to wonder where his visionary grandfather had gone. Did this happen to *all* old people? Did they all start slipping into a hole and then pulling the hole in after them?

"Pop, you're making the same kind of complaint every generation makes about the newer one. You've never been the kind of man to look backward. You've always been more interested in the future than the past. This isn't like you."

"Times change." Jamison tossed Luke's words back at him. "And I *am* talking about the future," the older man argued.

"There are all kinds of studies out now about what staring at screens are doing to kids' minds. That's why I wanted you to come in. I want you to see them. Read them. Open your damn mind long enough to admit that *maybe* I've got a point."

With that, Jamison turned to his desk and started riffling through the papers and files stacked there. Muttering beneath his breath, he checked everywhere, then checked again.

"I had it right here," he muttered. "Had Donna print it all out this morning." Facing Luke again, he said, "I can't find it right now and damned if I can figure out why—"

Luke frowned. "Doesn't matter."

"That's where you're wrong. Blast it, Luke, I don't want to be part of ruining a generation of children."

"Ruining?" Astonished, Luke stared at him. *"We're giving kids a step up, helping them learn to read—"*

"Their parents could do that by reading to them at night."

"Toddlers learn colors and puzzle solving with our games."

"They can do that with a box of crayons."

"God, you're a hardhead."

"First, I'm losing my mind, and now I'm just old and stubborn, is that it?" Jamison's eyes flashed. "Well, I can tell you I'm sharper than you are if you can't see the truth in what I'm telling you."

Luke shoved both hands through his hair. Maybe he hadn't really come to his grandfather's office. Maybe he was home in bed having a nightmare. Or maybe he'd taken a sharp left turn on the way here and had somehow ended up in hell.

His grandfather had always been on the current edge of everything. This about-face had really thrown Luke. He looked at Jamison's attitude now as not trusting Luke to take the helm of the company. As if he'd been indulging Luke and, now, was pulling the rug out from under him.

He took a deep breath, reminded himself that he loved the old man currently driving him bat-crap crazy and said, "You know what? We're just not going to agree on this, Pop. We need to stop hammering at each other over it. It's better if both of us just keep doing what we're doing."

Or at least what they had been doing the last couple of months. When Jamison first told Luke about his idea to scale back the tech division, Luke had argued until his head throbbed. He'd presented his case against the idea, which Pop had quickly dismissed. It hadn't been the first time they'd locked horns and fought it out, but somehow that argument had felt more... final than any of the others. When it was over, Luke had taken a stand and left the company to go out on his own. If nothing else, he was going to prove to his grandfather that he had faith in his own plans. Prove that tech toys really were the wave of the future.

"That's it? We just part ways? That's your final word on this?"

He met his grandfather's dark green eyes. It felt like the chasm between them was getting wider by the second. For now, Luke was going to concentrate on building his own tech toy company, Go Zone. "It is, Pop. The past can't build the future."

"You can't have a future *without* a past," Jamison pointed out.

"And the carousel keeps turning," Luke muttered. "Every time we talk about this, we say the same things, and neither one of us is convinced. We're on opposite sides of this, Pop. And there is no bridge. For me, it's better if I stay out on my own."

"Your grandmother cried last night. Over all of this."

Instantly, a sharp pang of guilt stabbed Luke but, then, he thought about it. Loretta Barrett was as tough as they came. His grandfather was sneaky enough to try to use his wife to win the argument. "No, she didn't."

Jamison scowled. "No, she didn't," he admitted. "She yelled some. But she could have cried. Probably will."

Luke blew out a breath and shook his head. "You're impossible."

"I'm doing what I have to do. You belong *here*, Luke, not running your own place."

And honestly, Luke had thought that Barrett Toys *was* his place. But things had changed with Pop's change of heart. With what felt to Luke as his lack of faith. His grandfather had always pushed him, believed in him. Trusted him. This felt like a betrayal, plain and simple. Luke's new company was small, but he had some great designers, just out of college, filled with ideas that would shake up the toy tech business. Luke was hoping to get manufacturing up and pumping out his new line by the end of the year.

This had all started because he'd been frustrated with his grandfather—but now, Luke was committed to making this work. Jamison might be willing to turn his back on progress, but Luke was greeting it with open arms.

"This is the *Barrett* toy company," Jamison reminded him. "A Barrett has been in charge since the beginning. Family, Luke. That's what's important."

That's what made all of this so much harder.

"We're still family, Pop," he reminded the older man—and himself at the same time. "And remember, you've got Cole here to run the business if you ever decide to retire."

"Cole's not you," Jamison said flatly. "I love the boy, but he hasn't got the head for the business that you do."

"He'll come around," Luke said, though he didn't really believe it. Hell, it's why Luke had been Jamison's choice to run the company in the first place. Cole just wasn't interested in the day-to-day of running a business. He liked being in charge. Liked the money. But he was a delegator, not a worker.

"You always were a stubborn one," Jamison muttered.

"Wonder where I got that," Luke said wryly.

"Touché." Nodding, his grandfather said, "Fine. You do what you have to do, so will I."

Luke hated having this simmering tension between him and his grandfather. Jamison Barrett was the rock in Luke's life. The old man had taught him how to fish, how to throw a fastball and how to tie a bow tie. He'd taught Luke everything about run-

ning a business and how to treat employees. He'd been there.
Always. And now, Luke felt like he was abandoning him. But
damned if he could think of a way to end it so that both of them
came out winning.

"Give my love to Gran."

He left before his grandfather could say anything else, closing the office door behind him. The company headquarters was
in Foothill Ranch, California, and most of the windows looked
out over palm trees, more buildings and parking lots. Still, there
was a greenbelt nearby and enough sunlight pouring through
the lightly tinted windows to make the whole place bright.

Jamison's secretary, Donna, looked up from her computer
screen. She was comfortably in her fifties and had been with
Jamison for thirty years. "See you, Luke."

"Yeah," he answered, giving his grandfather's door one last
look. He didn't like leaving the old man like this, but what
choice did he have?

Still frowning to himself, he asked, "Is Cole here?"

"Yep." Donna nodded toward a bank of offices across the
room.

"Thanks." Luke headed over to see his cousin. He gave a
brisk knock, then opened the door and stuck his head in. "How's
it going?"

"Hey." Cole looked up and smiled. Even in a suit, he looked
like a typical California surfer. Tanned, fit, with sun-streaked
blond hair and blue eyes, Cole Barrett was the charmer in the
company. He did lunches with prospective clients and took
meetings with manufacturers because he could usually smooth-
talk people into just about anything. "You here to see Pop?"

"Just left him." Luke braced one shoulder on the doorjamb
and idly noted how different Cole's office was from their grandfather's. Smaller, of course, but that was to be expected. It was
more than that, though. Cole's desk was steel and glass, his
desk chair black leather minimalist. Shelves were lined with

some of the toys their company had produced over the years, but the walls were dotted with professionally done photos of his wife, Susan, and their toddler son, Oliver—skiing in Switzerland, visiting the Pyramids and aboard the family yacht. Cole had always been more interested in playing than in the work required to make the money to do the playing.

Luke dismissed it all and met his cousin's eyes. "Wanted to warn you that he's still not happy about me leaving."

Cole leaned back in his desk chair and steepled his fingers. "No surprise there. You were the golden boy, destined to run Barrett Toys..."

Bitterness colored Cole's tone, but Luke was used to that. "That's changed."

"Only because you left." His cousin shook his head. "Pop is still determined to bring you back into the fold."

Pushing away from the wall, Luke straightened up. "Not going to happen. I've got my own company now."

Cole swung his chair lazily back and forth. "It's not Barrett, though, is it?"

No, it wasn't. A start-up company was fun. Challenging, even. But it wasn't like running Barrett's. He'd poured a lot of work and heart into the family business. But feeling as he did now, that his grandfather didn't trust him, how could he run Barrett's with any sort of confidence? "It will be," he said, with determination. "Someday."

"Right. Anyway." Cole stood up, slipped his suit jacket on and buttoned it. "I've got a lunch meeting."

"Fine. Just..." He thought about Pop, rooting around for those papers and looking confused about why he couldn't find them. "Keep me posted on Pop, will you?"

"Why?"

Luke shrugged. "He's getting old."

"Not to hear him tell it," Cole said with a short scrape of a laugh.

"Yeah, I know that." Luke nodded and told himself he'd done

what he'd gone there to do—try one more time to get through
to his grandfather. Make him see reason. Now it was time to
move the hell on. "All right, then. I've got a plane to catch. So,
say hello to Susan and Oliver for me."

"I will."

When he walked out, Luke didn't look back.

Jamison stood at his open office door and watched his grandson. An all-too-familiar stir of frustration had him falling back
into the old habit of jingling the coins in his pockets.

"You're jingling."

He stopped instantly and shot a look at his assistant.

"Didn't work, did it?" she asked.

"No one likes hearing 'I told you so,' Donna."

She shrugged. "I didn't say it."

"You were thinking it."

"If you're such a good mind reader," the woman countered,
"you should have known telling him that Loretta cried was a
mistake."

She had a point. No one who knew his wife would believe
she'd given in to a bout of tears.

"Fine," he grudgingly admitted. "You were right. Happy?"

"I'm not unhappy. It's always good to be right."

He scowled at the woman currently ignoring him as she busily typed up some damn thing or other. Donna had been with
him for thirty years and never let him forget it.

Shaking his head, Jamison shifted his gaze back to Luke as
he walked across the room, stopping to chat with people on his
way to the elevator. He was leaving, and Jamison didn't have
a clue how to get him back. So it seemed it was time for the
big guns.

"The woman you told me about. You still think she can help?"

Donna stopped typing and looked up at him. "Apparently,
she's pretty amazing, so maybe."

Jamison nodded. He wanted his grandson back in the company, damn it. How the hell could he ever retire if Luke wasn't there to take over for him? Cole was good at his specified job, but he didn't have it in him to keep growing Barrett Toys. Jamison needed Luke.

"Well, I tried the easy way," he murmured. "Now it's time to put on the pressure."

"Boss...if Luke finds out, this could all go bad in a huge way."

He dismissed her warning with an idle wave of a hand. "Then we'll have to make sure he doesn't find out, won't we? Make the call, Donna. I'll be waiting in my office."

"I've got a bad feeling about this," she said as she picked up the phone and started dialing.

Jamison turned to his office, but paused long enough to ask, "Where are those statistics I asked you to print out for me this morning?"

Frowning, she looked at him. "I put them on your desk first thing."

"You didn't move them?"

"Why would I do that?"

"Right, right." He nodded and tried to remember what he'd done with the damn things. Then something else occurred to him. "Okay, make the call. And Donna, there's no reason to tell Loretta any of this."

She rolled her eyes.

"I saw that."

"Wasn't hiding it," she countered.

"I am your boss, you know."

"Don't let it go to your head," Donna advised.

The next afternoon, Fiona Jordan walked into the restaurant at the Gables, a five-star hotel in San Francisco. The best part about owning her own business? She just never knew what would happen from day to day. Yesterday, she'd been working out of her duplex in Long Beach, California, and today, she was in a gorgeous hotel in San Francisco.

Smiling to herself, she took a breath and scanned the busy room.

White-cloth-draped tables and booths were crowded, and the hum of conversation, heavy silverware clinking against plates and the piped-in violin music streaming from discreetly hidden speakers created an atmosphere of luxury. There were windows all along one wall that afforded a spectacular view of the Bay, where the afternoon sun was busily painting a bright golden trail across the surface of the water.

But at the moment, the view wasn't her priority, Fiona thought as she did a more detailed scan of the room. She was here to find one particular person.

When she found him, her heart gave a quick, hard jolt, and a buzz of something hot and potentially dangerous zipped through her.

Luke Barrett. He had sun-streaked, light brown hair that was just long enough to curl over the collar of his dark blue suit jacket. Gaze focused on the phone he held, he seemed oblivious to the people surrounding him and completely content to be alone.

Fiona didn't really understand that. She liked people. Talking to them, hearing their stories—everyone had a story—and discovering what she liked about them. But she'd already been warned that Luke was so wrapped up in his work, he barely noticed the people around him.

So, she told herself, she'd simply have to be unforgettable.

Luke sat alone at a window table, but he paid no attention to the view. Fiona, on the other hand, was enjoying her view of him a little too much. Even in profile, he was more gorgeous than the picture she'd been given.

That buzz of something interesting shot straight through her again, and she took a moment to enjoy it. It had been a long time since a man had elicited that sort of reaction from her. Heck, she couldn't even remember the last time she'd felt a zing of interest.

Her gaze went back to his just-a-little-long hair and realized that it was an intriguing choice for a corporate type. Maybe Luke Barrett was going to be much more than she'd expected. But there was still the whole wrapped-up-in-his-phone thing to get past.

Fiona watched as a beautiful woman strolled by Luke's table, giving him a smile that most men would have drooled over—he didn't notice.

"Hmm." Realizing that meeting Luke Barrett might call for a little extra punch, Fiona turned toward the long sinuous sweep of the bar. She ordered a glass of chardonnay, gave the bartender a big tip and a smile, took a deep breath, and studied her target.

Then Fiona tossed her long, dark brown hair over her shoulder and started for his table. The short hem of her flirty black skirt swirled around her thighs and her mile-high black heels tapped cheerfully against the glossy floor. Her dark green long-sleeved blouse had a deeply scooped neckline, and gold hoops dangled from her earlobes.

She looked great, even if she was saying it herself, and it was a shame to ruin the outfit, but desperate times...

A waiter passed in front of her; Fiona deliberately stumbled, took a couple of halting steps, and with a slight shriek, threw herself and a full glass of very nice wine into Luke Barrett's lap.

CHAPTER TWO

LUKE'S FIRST INSTINCT was to grab hold of the woman who had dropped into his lap from out of nowhere. She smiled up at him, and he felt a punch of desire slam into his chest. When she squirmed on his lap, he felt that punch a lot lower.

"What the hell?" He looked into a pair of chocolate-brown eyes and realized she was laughing.

"Sorry, sorry!" She squirmed again, and he instantly held her still. "I guess I stumbled on something. Thank God you were here, or I'd have fallen onto something a lot harder."

He didn't know about that. He felt pretty damn hard at the moment. And wet. He felt wet, as the wine she'd been carrying now seeped into his shirt and pants. Even as he thought it, she half turned around, grabbed a cloth napkin and dabbed at the wine splashed across her blouse, then started in on his shirt. If she tried to dry his pants, he was a dead man.

"What'd you trip on?" He glanced down at the floor and saw nothing.

"I don't know," she admitted, then shrugged helplessly. "Sometimes I trip on air."

"Good to know."

She tipped her head to one side and long, dark brown hair slid across her shoulders. "Are you going to let me up?"

It wasn't his first thought. "Are you going to fall again?"

"Well, I'm not sure," she admitted with a grin. "Anything's possible."

"Then maybe it's safer if you stay where you are," Luke mused, still caught by the smile in those brown eyes of hers.

She started her fruitless dabbing at his shirt again. Not unlike trying to soak up the ocean with a sponge.

"Yeah," he said, taking the napkin from her. "Never mind."

"Well, I do feel badly about this," she said.

"Me, too."

"In all fairness, though," she pointed out, "I got plenty of the wine on my shirt, as well."

"And that should make me happy?"

She shrugged and her dark green off-the-shoulder shirt dipped a bit.

Instantly, his gaze dropped to the full swell of her breasts and he wondered if he'd get more of a look if she shrugged again. When he lifted his gaze to hers, he saw a knowing smile.

A waiter hustled up to them with several napkins, then just stood there as if unsure what his next move should be. Luke could sympathize.

Finally, the waiter asked, "Are you all right, miss?"

"Oh, I'm fine."

She was fine. He was being tortured but, apparently, no one cared about that.

"I'm so sorry, Mr. Barrett. Is there anything I can do?"

"No," he said grimly. "I think it's all been done."

"Well, there is one thing…" His mystery lap dancer spoke up. "My wine's gone." She held up the empty glass like it was a visual aid.

"And I know where it went," Luke muttered.

The waiter looked from Luke to the woman and back again. Still unsure. Still worried. Luke was used to that. He was rich. His family was famous. Most people got nervous around him.

And he hated that. So he forced a smile and said, "Would you get the lady another glass of wine, Michael?"

"Certainly. What were you drinking, miss?"

"Chardonnay, thanks. The house wine's fine."

Luke frowned and shook his head. "I think we can do better than that, can't we, Michael?"

The waiter grinned. "Yes, sir."

When the man left, Luke looked into those chocolate eyes again. "So, since you're sitting on my lap, I think it's only right I know your name."

"Oh, I'm Fiona. Fiona Jordan." She held out a hand to him.

He glanced at it and smirked. "I think we've already moved past a handshake, don't you?"

"I think we have," she said. "And since your lap is being so welcoming, maybe I could know your name? Last name Barrett, according to the waiter. First name?"

"Luke."

She tipped her head to one side and studied him for a long second or two. "I like it. Short. Strong. Sounds like a romance novel hero."

This had to be the strangest conversation he'd ever had.

Nodding, he confessed, "You found my secret. By day, I'm a tech-toy developer. But at night, I'm a pirate or a lord or a Highlander."

She gave him a wide grin, and that punch of desire hit him harder. "How is it you know so much about romance novels?"

"My grandmother goes through a dozen every week. I grew up seeing books with half-dressed men and women on the covers scattered around the house."

"A well-rounded childhood, then."

Luke thought about that and had to say, she was right. In spite of losing his parents when he was just a child, Luke's grandparents had saved him. They'd given him normalcy again. Made sure that though his world had been rocked, it hadn't been completely destroyed.

His lips quirked. "I always thought so."

"I envy you," she said simply, and before he could comment, the waiter was back.

Michael hurried up, carrying a glass of wine for Fiona and a refill of Luke's scotch. He set both glasses on the table and said, "On the house, Mr. Barrett. And again, we're very sorry about—"

"You don't have to apologize, Michael," Fiona told him. "I'm the clumsy one."

The man winced. "Oh, I wouldn't say clumsy…"

"That's because you don't smell like chardonnay," Luke put in wryly.

Michael nodded again before he scurried away.

"I think you scared him," Fiona said as she watched the man rush back to the bar.

"I think you're the one who scared him. Pretty women can have that effect on a man," Luke countered.

She turned back and literally beamed at him. "But not you?"

"I'm immune."

"Good to know," she said, smiling. "Does that mean I should give up or try even harder to be scary?"

"Oh, definitely keep trying." Luke grinned. Hell, he liked a woman this sure of herself. Well, to be honest, he just liked women. But a strong, gorgeous one with a sense of humor was right at the top of the list. And this one was more intriguing than most. It had been a long time since a woman had made this kind of impact on him. He laughed to himself at that thought, because she had landed on him with both physical and emotional impacts.

He took a quick look at the whole package. Long, dark brown hair, those chocolate eyes, a wide mouth, now curved in a smile, and a body that filled his mind with all kinds of interesting images. That green shirt looked great on her, and the full black skirt was short enough to showcase some great legs. The mile-high black heels just put the finishing touches on the whole picture. Oh yeah, she could be dangerous.

Even to a man who had no intention of getting into a "relationship," Luke loved women, and the occasional date or one-night stand was great. But he didn't have the time or the patience to devote himself to two passions right now. All of his focus had to be on his budding company. So meeting a woman like this one could be problematic.

"So…" Fiona spoke again, and Luke told himself to listen up. "Now that we're so comfy with each other, what brings you to San Francisco?"

"I don't know if *comfy* is the right word," Luke said wryly, shifting position a bit.

She reached for her wine, but Luke was faster. He handed her the glass. He wasn't going to risk another wine bath.

"What's the matter?" she asked. "Don't you trust me?"

"Since my shirt is still wet from your last glass of wine, I'm going to say no."

She laughed. "Well, that's honest, anyway. I like honest. But I have to say, I think it's time I moved to a chair."

He reached for his scotch and took a sip. The aged whiskey sent a slow burn through his body that couldn't even compare to the current blaze centered in his lap. "Yeah, maybe you should." He knew everyone in the restaurant had to be watching them, and Luke didn't give a flying damn. Fiona Jordan had broken up his afternoon and brightened a long, boring day, and he was going to enjoy it. In fact, he hadn't felt this…light since the day before with his grandfather.

Something about her made him forget the things plaguing him and, for that, he was grateful. Just before she'd dropped into his lap, he'd been going over and over again that conversation with Pop. Wondering if he could have handled things better. Hating that the two of them were at such odds.

But this woman with the brilliant smile and the gorgeous legs had changed that—for however long the feeling lasted.

She hopped up, and Luke muffled a groan as she took a seat across the table from him.

He had to admit he was breathing easier, even when she took a sip of her wine, then ran the tip of her tongue across her top lip to catch a stray drop. His gaze locked on that movement and yet one more sharp jab of heat stabbed him. He couldn't remember the last time a woman had attracted him so completely. And while warning bells were going off in the back of his mind, Luke ignored them all.

She took another sip of her wine, met his gaze across the table and asked, "So, what should we talk about?"

His eyebrows arched. "You want to have a conversation now?"

She shrugged. "You want to sit here in silence?"

She had a point. "Fine. Let's talk."

"Great." She took a sip of wine. "You start."

All he could really think about was what she was doing to him. Hard to come up with a conversational starter beyond *Let's go upstairs to my room.* "No. You start."

"Okay." She shrugged, and the bodice of her blouse dipped again. "What're you doing at the hotel?"

"At the moment, trying to keep my mind busy."

She grinned. "Let me rephrase. Are you from San Francisco?"

"No," he said. "I'm from Orange County. Newport Beach, specifically."

She grinned. "We're practically neighbors, then. I live in Long Beach. So, why are you here?"

"Business," Luke told her. "I'm here for the tech conference." Though he hadn't been enjoying it until she had dropped onto his lap. With all the thoughts racing through his mind—his grandfather, Barrett's, his own new company, he'd been silently stewing. She'd interrupted all of that.

"Ah." She nodded and gave a quick glance around the restaurant. "A conference. That explains all of the badges, not to mention the fact that everyone I see has their nose glued to a phone or computer."

He took a look, too, and had to admit that almost everyone in the dining area was reading a phone or scrolling on a tablet. Even at a table with six people sitting around it, all of them were busy with their own phones. He frowned a little, then shrugged it off. This conference was, as he'd said, for business.

"Guilty," he said, turning his gaze back to her.

"So if you're here for the conference, you're in the tech business, right?"

"I am." One of the reasons he came to these conferences was that here, he was surrounded by other forward-thinking people like him. People who understood that the future was in binary. "My company makes tech toys."

"Tech toys?" She tipped her head to one side. "What kind?"

She actually seemed interested, and there was nothing he liked more than to talk about the latest in tech toys. If Pop hadn't changed his mind, Luke would be even more eager to talk about them. He'd imagined steering Barrett's into the future. Drawing on their already trusted name in toys to introduce kids to the what was to come. Still, his new company would do all of that. It would just take longer to take off. To get recognition. Luke took the conversational thread and ran with it. "All kinds. From tablets that are user-friendly for toddlers, to gaming boards, video games and miniature robots and drones." He took a sip of his scotch. "We've got a full line of tech toys for every age."

She laughed again and the sound of it was like champagne bubbles.

"I barely understand my computer *now*. I can't imagine a toddler on one."

"You'd be surprised. Our test groups do very well at color and spatial relations and problem solving on the screen." He hadn't been able to convince his grandfather of that, of course. Because Jamison was concerned about pumping too much information into growing minds. But Luke believed that a young, open mind was far more likely to absorb information. And how was that a bad thing?

"There have been dozens of studies to prove that in children as young as one, the brain is like a sponge, soaking up information far faster than it will in the future."

She shook her head. "My best friend has a toddler whose main focus is eating the dog's kibble."

He laughed. "Maybe he needs a tablet."

"Maybe," she allowed. "Still, I'm amazed at the idea of babies on computers. But maybe I need a toddler to walk me through running my Word program."

Luke smiled at her.

"So, I guess 'tech toys' means you don't make bikes and dolls and things?"

His last encounter with his grandfather was still fresh in his mind, so his response was a little sharper than it should have been when he said, "No. The future isn't made up of dolls and bikes and Frisbees. It's in electronics."

She held up both hands in mock surrender. "Whoa. Okay. You convinced me. I give up."

Luke took a breath and blew it out again, reaching for calm. Wasn't her fault that his grandfather was suddenly retreating into the past. "Yeah, sorry. Sore spot. My grandfather and I have been going around and around about this."

"That has to be hard, disagreeing with family." She sipped at her wine. "Why are you?"

No way was he getting into all of that right now. "Long story."

She nodded as if she understood he simply didn't want to talk about it. But then she asked, "All right. But I'm still not convinced that tablets for toddlers are a good idea. Even tiny sponges need a teddy bear."

He smiled again, glad she'd dropped it. Back on safe ground, ground he knew like the back of his hand, he said, "There are plenty of companies that sell stuffed animals or dolls or whatever else you think a kid should have. But the future for kids today will be in technology, so shouldn't they get a jump as young as possible?"

She still looked unconvinced. "But toddlers?"

"Sure. If we can get children as young as two involved with electronics, their brains will develop faster, and they'll be more inclined toward the sciences. That's a win. For all of us."

"The sciences." She smiled. "Like making mud pies in the backyard?"

"You're a hard sell, aren't you?" He stared into her eyes and liked the feeling of being pulled in. A damn shame, he thought, that he could have a real conversation about what was important to him with a stranger—but his own grandfather wouldn't listen.

"I'm just saying that being comfortable with tech at a young age will make them more accepting of it later." As an example, he said, "We use colors and shapes and sound to get their interest." He was warming to the theme, as he always did. "They learn without realizing they're learning. Studies prove out that children who are challenged rise to the occasion more often than not."

"But aren't there just as many studies saying that it's not good to introduce small kids to tech too early?"

"You sound like my grandfather," he said.

"Thank you?" She laughed a little. "Not trying to argue, I just think that there are two sides to this and maybe your grandfather has a point."

Luke grumbled under his breath. It wasn't easy arguing for the future when everyone wanted to cling to the past. "My grandfather won't even listen to the arguments on this, so it's pointless to try any further."

"Have you listened to his side?"

Luke took another sip of his scotch and studied her. He was trying to decide if he should keep talking or change the subject. She took care of that for him.

"It sounds interesting," she said. "And a little scary."

Frowning, he sipped at his scotch. Now that too sounded like his grandfather's argument. "Why?"

"Because I like watching little kids pick dandelions or splash in mud puddles." She shrugged and took another sip of her wine. "They should be outside, running and playing. Seeing them staring at a screen instead just seems wrong. I mean, once you grow up, you're always on a computer. Why start before you have to?"

"Because it's fun?"

"If you say so." She shook her head and her gorgeous hair slid back and forth across her shoulders. "I have a love-hate relationship with my computer."

"You like email and the internet, right?"

"Sure. But I hate a full inbox. Drives me crazy."

"A full inbox means your business is doing well."

"Except for the spam."

He brushed that off. "Downside to everything."

He wondered why he wasn't as irritated with Fiona as he became with his grandfather when they had pretty much this same conversation. His phone buzzed, and Luke glanced at the screen before shifting it to voice mail. He wasn't in the position or in the mood to take a call from his grandfather.

"You don't have to get that?" she asked.

"Absolutely not."

"Okay, then." She set her wine down on the table.

His gaze dropped to her fingers sliding up and down the faceted stem of the glass.

Instantly, his body went rock hard again.

"So," he said abruptly, "since I'm pretty much trapped in this chair for a while, why don't you stay and have a late lunch with me."

She chewed at her bottom lip and with every tug of her teeth, Luke felt an answering tug inside him.

Finally, Fiona said, "I suppose that's fair, since I'm the reason you're trapped in that chair for a while."

"You are." He hadn't planned on company, but what the hell? Beautiful woman or doing email alone? Not really a contest.

"Okay, then." She crossed those great legs and swung her right foot lazily. Propping her elbows on the table, she leaned in and smiled. "Feeling better yet?"

He should have been. But he was still hard, and he missed the feel of her lush body plopped on top of his. That probably made him a masochist.

"Strangely enough, no."

A slow, wide smile curved her mouth. "Just what I was thinking."

Heat pulsed inside him and fed the flames keeping his dick at full alert. Hell, at this rate, he was going to have to hire someone to walk in front of him just to get out of the damn restaurant.

She picked up her wine, took a sip, then flicked out her tongue again to sweep away another stray drop from her top lip. Fire burning even hotter now, he thought.

"You're doing that on purpose, aren't you?"

Her mouth curved into a smile. "Is it working?"

"Too damn well," he admitted, and her smile spread further.

When the waiter brought menus, she flipped through hers until she got to the burgers.

Surprised, he asked, "A woman who's *not* going for a salad?"

She lifted her gaze to his and shook her head. "That's completely sexist. You know that, right?"

He shrugged the comment off. "Every woman I've ever taken to dinner ordered some kind of salad."

"Clearly, you're dating the wrong women." She closed the menu and folded her hands on top of it. "I'm an unapologetic carnivore. Burgers. Steaks. Love them all."

Nodding, Luke just looked at her, enjoying the view. "Good to know. And today? Burger or steak?"

"The San Francisco burger, hold the avocado."

"You don't like avocado?"

"Ew." Her features screwed up. "No."

"I don't know if I can have lunch with you after all," Luke said.

Her eyes sparkled. "So you have standards?"

"Doesn't everyone?"

"And avocado is one of them?"

"We live in California. Guacamole is a way of life here," Luke said.

"Not my life," she assured him. "I love Mexican food, but avocados are a deal breaker. It's a texture thing. They're too slimy."

"Have you tasted one?"

"God, no. I have standards, too." She grinned and Luke's insides stirred again.

The waiter came back, Luke gave him their order, then leaned back with his scotch to study the woman who had become the focus of his attention. Her bare shoulders made him think about sliding that pretty green shirt down her arms so he could feast on her breasts. His dick hardened even further, though he wouldn't have thought that possible, and his hands itched to touch her.

Fiona shifted beneath his steady stare and fought down the rise of heat threatening to engulf her. She seriously had not been prepared for the rush of something...*tantalizing* that she'd felt the moment she saw Luke Barrett. But how could she have been? All she'd had was his picture and a brief description of where she was most likely to find him.

No one had said his eyes were the color of the ocean on a summer day. Or that he was tall and muscular beneath that well-cut suit or that his hair was too long and sun-streaked. And there was no way she'd expected the deep timbre of his voice to rumble along her spine.

Mostly, though, she hadn't been prepared for the hot, throbbing ache that had settled between her thighs from sitting on his lap and feeling the hard press of him against her. Just remembering made her squirm a bit in her seat, as if to rekindle the sensation.

But she wasn't here to "kindle" anything. She was here because she'd given her word to someone. Taken a job. Made a promise. And Fiona always kept her promises.

She smiled because Luke looked at her as if he were trying to read her mind, and she was grateful he couldn't. Liking him was okay, liking him too much could jeopardize her job and that had to come first. She'd been offered a twenty-thousand dollar bonus if she succeeded. And she needed that money.

With an actual savings account, she could buy a car that didn't run on hopes and dreams and invest in her own business to help it grow.

"What are you thinking?" His question shattered the thoughts he was asking about.

Fiona had to scramble. "Just wondering how a man gets into tech toys," she said, and silently congratulated herself on coming up with that so quickly.

He took a sip of his scotch and set the heavy glass tumbler down again. "Started in the family business." He shrugged. "Recently I went out on my own."

"Really. Why?"

He gave her a suspicious look. "Why do you care?"

"I don't," she lied. "Just curious. Is this about your disagreement with your grandfather?"

"And why should I feed a stranger's curiosity?"

"Oh," Fiona said with a slow smile, "after what we've already shared, I don't think we're strangers anymore."

He laughed shortly and inclined his head. "Point taken. Okay, you're right. My grandfather and I couldn't see eye to eye."

"Isn't there a compromise in there somewhere?"

"Not with Pop. He prefers the past, and I want the future."

Basically what she already knew. "Sounds dire."

"No." One firm shake of his head. "Just business."

"Even with family?"

"Family adds another layer, but it still boils down to business." Frowning, he said, "My grandfather and I had a plan. He changed his mind, so I'm going ahead with the plan on my own. Simple."

"Is it? Simple, I mean."

"It will be," he said, nodding to himself.

He clammed up fast after that, and Fiona once again silently warned herself to go slowly. Carefully. His eyes were closed off, shuttered as if he'd erected a privacy wall around his thoughts. And she had a feeling that she'd never get past that wall by using a battering ram. He was clearly a private person, so that would make getting him to open up to her more difficult. And despite what he'd just said, she knew there was nothing simple about his situation.

Yet she had to wonder how he could shut out a grandfather who loved him. Fiona didn't have family. She had friends. Lots of friends, because she'd set out to *create* a family. She couldn't imagine turning her back on a grandfather who loved her.

Wistfully, she wondered briefly what that might be like and wondered why Luke couldn't see how lucky he was to have the very family he was at odds with.

Their lunch arrived then and they both went quiet as the waiter set the plates in front of them, then filled water goblets.

Luke had ordered the same burger she had, but *with* avocado. "Sure you don't want to try it?"

She held out one hand in a "stop" gesture. "Way sure."

"You could look at this as an opportunity to expand your horizons."

She laughed. "With an avocado?"

"It's a start." His eyes flashed and a new jolt of heat swept through Fiona.

"I think we could find a better place to start expanding those horizons," she said quietly. "Don't you?"

He looked at her for a long moment, the heat in his eyes searing every inch of her skin. "I can work with that."

CHAPTER THREE

BACK IN LAGUNA BEACH, Jamison walked into his house and strode directly into the living room. As always, he was struck at the silence in the big house. When Cole and Luke were young, there was laughter, shouting, the dogs barking and dozens of the kids' friends running in and out. Now that it was just him and his wife, Loretta, sometimes the quiet became overpowering.

The muffled voices from the television pulled him into the big room. Loretta was curled up in the corner of a couch, watching a flat-screen TV hanging on the wall above a fireplace, where gas flames danced over faux logs. She glanced at him and smiled, and Jamison felt that hard punch of love that always left him feeling off-balance.

From the first moment they'd met, almost sixty years ago now, Jamison thought with a jolt, he'd loved Loretta. She was the best thing that had ever happened to him and, as the years passed, that only became clearer to him.

Young people might think love was only for them, but Jamison was here to testify that flames didn't burn out, they only got warmer, steadier, and the love that fanned them, richer.

"Hi, hon," she said. "How was your day?"

"Frustrating," he admitted with a scowl and gave a quick look around the room. Usually, he walked in here and felt better.

Loretta had decorated the place in soothing tones of blue and greens that always reminded Jamison of the sea. Overstuffed couches and chairs, gleaming oak tables, and a stained-glass window on one wall that tossed colored patches of light onto the hardwood floor. It was a room made for relaxation but, today, he knew it wasn't going to help him.

Jamison walked to the wet bar across the room, poured himself a scotch and took the first gulp like it was medicine.

"Tell me what happened." Loretta hit the mute button and instantly, silence dropped onto the room.

"Still thinking about another fruitless argument with Luke yesterday."

"Oh, Jamie, for God's sake, let it go."

He stared at her. She was as beautiful as ever. Her short, stylish hair was a striking white now, but her blue eyes were as sharp as they always were. She wore the diamond stud earrings he'd given her for Christmas and some kind of loungy outfit of soft black pants and a pale gray top that was loose enough to hide what he knew was a body she kept in excellent shape. But the look in her pretty eyes was as frustrating as the rest of his day had been.

"How can I let it go?" He walked over, dropped onto the couch beside her and fixed his gaze on hers. "That boy was supposed to take over Barrett Toys. He was my future and, now, he's turned his back on everything to get kids hooked on technology."

She laughed, reached over to the closest table for her glass of red wine and took a sip. "You sound like a man on a horse-drawn cart complaining that his son wants one of those new-fangled cars."

"Not the same thing at all," he muttered, looking into his scotch glass as if searching for answers.

"Exactly the same." She straightened one leg and used her foot to nudge his thigh. "When you took over from your father, don't you remember how he lamented the end of the company because you wanted to make too many changes?"

He dropped one hand to her foot and lazily stroked it. That was different. His father had been stuck in the mud. No vision. No ability to *listen*. "Yes, but I didn't leave the company, did I?"

"And Luke won't either."

He snapped her a hard look. "He already has."

Loretta waved that away. "He'll be back."

"You sound damn sure of yourself."

"Not of me," she said. "I'm sure of Luke. Yes, he's off on his own right now, but that's not saying he'll stay there."

"If you'd heard him yesterday, you'd believe it."

"He needs to prove himself. Just as much as you needed the same thing about fifty years ago." She sighed a little. "He's as stubborn as you are. That's why the two of you butt heads so often."

"Thanks very much."

She ignored that and wiggled her foot. "Foot rub, please."

He snorted, but obliged.

Loretta sighed her pleasure, but then kept talking. "Like I said, Luke's proving something to you, I think. And until you can accept his ideas and trust him to do the right thing, neither of you is going to be happy. Meanwhile, until Luke comes back, you have Cole to help you out at the company."

"Cole." Shaking his head, Jamison said, "He just doesn't have the head for the company like Luke does. Today, Cole left early again. Took a lunch and then just went home rather than back to work. Said he had some to-do with Susan and Oliver." He paused before demanding, "What kind of activity does a two-year-old have that a father can't miss?"

She gave him a push with her foot. "That two-year-old is our great-grandson."

"And I love him, but Cole's not just that boy's father, he's a vice president of the company…"

"Spending time with his son is a good thing, Jamie."

"I know that, and it's not about that, really. In a family business, you should be able to take off time when you need to, to be with your kids. That's not what really bothers me." Shaking his head again, he muttered, "He doesn't give a flying damn about the business. Meetings at work, he's not paying attention. He's…indifferent. At the heart of it, he doesn't understand or care about what happens to the company and makes no effort to, either. He's just—"

"Just what?"

He looked at her and admitted the truth. "He's not *Luke*."

Studying him, she asked, "This isn't just about Cole's lack of vision and effort or even about Luke, is it? I mean, you're angry and hurt, but there's something else, too."

He scowled at her. "It's not easy being married to a mind reader."

"Thankfully, you have years of practice. So, stop stalling and spill it."

He rubbed at the spot between his eyes but didn't bother trying to ignore her. Jamison knew better than to evade anything as far as his wife was concerned. "I'm losing it, Loretta."

"What do you mean?"

He pushed her foot off his lap and stood up, clutching his scotch glass. "I mean, I'm forgetting things. It's been going on for a while, but lately, it seems to be getting worse."

She frowned a bit, but her voice was soft and easy as she asked, "What kind of things?"

One of the reasons he loved her as fiercely today as he had sixty years before was her inherent calm. Nothing shook the woman. Even when they'd lost both of their sons and daughters-in-law in one blindingly horrific plane crash, she'd been rocked only for a while. Because she had taken her pain and turned it into love she lavished on their grandsons, Cole and Luke.

Jamison was very glad of her stoicism today because by God, he needed it.

"Today, I couldn't find the statistics I had Donna print out for me on the new toy line. I put them on my desk and then a half hour later, they weren't there." Shaking his head, he muttered, "I must have moved them, but damned if I can remember doing it."

"Maybe Donna moved them."

"She said no."

"Well then, you were busy. Distracted."

"Maybe." Distraction only worked as an excuse for so long, though. And he'd been losing track of little things for weeks now. When would that change to the *big* things? Would he forget who he was? Forget Loretta? He ran one hand across the back of his neck and tried to still his racing thoughts. If there was one thing that terrified Jamison, it was the threat of losing *himself.* Of his mind slowly disappearing. At eighty, he'd prided himself on staying in shape, but there was nothing he could do about his memory. His ideas. His thoughts. If he lost all of that...

"You're worrying for nothing," Loretta said.

"It's not just the statistic reports," he countered. "Yesterday, after Cole and Susan went home, I couldn't find my damn car keys."

"That's not a new phenomenon," Loretta said wryly. "On our first date, you couldn't find them either, remember? You had to walk me home?"

He remembered and his smile proved it. "That was different. I did that on purpose to get more time with you."

"Jamison Barrett!" She slapped his arm. "I got in trouble for that because I was home so late."

"It was worth it," he said with a wink.

Her mouth worked as if she was biting back words trying to slip out. Finally, though, she admitted, "Yes, it was worth it. And, Jamie, you're worried now for nothing. You don't have Alzheimer's. You've just got too much on your mind."

"It's been happening for weeks, Loretta." He scowled at the admission. He hadn't wanted to worry her. Hadn't wanted to acknowledge that there might actually be something to worry about.

"You should have told me."

"I didn't want to talk about it. Now…"

"If you're that worried, go see Dr. Tucker."

His scowl deepened. "That's just admitting that I'm worried."

"You're driving yourself crazy over *nothing,* Jamie. I would have noticed if there was something wrong with you."

A splash of color from the stained-glass window fell on her, shading her hair and her features with pale, rosy light. He looked into her eyes and chose to believe her—because he needed to.

"You're probably right."

She laughed shortly, reaching up to cup his cheek. "After nearly sixty years together, you should know that I'm *always* right."

"True." He smiled. "What was I thinking?"

She moved into him, wrapped her arms around his waist and laid her head on his chest.

He tucked her in close with one arm across her shoulders and took the comfort she offered. And he thanked whatever lucky stars had given him this woman to go through life with. He'd needed this time with Loretta. This calm, soothing time when he could center himself again.

Which was why he didn't mention hiring the woman Donna had told him about.

Fiona stepped out of the shower the next morning and asked herself what the heck she was doing. She and Luke had spent the evening together, and then made plans to tour the city today.

"Shouldn't be doing this," she muttered. "Not supposed to be getting involved in a case. But how can I not? I have to talk to him, right?" And she really liked him, too. Which made all of this even harder.

"But at the same time, I have to get him to see his grandfather's side of things. Get him to talk to me about this, so I can present arguments he might listen to. Make him want to go back to the business, and I can't do that if I avoid him, right?"

Fiona turned the hot water off and took a second to just rest her forehead against the tiled wall. She'd flown all the way to San Francisco to meet him. To convince him... She couldn't exactly do that if she didn't spend time with him.

She flushed, just thinking about what had happened yesterday at their first meeting. She'd never been so blatantly sexual in her life. And wasn't sure how it had happened, beyond the instant attraction she'd felt for him.

"This has the chance of becoming a real mess," she muttered as she reached for a thick white towel and wrapped it around her still-dripping body. She used another one for her hair, then swiped the steamy fog off the mirror. That didn't help, though. Now she had to meet her own gaze and read the trouble in her own eyes.

Her big plan had been to meet him here, at the conference, where he was away from home. Talk to him, get to know him. Not sexually, just...friendly. Then when they got back home, maybe become his friend and ease him into seeing that his grandfather and the family company needed him.

"But I shot that plan down myself." Frowning at her reflection, she said, "This is really not good."

He was her job, damn it. She was supposed to be resolving his life, not throwing her own into turmoil. This was her job, and she was going to be professional. She had no business at all fantasizing about the most gorgeous man she'd ever seen. God, it was just embarrassing what had happened earlier. She never should have fallen into his lap.

When her cell phone rang, she thought of it as a break from her crazy-making thoughts. Then she saw the call screen and sighed. No avoiding this, either.

"Mr. Barrett," she said, forcing a smile into her voice. "I didn't expect to hear from you so soon."

Actually, she'd been hoping she wouldn't. But in her short

acquaintance with Luke's grandfather, she'd already learned the older man wasn't exactly patient. Still, she didn't have anything to report. Didn't have any news to give him. And she couldn't exactly share with the man that his grandson had set her body on fire.

"Ms. Jordan—is it all right if I call you Fiona?"

"Of course." She straightened the tower of a towel on her head, then with one hand, wiped the steam off the mirror again.

"Did you meet with Luke?"

"I did," she said, though she wouldn't be telling him how that first meeting had gone. She could just imagine. God, that would be mortifying. Yeah. That would be good.

Keep your mind off Luke. At least while you're talking to his grandfather.

"I'm meeting him in an hour. We're going to spend the day together." And she hoped to be able to get him talking about his grandfather again. Get this job back on track. Jamison Barrett had hired her to bring his grandson back into the family business, and she was going to do it. She'd never failed on a contract before, and she wouldn't this time, either.

Fiona's business, ICanFixIt, had been born out of her innate ability to solve problems. Not math, of course. Math was terrifying to her. But if someone lost a diamond ring, or a puppy, she could find it. If you needed tickets to a sold-out concert, Fiona could get them. Find long-lost relatives, she was your girl. Basically, Fiona could fix your problem, no matter what it was.

So, she wouldn't spoil her success record by failing this time.

"He's ignoring the conference in favor of you?" Jamison chuckled. "I'm impressed. Nothing my boy likes better than the technology business and being around others just like him. You must be a miracle worker after all."

"I wouldn't say that," she said, and frowned at her reflection.

"Well, from what my secretary, Donna, tells me, you accomplish the impossible all the time."

She winced. Yes. She had worked for Donna's sister Linda.

Fiona had found the daughter Linda had given up for adoption thirty years ago, and she'd helped the two women reunite. Which was how Jamison had found out about Fiona in the first place.

At the time, she'd had no idea that finding a long-lost daughter would be considered easy compared to what she was supposed to do now. From what she'd seen of Luke yesterday, not only was he gorgeous, ridiculously sexy and funny on top of it...he was also stubborn and determined to make his own company take off. She was on his side in that because she knew just how much her business meant to her.

But Jamison was her client, so her loyalties had to be to him.

"Mr. Barrett, I don't want you to get your hopes up too high," she warned quietly. Yes, she'd never failed before, but what was it her foster mom had always told her? *There's always a first time.* "I'm going to do my best, but your grandson seems very stubborn."

"He is," Jamison grumbled. "Got that from his grandmother."

Fiona almost laughed aloud at that. It was clear to her that Luke was more like his grandfather than either man would probably admit.

"This is the last night of the conference," he said next. "Luke will be flying home tomorrow, so I'll expect another update from you tomorrow night or the following morning at the latest."

"Of course," she said, and silently hoped that she would have some good news to give him. But from what she'd seen of Luke Barrett so far, Fiona had the feeling he wasn't the kind of man to make hasty decisions. He'd left the family business because he was convinced that it was the right move for him.

How was she supposed to change his mind over the course of a single weekend? Answer? She couldn't. It was going to take more than this weekend, which meant that she'd be seeing lots more of Luke Barrett.

She looked into the mirror and saw eager anticipation in her own eyes. Oh, not good.

"Fine, then. I look forward to hearing from you. Get it done." Jamison hung up a moment later, and Fiona set her phone down.

Staring at the woman in the mirror, she said, "This is just another job, Fiona."

When her own reflection rolled her eyes at that, Fiona knew she was in deep doo-doo. "No getting involved. No letting your hormones drive the car here. Get Luke talking about his family. Make him realize what he's walking away from. And when it's over...*you* walk away. Because if Luke discovers you were hired to meet him, convince him, he'll never speak to you again anyway."

So, it would be better for her if she simply didn't get attached in the first place...

By that evening, Luke felt like he was standing at the edge of a very high cliff. His body had been tight and hard since the moment Fiona had dropped into his lap the day before. Ditching the conference and spending time with her instead hadn't helped the situation any.

They'd played tourist all day, taking a cab down Lombard Street, checking out Golden Gate Park and stopping for a drink at a tiny pub at Fisherman's Wharf. Hell, if anyone had told him a week ago that he'd be playing tourist, he'd have laughed in their face.

But Fiona had wanted to see the park and the wharf, so he'd gone along. She'd checked out the sights and he'd watched *her*. The night before, his sleep had been haunted by images of her and now he had even more memories to draw on. Fiona, standing at the rail on the wharf as a sea wind tossed her hair and lifted that short black skirt. Her grin as their driver took them down the most notoriously twisted street in the world.

Not to mention the way her tongue had caressed the ice cream cone he'd bought her at the park.

He briefly closed his eyes and muffled a groan at *that* thought.

To distract himself while he sat in the bar and waited for Fiona to arrive for their dinner date, he opened his phone and checked his email. There were twenty new messages to go through and as he did, Luke shut out the rest of the room as if he were alone on an island.

The truth was, if he hadn't met Fiona, he'd have been bored out of his mind.

This conference had nothing new to offer him. Luke had already chosen his path, knew his own plans and had no interest in making changes to what was, in effect, a newborn company. He'd only come to San Francisco because he'd felt that he should make an appearance, talk to a couple of old friends. Then he'd met Fiona. She'd shaken him and he had no problem admitting that—at least to himself. She was smart and funny and confident and all three of those things, combined with that body and those eyes, had his mind wandering even while dealing with email.

"Not good." Luke shook his head to clear it. He had enough going on in his life right now and definitely didn't need the distraction of a woman—even one as intriguing as Fiona. Hell, he thought, maybe especially not one as intriguing as Fiona.

He had to focus on his company. No time in his life at the moment for a woman like her.

Blowing out a breath, he read the message from his assistant, Jack.

We've hit a snag in early production, boss. Peterson says they're backlogged and won't get to do the run of our new tablets in time for a Christmas release.

"Well, damn it." Frustration roared through him. Yes, to anyone else, talking about Christmas releases in February sounded ridiculous. But these things were always planned out months, if not years, in advance. Usually for just this reason. Something always went wrong.

This wasn't the first time Luke had had to deal with wrenches thrown into the works. At Barrett Toys and Tech, they'd often had to pull off last-minute miracles. Yes, his cousin Cole had supposedly been in charge of taking care of their production partners, but more often than not, that job had fallen to Luke. He'd handle it this time, too. Quickly, he fired off an email to Jack.

Tell Peterson we have a contract, and I expect him to honor it. Tell him I said to find a way. If he gives you any crap, I'll take care of it myself on Monday.

That would probably be enough to keep the man on track. If it wasn't, Luke would find someone else to do the job and word would spread that Peterson's Manufacturing couldn't be trusted to honor its schedules.

Focused now on his business, he answered a few more emails from marketing, engineering and design, then skipped the one from his grandfather. He knew damn well that Jamison would be telling him again that he should come back to the family business.

A quick ping of regret echoed inside him, but he ignored it. He loved that old man, but damned if he'd go back where his opinions weren't trusted. His new business wasn't just a company but a matter of pride. Luke wasn't going to walk away from it.

"Excuse me?"

A woman's voice from right beside him. One of the waitresses had already tried to freshen his drink twice before. He waved one hand at the table. "I don't need a refill, thanks."

"Good to know," the woman said, then added, "So do I have to fall into your lap again to get your attention?"

He went still before turning his head to look up at Fiona. If he'd thought she was stunning earlier in that short, flirty skirt, it was nothing to what he was thinking now.

She wore a dark red, off-the-shoulder dress that defined every curve in her body like a lover's hands. The dress was nipped in tightly at her narrow waist and the short, tight skirt stopped midway on her thighs. The black heels completed her outfit and made her legs look amazing. Instantly, he had a mental image of those legs locked around his hips while she pulled him deeper inside her heat.

And…just like that, he was too hard to stand.

Her hair was pulled back into a low ponytail that hung between her shoulders and her coffee-colored eyes sparkled as if she knew exactly what effect she was having on him.

"Have you seen enough?" she asked, "or would you like me to do a slow turn?"

If he saw her butt in that dress, it would finish him off. "Not necessary. Have a seat."

"Oh." She glanced toward the dining room. "I thought we were going to dinner. I am sort of hungry."

"Right. Carnivore. I remember." He nodded and as she sat down, he signaled for the waitress. "But that's going to have to wait until I can walk again."

Her mouth curved and he wanted nothing more than to taste it. "Again?" She smiled. "You're really good for my self-esteem."

"Yeah. Happy to help…" When the waitress arrived, Fiona looked up at her.

"Vodka martini, please. Dirty."

When they were alone again, Luke finished off the email he'd been composing. Anything to get his mind off what his mind wanted to stay on.

"Are we having a phone date?" Fiona asked, and her voice was so soft and sultry, he had to look up and meet her eyes.

"Should I get mine out of my purse?" She reached for the small black clutch she'd set on the table a moment ago.

"What? No. Just a little business I have to take care of."

"Uh-huh."

The waitress returned, set a chilled cocktail glass in front of Fiona and left again. Taking the stirrer from the glass, Fiona ate one of the three olives, then took a sip. "So business, anytime, anywhere?"

He tore his gaze from the email and glanced at her again, just in time to watch her put the second olive in her mouth and slide the stirrer between her lips.

Luke took a deep breath. "It's important."

"Oh, I'm sure." She sat back in the black leather chair and sipped at her drink. "Do you always do business after business hours?"

A little irritated with himself at how easily Fiona affected him, Luke concentrated on composing the email. "When I have to."

"You were working yesterday afternoon when we met, too."

"Things have to get done, whether I'm at the company or away."

"But today, you almost never checked your phone."

"Making up for it now," he said. It had been years since he'd gone most of the day without checking emails. But he hadn't been able to take his eyes off of her. It wasn't just a sexual pull he felt for her. He actually enjoyed listening to her, talking to her. It had been a long time since a woman had captivated him like this.

And right now, for Luke, that was off-limits. Fiona wasn't the kind of woman you walked away from easily. So, it was better to not get involved at all, right?

"So, you're never really off duty?"

"Not usually." He hit Send, and a response to his earlier message to Jack arrived. Dutifully, he clicked on it and smiled in satisfaction.

"What's the point in having your own business if you never have any time off?"

He lifted his gaze to hers and reached for his drink. "Clearly, you don't know how much is involved in running your own business."

"Not true. I just don't let my business interfere with my *life*."

He snorted. "This business *is* my life."

"Well, that's just sad," Fiona mused.

Luke stared at her. "Sad? I'm building a company from the ground up. That's not sad. It's exciting. Challenging."

"And sucking up everything around it like a black hole?"

He laughed shortly, looked back at the email he was writing to Jack. He finished it off, hit Send and then set his phone on the table beside him.

"Amazing," he said. "For a second there, you almost sounded like my grandfather."

Her eyebrows arched. "What every woman longs to hear."

"Not what I meant." Luke shook his head. "It's just that he's suddenly anti-technology."

"Oh, then I'm not like him at all," Fiona said, sipping at her drink again. "I like technology. I love email and texting with my mom who makes hilarious typos, and I'm very fond of my washing machine, car and television."

Nodding, he smiled. "Glad to hear it. That's what people don't get—including my grandfather. Tech isn't just computers or robots or drones. More than a hundred years ago, tech was the first airplane. It's about the future. Seeing it. Grabbing it."

"What about the present?"

"What?"

"The present," she repeated, giving him a knowing smile. "As in dinner? Can you walk yet?"

"As long as you don't sit on my lap again, I think we're good." He stood up, then walked around the table to pull her chair out.

She slowly rose, took a deep breath that lifted the tops of her breasts to dangerous levels and said, "I'll try to restrain myself."

And it wasn't going to be easy. She didn't have to actually touch him, Luke realized. Just looking at her was enough to feed a fire that threatened to burn him to ash.

Luke steered Fiona toward the hostess, then followed behind as the woman guided them to a table by a wide window. His gaze dropped to Fiona's butt and the way it swayed with her every step. He wanted his hands on her. Soon.

CHAPTER FOUR

"WE'VE SPENT THE day together and I still don't know why *you're* in San Francisco," Luke said.

True. She'd managed for most of the day to steer the conversation around to him. To keep him talking about his own company and, every once in a while, to bring up the grandfather who was so desperate to get Luke back into the fold.

Because she couldn't tell him what he wanted to know. Couldn't reveal that she had been hired to meet him and ease him back into his family. So, she was left with half-truths and outright lies. Fiona wasn't comfortable with them, but sometimes, there was just no other way.

"I'm actually here on business," she said.

His mesmerizing eyes locked on her, and she just managed not to shiver.

"Who do you work for?"

"Oh, I've got my own business." Fiona reached for her purse. She dug inside for the brightly flowered, metallic card holder that had been a gift from her best friend, Laura. Opening it up, she pulled out a card and handed it to him.

He looked at it and a quizzical expression crossed his face. She couldn't blame him. Most people had that initial reaction.

"ICanFixIt?" He lifted his gaze to hers, and Fiona gave another little jolt. His eyes had a sort of power over her she hadn't really expected—or found a way to combat, yet.

"Fix what?"

She shrugged. "Anything, really. If you need it fixed, I can do it."

He tucked her card into his inner jacket pocket in a move that felt oddly intimate. "That's fairly vague."

"What's vague? Actually, it's a perfect description of what I do."

"Explain."

Well, it wasn't the first time she'd had to give an explanation of what she did. Her business card really said it all.

"If someone's lost something or if they have something they need and can't get, then they call me, and I fix it."

"Easy as that."

It wasn't a question, but at the same time, it was. "I didn't say it was easy." Fiona smiled at him because, honestly, he looked so dubious it was going to be fun to prove him wrong. Plus, she still had flames licking at her insides when she looked into his eyes. There was definitely something happening between them that she hadn't counted on. That she hadn't expected at all. Was it going to complicate the situation? Absolutely. Oh sure, he was paying attention to her and that would help with her goal of convincing him to go back to his family business. But she wasn't a one-night kind of woman and, once he found out she'd set him up from their first meeting, that's all she would be relegated to. Was that going to change how she was feeling? Nope.

"Tell me something you've 'fixed' lately."

"Okay." She did a quick flip through her mental file folders and came up with a quick example.

"About two weeks ago, a woman called me for help finding her son's letterman jacket."

He laughed.

Fiona scowled at him. She wasn't really surprised at his re-action, but she was a little disappointed. Just because it seemed silly to Luke didn't mean that it wasn't important to the kid who'd lost his jacket.

"It seems like a small thing to you, but that boy worked really hard to earn his varsity letter. And his mom paid a lot of money for that jacket. Money she couldn't spare."

"But she could afford to hire you?"

Fiona grinned. "She made her son pay my fee out of his savings."

"Okay." He nodded. "Good for her. So how did you solve the problem?"

Pleased, Fiona continued. "I backtracked. Found out where he'd been, who he'd been with, if he'd stopped anywhere along his route."

He frowned again. "Sounds like a lot of work."

She shrugged that off. "You work hard, don't you?"

"Of course."

"So do I. Anyway," she said, "I went everywhere that Ryder went over a long weekend, because he couldn't remember where he was the last time he'd seen the jacket."

"Of course he couldn't."

She ignored that. "Really, it's amazing how many places a teenager can go in one weekend." Smiling now, she said, "I went to a hamburger stand in Bolsa Chica, a surf shop in Huntington Beach, a movie theater in Newport and a shake shack in Laguna. He was also applying for some jobs, so that took me back to Long Beach and then Palos Verdes, and I really hate driving over the Vincent Thomas Bridge."

He laughed again. "Why?"

"It's *huge*," she said. "Really long and really high, and I drive a Volkswagen Bug so when a truck gets close, I just picture myself sailing over the edge."

"You won't go over the edge. The railings are too high."

"Okay, then, being crushed."

"Reasonable," he admitted.

"Thank you." How very *kind* of him to admit she had a right to be nervous. A little irritated in spite of her attraction to him, she went on. "So, I talked to dozens of people, went through a lot of lost-and-found boxes, and finally found the jacket."

"I admit it. I'm intrigued. Where'd you find it?"

"At a girl's house." Grinning, Fiona picked up the martini she'd carried with her to the dining room and took a sip. "She'd seen the boy at a coffee shop in Long Beach where he was applying for a job. She goes to school with him, has a huge crush on him, and when he forgot the jacket after his interview, she picked it up."

"She just took it?" His expression said he was appalled.

"Well, she said she had completely planned to give it back to him at school, but instead, she held on to it. I do think she was going to give it back eventually, she just liked having it."

"So she stole it."

Fiona held up one finger for correction. "She rescued it."

"And held it hostage."

Laughing, Fiona shook her head. "There was no ransom, and I really think you're missing the point of this."

"Fine. Clue me in."

"The point is, I found the jacket. I returned it to the boy and his very grateful mother."

"And did you tell him about the girl who had it?"

Fiona winced. "Since she pleaded with me not to, no. I didn't. She was embarrassed."

"She was a thief."

Fiona tipped her head to one side and studied him. This was a side of him she hadn't seen before. Until now, he'd been charming, funny and just sexy as hell. His response now, though, painted a hard, unforgiving picture that was a little startling. "That's cold."

"Just a fact." He shrugged. "She took it and didn't return it."

"She was going to." Fiona was sure of it. Heck, she remembered being in high school and completely infatuated with the star of the baseball team. Who had, naturally, not been aware of her existence. She had understood what the girl was thinking, and Fiona had believed her when she'd sworn that she was going to give the jacket back. "So to you, facts are all that matter? No straying from the straight and narrow?"

"Is that so unusual? You're okay with people stealing things?"

"Of course not, but I'm willing to admit that people do things they regret—"

"Everyone does." His features darkened for a moment before he said, "Doesn't mean you don't have to accept the consequences."

"I'm all about responsibility, but a little understanding wouldn't hurt, either."

"Right and wrong. Period." He sipped at his drink and looked completely at ease with that pronouncement.

Well, that didn't bode well for her, Fiona thought. She'd started this—whatever it was between them—with a lie. She doubted he'd understand that.

"So, no shades of gray in your world?"

He shook his head. "Not really."

"Must be difficult being perfect in an imperfect world."

His lips curved briefly. "I didn't say I was perfect. When I'm wrong, I own it."

Her guess was, he didn't consider himself wrong very often. "And do you confess it?"

He didn't say anything, and Fiona could guess what that meant. No, he didn't. She imagined that apologies didn't come easy to a man so sure he was right all the time. So she used that moment to drive home her point. "Then why should this girl confess? Or have what she did pointed out? Who would gain? I returned the jacket. The boy was happy. His mom was happy. And the girl doesn't have to be worried about being teased or bullied at school over it."

"And did she learn anything?"

"I think so." In fact, she was sure of it. Fiona remembered

the horrified expression on the girl's face when she'd been tracked down.

"And that's your business?" he asked. "Tracking down jackets stolen by starry-eyed schoolgirls?"

"It's an example." This wasn't the first time someone had been dismissive of her business. But she bristled a little at his tone anyway. Feeling a little defensive now, she said, "I've helped people research their thesis, found a lost engagement ring, arranged for a band for a wedding and just a couple of months ago, I reunited a woman with the daughter she gave up for adoption thirty years ago."

And that case was the main reason she was here today. Of course, she couldn't tell Luke that. He might put things together if he found out that Fiona had done work for the sister of his grandfather's secretary.

His eyebrows arched. "That's impressive."

"Thank you. I know to some, my business might sound silly or not worth doing, even." Lifting her martini for another sip, she let the icy liquid cool the bubbles of insult in the pit of her stomach. It was ridiculous to take offense at Luke's remarks or outlook. It didn't matter what he thought of her business, did it? She'd faced the same thing from a lot of people over the years. It hadn't changed anything for Fiona.

She had a skill that she'd used in high school to make friends and, once grown, she'd honed her talents into a business that served a real purpose, and Fiona was proud of what she'd built. As proud, she was willing to bet, as Luke was of his tech business.

"But when it's your engagement ring that's missing, it's a big deal. Or when you manage to surprise your grandmother with tickets to a play she's been wanting to see." Fiona smiled at that memory. "It's not just the big things that are important, right? Sometimes, the small things in life mean the most."

"How did you get started in this 'business'?"

"You don't have to say it like that," she said. "As if it isn't a real company. I'm not as big as Barrett Toys and Tech, but I support myself and provide a service."

He gave her a slow nod. "Understood. So, how did you get started?"

"Kind of a long story…"

"I'll take my chances."

Fiona shrugged. "Okay, then. I grew up in a series of different foster homes." Before he could offer sympathy that she didn't want or need, she rushed on. "So that meant going to strange schools and always being the new girl."

"Rough."

"Especially for a teenager," she agreed, happy he hadn't gotten the pity gleam in his eyes that too many people did when learning about her background. It hadn't been easy, sure. But she'd survived. "So to make friends, I started offering help to people. Dog walking. Babysitting. Finding a pair of lost glasses. Tutoring football players. If it needed doing, I could do it."

He didn't say anything, just kept his gaze on her. She shifted a little uncomfortably under his steady stare but continued. "I went to community college, took business courses and turned my skill into a way to make my living."

"You still dog walking?"

"If someone needs it, sure. I also arrange for DJs for weddings, bounce houses for kids' parties, tours of movie studios…"

"And how do you pull that off?" He was curious, she could see it in his eyes, and she smiled.

"I've got a lot of friends with interesting jobs and we help each other out." She paused, then said, "I know that most of what I do doesn't sound important to you—or anyone else. But it's important to the people who hire me, and isn't that the point?"

He thought about that for a long moment, his gaze locked with hers. "Yes," he finally said. "You're right. It is."

His phone vibrated on the table and sounded like a rattlesnake in the brush. Fiona jumped, then frowned a bit when Luke reached for it. He glanced at the screen.

"This is business, just excuse me for a minute."

Times had changed, she reminded herself. Now no one thought twice about taking phone calls during dinner, or at a play or in the movies. And watching Luke, she could see his grandfather's point. Sure, technology was a great thing to have. It kept people connected—but it also had the ability to isolate them. If someone was more interested in a phone conversation than talking to the person he was with, why be with another person at all?

In spite of her annoyance, Luke's deep, rumbling voice sent shivers along her spine. His expressions shifted according to whatever the caller had to say. She could barely hear him, so she had no idea what the conversation was about. All she knew was that she was sitting opposite a gorgeous man who was more interested in his phone than in her. In the long run, that was probably best, she told herself. After all, she wasn't trying to make a romantic connection. She looked around the elegant dining room and saw that most of the people were staring at their phones.

It was a plague, she thought suddenly. And she was sympathetic to his grandfather's efforts to fight it… Strange that she'd never really paid all that much attention to people's dependency on technology until accepting this job from Jamison Barrett. She'd never paid much attention to people's love of technology simply because she was usually too busy. The evidence had been all around her all the time. Heck, she'd no doubt been guilty of it herself. Until today. As she sat there, waiting for Luke to hang up and look at her again, Fiona realized that she really liked him. Which had not been in the plan at all.

When Luke hung up, she said, "I propose a phone ban."

"Excuse me?"

"No more phones tonight. You took two calls earlier and

now this one." Shrugging, she said, "I suggest we both put our phones on the table and the first one to reach for it loses."

"Loses what?"

"The agreement."

His eyes sparked and she saw a definite gleam there that kindled the fires inside her to burn hotter and higher. Apparently, Luke Barrett thrived on competition.

"And what does the winner get?"

"Hmm. Good question. The pride of knowing they won?"

"Not much of an inducement to get me to ignore business calls," he said.

What would be enough? she wondered. She couldn't offer a cash prize because he was a billionaire; he wouldn't need her twenty bucks. Then an idea occurred to her that stirred up the flames inside to make them bright enough to read by.

"Okay," she countered as a dangerous thought occurred to her. "A kiss."

Well, she had his attention anyway. Kissing Luke Barrett was more tempting than she wanted to admit even to herself. And maybe that's why she'd suggested the prize. After all, she knew very well, that whatever was between she and Luke now, it wasn't going to go anywhere, so why not a kiss?

"One kiss?" He lifted an eyebrow, and she wondered how he did that. "One kiss isn't much of a prize."

"It is if you know what you're doing," she said.

His eyes darkened until they were the color of a stormy sea. "A challenge. I like it."

"So you agree? No phone. Winner gets a kiss."

"Then the loser gets one, too."

"True, but—"

"But," he said, "the winner chooses where, when, for how long and how deep."

Just hearing him say those words set up a low, throbbing ache and made her heart quicken into a beat that was wild and fierce.

And that was just *talking* about a kiss. Maybe this wasn't a very good idea.

"Deal?" He set his phone on the tabletop.

Fiona had one last chance to back out, but somehow, she just couldn't. Instead, she laid her phone beside his and the challenge began.

Dinner was good, but Luke hardly tasted it. All he could think of was the kiss that was coming his way. He'd wanted to taste her since the moment they'd met, and now it was so close, his mind was completely fixated.

His phone buzzed again. Third time in the last half hour, and he didn't even look at it. Instead, he met her gaze and saw the smile in those brown depths. She fully expected him to cave. To take the call, because she'd been seeing him do just that too many times. But Fiona Jordan had no idea just how determined he could be when he was focused on a goal.

And tonight, *she* was the goal. A temporary distraction? When he was back home, he could focus on his company. Here...

"I'm sorry to interrupt..."

Luke turned to look at a tall blonde woman in a slinky black dress standing beside a little boy clutching a stuffed green alligator to his chest.

After a brief glance at Luke, the woman looked at Fiona and smiled. "I'm really sorry, we'll only be a minute."

"It's no problem, Shelley," Fiona said, then looked down at the little boy. "Hi, Jake."

"Tank oo." He gave her a shy smile, snuggling up to his mom's leg as he rubbed his alligator across his cheek. "You find Dragon."

"Well, you're very welcome," Fiona told him with a grin. "He looks so happy now to be back with you."

Jake gave her a wide, two-year-old's smile and hugged the threadbare stuffed animal a little harder. "Me, too."

"I'm glad."

"He wanted to say thank you himself," Jake's mother said, "so when we saw you in the dining room, we had to come over."

"It's not a problem. I was happy to help."

"You have no idea how much you helped." Shelley smoothed one hand over her son's tousled blond hair. "He was heartbroken because Dragon was lost. He couldn't even sleep last night."

"Tank oo," the boy said again, then turned and scampered back to the table where his father sat, holding a baby girl with a bright pink ribbon in her hair.

"Seriously, thank you." Shelley shook Fiona's hand and left.

"Another satisfied client?"

Fiona smiled. "Jake lost Dragon yesterday somewhere in the hotel and, today, I saw his mom searching for it. But she was holding her baby and Jake was crying in his father's arms, so I volunteered to find it."

He frowned as he glanced at the happy little boy again. "We were together all day. When did you do this?"

She waved one hand. "When I went upstairs to change for dinner, I met up with them in the elevator."

Luke thought back. "You were only gone forty-five minutes. You found it that quickly?"

"This one was easy," she said. "They'd been at the pool most of the day, so I checked and found out the towels had been taken to the hotel laundry right after the family left the pool. Turns out, Dragon got lost in a bunch of towels. So, I went down there, and they let me look through the gigantic tubs of damp towels from the pool area that hadn't been washed yet and I found him." She shrugged. "No big deal."

Luke looked back to where the little boy was sitting, holding tightly to his alligator, and then turned his gaze back to Fiona. "To Jake it was."

She beamed at him. "You get it."

"Yeah," he said, now more determined than ever to win their

bet because there was nothing he wanted more than to kiss her senseless. To lose himself in her. "I think I do."

Her phone rang, a medieval-sounding tune, and still smiling, she automatically reached for it.

"You lose," Luke said.

She stopped, hand poised above her phone. The music finally ended as the call went to voice mail, but it was too late, and they both knew it. "Not fair. I was distracted."

Luke smiled, looked her dead in the eye and whispered, "Not nearly as much as you're going to be."

The promise of a kiss hung over the rest of their dinner date, and by the time they were finished and the bill was paid, Luke was strung tighter than a harp string. He'd never looked forward so much to a damn kiss. Hell, he'd been torturing himself since the moment she'd dropped into his lap. Knowing that he was finally going to get a taste of her was pushing him closer and closer to the edge.

"You know, we should probably talk about this…"

He had one hand at the small of her back, and he could have sworn he felt heat pouring from her body into his. "You're not trying to back out, are you? This was your idea."

They walked out onto the wide flagstone patio and walkway that wended its way through a gigantic garden before winding around the hotel itself.

"Yes, but—"

"But you thought you'd win," he finished for her and saw her mouth work as if she were biting back what she wanted to say. "Admit it. You thought I'd cave and grab for my phone."

"Well, of course I did," she said, tossing a quick look up at him. "Who knew you could be so…"

"Determined? Strong? Single-minded?"

"All of the above."

He grinned and kept her walking until they were in the deserted garden. The wind was whipping in off the ocean, and February in San Francisco could be downright cold. It seemed no one else was willing to brave the chill and that suited Luke just fine.

"It was a silly bet," she said.

"And yet we made it."

She stopped, looked up at him and narrowed her eyes. "You're enjoying this, aren't you?"

"So much," he admitted. He smiled at her, but that smile slowly dissolved as he *really* looked at her. That long dark hair was lifting in the wind and her brown eyes looked almost black in the moonlight.

If Luke had been looking for a romantic setting, he couldn't have picked a better spot. Trees swaying, flowers scenting the air, and the moon, shining out of a cloud swept sky, painting shadows on the grass. There were a few old-fashioned lamps made to look like gaslights sprinkled throughout the garden, adding splashes of gold in the darkness.

But it wasn't romance he was after, he reminded himself. He wasn't looking for a relationship, just to quench the fires inside. Lust was driving him. Pure need and a desire so all-consuming, he'd never known anything like it before.

"Are you trying to back out of our deal?" he asked quietly, keeping his gaze locked on hers so he could see if there was the slightest hesitation there.

"That would be awkward, since it was my idea in the first place."

"Not an answer," he said, his voice deepening with the need clawing at his throat. Still watching her eyes, he saw desire, irritation at herself for losing this little bet, but he didn't see "no." *Thank God.*

"No, I'm not trying to back out," she said, and took a deep breath as if steeling herself for a challenge. "You won, so it's your call. Just as we agreed."

He reached for her and slid his hands up and down her arms until she shivered under his touch. Her tongue swept out to lick her bottom lip, and everything in Luke fisted tight.

"I suppose if I were a gentleman, I'd let you squirm out of this..."

"But you're not a gentleman, are you?" she asked, tossing her wind-blown hair back from her face.

"Nope," he whispered, bending his head to hers.

"I'm glad," she murmured just before his mouth took hers.

The moment their mouths met, Luke knew he'd never be satisfied with a single kiss. The taste of her swamped him, filling every cell, flavoring his breath, fogging his mind.

She swayed into him and his arms came around her, one hand sweeping up her back to cradle her head in his palm. His fingers threaded through her hair, he held her still so he could drown in the sensation of having her with him at last.

It had been the longest day or two in his life. Being constantly tortured at her presence and not touching her had driven him crazy. And now he was determined to make the most of the kiss she'd lost to him.

Their tongues tangled together, and he swallowed her sigh. He devoured her, feeding the need within and spiking it to heights he hadn't known existed. She was more than he'd expected. More than he'd thought possible. And a part of him realized that made her dangerous to a man who wasn't interested in anything that lasted longer than a couple of weeks.

Who would have guessed she would be so addictive? The taste of her. The feel of her body, pliant and giving, pinned to his. The slide of her hair against his hand and the sound of her sighs. Everything about her demanded that he take his time. Everything he was told him to stop now while he still could.

Regretfully, Luke drew his head back and stared down at her. Her eyes were closed, her mouth still ready for the kiss to continue. Her breath heaved in and out of her lungs, and he saw her pounding pulse in the elegant column of her throat.

He couldn't seem to let her go. Her heat called to him. The need still gripping him erupted into a throbbing ache in his dick. All he could think about was sliding her dress down her shoulders, so he could bare her breasts to him. But damned if he'd act like a horny teenager in a public garden.

Slowly, she opened her eyes and looked up at him. Her tongue crossed her top lip, and she gave him such a sensuous, deliberate look, it was all Luke could do to keep from tasting her again.

"Wow."

He snorted. "Wow?"

Fiona took a deep breath, giving him a glimpse of her cleavage that only deepened the ache he felt. "Well, yeah. That was a really good kiss."

Luke grinned. No games. No playing or trying to pretend that kiss hadn't shaken both of them. Damned if he didn't like Fiona Jordan almost as much as he wanted her.

"Thanks," he said wryly, lifting one hand to stroke his fingertips along her cheek. "I try."

She patted his chest, then swept both hands through her hair. Taking another deep breath as if to steady herself, she blew it out in a rush. "It's appreciated. Seriously. So. Deal honored?"

Best bet he'd ever made. "Yeah."

"Then what do we do now?"

Images filled his mind, and heat roared through his bloodstream. He shoved them all aside, hoping she was thinking the same things. "Your call."

She looked up at him, smiled and said, "Ice cream."

"What?" That was so far off from where his mind was that he didn't know how to process it for a second or two. She went from a passion-fueled kiss hot enough to consume them both to...*ice cream*?

"I saw a great-looking creamery just a block or so from here."

Luke really didn't know what the hell to make of Fiona. He liked her. He wanted her. He worried about getting too close to her. But following her train of thought wasn't easy.

Still. Maybe ice cream would freeze the fires inside. Worth a shot.

CHAPTER FIVE

A COUPLE OF HOURS LATER, Fiona heard her best friend answer the phone and blurted out, "Help me."

"Who is this?"

Fiona choked out a laugh. "Laura, not kidding. I think I'm in deep trouble here."

Laura's tone changed instantly from teasing to worried. "What's wrong?"

Sighing a little, Fiona smiled to herself. She knew she could count on Laura Baker. Laura and her husband, Mike, owned the Long Beach duplex where Fiona lived. The Bakers had the three-bedroom unit and Fiona was up front in the one bedroom. From the moment Fiona had moved in a few years ago, the two women had bonded as if they'd known each other their entire lives.

And for Fiona that was a gift like nothing she'd ever known before. Oh, she had a huge circle of "friends" that she'd deliberately made along the way, to somehow fill the emptiness that never having a family of her own had carved into her heart. But finding Laura was like living her whole life alone and suddenly discovering she had a sister.

Like she'd told Luke, she'd grown up in a series of foster homes, bouncing like the proverbial Ping-Pong ball throughout Orange County. Until she was sixteen and was sent to Julie Maxwell. Julie was more than a foster mom. She had become *Mom*. She'd given Fiona the stability and sense of belonging that she'd always dreamed of. And when Fiona aged out of the system, Julie had insisted that she stay on at the house and go to school. Julie was the only real mother Fiona had ever known and she'd always be grateful.

She was just as thankful to have Laura in her life. Laura was short, blonde and, as her husband liked to say, *stacked*. She was also the most sensible human Fiona had ever known and the first one she went to with a problem. And she had a beauty to talk about this time.

"It's Luke Barrett. He's too sexy."

Laura laughed. "Is that even possible? Isn't that like too skinny? Too rich? Who ever heard of too sexy?"

Mike shouted in the background, "Thanks, babe!"

"Wasn't talking to you," Laura called back with a laugh, then asked Fiona, "What's going on?"

Fiona clutched the phone and paced aimlessly. Standing in this beautiful hotel room, all alone, she imagined that she was sitting next to Laura on her big leather sofa and immediately felt better. She stopped at the windows and stared out at San Francisco, draped in lights that made the city look magical at night. "This job. It's not turning out like I thought it would."

"Hold on." Then she called out to her husband. "Mike, bring me a glass of wine, will you?" Back to Fiona, she said, "I'm thinking I'm going to need one. Am I wrong?"

"Tell him to bring the bottle."

"Well, now I'm intrigued. Okay, I've got my wine. Travis is tucked into bed. I'm all yours. Talk."

So she did. While she continued to pace like a tiger in a too-small cage, Fiona told Laura everything that had happened from the moment she'd dropped into Luke's lap. Through it all, Laura only gave a murmured "Oooh" and a few sighs.

Finally, Fiona told her about the kiss that had singed every nerve ending she had and ended up with, "What do I do now?"

"Have sex?" Laura asked.

"Great idea!" Mike shouted, his voice coming clearly through the phone.

Fiona laughed again and felt the tight knot in her chest begin to dissolve. This is what she'd needed. To talk it all out with Laura. To be back in her "normal" zone. "I can't. It wouldn't be ethical. Would it?"

"Ethics, schmethics," Laura said. "Is he married?"

"No!"

"You're not either. So, what's the problem?"

"Um…" Fiona waved one hand in the air. "How about I'm lying to him? I'm working for his grandfather. This whole trip was paid for by Jamison Barrett just so I could convince Luke to go back to the family business."

"And did you take a celibacy pledge when I wasn't looking?"

"No, but—"

"Are you hoping that he's *the one* and you'll find happily-ever-after with him?"

Okay, she could admit that it wouldn't have taken much to imagine a perfect future with Luke as a gorgeous husband and father to a few beautiful kids. But that wasn't the point. Because the chances of anything like that happening were *way* out there.

"No, of course not, but—"

"Do you want him?"

Easy question to answer, given that her blood was still burning, and she could still taste his mouth on hers. "Oh, yes."

"So stop being so tortured. Go to bed with the man. Enjoy yourself." Laura took a breath, then said, "Let's face it. He's going to be furious when he finds out what's going on anyway. You've already said there's no future with the guy. So why not have the memory of great sex to help you through it?"

"Maybe he won't find out," Fiona argued. And really, if the

job went well, he shouldn't. He should just go back to the family business and pick up his life without ever knowing that the woman he spent a long weekend with was the reason why he'd changed his life around.

"He'll find out, sweetie," Laura said. "If you want something to stay secret, that's practically a guarantee that it won't."

"That's helpful." Fiona frowned as she caught her own reflection in the window glass. She hated the idea of Luke thinking she was a liar. That she'd felt nothing for him. Because despite her best efforts to remain professional, she couldn't help being drawn to him.

Laura sighed. "I think I'm going to need more wine. Fiona, do you like this guy?"

"I really do," she admitted, thinking back over the last couple of days. Luke was funny and gorgeous and smart, and men like that didn't grow on trees. "That's the problem, you know? I really do like him."

"Then enjoy him. Stop overthinking everything. Just accept this for what it is and appreciate it while it lasts."

Could she do that?

"Stop thinking," Laura said as if she could see the indecision written on Fiona's face. "Just relax for once and go with it."

She wasn't the most impulsive person in the world. And she definitely wasn't the one-night-stand kind of woman. Heck, it had been nearly a year since her last date. She liked to take her time. Get to know a guy before she had sex with him. Color her old-fashioned. But her personal rules seemed to be flying out a window when it came to Luke Barrett. She was so far out of her comfort zone, she couldn't even *see* it.

Luke Barrett was the kind of man who came along once in a lifetime. Fiona thought about him. Remembered that kiss. The way he felt pressed up against her. The fire in his eyes when he looked at her.

And she knew, trouble or not, she was going to risk it.

* * *

Late the next morning, Jamison Barrett was in his study at home. Church services with Loretta were finished and the rest of the day was his. He didn't quite know what to do with himself, though. In spite of his wife's assurances, Jamison was worried. If he was losing his mind, then he needed Luke back more than ever. And if Fiona Jordan failed at her task, Jamison didn't know how he'd manage it.

"Hey, Pop."

He looked up from his desk, startled to see his oldest grandson stroll into the room. "Cole? What're you doing here?"

"What do you mean?" Cole laughed a little uncertainly and tucked one hand into the pocket of his casual slacks. "We've had this planned for a week."

"Hello, Pop." Susan came in behind Cole, carrying Oliver, a blond boy with big blue eyes like his mother's and a smile just like Cole's.

"Susan!" Jamison came around the desk and scooped Oliver into his arms. "I wasn't expecting you and this little devil."

Susan smoothed her perfect hair and gave him a curious look. "I thought we were set for brunch today after your meeting with Cole…"

Jamison felt a hot jolt that he hopefully managed to hide. Oliver slapped both hands together in excitement and shouted, "Papa!"

Grinning at his great-grandson, Jamison set the toddler onto his feet and said, "Go see Nana in the kitchen. She's always got cookies."

The boy took off like a shot and not surprisingly, Susan was right behind him. How the woman managed to run in three-inch heels was beyond Jamison, but if there was one thing you could say about his granddaughter-in-law, she was devoted to her son.

When she and the boy were gone, Jamison turned to look at Cole. "Not that I'm unhappy to see all of you…but why are you here and what's this about brunch?"

Cole just stared at him for a long minute. "We've got a meeting scheduled for today about the new Christmas line, Pop."

Jamison frowned and shook his head. "That's tomorrow."

"No," Cole said softly, carefully. "It's today. You said you wanted to get it out of the way on Sunday so you could talk to marketing tomorrow at work."

Jamison scrubbed one hand across the back of his neck. He didn't remember saying that. Or even thinking it.

"And you said since we'd be working at the house, I should bring Susan and Oliver, and we'd do a Sunday brunch at the yacht club."

Jamison took a breath and held it. It was as if Cole were speaking Greek. He didn't remember anything about this. This didn't make sense. None of it did. A man didn't wake up one morning to find a giant hole in his metaphorical marble bag. Wasn't this something that slipped up on you? Weren't there small signs before big ones—like forgetting entire conversations?

"Are you okay, Pop?" Cole's gaze was steady and filled with the concern Jamison hated to see.

"Fine. I just forgot, is all." He was forgetting too damn much here lately, but he wasn't going to admit that to Cole. Or anyone else, for that matter—except Loretta, of course.

"You wrote it into your calendar last week."

Had he? Jamison searched his memory, but he didn't remember changing the meeting to Sunday. Worry coiled inside him like a snake. But just as quickly, he dismissed it. Damn it, he *knew* he'd set up that meeting for Monday. Irritated now, Jamison opened the calendar program on his computer. His home computer and his work unit were linked, so he could make changes or plans at either location.

Cole was the one who'd given him this program, telling Jamison that it would make his life easier. How in the hell going through a program was easier than a damn pen and paper was beyond him, but since it was a gift, Jamison had felt obligated to use it. "I know I wrote it down, boy. For tomorrow."

He scrolled through the program until he found what he was looking for and once he had, he felt worse than ever. There it was. *Sunday—Cole: Christmas line. Brunch with family.*

He swallowed back a knot of fear lodged in his throat. What the hell was happening to him? He never forgot a meeting. Hell, up until last year, he'd kept all of his appointments in his head and had never missed one.

Now he glared at the screen accusingly. As if it had somehow changed what he'd written.

"Pop?"

Cole's voice was hesitant, filled with distress, and Jamison hated it. He didn't need sympathy or concern. And he wanted it less.

"I'm fine," he insisted, in spite of the niggling doubts rattling through him. If there was a problem, he'd take care of it himself. The last thing he needed was people fluttering about him, treating him like a damn invalid—or worse. Pushing those thoughts aside, Jamison looked at his grandson and forced a smile he was nowhere near feeling.

Cole had his own wife and son to worry about. He didn't need to be thinking that his grandfather was on a slippery slope, balanced on one leg.

"Must have been too busy to notice," he said brusquely. "With Luke gone, I'm having to pick up a lot of slack in the company."

"You don't have to do it alone, Pop," Cole said stiffly. "I'm your grandson, too, you know. If you need help at the business, tell me. I can take over Luke's accounts. He's not the only one of us who grew up working at Barrett Toys and Tech."

Well, Jamison thought, he'd walked right into that one. It was a bone of contention for Cole that he wasn't stepping into Luke's shoes.

"I know that," he said, nodding. Cole was the oldest, but if truth be told, Luke was the more mature one. The one with the vision to see the company and where it could go. The fact that they were now arguing about that vision didn't matter. Cole was more about being in the moment rather than seeing the big picture, and that wasn't a trait that made for a good company president.

Still, he didn't need to get into all of that now. Looking at Cole, Jamison told himself that maybe he was being too hard on the boy. But he'd watched Luke and Cole grow up. He'd seen their personalities develop and though he loved them both, Jamison wasn't blind to their faults. Luke was always in the future, ignoring the present—and Cole was interested in a paycheck, but not the work.

"Maybe soon," Jamison hedged, "we'll have a talk about that." But if Fiona Jordan did the job he was paying her to accomplish, he wouldn't have to. Still, Cole knew nothing about that. "For right now, though, we'll go on the way we have been." He nodded and winked at Cole. "You never know, Luke might come back."

"Sure, Pop." Disappointment and frustration briefly crossed Cole's features, but an instant later, he'd buried whatever he was feeling beneath his usual smile. "We'll do it your way for now."

"That's good. So," Jamison said, sitting down at his desk again, "if you're ready, we can take care of this meeting right now."

"Okay." Cole took a seat, opened up his tablet and started talking.

Jamison listened. He really did. He even made notes when appropriate. But the back of his mind was filled with whispering voices, and none of them were comforting.

An hour later, Fiona somehow found herself on Luke's private jet, feeling like a peasant in a palace.

She was used to dragging herself through security, waiting at a crowded gate on uncomfortable chairs and then squeezing into tiny seats built for a butt a little smaller than her own.

This kind of luxury, she told herself as she looked at her surroundings, was going to make flying coach even more miserable in the future. There were two black leather sofas on either side of the sleek jet, and toward the front of the plane, a conversational group of six black leather chairs faced one another.

There were tables, reading lamps and a thick, plush white carpet on the floor. A flat-screen TV was on one wall and there were even fresh flowers in a copper vase that had been bolted to one of the tables. Slowly, she sank down onto one of the sofas and idly ran one hand across the cool, smooth surface, as if to convince herself she was really there and not dreaming.

Her gaze locked on Luke, talking with his own private flight attendant, the pilot and the copilot. She'd been introduced to all three of them when she'd come aboard and had even had a brief tour of the cockpit—an impressive and confusing wall of switches, lights and buttons.

And as distracted as she was by the plane and the luxury of not having to fight through a crowded airport, Fiona could barely take her eyes off Luke.

He wore a dark blue suit, pale blue shirt and scarlet tie. His hair, for some reason, kept capturing her attention. Too long for a businessman and too short for a surfer, and her fingers itched to touch it. His eyes were so blue, she felt as if she could drown in them. And when he turned his head to look at her, she felt a sharp jolt of electricity that set every nerve in her body sizzling.

It was that look that had kept her sleepless the night before. That *knowing* gleam in his eyes. Well, that and the memory of the kiss they'd shared in the garden. She had the distinct feeling she would remember that kiss even if she lived to be one hundred.

The feel of him pressed against her. The rush of his mouth on hers, his breath sliding into her lungs. The fire he'd kindled inside her had burned brightly all night, driving her half-crazy with an aching need that still throbbed with every beat of her heart.

Her gaze locked with his, Fiona realized she was sorry this weekend was over. It had started out as a job, but somehow it had become more than that. Now she was caught up in something completely different and she had no idea how it would end. Or where they would go from here.

When they were back in Orange County, she'd have to keep seeing him—that had been the original plan, after all. She still had to convince him to go back to the family company. But with that kiss, she had realized she wanted to keep seeing him because she simply wanted to. But sleeping with him was something else entirely. If she did and then he walked away at the end of the weekend, then she'd failed at her job. And there was still a big lie hanging between them that she really didn't want to think about. And what if he expected their weekend to end, well, with the weekend?

Too many thoughts were crashing through her mind at once and she instantly recalled Laura saying, *You always overthink everything.* Well, maybe her friend was right. Maybe it was time to stop thinking and just see what would happen.

A moment later, Luke walked toward her in long, almost lazy strides and Fiona's breath caught in her lungs. Honestly, the man was dangerous. Her heartbeat kept jumping into a fast gallop and that couldn't be healthy.

"We'll be cleared to take off in a few minutes."

"Okay." If she hadn't accepted his offer of a ride back to Southern California, right about now Fiona would have been sitting in the crowded airport waiting to be shuffled onto a jam-packed, uncomfortable plane. Not to mention, she wouldn't be with Luke. This was so much better. And so far out of her 'normal' world, she was a little off-balance. Of course, just being with Luke made her feel unsteady, so…

He helped her up, then drew her to one of the matching chairs. "We'll sit here for takeoff."

"A lot better than what I'm used to," she said, snapping her seat belt as she turned to watch him sit beside her.

He gave her a half smile that tugged at something inside her. "You can fly with me whenever you like."

"Well, that's a tempting offer," she mused, wondering if he meant it or if he was just being charming. Either way, it worked.

So strange, she thought, watching him. A few days ago, she didn't know him. Had never heard of him, really. And today, she was sitting beside him, feeling a tangle of emotions she'd never experienced before.

"I'm hoping so," he admitted, then turned to look at the woman approaching.

She was tall, wearing black slacks, a white long-sleeved blouse and a bright red scarf knotted at her neck. She was carrying two glasses of champagne and when she delivered them, she smiled. "Enjoy your flight. If you need me, Mr. Barrett, I'll be with the pilot as you requested."

"Thanks, Janice. We'll be fine."

So, he'd arranged for them to be alone. Oddly enough, that didn't make Fiona nervous at all. She took a sip of the bubbling wine and let the froth of it settle on her tongue for a moment before swallowing. Nope, not nervous. Eager, maybe.

The last few days had been so much more than she'd thought they would be. She'd gone there to do her job, but she'd never expected to be so drawn to Luke. So tempted by him. She'd never known a man who could turn her inside out so easily. Why did it have to be this man? They were separated not just by the lie that was hanging between them, but by the fact that she was in no way a part of his world. A world of private jets, for heaven's sake. No, sleeping with him would be a huge mistake.

Was it hot in the airplane, she wondered. Or was it just her?

Fiona took another sip of the cold champagne. "Oh yes. Definitely better than coach."

He grinned. "I told Janice we wouldn't be needing her after takeoff. It's only a ninety-minute flight, after all."

"Sure." Her mind was working, dancing, jumping from one thought to another. Ninety minutes could be a long time if you spent it wisely. Fly with him anytime? She doubted that would happen in the future. So why not take Laura's advice, stop thinking for a while, and just enjoy where she was and who she was with?

It wasn't like her at all to simply give in to her own wants and needs. She was more the type to think things through from every angle. Being impulsive was just counter to her nature. So why was she considering being just that?

Nerves rattled her, but Fiona tamped them down. If there were…consequences to pay, then she would pay them. Later. But if this weekend was all she would have of Luke Barrett, Fiona didn't want to waste it. For once in her life, she was going to leap without worrying about the fall. Just this once, she would take a chance. Risk it.

She felt the hum of the jet's engines as they revved, and the plane started taxiing to the runway. It felt as if she were doing the same thing. Moving inexorably forward.

"Once we're in the air," Luke said, leaning in closer to her, "I'll show you around."

She blinked at him. "There's more?"

He only smiled and then their plane was racing down the runway. Her heartbeat kept pace, thundering in her chest. Looking into his blue eyes was almost hypnotic. He could capture her with a glance. Her blood heated in her veins and she took another sip of the champagne to ease the fire. But nothing could do that.

The jet raced faster, then lifted into the air. As always, Fiona's stomach did a quick jitter, but this time, she had the feeling it was more being with Luke rather than her fear of flying.

A few minutes later, they were high above the banks of clouds she could see outside the windows. The jet's engines settled into a throaty purr that hummed in the background. Luke unhooked his seat belt, then held out a hand to her. She set her champagne aside and slipped her hand into his. He curled his fingers around hers and held on, and Fiona didn't mind in the slightest.

His skin next to hers made heat swarm through her and Fiona started a silent mantra, demanding that her hormones take a nap. They weren't listening to her, but she kept trying. Laura's advice aside, she couldn't help thinking that this connection she felt to Luke was not a good thing.

He was a job. He wasn't hers to care for or to dream about. If not for his grandfather, none of this would be happening. She still had to complete the job she'd been hired to do. What was she thinking even considering going to bed with him?

For heaven's sake, she'd known him about three days. Fiona couldn't remember a time when she'd been so willing to go with her instincts rather than planning something out. Still, it wasn't as if he was a complete stranger, was it?

A voice in the back of her mind said that the last three days, they'd been together almost nonstop. They'd talked more than most people did during weeks of getting to know each other. She liked him. A lot. And that worried her a little, because she had zero business building fantasies in her mind that centered on Luke Barrett. Just standing here, in his private jet, told her that much. They were from separate worlds. She had no place in the kind of universe he inhabited and no illusions about it, either.

Nothing in her life had prepared her for this man and she didn't think anything could have. He gave her hand a squeeze and her insides leaped into life again.

Take a nap, hormones, she thought to herself. *Take a nap.*

"And this is the bedroom," Luke said, opening a door to a room at the back of the plane.

"Handy," she answered, looking around. The room was small, but plush. A queen-size bed covered in a dark red duvet, twin tables and a television on the wall.

She looked up at him and knew there wasn't a chance in hell her hormones would be napping.

CHAPTER SIX

His gaze was locked on her, and Fiona felt the heat of it bathing her. The power of his stare was like a touch. She could *feel* him looking at her.

"The bathroom's right here," he was saying. "Though there's another up front by the cockpit."

"Right." She laughed a little, shaking her head. This was so far from her normal life it was as if she'd landed on a different planet. "Of course. A one-bedroom, two-bath plane. Sure."

He quirked an eyebrow. "Are you okay?"

"Honestly? I don't know." She glanced around the room, taking it all in before turning her gaze back on him. Was he really so used to living like this that he didn't even see how weird it was?

"I'm fine. It's just—usually when I fly, I call it luxury if the seat next to me is empty."

He shrugged and tucked his hands into his pockets. "Yeah, I can see that."

"But you've always lived like this."

Nodding, he said only, "Pretty much."

The plane's engines hummed beneath their feet and set up a vibration that echoed in her nervous system.

"My father was a pilot, so he liked having his own plane."

"Does he still?"

Luke's features tightened. "No. He and my mom died in a plane crash."

"Oh God. I'm so sorry." She didn't know which was worse, the pain in his eyes or the matter-of-fact way he'd said it. Fiona hadn't grown up with a family, and she knew how awful that had been. The emptiness, the wish for more, for love, to be wanted. Needed. But she couldn't even imagine the pain of *having* a family and then losing them like that.

"I was a kid," he said softly. "My cousin Cole's parents were with them. They were headed to Florida on a vacation and went down halfway there. No one survived."

Fiona didn't question her instincts this time. She just went with them. Wrapping her arms around his waist, she laid her head on his chest and simply held on. There was nothing she could say. No way to help. But she could see old pain in his eyes and hear it in his voice, and it was in her nature to try to offer whatever comfort she could.

When his arms came around her and Fiona's heartbeat jumped, she knew the decision she'd just made was going to lead to more than comfort.

Luke threaded his fingers through her hair and pulled her head back. Looking down into her eyes, he shook his head as if in wonder. "You're...unsettling."

She stared up at him, gave him a small smile and said, "Thank you."

He laughed shortly. "Figures you'd see that as a compliment."

Her heart jumped into a fast rhythm. "You really do say the nicest things."

He grinned, bent his head and kissed her. Fiona's mind scrambled so fast, it was a wonder she remembered how to breathe. They were standing beside a bed. In a jet. Alone.

Sex was bound to happen. Right? She'd already decided to go for it...to surrender to whatever was happening between them. And she vowed to not regret it later.

He deepened the kiss, and Fiona eagerly matched him. Her breath was coming short and hard. Her heartbeat raced and the blood in her veins was like lava. Every square inch of her skin felt as if it were on fire.

When he lifted his head and looked down at her, Fiona could see the same reaction on his face that she felt sure was stamped on hers.

"Are we doing this?" he asked, voice deep, quiet.

"I think we really are." Fiona shut down all her doubts.

Because none of that mattered right now. The only thing she could think was that she needed to touch him and be touched. She wanted to feel him deep inside her. She needed Luke Barrett in a way she'd never needed before.

And today, she was going to surrender to her own needs. This wasn't about anything but the current sizzling between her and Luke and Fiona wanted more than anything to indulge herself in him. Whatever came next…she'd worry about that when she had to.

A half smile curved one side of his mouth. "Really glad to hear that."

Then he kissed her again, and Fiona stopped thinking altogether. With his mouth on hers, his tongue stroking against hers, all she could do was *feel*. And there was so much, it was as if her brain were short-circuiting and she didn't miss it at all.

He tore his mouth from hers, tugged the hem of her red-and-white-striped boatneck shirt up and over her head, then tossed it aside. The cool air touched her skin and only enflamed it further. He stared at her black lace bra and sighed before flipping open the catch in front. Then his hands cupped her breasts and Fiona groaned.

His thumbs and forefingers tugged and pulled at her nipples, and she felt it all the way to her core. She was hot, achy and filled with so many needs she couldn't have named them all even if she could have spoken. Which she couldn't.

"I've wanted to touch you since that first day," he murmured, bending down to kiss her again. It was a hard, fast, desperate kiss that Fiona missed the moment it ended.

"Yes," she finally said, when she could gather enough coherent thought to form a sentence. "I remember how 'happy' you were when we first met."

He grinned. "You're about to find out that I'm a hell of a lot 'happier' right now."

"Promises, promises," she muttered as his hands dropped to the hem of her short black skirt. She'd always loved that skirt. Today, she thought it just might be her favorite piece of clothing.

Because it gave him quick, easy access to the one part of her body that was screaming for attention.

In seconds, his talented fingers had found the strip of elastic at her black panties and sent them sliding down her legs so she could kick them off. Then he cupped her with one hand and she instantly began rocking into his touch. She couldn't stop herself. Didn't want to stop. What she wanted was what he was giving her. A ride into oblivion. Release. And that thought alone kept her standing, moving into him.

One finger, then two, moved within her, stroking, caressing. His thumb found her center and rubbed that one, so sensitive bud until her eyes were wheeling in her head and breathing became an extreme sport.

If she had stood outside herself, she might have been embarrassed to be mostly naked, with a fully dressed man who was sliding his fingers inside her. But she wouldn't have changed anything.

Fiona felt as if she'd been primed for an orgasm from the moment she'd landed on his lap. So, it was no surprise when her body was suddenly on the broken verge of shattering.

Until he stopped.

Fiona blinked and stared up at him. "What? Why?"

"Nope," he said flatly. "You're not going there without me."

She watched him tear his clothes off, tossing his elegant suit to one side until he was naked and, she saw...*impressive.*

He unzipped her skirt and let it fall, then he tumbled her back onto the wide bed behind her and followed her down.

His hands claimed her body while his mouth took hers. Their tongues twisted and tangled together, breath sliding from one to the other of them. Fiona clutched at his shoulders and slid her fingertips down his muscular arms, loving the feel of him. The heat in his body that speared into hers.

She kissed him with everything she had and threw one leg over his hip, pulling that erection closer, closer. When the tip of him rubbed over her, she groaned and broke their kiss long enough to mutter, "For heaven's sake, do it. Do it now."

He reached to the closest table, opened the drawer and pulled out a condom.

"Handy," she murmured.

"I try," he countered.

In a blink, he had sheathed himself, and then he was kneeling between her thighs, holding her body open to his gaze. Fiona squirmed with impatience.

"I feel like we've been doing the whole foreplay thing for days," she whispered, looking up, into his summer-blue eyes. "Can we go for the big show now?"

He grinned. "Have I mentioned I really like your attitude?"

"Nope, but you can. Later."

"Right." He pushed into her body with one long, hard stroke.

She groaned. Fiona's head went back into the mattress and she stared blindly at the jet's ceiling as she adjusted to his size. He filled her completely, and she didn't know how she'd lived so long without having him inside her.

Then he rocked his hips against her, and everything got even better. A delicious friction built up between them as he moved inside her. He set a rhythm that she raced to keep up with. Her body was humming, her mind shutting down. She fought for breath, hoped her heart wouldn't explode and rocked her hips with his every movement. "More," she groaned. "More."

"Yes," he ground out. "Always more."

She was so close. So near the teetering edge of oblivion Fiona could almost taste it. Then he changed things up and threw her for a loop.

He sat back on his heels, drawing her up with him until she was straddling him. Eye to eye, they looked at each other, gazes locked as Fiona took charge of the rhythm. The pace. She moved on him, taking him deeper and deeper inside her and still it wasn't enough. She swiveled her hips against him, creating a new kind of friction that drove them both to the brink.

"You're amazing," he muttered, leaning in to take her mouth with his.

She licked her lips when the kiss was over, as if she could draw the taste of him into her.

His hands locked on her hips, guiding her, pushing her, helping her keep that wild, frantic rhythm at a breathless pace, because they were now caught together in a net of desperation. When the first splintering sensation jolted her, Fiona grabbed hold of him and kept moving, kept pushing herself higher and faster, riding that incredible pulse of pleasure that rocked her right to the bone.

While she shattered in his arms, she felt his release shake through him. His grip on her tightened; he clenched his jaw and kept his gaze fixed on her as if seeing her fed what he was feeling.

And when the crash was over, they fell to the bed, still locked together.

"Nice to keep a supply of condoms in the drawer," she murmured.

Luke grinned. "Yeah. I bought some this morning. Just in case."

She turned her head to look at him and Luke thought her eyes looked darker, deeper, somehow. Almost as if they were pulling him in. "So you thought I was a sure thing?"

"I hoped," he admitted, leaning in to get another kiss. God, the taste of her pumped through him with a life of its own. He'd just had her and he wanted her again. More than before because now he knew just how good it was.

"Good call," she said, and gave a lovely, long sigh. "That was…"

"Yeah. If we're this good in the air, imagine how good we'll be on the ground."

Her gaze snapped to his. "Will we?"

He smoothed her hair back, indulging himself by sliding his fingers through that soft, dark brown silk. "I'm not finished yet. You?"

She dragged her fingertips along his chest, and he sucked in a gulp of air. "No, I'm not finished, either."

"Like I said before. I like your attitude." He leaned over her and took one of her nipples into his mouth. He smiled against her at the quick catch of her breath. His tongue and teeth worked that dark pink bud until she was writhing beneath him and all Luke could think was how glad he was he'd bought the large box of condoms.

Then he lost himself in her again and stopped thinking entirely.

An hour later, Luke hooked one arm behind his head and said, "We'll be landing soon."

"Back to the real world."

"This isn't real?" he asked, turning his head to look at her. She was beautiful. Her eyes alone were enough to spellbind a man. And the minute that thought hit, he scowled to himself. Luke wouldn't allow that. In his world, the plan ruled all. And Fiona was definitely not a part of the plan. He wasn't spellbound and wasn't about to be, either. But he could appreciate a beautiful woman he'd just had the most incredible sex of his life with.

She grinned and he worried again. "This isn't *my* reality," she said. "It's a great place to visit, don't get me wrong. But when I get home, I've got to pay bills, answer emails and do some laundry. *That* is reality."

"I pay bills and do emails," he pointed out.

"And the laundry?"

He shrugged. "The housekeeper does it."

She laughed, and he liked the sound of it in spite of the fact that she was laughing at *him*.

"Of course she does."

Still frowning, he changed the subject, since he was suddenly *embarrassed* about having a housekeeper. If she found out he had a cook, too, she might laugh herself sick.

"Why don't you let me take you to dinner tomorrow night?"

"Really?" she seemed surprised, and frankly, so was he.

When they'd first boarded this plane, Luke hadn't planned on seeing her again once they got home. He wasn't interested in a relationship—he had way too much going on at the moment. But he didn't care for the thought of letting her go, either. Now, after that bout of incredible sex, he was even more interested in sticking around for a while. He didn't want to consider why. Refused to think of what that might mean. He wouldn't be distracted by emotional entanglements. This wasn't about emotion anyway. This was simple, beautiful lust, and he would stay with her until the desire for her had ebbed.

"Why not?"

"Well, for one thing, I've got a job tomorrow evening."

"Doing what?"

She studied him for a long second or two, then said, "Why don't you come over and you can go with me to my appointment? Then we can have dinner after."

Go with her. On what? A treasure hunt like she'd had the day before when she dug through wet towels to find a stuffed alligator? But even as he thought it, he realized he didn't care. "All right. It's a date."

"Great." She leaned over to kiss him, then smiled. "I'm just going to put my clothes on. Your flight attendant might guess what we were up to, but I'd rather she didn't see me naked."

He watched her snatch up her clothes and step into the attached bathroom. Luke wasn't sure why he'd agreed to go along on her job. He'd thought a nice dinner and then another great bout of lovemaking.

What had he gotten himself into here? And why didn't he care?

Late the next afternoon, Fiona and Laura sat in matching lawn chairs watching Travis chase a bright red ball across the lawn. The little boy's laughter spilled from him and floated behind him like soap bubbles on the air.

"So, he's coming over," Laura said.

"Yep."

"To go on your job with you."

"Yep."

"Okay, my question is, *why*?"

Fiona had wondered that, too. She'd thought it was going to be hard to stay close enough to him to complete her job for his grandfather. Instead, Luke himself had suggested meeting again. Was it the sex? Because it had been really great, but sex wasn't *everything*. "Because I'm irresistible?"

Laura laughed. "That must be it."

Fiona grinned. She looked at Travis, a two-year-old whose only problem at the moment was catching up to his favorite ball. Maybe Laura was right. Maybe she did overthink everything. Maybe she should take a clue from Travis and just focus on what was in front of her in the moment.

A soft wind swept over them and nodded the heads of the gem-colored pansies in Laura's flower bed. At the duplex next door, the Gonzalez girls sat on the porch, each of them playing on her own tablet. They, too, were focused on the moment. So the trick was to focus on what was *important* right now.

"I don't know why he wanted to see me again, but I couldn't say no. Not only is he gorgeous and funny and smart and *way* talented in bed, he's my job, too." She winced. "I can't believe I had sex with him."

"On a plane." Laura sighed and looked wistful. "I'm so jealous."

Fiona looked back at the Gonzalez kids again. They didn't talk to each other or laugh together or anything. They could have been twin statues for all the interaction happening between them. She sighed and shook her head.

Funny that she'd never noticed how many kids were glued to tablets before working for Jamison Barrett. The girls on that porch were ten and eight. Too young to be that wrapped up in a computer.

Frowning, Fiona made a mental note to point the girls out to Luke and to remember that he wasn't her "date." He was her job.

"This is crazy," she muttered. "*I'm* crazy."

"Yeah, probably," Laura mused. "But, Fiona, you never do anything wild or outrageous. Honey, you never take something for yourself. So maybe you were due."

She had a point, as much as Fiona hated to admit it. But that didn't let her off the hook, did it? Was doing something for herself enough of a reason to be with Luke? Was that fair to him? And what happened when he inevitably discovered the truth about their first meeting? She was lying to Luke about who she was and how she'd met him. He thought it was all an accident of fate. What would he say if he found out his grandfather had paid her to be there? Had arranged for her plane ticket and hotel room just so that she could convince him to come back to the company?

Wincing, she silently admitted she knew just what he'd say. *Goodbye.* So she had to remember that whatever was between them, it was temporary. An anomaly to her daily life. No more permanent than a sunset...beautiful, but quickly gone.

"Oh my... You know I love my honey," Laura whispered beside her. "But damn, Fiona..."

She didn't have to look to know that Luke had arrived. Laura's glassy-eyed stare was enough to alert her to his presence. Fiona was pretty sure she'd had the same expression on her face the first time she saw him. Still, she turned her head to watch the man approach.

He was wearing a suit again. Of course. She idly wondered if he even owned a pair of jeans. The suit was black with faint gray pinstripes. He wore a white dress shirt with a dark gray tie, and his too-long hair was ruffling in the sea breeze.

It was late afternoon, so the neighborhood kids were home from school. Somewhere down the street, a basketball thumped like the heartbeat of the neighborhood. Skateboard wheels growled across the sidewalks, and the sounds made her smile. At least *some* kids were outside and not staring at a screen.

"Hi!" Fiona stood up and walked to him, suddenly feeling very underdressed. Her beige ankle pants, yellow long-sleeved shirt and taupe Skechers really didn't hold up against that suit.

He slipped one hand to the back of her neck and leaned in to claim a quick, hard kiss. A zip of something amazing shot through Fiona like a whipcrack. A job, she thought frantically. He was a job. But even reminding herself of that fact didn't change what she was willing to risk just to be with him.

"I've been wanting to do that all day," he admitted.

A job and so much more.

"Well, don't be shy," she said. "Do it again."

He grinned and took advantage of the invitation.

Her head was spinning even as she gave herself a mental talking-to. Hadn't she just decided that she had to remain professional? Why was it that her best intentions flew out the window the minute she was close to him?

When she came up for air, Laura was standing right beside her. Her best friend was five inches shorter than Fiona's five nine, and her body was substantially curvier. Her wide smile was friendly, and her blue eyes were sparkling with interest and curiosity.

"Hi, I'm Laura. Best friend. Neighbor. Landlord." She held out one hand and Luke shook it.

"Nice to meet you," he said. "Luke Barrett."

"Fee!" Travis came racing up, grabbed hold of Fiona's legs and turned his face to her. "Up, Fee!"

"Right." She lifted him, sat him on her hip and said, "Luke, this is my boyfriend, Travis. He's the jealous type, so watch your step."

"I'll keep it in mind. He looks pretty tough."

"Oh, he is. Able to destroy a living room in less than ten minutes," Laura put in and scooped her son from Fiona.

"Maybe he could use something to keep him so busy learning he wouldn't have time for destruction," Luke said.

Now it was Fiona's turn to frown. Just the thought of this active little boy sitting in front of a computer tablet when he could be running in circles refocused her on the job at hand.

Fiona tugged at Luke's arm and pointed him at the house next door. The two girls were still there. Still staring at their screens. Still so absorbed with their tablets it was as if they'd forgotten they weren't alone.

"Busy like them, you mean?" Fiona asked. "That's Elena and Teresa Gonzalez. I'd introduce you, but they're zoned out. Being *busy*."

Luke looked at the girls and frowned thoughtfully. Fiona thought that maybe she'd scored a point. But whatever he was thinking, he didn't say. He simply shifted his gaze to her. "You ready to leave?"

Fiona let it go. For now. But she'd be talking to him about the girls and their technology again later. "Sure. Let me get my purse. I'll see you tomorrow, Laura."

"Have fun," her friend said, and headed off to get Travis's ball.

Luke followed her inside and stood practically at attention in her small living room. He looked around and she wished she knew what he was thinking. Fiona had no idea where he lived, but she knew that wherever it was, his place was nothing like hers.

Fiona's living room was painted a deep maroon and she'd

installed the white crown molding herself. Her windows didn't have curtains because Fiona hated them, but she had installed window shades that she pulled down at night for a little privacy. There was a green love seat and two club chairs covered in a fabric that boasted wild sprays of flowers, and a coffee table she'd found in a thrift shop. She'd sanded and painted the table a pale yellow, adding to the garden feel of the room.

"It's a nice place."

"Thanks." Her entire apartment was probably the size of his closet, but she loved the home she'd built for herself. Every room was a different color, and she'd filled the apartment with furniture she loved. So every time she walked into her apartment, Fiona felt satisfaction and a sense of...rightness she'd never known as a kid.

She reached over and turned on one of a pair of dented brass lamps she'd found at an auction, and soft light spilled into the room. "I just need to get my purse." She stopped and looked at him. "You don't have to wear a tie, you know. You could... loosen up a little."

He smoothed one hand down the gray tie and said, "I came straight from work. And my gray tie is my loose tie."

She grinned at the spark of humor in his eyes. He really was the whole package. Smart. Funny. And so sexy it took her breath away. "Is that right?"

"Oh yeah." He nodded solemnly. "Red ties? Power. Navy? All business. Gray? Casual and loose."

"Wow, I didn't know they made a tie for 'casual.'"

"Now you do." He checked his watch. "What time is your appointment?"

"Twenty minutes or so. But he's in Seal Beach. It won't take long to get there."

"He?" Luke lifted one eyebrow. "What're you doing for 'him'?"

"It's a secret." Fiona smiled, grabbed her purse and headed for the door. "Let's go."

CHAPTER SEVEN

WHATEVER LUKE HAD been expecting, this wasn't it. The "him" in question was seventeen, extremely tall and gangly, with a hank of hair that kept falling over his eyes, and he was going to his first prom in a few weeks. He needed to know how to dance.

"Ow!" Fiona hopped a little after the boy stepped on her foot for the third time.

Luke winced. This was painful to watch. How the hell did Fiona make a living doing all of these short-term jobs? Teaching a kid to dance. Finding an alligator. Now she'd probably be limping for a week.

"I'm never getting this."

"You're doing fine, Kenny," she said to the boy, who towered over her. "You just have to relax."

"How can I relax when I'm worried about stepping on you? I can't do this. I'll break Amber's foot." He shook his head and held both hands up. "I'll just stick to the fast dances."

Luke sighed and shook his head. He'd been watching this disaster for a half hour now, and he had to wonder how this kid was the star of the basketball team. He had zero rhythm. He was too tense, too. He held on to Fiona like she was a live grenade about to explode. He was probably more relaxed on the court, Luke thought. Hell, he'd have to be.

"Okay." He stood up and walked to Fiona. "Let's try something else." Talking to Kenny, he said, "You just sit down and watch." To Fiona, he added, "We'll show him how to do it."

How he'd gotten into this, he wasn't sure. Luke had thought about Fiona all day. What he'd wanted was to get her alone on a flat surface somewhere. Instead, he was slow dancing for a teenager in his parents' den.

"Oh, good idea," she said, and gave Kenny an encouraging smile. "Watch us for a minute or two, then we'll try again."

"It's useless." He swung his dark brown hair out of his eyes and scowled.

"Only if you quit," Luke said. Taking Fiona in his arms, he looked into her eyes, but his words were for Kenny. "Hold her closer."

"I can't hold on to Fiona like that. It's too weird, man."

"You're practicing," Luke reminded him. "You'll want to hold Amber close, right?"

"Well, yeah…"

"Okay. Hold her close." He pulled Fiona in tightly to him. "Put your feet in place before the music starts—on either side of one of her feet."

Kenny studied him. "Okay…"

"You don't have to be fancy about it. Going in circles will get the job done for you." Luke started moving and paid no attention to Fiona's bright smile. She was enjoying this. Well, surprisingly enough, so was he.

The music played and Luke moved with it. "Listen to the beat and keep up with it. Slow or fast, if you stay with the beat you won't look uncoordinated."

"Hey!" Kenny the basketball star was offended.

"And you'll notice, I'm not stepping on her feet because I'm barely lifting mine."

"Yeah. That works…" Kenny nodded and looked a little less defeated.

"Her steps will follow yours in the dance. It's just instinct.

You act like you know what you're doing, and it'll be fine." Of course, teenage hormones would be soaring. And he knew that because holding on to Fiona like this with the slow music streaming from the speakers on the wall made him want to pick her up and carry her out to the car.

Which meant, he told himself, lesson over. Luke stepped back and motioned to Kenny. "You try it now."

Fiona grinned at him, then gave Kenny an encouraging smile. "You can do this. And you'll be glad you did."

Kenny shrugged. "It's your feet."

"I'll risk it."

Luke stood aside and watched as Kenny did just as he'd been told. Fiona smiled up at the boy and, as the music played and they began to dance, Kenny visibly relaxed. It wasn't exactly an old Gene Kelly movie, but it was good enough for prom, and now the kid knew he could dance with his girlfriend without permanently maiming her.

The song ended and Kenny dropped Fiona like she was on fire. "That was awesome." He grinned and flashed a look at Luke. "Thanks, man. That works."

"You did fine."

Fiona asked, "Do you want to try it again? Just to make sure you've got it?"

"Don't have to. What he said made sense and now I know I can do it. Just plant my feet before the music."

"Excellent," Luke said.

"Okay, then." Fiona reached up and gave the kid a hug. "Lesson over. Have a great time at the dance, Kenny."

"I will now. Thanks." He jerked his hair out of his eyes and looked at Luke again. "Thanks. Really."

"You're welcome." He held out a hand and the kid shook it with a hard grip. "Have fun."

After Fiona collected a check from Kenny's grateful mother, they were outside on the front walk. Streetlights were on, casting pale white glows into the darkness. A crisp sea breeze kicked up and Fiona shivered. Automatically, he dropped one arm around her shoulders and pulled her in close.

"That was nice," she said. "What you did for Kenny."

"It was more for Amber. And you." He snorted. "I couldn't take it anymore. If I hadn't stepped in, you would have ended the night in a cast."

"It wasn't that bad." She laughed, though, and he liked the sound. "It's hard to teach a guy the guy's moves, so thanks for helping out."

"You're welcome." He looked down at her and felt his body stir again. Hell, since the moment he'd met this woman, his body had been like stone. "Not hard to sway back and forth and move in a circle."

She grinned at him. "It meant a lot to Kenny."

"Uh-huh." He couldn't have cared less about Kenny and his plans for a night of dancing and who the hell knew what else. What he'd done, he'd done for Fiona. To see that smile he was currently basking in.

He didn't like knowing that she was becoming more important to him than he cared to acknowledge. But even if his mind shied away from that thought, his body had no trouble admitting it.

"So?" she asked, and Luke was ready for any suggestion that would get them alone and naked. "Dinner. How about a burger?"

Her eyes sparkled and her lips were curved in that smile that drove him crazy. Not the idea he'd had in mind, but it'd do. For now.

The next morning, Fiona called Jamison Barrett on the direct number he'd given her. She had to report in on her weekend with Luke. Of course, she has no intention of telling the older man about what had happened on the plane. Or last night in her apartment, for that matter. She shivered a little at the images flooding her mind and knew she'd never be able to sleep in that bed again without Luke's memory joining her.

Jamison answered and Fiona jumped.

"Yes?" He sounded distracted. Maybe that was a good thing.

"Mr. Barrett," Fiona said, rising to walk across her living room. "This is Fiona Jordan."

"Hmm? Oh. Yes. Yes. Fiona. Hello."

Frowning, she stared out at the sun-washed street. "I just wanted you to know that the weekend with Luke went very well, and I think I'm making headway."

"That's good."

His voice sounded odd to her. Less confident. The last time she spoke to him, Jamison had been brisk, impatient. Now it seemed as if he wasn't even interested in what was happening with Luke. Was he having second thoughts? Was he sorry he'd hired her in the first place?

Because Fiona could completely understand regrets. She regretted ever lying to Luke. But she couldn't be sorry she'd taken this job, because if she hadn't, she never would have met him, and she couldn't even imagine not knowing him.

How did this whole situation get so confused and tangled up? Luke loved his grandfather but couldn't work with him. Jamison loved his grandson but couldn't compromise. And Fiona? Fiona was in the middle, unsure which way to turn.

Still, she tried. "I'm seeing him again today and—"

"Right. You just get it done and we'll talk then. All right? Thank you."

He hung up and Fiona took the phone from her ear to stare at it. For a man who was so determined to win his grandson back, he seemed decidedly uninterested in hearing the report he had asked for. What was going on?

When Jamison hung up, Fiona went straight out of his mind. He had bigger problems at the moment. He stared at the contract in front of him and felt panic clawing at the edges of his soul.

His signature was on the bottom line, but damned if he remembered signing it. "Why the hell would I order skateboards from a new company when I've already got Salem's boards?"

Didn't make sense. But then, lately nothing was making sense, and Jamison felt a fresh stir of fear. And he didn't like that, either. He'd faced a lot in his lifetime. He lost his father in a world war, the loss of his sons. He'd fought his way through bad times before and he would this time, too.

He knew Cole was worried about him. And it wouldn't be long before he saw the same look of concern on Loretta's face, too. Jamison didn't think he could stand that. Maybe it was time to talk to his doctor. Get to the bottom of this. Bill Tucker was a no-nonsense kind of man. He'd be straight with Jamison. And maybe, he admitted silently, that was why he hadn't gone to see him yet. He was afraid of what Bill might have to say.

Loretta claimed it was nothing, but he couldn't help worrying. He'd seen friends diagnosed with dementia. He'd watched them slowly fade away until there was nothing of them left, and it terrified him to believe that might be happening to him.

"Pop?" Cole poked his head in the door.

"Yes." He looked up. "What is it?"

"I wanted to ask you about the order for basketballs you canceled."

"What? I didn't cancel an order." Did he?

Cole stepped into the room and his features were twisted into a mask of worry that ate at Jamison's insides. "I just got a call from Adam Carey, and he says he got the cancellation late last night."

"Last night?" Shaking his head, Jamison jumped to his feet. That should be proof that he wasn't doing this. That he hadn't lost his mind. "I was out with your grandmother last night. We went to the club for dinner..."

Cole winced and handed out the email he'd printed out. "Adam forwarded the email to me, Pop. It's definitely from you. Went out about ten last night."

Jamison studied it and an icy ball dropped into the pit of his stomach. It was from his email address. Canceling an order. But he didn't do it. Crumpling the paper in his fist, he looked at Cole. "I didn't send this."

"Pop..." Cole scrubbed one hand across his neck and looked as if he wished he were anywhere else.

Jamison knew the feeling.

"Damn it, boy, stop looking at me like I'm dying."

"I don't like this, Pop."

"Well, neither do I. Look, I don't know what's going on here, but I didn't send this." He tossed the offensive wad of paper into the trash, then sat down behind his desk again. "I'll call Adam. Set things straight."

"Good luck. He's pretty pissed."

"I said I'll take care of it." He looked back at the file on his desk, silently dismissing Cole. But his grandson didn't leave.

"Pop, do you think maybe we should talk to a doctor?"

"We?" Jamison speared his grandson with a steely look. Damned if he'd be treated like a slobbering old fool. "You having a problem you didn't tell me about?"

Cole took a breath. "Fine. You, then. Pop, you seem to be having some trouble lately, and I want you to know that I'm here." The younger man moved closer, leaned both hands on the edge of the desk and said, "I can take over for you. Handle things while you take a break. Maybe you just need a long rest."

If what he was hearing was simple familial concern, then Jamison should have been touched. But he knew that there was nothing Cole would like better than stepping into the CEO job. He'd been angling for it for years.

"How long a break, Cole? Forever?" Jamison loved his grandson, but he knew Cole's ambitions far exceeded his talents.

"You know, I'm not saying that." He pushed up from the desk. "But with Luke gone, I'm the one you can trust to take over. Pop, I'm here. Use me."

Irritation rushed in and was swamped by regret for thinking badly of Cole. Sure, he had a lot of ambition, but so had

Jamison at his age. It wasn't Cole's fault now that his grandfather's brain was taking a vacation. "I know that. And I appreciate it. But I'm not ready to quit. And we don't know that Luke's gone for good, either."

Cole pushed one hand through his hair in frustration. "Luke isn't your only grandson, Pop. He isn't the only Barrett who's worked at the company since he was a kid. He's not the only man who could run this company."

There was a lot of bitterness there. More than he'd suspected.

"You're getting worked up for nothing, Cole." Jamison shook his head and tried to understand that Cole's jealousy of his cousin was probably Jamison's fault. He'd always favored Luke because he'd seen himself in the boy. He knew that Luke was the one to run this company into the next generation. Cole was good at what he did, but he wasn't qualified to be the CEO.

It was never easy to admit unpleasant truths, but Jamison had faced it years ago. Cole, though, would never accept his own limits. Then again, maybe he shouldn't. If a person started putting limitations on what he thought he could do, then he'd never do anything.

"Am I?" Cole threw both hands up in complete exasperation. "I'm tired of being overlooked in favor of the man who left the company. Luke left. He walked out on you, Pop, and you *still* prefer him? I'm *here*. I stayed. I'm the one who gives a damn about the company. And you."

"I know." Jamison forced a smile. Truth be told, he wasn't up for a conflict right now. There were too many worries riding his possibly failing brain. Plus, he was already at war with one grandson. Did he really want another one?

"You're a good man, Cole," he said, hoping to placate him. "And I know you'll be there for me if I need you to step in. I just don't need it yet."

Clearly still irritated, Cole said, "You sure about that? You're losing it, Pop, and we both know it."

"No," he said flatly. He wasn't about to share his worries with

Cole and get the man even more worked up than he already was. "We don't. Now I've got work to do and I'm sure you do, too."

"Fine." Cole shook his head and blew out a breath. "Call Adam. Straighten it out. I'm meeting Susan and Oliver at the yacht club for lunch. I'll probably just go home from there."

Jamison nodded, unsurprised. But he couldn't help thinking, *there,* Cole. That's why you're not the one. You leave in the middle of the day. Nearly every damn day. Jamison was all for spending time with your family, but there were responsibilities to be taken care of as well. Cole ran himself ragged trying to make Susan happy and paid little if any attention to the business that's keeping them both living in their mansion in Dana Point.

Cole stormed out, and Jamison rubbed his aching temples. If Luke didn't come back, he didn't think the company would survive. Hell, at this point, he wasn't sure *he* would survive.

And on that happy thought, he picked up the phone, dialed a number and said, "Adam? Jamison Barrett here. What's all this nonsense about a canceled order?"

Fiona loved the beach in winter. The sand was empty but for a few die-hard souls and the waves only called to the most dedicated surfers. In February, the sea looked slate gray and the wind that blew past them was sharp and icy. The waves crashed on the shore, then slid back where they'd come from in lacy patterns they left behind on the wet sand.

She tipped her face into the wind and smiled. The only thing better than taking a winter walk on the beach was having Luke with her.

"I can't believe this is your view. Every day." She took a deep breath, drawing the damp sea air deep inside her. Holding her hair down, she looked up at him. "If I lived here, I'd be down on the beach every chance I got."

"Don't have many chances." He tucked a piece of her hair behind her ear and trailed his fingers down her cheek. Fiona shivered at his touch and wondered if she always would.

"Work keeps me busy," he added with a shrug.

"And your phone…" Her tone was teasing, but her words weren't.

He scowled at her. "I left it back at the house, didn't I?"

"And is not having it driving you crazy?"

"No. *You* are."

She smiled. "There you go, saying nice things again."

"I don't know what it is about you, Fiona." His gaze moved over her features before settling on her eyes. "When I'm with you I have to touch you. When I'm not with you, I'm thinking about you."

"I feel the same way," she said softly.

He pulled her into his arms and Fiona went willingly. Being with him now was worth the price she would eventually have to pay. Reaching up, she cupped his cheeks in her palms and told herself that later on, she wouldn't regret this time with him. If memories were all she was going to have, then she wanted a lot of them burned into her mind so that she'd never forget a moment of the time spent with Luke. She'd never taken something for herself. Not like this. And when this time with Luke was over, she might never feel like this again.

He turned his face into her palm and kissed it, sending pearls of heat tumbling through her. Fiona was in such deep trouble, and she didn't care. What she felt for Luke was so unexpected, such a gift, she couldn't turn away from it.

"How about we go back to my house?"

They'd stopped at his house for a drink after seeing a movie she couldn't even remember. And now all she could think was, she wanted to be inside, where people couldn't see them. Inside, where she could touch him and be touched.

"That sounds good," she said, and turned with him to walk back across the sand.

At night, his home shone like a jewel. It was right on the beach and built as if it belonged in Spain. The arched windows, the red-tiled entrance, and the trailing vines and flowers that swept across the second story all spoke of sun-drenched days and long, warm nights.

"I love your house."

"I did, too."

"Did?" She turned her face up to his.

"Yeah, I'm moving," he said. "To a cliff view where thousands of beachgoers aren't in my front yard every summer."

He had a point. The beach in winter was secluded, quiet. But the same spot in summer would be noisy and crowded and— still beautiful. "I suppose I can understand that, but I would miss the beach..."

He pulled her in close, one arm around her shoulders. "At the new house, there's a path down to the sand. And the house is close to my grandparents. They're getting older and—"

She stopped, drawing him to a stop, too. "You won't work for your grandfather, but you'll move to live closer to him?"

He stepped back and shoved both hands into his pockets—he did own a pair of jeans and looked spectacular in them. Squinting into the wind, he said, "Just because I left the company doesn't mean I left the family."

Why couldn't he see that his grandfather was convinced that that was exactly what it meant? To Jamison Barrett, the toy company was an extension of the family. Having Luke walk away from it made Jamison feel he was leaving *them* behind as well.

"So why do you insist on staying away from the company? That *is* your family, isn't it? Why not just work through your problems with your grandfather?" Fiona looked at this conversation as an opportunity she had to take advantage of. "Like you said, they're getting older. Why not compromise?"

He seemed to think about it for a long moment before answering. The wind ruffled his hair; moonlight glittered in his eyes when he met her gaze. "Because I've got to prove this to Pop. And maybe," he said, "to myself, too. I'm right about the technological future."

"But it's Barrett Toys and *Tech*. Isn't he already compromising with you?"

"No." His features went hard and closed. "It's compromise on his terms. He'll toss me a bone, but we'd still be doing things his way. He wants to dial the tech back while I believe it should be expanded." He looked at the churning sea and talked almost to himself. "Kids today are hungry for more and more tech. Why wouldn't we want to get in on giving it to them?"

"Oh, Luke. Just because a kid wants something doesn't mean they should have it."

He whipped his head back to look into her eyes. Surprise etched on his face, he asked, "You're on his side in this?"

"I'm on nobody's side," she assured him, holding up both hands in a peace offering.

"Thanks," he muttered.

She wanted to sigh. Any other time, she'd be happy to be on his side. But in this case, Fiona thought his grandfather had a point. "I'm just saying that because something is new and shiny doesn't make it better. Like you said yourself, technology isn't going away. It's the future. Why do kids have to learn it when they should be out playing baseball or surfing or whatever?"

"Because tech is part of the society that they're growing up in. Adapting young means they'll be more flexible when tech keeps changing," he argued.

A couple holding hands walked past them but neither of them noticed. Fiona couldn't look away from Luke's eyes. This was her chance to talk to him about the rift between him and his grandfather. Yes, it was her job to convince him, but more than that, she knew what it was like to not have a family. She didn't want to watch him throw away what she'd never had.

"Did you know," she asked quietly, "that doctors are actually seeing cases of severe language delays due to screens?"

That statement caught him off guard. "What?"

Fiona had done a lot of reading on this subject, and there were studies that supported both Luke's and his grandfather's opinions. But if you were dealing with the *chance* of doing permanent harm to a child's mind, wouldn't you take the more careful route?

"You said it yourself, there are a lot of studies—good and bad—being done. Well," she said, "I saw an article about it, and I thought it sounded weird, so I read it. Apparently, small children who spend many hours a day on screens—phones, tablets—don't develop normal language skills. Their brains are being rewired."

Luke frowned and shook his head. Bracing his feet wide apart, he folded his arms across his chest and shook his head. "I can point you to studies that say the exact opposite."

"I guess," Fiona said. "But it's scary to think about, right? This article said some toddlers have had to seek speech therapy to make up their delays. And teenagers are spending eight to twelve hours a *day* online."

His frown deepened and she wouldn't have thought that possible. "Anything can be bad if overdone."

"True." Fiona laid one hand on his forearm. "But see, that's the thing. They're kids. They're going to overdo. And according to this article, most parents are unaware of the negative consequences for their kids spending so much time on screens."

His stance relaxed a bit, but his eyes narrowed on her in suspicion. "Fiona, what are you up to?"

Slow it down, she told herself. Shaking her head, she said, "Nothing. Honestly. It's just that we've been talking about this since we met, and I decided to research it. Some kids are being digitally distracted from the real world."

"And you think that's what I'm doing?"

"Not deliberately, of course not."

The wind slapped at them both, whipping her hair across her eyes, and she pushed it free. Luke stood in front of her like a glowering giant, readying for battle. "We're selling screens. Tablets. We're not even trying to get into the video game market."

"But you sell reading games and swirling color games for

toddlers," she argued. "Isn't that priming them to want to play as much as they can, and to want more involved games later?"

"Maybe." That glowering frown deepened. "I hadn't considered it, but I guess there is a case to be made for what you're saying."

"Luke, why don't you talk to your grandfather about all of this? I'm trying to see both sides and maybe your grandfather is feeling that his company is about family. And that you're walking away not just from the business, but from him. You never know. He might be more willing to compromise now that you've been gone for a while."

"No. Pop knows I love him. This isn't about that." He snorted and started walking toward the house again. "I'm willing to give on a couple of points you made. And I'm going to look into the research more deeply. But when it comes to my grandfather, you're wrong, Fiona. You don't know him like I do."

Fiona had to hurry her steps to keep up with him. Had she pushed too hard, too fast?

"People change, Luke."

"Not him, Fiona." His voice was low and almost lost in the driving wind and the throaty roar of the ocean. "I'm not saying you're completely wrong."

That was something, she told herself, so she gave him more to think about. "That article I read, it had a lot of really interesting points. The doctor wrote that screens are bad for kids, because they *need* to communicate face-to-face with other people. That it's essential for their social and emotional development."

He stopped right outside his home's enclosed patio. Plexiglass panels lifted off what looked like adobe but was probably stucco walls, to allow the view while protecting people on the patio from the fierce wind. There were chairs and tables and even a pizza oven tucked into one corner of the patio. But at the moment, all Fiona could see was Luke.

He tipped his head to one side and stared at her. "Did you *memorize* this article?"

She winced. "Sounds like it, doesn't it?"

"Sounds like you're trying to convince me that my grandfather's right."

Fiona stepped in close to him and laid one hand on his chest. "In a way, I guess I am."

He curled his hand around hers and held on. The faint wash of lights from his house fell across them. From somewhere nearby, a stereo played, and music drifted almost lazily on the wind.

"He's not right to turn his back on the future," Luke said softly.

"No, he's not." There must be a compromise, but he and his grandfather had to really talk to find it. "I'm not saying you're completely wrong, or that he's completely right. I'm just saying that maybe the world has enough room for technology *and* teddy bears. Imagination is important, too, right?"

"Of course it is," he agreed with a half-smile. "But my toys don't destroy imagination."

"No, but your designers make such great games and tech toys, the kids don't have to use their *own* imaginations because your guys did it for them." She moved in closer and hooked both hands behind his neck. "Maybe there's a middle ground."

"If there is," he muttered, as his arms snaked around her waist, "I haven't found it yet."

Tipping her head to one side, she met his gaze and asked quietly, "Have you really looked?"

He stared into her eyes for what felt like forever. She couldn't read his thoughts, but the expression on his face clearly said he wasn't happy. Finally, he said, "No, I guess I haven't. I was so busy trying to prove I was right, I never really thought about meeting him halfway. Or even if there *is* a halfway."

She smiled at him and told herself not to celebrate. This didn't mean he'd go back to his family company. But it did mean he was willing to consider his options and maybe that was enough.

"You could talk to your grandfather..."

Nodding, he admitted, "I do miss that old hardhead."

She grinned. "I envy you your family, Luke. I never had that. When I was a child, I would have given anything for a family of my own. And, like you just said, he's getting old. Do you really want to let this keep you apart until it's too late to fix it?"

His features tightened, and she could see that she'd given him more to think about. She was glad. Everything she'd said hadn't just been to serve this job. After Jamison hired her, Fiona had done research on kids and electronics, and some of the statistics had worried her.

She knew Luke was excited about this road he was on, but she thought that maybe he hadn't considered all the ramifications of pushing kids too hard into a digital world. If he was going to rethink some of his opinions, that was a good thing.

And maybe, she thought wistfully, one day, he'd look back on this time with her and smile. Maybe he wouldn't hate her once he'd found out she'd lied to him. Maybe...

"Why am I listening to you?" he asked, shaking his head.

"Because you're brilliant and insightful?"

"Yeah," he said, bending his head to kiss her. "That must be it."

CHAPTER EIGHT

THE TASTE OF her put everything else out of Luke's mind.

He liked talking to her. Even liked arguing with her, because she wasn't afraid to state her opinion and then defend it. She made him laugh. Made him think. Even about things he didn't want to consider.

But there was nothing like touching her. The rush of heat that overtook him every damn time kept him coming back to her. He didn't want or need a relationship. But for now, he needed Fiona.

He'd never meant for this—whatever it was between them— to continue beyond that long weekend in San Francisco. But the more time he spent with her, the more time he wanted with her. That thought should have worried Luke, and maybe it would. Later. But at the moment, all he could think was to feed the need devouring him.

Luke lost himself in Fiona just as he did every time he kissed her. Her scent, her taste, the hot, lush feel of her body pressed to his. He wanted it all. Wanted her more every time he had her.

Even with the icy ocean wind pummeling them from all sides, even with the lights of the house illuminating them for anyone to see, even with the fact that she'd just shot down some of his theories on technology for kids, he wanted her.

This kiss in the night wouldn't be enough. Tearing his mouth from hers, he looked down into chocolate-brown eyes that were swimming with passion and the kind of need that was nearly choking him.

"Come inside with me," he said, voice low and tight.

"Yes." She leaned into him more fully. "Oh, yes."

He gave her a quick grin, then grabbed her hand and tugged her along behind him. Across the patio, through the front door, and locked it after them. Up the stairs on the right to the landing and then down the hall to his bedroom.

Luke pulled Fiona into the room, then kicked the door shut behind them. She was laughing. Damn it, she was laughing and something inside him turned over. That wide smile, her bright brown eyes sparkling with humor and heat.

Of course he wanted her.

"In a hurry?" she finally asked, moving into his arms.

"Damn right I am," he assured her, pulling her in tight, using his hands, up and down her back to mold her body to his. He held her against his aching groin so she could feel exactly why he'd nearly run her legs off to get to this room with its massive bed.

"Me, too," she said, sliding her hands across his chest until he grabbed those hands and held them in a tight grip.

While they stood there, she looked around quickly. "I like your bedroom."

He knew what she was seeing. Pale gray walls, bookcases, flat-screen TV, forest green duvet covering his massive bed, and wide windows that overlooked the ocean. Because of those windows, Luke reached over and hit a switch on the wall. Instantly, heavy, dark green drapes slid soundlessly across the windows, throwing the room into darkness.

"Wow. A housekeeper. A cook. And you don't even have to close your own curtains," she whispered.

He grinned. "I did flip the switch."

"You're right. You're practically a frontiersman." She laughed again and everything in Luke fisted.

"Enough talking," he announced, and picked her up. She was tall, which he liked, and curvy, which he *really* liked, and she felt great in his arms.

He dropped her onto the bed and that amazing laugh bubbled out of her again. He'd never been with a woman who laughed before, during and after sex. He liked it. It was somehow *more* because of that ease, that companionable laughter.

Luke switched on a bedside lamp because damn it, he wanted to see her. She lay stretched out across the bed like a beautifully wrapped present. Her black slacks and green long-sleeved shirt were like the wrappings, and he couldn't wait to undo it all.

As he watched, she undid the buttons on her shirt and then sat up to shrug it off, leaving behind only a pale pink lace bra that barely covered the breasts he wanted to indulge himself in.

"You're amazing," he muttered.

"I'm happy you think so," she whispered.

Luke tore his clothes off and tossed them onto a chair in the corner. Her eyes widened as she looked at him, and the expression on her face only fed the fires building inside him. Reaching down, he unhooked her slacks and slid them down and off her beautiful legs. The pale pink panties were next, and she lifted her hips to help him get them off. And then she was there, spread out before him like a feast.

Luke didn't waste a moment. He dragged her closer, then took her with his mouth. She gasped, lifted her hips again and cried out his name.

Sweetest sound he'd ever heard. Luke took his time, tasting, licking, nibbling at the core of her. Her heat swamped him, her shrieks and groans fed the need to give her more. To take more. He drove her to the ragged edge, while her fingers threaded through his hair and held his head to her. His hands cupped her butt and squeezed, his tongue swept over her innermost depths, and when he felt her nearly ready to shatter, he stopped.

"No, don't. Don't you dare leave me hanging like this." She lifted her head and fired a hard stare at him.

He grinned at her, then with a quick move, flipped her over onto her stomach. "Just getting started, Fiona."

She whipped her hair out of her face and looked back at him over her shoulder. "You're making me crazy."

"Well, it's about time. You've been doing that to me since we met."

Amazingly enough, she laughed again, and Luke told himself there was no one else like her. But who had time for revelations now?

"Up on your knees, Fiona..."

She stared at him for a long moment, then licked her lips in anticipation and did what he asked.

Still holding her gaze, he inched back off the bed and stood there a second or two before pulling her back toward him. When her butt was close enough, he smoothed his palms over it, squeezing, kneading, until she was moaning his name and rocking her hips in a futile search for the release he kept denying her.

Luke grabbed a condom from the bedside drawer, sheathed himself, then pushed himself deep inside her. Instantly, he groaned, and she gave a soft sigh of completion. It wasn't enough. It would never be enough. Being inside her heat, a part of her, yet separate, felt right. But the aching need to shatter pushed at him and Luke responded.

Again and again, he took her. He held her hips steady and moved his own, claiming her body, giving her his. He set a rhythm that she eagerly raced to meet. The only sounds in the room were their combined groans and the beautiful slap of flesh against flesh.

Luke gave himself over to the sensations pouring through him. He looked at her, listened to her and let her reactions multiply his own. When her gasping cries and shuddering body told him she was about to climax, he pushed her harder, faster until she called out his name on a high, thin scream and shattered in his hands.

A moment later, Luke let himself find the same shaking release, and he knew that nothing else would ever compare to what he shared with Fiona.

And as he swept her up into his arms, then lay down on the bed with her cuddled in close to his side, Luke realized that that admission should scare the hell out of him.

Later that night, Fiona stopped at Laura's because she had to talk to someone. Having that argument with Luke, fighting to make him see her side—his grandfather's side—had been nerve-racking. If she didn't push hard enough, nothing changed. If she pushed too hard, she'd lose him—even before she'd managed to complete her job and get him to go back to his family.

Then being with him, making love in that beautiful beach house, wrapped in his arms, feeling her own world shatter again and again. The whole night had filled her with an anxiety she didn't know how to deal with. She wanted this to be forever. And she knew it wouldn't—couldn't be. Because to stay with him, she'd have to confess to her lie. And if she did that, she'd lose him anyway. His was a world of black-and-white, right and wrong. And lying was wrong.

Mike answered the door. "Hey, Fiona."

He was wearing worn jeans and a black T-shirt. His hair was rumpled and whiskers stubbled his jaws.

"Hi, Mike. Sorry it's so late." Not really all that late. About eleven, but she still felt guilty for showing up out of the blue. Especially since Mike worked construction and would be out of the house at the crack of dawn.

"No problem." He pushed the screen door open and waved her inside. "Laura's in the kitchen baking cookies."

When Fiona looked at him in confusion, he shrugged.

"I don't ask why anymore." Smiling, he said, "Go on back. Have a cookie."

"Right. Thanks." She walked through the living room and found Laura, as promised, taking a tray of cookies out of the oven. Fiona wasn't even tempted to grab one, which only proved how torn up she was inside.

Laura looked up and blew a lock of hair out of her eyes. "Hey, you're home early. Usually when you're with Luke it's a lot later—or even," she said with a grin, "the next morning."

"I've got an early job in Lakewood tomorrow."

Laura nodded. "Cookie?"

"No, thanks." She slid onto a barstool beneath the island counter.

"Uh-oh. If chocolate chip cookies can't tempt you, something is seriously wrong."

"Pretty much." Fiona braced both elbows on the granite counter and covered her face with her hands. Too many different emotions were stirring inside her at once. The memory of being with Luke made her blood burn, but the memory of talking to him, trying to make him change his mind about his family, his business, made her want to come clean. Her lie of omission was tearing at her. "It's a mess."

"Start talking." Laura set the hot tray onto the stove top to cool off, then went for a bottle of wine in the fridge. She poured two glasses, handed one to Fiona, took a sip of her own and waited.

"I don't even know where to start." She was in so deep now, she couldn't imagine a way out. Even if she told Luke the truth now, would it be enough to make up for lying to him for so long?

And wouldn't it put him and his grandfather at odds, too, if he found out the older man had hired someone to bring him back to the business?

Fiona stared at the sunlight-colored wine and finally drank some, if only to ease the tightness in her throat. "It's Luke."

"Yes." Laura leaned both elbows on the countertop. "I cleverly deduced that. What about him?"

Fingers absently twirling the stem of her wineglass, Fiona muttered, "I think I've about convinced him to make up with his grandfather."

"That's good news," Laura said, until Fiona's gaze met hers. Then she added, "Or not."

She gave her friend a strained smile. "No, it is. It really is. I mean, that is why his grandfather hired me. So that's good. But, Laura, there's a problem."

"You're in love with him."

Gaping at her best friend, Fiona could only nod. "I don't know how you know when I only just figured it out myself on the way home."

Laura patted her hand. "Oh, Fiona, it wasn't hard. You light up when you see him. You talk about him all the time. And you look at him like I look at Mike."

"Oh God." She scooped one hand through her still-wind-blown hair and took another drink of her wine. "This wasn't supposed to happen."

"Everybody says that." Laura took another sip of wine and shrugged.

"This is different, though." Shaking her head, she had another sip of wine and felt the cool slide through her system. "This started out as a job. I wasn't supposed to care about him, let alone *love* him. Plus, I've been lying to him, Laura. Right from the beginning."

She shrugged. "So tell him the truth."

"I can't do that."

"Why not? It's not exactly a wild idea."

Probably not to most rational people, but Fiona was feeling far from rational at the moment. "But if I tell him, I'll lose him. Not to mention that he'd be furious with his grandfather and how can I do that? Luke has hard lines between right and wrong, and a lie from me is going to fall on the 'wrong' side for sure."

"Hard lines get erased or moved all the time."

"Not by Luke."

Laura set her glass aside. "Sweetie, if you don't tell him, you've lost him anyway. You'll never really have him because you'll have that lie between you and it will make you crazy."

She was right, and Fiona really didn't want her to be right.

"Or worse, what if his family tells him what's been going on? What if he makes up with his grandfather and the old man brags about how he hired you to make it happen?"

Well, that was a horrifying thought. Fiona didn't believe Jamison would do that, because he wouldn't look good, either. But it could happen; her secret wasn't safe.

"Telling him the truth is really your only shot."

"And I really don't want it to be," Fiona admitted. God, she could still feel Luke's arms around her. Taste his mouth on hers. The thought of losing him now was almost more than she could take.

"Honey, I know that." Laura turned and grabbed two still-warm cookies off the tray and handed one to Fiona. "But at least once it's done, you'll know where you really stand."

Fiona took a bite because she felt obligated, but as good a baker as Laura was, the cookie tasted like sawdust. Fiona didn't have to find out where she would stand when she told Luke the truth. She knew exactly where she would be standing.

On the outside looking in.

By the following afternoon, Luke was more torn than ever. He left work early because he just couldn't concentrate. Fiona stayed in his mind all the time now. Not just images of her, or the memories of incredible sex. It was her words haunting him, too. Everything she'd said the night before kept echoing in his brain, forcing him to sort through too many thoughts at once, struggling to make sense of everything and find the right path to take.

It wasn't just Fiona, either. Since meeting her, he'd become more aware, somehow. He'd noticed how people were attached to their phones. He saw little kids in restaurants, eyes on screens filled with laughing cartoon characters or brightly colored patterns. He realized that technology, while a boon to civilization—which he still believed—also had a downside.

It could keep families from staying connected.

Standing on his patio, staring out at the ocean, Luke had to wonder if his brilliant idea to hook small children on technology was the right path to take. He still believed technology was the wave of the future and that he wanted to be a part of it.

But everything Fiona had said to him the night before had sparked enough concern that he'd done more research of his own—all morning. And what he'd found had him second- and third-guessing himself. She'd been right about all of it. Kids were getting more and more isolated. Teen anxiety and depression rates were up, and toddlers were turning up with language delays after spending too much time with screens and not enough time talking with the grown-ups caring for them.

Scowling now, he took a sip of coffee and watched a lone surfer grab a wave and ride it to shore. "Another thing Fiona was right about," he muttered. "I'm going to miss being right on the ocean like this."

But wasn't that quandary a lot like his other problem at the moment? To live on the beach meant putting up with thousands of strangers staring in his windows or tossing trash onto his patio. Like being too involved with electronics cost a kid his own imagination. His own dreams.

He was moving to a cliffside house to protect his privacy. He was giving up what looked great for the right to make his life what he wanted it to be. Shouldn't he give his customers the same chance? By pushing tablets and screens on small children, wasn't he metaphorically tossing trash onto their patios?

"Damn it, Fiona." He gulped at his coffee and felt the burn as it scalded its way down his throat.

Do you really want to let this keep you apart until it's too late to fix it?

Her words had been circling his brain for hours.

Of course he didn't want Jamison to die with this stupid argument between them. Hell, he didn't want Jamison to die, period. And Luke was half convinced the old man was immortal. He was always so strong. So confident. So totally in control.

And Luke had turned out just like him. No wonder they clashed. Neither one of them was willing to give an inch. Back either one of them into a corner and they'd fight like mad to hold on to what they thought was right. Which meant that neither of them had ever learned how to bend.

On that thought, Luke pulled his phone from his back pocket and hit speed dial for his grandfather's office.

"Barrett."

"Cole?" Luke asked, recognizing his cousin's voice instantly. "What are you doing answering Pop's phone?"

"Pop's not here today," Cole said. "He took a personal day."

"Has there been an apocalypse nobody told me about?" Luke frowned at the phone. "Pop never takes a day off."

Cole sighed heavily. "He's eighty years old, Luke. For God's sake, can't the man take a nap without your say-so?"

"He's *napping*?" Something was wrong. Jamison lived on about five hours sleep a night. Always had. And he had more energy than any ten men. Naps? Personal days? This was not Jamison Barrett.

"Did you expect him to live forever?" Cole countered. "He's an old man. You left and that changed everything for him. But I'm still here so I'm helping out."

That stung. Mostly because it was true. "Fine. Is he at home?"

"Yes, and don't call him."

"Excuse me?" Anger buzzed around like a hornet inside his mind.

"He needs the rest, Luke. He doesn't need you calling to argue with him again." Cole took a breath and said, "Look, I didn't want to say anything, but Pop's furious with you. Feels like you deserted him."

Regret and pain tangled together inside him, but Luke didn't argue with Cole. What would be the point? Besides, it wasn't his cousin he had to talk to. It was Pop.

"Just leave him be."

More emotions gathered inside him, nearly choking him. Since when did Cole call the shots not only for the company but for the family? "Yeah, thanks. Think I'll talk to him anyway."

"You would," Cole said. "Never think about the old man. Just do what Luke wants. That sounds right."

There was more bitterness than usual in his voice and Luke wondered what else was going on. "What's your problem, Cole?"

"Same as always," his cousin said. "You." He hung up before Luke could say anything.

"Well, damn. Things have gone downhill fast." He'd talked to his grandfather just before the San Francisco trip and he'd been fine. Pissed off, but fine. A little more than a week later, to hear Cole tell it, Jamison was at death's door and Cole was the new sheriff in town.

Luke turned his face into the wind, hoping that the icy air would sweep away all the conflicting, troubling thoughts. Naturally, it didn't work. He had some things to do, but when he was finished, he'd be going to his grandparents' house to settle things.

Jamison had had enough. Damned if he'd sit back and wait for the proverbial ax to fall. He had always been a big believer that it was better to *know* something than to worry or guess about it.

And the last straw had been that contract that he'd supposedly signed. He knew damn well he hadn't. So what the hell was going on with him?

"I hate doctors' offices," he muttered. Impersonal, almost terrifying places that were cold, clinical, where the pale green walls seemed to have absorbed years of worry and then echoed it back into whoever happened to be in there. He shot a dirty look at the examination table and stayed right where he was in the most uncomfortable chair in the world. "I hate being here."

"Hey, me, too." Dr. Bill Tucker walked in, closed the door

and then sat down on a chair opposite Jamison. "What say we blow this place?"

Jamison grinned in spite of the situation. Bill Tucker had been his doctor for twenty years. Somewhere in his sixties, Bill had gray hair, kind brown eyes and a permanent smile etched onto his face. Not one of those plastic *it'll be all right* smiles, but a real one. And today, Jamison needed to see it.

"What's going on, Jamie? Didn't expect to see you until your physical in a couple months."

"This couldn't wait." God, he hated this. Hated thinking he was losing his mind. Hated even more that someone might be trying to *convince* him he was going crazy.

Jamison had created what he'd always thought of as a family atmosphere at Barrett's. Had one of the people who'd worked for him for years turned on him? Why? It was the only thing that could explain what was happening to him, though he hated to consider it.

Bill gave him a rare frown. "Okay, tell me."

Jamison did, and as he told the story, he began to feel better. More in control. He wasn't being a passive observer to his own destruction anymore. He was finally doing something about it.

By the time he was finished, Bill wasn't smiling, but he didn't look worried, either.

"Jamie, that's a strange tale." He sat back and seemed to be mulling over his thoughts. "I don't think you've got anything to worry about, but we'll do some tests. Starting with the SLUMS cognitive test."

"Slums?"

Bill smiled again. "It's an acronym for the Saint Louis University Mental Status test. It's fast and will give us an idea of whether or not further testing will be necessary."

Worry erupted in his belly again, but this time Jamison pushed it aside. He was done agonizing without information. If there was something wrong, he'd fix it. Or find someone who could.

"Fine. When do we start?"

Bill nodded sharply. "I'll go get the test, and we can start right away."

Alone again, Jamison went over the whole strange story in his mind and tried to figure out exactly when things had started going badly. He couldn't pin it down to a specific day, but he knew damn well that he'd been fine a couple of months ago.

"And I'm fine now, too."

He needed to believe it, because anything else was just unacceptable.

Fiona had spent the morning tracking down a band that had once played at her client's high school dance, because the client wanted the same band to play at her wedding. In the last few years, that band had built an audience and, now, it spent a lot of time on the road, opening for bigger acts. Fiona's client knew the odds of making this happen were long, but she really wanted it because she and her fiancé had met at one of those school dances.

It should have taken forever, but Fiona had a friend in the business who gave her the number of the band's agent.

Once she explained the request to the woman, she put Fiona in touch with the band's lead singer. He was so flattered at the request, he not only agreed to do the wedding, but he wasn't going to charge them a thing. Especially after Fiona pointed out to him that a story like this was publicity gold.

The bride was ecstatic at the news, but once that call had been made, Fiona was left with her own troubling thoughts again. She had to tell Luke the truth. But before she did that, it was only fair that she let Jamison Barrett know what she was planning. She hoped he would understand, though she knew he might not, since Luke would be furious not only with her, but with his grandfather.

But there was no other choice. If she wanted a chance at

long-term with Luke, and she did, then she had to remove the lie standing between them like a solid wall.

She didn't have to meet her next client for an hour, so there was no time like now to get the chat with Jamison over and done.

Fiona dialed, took a deep breath and let it out when a familiar voice said simply, "Fiona."

"Yes." As usual, she paced aimlessly in her apartment and for the first time, wished for more space. Wished she were at Luke's house so she could simply walk out onto the sand and feel the wind in her face.

"Now isn't the best time." His voice was short. Tense. "But I'll be calling you tomorrow to talk about a new job."

"What?" She hadn't been expecting that at all. He sounded better than he had the last time she spoke with him, and she was glad of it. But it was the current job she had to talk to him about. "Mr. Barrett..."

"Sorry, Fiona, no time." He hung up and Fiona was left hanging again.

"Now what?" she muttered darkly.

He had "no time" to hear about the job he'd hired her for? That didn't make sense. And he wanted to hire her for something else? What was going on with Luke's grandfather? And oh boy, did she wish she could talk to Luke about all of this. But she couldn't. Because of the lies.

Which brought her back to: she had to tell Luke everything and try to explain. Just the thought of that turned her stomach and made her regret ever getting into this in the first place. Although if she hadn't accepted the job from Jamison Barrett, she never would have met Luke at all.

God, she had a headache.

If she didn't tell Luke soon, he might find out on his own. And that would be worse. But if she did tell him without first telling his grandfather, that wouldn't be fair to the older man.

She was still caught. Trapped. In her own lie.

CHAPTER NINE

"Mr. Barrett. I didn't expect you here today."

Luke glanced at the other man. One of his top marketing guys, David Fontenot, was tall, blond and tanned. As the head of market research for Luke's new company, Dave ran the focus groups brought in to try out their new products. He knew how to read the kids' reactions to the tech they were introduced to and knew exactly how to push those products in the best markets.

"I wanted to come and watch the focus group for myself this time." He'd been getting reports, of course, from Dave himself, the observers, designers, graphic artists. But given the conversation he and Fiona had had the night before, Luke had decided it was time to get some firsthand information.

"Sure." Dave waved one hand down the hall and started walking. "I'll show you where you can sit and watch. We've got a group of six kids for today."

"How old?"

Dave winced, then laughed. "This is the toddler bunch. I'll tell you right off that getting the younger kids to settle down and pay attention is a little like trying to herd cats."

Luke lifted one eyebrow. "Aren't the tablets supposed to do that? Engage young minds, get them to learn?"

"Of course. Sure." Dave spoke quickly, explaining. "But first, we have to get them to notice the tablets. And the truth is, I think the toddlers scare Andy—he's our guy in the room. They're a little overwhelming—"

"So get someone else in there."

He laughed and shook his head. "Yeah, that's the thing. Mr. Barrett, we can't get anyone else to volunteer to be in the middle of toddlers. The older kids? No problem. Plenty of volunteers." He shrugged. "Andy will get the job done, though. I promised him I'd buy his coffee for a week."

"Good bribe," Luke said, approving.

"Not for me, since I'll be paying, and he drinks a lot of coffee." Dave opened a door at the end of the hallway and showed Luke into a tiny room with four empty chairs. "You can stay here. This is one of three observation rooms."

"Thanks." Luke didn't usually come down here to the satellite office in Irvine. Marketing, research and design were located here but he was able to stay on top of everything through email and phone calls.

He checked his watch. "When does it start and how long will it last?"

Dave took his phone out to check the time. "The kids will be going inside any minute and with the toddlers, we don't go longer than a half hour." He shrugged and grinned. "By then they want a drink or a nap or a banana."

For participating in the focus groups, the kids would get a toy and their parents received gift cards for any restaurant they chose. And hopefully, Luke and his team would get the information they needed to perfect their toys and tablets.

Dave nodded. "There they are now."

Luke watched six tiny kids race into the room. The area was filled with beanbag chairs, small tables littered with paper and crayons, and of course, his company's toys and tablets. For toddlers, the tablets were practically unbreakable and came in cases that were in bright primary colors.

Andy, the volunteer who apparently wished he were anywhere else, did his best to steer the kids toward the tablets, and four of the six complied. They turned on the tablets, and bright patterns and storyboards sailed across the screens. Those four toddlers immediately sat down to study the program playing, and Luke watched as they settled down and focused on the screen pattern.

The other two kids, though, chased each other around the small play area while Andy tried unsuccessfully to corral them.

Luke smiled to himself at the sound of the giggles streaming through the speakers. Two out of six were playing, coloring, jumping onto the beanbag chairs. And he suddenly remembered Laura's son, Travis, running across the yard chasing a ball while the neighbor kids sat on a porch lost in their screens.

He could almost hear Fiona's voice in his ear, talking about kids playing, using their imaginations. He could see her eyes, staring up into his, and he heard her telling him to take a chance at compromise with his grandfather.

She was right, he thought, and felt a twinge in his heart he hadn't expected.

And as he continued to study the kids, he realized there was a stark difference between those four children, mesmerized by the flashing colors and dancing bears—and the two free spirits now trying to color Andy's khaki slacks.

He stayed through the whole half hour and when he left, he found Dave. "Tell Andy the company's buying his coffee for a month. He earned it."

Laughing, Dave went back to work, and Luke stepped into the afternoon sunlight. His mind was racing, bouncing from one thought to the next as he began to rethink his own opinions on kids and tech.

Maybe it was time to go see Pop.

Jamison felt better than he had in weeks.

Except for the fury.

"Loretta," he snapped, "*someone* at the company's been try-ing to gaslight me and doing a damn fine job of it."

It infuriated him that he'd bought into the whole thing. He should have had more confidence in his own damn mind. But whoever was behind this had counted on him reacting just as he had. As you got older, there was no greater fear than losing your marbles. Forget *anything* and the word *Alzheimer's* sailed into your brain along with the terror that word invoked.

"There has to be another explanation," his wife said from her chair in his study.

"Like what?" He tossed both hands up and shook his head fiercely. "Some stupid practical joke that nobody laughed at? What other possible explanation is there except that someone wanted me to think I was losing my mind?"

Since taking that SLUMS test at the doctor's office, Jamison knew his mind was as sharp as ever. Bill hadn't even bothered with other tests once he'd seen the results. The doctor had sent him home with a clean bill of health, thank God. But now he was forced to get to the bottom of a mystery.

Idly, he jingled the change in his pants pockets until the sound began to rattle him. He stopped, stared into space and tried to get a grip on the anger surging through him. Even Loretta's calming nature couldn't quell it. Not this time.

"Jamie," she asked, "who would do it?"

"I don't know," he admitted, shooting a glance at his wife. The not knowing was gnawing a hole in his gut. At this rate, he'd have his mind but would soon gain an ulcer.

Outside, the winter sky was as dark as Jamison's thoughts. He'd been betrayed. By someone he trusted. And that was a hard thing to accept.

"By God, most of our employees have been with us more than twenty years," he murmured. "Why suddenly would any one of them turn on me like this?"

Loretta folded her arms across her chest and hugged herself tightly. Shaking her head, she said, "It can't be someone we know."

"It has to be," Jamison countered. He knew what she was feeling, because he was feeling the same thing. Neither of them wanted to believe that someone they'd known and trusted for years would do something like this. But it was the only answer. "Who else would know how to forge my signature? Or do any of the other things that were done to me? It's someone close to me."

He paused. "Donna?"

"Oh, please." Insulted for the woman who had been their friend for decades, Loretta said hotly, "You might as well suggest it's Cole as Donna. I'll never believe she is capable of this."

"But we can say that about everyone at the company." He scrubbed one hand across the back of his neck. "Tim in marketing? Sharon in accounting? Phillip in purchasing? I'll tell you the truth, Loretta. This is a damn nightmare."

Loretta stood up, walked to her husband and wrapped her arms around him for a quick hug. "We'll find out what's going on."

He patted her back. "It won't change anything, but damn right we will. Someone in my own damn company was trying to sabotage me. Get me thinking I was senile or something. I need to know who." He thought about it for a minute. "I can't come right out and ask anybody, because they'd all deny it. So, we'll have to be sneaky about it."

"I hate this," Loretta murmured, stepping back from him to stare into his eyes.

"So do I," Jamison admitted. "But it has to be done, and there is one person who might be able to get to the bottom of this. Fiona Jordan."

"Who's that?" Loretta asked.

"How do you know Fiona?" Luke demanded.

Luke stared at his grandfather and, to his credit, the old man didn't look away. But he knew his grandfather well enough to see the shock and shame glittering in his eyes. As if it were a living, breathing entity in the room, Luke sensed *guilt* hovering right behind his grandfather as if trying to go unnoticed.

"Luke, sweetheart, it's so good to see you!" Loretta smiled and gave him a hug.

"Hello, Gran." He held on to her for a moment, then let her go and fired another hard look at the man who'd raised him.

Jamison Barrett was a law unto himself. He did what he thought was right and didn't care what anyone had to say about it. But Luke knew him too well to be thrown by the bravado in the old man's eyes. There was something here, and he wasn't leaving until he found out what it was.

"Good to see you, boy."

"Uh-huh. How do you know Fiona Jordan, Pop?" Luke kept his gaze fixed on the older man's. He saw the flash of unease in Jamison's eyes and knew that whatever was coming, he wasn't going to like it. In his own head, Luke was putting things together quickly and he didn't like what he was finding.

Meeting a gorgeous woman at a tech conference in San Francisco when she had no real reason to be at that hotel? She'd said she was there on business, but what were the odds of someone in Northern California hiring a woman from Long Beach to do anything?

He smelled a setup.

Betrayal snarled inside him. Were Fiona and Pop conspiring together against him? God, he was an idiot. Fiona had been lying to him all this time. What the hell else had she lied about?

"Well," Jamison said, and jingled the change in his pocket.

Luke frowned. The jingling was a nervous habit when Jamison was trying to think or when he was uneasy.

"Fiona did some business for Donna not too long ago. Found her sister's long-lost daughter."

"It's true," Loretta said, laying one hand on her heart. "It was lovely to see Donna's sister Linda so happy after all those years."

Fiona had told him about that job. She hadn't mentioned that she'd done it for his grandfather's secretary's sister. All the time they'd talked about Jamison and she'd never once mentioned that she had a connection through Donna?

Coincidence? Luke didn't think so.

"Right. So, you didn't hire her?" Luke asked.

The change jingling got louder. Jamison rocked on his heels and did everything he could to avoid eye contact.

"You did, didn't you?" Luke pushed one hand through his hair in frustration. "You hired her. You sent her to San Francisco to ambush me."

His grandfather rubbed his jaw.

"My God, Pop. What the hell won't you do to get your way?"

"Jamie?" Loretta asked warily, "Is he right? Did you do something you should be ashamed of?"

Jamison looked from one to the other of them and even through the anger spiking inside him, Luke could see the old man trying to find a way out of this.

Luke wasn't going to let him. "Damn it, Pop, just admit that you did it. You hired Fiona to seduce me into coming back to the company."

"What?" He looked genuinely shocked at the accusation. "I did not. I hired her to get you to come back, yes. If you were seduced, that's on you."

"Jamie, how could you?" Loretta gave her husband a smack on the arm.

"What else could I do?" he argued. Pointing at Luke, he continued, "The boy wouldn't listen to me. I was afraid he'd never come back, and I needed him."

"You're unbelievable." Luke could hardly talk. He was furious. He'd been used by his family, lied to by his lover. His stomach was in knots, and his heart was hammering in his chest.

What the hell was going on here?

"You left me no choice."

"The choice was to butt the hell out."

Jamison waved that away. "That wasn't going to happen."

"Of course not." Through the rage, the sense of betrayal, Luke could admit that he should have seen this coming. His grandfather would always do whatever he had to do to get his way. He'd been doing it his whole life. Hell, he'd taught Cole and Luke both to go after what they wanted and never take no for an answer.

It had never occurred to Luke, though, that meeting Fiona was anything other than a happy accident. Had she *planned* to fall into his lap? Was the sex all about the job? Did she sleep with all of her clients or targets?

Damn it, he'd fallen for her whole act. That laugh of hers. Her eyes. Her kiss. He'd *listened* to her. Respected her opinion, and it was all a lie. Hell, for all he knew, she loved the idea of tech for kids, and everything she'd said to him about it had been scripted by his grandfather. He'd actually been tempted to build something with Fiona. In spite of not wanting a relationship, he'd been leaning toward breaking that personal rule. And this is what it got him.

"This is low, Pop," he ground out, gaze pinning the older man. "Even for you."

Jamison didn't like that and scowled to prove it. "If you'd just listened to me."

"Jamie, you never should have done this," Loretta snapped, glaring at the man she loved. "Apologize this instant."

"Damned if I will. I did what needed doing." Jamison shot a hard look at his grandson. "I'm eighty years old, boy. You think I'm going to live forever? If you don't come back, the family company will go under."

"Oh no," Luke told him. "You don't get to lay this on me. Cole is more than ready to take it over."

"We both know Cole couldn't do the job. It's *you* I needed, and you damn well knew it when you walked out." Jamison was just as mad as Luke. and the two of them stood there glaring at each other.

"I left to prove something to myself. And to you," Luke snapped. "I didn't do it to ruin your plans—"

"Well you did anyway."

"Jamie!"

"They were *your* plans," Luke argued. "Not mine."

"And that's what this is about? A tantrum? You don't like taking orders, so you just run off?"

"Jamie, stop," Loretta ordered.

"I didn't run. I left. You know the irony is," Luke countered, gritting his teeth and narrowing his gaze on the man he admired more than anyone else in his life, "I was actually coming here today to say maybe you were right. Maybe we should work together at the family company. Find a compromise."

Jamison's eyes lit up.

"*Then* I find out you set me up."

"Oh hell," Jamison argued, "that doesn't change what you've come to believe, does it? True is true no matter how you come to it."

Loretta sighed. "Jamie, I'm so disappointed in you. You can't run our boys' lives no matter how much you want to. What were you thinking?"

He turned on his beloved wife then. "I was thinking that I heard my wife crying in the shower when she thought I couldn't hear her over the water running."

Luke snorted. "Gran doesn't cry." Then he looked at her and saw the truth on her face. "You *cried*?"

Frowning at Jamison, she stabbed her index finger at him. "You shouldn't have said anything. That was private. And stop listening at the bathroom door, it's rude."

He went to her, rubbed his hands up and down her arms and said, "I was worried about you, is all. And I knew I had to get him—" he jerked a thumb at Luke "—back for both our sakes."

Luke shoved his hands through his hair. He was angry and regretful and furious and guilty and realizing that maybe he'd had a huge hand in all of this happening. He hated thinking that

Gran had been brought to tears over what he'd done. He owed her better than that. And Pop had only done what he'd always done. Rush in to handle a situation the best way he knew how.

That might excuse his grandfather, but it sure as hell didn't excuse Fiona. She'd lied to him. He felt like a damn fool. Every minute of time he had spent with her had been bought and paid for by his grandfather.

She had come to mean a lot to him. Now he had to face the fact that all of that was a lie as well. Where that left him, he didn't know.

Shaking his head, Luke promised himself to take this up with her later. He would have the truth. Finally. From everyone. For now, there was his grandfather to deal with.

Taking a deep breath, Luke shoved his hands into his pants pockets and stared at the old man watching him warily. "Leaving all the rest of it alone, what are you hiring Fiona for now?"

Jamison eyed him. "Does this mean you're back?"

"God, you're a hardhead." Luke threw both hands in the air. "Even when I find out what you've been doing all you're interested in is, *am I coming back?*"

"Well, why wouldn't I want to know? That's what it's all been for. So, are you?"

Blowing out a breath, Luke said only, "It means I'm here now, and I haven't left even though I'm so mad at you I can't see straight."

Clearly insulted, Jamison muttered, "Well, that seems an exaggeration."

"Jamie!" Gran slapped one hand to her own forehead in clear exasperation and, suddenly, Luke felt all kinds of respect for the woman who could put up with Jamison Barrett for nearly sixty years.

Scowling, Jamison admitted, "Fine. We'll leave it for now. As to your question, I need Fiona to find out who's been trying to drive me out of my mind." He was jingling again.

"What are you talking about, Pop?"

Jamison started talking then, words rushing together, and with every word his grandfather said, Luke's anger became cold as ice. Who the hell would torture an old man like that? Make him doubt himself?

Too many lies, he told himself. Too many people who couldn't be trusted. He'd find who had been trying to destroy Pop. He'd even use Fiona to get it done.

But first, he was going to have a talk with the woman who'd been lying to him from the moment they met.

Fiona finished typing up three résumés for new clients, then baked a pan of brownies for a neighbor's birthday party and ended the day by returning a lost dog to its very happy owner. Of course, she still had to design baby announcements and one save-the-date card for two other clients, but those jobs would be fun.

She loved the creativity of what she did and, mostly, she loved being busy. Because at the moment, keeping her mind occupied meant she didn't have time to worry about what would happen when she talked to Luke.

Fiona had tried to make plans for exactly *how* to tell him the truth. No matter what she came up with though, it didn't sound right. Over a drink? During dinner? After sex? She wouldn't want to tell him *before* sex, or it might not happen again.

The sad truth was, she didn't want to tell Luke at all. In her fantasies, her lies were buried, Luke loved her, and they lived happily ever after. But fantasy rarely had anything at all to do with reality. So, she was left with her only choice.

Confessing all and watching him walk away.

When she pulled into the driveway that afternoon, it seemed almost cosmic, then, to find Luke sitting on her front porch, waiting for her. Her stomach jumped and her heart gave a hard leap in her chest.

He wore one of his amazing suits, with the top collar button of his shirt undone and his dark green tie hanging loose.

He had one arm resting on his upraised knee and as she approached, he narrowed his gaze on her until she felt as if she were under a microscope.

"Luke? I wasn't expecting to see you tonight."

"Yeah. Thought I should come by and tell you that I talked to my grandfather today."

Her heartbeat skittered into a frantic beat. She swallowed hard and forced a smile. "That's wonderful. Did you work everything out?"

"Not nearly." He stood up and loomed over her, forcing Fiona to tip her head back to meet his gaze. "But you'll be happy to know that Pop is planning on hiring you again since you did such a great job with *me*."

Did the earth open up under her feet? Is that why she felt that sinking sensation? Staring into his eyes, she wanted to look away, but didn't. She saw the accusation, the anger, there and knew this talk was going to be every bit as bad as she'd feared it would.

"Oh God. Luke... I wanted to tell you—"

"But you just couldn't find the time?" Sarcasm and a hard expression.

Fiona shook her head, dug in her purse for her keys and said, "Just let me open the door. Come inside. I'll explain everything."

She squeezed past him and he didn't budge an inch.

"Can't wait to hear it."

She felt him behind her. Judgment and anger were rolling off him in thick waves, and she couldn't even blame him. Her hands shook so badly she couldn't get the stupid key into the stupid lock. But maybe part of that was psychological. She knew that the minute they were inside, the argument would start, and the end of her relationship with him would arrive.

"Let me do it." Luke reached around her for the key. She gave it to him; he slid it home and opened the door. He was right behind her as she stepped into her house.

Fiona dropped her purse onto the closest chair, braced herself and turned to face him. "I know you're angry…"

"Oh," he assured her, "angry doesn't even come close to describing what I am right now."

One look into his eyes told her that. The cool blue was glinting with too many emotions to sort out. But his fury was obvious in the way he moved and stood.

"You have every right to be mad."

"Thanks so much."

She winced at the ice in his voice. "I was going to tell you myself tomorrow, Luke."

"Easy to say now."

"I know, but it's true." He wouldn't believe her, she knew. But then, why should he? "I hated lying to you."

"But you did it anyway. Impressive."

Fiona ignored that. "Yes, your grandfather hired me. I couldn't tell you that. Jamison was my client and I owed him confidentiality."

"And what did you owe me?"

"Luke, at first, it was just a job, but the moment I met you—"

"Let me guess," he said sarcastically. "Everything changed for you."

Helplessly, she threw her hands up. "Well, yeah."

"Don't, Fiona." He stopped her before she could say more. "Just, don't. My grandfather paid you to talk me into going back to the family business. Everything else was just part of the dance."

His voice was cold and hard, and she couldn't even blame him. But oh, standing here with him, so close, but so far away from each other, was even worse than she'd imagined it would be.

"Not everything."

"Right. So, do you sleep with all your targets, or was I just lucky?"

She sucked in a gulp of air at the insult. He was hurting. He was pissed. He felt betrayed. Of course he was going to strike back. "I'm going to let that go because I know you're furious."

"Tell me, just how much did you charge the old man for having sex with me?"

Her head jerked back as if she'd been slapped. "He didn't pay me to care about you. Didn't pay me to sleep with you."

"Good, because we didn't do much sleeping, did we?"

Okay, she was willing to give a lot here because she was the one who'd screwed this all up. As soon as she'd realized she was coming to care for him, she should have told him everything. Should have been honest with him no matter what it had cost. But there was a limit to how much offense she was willing to put up with. Her own anger started as a flicker of heat in the pit of her stomach and quickly spread until she was swamped with it.

"You know what?" she snapped, taking a step toward him. "Insulting me isn't the answer here. Yes. I lied. Yes, I'm a horrible human being. But I didn't have sex with you for money."

"And I should believe you because you're so honest." Sarcasm dripped from his tone and if anything, his eyes became even icier.

"Do or don't," she said hotly. "That's up to you. But I'm not going to keep taking this from you, Luke. Are you so perfect that you've never done anything you regret? Are your hard lines of right and wrong so deeply drawn that you can't see that other people make difficult choices and don't always make the right ones?"

"Are you seriously trying to turn this around on me?" he countered.

"I didn't say that. I'm willing to take the blame for all of this—even though *you're* the one who put your grandfather into a situation where he felt the only way to solve it was to hire a stranger to talk to his own grandson!"

She enjoyed seeing a quick flash of guilt in his eyes, but it was gone an instant later.

Fiona felt bad about this whole situation. She had all along, but she wasn't going to stand there and not defend herself.

"I didn't decide to sleep with you easily. I've never done anything like that before. Heck, I've never slept with anyone as quickly as I did with you." She'd known all along that this was coming. She'd taken something for herself, for her own needs and desires and now, the bill was due. She had to accept the consequences, no matter how difficult. "And I wanted to pretend, I guess, that there was more between us than there was. I only had sex with you because I cared about you."

"Right."

"Do you think I could fake that? What we felt when we were together?" That hurt. Looking into his eyes and seeing only anger flashing there might have made it a little easier. But she saw pain there, too, and that told her he was having as hard a time with this as she was.

"How the hell do I know? You're a damn good liar."

"Now who's lying, Luke?" She met his gaze and stared him down. "I was there. I felt your response to me, and I know you were feeling everything I did."

"You don't know anything about me, Fiona," he said, bending lower so their faces were just a breath apart. "If you did, you wouldn't have lied to me."

"Yes. I lied. But not about everything."

"I don't believe you."

"Was it so wrong for me to be with you? To let myself feel? Think what you want to, you will anyway." She moved in closer to him, tipped her head back and met that icy blue stare unflinchingly. "But I took that job from your grandfather because it was for *family*." Even saying that word had tears burning at the backs of her eyes. "I never had what you turned your back on. I had exactly one person in my life who loved me. One. That's more than I ever thought I'd have.

"But you had a whole family who loved you. You had everything I used to dream about having and still you walked away from it all. You crushed your grandfather."

He snorted, but his expression said he worried she was right. "That old man is indestructible."

Sadly, she shook her head. "No one is, Luke. Jamison depends on you. Loves you. He's proud of you."

"This isn't about Pop," he pointed out.

"Part of it is," she countered. "He didn't want you to know that he'd hired me because he knew you would never listen if you did. So, this is mostly about you, Luke. You walked out on the people who loved you most. Well, your grandparents want you to come home. And I think you should."

"I think what I do is none of your business."

"Yes, you've made that clear enough." His words were like another slap, only this time to her heart. Fiona loved a man who would always see her as a liar. He would never understand what had driven her to be with him, even knowing that it was impossible for it to last. So, it was over. And emptiness rose up inside her like an incoming tide.

But he was still standing there, staring at her, and she couldn't help wondering why he hadn't left. Why hadn't he stormed out, taking all of his righteous anger with him?

"Is there more?" she asked. "Have any other insults you'd like to toss around?"

"Quite a few, actually," he said tightly. "But I'll pass. Instead, I have another job for you from my grandfather."

"No, thank you. Go away." She wanted nothing more to do with the Barrett family.

"I think you owe me one," he said and that had her snapping him a look.

"How do I owe you anything?"

"Lies have a price, Fiona, and you told a boatload."

She took a step back from him because she couldn't stand being so close and not being able to touch him. Even now, her heart yearned for him and everything in her ached to wrap her arms around him and hold on. So, a little space between them was a very good thing.

"Fine. What does he want?"

"Someone at the company has been trying to convince Jamison he's crazy." Luke scowled at the thought. "Hiding things from him, canceling orders, ordering other things. They had him convinced he was sliding into dementia. He wants you to look into it. Do what you do. Talk to people. Find out who's behind it."

That was terrible, and now she at least knew why Jamison had sounded so unsure of himself that time on the phone. Who would do something so vicious and heartless?

"I'll do it," she said. "Only because I like your grandfather."

"Fine. Let me know when you have something."

He couldn't have been more distant. His beautiful eyes were shuttered. His voice was clipped and raw. And still, she loved him. Knew she'd never love anyone else like this. Everything in Fiona ached to say the words. Just once, she wanted to say them and mean them and it didn't matter to her if he dismissed them, because he'd already dismissed *her*.

He opened the door, and Fiona knew she had to tell him because who knew if she'd ever have the chance to say those words again and really mean them. Her heart hurt because her best chance at a happily ever after was about to walk out her door. How could she not tell him how she felt?

"Luke."

He looked at her.

She took a breath and let it out again. "I only had sex with you because I fell in love with you."

His eyes flashed, and his mouth worked as if he were biting back words that were trying to tumble out.

"I just wanted to tell you that," Fiona said. "Because I've never said those words before, and I don't know if I'll ever have the chance again."

Still he didn't speak, but his gaze was fixed on her. It didn't matter if he responded or not. She hadn't said those magical words for his sake, but for her own.

"But when this job is done," she said quietly, "I never want to see you again."

CHAPTER TEN

LUKE HADN'T SEEN Fiona in a week, and he missed her, damn it.

He shouldn't. She'd become the very distraction he had been trying to avoid. She'd lied to him from the beginning. Every conversation. Every laugh. Every kiss. Every... It was all built on lies.

And still, he wanted her. Thought about her. Missed her.

"Where's your mind, boy?" Jamison's voice cut into his thoughts, and Luke could have kissed his grandfather for the distraction.

"Right here," he said, looking at Pop from across the dining room table.

His grandparents' house hadn't changed in years. And somehow that was comforting since everything else around him seemed to be a swirling vortex of chaos. For the last week, Luke and Jamison had worked here, at the house, coming up with a compromise. Luke believed that this time, they'd be able to find a way to walk a line between the past and the future, while encouraging kids to get outside and have adventures again.

It would have been easier to do all this at the office, but until they found out who was behind the mental attacks on Jamison, they weren't announcing Luke's return. Not even to Cole, because he'd never been very good at keeping a secret.

"Are you sure you want to keep your group of people working on the tech division?" Jamison shook his head and checked one of the papers strewn across the table. "Might be easier to fold them into the division we've already got."

"No," Luke said. He was willing to go back to Barrett. Thought it was a good idea, actually. But though the tech part of the business would be taking a back seat to more standardized toys, he wanted his hand-picked crew working on the technological side of things. Whatever tech toys they *did* produce would be top of the line.

"My people have some great ideas, and I'd like them to keep working on those right where they're at for now. We'll call it a research division of the company. Maybe later, we can revisit."

Jamison looked at him for a long moment, then nodded, satisfied. "All right, then. We can talk about next year's lineup."

"That's fine, Pop." Better to focus. To think about work—that way thoughts of Fiona couldn't slip in to torture him.

"Have you heard from Fiona?"

He muffled a groan because it seemed he couldn't avoid thinking or talking about Fiona. "No. You?"

"Nothing," Jamison muttered, and tossed his pen down in disgust. "I was hoping she'd have something by now. I need to know who was doing that to me, Luke. Need to get rid of them so I can move forward knowing that everyone working for me is really working *for* me."

"I get it." Luke wanted to know, too. And then he planned on having a long chat with whoever had tried to submarine his grandfather.

"Well, then, call her, boy. Find out what she knows."

Luke went still. "She'll call when she has something."

"Is there a reason you're suddenly not interested in talking to the woman?"

Luke just stared at him for a long moment. "Yeah. She lied to me."

"They weren't her lies, they were mine."

Snorting, Luke shook his head. "Not all of them."

"The problem here is, you care for her."

"Nope, that's not it." Luke picked up the graphic sample of their fall ads. "What do you think about this? I'm thinking my graphic designer could find a way to make this stand out more."

"I'm thinking you're avoiding the subject."

"Good call," Luke told him. "So drop it."

"I would, but I like the girl."

Leaning back in his chair, Luke glared at him. "This time I'm just going to say it. Butt out, Pop."

"Well now," Jamison said with a wink, "we both know that's not going to happen."

Reaching for the coffee carafe, Luke poured himself another cup of the hot black brew and tried to ignore the older man across from him.

"When I met your grandmother, I knew right away that she was the one." He smiled to himself as if looking back through the years. "You know how?"

"No." But he guessed he was about to find out.

"Because she made me laugh," Jamison said. "She made me think. She made me a better man just by being around me."

Luke frowned at his coffee. He didn't want to hear this because it struck too close to home. Wasn't that exactly what Fiona had done for him? Hadn't she, just by being herself, made him reconsider everything he'd thought he'd believed?

Didn't her laughter make him smile? Her touch make him hunger? Her sighs feed something in his soul that had been empty before her?

He remembered the look on her face when he'd confronted her. Remembered the shock and the pain in her eyes when he'd suggested she'd had sex with him because it was her *job*.

Okay, yes, he'd been a colossal jerk, and she'd called him on it. But in his defense… Screw it, there was no defense.

Jamison was watching him, and the old man was way too cagey for Luke's liking. Whatever had been between him and

Fiona was over. Whether it was her lies or his accusations, it was over and done now.

"Let it go, Pop. *Please*."

"Fine," he said, nodding. "For now."

At this point, Luke was willing to accept that.

Two days later, Fiona knocked on the front door of Luke's home. The roar of the sea seemed to match her thundering heartbeat, and the icy wind was the same temperature as her cold hands. Her stomach was a twisting, swirling mess and it felt like every cell in her body was on high alert. She felt brittle. As if she might shatter into pieces at any moment.

She'd completed her job, and though they might not like the answers she was offering them, once this task was done, the Barrett family would be out of her life for good. And that thought chilled her far more than the wind could.

The door swung open and there he was, just inches from her. Fiona took a deep breath to steady herself, but it didn't do any good. How could it, when all she had to do was look at Luke Barrett and her knees got wobbly and her heart began racing?

He wore a tight black T-shirt and worn jeans that rode low on his hips. He was barefoot and his hair was rumpled, making her wish she had the right to run her fingers through it. But those days were gone for good.

Still, she was glad she'd taken the time to dress for this meeting. She wore a dark green shirt with cap sleeves and a scoop neckline and the kicky black skirt she'd been wearing when she first dropped onto his lap. She knew the choice had been a good one when she saw his eyes flare dangerously.

"Fiona."

His voice sent a whisper of sensation drifting along her spine.

"Hello, Luke. I finished looking into your grandfather's problem."

One eyebrow lifted. "And?"

"And," she repeated, "I want to talk to you about it."

His gaze felt like a touch. It was intimate and distant all at once.

He opened the door wider, and she walked inside, being careful not to brush against him. How strange this was, she thought. They'd been as close as any two people could be and, now, they were less than strangers.

She knew her way around, so she walked directly into the living room. There were moving boxes everywhere, and her heart felt a sharp stab of regret. He was getting ready to leave this house and though she knew he was moving, she had no idea where. So, she'd never be able to find him again. That thought was a lonely one, but at the same time, she supposed it was for the best. Now she couldn't be tempted to drive past his house like some sad stalker, hoping to catch a glimpse of him.

Turning to face him, she handed him a manila envelope and when he opened it, she started talking. "I have a friend who's a computer genius."

"Of course you do."

She ignored that. "With Jamison's permission, he hacked into the system at Barrett's and tracked everything he could. There were what he called 'footprints' left behind and when he followed them, he found the person responsible for hurting your grandfather."

Luke looked at the papers, then lifted his gaze and shook his head. "This can't be right."

"It is," she assured him. "We checked everything twice, to make sure. I'm sorry, Luke."

His gaze hardened instantly, and she was sad to see it.

"I don't want another apology."

"I'm sorry about *this*." Fiona straightened up, squaring her shoulders, lifting her chin. "As for the other thing, I've already apologized once, and I won't do it again."

"Is that right?"

"Yes, Luke." She moved in close enough that she could see every shift of emotion in his eyes. "Normal people screw up and when they do, they apologize, are forgiven and the world goes on."

"So now this is my fault." He snorted and shoved the paperwork back into the envelope.

"I didn't say that." Sighing, she shook her hair back behind her shoulders. He wouldn't bend. Wouldn't understand that what she'd done had been hard for her. That it had torn at her. That it was more complicated than black-and-white. It wasn't that he *couldn't* forgive her. He chose not to. "I don't think you'll ever find anyone perfect enough to live in your idealized world, and that's a shame."

He stiffened, and his features went cold and hard. "I didn't ask for your sympathy, either."

"Too bad. You've got it anyway." She paused to steady herself so she could say and believe the hard truth. "It's over, Luke. No matter who's at fault, it's over. I know that and so do you. That's really the only thing that counts now."

She took one long last look into those summer-blue eyes of his, then left while she still could.

"I'm sorry about this, Pop." An hour later, Luke watched his grandfather read over the paperwork Fiona had given him, and he could have sworn he saw the old man age right before his eyes.

And Luke could have punched his cousin in the face for that alone.

"Can't believe Cole would do all of this," Jamison muttered. "I never would have guessed it was him. Which is why, I suppose, he was able to do it."

"There must be a reason," Loretta mused aloud, as if trying to reassure herself.

There was a gas fire dancing in the hearth against the February cold, but it didn't do a thing to mitigate the chill sweeping through his grandfather's living room. The cozy furniture, the warmth of the decor, all seemed covered in a thin layer of ice brought about by Cole's betrayal.

"It's his ambition," Jamison murmured, sitting back and rubbing one hand across his jaw. "His and Susan's. That woman's always pushing Cole for more. I'm not excusing him, mind you. What he did, *he* did. But I am saying he's probably been feeling some pressure."

He looked at Luke. "The way I treated you—favored you over him—probably had a lot to do with it, too."

"No," Luke said. He'd been going over and over this since the moment Fiona had given him the proof of Cole's deception. "You're not taking the blame for this, Pop. What Cole did, he did on his own. If he wanted more responsibility at the company, then he damn well should have earned it. You know as well as I do that he loves the paycheck, he just doesn't want to work."

"He doesn't get to slide on this. You should call the police."

"And tell them what?" Jamison countered with a choked laugh. "That my grandson was gaslighting me? No. This is family, and that's how we'll handle it."

"I agree, Jamie." Loretta's voice was soft but firm.

Luke looked at them both and didn't get it. Cole had hurt the man who'd raised him, loved him. Cole had done awful things, so how could he ever be forgiven for it? Fiona was wrong, he told himself. An apology didn't mean forgiveness, and it certainly didn't mean anyone would forget what had happened.

But this wasn't his call.

"Fine," he said finally. "We'll do it your way. What's the plan?"

"We'll be having a family dinner here tonight," Jamison said, with a glance at his wife to make sure the idea was all right with her. At Loretta's nod, Jamison said, "We'll talk then, and I'll handle Cole."

"I'm sorry it all went to hell. I liked Luke."

"Me, too," Fiona said with a wry smile. She'd relived that

last argument, the one they'd had the week before, almost daily. She kept coming up with things she should have said, should have done. Would it have changed anything? Probably not, but he might have at least understood.

For a week, she'd tortured herself while gathering information for his grandfather. Now that job was done, and it was time to admit that whatever she'd had with Luke was just as finished.

"He might come crawling back," Laura mused.

"Luke? Crawl?" Fiona shook her head and laughed. "That would be something to see. But it would never happen. He's too proud. Too sure of himself and too wrapped up in his boldly black-and-white, right-and-wrong world. He'll never forgive me for lying to him.

"And though I'm sorry it was necessary, I can't completely regret it, because if I hadn't agreed to keep my identity and purpose a secret, I never would have met him in the first place. God. Isn't this a pitiful rant?"

"I've heard worse."

Fiona laughed a little. "That's something, I guess." She reached for a cookie, pulled off a few crumbs and said, "What am I supposed to do now, Laura?"

Her best friend reached across the table, patted her hand and said, "What you always do. Live. Work. Smile."

Fiona's eyes filled with tears. That all sounded impossible at the moment. "It hurts to breathe."

Laura cried with her. "I know, Fee. It's going to for a while. That's why we have wine and cookies."

Briefly, Fiona's lips curved. "And friends."

Then dutifully, she took a bite of her cookie and washed it down with wine.

When Cole and his family arrived, Jamison braced himself. He still didn't want to believe that the boy he'd loved and raised had tried so hard to convince him that he was losing his mind.

That was a stab to the heart that was going to take some time to get past.

But he would get past it. This was family and, despite the current circumstances, Jamison knew Cole was a decent man. Underneath his jealousy of Luke, his blind ambition and desire to take over the company to prove to himself he was just as good as, if not better than Luke, Cole was just a man looking for something he couldn't find.

Jamison hurt for him, but his anger and disappointment were just as vibrant as the pain he felt. He needed to make Cole accept that actions have consequences.

Cole needed to be reminded of what was truly important.

Carrying his son Oliver into the room, Cole was followed by Susan, just a step or two behind them. Cole was wearing khaki slacks, a red polo shirt and loafers while Susan looked as she always did. As if she'd just stepped out of a fashion magazine— cool and beautiful. Oliver, of course, was the shining, smiling boy he was supposed to be. And Jamison meant to keep him that way. Damned if he'd destroy the boy's father to make a point.

Jamison noticed the moment Cole spotted Luke standing at the wet bar in the corner, and Jamison frowned to see the hard resentment on Cole's features. Yes, Jamison told himself. No matter what else, he had to take partial responsibility for this mess. He'd favored Luke and, in doing so, he'd shortchanged Cole. He hadn't meant to. He'd only responded to the boys as their nature—and his—had demanded. But that had been a mistake. Maybe if he'd expected more of Cole, Jamison would have gotten it.

What was the old saying? *People will rise or fall according to your expectations of them.*

In that, he'd let Cole down.

He was about to make up for that.

"Luke," Cole said flatly. "I didn't expect to see you here."

"I'll bet," Luke muttered.

Jamison shot him a quelling look, then said, "Susan, why

don't you take Oliver back to Marie? She's made his favorite cookies today and that will give us all a chance to talk."

Their cook loved little Oliver, so Jamison knew the boy would be looked after while the adults had a serious discussion.

"All right." Susan did as asked, and Cole sat down on one of the sofas.

"Want a drink?" Luke asked from the corner.

"Yeah. Scotch."

Loretta took Jamison's hand and gave it a squeeze as he stood up and walked across the room to stand by the fireplace.

Luke delivered Cole's scotch, then took a seat in an armchair near his cousin. Jamison watched them all.

Luke was tense, Loretta was miserable, Cole was clearly uneasy and Susan, when she reentered the room, looked tranquil. That wouldn't last much longer.

Jamison had done plenty of unpleasant things in his life, but none of them, he thought, compared to this single moment. He loved Cole, but Jamison had been through a nightmare the last few weeks and his grandson was the reason why. That had to be addressed, like it or not.

Cole shot a look at Luke, then turned to his grandfather. "What's going on, Pop?"

"I know what you've been up to, Cole." He kept his gaze fixed on Cole's, so he saw when the man flinched, and it damn near broke Jamison's heart. Yes, he had known it was true. But seeing it on Cole's face just made it so much more painful.

"I don't know what you're talking about."

"Don't lie to him," Luke muttered. "Don't make it even worse."

Cole snapped, "Stay out of this. Why are you even here? You *left*."

"I came back."

"What?" Susan finally spoke and the shock in her voice said volumes.

Jamison knew she'd been counting on her husband taking

over the company. Susan wasn't a bad person, but she was a social climber and having her husband as the CEO of a billion-dollar company would be right up her alley.

Cole ignored his wife and turned to Jamison. "You mean, he's back at the company? All is forgiven? Just like that?"

"Just like that," Jamison said, and lifted one hand to Luke, silently telling him to keep quiet. This was for Jamison to do, as much as he wished he didn't have to. "You have anything to say about this, Cole?"

"If you're talking about Luke sliding back into the fold, then yeah. I've got things to say."

"You should be more concerned with yourself than Luke," Jamison told him shortly. "I told you. I know what you've been doing to me."

"Pop—"

The room was so quiet it was as if everyone in it had taken a breath and held it. "I've got evidence, so don't bother denying it."

CHAPTER ELEVEN

COLE TOSSED HIS scotch down his throat, then set the glass on the table in front of him. "I won't. What would be the point?"

"You bastard," Luke muttered.

"That's enough, Luke." Jamison's heart was aching as he looked at his oldest grandson. "Why, Cole? Just so you could take charge?"

"Why shouldn't he?" Susan asked. "He's your grandson, too."

"He is." Jamison nodded. "But as of today, he's not a vice president at the company any longer."

"You can't do that." Susan jumped to her feet and faced Jamison.

"Yes, he can." Cole gave his wife a steely look, then stood up. He looked directly into Jamison's eyes and said, "I did it. And I swear a part of me thought it was for your sake, too, Pop. Force you to slow down. Retire."

"By making me think I was losing my mind?"

To his credit, Cole flushed and shifted his gaze.

Jamison wasn't nearly finished. "You gave me more than a few hard days. But you made your Gran worry *for* me and that I won't allow."

Cole looked at Loretta and even from across the room, Jamison could read the man's shame. "I'm sorry for this, Gran."

Sadly, she nodded. "I know you are, Cole."

"I don't know that," Jamison said brusquely and waited for Cole to look at him again. "But I'm going to believe that you mean it because I want to. And more importantly, because I need to."

Cole nodded and squared his shoulders. He never again looked at Luke and that, to Jamison's mind, was telling. He was standing on his own and taking it, maybe for the first time in his adult life, and Jamison was glad to see it.

"I am sorry, Pop."

In Jamison's eyes, Cole was still a young boy, devastated at the loss of his parents, coming to live with his grandparents, trying to find his way and failing more often than he succeeded. He'd never been as sure of himself as Luke and, after a time, that had begun to eat at him. Maybe if Jamison had tried to address what Cole was feeling earlier, none of this would have happened.

Loving Cole didn't stop just because he'd been a damn fool. But love didn't mean there'd be no consequences.

"You're not going to be running Barrett's, Cole. You're not going to be trusted with much of anything at the company. Not until you prove yourself to me."

"I understand."

"I don't." Susan nudged her husband, and Cole turned to glare at her.

"Quiet," he said tightly. "Just, be quiet, Susan."

"But it's not right."

"*Stop.*"

Shocked, she closed her mouth, but her eyes were screaming.

When he had quiet again, Jamison said, "You'll be working with Tony in janitorial."

"*What?*" Susan exclaimed again, and Jamison almost enjoyed watching her stunned expression.

But Cole didn't even flinch, and Jamison gave him full points for that.

"You'll work there until Tony is convinced that you're ready to move up to research. From there, you'll move through the company, earning the respect of every one of our employees."

"I understand." Cole's teeth were gritted and his voice strained, but he didn't argue.

"I hope you do. But, so we're clear on this, Cole," Jamison said, "you'll take the time to learn everything there is to know about this company, to understand every detail *and* the big picture, or you'll be fired."

Stiffly, he nodded.

"This is my offer to you, Cole." Jamison looked only at Cole. It was as if the rest of the room had disappeared. He had to reach his grandson, and this was the only way he knew. "Work your way back up. Earn my trust again. But ultimately, the choice is yours.

"You can do this my way or you can leave the company and strike out on your own."

Cole turned to look at his wife, then slanted a look at Luke, who'd been so still, so quiet, Jamison had almost forgotten he was there.

"I'll stay," Cole said, and lifted his chin. "I'll do whatever I have to do, Pop. And I'll earn your trust again."

"I look forward to that." Nodding, Jamison walked to Cole and stopped right in front of him. "Just so you know, no more yacht club memberships, and your salary won't be a vice president's."

"Oh, now—"

Cole simply ground out, "Susan…"

"I'll see that you can stay in your house," Jamison added, and that mollified Susan a bit. "For Oliver's sake. I don't want my great-grandson uprooted because his father was a damn fool."

"Thanks." Cole swallowed hard and nodded. "It's more than I deserve. And I know that."

Jamison looked into his grandson's eyes for a long minute and was relieved to see what he'd hoped for. Real contrition. Real shame. And a determination that he'd never really seen there before. This might turn out to be the best thing that had ever happened to Cole. Jamison hoped so.

"What you did was bad, Cole," Jamison said, and reached out to clap one hand on the other man's shoulder. "But I love you. Nothing you do can change that."

Hope shone in Cole's eyes before he said, "Thank you for that, too. I'll prove myself, Pop. Even if it takes a decade."

"Good." He squeezed Cole's shoulder and the gratitude in his eyes almost undid Jamison. "Now why don't you take your family home so you and Susan can talk about your new situation."

"I will." He walked to Loretta and bent to kiss her cheek. She patted his hand and gave him an encouraging smile.

When he passed Luke, Cole nodded. Finally, he took Susan's arm and steered her from the room. Jamison dropped onto the nearest couch and sighed, exhausted from the emotional turmoil. "That's not something I ever want to do again."

"I'm just going to the kitchen to see Oliver before they leave." Loretta hurried from the room, leaving the two men alone.

"That's it?" Luke asked. "Start him at the bottom and work his way back up?"

Still tired, Jamison slanted a look at his other grandson. "It's a lesson for him, Luke. The last time he worked janitorial was when he was sixteen. Just like you." Jamison rubbed his eyes trying to ease the headache settled behind them. "For a man like Cole, starting over is the hardest thing for him to face.

"The fact that he accepted it is a good sign. Of course we'll have to see if he actually follows through."

"I think he will," Luke admitted reluctantly.

"Why?"

"He was shocked when you called him on what he'd done. I don't think he ever considered that he'd get caught."

"True."

Frowning to himself, Luke added, "But once he knew you had him, he stood up to it. I'll give him that."

"Sounds like you're easing up on him."

Instantly, Luke shook his head. "Nope. For what he did, there is no forgiveness."

"Oh hell." Jamison pushed out of the chair and walked to the wet bar. He poured himself a scotch and took a sip. "All of us need forgiveness now and then."

"And then it's all good? Slate clean?"

"The slate's never clean," Jamison told him. "Hell, the slate doesn't even start out clean. There's always dust or something on it. And when we wipe away the bad stuff, there's a shadow, an echo of what's been there before. But that's all there is. Just a shadow. And we're free to write on the slate again—good or bad."

Luke stared into his glass and the expression on his face told Jamison he was thinking about his own "slate." Jamison had a feeling he knew what Luke was thinking about and being a man who always had an opinion and didn't mind sharing it, Jamison started talking again.

"Fiona's a miracle worker, I swear."

Luke's gaze shot to his. "I suppose. She came through this time, anyway."

"Came through with you, too," Jamison said.

"By lying? Sure." Luke took a sip of his scotch and sat there glowering like a gargoyle.

"Lies are slippery things," Jamison mused as if to himself. "I tell them and say your Gran looks good in that ugly blue dress she loves, and she kisses me. Cole tells them, and it destroyed what he most wanted. Fiona tells them, and you're back with the company where you belong."

Luke just stared at him. "You're not exactly subtle. You know that, right?"

Jamison chuckled. "Wasn't trying to be. What Fiona did, she did because I hired her. She couldn't exactly show up and tell you why she was there, could she?"

"She could have told me later. After—"

"Maybe she was afraid you'd take it badly," Jamison said wryly.

"Maybe," Luke allowed, still staring into his scotch as if searching for answers in that amber liquid. After a long minute or two, he said, almost to himself, "And maybe there's no forgiveness for what I said to her once I knew the truth."

"Both of my grandsons…damn fools. There's only one way to find out if she'll forgive you." Luke looked at him and Jamison blurted out impatiently, "For God's sake, boy, go and get her. Convince her to take a shot on you."

A brief smile curved Luke's mouth. "And start over with a clean slate?"

"Write a new story."

The next day, Fiona realized she was doing just what Laura had advised.

She lived. She worked.

She wasn't smiling yet, but she'd get there. Eventually.

"And you're helping, aren't you, George?" Fiona bent down to frame the giant dog's face. A Bernese mountain dog, George weighed a hundred and twenty pounds and was living under the delusion that he was a lap dog.

George lifted one huge paw and laid it on her forearm. Fiona staggered a little but found a small smile just for him. Dog sitting was one of the jobs she most loved doing. Having George in her house for the next week while his family was at Disney World would give her comfort and company.

"You're such a good boy," she said, and gave his big head another brisk rub. "You want to go for a walk?"

George barked and wiggled all over. Thankfully, Fiona had already taken all the breakables off low tables so his swishing tail couldn't do much damage.

"I'll take that as a yes," she said and picked up the leash. Hooking it to his collar, she grabbed a couple of poop bags, just in case, and opened the front door.

"Hello, Fiona."

Her heart stopped. Actually stopped.

When she took a sudden deep breath, it started again and almost made her dizzy. The one person in the world she never would have expected to find on her porch was standing there staring at her.

"Luke?"

As if sensing her distress, George stepped in front of her, looked up at Luke and growled from deep in his throat.

Luke took a step back. "Whoa. You have a pony now?"

A short, sharp laugh shot from her throat. "This is George. I'm dog sitting for a neighbor." Looking down at the big dog, she ran one hand over his thick neck and smooth, beautiful fur. "He's very protective. It's okay, George. Luke is a...*friend*."

The dog calmed down, but Luke said, "Am I? A friend?"

She shrugged, not knowing what to make of this. "He knows that word, so he'll calm down."

"You didn't answer the question, Fiona."

"I don't know the answer, Luke." She didn't know anything. Obviously. She hadn't expected to ever see Luke again, yet here he was. His hair was a little longer now, and his summer-blue eyes were locked on her. He wore one of his perfect suits and managed somehow to look both businesslike and dangerously attractive.

She was trying to get over him. To let go of him and everything that might have been. Having him show up at her house wasn't exactly helping.

"He needs to take a walk," she said, stepping outside with George and forcing Luke to step back farther. She closed her door and stopped again when Luke stood in front of her.

"Can I go with you?"

She wanted to shout *yes!* Because she'd missed him so much. Missed talking to him, looking at him, kissing him, laughing with him, kissing him, curling up next to him, their naked bodies still warm from the sex that haunted her with detailed, torturous memories.

Apparently, Luke saw her indecision, because he said, "I need to talk to you, Fiona."

That decided her. "What's left to say, Luke?"

Sunlight drifted through the branches of the trees and a soft, cold wind slid past them.

"A lot, I think. Will you listen?"

She looked into his eyes and tried to decide why he was there. What else he might want to say to her? And finally, Fiona realized that the only way to get through this was to get it over with.

"Walk and talk," she said, and let George pull her down the walkway to the sidewalk out front.

George was in seventh heaven, sniffing at every tree, every blade of grass. He turned his face into the wind, shook his head and kept going. Thankfully, he had been well trained for the leash because if she'd had to hold him back, Fiona never would have been able to.

"Pop settled the situation with Cole," Luke said, and she glanced at him.

"I'm glad."

"He didn't fire him." Luke frowned a bit at that. "I thought he should have, but Pop wouldn't hear anything about it."

She shrugged. "He's family." And Fiona, who had never had

a family of her own, understood the importance of that relationship. Knew what a gift it was and how hard it would be to deny.

"Yeah. He's been seriously demoted, though. He has to work his way through every department in the company, earning respect along the way, before he'll be allowed back in completely."

"He'll do it," Fiona said firmly.

"You're so sure?"

"I am. He knows now what he almost lost. He'll fight to get it all back." That's what she would do.

"Can he?" Luke asked.

She looked up at him when George stopped to mark a tree.

"Of course. Your grandfather loves him. Love doesn't just stop one day because things get hard or ugly."

"I'm glad to hear you say that."

Luke took her arm and turned her to face him. God, he'd missed her. Just being beside her. Looking into her warm chocolate eyes. The only thing missing was her smile and he knew that *he* was the reason behind that. It killed him now to remember what he'd said to her. How he'd treated her.

And he knew how Cole must have felt standing before their grandfather. Unsure of whether he'd be forgiven—or even if he deserved forgiveness.

Suspicion flashed in her eyes. "Why?"

"Because I need you to forgive me, Fiona. I said some really crappy things to you." Which didn't even start to cover it. "I'm sorry for it. Maybe I was looking at things like you said, black and white, right and wrong, and I forgot—or didn't want to know that there are shades of gray, too. My view was so narrow I couldn't see what I was missing. I looked at my job, my family, my company in a single vision and didn't notice that other things were there, too.

"And I saw your lies and didn't look for more. I should have. You're the one who opened me up, Fiona. Taught me to look beyond the obvious and I should have done that with you, too. I want you to know I didn't mean a word of what I said before. I was just—"

"Furious? Hurt?"

"Both," he admitted.

"I understand that. So yes. I forgive you."

"Thank you." He smiled. "And now I can tell you that the main reason I came here today was to hire you for another job. I've lost something important."

"Oh."

Disappointment shone in her eyes, and Luke felt like an ass. At the same time, a flicker of hope rose up in his chest.

After a second or two, she asked, "What did you lose?"

"My heart." Luke watched her reaction and saw confusion there now, which was way better than disappointment. "My heart's been lost since the moment I met you."

Her eyes widened and her breathing quickened. All good signs. Then she asked, "Are you sure you had one to begin with?"

One corner of his mouth lifted briefly. "A fair question. And yes, I'm sure. It was a hard ball of ice in my chest and when I lost it, warmth came back." He kept his gaze locked on hers, searching for what he wanted, *needed* to see. "I didn't even recognize it for the gift it was," he admitted. "I didn't appreciate that warmth until it was gone, and the ice was back."

"Luke..."

He cut her off. "I'm not saying it'll be easy to find my heart. Might take years. Might take forever. Are you willing to take on a long-term job like that?"

George tugged on the leash, clearly impatient with the humans interfering with his walk. Fiona laughed and the sound swept through Luke like a warm breeze. He'd missed it. He'd missed so much.

"I don't know, Luke," she said, shaking her head. "I want to believe you, I really do."

"Then do it." He took the leash from her hand, looked at George and said firmly, *"Sit."*

Once the dog complied, he turned back to her. "I was an ass, Fiona."

"No argument."

He snorted. "I deserve that. I was wrong. If it weren't for the lies you told for my grandfather, I never would have met you and—" He shook his head. "I can't even imagine not knowing you. Not loving you."

She sucked in a gulp of air. "Love?"

"Yeah," he said, rubbing the backs of his fingers against her cheek. "Surprised me, too. And maybe that's why I was acting like such a jackass. I'd never been in love before, so I didn't appreciate it. Didn't really recognize it. But I do now.

"I love you, Fiona. I want you. I need you. But mostly, I can't even picture living my life without you."

Fiona sighed and he hoped it was with happiness. But he kept talking because he couldn't take the chance of losing her now.

"I'm asking you to marry me, Fiona."

"Oh my God." She staggered back a step, and he tightened his grip on her. "I can't believe this."

"Believe it. Believe me," he urged. "I want to marry you. I want us to have that family you used to dream of having. Kids, Fiona."

She inhaled sharply, her heart clenching as he offered her... everything.

"I want us to build something amazing together. And I really hope you want all of that, too."

Lifting one hand to cover her mouth, her gaze was locked with his and he saw what he'd hoped to see in those dark brown depths. Love. Acceptance. Forgiveness.

And Luke took his first easy breath in more than a week.

She reached up and cupped his cheek in her palm, and the heat of her touch slid through him like a blessing, easing away the last of the chill that had been with him since he'd sent her away.

"I want all of that, too, Luke. I do love you. So much."

He let out a breath he hadn't realized he'd been holding. "Thank God."

"I want you, too. I love you, Luke. Maybe I have right from that first day. And I'd love to build a family with you." Tears glimmered in her eyes, making them shine with hope and a promise for the future. *Their* future.

The big dog wandered over, leaned against Luke's leg and nearly toppled him. When he would have snapped at the beast, George looked up at him with adoration. Luke sighed and petted him before digging into his pants pocket for a blue velvet ring box.

Fiona saw it and gasped.

"I don't understand the shock," he said, smiling. "I proposed, you accepted. A ring is traditional."

She laughed. "I know, it's just…this is all so not what I expected to happen today."

Luke opened the box to show her the ring he'd chosen for her. A huge dark emerald surrounded by diamonds winked in the afternoon sun.

She looked up at him. "It's beautiful."

He took the ring from its perch and slid it onto her finger. "When I saw it, it made me think of that dark green shirt you were wearing the day we met. The day you fell into my lap and completely changed my world."

A lone tear escaped her eye to roll down her cheek. He caught it with a fingertip and kissed it away.

"This is the most romantic thing that's ever happened to me," she said, lifting her gaze from the ring to the man who'd given it to her.

"Even with George here?"

At the sound of his name, George barked and looked from one to the other of them, a smile on his face as if he were in on the secret.

"Especially with George here," she said, laughing. "Which reminds me, I always wanted a dog."

"Deal," he said, then stroked the big dog's head. "Maybe George has a cousin who needs a home."

If not, Luke would find one. A dog like George. To always remind him of this day. This moment. When Fiona loved him.

"You're offering me everything I ever dreamed of," Fiona said softly. "Someone to love and be loved by. Someone to make a family with. Someone who will always be there, standing beside me."

"All of that and more, Fiona." He swore it to her and to himself.

She went to him and hooked her arms around his neck, holding on tightly as if afraid he might slip away. But she didn't have to worry, Luke told himself as he held her just as close. He'd never lose her again.

He pulled his head back then and grinned at her. "Oh, there's something else, too. Jamison wants to see you."

"About what?"

"Something about keeping an eye on Cole for a while to make sure it's all working out with him."

"Do you think it will?" she asked, still holding on to him, staring into his eyes.

"I know it will," Luke said. "He got a second chance. Pop loved him enough to forgive him. To start over. Cole won't blow that chance."

Still looking up at him, Fiona asked, "And we've forgiven each other, so the same thing holds true?"

"We've got a clean slate, Fiona," Luke said. "No echoes, no shadows. Just a brand-new story we get to write. Together."

She grinned. "What does that mean?"

It meant, he thought, that shades of gray were beautiful.

"I'll tell you later," he promised. Then he kissed her and his world came right again. Everything was good. Everything was...perfect.

* * * * *

The Rancher's Promise

Brenda Harlen

WESTERN

Rugged men looking for love...

Brenda Harlen is a former attorney who once had the privilege of appearing before the Supreme Court of Canada. The practice of law taught her a lot about the world and reinforced her determination to become a writer—because in fiction, she could promise a happy ending! Now she is an award-winning, RITA® Award–nominated nationally bestselling author of more than thirty titles for Harlequin. You can keep up-to-date with Brenda on Facebook and Twitter, or through her website, brendaharlen.com.

Books by Brenda Harlen

Harlequin Special Edition

Match Made in Haven

Claiming the Cowboy's Heart
Double Duty for the Cowboy
One Night with the Cowboy
A Chance for the Rancher
The Marine's Road Home
Meet Me Under the Mistletoe

Montana Mavericks: What Happened to Beatrix?

A Cowboy's Christmas Carol

Montana Mavericks: Six Brides for Six Brothers

Maverick Christmas Surprise

Montana Mavericks: The Lonelyhearts Ranch

Bring Me a Maverick for Christmas!

Visit the Author Profile page
at millsandboon.com.au for more titles.

Dear Reader,

The sun is shining, birds are chirping and flowers are blooming—all signs that spring is in the air.

After a long, cold winter, I'm always happy to put away the bulky coats and heavy boots, eager to go outside and feel the warmth of the sun on my face and breathe in the fragrance of fresh cut grass. (Apologies to those who suffer seasonal allergies, but it's one of my favorite scents this time of year!)

Spring has long been celebrated as a season of awakening and renewal, as Lindsay Thomas is about to discover... The single mom's heart went into hibernation after the death of her husband more than two years earlier, and then it was roused by an unexpected New Year's Eve kiss from Mitchell Gilmore.

Lindsay and Mitchell have been friends for a long time, and both are wary about changing the nature of their relationship. But as winter gives way to spring—and with the help of Lindsay's two adorable children—that longtime camaraderie just might begin to blossom into something more...

I hope you enjoy this return to Haven, Nevada, and Lindsay and Mitchell's story.

Happy reading!

Brenda Harlen

PS: For up-to-date information on my new releases (or to discover my backlist titles), check out my website, brendaharlen.com, or follow me on Facebook.

For Susan Litman, who has been with me from the beginning, helping to make every one of my stories better—and reminding me to breathe when I forget. Thank you for everything!

PROLOGUE

LINDSAY DELGADO WAS ten years old when Mitchell Gilmore asked her to marry him.

She accepted his proposal because they were friends, and she figured that if she had to marry someone, it should be someone she actually *liked*. Then he gave her a plastic ring with a purple flower on it that he got for twenty-five cents out of a vending machine at Jo's Pizza, and they sealed their deal with a kiss.

It was her first proposal and her first kiss.

Now, fifteen years later, it was finally her wedding day.

And though she was wearing a sparkling diamond on her finger now, she still had that plastic token, usually tucked in the secret bottom compartment of her jewelry box.

Sentimental nonsense, her great-aunt Edna would say.

And maybe she was right.

But Lindsay didn't care, because she'd always love the boy who'd given it to her.

She turned to face the mirror and brushed her hands over the tulle skirt of her off-the-shoulder wedding gown. Saying yes to her soon-to-be-husband's proposal had been a lot easier than saying yes to the dress, and she must have tried on a hundred different styles before deciding the simple ball gown with lace at the hem was "the one." She'd originally dismissed the suggestion of a veil—until her mom had offered the one she'd worn at her own wedding and then carefully packed away in the hope that she might have a daughter who wanted to wear it one day.

"It can be your something old and something borrowed," Marilyn Delgado said. (Apparently, Lindsay got her sentimentality from her mother's side of the family.)

She'd nodded, unwilling to confess that she already had something old: the purple plastic flower ring that she'd secured to the hem of her skirt with a few loops of thread.

"Are you ready?" her sister asked now, offering the arrangement of garden roses, ranunculus, hellebores, freesia and gardenias to the bride.

Lindsay accepted the flowers as a brisk knock sounded on the door and then her father stepped into the room.

It was time.

A kaleidoscope of butterflies took flight in her tummy, swirling and twirling.

"Lindsay…oh my." His moss-green eyes—a dreamy shade inherited by each of his daughters—grew misty. "Look at you… you look like a princess bride."

"Thanks, Dad." And though she didn't think she'd ever seen a more handsome hero on the cover of any romance novel than Jackson Delgado in his classic black tuxedo with a gardenia boutonniere pinned to his lapel, the sudden tightness of her throat prevented her from expressing the thought aloud.

Behind her, Kristyne cleared her own throat. Loudly.

Their father's lips curved in an indulgent smile as his gaze shifted to his younger daughter.

Lindsay smiled, too, grateful to her sister for defusing the emotional powder keg moment so that she wouldn't walk down the aisle with mascara smeared under her eyes.

"Yes, I see you, too, Kristyne," Jackson assured her.

"Just checking," the taffeta-clad maid of honor said with a dramatic sniff.

"And you look almost as beautiful as the bride," their father noted.

"I can't wait until I *am* the bride," Kristyne said, perhaps a little wistfully. "Of course, Gabe has to propose first."

"Don't be in such a hurry," Jackson admonished. "You're young yet."

"Are you saying that I'm old?" Lindsay couldn't resist teasing him.

"I'm saying that your groom is growing old, waiting for the two of you to stop yakking so we can get this show on the road," he said, deftly sidestepping the loaded question.

"Well, let's not make him wait any longer," the bride said.

Kristyne grabbed her own flowers, then brushed a quick kiss on her sister's cheek. "Love you."

"Love you, too," Lindsay managed, though her throat had tightened up again.

As the maid of honor headed out of the room, Jackson bent his arm, and Lindsay tucked her hand into the crook of his elbow.

The organist was playing Pachelbel's "Canon in D" and Kristyne waited for her cue, then began to make her way down the aisle.

"You're trembling," Jackson murmured softly, looking at his daughter with concern.

"I'm a little nervous," she admitted.

"Are you ready to do this? Because if you're having second thoughts, we can turn around and walk right out that door over there," he said.

He'd let her do it, too.

Lindsay had no doubt about that.

Over the past several months, her dad had grumbled—mostly good-naturedly—about what this wedding was costing him, but if she told him that she wasn't one hundred percent certain she was doing the right thing, he would tell her to wait until she was. Because marriage was forever and when she made her vows, she needed to feel confident in every word.

From this day forward...till death do us part.

"Linds?" he prompted.

"I'm ready," she said, hoping she sounded more confident than she felt as the organist transitioned to Wagner's "Bridal Chorus."

She drew a deep breath and peeked around the corner, looking toward the front of the church. She caught Mitchell's eye and, when he winked at her, the butterflies in her tummy immediately settled.

Then she walked down the aisle to marry his best friend.

CHAPTER ONE

New Year's Eve
Eight years later

"I DON'T KNOW why I ever agreed to go to this stupid party," Lindsay muttered, staring at the clothes strewn all over the floor of her bedroom.

But she did know.

She'd been goaded into it by her sister, who'd argued that nothing said "grieving widow" more clearly than staying home and eating a tub of ice cream by oneself on New Year's Eve.

Of course, Lindsay *was* a widow and, in her mind, entitled to indulge her penchant for frozen deliciousness every now and again. (And sometimes more frequently.)

Except that was what she'd done the previous New Year's Eve. And the one before that. And even she had to admit that three years in a row might push her beyond "grieving" to "pitiful," and what kind of example would that set for her children?

So when her oldest and dearest friend told her that he had an extra ticket for the "Cheer for the New Year" party at Diggers' Bar & Grill and asked if she wanted to go, she'd impulsively said yes. She could have used her kids as an excuse to decline, but she knew that Suzanne and Arthur Thomas, always happy to spend time with their grandchildren, would be overjoyed to keep Elliott and Avenlea for the night.

And they were. In fact, they didn't even ask why their daughter-in-law needed someone to watch the kids. Of course, she'd told them anyway, wanting to ensure that they knew she wasn't going on a date but just spending a few hours out with Mitchell Gilmore.

"Have a good time," her mother-in-law said, practically shoving Lindsay out the door after she'd exchanged hugs and kisses with her son and daughter.

"Happy New Year," her father-in-law added with a wave.

"You, too," Lindsay said. "And thanks again."

But she was talking to the door.

As she drove the short distance from her in-laws' house to her own, she tried to muster some enthusiasm for the night ahead.

She had no doubt that Elliott and Avenlea would have a great time with Gramma and Grampa T—as they were known to distinguish them from her own parents, Gramma and Grampa D. The Thomases were wonderful grandparents who always planned activities to entertain and engage them. In fact, the presence of both sets of grandparents in Haven had been a major factor in Lindsay's decision to move back to her hometown after her husband's funeral.

Losing Nathan in a small plane crash on his way home from a business trip had been a shock. The suddenness and unexpectedness of it had made Lindsay wonder and worry about what might happen to Elliott and Avenlea if they stayed in Moose Creek and something happened to her. Sure, she and Nathan had made friends in the almost six years that they'd lived in Alaska—good friends, even—but she wanted to be near family.

And then, barely eleven months after she'd brought her children home to Haven, her parents had moved to a warmer climate for their retirement. Actually, they'd made the decision to move two years prior to that, after a particularly harsh winter that had taken a toll on Marilyn's arthritic joints. Then they got the call from Lindsay, telling them that Nathan was dead.

So Marilyn and Jackson had put their plans on hold to be in Haven when their eldest daughter came home, to offer her support and comfort and much needed help with her preschool-aged son and infant daughter. But even in the midst of her paralyzing grief and mind-numbing exhaustion, Lindsay could see that her mom struggled through the cold weather months. When she summoned the courage to ask if they'd ever considered moving south, they admitted that they'd already bought a condo in a retirement community in Arizona. They were just waiting for Lindsay and Elliott and Avenlea to be settled before they called the real estate agent to put a sign on the front lawn.

The decision to buy her parents' house had been an easy one for Lindsay. She had so many happy memories from her own childhood at 355 Winterberry Drive that she was pleased by the prospect of raising her own kids there. When Kristyne learned that her sister was buying it, she'd threatened to start a bidding war, but Lindsay knew she was only teasing. In fact, Kristyne and her husband, Gabe, had already bought a house of their own on Sagebrush Lane, only a few blocks away.

As Lindsay had passed their street on her way home, she'd considered FaceTiming her sister for help figuring out what to wear to the party. But she'd resisted, because she was trying really hard to stand on her own two feet, to prove to her friends and family that she could. That more than two years—actually two years, three months and seventeen days—after her husband's sudden death, she was finally moving on with her life.

If only she actually believed it was true.

Because staring at the entire contents of her wardrobe, haphazardly strewn over her bed and across the floor, she started to cry. Tears of grief and frustration and anger, because yes, it had been twenty-seven months and seventeen days, and she was still mad at her husband for leaving her. And yes, she knew it was completely irrational and patently unreasonable to blame him for his death, but she didn't care. They'd made promises to one another and plans for their life together—so many plans that would never come to fruition now, because Nathan was gone.

...till death do us part.

She sank to the floor and hugged her knees close to her chest as her shoulders shook and tears streamed down her face.

Damn you, Nathan. How could you do this to me? How could you leave me to raise our babies alone?

Of course, their children weren't babies anymore.

Elliott was five and a half already and Avenlea would turn three in May—coincidentally the same age that Elliott had been when she'd had to tell him that his daddy was gone. It hurt Lindsay to realize that his memories of his father were fading every day, and even more so to know that her daughter didn't have any. But there was a picture in a silver frame on her dresser to ensure Avenlea knew that she'd been loved by her daddy.

In the photo, the three-month-old was sleeping contentedly in Nathan's arms. It was a candid shot that Lindsay had snapped with the camera on her phone when she happened to be walking by. Nathan had no idea that she'd paused in the doorway to capture the moment, and the picture of her husband smiling down at their baby girl with a look of unmistakable love and pride was one of her absolute favorites.

It was also one of the last photos she had of father and daughter, because he'd been killed only a few weeks later, on his way home to his family after one of his short albeit frequent business trips.

The amount of travel required for his job as a project manager at Moose Creek Mining sometimes left Lindsay feeling like a single parent, but she couldn't really complain when his income allowed her to stay at home full-time with Elliott and work toward her Masters of Library and Information Science degree. Then she'd gotten pregnant with Avenlea, and the prospect of putting her education to use seemed further away than ever. She loved being a mom and she was happy at home with her children, but being the primary—and sometimes exclusive—caregiver wasn't always easy.

They'd had a brief argument before he left for that fated trip. She couldn't even remember what it was about anymore. Something silly, no doubt. But they'd talked later that night, after he'd checked into his hotel in Anchorage, and he'd told her to forget it, assuring her that he already had. Still, she'd planned a special dinner for his return, wanting to make it up to him. Buttermilk fried chicken and roasted potatoes and creamed corn—all his favorite foods. But he'd never made it home for that meal...

Her phone chimed, jolting her back to the present.

Mitchell, she guessed, even before she glanced at the screen to read the text message.

Are you ready?

She wiped her hands over her wet cheeks and glanced around at the various and numerous outfits she'd considered and rejected for the party. And though she felt just the teensiest bit guilty for canceling at the eleventh hour, she sent her response:

I'm sorry, but I'm not going to be able to make it tonight.

The guilt weighed a little heavier when she read his immediate reply:

Are you okay? Are the kids okay?

Yeah, we're all good. They're with their grandparents. I just don't feel up to going anywhere.

It took him a little longer to respond to that, so she was surprised when the next message that came through was simply two letters:

OK

She waited for something more—an attempt to persuade or cajole or otherwise change her mind, but apparently that was all her longtime friend intended to say on the subject. So Lindsay allowed herself to breathe a sigh of relief, even as she worried that he might be mad—and justifiably so.

Her best friend since second grade, Mitchell had been there for her in more ways than she could count since she'd moved back to Haven. And in all that time, he hadn't asked anything of her other than that she attend the annual New Year's Eve party at Diggers' with him.

She wanted to go, to be there for him as he'd been there for her, but she wasn't ready to subject herself to the stares and whispers that, even after more than two years, had yet to completely subside. She was hardly the only widow in town, but she was "so young" to be on her own—and raising "two adorable children," too. Really, it was "so tragic" that her husband had been taken in the prime of his life, and how was she doing?

Lindsay would force a smile and respond that she was doing just fine, thank you, even when it had been a blatant lie. Because admitting that she was barely holding on to the fraying end of her rope would have been uncomfortable for everyone. Only two people—Kristyne and Mitchell—had known the truth.

They were the only two people she could always be completely honest with, which was why she felt guilty about lying to Mitchell tonight. But it was for the best. Because although she was doing much better now, today was not a good day, and she knew that he would have a much better time at the party without her.

She froze when the doorbell rang and silently berated herself for assuming that his "OK" meant that he'd accepted her decision to stay home tonight. But she had no intention of letting herself be persuaded or cajoled, so she stayed right where she was, on the floor of her bedroom, waiting for him to give up and go away so that she could binge on the tub of rocky road ice cream she knew was in the freezer.

Mitch wasn't at all surprised when Lindsay bailed on their plans for the evening. Truthfully, he'd been more surprised that she'd ever said yes in the first place. And while the party was always fun, he'd known that the odds of him and Lindsay actually making it there were slim to none.

He wasn't concerned when she didn't answer when he rang the doorbell. She was nothing if not stubborn and obviously didn't want to talk to him about her reasons for breaking their plans. And though he knew her refusal to come to the door was hardly an emergency, he didn't hesitate to use the key she'd given to him in case of one.

He took off his boots inside the door before making his way to the kitchen to put the bottle of champagne he'd brought in the refrigerator. The house was quiet, confirming that the kids were gone. Proof that she hadn't planned to stand him up, which made him feel a little bit better about the fact that she'd done so.

Was it his fault? Had he pressured her to say yes? He tried to respect the fact that she was grieving, but Nate had been gone for more than two years now, and Mitch couldn't help but worry sometimes that Lindsay was barely living.

"It's just me, Linds," he called out so that she wouldn't be startled by the creaking stairs as he made his way to the upper level.

She didn't say anything, but he thought he heard the exhale of a weary sigh from what he knew was her bedroom.

He paused in the doorway when he saw her sitting on the floor, her chin propped on her knees. Her long blond hair spilled over the shoulders of a fuzzy red sweater she wore with black leggings, and her face was streaked with tears.

His heart ached for her, but he kept his tone light when he said, "I was wrong."

She lifted beautiful moss-green eyes to look at him then. "About what?"

"I didn't think there was an emergency, but apparently a hurricane passed through here."

She managed a weak smile as her gaze surveyed the disaster zone that used to be her bedroom. "I can see why you might think that," she acknowledged.

"Not a hurricane?"

She shook her head.

"You stuffed your closet too full and it vomited all of its contents?" The drawers of her dressers were open, too, and mostly empty.

That got another subtle head shake.

"I was trying to find something to wear to the party," she finally confided.

"You want some help with the cleanup?" He didn't wait for a response before crouching to pick up the nearest garment, a blue velvet dress with long sleeves and a ruffled skirt.

She sighed again and pushed herself to her feet. "You shouldn't be here, Mitchell. You should be at Diggers'."

"We made plans to celebrate the New Year together," he reminded her.

"I don't feel much like celebrating."

"Then we'll not celebrate together."

"I'm in a seriously lousy mood," she warned.

He was pretty sure her mood was *sad* rather than *bad*, and, as her friend, he refused to let her wallow.

"Look at your feet," he suggested.

Her brows drew together. "What?"

"Look at your feet," he said again.

Though her expression remained skeptical, she tipped her head down and the corners of her mouth slowly lifted.

It wasn't quite a smile, but it definitely wasn't a frown.

"See? Red-nosed reindeer socks make everything better."

"Avenlea loves these socks," she confided, wiggling her toes.

"Who wouldn't?" he agreed, reaching for a discarded hanger for the dress.

"Don't." She tugged the garment out of his hand and tossed it toward the chair in the corner.

Her effort fell short, and the dress slid off the edge of the seat to pool again on the floor.

"Donation pile?" he guessed.

She nodded. "For the women's shelter."

He didn't mean to pry, but he wanted to understand what had led to the pillaging of her wardrobe. "It doesn't fit? You don't like it anymore?"

Now she shook her head. "The last time I wore it was to a Christmas party...with Nathan."

"Ahh."

He moved to pick up the discarded garment and drape it over the chair.

"And this one?" he asked, shaking out a sleeveless black dress that had been crumpled into a ball.

"I bought that one for the funeral." She swallowed. "I don't even know why I still have it. It's not like I was ever going to be able to wear it and not think, 'this is the dress I wore to my husband's funeral.'"

"I'm sorry," Mitch said gently. "I didn't realize my invitation was going to lead you into a minefield of memories."

"It's not your fault," she told him. "The closet was obviously overdue for a cleaning, and it's been a while since I've had a meltdown so that was probably overdue, too."

"You should have called me—I would have been here for you."

"I know," she said. "But I generally prefer to have my meltdowns in private."

"Are these meltdowns a regular occurrence?" he asked, sincerely concerned.

"No. In fact, I haven't had one like this since... June."

The day of her wedding anniversary, he'd bet.

"So…are you keeping any of this stuff?" he wondered.

"Yeah, but—" she waved a hand dismissively "—I'll deal with it later."

"Why don't we deal with it now? Then when you want to fall into bed tonight, you'll actually be able to find it."

With a sigh of resignation, she scooped up a sweater and began to fold it.

He held up a sparkly silver top for her consideration.

"Donate," she said.

Yoga pants went into the dresser; button-front shirts were hung in the closet; a lacy nightgown was snatched out of his hand.

"If you really wanted to be helpful, you'd go to the party," Lindsay said, tucking the intimate garment into a drawer.

"How would that help?" he wondered aloud.

"By allowing me to maintain the illusion that I didn't completely ruin your New Year's Eve."

"You haven't ruined anything," he assured her.

"I'm just not ready," she said quietly. "I know I should be… it's been more than two years…but I'm not."

"Grief doesn't operate on any particular schedule," he said, drawing her into his arms. "If you're not ready, you're not ready, and you don't have to apologize for that."

He stood six inches taller than her five-feet four-inch frame, and she dropped her forehead against his chest, her voice muffled against his shirt when she said, "Why are you being so understanding?"

"Nate was my friend, too," he reminded her. "And every once in a while, someone will say or do something that reminds me of him and I'll smile at the memory…and then I'll remember that he's gone and curse at the unfairness of it all. I can only imagine how much worse it must be for you, because he was your husband and the father of your children."

"I teared up in The Trading Post a couple weeks ago," she

admitted. "In the cereal aisle, when I told Elliott to pick a cereal, and he grabbed a box of shredded wheat."

"I've never heard of a kid choosing shredded wheat," he admitted.

"He'd never had it before, but I think he recognized the box, because it was Nathan's favorite. In the winter—which was about eight months of the year in Moose Creek—he liked it with warm milk. And heaping teaspoons of sugar."

"So...did you buy the shredded wheat?"

"I did," she confirmed. "And then I went back the next day to get a box of Kix, because Elliott decided that shredded wheat was gross."

Mitch chuckled. "I wouldn't disagree with that."

She moved out of his arms then and reached down to pick up a T-shirt. "You're not going anywhere, are you?"

"Not before midnight," he told her.

"Not even if I kick you out?"

"You can try," he said. "But I'm bigger and stronger than you."

"You're also single," she pointed out, as she folded the shirt and tucked it into a drawer. "Which is why you should be out tonight, dancing and flirting with pretty girls."

"I'd rather be here with you," he said, and immediately winced at the backhanded compliment.

But Lindsay laughed. "I've never had to worry about keeping my feet on the ground around you."

"What I meant to say is that I'd rather be here with the prettiest girl in town."

She shook her head, but she was smiling. "What I am, right now, is hungry. Why don't you call Jo's and order a pizza?"

"Because everybody—and all of their cousins—orders pizza from Jo's on New Year's Eve, and I don't want to wait three hours to eat."

"Pizza in three hours beats no pizza at all," she said philosophically.

"I have a better idea," he said. "How about I go down to the kitchen and forage for food while you finish up in here?"

She nodded. "That works."

He started toward the door.

"Mitch?"

He turned back again. "Yeah?"

"Thank you...for knowing I needed your company even before I realized it myself."

"I'll always be here for you, Linds."

It was a promise he felt confident that he could keep.

Because he'd gotten over his teenage crush on her a lot of years earlier—he was almost certain of it.

CHAPTER TWO

LINDSAY FOLLOWED THE rich scents of tomato, garlic and oregano into the kitchen, her lips curving automatically when she saw Mitchell standing by the stove. She imagined any woman would smile to see a good-looking guy cooking dinner—and she had to admit, her best friend had grown up gorgeous.

The stereotypical tall, dark and handsome description fit him as well as the dark jeans, button-down shirt and vest he wore, but he was so much more than that. Along with the strong, hard body of a rancher, he had a gentle touch and a generous heart. She'd loved him for almost as long as she'd known him, and it was no wonder that her children loved him, too.

"I see you found the pasta sauce in the freezer."

He dropped a handful of spaghetti into the pot of water already boiling on the stove. "Lucky I did," he said. "Because your fridge is woefully empty."

"I forgot to stop at the grocery store today," she confided. "Plus, I thought we'd be eating at the party."

"Well, I did put out some snacks, in case you wanted to nibble on something while we're waiting for the pasta to cook."

He'd opened a bottle of her favorite cabernet sauvignon, too, she noted, and poured two glasses.

It wasn't surprising that he was as comfortable in her home

as his own. Especially considering that the house in which she was now living with her kids was the same house she and her sister had grown up in, and Mitchell, as one of her best friends, had spent plenty of time there with her, working on homework together or just hanging out. And since her return to Haven, they'd easily fallen back into their old routines, almost as if she'd never left.

She picked up one of the glasses and perused the appetizer plate as she sipped her wine. "You cut up string cheese?"

"Woefully empty," he said again.

She nodded an acknowledgment.

In addition to the circular chunks of cheese, he'd peeled one of the strings into thin strands and arranged them into a shape that looked something like a flower, added a pile of goldfish crackers to the plate, a glass ramekin of pimento-stuffed olives and a handful of slightly shriveled grapes.

Lindsay popped an olive into her mouth. "I bet you'd kick butt on *Chopped*!"

"What's that?"

"A TV show where chefs compete to incorporate four mystery ingredients into appetizers, main courses and desserts."

"Is that your idea of entertainment?"

"A mom cannot live on Nick Jr. alone," she told him.

"You never heard of ESPN?"

She pursed her lips, as if racking her brain. "It rings a bell."

Of course it did, because before she and Nate had moved to Moose Creek, Mitchell had been a fixture at their place, hanging out to watch the game, regardless of who or what was playing.

"The Sun Bowl was a good game this afternoon."

"I had a date with my closet this afternoon," she reminded him, as the timer buzzed.

"Based on what I saw—" Mitch turned off the burner and dumped the contents of the pasta pot into a strainer "—I think you should consider a new relationship."

"Or at least a new wardrobe," she said, spooning sauce on top of the plate of pasta he passed to her.

Mitch did the same with his own, then took a seat across from her at the table.

"To old friends and the New Year," he said, lifting his wine goblet.

She tapped her glass against his, then sipped her wine.

Mitch sampled his pasta. "Mmm...this is really good sauce."

"Nonna Delgado's family recipe," she said, as she sprinkled parmesan cheese over her plate.

"Judging by the stack of containers in your freezer, you plan on eating a lot of spaghetti this winter."

"It's one of Elliott and Avenlea's favorite foods," she said. "But those containers aren't all pasta sauce. There's also chili, beef stew and shepherd's pie."

"When did you find time to make all of that?" he wondered.

"It wasn't me—it was my mom. I swear she thinks we'd live on takeout if she didn't cook for us every time she visits."

"Or maybe she just likes to take care of you," he suggested as an alternative.

"And feels guilty that they moved away after I moved back home," she said, stabbing a chunk of pepper with her fork. "Either way, I don't argue with her about it, for fear that she might not feel inclined to stock my freezer."

He chuckled as he twirled his fork in his spaghetti. "I don't think they moved away because you came home—they were already getting the house ready for sale before...before you came back."

She didn't miss the pause and suspected that he'd been thinking "before Nathan died." But of course he didn't say it. Because most people tried not to remind her that she'd lost her husband, as if that might somehow allow her to forget. As if she didn't wake up every morning aware that she wasn't a married woman anymore but a widow and single parent to two young children.

"I know," she admitted now. "And maybe I should feel guilty

that they put their plans on hold to stay through that first year for me and the kids, but I don't, because I'm not sure that I would have been able to manage without them or Kristyne or you."

"I don't know what I did," he said modestly.

"You were—and *are*—here for me. And for Elliott and Avenlea."

"That part's easy," he said. "They're great kids. And you're not so bad, either."

She smiled at that, then her expression turned serious again. "I'm sorry you're missing the party tonight."

"I'm not," he said.

"You didn't want to go?" she asked, surprised.

"Not as much as I wanted *you* to go," he clarified. "Because I'm pretty sure you haven't had a night out in more than two years."

"Not true," she said, as she pushed aside a slice of mushroom. "I was at Ridgeview Elementary School for the Season of Wonder holiday concert just a few weeks ago."

He chewed on a piece of sausage. "I meant a night out without your children."

"Yeah, it's been a while since I had one of those," she admitted. "But a night *in* without my children could be nice, too."

"Except that you're wondering what they're doing right now, aren't you?"

She glanced at her watch. "I don't have to wonder. Right now Elliott is watching the original *Cars* movie on Disney Plus with Grampa while Avenlea is snuggled with Gramma for story time."

"Or maybe they're both slurping Pepsi through Red Vines and jumping on the sofa like it's a trampoline," he teased.

"You just got yourself taken off the approved babysitter list," she told him.

"If there's a list, I'm at the top of it," he said confidently.

He was right, because Elliott and Avenlea absolutely loved hanging out with "Uncle Mitch," especially at the Circle G

Ranch where he lived and worked. And since the local minor hockey association had started its season in October, he'd taken Elliott to the ice rink at the community center for his hockey school session almost as often as she had. Which she really appreciated, because Avenlea hated being at the rink. Watching her brother push a puck around with his stick was *not* the little girl's idea of fun.

"Seriously, though, I feel lucky that Suzanne and Arthur make such an effort to enjoy their time with Elliott and Avenlea," she said. "Suzanne had a whole afternoon of activities planned for them—including crafts and games and special snacks."

"No wonder the kids love going over there."

"I always enjoyed visiting my grandparents' house when I was a kid," she said, smiling at the memory. "They had a closet under the staircase that was filled with toys and games for us to play with. And Grandma always made cookies that we got to eat fresh out of the oven. I still think of her whenever I have a warm chocolate chip cookie with a cold glass of milk."

"My grandmother says it's easier being a grandparent than a parent, because you don't have to worry about enforcing rules and can just enjoy being together."

"That's probably true," she acknowledged.

"And now she's a great-grandmother times six—with two more great-grandbabies on the way," he said, referring to his cousin Haylee's twin pregnancy.

"I love my kids," she said sincerely. "But I'm so grateful they came one at a time."

They continued to chat comfortably about various and numerous topics while they finished their dinner and then tidied up the kitchen. Afterward, they took their glasses and the bottle of the wine to the living room, where Lindsay turned on the fireplace and Mitchell found a television broadcast of the New Year's Eve celebrations from Las Vegas. She plugged in the Christmas tree lights, too—"just one last time"—since the decorations would come off it the next day and the tree put out for pickup by the town, to be mulched for local naturalization projects.

"This is nice," she said, stretching her legs out toward the flames that ignited at the flick of a switch. Growing up, the fireplace had burned real wood and Lindsay still shuddered to think of the spiders she'd seen scrambling over the logs in the woodpile—or worse, felt crawling across her hands—when she and Kristyne were sent out to restock the bin.

"It is," he agreed.

"And quiet," she said.

He chuckled. "Do you want me to turn up the volume on the TV?"

"No. I'm happy to enjoy the quiet for a change." She reached for her wineglass again, surprised to discover it was empty.

Mitch picked up the bottle and refilled it for her.

She settled back against the sofa again and sipped her wine.

"So…are you ever going to tell me what happened with Brittney?" she asked, referring to the girlfriend he'd split up with just before Thanksgiving.

He shrugged. "It's hardly a big secret—we just realized that we wanted different things out of the relationship."

"She wanted to get married and you didn't?" Lindsay guessed.

"She wanted to at least know we were moving in that direction and I wasn't sure that we were. Not after only six months together."

"Making a commitment after six months might seem hasty when you're twenty," she said. "But half a year should be enough time to figure things out when you're thirty-three."

"You're right," he agreed. "And I figured out she wasn't someone I wanted to spend the rest of my life with, but we parted on good terms."

"I guess that's fair. But you shouldn't be too picky," she cautioned. "There probably aren't many—if there are *any*—single women left in this town that you haven't already dated."

"Thankfully, the world is bigger than Haven," he said lightly.

Lindsay sipped her wine as she watched the fire.

"So…who is she?" she asked, after another few minutes had passed.

He frowned. "Who is who?"

"The woman who's getting in the way of you committing to anyone else."

"There's no other woman," Mitchell told her.

Ordinarily she would respect his boundaries and let the subject drop, but the wine had made her feel brave. Plus, she really wanted to know. Because he was a great guy, and she honestly didn't understand why he was still single.

"Is she married?" she pressed, unpersuaded by his denial. "Is that why you're not with her?"

He sighed. "You don't give up, do you?"

"No," she agreed readily. "Because I want you to be happy. You deserve to be happy."

"I am happy."

"Really?" She didn't even try to hide her skepticism. "Because you're hanging out with a widowed friend on New Year's Eve when you could be at a party."

"Yeah, but I got a free meal," he pointed out.

"Does it count as a free meal if you did the cooking?" she wondered aloud.

"Does it count as cooking if all you do is heat water to boil pasta?" he countered.

"In my book it does," she assured him. "Plus, you defrosted the sauce."

"Yeah, that was a challenge. Seriously," he said, when she laughed. "Your microwave has more bells and whistles than the control panel of a jumbo jet."

"When have you ever seen the control panel of a jumbo jet?" she challenged.

"I watch TV," he told her.

"Well, I think you did a great job with dinner," she said, letting her head drop back against his shoulder. "And it was a definite treat to sit down to a meal that someone else had cooked."

"I'm glad you enjoyed it."

"So...what about you?" he asked, after several more minutes had passed. "Have you thought about dating again?"

"Me? No." She shook her head emphatically.

"Why not?"

She twisted the rings on the third finger of her left hand—a constant reminder of the vows she'd exchanged and the husband she'd lost. "Because I'm a widow with two kids."

"Elliott and Avenlea aren't going to scare off any potential suitors."

"You're right," she agreed. "I'm the one who'd scare them off. I'm a mess."

"Yeah, but you're a hot mess."

She laughed at that. "Thanks... I think."

"And I happen to know at least one former classmate who's solely focused on the hot part."

"Really?" She sounded more surprised than curious.

He nodded. "I was at Jo's recently with some of the guys from high school and Austin Saddler expressed an interest in asking you out."

"Did he give you a note to pass on to me?"

"No, but he said I could give you his number."

"I'll pass," she said. "And isn't he married to Lianne Glover?"

"He *was* married to Lianne," he confirmed. "They've been divorced about three years now."

"I hadn't heard," she said.

"You weren't here," he pointed out. "Anyway, it was a fairly amicable split."

"If there is such a thing."

He shrugged. "They've got a seven-year-old son together and seem to be making things work for Hunter's benefit."

"Well, good for them," she said, still sounding skeptical. "But I'm not interested in dating anyone right now and, even if I was, I'd never go out with the guy who threw my favorite Beanie Baby into a tree at Prospect Park."

"I forgot that was Austin," he said, though of course he remembered the incident.

"Well, I didn't," she assured him. "And I didn't forget who climbed the tree to get Tracker the Bassett Hound back for me, either."

She reached out then to trace her fingertip along the inside of his forearm, where she knew there was a jagged three-inch scar—courtesy of the branch that broke when he was in the tree, hastening his descent and gouging his flesh.

"You cried when you saw the blood," he remembered, wanting—*needing*—to focus on something other than the completely inappropriate way his blood heated in response to her gentle touch.

Was it the wine? The occasion?

Why was he suddenly aware of Lindsay as a woman instead of simply the friend she'd always been?

She lifted her gaze to his then, her eyes twinkling with humor. "I cried because you got blood on my Beanie Baby."

"I did not," he denied. "I tossed it down to you from the tree, and *then* I fell."

"My hero," she said lightly.

"I'm nobody's hero," he assured her.

"You're mine," she insisted. "For a lot more reasons than rescuing Beanie Babies."

Before Mitchell could respond to that, Lindsay's cell phone buzzed against the table.

"The only person who ever calls me after nine o'clock is you," she noted, automatically picking it up to glance at the screen. "It's my in-laws."

She was already swiping to answer the call. "Hello?"

Mitchell started to rise, probably wanting to give her some

privacy for the conversation, but she touched a hand to his arm again, a wordless request for him to stay.

"Hi, Mommy."

"Elliott." Lindsay exhaled a sigh of relief when she heard her son's voice. "What's going on? Why are you still awake?"

"I couldn't go to sleep without sayin' g'night." His earnest claim melted her still-beating-too-fast heart into a puddle at her feet.

"Does Gramma know you're calling?"

"No," he confessed in a whisper. "She's downstairs, watchin' TV with Grampa."

"So you snuck out of bed and into Gramma and Grampa's room to use the phone?" she guessed.

"I 'membered your number," he said, a hint of pride in his voice. "But I didn't hafta know it, cuz it's programmed into Gramma's phone."

"Well, I'm glad you called," she told him sincerely. "Because I don't think I would have been able to go to sleep without saying good-night, either."

"G'night," he said, getting straight to the point now. "I love you, Mommy."

"I love you, too, baby. Now go to bed and have sweet dreams and I'll see you in the morning."

"Are you comin' for breakfast?" he asked. "Gramma's gonna make pancakes."

"I don't know that I'll be there early enough for breakfast," she said, because she was looking forward to the rare opportunity to sleep in (or at least try!) and not be up with her kids at 6:00 a.m.—even if she was skeptical of it actually happening. "But I'll definitely be there before lunch."

For the past several months, Elliott and Avenlea had spent one night a month at their grandparents' house, because Suzanne had asked and because Lindsay's grief counselor had told her that it was important to nurture her children's independence as well as her own. Apparently, wanting to hold on tight wasn't uncommon after the loss of a loved one, but it wasn't healthy. So Lindsay had reluctantly agreed to a first sleepover at Gramma and Grampa T's—and the kids had loved it.

She hadn't loved it, but she'd survived it—even if she hadn't managed to sleep a wink because the house just felt too empty without Elliott and Avenlea. But they'd been so excited to tell her about their adventures when they came home that she couldn't deny it had been good for them.

For Arthur and Suzanne, too, who'd been devastated by the loss of their only child and were grateful to spend one-on-one time with their grandchildren, the only part of Nathan they had left. And when Lindsay had suggested that the kids might enjoy having one sleepover a month at Grampa and Gramma T's, Suzanne had been so happy and grateful, she'd actually cried.

So Lindsay had forced herself to stick with the schedule, no matter that she usually woke up in the middle of the night when the kids were away, her heart pounding with an irrational but undeniable fear inside her chest that they were gone. After which she'd end up in Elliott's bed, with one of Avenlea's teddy bears clutched against her chest. Even if she didn't manage to fall back to sleep, the worst of the fear would fade as she counted the hours until morning, when she could pick them up to bring them home again.

"Everything okay?" Mitchell asked, as his own phone pinged to signal a text message.

She nodded. "Elliott just wanted to say good-night."

He scanned the message and swiped to close the screen again. "And MG wanted to tell me that he was spending the night at Paige's so I shouldn't expect him at the ranch too early in the morning."

"Because of course your brother would want to rub it in that he's got a woman and you don't," she teased.

"Something like that," he acknowledged.

"So—are there wedding plans in the future for MG and Paige?"

He shook his head. "I don't think he's ready."

"Sounds like I've heard this before," she mused. "Maybe the unwillingness to commit is a Gilmore trait."

"More likely he never got over being dumped by Hope Bradford."

"The girl he dated in high school? The one who moved to LA to become an actress?"

He nodded.

"But that was—" she did a quick mental calculation, though not as quick as she would have done before her third glass of wine "—at least eighteen years ago."

"When Gilmores fall, they fall hard and forever."

"That's actually kind of romantic," she said. "Even if it makes me a little sad for Paige."

"I don't think you need to worry about Paige."

"What about you?"

"What about me?" he asked warily.

"Should I worry about you? Why haven't you dated anyone since you broke up with Brittney?" And then, as if the thought had just occurred to her, "Is it my fault?"

He frowned at that. "What do you mean? Why would you think it's your fault that I'm not dating?"

Lindsay shrugged. "Since I moved back to Haven, you've been spending a lot of time with me and Elliott and Avenlea. Anytime I need something, you're here—even when I don't realize I need someone, you're here. It must be hard to be there for anyone else when you're always holding the hand of your best friend's widow."

"You're more than my best friend's widow," he said. "You're my friend, too. In fact, we were friends long before Nathan Thomas moved to town."

She nodded. "But that doesn't give me the right to monopolize so much of your time."

"If there was someone else I wanted to be with, I would be," he assured her.

"Well, I'm glad you're here. It's nice having someone—an adult—to talk to at the end of the day. Usually my night ends with the latest adventures of *Brady Brady*," she said, naming the title character of the series of beginning reader books that Mitchell had given to Elliott for his birthday.

He grinned. "He still likes those stories?"

"They're his favorite," she assured him. "So much so that I could probably recite *Brady Brady and the MVP* without opening the cover of the book."

"I think I've read that one, too," he said. "Though not as many times as *Goodnight Moon*."

"That's a classic," she noted.

They continued to chat until the bottle of wine was empty and the clock had inched close to midnight. Then they opened the bottle of champagne that Mitchell had brought, and when the fireworks shot into the sky over the Vegas strip, they wished one another a happy New Year and tapped their glasses before sipping the bubbly.

He leaned forward to give her a customary kiss on the cheek at the same moment Lindsay turned her head to peck his cheek.

Their lips collided.

The contact was fleeting, but the impact was startling. It wasn't just her mouth that tingled, it was every part of her, from the top of her head to the tips of her toes, and especially the parts in between.

For so long, she'd known nothing but emptiness and grief. Now, suddenly, there were other emotions coursing through her system. Surprise. Awareness. Desire.

The feelings were unexpected but not entirely unwelcome.

She looked at Mitchell, trying to gauge his reaction to the accidental kiss, wanting to know if he was experiencing any of the same emotions.

His expression was guarded, and perhaps a little wary.

But she saw something else in the depths of his dark brown eyes, too. Something that almost looked like a flicker of interest.

He held himself perfectly still, as if waiting to take his cues from her, to let her decide what happened next.

What happened next was that she took his champagne glass and set it down beside her own, then she leaned forward and kissed him again.

CHAPTER THREE

IF THE FIRST kiss had been a surprise to Mitch, this second one was a revelation. Not only because it was the result of deliberate action on Lindsay's part, but also because it was so unexpectedly and unbelievably hot. The way her mouth moved against his with both urgency and intensity, it was as if she wanted nothing as much as she wanted to kiss him. Which worked for him because, in that moment, he wanted nothing as much as he wanted to kiss her.

He'd always believed that kissing was one of the more pleasurable things a man could do with his mouth, and often a prelude to so much more. But not since he was a teenager had he found so much enjoyment in a simple kiss, and he knew he would have been perfectly content to stay right where he was, all night, just kissing her.

But Lindsay wanted more, and she telegraphed her desire by sliding her tongue between his lips and into his mouth. The already hot kiss became an inferno, making him burn with yearning. She hummed, a soft sound of satisfaction low in her throat that stoked the fire inside him.

And then somehow, without him having a clue how it happened, she was in his arms, straddling his lap. Her hands were linked behind his head, her soft breasts were pressed against his chest and her hips were rocking against his in a way that had all the blood rushing out of his head.

As if of their own volition, his hands moved to caress her thighs, the curve of her buttocks, and he said a silent prayer of thanksgiving to whatever celebrity had popularized leggings because the thin, stretchy fabric left nothing of her curves to his imagination.

And yes, he'd imagined her just like this, wanted her just like this. Even when he knew he shouldn't. At first, because they were friends and he worried crossing that line might interfere with their friendship. And later, because she'd chosen Nathan, and fantasizing about his best friend's girlfriend was a violation of the bro code.

Not only had she chosen Nate, she'd married him. Then they'd moved twenty-five hundred miles away and had two beautiful children together. And the only reason she was here now—and he was here now—was that Nathan was dead.

He would never be more than her second choice, if he was even that.

The realization should have doused his passion, but it was difficult to care where he might rank on her list when she was all over him. Even if he'd been last, it only mattered that she was with him now. Rocking her pelvis against his, creating a mind-blowing friction that pushed him dangerously close to the edge of rapture.

He let his hands explore higher, stroking the sides of her torso, skimming the curve of her breasts. She sighed into his mouth and started to rock faster, threatening the tenuous grip he had on his self-control.

If she'd been anyone else, he'd be tugging her sweater over her head and dragging those stretchy pants down her legs in anticipation of satisfying what was apparently a mutual and almost out-of-control desire.

But she wasn't anyone else—she was *Lindsay*.

And no matter that she was the one who'd made the first

move, he couldn't help but feel as if he was taking advantage of his friend. A friend who was still grieving the loss of her husband.

Dammit.

That was why he was desperately trying to maintain his slippery hold, so that the almost out-of-control desire didn't spiral completely out of control. That was why he grabbed hold of her gyrating hips and, gently but firmly, shifted her away from the danger zone.

She whimpered, a soft sound of protest that tempted him to throw caution to the wind and ease Lindsay onto the soft rug by the fire and finish what they'd started.

Then she opened her eyes, and it took only a fraction of a second for the haze of desire to clear and reality to come into focus again.

"Ohmygod." She lifted a hand to her mouth, her fingers pressing against lips swollen from their kiss. He could see the remorse and regret in her moss-green eyes, but he didn't want to hear her say that she was sorry for kissing him.

So he spoke first, before she could. "Happy New Year."

She seemed surprised by his willingness to downplay the intimacy of what they'd shared, but he thought she looked relieved, too. Grateful that he wasn't making a big deal out of the mind-numbing lip-lock.

Her hand dropped away from her mouth.

"Happy New Year," she echoed.

Which should have signaled a return to the status quo—except that she was still in his lap, those talented, tempting lips within easy reach if he just leaned forward—

He cleared his throat. "And since it's after midnight now, I should probably be on my way, because there are morning chores to be done on the ranch even on New Year's Day."

"Oh. Right. Of course," she said, sounding just a little bit flustered.

And then she seemed to realize she was still straddling him, because she quickly scrambled out of the way so that he could stand.

Lindsay could feel the heat in her cheeks as she followed Mitchell to the door, waiting for him to say something more—or something at all—about the kiss they'd shared. But he seemed engrossed in the act of pulling on his boots, then putting on his jacket—or maybe he was totally unaffected by what had happened between them in the family room (hard evidence to the contrary!) while she was completely churned up inside.

"Is that really all that's on your mind?" she finally asked. "Morning chores?"

"No." He took his time zipping up the front of his jacket before he looked at her. "Not all."

There was something there—a flicker in the depths of his gaze that might have been desire—that made her think he wasn't as totally unaffected as he wanted her to believe. But then it was gone, leaving her to wonder if maybe she'd only imagined it.

She swallowed. "Do you think we should talk about what just happened?"

"It was just a kiss, Lindsay," he said tersely. "I don't think there's anything to be gained from talking about it."

"Just a kiss," she echoed. So maybe she had imagined that flicker, but she hadn't imagined his response to her kiss, even if he had been the one to end it. "You're right. Why make a big deal out of something that was obviously nothing?"

"I didn't say it was nothing."

"Well, you're acting like it was nothing." And it was a blow to her pride—at the very least—that he was so easily walking away from something that had shaken her down to her toes.

"Would it make you feel better if I told you that I was hanging on to my self-control by a thread?"

"No… Maybe. If it was true."

He looked at her then, with so much heat in his gaze that it reignited the embers of the fire low in her belly.

"Or we could just pretend it didn't happen," she suggested as an alternative.

He nodded slowly. "That might be for the best."

"Okay," she agreed, not entirely sure if she was relieved or disappointed by his response.

Mitchell paused with his hand on the doorknob. "Are you going to be okay now?"

She felt her cheeks flush. "The champagne might have muddled my judgment for a few minutes," she said, aware that her prim tone was a stark contrast to the passion she'd exhibited on the sofa. "But I promise you, I'm not going to have another meltdown just because we shared a kiss that we just agreed to pretend never happened."

"I was actually referring to the fact that you'll be alone tonight because Elliott and Avenlea aren't home."

"Oh. Right." Her cheeks burned hotter. "Yes. I'm fine. I'll be fine. Okay, I'm a little bit flustered. And maybe a little bit tipsy from the champagne."

"You had a few sips. Plus the better part of a bottle of wine," he acknowledged.

"It's the bubbles," she said. "They go straight to my head every time."

He nodded, apparently willing to accept the excuse if it made her feel better. "Make sure you drink lots of water before you go to bed."

"I will," she promised. "Drive safely."

Lindsay stood at the door, watching through the sidelight as Mitchell made his way to his truck. When he'd driven away, she leaned her forehead against the cold glass, as if that might cool the heat still churning in her veins.

Oh. My. God.

She'd kissed Mitchell.

Not just kissed him, but climbed into his lap and wrapped herself around him, practically begging him to take her right then and there.

Of course Mitchell, being the gentleman that he was, had declined her alcohol-fueled invitation.

But maybe it was unfair to blame the champagne for her behavior—and his response. Maybe the bubbly had lessened her inhibitions, but it was the first touch of his lips that had compelled her to throw caution to the wind.

And maybe his rebuffing of her attempted seduction wasn't about his morals so much as an indication that he hadn't been tempted by her aggressive efforts at seduction. He'd been turned on—from where she'd been sitting, there'd been no doubt about that!—but not sufficiently aroused to want to take her to bed.

Or on the sofa.

Or anywhere else, apparently.

She huffed out a breath, fogging the glass.

She should be grateful to Mitchell for putting on the brakes. For understanding that she was dealing with a lot of emotions and not thinking clearly.

But she didn't feel grateful.

She felt rejected and foolish and more than a little bit guilty. Guilty that she'd been unfaithful to the husband who'd been gone for more than two years. Guilty that she'd taken advantage of a man who'd always been there for her.

But mostly, with this newly awakened desire still churning in her veins, she felt alive.

And confused.

Because the man who'd awakened that desire was one of her oldest and dearest friends.

Of course, her old friend was an incredibly good-looking man with a hard body and a quick smile that made women sigh and yearn. He was also a member of the wealthy and successful Gilmore ranching family and one of the most sought-after bachelors in town. Lindsay didn't think there was a woman in Haven who hadn't secretly crushed on Mitchell or his brother Michael—better known as MG—and quite likely one or more of their cousins, too.

But Liam and Caleb were both happily married now, leaving the single women who wanted to nab a Gilmore to scramble for the affections of Mitchell and MG. And while the brothers were happy to spread their affections around, neither had given any indication that he was ready to settle down.

Not that Lindsay was looking for a relationship. She was still trying to wrap her head around the surprising realization that she could be attracted to a man who wasn't her husband. Though she'd been certain a part of her had died when Nathan did, apparently it wasn't any of those all-important female parts.

She would always miss Nate, and she'd always be sad that he'd miss so many milestones in each of their children's lives. But she'd moved on—or was at least moving in that direction. She didn't cry herself to sleep anymore—except on Nathan's birthday and their anniversary and the anniversary of the plane crash that killed him. And okay, she'd cried after her shopping trip when Elliott had asked her to buy shredded wheat.

Not just because she missed him, though she did every day, but because she felt so alone. It wasn't only on birthdays or anniversaries that she was cognizant of his absence; it was that there was no one to share the trials and triumphs of everyday life. Whether it was something as simple as Avenlea asking to use the potty or as complicated as figuring out what wrench to use to fix a leaky pipe—and then calling the plumber.

She was getting used to being on her own, but that didn't mean she liked it. And though her kids kept her busy during the day, there were a lot of long, lonely hours between their bedtime and her own. It was during those hours that she missed Nathan the most, that she started to think maybe she wouldn't mind meeting someone new.

Then morning would come, and she'd get busy with the kids and disregard the notion again. Because she barely had two minutes to brush her teeth before she rushed out of the house, never mind time for a romance.

Maybe she could revisit the possibility when they were older, but right now she couldn't imagine it happening. New relationships simply required too much time and attention that she didn't have.

Unless it was a new romance with an old friend.

No. Absolutely not. She refused to consider it.

Sure, she and Mitchell would be able to skip all of the getting-to-know-you stuff that dominated the beginning of a relationship, but she suspected that Mitchell—having recently broken up with Brittney—wasn't looking for a relationship any more than she was.

And even if she was looking for a romance, it would be a mistake to look at Mitchell, because he was one of her best friends. He was the one person who'd been there for her at every point in her life—not just from the day she'd married Nathan to the day she'd buried him, but countless days before and after and in between. And she wasn't going to risk that friendship for anything.

The frigid wind slapped at his face and burned in his lungs when Mitch stepped outside into the bitter cold early morning of January 1.

"Happy freakin' New Year to me," he muttered, as he tucked his chin into his collar and shoved his hands deeper into his pockets.

His breath puffed out in clouds and his boots crunched in the snow as he trudged toward the barn. Because, as he'd remarked to Lindsay the night before, animals needed to be fed and watered every day of the year, no matter the weather or temperature or even the disposition of the rancher.

Fortunately, between him and his brother and their cousins, there were plenty of capable hands to share the work. Unfortunately, he'd drawn the short straw and ended up with morning chores on New Year's Day.

Which shouldn't have been any worse than any other cold winter morning, because he hadn't been out particularly late nor overindulged the night before. But he'd tossed and turned for a long time before falling asleep, and it seemed as if he'd only just done that when his alarm started screeching at him to wake up again.

The single cup of coffee he'd gulped down before heading out of the former bunkhouse that he now shared with his brother—when MG bothered to sleep at home—hadn't provided enough of a caffeine kick to compensate for his lack of sleep, and the Tylenol he'd swallowed had done nothing to diminish the pounding in his head.

He wasn't hungover. He'd only had two glasses of wine with dinner and, several hours later, half a glass of champagne, because he knew he was driving. Lindsay had polished off the rest of the bottle of wine, so maybe he should cut her some slack with respect to what had happened the night before.

Of course, nothing had really happened.

Nothing except that they'd shared one incredibly hot kiss that had made him want so much more.

It wasn't her fault that she'd gotten him all stirred up—it was the wine that had fueled her actions.

And the press of her sexy body against his that had revived his long-dormant fantasies.

Sure, he'd thought about kissing her before last night. But that was years ago, when he was a teenage boy who suddenly discovered that one of his best friends was a teenage girl with curves in all the right places. But even then, he'd been reticent to act on what he was thinking. Maybe too reticent—but that was water long under the bridge.

He'd kissed a lot of girls in his thirty-three years—more than his fair share, some would say—but he'd never made a move on Lindsay. Well, not since he'd proposed to her when they were both ten years old, and that quick peck—and immediate recoil—hardly counted as a kiss. Obviously they'd both learned a lot since then, but never would he have imagined that a single kiss could generate so much heat and passion.

Thinking about it now, he realized that she probably hadn't

kissed a man since her husband died—more than two years earlier. And he would bet the ranch that she hadn't been intimate with one. Maybe she took care of her own needs—and he definitely didn't want to let his mind wander too far down that tantalizing path—but from his perspective, a solo adventure was never as satisfying as one with a partner.

"Here you are," MG said, jolting Mitchell out of his prurient fantasy and back to the present as he sauntered into the barn—conveniently *after* Mitch had finished mucking out the stalls.

He wiped a hand over his sweaty brow. "Where else would I be?"

MG shrugged. "You were MIA last night."

"I wasn't MIA," he denied.

"Well, you didn't show up at Diggers' after you'd said you'd be there."

"Change of plans," he said, rolling back his shoulders and arching his back to stretch out the tight muscles.

"You hung out with Lindsay and the kids at her place, didn't you?" his brother guessed.

"Actually, the kids were with their grandparents."

"So just you and Lindsay," MG mused thoughtfully. "Now I get why you skipped the party."

"There's nothing to get," Mitch told him. "Lindsay didn't feel like going out, so we stayed in."

His brother nodded. "Because you wanted to make your move without half of the population of Haven watching."

"I did *not* make a move."

And it was true.

Lindsay had made the move, but he wasn't going to share any of that with MG, who would somehow twist the details to rib him mercilessly—because that's what brothers did.

Now MG shook his head. "Nathan's been gone for more than two years. What are you waiting for?"

"She's my friend," he reminded his brother—and himself.

"She's also incredibly hot. And if you try to tell me you don't see her that way, you're either lying or in denial because I know how hard you crushed on her in high school."

"Maybe I did," he acknowledged. "But that was high school, and I got over my crush a long time ago."

"Did you?" MG pressed.

"I stood up for her husband at their wedding," he reminded his brother.

"And got drunk that night."

"As if you've never overindulged at a party," he scoffed.

"You got drunk again the night before they moved to Alaska," MG pointed out.

"That was eight years ago—how could you possibly remember something like that when I don't even remember what I was doing eight years ago?"

"You only wish you could forget," MG said. "I remember because I saw how it gutted you to say goodbye to her, knowing she was moving twenty-five hundred miles away and not knowing if she'd ever come back."

Uncomfortable with his brother's insightful assessment, he turned the tables. "You've been reading mom's romance novels again, haven't you?"

"As if you didn't read them, too," MG retorted.

Of course his brother knew that he had, because they'd passed the books back and forth when they were younger, giggling—and yes, aroused—by the explicit and intimate details.

"There was some good stuff in those books," he acknowledged. "I learned a lot from the love scenes."

"Is that where you learned to sidestep uncomfortable questions, too?"

"I don't recall a question—just you spouting some made-up nonsense about my supposed feelings way back when."

"Okay, let's skip to the present," MG said.

"Let's," Mitch agreed, with false enthusiasm.

"On New Year's Eve this year, when you had the opportunity to be at a party with an assortment of beautiful, single women, you chose to spend a quiet night at home with Lindsay instead. And somehow, I'm supposed to believe this is proof that you're no longer carrying a torch for her."

"Did they bring in a bus from out of town? Because the last time I checked, there weren't that many beautiful, single women in Haven."

"You mean, that you haven't already dated," MG clarified, as Olivia muscled open the door and led Dolly, her palomino mare, into the barn.

"Or you haven't," Mitch countered, with a nod to acknowledge their sister's presence. "And if you want to talk about torches—yours has been burning bright for eighteen years."

"Are we talking about Hope?" Olivia asked, referring to MG's long-ago girlfriend who'd left Haven to pursue an acting career in Hollywood when she was seventeen years old.

"No, we're not talking about Hope," MG said firmly. "And Mitch is full of the stuff he shoveled into that wheelbarrow."

"So you don't have your DVR set to record every episode of *Rockwood Ridge*?" their sister challenged as she removed the horse's saddle and bridle.

"It's a good show," MG said, in defense of the popular weekly drama in which Hope played a recurring role.

"Uh-huh," Mitch agreed, as Olivia carried her equipment to the tack room. "But most people erase an episode after watching it. You save them until you can buy the season on DVD."

"Don't even try to deny it's true," Olivia said, rejoining their conversation. "Because Grams told me that she borrowed Season Two last week, because the finale is one of her favorite episodes. You know—the one where Lainey Howard, played by Hope Bradford, walks down the aisle to marry Thorne Chesterfield."

"I don't recall anyone inviting you to join this conversation," MG grumbled.

"I'm the little sister," she acknowledged. "If I had to wait for an invitation, I'd still be waiting."

"Why were you out so early this morning?" Mitch asked, steering the conversation in another direction to defuse the rising tension between his siblings.

"It was my New Year's resolution for both me and Dolly to get more exercise," she announced proudly.

"Wonder how long this one will last," MG said.

She huffed out a breath. "You could at least give me credit for making a resolution—I bet you didn't."

"Resolutions are for people who want to change," MG said. "I'm perfectly happy with my life just the way it is."

"Now who's in denial?" Mitch asked.

"I am happy with my life," his brother insisted.

"Paige isn't," Olivia noted. "We all saw her face at Christmas when she opened the box with The Gold Mine logo on the top and found earrings instead of a ring."

"They were diamond earrings," MG pointed out.

"Still not what she was hoping for."

"Well, she should have known better than to think that I'd ever propose with my whole family looking on," he said.

"She should know better than to think that you're ever going to propose—period," Mitch said.

"Because when Hope left town, she shattered his heart into a thousand pieces," Olivia noted.

"Ouch," Mitch said.

"But what's your excuse?" his sister asked, turning on him. "You've never let anyone get close enough to break your heart because you're still holding out hope that Lindsay will suddenly wake up one day and realize that she's in love with you."

"What do you know about love?" MG challenged.

"I know enough to tread cautiously," she said. "Because what I've learned from everyone around me is that when Gilmores fall in love, it's a life sentence."

It was the same sentiment that Mitch had expressed to Lindsay the night before—and why it was lucky that he wasn't in love with her.

CHAPTER FOUR

"I'M SORRY," LINDSAY said when her brother-in-law opened the door in response to her knock. "I know it's early, but I really need to talk to Kristyne."

Gabe Berkeley appeared to consider the request as he perused the tray of coffee cups she held in one hand and the paper bag in the other.

"I don't see a box with Sweet Caroline's logo on it," he said, sounding disappointed that, whatever might be in the bag, it obviously wasn't one of his favorite treats—apple fritters from the local shop.

"The bakery's closed today," she told him.

"Imagine that," he said dryly, stepping aside so that she could enter. "Almost as if New Year's Day was a holiday or something."

She chose to ignore the barb as she set the bag and tray on the small table beside the door so that she could remove her boots. "But The Daily Grind was open, and they had s'mores muffins."

"Those are your sister's favorite, not mine."

Gabe disapproved of the concept of dessert for breakfast—apple fritters being the sole exception to his healthy eating rule.

"And she's the one carrying the baby," she pointed out.

"Which is why I already made her a spinach omelet for breakfast," her brother-in-law said.

"Then there's no reason you should object to her having a muffin for dessert," she pointed out reasonably.

"Is that decaf?" he asked, shifting his attention to the trio of cups in the tray.

"Only Kristyne's. You and I get the good stuff."

He flashed a quick grin. "Okay, you're forgiven for showing up before nine a.m."

She pried the cup marked with a B—indicating the coffee was black—out of the holder and offered it to him.

"And what did you have for breakfast?" he asked.

"I'm going to have a muffin."

Her brother-in-law shook his head. "I'll make you an omelet."

"Well, if it's not too much trouble," she said, smiling hopefully.

"Not at all. It's just beating some eggs."

"Thank you." She took one of the muffins out of the bag and balanced it on the lid of his coffee cup. "Cinnamon apple."

"I'll give you an A for effort," he decided.

She smiled and kissed his bristly cheek. "Happy New Year."

"Kristyne's in the solarium," he said. "I'll bring your omelet in when it's ready."

Lindsay made her way to the back of the house and the room with three walls and a ceiling composed of glass to welcome in the natural light. The decor her sister had chosen suited the setting: white wicker furniture with floral cushions, big ceramic pots filled with tropical plants and even a freestanding water wall. It was a room designed for rest and relaxation, and Lindsay knew that her sister spent a lot of time there, especially when her musician husband was busy writing or rehearsing in his soundproofed room above the garage.

"I thought I heard your voice," Kristyne said, when Lindsay stepped around an enormous banana plant and into view.

The expectant mom was wearing a tunic-style sweater and

stretchy leggings with thick, fuzzy socks on her feet. Her honey-blond hair was piled on her head in a messy bun and her face, devoid of makeup, was glowing with happiness.

"You heard my voice and didn't even get up to say hi," Lindsay chastised teasingly, as she bent to kiss her sister's cheek.

Kristyne looked pointedly past her swollen belly to her legs, stretched out in front of her and propped up on the wicker coffee table. "The doctor has encouraged me to put up my feet as much as possible over the next couple of days to alleviate the swelling in my ankles, and Gabe is policing her directions."

"You assured me that everything was good at your last appointment."

"Everything *is* good," Kristyne insisted. "I'm fine, aside from some very mild edema."

"You should be drinking water," Lindsay noted, even as she reluctantly handed over the coffee her sister was gesturing for.

"I've been drinking water." Kristyne indicated the half-full sports bottle on the side table. "But I desperately want coffee—even if I know it's decaf."

Lindsay sat sideways on the sofa, so that she was facing her sister. "How are you feeling otherwise?"

"Fat."

Unable to resist, she reached over to gently rub the curve of her sister's belly. "You're not fat, you're pregnant."

"To-may-to, to-mah-to."

Kristyne opened the bag Lindsay offered, her gloomy expression brightening when she saw what was inside.

"But I really can't complain," she continued. "Gabe has been waiting on me hand and foot—and keeping the house tidy, too."

"Enjoy it while you can," Lindsay advised. "Once the baby is born, a tidy house will be a distant memory, you'll both be running ragged and you'll lament the days when you could actually close your eyes and relax for *just ten minutes*."

"I can't wait," Kristyne assured her. "I feel as if I've been pregnant forever."

"Be grateful you're not an elephant. They carry their babies for eighteen-to-twenty-two months."

"Maybe I am an elephant. I probably weigh as much as one these days. But I'm going to eat this muffin anyway," she said, tearing off a piece, "while you tell me about the party last night. And don't spare any details."

"Isn't one party pretty much the same as the next?" Lindsay hedged.

"Yeah, but since I didn't go out last night, I need to live vicariously through you." She popped the bite of muffin, rich with chocolate chunks and marshmallow bits, into her mouth and closed her eyes on a blissful sigh. "Mostly I want to know who went home with whom after the clock struck twelve."

"Then you're going to be disappointed, because I don't have those kinds of details," she confessed.

Her sister's eyes popped open again. "Don't tell me you skipped out before midnight." Then her gaze narrowed. "And don't you dare tell me you didn't go."

Lindsay sipped her coffee.

Kristyne sighed. "Oh, Linds. You didn't go, did you?"

"I *wanted* to go," she said. "But I didn't have anything to wear."

Which had seemed like a perfectly reasonable explanation the day before but now sounded like a hollow excuse—just like the other hollow excuses she'd manufactured to decline various invitations over the past two years. But she'd honestly intended to follow through when she'd said yes to Mitchell's invitation for New Year's Eve—right up until it was time to get ready for the event.

"That ranks right up there with 'I had to wash my hair' at the top of the list of Lamest Excuses of All Time."

"It's the truth," Lindsay said.

"You could have borrowed something from my closet," Kristyne told her. "God knows, none of my party clothes fit me anymore."

"Except that I didn't look in my closet until after I'd dropped Elliott and Avenlea off at their grandparents' house, and by then it was too late to consider other options."

"So you spent New Year's Eve alone?" Kristyne immediately shook her head, answering her own question before her sister could respond. "No. Mitchell wouldn't let you do that."

"No," she agreed. "Though I hate knowing he missed the party on my account."

"So what did you guys do?" Kristyne prompted.

"We ate spaghetti and watched the celebrations in Vegas on TV."

Her sister shook her head. "I don't think so."

"Excuse me?"

"I'm not saying you didn't have dinner and watch TV," she allowed. "I'm saying something else happened...something that brought you to my door the morning after."

"I think she came for a free meal," Gabe said, entering the room with a tray.

"Yours wasn't the only breakfast offer I had," his sister-in-law told him.

Kristyne waggled her eyebrows. "Do tell."

Lindsay rolled her eyes as she accepted the tray. "Suzanne was making pancakes this morning."

Her sister sighed, obviously disappointed. "That's *not* where I thought this was going."

"But this looks even better than pancakes," Lindsay said, eyeing the fluffy omelet filled with baby spinach and parmesan cheese and served with a side of sliced tomato. "Thanks, Gabe."

"You're welcome," he said. "And since I obviously interrupted a conversation about something that, truthfully, I don't want to know, I'll leave you two to chat."

Lindsay picked up the fork—on top of the neatly folded napkin beside the plate—and dug into the eggs.

"You really did luck out when you married him," she said.

"Not only is he a hunky musician who loves you beyond belief, the man has serious kitchen skills."

"Nathan wasn't much of a cook, was he?" Kristyne asked, because she'd never been one of those people who tiptoed around saying his name, understanding that Lindsay's life with Nathan was something she needed to talk about, to remember.

"He was good at a lot of things, but cooking wasn't one of them." Probably because he'd made no effort to learn how to cook, preferring to let his wife be responsible for planning and preparing their meals. "Unless throwing steaks or burgers on the grill counts as cooking," Lindsay added. "He was happy enough to do that if I asked, but chop up vegetables to make a salad to go with the steak? Never."

"You should have expected that," Kristyne noted. "Considering he grew up with parents in traditional gender roles. Whereas Gabe was raised by a single father, so he knows a man is capable of doing it all—and he does."

"Even laundry?" Lindsay asked curiously.

"You should see the man wield an iron," her sister said.

"You're kidding."

Kristyne shook her head. "I'm not," she promised. "He even irons *my* clothes."

"That's impressive. Not quite as impressive as this," she said, lifting another forkful of eggs. "But still."

"Getting back to last night..." Kristyne prompted.

Lindsay took her time chewing, savoring the fluffy omelet— was that a hint of nutmeg she tasted?—and buying herself time to figure out what to say. Which she probably should have done on the drive over here, since the purpose of this visit was to talk to her sister. But it was a short drive, and Lindsay had a lot of tangled emotions to unravel.

She washed down the egg with a mouthful of sweet coffee before confessing: "Last night, when the clock struck twelve and fireworks exploded to fill the Vegas sky with light and color... I kissed Mitchell."

"So?" Kristyne was clearly unimpressed. "Everyone kisses everyone on New Year's—it's like a smooching free-for-all."

"No," Lindsay said. "I mean I *really* kissed him."

Her sister nibbled on another bite of muffin while she considered this revelation. "And then?"

And then Lindsay had climbed into his lap, pressed every part of her body against every part of his and almost come apart as a result of the delicious friction they'd generated together even with all their clothes on.

But there was no way she was going to share *those* details with her sister. Not because Kristyne wasn't a trustworthy confidante, but because Lindsay wasn't comfortable acknowledging the true extent of her shameless behavior. Kristyne wouldn't judge her but Lindsay was definitely judging herself.

"What do you mean—*and then*?" she asked. "Isn't that shocking enough?"

"The only shocking part is that it's taken this long for you two to hook up," her sister said.

"We didn't hook up," she denied. "And what do you mean—it's taken this long?"

"Please. The two of you have been dancing around your feelings forever."

"What feelings?" She was sincerely baffled by her sister's matter-of-fact statement. "Mitchell is one of my best friends. And he was Nathan's friend, too."

"Which is probably what held him back from making a move before last night," Kristyne acknowledged.

Lindsay swallowed another mouthful of coffee as she considered her sister's theory. But the fact was, he still hadn't made a move—she was the one who'd kissed him, forcing him to extricate himself from an awkward situation.

"So...how was the kiss?" Kristyne prompted. "Was it sweet? Sexy? Did it make your toes curl?"

Lindsay couldn't remember the last time she'd been kissed like Mitchell had kissed her. Of course, when you were married with a preschooler and an infant, you didn't waste a lot of time on foreplay. Moments of intimacy didn't have to be few and far between, but they were often quick and unexpected. As a result, she'd almost forgotten how much pleasure could be found in a kiss—until last night.

"It made my toes curl and my heart pound and all my other parts ache," she confided.

Her sister smiled. "That's the very best kind of kiss."

"Except that it never should have happened," she said.

"Why would you say that?" Kristyne asked, mystified.

"Because a kiss like that changes everything."

"Isn't that the point?"

Lindsay shook her head. "I don't want our relationship to change."

"Obviously you do, or you wouldn't have kissed him," her sister pointed out.

"I wasn't thinking straight," she said. "We had wine with dinner...and then champagne."

"The alcohol might have lessened your inhibitions," Kristyne acknowledged. "But it didn't make you do anything you didn't want to do." She wiggled her eyebrows. "And you want to do Mitchell Gilmore."

"I don't." She huffed out a breath. "I can't."

"You can and you should. Nathan's been gone for more than two years," her sister pointed out gently.

Lindsay nodded, her throat tight.

Twenty-seven months and seventeen days, in fact.

Or was it eighteen days now?

She sucked in a breath, stunned to realize that she might have lost track of the number.

Not that she'd been counting on purpose. It was more that she'd been focused on getting through one day at a time, and after that first day came a second day and then a third...

"It's okay to move on with your life," Kristyne said gently.

"I have moved on."

Her sister shook her head. "Moving isn't the same as moving on."

Lindsay considered that as she swallowed another mouthful of coffee, no longer tasting the sweetness.

"If you'd really moved on, you wouldn't still be wearing your wedding rings."

She automatically looked down at the emerald-cut diamond solitaire and matching embossed gold band on the third finger of her left hand—proof of her identity as Nathan's wife. "When we got married, I was sure it was forever... I never imagined that I'd take my rings off."

"And you don't have to take them off now," Kristyne said. "But you should think about why you're still wearing them. Is it habit? Is it because you still feel married? Or is it because they protect you from opening your heart again?"

It was an insightful question, and Lindsay realized that her answer might be all of the above.

Mitch spent the rest of the morning with his cousin Caleb, delivering grain to feed boxes to supplement the winter diet of the Circle G cattle. When they were done, Caleb rushed home to his wife and baby, and Mitch went to the empty bunkhouse and made himself a sandwich. After lunch, he considered taking a nap but opted for a walk instead.

He might not have thought he had a destination in mind when he headed out into the cold again, but he wasn't at all surprised to find himself standing in front of his childhood home only a few minutes later.

He knocked the snow off his boots outside the side door, wiped the soles on the thick coir mat, then hung his coat and hat on the hooks inside the mudroom.

"I don't often see you here in the middle of the day," Angela Gilmore remarked when Mitch made his way to the kitchen.

"Am I interrupting?" he asked.

"Of course not," his mom said. "I'm just making bread—we can chat while I knead."

He reached into the cupboard above the coffee maker for a mug. "Do you want coffee?"

She shook her head. "No, thanks. I've had my quota for the day."

Mitch filled his mug from the carafe on the warmer.

"So what's on your mind?" she asked.

"Do I really only come here when there's something on my mind?"

"Or nothing in your belly," she teased. "And since it's too late for lunch and too early for dinner, I figured you wanted to talk."

"I wouldn't say no to something from that jar on the counter," he said, referring to the ceramic Cookie Monster container that had sat in the same spot on the counter for as long as he could remember—and was always guaranteed to have some kind of homemade goodies inside.

"Help yourself," she told him.

He lifted Cookie Monster's head and reached inside, then pulled out a handful of chunky peanut butter cookies.

Angela sprinkled flour on her board, then scooped the dough from the bowl and turned it out, creating a puff of white dust. It would have been easier—and maybe even cheaper—to buy a loaf at The Trading Post, but for as long as Mitch could remember, his mom had made her own bread, and the yeasty scent of a freshly baked loaf always reminded him of her kitchen.

He nibbled on a cookie, savoring the soft and chewy treat, and washed it down with coffee, strong and black, while she began to knead.

"Do you ever use that mixer Dad bought for you?" he asked as he watched her fold and press the dough.

"Kneading by hand is better for bread," she said, then grinned. "And better for my arms, too."

"So it's not that you don't use it because a kitchen appliance is a lousy anniversary present?"

She chuckled softly. "No. While I would generally agree that jewelry is a safer choice, I know very well how much that fancy mixer cost because I'd been eyeing one for some time.

"And yes, I use it to cook for your dad, so he reaps the benefit of his gift to me. But I bought him tickets to a Dodgers game expecting that he'd take me with him," she pointed out. "Because after thirty-nine years of marriage, we know one another pretty well."

"And even after thirty-nine years, Dad tells the same story on your anniversary every year—about the day you first met."

She smiled at that. "He does like that story."

"Is it true? Did you really fall in love at first sight?"

"There was an immediate attraction," she acknowledged. "But love, real love, doesn't happen in an instant. It's like growing a flower from a seed. The blossom doesn't appear overnight—it needs tending and nurturing."

He considered that as he chewed on another cookie.

"Is there any particular reason you were thinking about the story now?" she asked.

"Olivia was giving me a hard time earlier because I've never had my heart broken."

"Which only proves that your sister doesn't know everything," Angela noted.

He lifted his mug to his lips and sipped his coffee.

"Because I was there at the church when Lindsay and Nathan exchanged their vows, and I saw your heart break," she continued, her tone gentle.

"It might have cracked a little," he conceded. "But that crack healed a long time ago."

"I hope that's true," she said. "Because you've been spending a lot of time with her since she came back. Not just with Lindsay but Elliott and Avenlea, too."

"They're great kids."

"Great kids who don't have a dad, and who might already be

looking at you as a father figure," she cautioned, folding and turning the dough again.

He swallowed his last mouthful of coffee. "Are you suggesting that I should spend less time with them?"

"Of course not," she immediately replied, sprinkling a little more flour onto the dough. "But I'd be lying if I said I wasn't worried that you might end up with your heart broken again."

"Cracked," he reminded her. "And I got over my feelings for Lindsay a long time ago."

"Maybe," she said. "But I guarantee that whatever barriers you've put up around your heart won't hold up for long—especially not against those kids."

If it was a warning, it had come too late—Elliott and Avenlea had already taken hold of his heart, and there wasn't anything Mitch wouldn't do for either of them.

Truth be told, there wasn't anything he wouldn't do for Lindsay, either. Because he loved her, too, but in a strictly platonic sense this time.

One incredibly steamy New Year's Eve kiss notwithstanding.

CHAPTER FIVE

ARTHUR THOMAS—a semi-retired district court judge—and his wife, Suzanne—a lawyer-turned-homemaker—lived on Miners' Pass, part of a newer development in the most affluent part of town. Their house was two stories of stone and brick with lots of windows and professionally landscaped grounds, and the judge's home office had a bay window that allowed him to see anyone coming or going. Obviously he saw Lindsay coming, because he opened the door before she could knock.

Though her father-in-law was almost seventy, he was a good-looking man with thick salt-and-pepper hair, deep blue eyes beneath bushy eyebrows and a trim physique that he maintained through regular use of the home gym and—in the summer months—frequent rounds of golf.

Lindsay used to tease Nathan that one of the reasons she'd married him was that she knew he'd still be handsome when he got older because he looked so much like his dad. Of course, Nathan never had a chance to get older, dying a few weeks shy of his thirty-first birthday.

"Happy New Year." She kissed Arthur's cheek as she stepped inside the door. "Are you so anxious to get rid of the grandkids that you've been waiting and watching for me?"

He chuckled. "Of course not. I just happened to see your car turn into the drive."

"You weren't in your office working on the holiday, were you?"

"I was," he confided. "I promised to deliver my judgment in a civil action on the first day back, and apparently it's not going to write itself."

"So much for retirement, huh?"

"I'm only partially retired," he reminded her. "Suzanne's idea, because she worried that I wouldn't know what to do with myself. At least that's what she said. Truthfully, I think she was more worried that I'd be in her way all the time."

"There might be some truth in that," Lindsay acknowledged, aware that her mother-in-law was very Type A and had specific schedules and routines that she didn't like to have interrupted—unless it was for the opportunity to spend more time with her grandchildren.

"Anyway, I'm sure you didn't come here to chat with me. Elliott and Avenlea are in the dining room, finishing up their breakfast. Or they *were* in the dining room," he amended, as Elliott—apparently having heard his mom's voice—came racing around the corner.

"Mommy! Mommy!" He practically flew down the hall toward her, his little sister close on her heels.

"Mommy! Mommy!" Avenlea echoed.

Lindsay's heart filled with joy as she knelt to catch them both in her arms and squeeze them tight. She planted noisy kisses on their cheeks as she breathed in the familiar scent of baby shampoo...and maple syrup.

Obviously they'd had their pancakes for breakfast.

"Were you good for Gramma and Grampa?" she asked.

"Uh-huh," Elliott said.

Avenlea nodded her head, her lopsided pigtails bobbing.

"So good Gramma made pancakes. With chocolate chips."

"Chocolate chip pancakes, huh? Your gramma must love you an awful lot."

There were more head bobs then as Suzanne came down the hall from the kitchen at the back of the house, where the doors opened up onto a gorgeous interlocking brick patio for outdoor dining, weather permitting. The sixty-seven-year-old looked at least ten years younger, with sable-colored hair stylishly cut in a long bob and makeup immaculately applied. She was fond of sweater sets and neatly pressed trousers and always looked as if she was ready to walk into a PTA meeting even if she was spending the day at home.

Lindsay was suddenly aware of the contrast of her own outfit—a baggy sweater with jeans frayed at the cuffs.

Suzanne greeted her daughter-in-law with a smile and an air kiss. "Coffee's fresh, if you've got time for a cup."

Lindsay thought about the mountain of laundry waiting at home along with a ridiculous number of holiday decorations that needed to be taken down and packed away for next Christmas. And then she thought about how lucky she was to have in-laws that she sincerely enjoyed spending time with. And because the dirty clothes and garlands and wreaths and nutcrackers would still be there when she got home, whether that was in ten minutes or an hour, she said, "Coffee sounds great."

"Did you want some pancakes?" Suzanne asked, leading the way to the kitchen. "It will only take me a minute to heat up the leftovers."

"Thanks, but I already had breakfast."

"Coffee—even with lots of cream and sugar—doesn't count as breakfast," her mother-in-law admonished, aware that Lindsay was frequently guilty of substituting coffee for the morning meal.

"I know," she admitted, as she dropped another teaspoonful of sugar into the cup that Suzanne had set in front of her. "But I stopped by to see my sister this morning, and Gabe made me an omelet."

"You did get an early start, then," Suzanne noted.

"I don't sleep well when the house is empty," she confided.

And she'd hardly slept a wink the night before, not because Elliott and Avenlea were gone but because she couldn't stop thinking about the fact that she'd kissed Mitchell. And when she'd finally managed to fall asleep, she'd dreamed of him—but in her dreams, they'd done a lot more than share a few kisses.

"How is Kristyne?"

Suzanne's question jolted Lindsay out of her reverie. "She's good. Impatient, but good."

Her mother-in-law smiled at that. "She isn't due until the end of February, right?"

Lindsay nodded. "The twenty-fifth."

"Expectant moms are always so anxious to hold their babies in their arms," Suzanne acknowledged. "And all too soon, our babies are grown and we never realize we're holding our child for the last time, until he won't let himself be held anymore."

Lindsay reached across the island and squeezed her mother-in-law's hand. "And then you have grandkids—and you get to do it all over again."

Suzanne blinked away the moisture that had filled her eyes and forced a smile. "You're right. Grandkids are a blessing and a second chance."

"Grandparents are a blessing, too," Lindsay assured her. "I hope you know how much Elliott and Avenlea enjoy spending time with you and Arthur."

"We're happy to have them anytime," Suzanne said. "In fact, we were thinking—*hoping*—that you might agree to let them stay with us two nights a month instead of just one."

Lindsay's instinct was to say no—because she hated how empty the house seemed when her kids were gone. But that was a purely selfish reaction, especially considering how much Elliott and Avenlea enjoyed their sleepovers with Gramma and Grampa T.

"It would be a treat for us—and a break for you," her mother-in-law continued, to press her case.

At the library, Lindsay sometimes overheard female patrons talking to their friends about how they were desperate for a break from being a mom 24/7. She couldn't really relate to their frustration, because being a mom was all she had left now. But although her kids were everything to her, she knew that they needed to be given opportunities to experience and explore the world outside 355 Winterberry Drive.

"I'll look at their schedules and see what we can work out," she promised.

"Thank you," Suzanne said gratefully. "Now tell me about the party."

"I didn't end up going," she admitted.

"Then you should have come here," her mother-in-law said. "No one should be alone on New Year's Eve."

"I wasn't alone," she said. "Mitchell stopped by."

"I'm glad," Suzanne said.

And Lindsay knew that she meant it, but she couldn't help wondering if her mother-in-law might feel differently if she knew about the kiss that Lindsay had planted on Mitchell at midnight.

"You've been friends a long time," her mother-in-law acknowledged. "Arthur used to refer to you and Nate and Mitch as the Three Musketeers."

Lindsay nodded, smiling a little at the memory.

It was true that when the Thomases had moved to town— or back to town, in the case of Suzanne, who'd grown up on Sterling Ranch in Haven but moved away to go to college— during the summer before seventh grade, Nathan and Mitchell had quickly become friends. Nathan wasn't too happy to share his new friend with a girl, though, and he'd balked at Mitchell's insistence on inviting Lindsay along whenever they made plans. But Mitchell had stood firm, because he and Lindsay went much further back, to the first day of second grade, after her family had moved to Haven.

Aware of her status as "the new kid," Lindsay had been outside at recess, quietly watching different groups of kids playing hopscotch and dodgeball and spinning in Hula-Hoops, wondering which group might eventually let her join in. But for now, they were all keeping their distance, and she was alone eating her Oreo cookies when the dodgeball got away, bounced near her feet, then smacked her in the nose.

Cody, whom she'd already pegged as a bully when she saw him shove his way in front of Sonja in the line for the drinking fountain, pointed and laughed, apparently finding it funny that the new girl was crying *and* bleeding. Tristan, who'd thrown the ball, ran over to retrieve it, mumbling a cursory apology before racing back to his friends. But one of those friends walked away from the circle to take her to the first-aid room.

"I'm Mitchell," he'd said, introducing himself while they waited for the school nurse.

"I'm Lindsay."

Which, of course, he knew because the teacher had introduced her to the class, asking the other students—most of whom had been in school together since kindergarten—to make her feel welcome.

He waited outside while she was examined, and by the time she'd been cleaned up and given a baggie filled with ice to hold against her swollen nose, recess was over. But Mitchell invited her to play dodgeball with them when everyone went out again after lunch, and she had the distinct pleasure of being the one to knock Cody out of the circle.

After that, Lindsay and Mitchell were almost inseparable. When a teacher told the class to "find a partner" for cooperative assignments, they automatically looked for one another. When Mitchell didn't want to read the book he'd been assigned for a report, Lindsay had read it with him; and when she struggled with fractions, he helped her figure it out.

Then Nathan Thomas moved to town, and their relationship dynamic had changed.

* * *

"Can we watch *Paw Patrol*, Mommy?" Elliott asked, almost before they were in the door back at home.

The show about search and rescue dogs working together with a young boy to keep Adventure Bay safe was his absolute favorite—an affinity that was reflected in much of his wardrobe and most of his toy box. When she was a kid, she'd memorized the TV schedule so that she knew which of her favorite programs came on at which day and hour. Now it seemed as if everything was available for streaming all the time. But because there had been rare occasions when service was offline, she also had a collection of backup DVDs in reserve to avoid potential meltdowns. Of course, if the power went out, they were all doomed.

"Can we get inside first and unpack your sleepover stuff?" she suggested.

"Then can we watch *Paw Patrol*?"

"Actually, I was thinking maybe we could play a game after I get the laundry started," she suggested, because she tried to limit their screen time as much as possible. "How about Pop-Up Pirate?"

Elliott made a face. "We played lotsa games with Gramma and Grampa T."

So she let them watch TV, because she knew the program would keep them occupied while she took the ornaments and garland and lights off the Christmas tree. She got started on the laundry, too, making sure that the first load included Elliott's new *Paw Patrol* hoodie, because she knew he'd want it for his first day back at school—only three days away.

Of course, he'd need a lunch for school, too, which meant that she definitely needed to get to The Trading Post tomorrow to stock up on the kids' favorite treats and other essentials. It was a challenge to send a sandwich that he would eat because, like most kids, he was most fond of PB&J, but there was a child with a peanut allergy in the class so it was crucial that all parents sent only peanut-free lunches to school.

Another thing that Elliott liked were the prepackaged lunches with crackers and meat and cheese that he could then stack together, so she tried to keep a couple of those on hand for those days when she realized she'd forgotten to pack his lunch. At other times, she made her own, substituting grapes or apple wedges for the candy treat.

So she pulled her phone out of her pocket and started to make a list: bread, milk, eggs, OJ, meat, cheese, crackers, yogurt tubes, apple sauce. Of course, she'd add a lot more items to her cart as she pushed it around the store, but having a list helped to ensure she didn't forget any of the essentials.

Her phone pinged, signaling receipt of a text message while she was adding to her list, and her heart actually skipped a beat when she saw Mitchell's name pop up at the top. It was both a ridiculous and juvenile reaction, considering that she and Mitch had exchanged thousands—probably tens of thousands—of text messages over the years, and never before had she reacted in such a way.

But never before had he kissed her so thoroughly that she could barely remember her name the next day.

She tapped to open the message.

OK if I pick up pizza and bring it over for dinner?

He wanted to come *over*?

Her heart skipped another beat at the prospect of seeing him again so soon, but she wasn't sure if it was anticipation or apprehension. And how screwed up was that?

Because she *always* looked forward to seeing him. She was always happy to hang out with a friend who knew her better than almost anyone else and loved her anyway. And she knew that he did love her—just as she loved him, in the enduring but purely platonic way of two people who had been friends forever.

Now they were friends who'd shared a steamy kiss while locked in a passionate embrace, and she needed some more time to figure out what that meant for their relationship going forward. Because pretending it hadn't happened wasn't working so well for her.

But if she told Mitch that she didn't want him to come over, then he might think she was making a big deal out of what had happened the night before. And as he'd pointed out, it was just a kiss. And maybe a little bit of touchy-feely stuff along with the kissing, but certainly nothing that warranted getting her panties in a twist.

Except that just the memory of that kiss was almost enough to make her panties melt.

So she pushed the memory aside and refocused her attention on his message, determined to reply as if nothing of any significance had happened between them.

Depends. Are you planning to share?

He responded with an eye roll emoji followed by:

Of course.

She answered:

In that case...yes!

Be there around 6.

Sounds good.

And then, because she was in the laundry room, she wondered if she should change her clothes.

But why would she?

There wasn't anything wrong with what she was wearing.

In fact, the jeans and turtleneck sweater were perfectly appropriate for an afternoon at home with her kids.

Maybe the sweater was a little big and not at all flattering to her figure, but she didn't need to try to make herself attractive just because a friend was coming over.

Besides, Mitch had seen her looking a lot worse. Such as when she'd had dental surgery to remove her impacted wisdom teeth. Despite telling him that she didn't want visitors—because she didn't want anyone to see her with her jaw swollen and bruised—he'd shown up at the door with flowers. He'd even stood stoically by with the bucket while she vomited the remnants of the anesthetic out of her system.

He was there, too, the first time she got drunk—cautioning her to slow down on the cosmopolitans she was gulping like Kool-Aid because they tasted so good and because she wanted to seem as sophisticated as Carrie Bradshaw and her friends. Of course, she hadn't listened to his warning, and a few hours later, he'd held her hair back while she'd puked into the bushes outside Diggers'.

Apparently throwing up was a common theme running through her worst moments.

And considering those moments, it was unlikely that Mitchell would be fazed by the coffee dribbled on her sweater, above the right breast. Except that the stain did draw attention to her breast, which she didn't want to do. Especially when just the memory of his hands skimming up her torso and brushing the sides of her breasts was enough to make her knees weak.

She dropped her head into her hands and muffled a frustrated scream.

This was ridiculous.

She was being ridiculous.

Mitchell had been her friend forever. Whatever had happened between them the night before—and it really was just a kiss—didn't have to change anything.

Not if they didn't want it to.

She tugged the stained sweater over her head and added it to the pile of dirty laundry on the floor, then grabbed another sweater from the basket of clean clothes. This one was a V-neck in smoky gray cashmere—a Christmas gift from Kristyne and Gabe.

"What's for supper? I'm hungry," Elliott said, when she came out of the laundry room with a basket of clothes to be put away.

"I hun-wee, too," Avenlea chimed in.

"Uncle Mitch is going to bring pizza for supper," she told them.

"Yay!" Her son punched his fist in the air.

"Yay!" His little sister echoed the sentiment and mimicked the action.

"Just cheese?" Elliott asked hopefully.

"I don't know," she said.

But she suspected that Mitchell would get a small pizza with just cheese, because he knew that's what the kids preferred. And he'd bring one with pepperoni, black olives and hot peppers, because that's what she liked—even if she'd forgotten her own preferences for a while.

She'd given up olives on her pizza when she was dating Nathan because he'd hated them with a passion and she'd really liked Nathan, and it seemed like a small sacrifice to make to be with him. After they'd been dating a while, she'd suggested that they could get olives just on half, but he'd shuddered at the possibility that one might accidentally be dropped on *his* "just pepperoni" half of the pie.

And although she'd occasionally grumbled that she missed having black olives on her pizza, she would have given them up forever if it meant she could have her husband—and Elliott and Avenlea could have their dad—back.

CHAPTER SIX

SHARING A CASUAL meal and easy conversation with Lindsay in the presence of her kids seemed to Mitch like the perfect opportunity to restore the status quo—if only he could stop thinking about the night before and how great it had been to finally kiss her. But she wanted to pretend it had never happened, so that's what he was determined to do.

Did that make him a hero or an idiot?

He didn't have a clue.

But he had pizza—so he grabbed the boxes off the passenger seat and headed toward the door.

"Uncamitch! Uncamitch!" The enthusiastic greeting came from Avenlea, who raced toward the door, blond pigtails bobbing and green eyes twinkling. She launched herself at him, confident he would catch her despite the pizza boxes he balanced on one hand.

Of course he did, easily scooping up the adorable little girl with his free arm. She rewarded him with a smacking kiss on the cheek.

"Pizza! Pizza!" was the chorus from Elliott.

"Can you tell they're happy to see you?" Lindsay asked, taking the boxes from him as he shifted the little girl onto his hip.

"Me or the pizza?" he wondered.

"Probably both," she acknowledged with a smile.

But it was a slightly dimmer version of her usual vibrant smile, making him suspect that forgetting about that midnight kiss was going to take some effort on both their parts.

Thankfully, the presence of Elliott and Avenlea didn't allow for awkward pauses or strained silences.

"Is it cheese? Did you bring us cheese pizza?" Elliott wanted to know.

"The small box is just cheese, for you and Avenlea," he confirmed.

The little girl tipped her head back against his shoulder and looked at him adoringly. "I wuv you, Uncamitch."

It was a common refrain from a child who freely expressed her love to everyone around her, but still it made his heart melt. Every. Single. Time. "I love you, too, Princess Avenlea."

She giggled at the nickname he'd bestowed upon her when she'd dressed up as Cinderella for Halloween the previous year. Lindsay had balked at her daughter's choice when the little girl grabbed hold of the blue dress in the costume store and refused to let go. Not that she objected to the idea of her daughter wanting to be the storybook character; she just would have preferred that Avenlea dress up as the scullery maid version rather than the transformed princess. Because, as she'd tried to explain to the toddler, it was important to understand that she'd have to work hard to get what she wanted in life and not expect a handsome prince to give her the keys to the kingdom.

But Avenlea wanted the fancy dress and sparkly crown. And when Mitch pointed out that Elliott had been allowed to pick a firefighter bulldog costume without getting a lecture on the perils of believing dogs could wield fire hoses, she'd finally relented.

"If Her Highness and her adoring subject would like to come to the table, dinner is served," Lindsay said.

Mitchell grinned and carried Avenlea to the kitchen, setting her in her booster seat and buckling the belt around her waist.

The routine was familiar and easy, and almost convinced him that their efforts to restore the status quo could be successful.

"I wanted to make a salad to go with the pizza," she said, as she poured glasses of milk for Elliott and Avenlea. "But The Trading Post was closed today, so my fridge is still as empty as it was last night. Emptier, actually, because Elliott and Avenlea ate the last cheese strings while they were watching *Paw Patrol* this afternoon."

"The great thing about pizza is that it's a perfect meal all by itself," he told her, as he lifted a slice from the larger box and set it on her plate.

"I don't know that the USDA Food Guide would concur," she said, peeling an olive off her slice and popping it into her mouth. "But it certainly tastes good."

"I wike Jo's p'za," Avenlea said.

"Like," she said, emphasizing the *L*.

"Wike," her daughter said again, nodding.

"I think you're focused on the wrong word in that sentence," Mitch remarked. "You should have noticed that she didn't say she likes pizza. She specified Jo's pizza. Not yet three years old, and she already has a discerning palate."

"Except that she's only ever had Jo's pizza," Lindsay said.

"Nuh-uh," Elliott said, speaking around a mouthful of dough and cheese. Catching his mother's eye, he quickly chewed and swallowed before continuing. "Gramma T made it once—from itch."

"Itch?" A smile tugged at the corner of Lindsay's mouth. "Do you mean scratch?"

"Yeah, that was it," her son agreed. "She promised it would be better than Jo's, cuz it was homemade." He shook his head then. "It wasn't."

"How did I not hear about this before now?" she wondered. Elliott shrugged.

"Did Avenlea like it?"

Her son shook his head again. "She took one bite, spit it out and asked for Jo's."

"Definitely a discerning palate," Mitch said, as the little girl took another big bite of her pizza. "And now you know why Suzanne didn't tell you the story."

"That could be," Lindsay agreed, reaching into the box for a second slice. "And thank you for this—I didn't realize how hungry I was until I started eating."

"Because you don't slow down long enough to eat half the time," he noted.

"I did miss lunch today," she confided.

"But I'll bet Elliott and Avenlea didn't."

"How could I ever forget to feed them when they're constantly telling me they're hungry?"

"So why didn't you eat when they did?"

"Because I was taking down Christmas decorations. And I wasn't in the mood for a peanut butter and jelly sandwich."

He shook his head. "I hope you're planning on grocery shopping tomorrow."

"We'll be waiting outside The Trading Post for it to open."

"And what will you have for breakfast before you go?"

"Leftover pizza?" she suggested hopefully.

He laughed even as his hand instinctively lifted toward her face. "You've got sauce—" he brushed his thumb over the spot beside her mouth "—here."

It was the automatic gesture of a friend who felt comfortable letting her know when she had spinach in her teeth or an unknown substance on the butt of her pants after a trip to the park.

But this time, Lindsay's breath caught as her eyes locked with his. And Mitch's pulse thrummed beneath his skin, vibrating awareness through every inch of his body. And suddenly, neither of them was able to pretend the kiss had never happened.

His gaze dipped to her mouth, remembering the silky texture of her lips, the seductive flavor of her kiss, the sweet torture of her soft curves—

"Avenlea's got sauce on her face, too," Elliott said, breaking the sensual spell that had wrapped around them.

Mitch drew back, exhaling a shaky breath, and looked at the little girl who, sure enough, had red smeared around her mouth almost from ear to ear.

"I think someone's definitely going to need a bath after dinner," Lindsay said.

"Me! Me!" Avenlea said.

"Yes, you," her mom agreed.

"Not me," Elliott said.

"Just because you don't have pizza sauce all over your face doesn't mean you can skip your bath."

"But I had a bath last night at Gramma and Grampa T's."

"Well, then, I guess you won't need another one until Valentine's Day."

"Really?" he said, sounding hopeful.

"Not really."

He sighed wearily.

"Come on," she said. "Let's get the kitchen tidied up and get you two ready for bed."

"Can't we stay up a little bit longer?" Elliott pleaded.

She shook her head. "We've been a little too lax about your bedtime over the holidays, and we need to get you back on schedule to get ready for school."

"I don't even know what *lax* means," Elliott protested.

"It means relaxed."

"But you always say it's good to relax."

"About some things," she agreed. "But routines are important, too."

"Why can't a later bedtime be part of the routine?"

Honestly, the kid had some impressive negotiating skills for a five-year-old.

"You already have a later bedtime than your sister," Lindsay pointed out.

"Because she's still a baby."

"Am not," Avenlea protested, though her words might have been more convincing if she hadn't had to take her thumb out of her mouth to reply.

"Are too," Elliott insisted.

"When do you go back to school?" Mitch asked, in an effort to avoid the familiar "am not/are too" sibling argument that he knew from experience with his own brother and sister could go on in perpetuity.

"Monday," Elliott said, obviously excited about returning to school and seeing his friends.

Of course, all kids loved school when they were in kindergarten, and according to his cousin's wife—who was Elliott's teacher this year—the new play-based curriculum meant that most kids were having so much fun they didn't even realize they were learning.

"I wanna go to 'chool," Avenlea said.

"I know," Lindsay acknowledged. "And when you're four, you will."

"And when you're fourteen, you'll be saying, 'Do I hafta go to school?'" Mitch told her.

Avenlea's little brow furrowed as she considered his warning.

"In the meantime, you get to go to swimming school," her mom reminded her.

"I wike swimmin'."

"And you're getting to be a really good swimmer," Lindsay said encouragingly.

"Uncamitch swim wif us."

"Uncle Mitch will be working when we're at the pool."

Avenlea shook her head. "Swim at Uncamitch's."

"Could she be talking about the pond at the Circle G?" Mitch wondered, though doubtful that the little girl would recall an event that had taken place five months earlier.

"Do you remember going swimming at the ranch last summer?" Lindsay asked.

Now Avenlea nodded. "Wif Uncamitch."

"Yes, we did," her mom agreed.

"But the water in the pond is frozen right now, because it's winter," Mitch explained. "You might be able to skate on it, but you can't swim in it."

"'Kate at Uncamitch's?"

"You want to learn how to skate?"

She nodded again. "Wike Ew-ee-it."

"Well, it's going to take a few lessons before you can skate like Elliott," he said. "But we can get you out on the pond, if you want."

"Want," she confirmed.

"Do you know what I want?" Lindsay asked her, as she unbuckled her daughter's safety strap.

"Go 'katin'?" Avenlea guessed.

"No." Her mom lifted the little girl into her arms. "I want *you* to have your bath and get ready for bed."

"But I not s'eepy." The little girl's protest was followed by a big yawn as she dropped her head onto Lindsay's shoulder.

The pizza had been a good idea, Mitch decided, as mom and daughter headed upstairs for bath time. After twenty-five years of friendship, he knew Lindsay well enough to know that if he gave her too much time and space to think about the kiss they'd shared, it would end up becoming a big thing between them. Plus, as he'd remarked to his mother earlier, she had great kids, and he really enjoyed spending time with them.

When he sat down at the table for the meal, it was almost too easy to imagine that they could be a family. But as he relaxed on the sofa, near where Elliott was driving his Matchbox cars around on his play mat designed to replicate a city center, complete with roads and greenspaces and buildings, there was no ignoring the fact that Lindsay's kids were also Nathan's kids.

Elliott was the spitting image of his dad, with Nathan's curly dark hair, narrow face, thick brows and straight nose. It was only his eyes that he'd inherited from his mom—both the shape and the mossy-green color. Avenlea, on the other hand, was every inch her mom's daughter, with the same pale blond hair and green eyes, and a sweet smile that never failed to tug at his heart.

While Elliott played with his cars, he regaled Mitch with stories about his Christmas holidays, about how Gramma and Grampa D came to stay for two whole weeks, and Gramma made cookies that she let them decorate with colored icing and sugar, and Grampa took them sledding. And about their visit to the fire station to see Santa Claus—and how Avenlea was too scared to sit on Santa's lap until Mommy went with her. (Mitch would love to see a picture of that!) They even made a trip to the antiques and craft market so that they could pick out presents to wrap and put under the tree for Mommy. Avenlea picked out a pair of fuzzy socks with reindeer faces on top of the feet—obviously the same socks that she'd been wearing the day before—and Elliott got her a book with blank pages that she could write in.

Mitch knew that Marilyn and Jackson Delgado had been in Haven until the thirtieth, and then flown back to Phoenix for the New Year's party at the community center in their retirement village. He'd enjoyed a brief visit with them the day before Christmas Eve, when he stopped by to drop off his presents for the kids. Though they seemed confident that they'd made the right decision when they'd moved south, Marilyn confided that they missed the grandchildren like crazy. Thankfully, they were able to keep in touch via Skype, so they could see Elliott and Avenlea rather than just talk to them. They'd also told him that they were planning to come back again in February—or March—depending on when Kristyne had her baby, and then again in the summer for a few weeks, as they'd done the previous year.

"Did you get new cars for Christmas?" Mitch asked, as Elliott took inventory of his fleet.

"Gramma gave 'em to me yesterday. They used to be my dad's."

"It looks like a pretty cool collection," he noted.

"This is a Camaro," Elliott said, pointing first to a yellow sports car and then a candy-apple red vehicle. "And this is a classic Mustang."

"What's this one?" He picked up a green van with a mostly faded but familiar logo on the side panel.

The boy shrugged.

"I think it's the Mystery Machine," Mitch told him.

"What's that?" Elliott asked.

"You don't watch *Scooby Doo*?"

"Who?"

He sighed and returned the vehicle to its place in the specific arrangement on the floor. "Kids these days have no idea what they're missing."

"Don't you mean meddling kids?"

Mitch grinned as he glanced up to see Lindsay had returned. "See? Your mom knows her classic cartoons."

"*Classic* is just a fancy word for old," Elliott said.

"Who told you that?" Lindsay asked him.

"Gramma T."

"Well, it's not really that simple," she said.

"But in this case, it's true," Mitch acknowledged.

"Anyway, it's time for you to put all your *classic* cars away and have your bath," Lindsay said to her son.

"And it's probably time for me to head out," Mitch said, not wanting to overstay his welcome.

"Actually, if you're not in a rush..." Lindsay began.

"What do you need?"

"Avenlea has requested that you read her bedtime story tonight."

"Me?" he asked, surprised.

She shrugged. "She likes the way you do the voices for the characters in *The Gruffalo*."

"And that stings your pride, just a little bit, doesn't it?" he teased.

"That she wants you to read about a monster with a poison-ous wart on his nose?"

"Okay, that stings more than a little."

She laughed and nudged him with her shoulder as they walked side by side up the stairs together.

And if he felt as if he was walking in his friend's shadow, well, that was his issue to deal with on his own time.

Three days later, Lindsay was standing outside the fence that bordered the kindergarten play area, waving to Elliott as he raced to line up in response to the bell. Her son, happy to be back at school with his friends, never looked back.

"It's hard, isn't it?"

She turned to the man she hadn't realized was standing be-side her, his hands tucked into the pockets of a blue ski jacket. He had short, light brown hair, with just a hint of gray at the temples and brown eyes with crinkles at the corners. He looked vaguely familiar—no doubt she'd seen him at drop-off or pickup before, though she was certain they'd never been introduced.

"I'm sorry?"

"I was just remarking how difficult it is, to watch your child race off into the world," he clarified. "On the one hand, you're proud that they have the confidence to tackle the unknown. On the other, you can't help but feel a little superfluous, because you've done your job as a parent so well that they don't need you every minute of every day anymore."

"Nailed it," she admitted.

"A word of warning," he told her. "It's even harder when it's your youngest—or only—child." He inclined his head toward Avenlea, the little girl's mittened hand clutched tightly within her own. "At least you've still got one who sees you as the cen-ter of her world."

"How many kids do you have?"

"Three. Mason's the youngest."

"So he has older brothers or sisters who can look out for him as he navigates the perils of kindergarten?"

"He's got one of each, but they're not here. They're in high school."

"Oh."

He nodded. "My wife and I started young, and Mason was an effort to restore the dying spark in our marriage." He shrugged. "We're divorced now, but we got another great kid out of the deal. Or maybe I should say that *I* got another great kid, because she lives in Colorado now where she manages some posh ski resort, and I'm here with the kids."

"I'm sorry—not that you got custody," she hastened to clarify. "About the divorce, I mean."

He shrugged. "It wasn't how I envisioned things working out when we got married. Then again, I don't imagine you ever thought you'd end up a young widow, either."

"Obviously someone's been telling tales outside of school," she remarked lightly.

"I saw you at the holiday assembly and asked Debby Jensen who you were," he confided now. "She told me about the passing of your husband. That's why I told you about my divorce. I don't usually dump that information on a stranger at a first meeting, but I wanted to put us on equal footing."

"Thank you?"

He smiled. "By the way, I'm Parker Ross. Dad of Mason, who's in Mrs. Gilmore's class with your son, Elliott."

"Lindsay Thomas." She shook the proffered hand. "But of course, you know that already."

"I do," he confirmed.

"And this is Avenlea," she said, introducing her daughter.

"It's nice to meet both of you." He glanced down at the little girl. "Do you have time for a cup of coffee, Avenlea? Or do you have places to go?"

The little girl made a face; he laughed.

"Hot chocolate?" he suggested as an alternative.

Avenlea nodded.

"Unfortunately, we do have places to go," Lindsay said. "Avenlea's got a swimming lesson this morning and we need to get over to the community center or we're going to be late."

"Maybe another time?" he asked.

"Maybe," she agreed, meaning "probably not ever."

But then she considered that her explosive reaction to a simple kiss on New Year's Eve might have been a sign that she was ready to move on. And since she and Mitchell had agreed to pretend the kiss had never happened, if she ever wanted to be in a relationship again, she was going to have to put herself out there.

So what if there were no immediate sparks with Parker? Since when were sparks required to enjoy a hot beverage with someone?

"Actually, let's change that 'maybe' to a 'definitely,'" she decided.

"Yeah?" He flashed a quick grin. "You say when and where."

"Wednesday morning, ten-thirty at The Daily Grind?"

"I'll be there," he promised.

"You don't have to check a work schedule or something?" she asked curiously.

"Want to be sure I'm gainfully employed before coffee leads to dinner?" he teased.

"I'm sorry," she immediately apologized. "That was rude, wasn't it?"

"Not rude," he said. "Just not very subtle."

"I'm sorry," she said again. "I'm not very good at this."

"Making conversation?" he teased.

"Meeting new people," she clarified.

"It's not one of my strengths, either," he confided. "And in the interest of alleviating any concerns, I'll confirm that I do have a job. I work in IT support from home, so my hours are completely flexible."

"That's lucky," she said.

"Very," Parker agreed. "Because it means I can take a coffee break at ten-thirty Wednesday morning."

"I'll see you then," Lindsay promised.

CHAPTER SEVEN

LINDSAY HAD ALWAYS believed that the library was a magical place. As soon as she was able to read and discovered the power of words to transport her to different worlds, it had become her favorite place to visit. It was always quiet, it smelled like books and it was filled with stories. So many wonderful stories.

Library Day—always capitalized in her mind—had been her favorite day at school, because she'd return a book that had been read and reread countless times and take home a brand-new one to read and reread. She enjoyed all kinds of stories— nonfiction and fiction—because it was as interesting to read about real people as imaginary ones.

The Magic Tree House books had been some of her favorites when she was younger, and they were still a popular item in the library catalog today, albeit less so than *Junie B. Jones* and *Ready, Freddy!* But as she perused the stacks in the children's section, searching through familiar authors such as Sandra Boynton, Beverly Cleary, Roald Dahl, Robert Munsch, Shel Silverstein and Dr. Seuss, she found herself reflecting on the chain of events that had led to her opportunity to work at the local library.

She'd been lucky, when she came back to Haven, that Hazel Hemingway—who'd been the librarian for a lot longer than

Lindsay had been alive—was ready to cut back her hours. Maybe *lucky* wasn't the right word, considering the reason for Lindsay's return, but it had at least been fortuitous timing.

Of course, being a working mom meant having to put her daughter in day care—and her son, too, when he wasn't at school. Her mother-in-law had tried to convince Lindsay to let Avenlea stay with her, but Lindsay believed it was important for the little girl to be with kids her own age, to learn to play and share.

"Is everything okay?" Quinn asked. "You seem a little distracted this morning."

"Sorry," Lindsay apologized automatically as she pulled *The One in the Middle is the Green Kangaroo* off the shelf and added it to the growing pile on the table where Avenlea sat with a box of fat crayons and some coloring pages, pretending she was at school "wike Ew-ee-it."

Since Lindsay had started working at the library, she'd become good friends with Quinn Ellison—the driver of the local bookmobile who lived in Cooper's Corners. The twenty-nine-year-old loved meeting people of all ages and backgrounds— even those who wondered why she didn't seem to have any greater ambition in life than to drive around with a bus full of books. Of course, those people didn't realize that Quinn's part-time driving job was really just a hobby for the bestselling novelist.

"Don't be sorry—tell me what's going on," her friend urged.

"It's nothing," she said.

"Let me be the judge of that," Quinn advised with a wink. "You never know what might be fodder for my next book."

"I guarantee that nothing about my life would interest your readers."

"Even the writer is growing bored now, so spill."

"Okay," Lindsay agreed. "When I dropped Elliott off at school this morning, one of the other parents—a dad—asked me to go for coffee."

"Did you say yes?"

She nodded.

"So you've got a date," her friend said, grinning. "Good for you."

"Is coffee a date?" Lindsay wondered.

"It's a date," Quinn insisted. And then, "Is he cute?"

"I'm not sure that *cute* is a word that should be applied to anyone over the age of thirty," she cautioned.

"Which doesn't answer my question."

"He's kind of handsome, I guess."

Her friend rolled her eyes. "You guess?"

"He *is* handsome," she said. Maybe he wasn't quite as tall as Mitchell, and his shoulders weren't nearly as broad as the rancher's nor his jaw as strongly defined and…why was she comparing Parker to Mitchell? Even if her friend was one of the hottest bachelors in town, and probably the absolute best kisser and—

Aargh! She really needed to stop thinking about Mitchell!

"And he has a nice smile," she said, refocusing her thoughts on Parker.

"So when is this date?" Quinn asked. "And where?"

"Wednesday. The Daily Grind. But now I'm wishing that I'd agreed to have coffee this morning so I wouldn't have to spend the next two days thinking about it."

"Why didn't you agree to coffee this morning?"

"Because Avenlea had a swimming lesson."

"Which I'm sure she would have happily sacrificed in the interest of romance."

"Have you met my daughter?" Lindsay asked dryly.

Quinn chuckled. "I have, and I know that she can be bribed with chocolate."

Avenlea's head shot up. "Choc'ate?" she asked hopefully.

"See?" Quinn said to Lindsay, as she pulled a treat-size Kit Kat out of her pocket.

The little girl held out the hand not holding the red crayon. "P'ease?"

Quinn gave her the chocolate. "But you have to save it until later, when Mommy says, okay?"

"'Kay," Avenlea promised.

Lindsay shook her head as she continued to help her friend collect the books on a list carefully curated to reflect the preferences of her regular patrons, who ranged in age from two to ninety-two.

"Well, at least you said yes to Wednesday," Quinn said. "Because you have to take the first step sometime."

"Says who?" Lindsay challenged.

"Says me." Her friend's tone was firm. "You're too young to spend the rest of your life alone."

"It's hard to be alone with a five-year-old and almost-three-year-old in the house," Lindsay pointed out. "I can't even shower without one of them interrupting."

"You know what I mean," Quinn chided. "Plus, your kids are eventually going to grow up and move out, and then you really will be alone."

"I think I've still got a few years before that happens," she said dryly.

"A few," her friend agreed. "So...what time do you want a fake emergency text on Wednesday? Around ten forty-five?"

Lindsay frowned. "Why would you send me a fake emergency text?"

Quinn shook her head. "You really have been out of the dating game a long time, haven't you?"

"Only because Nathan and I both agreed not to date other people while we were married," she remarked dryly.

"The fake emergency text is sent so that the friend on the date has an excuse to escape if the guy is a disaster."

"It's *coffee*," Lindsay said again. "The only disaster I can imagine is if The Daily Grind is out of whipped cream for my café mocha."

"Whipped cream on a first date?" Quinn shook her head. "I didn't realize you were such a brazen hussy."

"But now I'm wondering what kind of fake emergency you might come up with," she said, ignoring her friend's comment. "Just in case you do text me around ten forty-five on Wednesday about a real emergency."

"Work-related emergencies are usually best, to avoid the potential of creating any real panic." Quinn's ready response convinced Lindsay that she'd done this before.

"What kind of work-related emergency happens at the library?" she wondered.

Quinn turned to look at the shelf of books behind her. "Right here," she said, her finger sliding across the adjacent spines of two books. "*Ramona the Pest* should come after *Ramona the Brave*. These books are clearly out of order, and without order, there is only chaos."

"They're not in strict alphabetical order," Lindsay allowed. "But the Ramona series is in chronological order."

"Chaos," Quinn said again, making Lindsay laugh.

She had a date.

Only four days after she'd kissed him, Lindsay apparently had agreed to a date with someone else. Another single parent from the school, or so Mitch had been told.

He mulled over the information, not sure how he was supposed to feel about it. Not sure what to think about the fact that he'd suffered through four days of cold showers because of the kiss-that-never-happened while she'd suddenly decided that she was ready to start dating.

But maybe he should hear Lindsay's side of the story before jumping to conclusions...

"What brings you into town on a Monday afternoon?" Lindsay asked, as she handed him the mug of coffee she'd made in her single-serve brewer when she saw his truck pull into the driveway.

"I had to pick up a few things at the hardware store," he said.

Actually the trip to the store had been a ruse to explain his trip into town, but she didn't need to know that.

And though he was a little disappointed to miss seeing Avenlea—who'd gone down for a nap just before he arrived—he was glad to be able to talk to Lindsay without interruption.

"You know this isn't the hardware store, don't you?" she teased.

"I also figured, since I was in town, I'd stop by to see how you were doing," he continued, his tone as casual as his leaning-against-the-counter pose.

But maybe his tone was *too* casual, because her eyes narrowed suspiciously. "Did you think I was going to fall apart because my son went off to school this morning?"

"Again, you mean?"

He was referring, of course, to Elliott's first day of school in September, when she'd sobbed against his shoulder after her son had disappeared into the hallowed halls of kindergarten with eleven new classmates. Because yes, he'd been there, having anticipated that it would be an emotional day for Lindsay and not wanting her to have to face it alone.

"Maybe my eyes watered a little as he waved goodbye, but I did not fall apart."

"Progress," he said, nodding approvingly. "And how was Avenlea?"

"She was fine today."

Unlike that day in September, when she'd cried harder than her mom because she wanted to go to school with her beloved brother.

"But I was smarter this time," Lindsay continued. "I let her pack her backpack with some school supplies and, after her swimming lesson, we went to the library and pretended it was a classroom, because she wants to do everything Elliott does."

"I was the same with MG," Mitch said. "It's hard being the younger sibling."

"So why don't you have more sympathy for your younger sister?" she wondered.

"Because my sister is a nosy, interfering tattletale." Which didn't mean he didn't love her and wouldn't do bodily harm to anyone who ever hurt her.

Lindsay laughed softly. "You do know she's not ten years old anymore, right?"

"I know. But she's still a nosy, interfering tattletale," he said, still irritated about the observations she'd shared in the barn on New Year's Day.

"What did she do now?" she asked.

He shook his head. "It's not important."

"But now my curiosity's piqued," she said.

"She was riding MG about his Christmas present to Paige." Which only skimmed the surface of their conversation that morning, but he figured it was enough information to satisfy Lindsay's curiosity.

"The earrings?" she guessed.

At his quizzical glance, she shrugged.

"Paige was wearing them when I ran into her at The Daily Grind last week. I commented on how pretty they were, and she said MG gave them to her."

"Well, Olivia seems to think that Paige was expecting a ring."

"I'd guess that she was probably *hoping* for a ring," Lindsay said. "But she was happy with the earrings."

"Which proves again that my sister doesn't know everything," he said.

"Just enough to get under your skin," she remarked with obvious amusement.

He waved a hand dismissively. "That's enough about Olivia. Tell me...did anything else interesting happen today?"

"Not really," she said. And then, "Ohmygod—you heard, didn't you?"

"If you're referring to your coffee date with the dad of the peanut allergy boy, then yes," he acknowledged.

"How?" she demanded. "And how do you know his son is the one with the peanut allergy? I didn't even know that."

"Caleb told me," he said.

"I'm guessing Caleb heard from Brielle," she said, naming his cousin's wife, who happened to be the kindergarten teacher. "But how did she know?"

"I'd think it's policy for teachers to be informed of potential medical issues."

She rolled her eyes. "I wasn't asking how Brielle knew about the allergy but how she heard about my plans to have coffee with Parker."

"Her TA heard it from the crossing guard who stands near the kindergarten gate."

"Sometimes I really hate this town," she muttered.

"So it's true," he said, his heart sinking as he accepted the fact. "You've got a date."

"It's *not* a date," she said. "We're meeting for coffee at ten-thirty in the morning."

"It's not the time but the intent that matters."

"Well, I don't intend to let myself be seduced over a café mocha," she told him.

"But if you were having mimosas, all bets would be off."

Her gaze narrowed.

He immediately held up his hands in a gesture of surrender. "Sorry."

"Do you have a problem with me having coffee with Parker?"

Yes.

"Of course not," he said. "I think it's great that you're getting out and meeting new people."

Thankfully, she took him at his word.

And he should have been happy for her, pleased that she was finally ready to move forward with her life after mourning the loss of her husband for more than two years. She was too young to give up on the possibility of romance, too passionate to resign herself to sleeping alone.

But the thought of her kissing another man like she'd kissed him—of another man's hands touching where his hands had touched—left him feeling decidedly *un*happy.

One of the benefits of living at the Circle G was proximity to his parents' house and the fact that they didn't mind if he stopped by at dinnertime to join them for the evening meal. In fact, he'd guess that his mom usually planned on having her whole family around the table because there was always more than enough food for everyone—plus leftovers that she'd package up for him and his brother to take back to the cabin they shared.

But he didn't eat breakfast and lunch with his parents, which meant that either he or MG had to venture into town every now and again to buy groceries. It was his turn to do the shopping this week, and he moved purposefully through the store with the list in hand until he ran into Frieda Zimmerman in the produce section, and she pulled out her phone to show him the latest video of her grandson taking his first steps. Then he spent a couple of minutes chatting with Estela Lopez, who had a big box of dog biscuits in her cart despite the fact that she'd lost her canine companion a few years earlier, because she liked to have treats on hand for the other dogs who walked through her neighborhood. He got away with exchanging waves with Deanna Raitt, a longtime server at Diggers', who was arguing with someone on her phone about the difference between Italian and French bread.

One of the things Mitch really liked about living in Haven was that neighbors looked out for one another. One of the things he disliked was that everyone knew everyone else's business. But a lot of the families who'd settled the town had been friends for generations—or, in the case of the Gilmores and Blakes, enemies. In the past few years, though, a slew of romances and reunions had brought the two families together, finally and deeply burying the hatchet on the age-old feud.

He was in the frozen food section, near the end of his list, when he noticed that his brother had scrawled an extra item on the bottom.

Oyster sauce?

What the heck was MG going to do with oyster sauce?

And where would he even find oyster sauce?

Was it a condiment? Or a seafood?

A quick Google search on his smartphone had him turning to head back to the condiments aisle when he found himself cart to cart with Heather Dekker. He and Heather had gone to school together—when her last name was Foss—and while they hadn't made an effort to keep in touch after high school graduation, it was inevitable that their paths occasionally crossed around town.

She had her little girl with her today, an adorable toddler with dark curls and big blue eyes. The child's shirt announced "I'm a Unicorn" and the sparkly crown on her head identified her as "Birthday Girl."

He remembered that she had an unusual name, but as he was completely blanking on it right now, he simply said, "I'm guessing it's someone's birthday today."

The little girl nodded enthusiastically, the movement causing the crown to slip on her baby-soft hair.

Heather adjusted the decoration on her daughter's head as she said, "Can you tell Mr. Gilmore how old you are, Silver?"

The child stretched out her arm with two fingers splayed wide.

He remembered the whispers that followed Heather's hasty marriage to James Dekker—an insurance agent at the company where she also worked. Whispers that started up again when she gave birth to a baby girl only five months later.

Mitch hadn't given it a second thought at the time. It wasn't any business of his if she was pregnant when she got married. And he didn't think anyone expected a woman to be a virgin when she exchanged her vows these days, especially one who'd been married before.

And though he wasn't judging, now that he was looking at her little girl, there was something about her...

"Two years old, huh?" he said.

Heather busied herself rearranging some items in her cart. Was she avoiding his gaze? Or simply concerned that her eggs had somehow gotten trapped beneath a bag of apples?

"Da! Da!" The little girl stretched her arms up as a man Mitch recognized as Heather's husband came down the aisle to join his family.

The dad unbuckled the belt that secured her in the cart and lifted her into his arms.

James Dekker nodded to Mitch before asking his wife, "Did you get everything on the list?"

"Everything except the ice cream," she said. "I didn't know how long it was going to take you to get the cake, and I didn't want it to melt."

"I'cweam!" Silver chimed in, clapping her hands. "I'cweam!"

"Yes, we're going to get ice cream," her mom promised.

"Ask for chocolate," Mitch said in a stage whisper to the birthday girl. "It's the best."

"If by *best* you mean *messiest*, I'd have to agree," Heather said dryly.

"I like chocolate," her husband chimed in helpfully.

As the Dekkers debated ice cream flavors, Mitch moved on in search of oyster sauce.

But as he searched the aisles, he kept picturing the little girl. And wondering why her gaze seemed disturbingly familiar.

CHAPTER EIGHT

"THE BIG HAND'S almost on the three now." Elliott already had his coat and boots on, clearly impatient to be on his way to the arena. "We always leave when the big hand's on the three."

"I know," Lindsay said wearily. "But I don't think we're going to make it today."

"How come?"

"Because Avenlea's sick."

The little girl's fever seemed to come from out of nowhere. All morning she'd been her usual happy and chatty self, but by lunchtime she'd become listless and she'd barely touched the grilled cheese sandwich Lindsay had put in front of her. Afterward, she'd crawled onto the sofa with a picture book and fallen asleep. When Lindsay checked on her a few minutes later, her cheeks were flushed and warm, and a quick scan with the thermometer confirmed her fever.

Lindsay hadn't panicked. She'd been a mom long enough now to know that kids got sick—and often. But her daughter's unexpected ailment meant that Lindsay was going to have to call in reinforcements to ensure Avenlea was taken care of and Elliott made it to his weekly on-ice hockey skills session.

Two hours later, her options were exhausted and so was she. Though she had an excellent support network, it turned out that all of her usual helpers were otherwise occupied today. Arthur was at a law conference in San Diego and Suzanne had opted to go with him this trip; Gabe was at prenatal class with Kristyne; and Monica Renaldi, her next-door neighbor, had a husband currently undergoing chemotherapy treatments, and Lindsay had no idea if Avenlea's fever represented something contagious.

"It's not fair," Elliott said now. "Why do I have to miss hockey because Avenlea's sick?"

"Because I can't take her to the arena when she's running a fever," she explained patiently.

"Then Grampa can take me," he said.

"Grampa and Gramma are in San Diego and Uncle Gabe and Aunt Kristyne are busy."

"Did you call Uncle Mitch?"

"No," she admitted. "Because even if he was available to take you, by the time he drove all the way here from the Circle G, your session would be over."

"But it's skills competition day," Elliott said.

She winced, having forgotten about the monthly competition that allowed the kids to show their coaches what they'd learned—and sent everyone home with a medal.

"I'm sorry," Lindsay said sincerely.

But her son didn't want to hear excuses or apologies.

"It's not fair," he said again, kicking the bag of equipment waiting by the front door before he stomped up the stairs to his room.

Lindsay should probably reprimand him for his behavior, except that she understood his disappointment and frustration. Unfortunately, understanding wasn't going to get him to the rink.

She checked Avenlea's temperature again, relieved to discover that the children's Advil seemed to be doing the trick and her daughter's temperature was moving in the right direction.

She heard Elliott clomping down the stairs again and exhaled a grateful sigh that he wasn't going to sulk in his room all afternoon. Maybe she'd offer to pop a bowl of corn and put on his favorite *Paw Patrol* DVD for them to watch together. It wouldn't be as much fun for him as hockey school, but she didn't think it was too bad as a consolation prize.

"Hey, El, I was thinking…" Her words trailed off when he walked into the room, holding the cordless phone out to her.

"Uncle Mitch wants to talk to you," he said.

She gave him her best "disapproving mom" look. "You called Uncle Mitch?"

"I wanna go to hockey," he said, unchastened.

Lindsay took the phone even as she made a mental note to have a chat with her son about going behind her back later. "Hello?"

"I've already told Elliott to start getting dressed—everything but his skates. I'll be there to pick him up in fifteen minutes."

"You really don't have to come into town—"

"I was already on my way," he said.

And Elliott was already pulling equipment out of his hockey bag.

"Then I guess we'll see you in fifteen minutes," she said. "Thank you."

An hour and a half later, Mitch walked out of the arena with a sweaty—and mostly happy—little boy. But he noticed that as they drove and got closer to Winterberry Drive, Elliott's apprehension seemed to grow.

"You're worried that your mom's mad, aren't you?" he guessed.

"She *is* mad," Elliott said.

"Why do you think she's mad?"

"Because I called you without asking to use the phone," he admitted. "But if I'd asked, she would have said no."

"I don't think that's an argument in your favor," Mitch warned.

"Maybe she won't be mad if I give her my medal," Elliott said, glancing down at the silver-colored plastic disc on a ribbon around his neck.

"I think your mom will be happy to see your medal. I think she'd be even happier if you acknowledged that you were wrong to go behind her back to call me and apologized."

"But I'm not really sorry," Elliott confided. "Because if I didn't call you, I would have missed hockey."

Well, Mitch thought as he pulled into Lindsay's driveway, at least the kid was honest.

"Don't forget to hang your equipment up," he said, as he followed Elliott into the house.

"I will," the boy promised, kicking off his snow boots. "I wanna see Avenlea first."

"She's sleeping," Lindsay whispered, joining them in the foyer.

"I'll be quiet," Elliott said, hanging his coat on the child-height hook inside the closet before tiptoeing into the living room.

His sister had kicked her blanket away, so that it was hanging off the sofa. Elliott picked it up and carefully draped it over Avenlea, tucking it into the cushion behind her. Then he pulled his medal over his head and carefully placed it on the pillow beside her.

Mitch glanced at Lindsay, who was watching the scene with a small smile on her face. "How am I supposed to reprimand him now?" she asked quietly.

"You're a mom," he reminded her with a wink. "You'll figure out a way."

"I appreciate your faith in me," she said wryly. "Although, for the record, I'm not too thrilled with you right now, either."

"What did I do?" he asked, bewildered by her remark.

"You undermined my authority."

"That wasn't my intention."

"I know, but it was the result," she said. "All the parenting books I've read talk about how it's important for moms and dads to present a united front. Obviously Elliott knows that you're not his dad, but now, whenever he doesn't like what his mom says, he's going to think it's okay to ask Uncle Mitch."

The pointed reminder that he wasn't the boy's father hit its target, and she was right to call him out for overstepping. "I'm sorry."

"I'd be a lot madder if I didn't believe that," she said.

Elliott returned to the foyer then. He looked up and, catching his mom's eye, away again quickly. "I've gotta hang up my equipment."

She nodded. "Make sure you put your Under Armour in the laundry basket."

"I know."

"Just a heads-up," Mitch said to Lindsay, when Elliott had dragged his hockey bag to the laundry room to unpack it, "he wants to play real hockey next year."

"What's not real about what he does on the ice every week?" she asked.

"He means on an actual team, with practices and games."

She sighed. "I figured this was coming, but I was hoping to put it off another year."

"Why don't you want him to play on a team?"

"It's not about what I want," she said. "It's that the closest team is in Battle Mountain, and I'm not sure I can manage getting him to a practice and a game every week."

"You manage by asking for help," he told her.

"I do ask for help," she said.

"You didn't today."

"I did," she insisted. "I went through everyone on my list."

"Except me," he noted.

"Because I assumed you were at the Circle G, and by the time you drove all the way into town to pick up Elliott and then drove to the community center and got him dressed and on the ice, his session would be over."

It made sense, and yet he had to wonder: "Is that the only reason?"

"Why would you think there's another reason?" she hedged.

"Maybe because things have been awkward between us since New Year's Eve," he pointed out.

She sighed, but she didn't deny it. "I really hoped they wouldn't be."

"Obviously pretending that nothing happened isn't working," he said.

"So what are we supposed to do?" she asked warily.

He shrugged. "Maybe we should acknowledge that we're attracted to one another and, instead of dating other people, try dating each other."

And where had *that* come from?

Clearly there was a miscommunication between his brain and his mouth, because *that* was not what he'd intended to say.

But now that the words were out there, he decided that it wasn't an entirely horrible idea.

"And if it didn't work out?" Lindsay asked.

Then she shook her head before he had a chance to answer, because apparently she thought it was a horrible idea.

"I'd lose my best friend, and that's just too big a risk," she said, responding to her own question.

He took her hands in his. "You wouldn't lose me, Linds."

"How many of your ex-girlfriends do you keep in touch with?" she challenged, unconvinced.

"That's not really a fair question, because I haven't dated anyone I was friends with first."

"Because you know that dating a friend is a bad idea," she surmised.

More likely because he didn't have a lot of female friends, though he didn't admit it aloud because he didn't think it was a point in his favor.

"Anyway," he said, deciding to steer the topic of conversation back around again rather than beat his head against the wall, "hockey registration opens in a few weeks."

"I'll look into it," she promised, sounding less than enthusiastic.

"I think what you're really afraid of is that Avenlea's going to want to play, too," he said, only half teasing.

"I'm not afraid, I'm resigned," she said. "She already wants to do everything her brother does. The only reason she's not already taking skating lessons is that she's too young."

"Is that why she's in Tiny Tumblers?" he asked, referring to the introductory gymnastics program she'd been participating in for the past several months.

"That and I needed her to have a safe outlet for all her energy so that she's not bouncing on the furniture. But she'll have to miss it tomorrow," Lindsay realized. "Although she seems to have rebounded, I think we'll stay home—just to be safe.

"I talked to my mom when you were at the rink," she continued. "And she thinks Avenlea might finally be getting her second molars—which is the first thing I should have considered when I saw her red cheeks."

"The important thing is that she's rebounded," Mitch said. "And that Elliott didn't miss hockey."

"I still feel as if I should ground him for using the phone without permission."

"If he'd asked, would you have said yes?"

"No. For the same reasons that I gave him when he asked if I'd called you." She closed her eyes and exhaled a weary sigh. "I hate having to be the bad guy all the time."

"You're not the bad guy," he assured her. "You're a single parent doing the best that you can—which, by the way, is a pretty awesome job from my perspective."

Lindsay managed a smile. "I'm not sure my kids would agree with that, but thank you for saying so."

And then, in an obvious effort to shift the topic of conversation, she asked, "So why were you on your way into town when Elliott called?"

"Oh, crap." Mitch glanced at the time displayed on his phone. "I was supposed to do a favor for someone."

"Did you at least call to tell her that you were going to be late?"

He frowned. "I never said the someone was a her."

"You also never gave a name, which you would have done if it was a him."

"You're right," he acknowledged. "The someone is Brittney who, incidentally, I dated for several months last year and yet somehow managed to maintain a friendly relationship."

"And what's the favor you're supposed to do for Brittney?" she asked curiously.

"She's having trouble with a closet door sticking and asked if I could take a look at it."

"Bedroom closet?" Lindsay guessed.

"I have no idea."

"And no clue."

"What's that supposed to mean?"

"Your *friend* Brittney wants to get back together."

"No, she doesn't."

"The stuck closet door is totally a ploy to get you over to her place so that she can get you into bed."

"Well, that's not happening," he said.

And then it was his turn to signal a topic of conversation was closed, which he did by asking, "How was your coffee date last week?"

She feigned shock at the question. "You mean you didn't get all the details from the barista's cousin's best friend's sister?"

"She was surprisingly tight-lipped about the encounter," he said, his own lips twitching as he fought against a smile.

"Or maybe there wasn't much to say," Lindsay said.

"Was it just coffee? Or did you go wild and have a dough-nut, too?"

"Just coffee," she said. "Actually, I had a café mocha, so I guess I went partially wild. Parker had regular coffee and a chocolate peanut butter banana croissant."

"So…are you going to see him again?"

She nodded. "We're meeting for coffee again in a couple of weeks."

"Coffee again?" he asked, surprised—and secretly relieved. "I guess that means there were no sparks, huh?"

"Why would you say that?"

"Because if there were sparks, you'd be progressing from coffee to dinner—or at least lunch," he said.

"We had a very pleasant conversation," she said, a little defensively. "And anyway, sparks are overrated."

"Which isn't at all what you'd be saying if there were sparks."

"Maybe you're right," she said. "But the fact is, there's only one guy who ever made my heart race with just a look."

"Nathan." He winced, feeling suddenly guilty for teasing her.

But she surprised him by shaking her head. "No. Don't get me wrong—I loved Nathan with my whole heart, but the attraction between us took a while to develop."

"Then who?" he asked.

She shook her head again, refusing to meet his gaze. "Forget I said anything."

"You can't say something like that and expect me to not want to know," he chided.

"Well, I'm not going to tell you."

"Why…" His words trailed off as an unlikely possibility teased his mind. "Wait a minute—was it me?"

"It was a long time ago," she said, her cheeks turning pink.

"It was me," he realized, stunned.

"I was fifteen," she said, a little defensively, "with all those teenage hormones running rampant through my system, and we spent a lot of time together that summer."

"We spent a lot of time together in almost every season."

"Thankfully puberty wasn't an issue every season."

"So…that summer," he prompted.

The color in her cheeks deepened. "I can't believe I'm telling you this."

"You haven't really told me anything yet," he pointed out to her.

"We were sitting shoulder to shoulder in the movie theater, sharing a tub of popcorn…and you smelled so good…and when you leaned down to whisper something to me, the warmth of your breath on my ear sent sparks dancing in my veins."

"It was *Spider-Man*," he said, proving that his memory of that day was as clear as hers. "The first Tobey Maguire one."

She nodded.

"I'd just gotten my license and had to beg to borrow my dad's truck to drive into town to pick you up." She'd been wearing low-rise jeans with a cropped top, so that a couple inches of tanned midriff were exposed, with gold hoop earrings and shiny gloss on her lips.

"And my mom insisted that we take Kristyne with us, because she wanted to see the movie, too," Lindsay said.

"But you wouldn't let her sit with us, so she sat two rows back and threw popcorn at us."

She smiled at the memory. "Good times."

"I wish I'd known that you felt sparks," he said.

"It was a long time ago—and the feeling was obviously one-sided."

"Why would you say that?"

"Because only a few months later, when I told you that Nathan had invited me to go to the prom with him, you said that I should accept his invitation."

"What was I supposed to say?" he demanded. "Should I have told you that Nathan knew I was planning to ask you and he asked first, because everything was always a competition with Nathan?"

Her jaw actually dropped open at this revelation, but she pulled it up again to respond. "You were going to ask me to the prom?"

"And that was a secret I'd planned to take to my grave," he said, then immediately winced at the insensitive phrasing. "I'm sorry. I didn't mean it that way."

She winced, too, but then she drew in a breath and fluttered her fingers, waving off his apology. "You were going to ask me to the prom?" she said again, determined to get an answer to the question.

"Yes," he finally admitted.

And he'd told Nate—in strict confidence—about his plan, because he thought his friend, who already had something of a reputation as a ladies' man, might have some advice for him.

"My advice is to ask someone else," Nate said.

"Why not Lindsay?"

"Because you don't have a hope in hell of getting past first base with Lindsay. And why would you spend two hundred bucks on prom tickets unless you think there's a chance you'll get to see what your date's wearing under her dress?"

"Because I like her," he said, unwilling to be dissuaded.

Nate shrugged. "I'm probably going to take Heather, even though we've already done it a few times."

Which Mitch knew, because Nate boasted about it every time it happened.

"But…why didn't you?" Lindsay asked, seemingly baffled by his reticence. "You had to know I would never say no to you."

"But I didn't want you to say yes because it was an invitation from a friend—I wanted you to say yes because you wanted to go with me as much as I wanted to go with you. Because you felt about me the way I felt about you."

"How did you feel about me?"

"I liked you. A lot."

"I had no idea," she admitted.

"I didn't want you to know," he said. "I didn't want our relationship to get weird."

"You mean like now?"

He managed a wry smile. "Yeah. And anyway, I was sure the crush would fade away if I just ignored it."

"Obviously it did," she said.

"Eventually," he agreed. "But when you kissed me on New Year's Eve, it was like the realization of a dream I've had since I was fifteen years old."

"I'm glad I didn't know that beforehand," she said lightly. "That kind of pressure might have been intimidating."

She was joking, of course, steering them back to familiar ground where they were friends with a long history that he now knew included some surprising feelings on both sides.

But they'd both moved on from those feelings a long time ago, and he'd be a fool to acknowledge that one kiss had stirred up his desire again.

"This is a nice surprise," Lindsay said, opening the door for her sister the following Saturday morning.

"I brought treats," Kristyne said, holding up the box from Sweet Caroline's.

"Another nice surprise." She looked past her sister. "Where's Gabe?"

"Closed up in his music room at home. Practicing for his upcoming studio session."

"Does he know you left the house?"

"I didn't sneak out," Kristyne said dryly.

"Well, the way he's been hovering like a hummingbird at a feeder since your last doctor's appointment, I thought I should ask."

"And I had another appointment this week and the doctor assured us both that everything is fine," her sister told her.

While Kristyne was hanging up her coat, Lindsay called into the family room to Elliott and Avenlea to let them know their aunt was there—with treats.

"Auntiekwisty!" Avenlea called out, racing to greet her beloved aunt. After a quick hug, she drew back and gently patted Kristyne's round belly. "Hi, Baby."

"Baby says hi back," the expectant mom told her.

Avenlea giggled. "Baby can't talk."

"Right here," Kristyne said, moving her niece's hand to the side. "Do you feel that?"

The little girl nodded, her eyes wide.

"That's the baby's way of saying hi."

Avenlea still wasn't entirely convinced. "We-wy?"

"Uh-huh. Of course the baby's favorite time to chat is three o'clock in the morning. Or when I've got a full bladder—which seems like always these days."

"You bwin' tweats?" Avenlea asked, proving that her interest in the baby wasn't as keen as her sweet tooth.

Elliott had bypassed his aunt completely in favor of the bakery box on the table—until he caught his mother's eye.

"Thanks for the treats, Aunt Kristyne."

"You're welcome," she said. "But you have to save some for your sister and your mom and me."

"An' me," Avenlea piped up.

"You're the sister," Elliott told her, adding a dramatic eye roll to express his exasperation.

"Oh."

"I'm a sister, too," Kristyne said, as Lindsay poured milk for the kids.

Elliott appeared skeptical of this information. "You're our aunt."

"Because I'm your mom's sister—and she's mine."

The little boy still looked perplexed as he bit into a jelly-filled doughnut.

"We'll sort out the family tree next week," Lindsay promised.

When Elliott and Avenlea had finished their snack and had their hands and faces washed, Lindsay sent them off to play so that she and Kristyne could chat over cups of chai tea that she'd brewed.

"You mentioned a doctor's appointment this week," she said, sitting down across from her sister. "Did you have another ultrasound?"

"I did."

Lindsay surveyed the contents of the box, trying to decide between a lemon meringue tart and Boston cream doughnut. "Boy or girl?"

"Not telling," Kristyne said.

Knowing that her sister had a fondness for Boston cream and because there was only one in the box, Lindsay opted for the tart.

"Because you don't know," she deduced. "If you did, you wouldn't be able to keep it to yourself."

"You're right," her sister admitted. "And I thought I wanted to know, but at the last minute, when the tech was ready to tell us, I said no. Which is silly, right?"

"Why is it silly? Lots of expectant parents prefer to wait until delivery to find out."

"I just think it would be so much easier to prepare if we knew."

"You *are* prepared," Lindsay reminded her. "The nursery is painted, the furniture is in place, the dresser is filled with diapers and onesies and sleepers—and I've got plenty of newborn clothes for boys *and* girls, ready to go as soon as you tell me what you need."

"You're right," Kristyne said. "I think it's the name that's the problem. I'm tired of referring to my baby as 'him or her' or 'he or she.' I want to be able to say Jack or Jill."

"I gave you a book with more than ten thousand baby names and those are your options?"

Her sister laughed. "No, they're just random examples. Although Jack is on our short list of boys' names."

"Dad would love that," Lindsay said.

Kristyne absently rubbed a hand over her belly as she nibbled on the Boston cream.

"Why do I get the feeling there's more on your mind than baby names?" Lindsay asked.

"I'm a little worried about Gabe's upcoming trip to LA,"

her sister admitted. "And that he might not be here when I go into labor."

Lindsay was worried, too, though probably for different reasons. But there was no way she was going to add her concerns to those already weighing on Kristyne's mind. "His trip is next week, isn't it?"

"It's been bumped back two more weeks," her sister said.

Which meant two weeks closer—and now very close—to Kristyne's due date.

"You don't have to worry," Lindsay said confidently, even as she crossed her fingers under the table and said a quick and silent prayer that her sister's husband would return on time and, more important, safely. "He'll be back."

"How do you know?"

"Because there's no way he's not going to be there to help bring your baby into the world," she promised.

And because—the crash that killed Nathan notwithstanding—flying was the safest mode of transportation.

"Plus, and I know you don't want to hear this," Lindsay continued, "but first babies are almost always late."

"Yeah," Kristyne rubbed a hand over her round belly. "I definitely don't want to hear that."

"Elliott didn't come until a full week after my due date," she said, choosing to focus on the labor process rather than her brother-in-law's travel.

"That does make me feel a little bit better about Gabe's trip—and a little bit like this pregnancy is going to go on forever. But just in case...would you be my backup labor coach?"

"I'll give you all my Boston cream doughnuts forever if I get to be there when my first niece or nephew is born," Lindsay promised.

And added a silent vow to be there for her sister always, no matter what.

CHAPTER NINE

LINDSAY WAS SETTING up for the Toddlers and Tots story time, positioning thick, colorful pillows in a semicircle on the floor facing the storyteller's throne—an old red velvet wing chair that someone had donated to the library long before she started working there. Quinn, hanging out at the library as she was in the habit of doing when she was struggling with her writing, had wandered over to the adult section to browse the stacks when Lindsay began checking in parents and children for story time Wednesday morning.

Reading aloud and sharing her love of stories with little ones was one of her favorite parts of the job. An added bonus was that she got to meet a lot of parents and the young children who would go to school with Elliott and Avenlea.

"Heather Foss." She smiled, genuinely happy to see the classmate she'd lost touch with a lot of years earlier, even before she and Nathan had moved away. But she would have recognized Heather anywhere, because the woman looked just as fabulous as she had ten years earlier. Her platinum-blond hair was shorter now and there were laugh lines at the corners of her eyes and mouth that hadn't been there a decade and a half earlier, but otherwise she looked the same. "It's great to see you. How are you doing?"

The other woman's answering smile was thin. "It's Heather Dekker now."

Lindsay winced inwardly at the faux pas even as she nodded. "Of course. I saw your name on the story-time registration." She scanned the list on her tablet again and tapped to check the attendance box. "Here you are—Heather and Silver. Oh, that's a beautiful and unique name."

"Thank you. It's something of a family name…on her dad's side," Heather said.

Lindsay turned her attention to the little girl clinging tightly to her mother's hand. "Welcome to story time, Silver."

The child offered a shy smile even as she ducked her head a little.

"How long have you worked here?" Heather asked.

"I just started in the fall. Part-time," Lindsay explained. "Tuesday and Thursday mornings, full days on Wednesdays and one Saturday a month. It's a great schedule, because I can take Elliott to school in the morning and pick him up again at the end of the day, and it means Avenlea only has to be in day care part-time."

"You have two kids?"

She nodded. "How about you?"

"Just Silver for now," she said, loosening up enough to smile down at her daughter. "But she's going to be a big sister in about six and a half months."

"Congratulations," Lindsay said sincerely.

"Thanks." Heather hesitated briefly then before saying, "I should have reached out when I heard about Nathan's passing… to tell you that I was sorry for your loss."

It was what most people said when she saw them for the first time after her husband's passing. And in the early days, the words had always hit her like a sucker punch to the gut, knocking the air out of her lungs and making her knees want to buckle. But with each day that passed, the grief faded a little more and she got a little stronger. Now the words caused no more than a slight twinge—bittersweet proof that she was healing.

"Thank you," she said.

"It can't be easy, raising your children without a dad," Heather acknowledged hesitantly.

"It's the reason we came back to Haven," she confided. "Because Nate's parents are here, and my sister and her husband, and Mitchell, of course."

"You and Mitch are still friends?"

Lindsay nodded.

"That's good," Heather said, though her tone was dubious. "Well…we should go find a place on the carpet."

"And quick, before it's standing room only," Lindsay said, obviously joking.

Heather offered another thin smile before moving toward the circle with her daughter.

"That was weird," Quinn remarked, as Heather and Silver went to join the group of moms and toddlers already seated in a semicircle facing the storyteller's throne.

"You thought so, too?" Lindsay said.

Her friend nodded. "You two have some kind of history?"

"We went through school together," Lindsay acknowledged. "But before today, I hadn't seen her in… I couldn't even tell you how many years."

"Friends who lost touch?"

"We didn't hang out together, but we weren't *not* friends," she said. "In fact, she dated my husband—a long time before he was my husband."

"Did you steal her from him?" Quinn asked, only half teasing.

"Of course not!" she immediately denied.

"Then why are you frowning?"

Lindsay deliberately relaxed her facial muscles, smoothing her brow. "I guess I did date him right after he broke up with

Heather," she acknowledged. "But that was more than sixteen years ago."

"Some people know how to hold a grudge," her friend noted.

Lindsay shook her head. "It's not as if Nathan broke her heart. In fact, she tied the knot with some guy she met at college before me and Nate got married. Actually, I think she might have been separated—or maybe even divorced—before our wedding.

"Her current husband, James Dekker, is her third. And it's a third marriage for him, too. But they say the third time's the charm."

"Who's they?" Quinn wondered aloud. "And how is it that you were gone for more than five years and you still know what's going on with everyone in this town before I do?"

"I stop at The Daily Grind every morning before work," she explained.

"Where the coffee is hot and the gossip is hotter," her friend acknowledged.

"See what you miss out on when you get your java from Sweet Caroline's instead?"

"You're the one missing out. Sweet Caroline's pastries put The Daily Grind to shame."

"Obviously, you haven't had the s'mores muffin from the coffee shop," Lindsay told her.

"There's no way it can compare to the chocolate peanut butter banana croissant at the bakery."

"That's what Parker had when we met for coffee—he said they're addictive."

"They are," Quinn confirmed. "I can't walk past Sweet Caroline's without popping in to get one. Or two. Because even a day old, they're delicious."

"Enough talk about muffins and croissants," Lindsay said. "My stomach is starting to rumble and it's still two hours until my lunch break."

"Did you brown bag it today?"

She nodded. "But I didn't pack anything that won't keep until tomorrow, if you were planning to stick around."

"I've got some research to do," Quinn said. "And I've been craving a Diggers' buffalo chicken wrap with spicy fries."

"Go do your research and stop making me think about food," Lindsay said, shooing her friend.

Quinn started to go, then paused to ask, "What story are you reading today?"

She glanced at the book on top of the desk and sighed. *"The Very Hungry Caterpillar."*

Her friend walked away laughing.

When Elliott was promoted from "hockey skills" to "hockey school," his sessions changed from Saturday afternoons to mornings. Lindsay had not been thrilled with the new time slot, and Avenlea was even less so—a fact that was evident to Mitch when he joined the mom and daughter watching the activity on the ice.

"Someone looks like a grumpy pants this morning," he remarked, as he lowered himself onto the seat beside Lindsay.

"Early mornings in a cold arena are not my idea of fun," she told him.

He chuckled. "Actually, I was referring to your daughter."

"Hers, either," she acknowledged.

But the little girl had spotted "Uncamitch" and was already crawling across her mom's lap to get to him.

She eyed the tray of to-go cups in his hand with wide eyes. "Did you bwin' hot choc'ate, Uncamitch?" she asked hopefully.

"You know I did," he said.

He pried the small cup out of the tray and removed the stirrer from the opening in the domed lid so that she could sip from it.

"Half hot chocolate, half cold milk," he told Lindsay, so that she wouldn't worry about her daughter burning her mouth.

"What do you say to Uncle Mitch?" Lindsay prompted.

"I wuv you, Uncamitch."

Lindsay laughed softly. "Try 'thank you, Uncle Mitch.'"

"Thank you, Uncamitch," the little girl dutifully intoned.

"Thank you, Uncle Mitch," Lindsay echoed, as he handed her a large cup of hot coffee.

She took her first sip, then sighed with blissful pleasure. "Café mocha," she realized. "What did I do to deserve this?"

He shrugged. "I know how much you hate early mornings in a cold arena."

"You really are the best," she told him.

"That's what all the women say," he said with a wink.

She nudged him with her elbow, a little harder than would be considered playful, making him grunt as she connected with his ribs.

"You had your chance to be one of those women and you turned it down," he reminded her.

"Speaking of those women—did you ever get over to fix Brittney's closet?"

"No," he admitted. "Apparently Brett Tanner is fixing her doors these days."

"So I was right," she said triumphantly.

He shrugged. "Since I never made it over to her place that night, I guess we'll never know."

"You know," she said. "You just don't want to admit it."

Instead of confirming or denying, he turned his attention to the kids on the ice, picking Elliott out of the crowd right away. "His skating is really coming along," he noted.

"He's making progress," she acknowledged. "But he's not very intuitive on the ice."

"Does he have fun?" Mitch asked.

"He loves it."

"Then that's all that matters."

"You're right," she said. "It's just…"

"It's just what?"

She sighed. "Nathan would get so frustrated with him. He had Elliott on the ice as soon as he was big enough for skates, determined to make his son into an even better hockey player than he'd been. But it doesn't come naturally to Elliott."

"Nate was pretty serious about hockey...until he discovered girls—I mean *you*," Mitch quickly amended.

"You don't have to revise history on my account," she told him. "I was there. I know he earned his reputation."

Which was only one of the reasons Mitch had been concerned when Nate and Lindsay first hooked up. He'd been certain that Lindsay would end up with her heart broken if she was foolish enough to fall in love with Nate. He'd never anticipated that Nate would fall first.

"Since you brought up the subject of Nathan's past," Lindsay began.

"Did I?" he asked warily.

"Something strange happened at the library the other day," she continued.

"What's that?"

"Heather Foss—now Heather Dekker—came in for story time with her daughter."

"Why is that strange?" He kept his tone casual, ignoring the uneasiness that skittered down his spine.

"The strange part is the way she acted," Lindsay said. "I know we were never the best of friends, but we were friendly. And at the library, she really wasn't."

"You're probably reading something into nothing," he said.

"I don't know...even Quinn remarked that it was odd."

"It's Quinn's job to make stuff up," he reminded her.

"One of the reasons she's such a good writer is that she has keen observation skills," Lindsay pointed out. "Anyway, she asked if I stole Nathan from Heather in high school, which got me wondering if maybe I did."

He laughed. "Are you seriously worried about something that happened sixteen years ago?"

"Did I steal Nathan from Heather?" she pressed.

"No," he said. "At least, not on purpose."

She frowned at that. "Are you saying that I *accidentally* stole him?"

"I'm saying that Nate wasn't the type of guy to let obstacles stand in his way, and when he decided that he wanted to go out with you, he dumped Heather.

"But I can't imagine that she's still holding a grudge over that," he was quick to assure her, when he saw the stricken expression on her face. "It's more likely that she was just having an off day."

"Maybe," Lindsay allowed. "And speaking of off days...how did you wrangle the day off?"

"MG owed me a favor."

"And you called it in so that you could drive into town to sit in a cold arena on a Saturday morning?"

"It beats sitting in a cold saddle with the icy wind in my face riding fence in the back forty," he told her.

"I guess it's all a matter of perspective, isn't it?" she mused. "Anyway, we're heading to The Trading Post when Elliott gets off the ice. He asked if I would make lasagna this weekend, so that's our plan for dinner tonight, if you want to join us."

"That sounds great, but I've actually got plans tonight," he said. "Any chance you can save the lasagna for tomorrow?"

"Wait," she said, holding up a hand. "You skipped over the mention of plans really fast...do you have a date tonight?"

"I'd rather not put a label on it, but that one probably fits," he admitted.

Lindsay knew that she should be happy for him. A good friend would be pleased to hear that he'd met someone he was interested in pursuing a relationship with. A good friend would want to hear all about his plans and eventually even meet the object of his affection.

And if she wasn't actually happy about his news—and she'd think about the reasons for that later—the least she could do was fake it.

"That's great," she said brightly. "What's her name? Where'd you meet her?"

"Her name's Sheridan, and I'm meeting her at Diggers' tonight," he said, sounding less than enthused by the prospect.

"A blind date," she noted, surprised.

"Sort of." He shrugged. "She's a friend of Paige's, so MG and Paige and me and Sheridan are having dinner together."

"Well…that's great," she said again.

"Maybe you should say *great* a third time to convince me," he suggested in a dry tone.

"Sorry," she said. "I was just caught off guard. But it *is* great, because you're a terrific guy and you deserve to share your life with someone special."

"It's just dinner," he said dismissively.

"Every relationship has to start somewhere," she pointed out.

"So does tomorrow night work for the lasagna instead?" he prompted.

"Sure," she agreed. "But why don't we confirm in the morning? Just in case."

"In case of what?"

Was he really that obtuse?

"In case you really hit it off with Sheridan and want to see her again tomorrow night," she explained.

He shook his head. "Even if we did hit it off, that kind of eagerness screams of desperation," he told her. "I'm a firm believer in waiting at least three days after a date to reach out."

"And while you're waiting three days, she might be getting a dozen hits from Tinder or Bumble or OkCupid and decide to move on without you," Lindsay said, not sure if her words were intended as a warning to him or reassurance to herself.

"Why would she agree to have dinner with me if she's looking for someone through online dating sites?" Mitchell asked, sounding more curious than concerned.

"Because she's a woman who wants to be in a relationship

and Haven isn't exactly a booming metropolis?" Lindsay suggested.

Instead of arguing the point he asked, "How do you know so much about online dating?"

"My world might revolve around my children, but I get out and talk to people," she said.

"By people you mean Quinn," he guessed.

She sighed. "Is my world really that small?"

"It's hardly a booming metropolis," he said, teasing her with her own words.

"My point is, if you have a good time tonight, you should give her a call tomorrow...unless you wake up with her, in which case a phone call probably won't be necessary—and might even be weird."

"This conversation is weird," he decided.

"It shouldn't be," she said, though she couldn't deny that it was. "Didn't we promise one another that we wouldn't let things be weird?"

"It's not weird because I'm discussing my dating prospects with you after what happened on New Year's Eve," he told her. "It's weird because it's not something I'd usually discuss with *anyone.*"

"Not even your brother or one of your buddies?"

"No," he said firmly.

"How did this double date get set up if you didn't talk to MG about it?" she challenged.

"He said, 'You got any plans for Saturday night?' I said, 'No.' He said, 'Paige has a friend she wants you to meet.' I said, *'Hell, no.'* He said, 'I've been told to make sure you're there, so I need you to be there.' And I said, 'Okay.'"

"You didn't ask any questions about Paige's friend?" she asked incredulously.

He shrugged again. "I figured I'd learn everything I need to know when we're at dinner."

"Do you at least know her last name, so you can check out her social media?"

"No. And even if I did, I wouldn't tell you, because I don't want *you* checking out her social media or—worse—making contact with her."

"I wouldn't do that," she protested.

He gave her a look.

"Probably not," she amended, as the kids on the ice, exhausted from their workout, funneled toward the open door to retreat to their dressing rooms. "But you can't blame me for looking out for you."

"I can look out for myself," he assured her.

She shook her head. "You don't realize what a catch you are."

His brows lifted then. "You think I'm a catch?"

"We're not talking about me—we're talking about Paige's friend with the baited hook."

"Here's a better idea—" he rose from his seat "—let's stop talking about this altogether."

"Where are you going?"

"To help Elliott with his skates and equipment," Mitchell said, and made his escape.

"I didn't expect to have to share the TV with you tonight," Mitch remarked, carrying two bottles of beer into the living room where his brother was already settled on the sofa with a game on TV the following Friday night.

"I do still live here," MG told him.

"Do you? I wasn't sure."

"Ha ha." He accepted the bottle of beer his brother offered. "You know I never spend more than two consecutive nights at Paige's place."

"Why is that?" Mitch wondered, twisting the cap off his own bottle.

"Because I don't want her to start to think that we're living together."

"Because that would be a bigger commitment than you're willing to make."

"It's a slippery slope," MG noted. "Although, unlike you, I can at least commit to a second date."

"You're talking about Sheridan," he guessed.

"You been on any other first dates lately?"

"Not lately."

"She told Paige that she really liked you."

"I think her opinion changed dramatically when Paige told her that the Circle G is one of the biggest cattle ranches in Nevada."

"So?"

"So there was no real chemistry between us."

"Sometimes it's hard to gauge chemistry across a dinner table—especially when there are two other people there."

"I'm not interested," Mitch said bluntly.

MG shrugged. "Okay, then."

"You're not going to try to maneuver us together again?" he asked, wary of his brother's easy acquiescence.

"I promised Paige that I'd get you to the restaurant. I didn't promise that you'd hit it off with her friend," MG said.

"Okay, then," Mitch echoed, and tipped his bottle to his lips again.

They watched the game in silence for several minutes before MG said, "Something else is on your mind."

"What?"

"Vegas just scored a short-handed goal and you didn't even blink, so I figured your mind must be on something other than the game."

"Yeah," Mitch admitted.

But he wasn't sure if he should say anything more than that. He wasn't even sure there was anything to say.

Over the past month, he'd tried to ignore the alarms that clanged in his head whenever he thought about the encounter with Heather at The Trading Post. But since Lindsay had shared the details of her interaction with Heather at the library, those alarms had been harder to ignore.

"Good talk," MG said, after a long moment had passed without his brother elaborating on his single word response.

Mitch managed a wry smile. "Did you ever find yourself in a position of knowing something that you didn't want to know?"

"Sometimes ignorance is bliss," his brother agreed.

He nodded and swallowed another mouthful of beer.

"Does this have something to do with Lindsay?" MG asked.

"Why would you think that?"

"Because anytime you get twisted up over something, it has to do with Lindsay."

"Actually, it's about Nathan," he said.

"Who was Lindsay's husband," his brother pointed out.

As if he might have forgotten.

After another minute passed, MG asked, "Did he cheat on her?"

Mitch frowned at the question. "That came from out in left field."

"Hardly," his brother scoffed. "The guy was a total player before Lindsay."

"But he changed when he fell for her," he felt compelled to point out. And it might have surprised Mitch, but there was no denying it was true.

"Maybe," his brother said dubiously.

"What do you know that I don't?"

"I don't *know* anything," MG denied. "But I did see Nate at Diggers' that weekend he was home for his mom's birthday."

"And?" Mitch prompted.

"He was with Heather Foss. Or Dekker. Or whatever her name was at the time. And they were all over each other at the bar."

"You never told me that," Mitch said, surprised by his brother's silence then more than his revelation now.

MG slowly curled his hand into a fist and stared at his knuckles. "I didn't tell you because I didn't want to have to bail you out of jail after you beat him to a bloody pulp. I figured the fat lip I gave him made the same point but without the necessity of a police presence."

"You got in a fight with Nate at Diggers'?"

"It was outside," MG said. "You know Duke has a strict rule about fighting in the bar. And it wasn't a fight—I hit him once but he never hit back, probably because he knew he deserved it."

"You're right, I would have beat him bloody," Mitch said.

"And I would have bailed you out, but I'm glad I didn't have to."

"The question now is—do I tell Lindsay?"

"She won't thank you if you do," MG cautioned.

"I know," he agreed. "It just seems like a really big secret to keep."

"And a really big secret to tell."

Mitch swallowed his last mouthful of beer.

"Nate's gone—all she's got left are her memories, and if you tell her that he picked up with his ex-girlfriend when he was in town, all those shiny, happy memories will be tarnished forever."

And maybe, if that's all that had happened, Mitch might have been able to let it go.

"Heather's little girl turned two in January," he told his brother.

MG considered this for a beat, then swore, proving that he could do the math and knew what the answer was when two-plus-two equaled a baby nine months later. "So possibly a bigger secret than I realized."

"Do you still think I shouldn't tell her?" Mitch asked.

"I think that once the words are spoken, they can't be taken back."

"But if she hears about it from someone else and later finds out that I knew and didn't tell her, she might never forgive me."

MG lifted his beer as if offering a toast. "Welcome to the space known as 'between a rock and a hard place.'"

"I need a spa day," Quinn announced, dropping a stack of books on the checkout counter.

"Deadline crunch?" Lindsay guessed, as she began scanning the items.

"Am I that predictable?"

"You do tend to get stressed when you have a book due," she told her friend.

"In six weeks," Quinn said. "I only have six weeks to wrap up the story and catch the bad guy."

"And you'll do it," Lindsay said confidently, because Quinn's ability to deliver was as dependable as her panic. "But if you need some extra incentive to push through, make an appointment at Serenity Spa for the day after your manuscript is due as your reward."

"That's a good plan," Quinn agreed, scrolling through the calendar app on her phone. "Is April second good for you? It's a Friday—and you're off Fridays, right?"

"I don't work here on Fridays," she agreed. "But I still have two kids that need to be taken care of—and only one is in school during the day."

"I'm sure your mother-in-law would be happy to spend a few hours with Avenlea."

"She would, but I'm not the one who needs a spa day," Lindsay pointed out.

"You have two kids," Quinn said, echoing her words. "You probably need a spa day as much as I do."

The idea was certainly tempting. "Well, I wouldn't mind a pedicure," Lindsay said, as she finished scanning the books. "And I've got a gift certificate." Actually, she had two of them, because Suzanne and Arthur had given them to her for her birthday the past couple of years.

"Mark it in your calendar," Quinn said. "April second—spa day."

Lindsay did as directed and realized that she was sincerely looking forward to an afternoon of relaxation and fun with a girlfriend—yet more proof that life did go on.

CHAPTER TEN

AFTER HIS BLIND date with Sheridan had turned out to be a dud, Mitch didn't know why he let his sister talk him into agreeing to another setup—this time with a woman who'd recently joined the same yoga studio. Olivia had not only insisted that he meet Karli but that he take her somewhere nice, so he'd made a reservation at The Home Station, the only upscale restaurant in town.

Karli was as attractive as his sister had promised, with auburn hair and whiskey-colored eyes and a sprinkle of freckles across her nose. She was also tall—probably close to six feet in the high-heeled boots she wore with a dark purple sweater dress. And smart, with a civil engineering degree with specialization in environmental and water issues from Northwestern Michigan College.

"How did you end up in Haven?" he wondered.

"I came to town to do an environmental assessment for Blake Mining."

"So it's a short-term assignment?"

"I thought so," she said. "But there's the possibility of it becoming a permanent position, if they're happy with my work and if I want to stay." She smiled at him then. "And I've seen a lot to like about this town so far."

The date seemed to be off to a promising start when a short chirp sounded from his phone.

"Sorry." He reached into his pocket for the offending device. "Just let me turn off my notifications so..."

His words trailed off when he saw the message.

Kristyne's in labor and Gabe's in LA.

The unasked question from Lindsay was, could he watch Elliott and Avenlea so that she could go to the hospital with her sister, as they'd previously discussed?

He immediately replied:

Be there in 10.

"Is something wrong?" Karli asked.

"I'm sorry," he said. "I have to go. The sister of a friend of mine is having a baby, and I promised I'd watch her kids so that she could coach her through labor."

"I like kids," Karli said. "I'd be happy to babysit with you."

While Lindsay had seemed cool about him dating, he was pretty sure she wouldn't approve of him bringing a woman he'd just met into her home to help take care of Elliott and Avenlea. Truthfully, he wasn't comfortable with that scenario, either.

"Thanks, but you should stay and order dinner," he said, already pushing his chair back from the table. "The food here is really good, and I'll leave my credit card with the maître d' to cover the check."

And then, without waiting for her to respond, he was gone.

"That was quick," Lindsay said, when she opened the door in response to his knock.

"I told you I'd be here in ten."

"And you made it with—" she glanced at her watch "—just about thirty seconds to spare."

He lifted his brows when he heard a beep from the kitchen. "Were you timing me?"

She laughed. "No. That's the oven signaling that it's pre-heated. We were late getting home from the children's museum in Battle Mountain and I was just about to put chicken fingers in for the kids' dinner."

She turned toward the kitchen, but he caught her shoulders and steered her back around again.

"Your sister's waiting for you," he reminded her.

"I know, but—"

"Auntiekwisty's havin' a baby!" Drawn away from her toys by the sound of their voices, Avenlea bounced into the foyer to make the announcement.

"I hope it's a boy," Elliott said, joining them.

"Giwl!" Avenlea countered.

"Boy or girl, your aunt Kristyne will be having her baby at home if your mom doesn't leave right now," Mitch said.

Lindsay swallowed. "You're right. I have to go. Just let me—"

"You've got your keys and your purse," he noted. "That's all you need. I can handle things here."

"I know," she said again, bending to give her children a quick hug. "Thank you."

So while Lindsay headed back to Battle Mountain, to the hospital with her sister this time, Mitch cooked the chicken fingers. He even cut carrot sticks and cucumber slices to go with them, because Lindsay believed it was important for the kids to have vegetables at every meal. And because he knew Elliott and Avenlea liked to dip, he squirted little pools of barbecue sauce and ranch dressing on their plates.

When it was time to eat, Avenlea's previously discerning palate proved that it was either confused or adventurous, because she chose to dip her chicken in the ranch dressing and her cucumber in the barbecue sauce. Of course, this caused her brother to make gagging noises, but Mitch quickly silenced Elliott's criticism, pointing out that everything was going to the same place.

It was what his mom had always said, insisting that as long as kids were eating—and what they were eating wasn't harmful to them—there was no reason to worry about unconventional food choices. No doubt that was why leftover pizza was still one of Mitch's favorite breakfast foods.

After dinner was finished, he enlisted Elliott and Avenlea to help clear the table and put their plates and cups in the dishwasher. Then they washed up and got their pajamas on, ready for bed.

"But we don't have to go to bed right now, do we?" Elliott asked.

"Not right now," Mitch agreed.

Though he'd forgotten to verify bedtimes with Lindsay before she left, he didn't think it would be a big deal if they were a little bit later for one night. And yes, he could have sent her a text message to ask, but he didn't want to take her focus away from her sister.

She'd checked in with him, though, when they got to the hospital, and again to tell him that Kristyne was four centimeters dilated. He didn't know if that was good or bad and, truthfully, he didn't want to think about it too much. He couldn't be a rancher if he was squeamish about the process of birth, and he'd witnessed more calves and foals being born than he could possibly remember—and even a couple litters of kittens. But baby cows and horses came when they were ready, and it was most often a completely natural process. Human beings tended to make everything more complicated, and Mitch preferred not to think about the details of Lindsay's sister expelling a baby from her birth canal.

Of course, as soon as he'd decided not to worry about strict adherence to the children's usual nighttime schedule, his phone chirped with another message.

Bedtime is 7 for Avenlea and 8 for Elliott (usually) ;)

He replied:

I'll make sure they brush their teeth after they finish their Red Vines and Pepsi.

And jumping on the furniture?

They got bored with that already. Now we're in a fort made out of sofa cushions.

He immediately followed that up with another message:

Question—was the green marker stain always on the flow-ered chair cushion?

Her reply was quicker than he'd expected:

I'm going to assume you're joking because I'm off to track down more ice chips for my sister who's busy trying to have a baby while you're practicing your stand-up comedy routine.

Are you laughing?

She didn't respond, which he took to mean that she was ei-ther not amused or preoccupied with her search for ice.

So he settled the kids in front of the TV to watch an episode of their favorite (and mom-approved) program on Nick Jr. While they were engrossed in the animated adventures of rescue hero canines, he searched on his phone for current hockey scores and discovered there was a game on—he glanced at the clock on the wall—right now.

"Can we watch one more? Please, Uncle Mitch?" Elliott asked, when the episode ended with—surprise!—the Paw Pa-trol saving the day.

"P'ease?" Avenlea beseeched.

"Not tonight," he said. "It's already past your usual bedtime and the Golden Knights are playing the Dallas Stars."

"Can I watch the game with you?" Elliott asked.

"Past your bedtime," Mitch said again.

"But my bedtime is later than Avenlea's," the boy reminded him.

"You can stay up until the end of the second period," he relented, since it was just about to start.

Avenlea poked out her lower lip, clearly unhappy with what she saw as favored treatment of her brother.

"And you can pick two stories to read before lights out," he said, not above bribing her to turn that frown upside down.

It worked.

Avenlea skipped happily up the stairs to choose her books.

While she was sorting through the titles on her bookshelf, Lindsay texted again:

And don't let Avenlea con you into more than one story.

Too late.

Of course, it took the little girl almost as long to pick the books as it did for him to read them, but he finally closed the cover on *Lovabye Dragon*, pulled her covers up under her chin, kissed her forehead and wished her "sweet dreams."

He'd just settled back on the sofa with Elliott—eight minutes already gone in the first period—when the phone rang.

Though Lindsay had considered giving up the landline (with the same number he'd memorized when they were in grade school, before everyone and their brother had cell phones), she was reluctant to do so "in case of emergency." He considered letting the call go to voice mail, but he didn't want the ringing to disturb Avenlea, who was hopefully, finally, asleep.

"It's probably Gramma," Elliott told him. "She's the only one who calls that number."

"Gramma D or Gramma T?" Mitch asked. Not that it mattered—he was going to answer the phone regardless.

"T," the boy responded. "Gramma D calls on the computer." He grabbed the phone on the third ring. "Hello?"

"I'd like to speak to Lindsay, please."

Elliott had guessed correctly—it was Gramma T.

Mitch probably would have recognized Suzanne Thomas's voice even without the boy's forewarning, but she obviously didn't recognize his. Or maybe she just didn't expect him to be answering Lindsay's phone.

"She isn't here right now, Mrs. Thomas, but I'd be happy to take a message," he said.

"Where is she?" Suzanne asked, sounding perplexed by the possibility that her daughter-in-law would be anywhere but at home with her children.

And while he wouldn't have freely given the information to anyone else, he figured it was a safe bet that Suzanne knew Lindsay's sister was near her due date. "She's at the hospital with Kristyne."

"Her sister's having her baby?"

"That's the plan."

"But…who's watching Elliott and Avenlea?"

"I am, Mrs. Thomas," he said, torn between amusement and exasperation. "That's why I'm here."

"But…surely you have better things to do on a Saturday night than babysit," Suzanne said. "Lindsay should have brought the children here."

"I think Lindsay was eager to get to the hospital and I happened to be in town," he said, not wanting Elliott and Avenlea's grandmother to feel slighted by the arrangements that had been made.

"Still, she should have called me and Arthur," Suzanne said. "After all, we're the grandparents."

"And I'm one of the godparents," he reminded her—the other one being Kristyne, who was otherwise occupied at present.

"I'm sorry. I didn't mean to imply that you aren't capable," she said. "I just worry that Lindsay relies on you too much, that she sometimes takes advantage of your affection for her—because she was married to your best friend."

"You don't need to worry about me," he assured her, not fooled for a minute by her fake apology or concern.

"Well, just let Lindsay know that I called," she said.

"I will," he promised, and went to watch the last five minutes of the second period.

Elliott went up to bed without further protest when the buzzer sounded, obviously tired out and ready to call it a day. In fact, he was drifting off before Mitch finished reading his chosen bedtime story.

But Avenlea woke up midway through the third period, asking for Mommy. Though Mitch wasn't sure Lindsay would approve, he took the little girl down to the family room to snuggle with him while he watched the end of the game.

Just when her eyes started growing heavy again, Elliott woke up and made his way back downstairs to ask if there was any news from the hospital. Realizing that his sister was awake, of course he insisted on staying up, too. And that's how Mitch ended up sandwiched between them on the sofa.

Lindsay was exhausted—both physically and emotionally—when she slid behind the wheel of her SUV to make her way home. But witnessing the miracle of her niece's birth had brought back so many memories, and she sat in the parking lot for a long while letting the tears stream down her face as memories flooded her heart.

It was the middle of the night when Lindsay had gone into labor before Elliott was born, so of course Nathan was there for that. Her contractions started almost immediately after her water broke, and so they put her overnight bag—already packed because she was a week overdue—into the SUV and headed to the hospital in Fairbanks. It turned out there was no reason to hurry—their son wasn't born until sixteen hours later.

Two and a half years after that, Avenlea decided to make her appearance in the middle of the day precisely on her due date—when her dad was at work and tied up in an important meeting. Thankfully they lived next door to a wonderful couple who had a son a few months older than Elliott, and Tammy offered to stay home with both the boys while Rita drove Lindsay to the hospital. Nathan had met her in the delivery room, arriving just in time to cut the umbilical cord.

She'd cried then, too. Overwhelmed by love for her daughter. Grateful and relieved that her husband had made it to the hospital in time to share at least part of the experience. And frustrated—and maybe even a little bit angry—that he'd come so close to missing the monumental event.

He'd promised her then that he would always be there for the important moments, and though she knew it wasn't a promise he ever wanted to break, he'd done so anyway. An undiagnosed mechanical issue with a plane flown by an inexperienced pilot had taken his life and so much more. So while Lindsay was overjoyed for Kristyne and Gabe, and excited about the beautiful new addition to their family, she was also all too aware that happiness could be fleeting and there were no guaranteed tomorrows.

Wiping the tears from her cheeks, she sent a quick message to Mitch to let him know she was on her way home. When he didn't reply, she guessed that he'd probably fallen asleep on the sofa, watching some game or another on TV.

Half an hour later, she toed off her shoes by the door and set her purse inside the coat closet, then quietly made her way to the family room. Sure enough, the TV was on, tuned to one of those all-sports channels that had likely shown a Golden Knights game earlier but was now recapping all the action from around the league that night. She expected that Mitch would be stretched out on the sofa, making use of the blanket and pillow she'd left for him. Instead, he was asleep sitting up, with her son tucked against one side and her daughter the other.

And the heart that had taken an emotional beating over the past several hours filled with so much joy it actually felt as if it was pressing against her ribs.

Because life was good, she realized.

And Mitchell was a good man who filled so much of the void that had been left after Nathan's death—a friend whose support meant the world to her. And even if the memory of his kiss was enough to make her knees weak and her body yearn, their friendship was too important to her to risk for the chance of something more.

She moved closer and carefully picked up Avenlea, trying not to disturb Mitchell. Of course, he immediately woke up when the weight of the sleeping child was lifted away from his side.

"You're home." His voice was rough and his eyes clouded with sleep.

"No, you're dreaming," she whispered teasingly.

"If I was dreaming, you'd be naked," he countered.

Warmth rushed to her cheeks, and a different kind of heat stirred in her belly.

"Sorry," he apologized gruffly. "My brain is still half-asleep."

"Luckily both Elliott and Avenlea are completely asleep," she said. And too young to understand, even if they'd happened to overhear his comment.

However, the implication of his teasing words was as clear to Lindsay as the awareness that suddenly sparked between them again. But with her sleeping daughter in her arms, this was neither the time nor the place to let her thoughts meander down that path.

She started to nudge Elliott awake, because he was getting too heavy for her to carry, but Mitchell halted her effort.

"I've got him," he said.

"Are you sure? I thought you were still half-asleep yourself."

"I'm awake now," he assured her.

So he carried Elliott up the stairs and tucked him into his bed, while she did the same with Avenlea. Of course, she checked on Elliott, too, because that was part of her usual nightly routine. She saw *Brady Brady and the Runaway Goalie* on the nightstand, and knew that Mitchell had read with him before he'd gone to sleep, understanding the importance of their nightly routines even when there was a hockey game on TV.

She'd wondered, more than once, how it was possible that he wasn't already married with half a dozen of his own kids running around the Circle G. Because it was obvious to Lindsay that he was meant to be a dad.

He'd be quite a catch as a husband, too, for whatever lucky woman managed to snag him. He was handsome, charming, sweet, sexy—and she hoped that someday he'd find someone who could appreciate all of his wonderful attributes and what a truly great guy he was.

As for herself, she needed to stand on her own two feet, to prove to him that she could. He'd done so much for her over the past two years that she'd become dependent on him, and that wasn't fair. Despite the fact that he'd always looked out for her, he wasn't responsible for her.

She wasn't a child anymore who needed a friend to walk her to the nurse's office for a Band-Aid when she fell down in the playground and skinned her knee. Or a naive teenager who didn't know what Jeremy Falconi had in mind when he invited her to eat lunch with him in the back seat of his new Mustang. And yeah, Mitch had saved her then, too.

Maybe she should have been embarrassed to be caught fending off Jeremy's grabby hands, but she'd been too grateful to Mitch for yanking open the car door and pulling her out of harm's way to feel any shame. Not until Nathan, coming upon the scene a split second later, had made fun of her innocence and naivete. In response to which Mitchell had told him to shut the hell up.

She knew that Nathan hadn't meant to be cruel, but his mockery had stung and Mitchell's defense had soothed. Much later, Nathan would acknowledge that he'd been a bit of an ass to her in high school because he'd liked her but hadn't wanted her to know it. He'd certainly succeeded in that regard. In fact, he'd done such a good job that she'd sometimes wondered how it was possible that she and Nathan, who could hardly stand one another, could both be friends with Mitchell.

And then, seemingly out of the blue, Nathan had asked her to go to the junior prom with him.

She'd been so shocked by the invitation, she'd actually stammered while trying to come up with a reply. In the end, she'd told him that she had to check with her mom before she gave him an answer, but the truth was, she'd wanted to check with Mitchell.

Because she hadn't really dated anyone before then. She'd occasionally gone out with a group of friends and sometimes one of the guys would express an interest in "going somewhere a little more private," but she'd declined all those invitations, feeling more comfortable in the crowd—where Mitchell was close by.

She'd been even more wary after the incident with Jeremy Falconi, and if she liked someone, she'd ask Mitchell's opinion, wanting to know if he was a good guy or if she should steer clear. He usually advised her to steer clear, claiming that even the good guys were "not good enough for you." Every single time, he came up with some reason that she shouldn't go out with a guy she was interested in.

Until Nathan.

Was it true that he'd only asked her to the prom because he'd known that Mitchell intended to ask her?

Whatever his reasons, she was glad she'd said yes to his invitation, because he'd been charming and sweet and she'd fallen just a little bit in love with him that first night. And even if she'd known then that their time together would be limited, she wouldn't change a minute of it, because without Nathan, she wouldn't have Elliott and Avenlea, and they were her everything.

Making her way back down the stairs again, she found Mitchell in the kitchen and the kettle just starting to boil.

"Since when are you a tea drinker?" she asked curiously.

"It's not for me, it's for you," he said. "I figured you'd be pretty wound up after all the excitement at the hospital and my mom swears that a cup of chamomile tea—which you conveniently had in your cupboard—helps her relax and sleep."

"You're always taking care of me," she remarked, as she dropped into a chair at the table.

"It's just a cup of tea," he said.

But it wasn't.

He'd done so much for her, and not just tonight, and she knew there was no way she could ever repay him.

"Boy or girl?" he finally asked, as he poured boiling water over the tea bag in her favorite mug.

She smiled. "Girl. Harper Rose. Eight pounds twelve ounces and twenty-two inches."

"Is that big?"

"Bigger than both of mine," she said. "Elliott weighed in at seven twelve and Avenlea was seven seven—with a bonus of three stitches for me."

He winced and quickly changed the subject. "Did Gabe make it back in time to see his daughter born?"

"He walked into the delivery room just as the doctor gave Kristyne the okay to start pushing."

"And then you got kicked out?" he guessed, setting the mug of hot tea in front of her.

"No." She smiled again. "They let me stay. And it was so amazing." She blinked away the moisture that filled her eyes. "And yes, I know I've been through childbirth before, but it was still an incredibly beautiful and emotional experience.

"So thank you," she said. "It was easy for me to focus on my sister tonight and not worry about Elliott and Avenlea, because they were with you."

"So texting to check in every ten minutes is what you do when you're not worried?" he teased.

"The texting was more to pass the time, because not much was happening in the beginning," she explained. "And I shared our messages with Kristyne, to distract her."

"From the pain of nothing happening?" he asked dryly.

"Even in the early stages, it's called labor for a reason." But Lindsay knew that her sister had been worried, too, about Gabe getting there on time. Or at all. And while she'd done her best to keep her mind off her husband's absence, she'd been as relieved as Kristyne when he finally arrived.

"Well, I appreciate your faith in me," Mitch said now. "Unfortunately, your mother-in-law doesn't share it."

"Suzanne called?" Lindsay guessed.

He nodded. "And wanted to come over when she found out that you'd left me in charge."

"She just wanted an excuse to come over and see the kids," she said, lifting her mug to blow on the hot tea.

"Maybe." He sounded doubtful, but moved on then to ask, "Did you get something to eat at the hospital?"

She shook her head. "No."

"Why not?"

"Because the hospital has a 'nothing by mouth' policy for women in labor, in case they need to be sedated, and I didn't want to eat in front of my sister."

"But you could have snuck down to the cafeteria for a snack."

"Is that a guy thing?" she asked. "Because that's exactly what Nathan did when I was in labor with Elliott. Although he didn't sneak—he outright told me that he was going to the cafeteria to get a sandwich, because he was hungry. *I* was the one in labor for sixteen hours, but *he* was hungry."

He opened the cookie jar on the counter and pulled out a handful of cookies, setting them on the table in front of her.

"You're not you when you're hungry," he said, borrowing a popular candy bar slogan.

She laughed as she broke off a piece of cookie and popped it into her mouth. "So how was your dinner?"

"I taught Elliott and Avenlea a new word when we were eating," he told her.

"Did you swear in front of my kids?"

"Of course not," he said indignantly. "Their new word is crudités, which we had with our chicken fingers."

"You mean raw veggies?"

"Yeah, but they're listed as crudités on the menu at The Home Station," he told her. "So when Elliott complained about having to eat carrot sticks and cucumber wheels, I explained that they were actually French hors d'oeuvres—and if he wanted *crème glacée* for dessert, he had to eat his crudités."

"Two questions," she said. "One—when were you at The Home Station?"

"Tonight, actually," he admitted. "That's where I was when you texted about Kristyne."

"You were on a *date*?" She stared at him, horrified. "Why didn't you tell me that you were on a date?"

"Because it wasn't as important as the fact that your sister was going to have her baby."

"I could have asked Mrs. Renaldi to come over to stay with Elliott and Avenlea."

"They like me better than Mrs. Renaldi," he said.

"They like you better than everyone," she agreed. "Even me sometimes."

"That's because I'm cool Uncamitch." He said it as one word, the way that Avenlea did. "And you're the parent who has to enforce rules and bath schedules and bedtimes."

"Isn't that the truth?" Then she shook her head. "But you're not going to distract me that easily."

"Is that what I was doing?"

"Tell me about her," Lindsay said, still baffled—and secretly pleased—by the realization that he'd ditched his date when she'd texted him.

"I don't know very much," he hedged. "We didn't make it too far past the basic introductions before you texted."

"You could start with her name," she suggested.

"Karli, with a *K* and an *i*," he said. "Who recently moved here from Colorado, with a *C* and an *o*."

She lifted her brows.

He shrugged. "That's how she introduced herself."

"Does Karli with a *K* dot the *i* with a heart?" she wondered aloud. Then, immediately apologized. "I'm sorry. That was snarky and unfair."

"It was," he agreed. "Especially considering that you're the one who's been pushing me to open myself up to the possibility of a relationship."

"You're right. I'm sorry," she said again. And if she'd had second thoughts about the decision when she'd learned that he actually was dating other women, well, it was too late to change her mind now.

Wasn't it?

"Anyway, you said two questions," he reminded her. "And that was only one."

"Right." But she was still trying to wrap her head around the fact that he'd run out on a date to babysit her kids. Which she sincerely appreciated but didn't imagine was going to increase his odds of getting another date.

"Second question," he prompted again.

"Did you let Elliott and Avenlea eat the last of my rocky road ice cream?" she asked.

"They had vanilla with caramel sauce and sprinkles. Lots of sprinkles."

The way he specified *they* made her eyes narrow. "Did *you* eat all of my rocky road ice cream?"

"There really wasn't much left," he said in his defense, offering another cookie to her.

She playfully snatched it out of his hand. "You owe me ice cream."

"And I'll buy you some—as soon as I get my babysitting money," he promised.

She smiled as she bit into the cookie, appreciating his sense of humor as much as his camaraderie.

And reminding herself again that friendship was enough.

CHAPTER ELEVEN

"I WAS GLAD—if a little surprised—that you called," Karli said, as The Home Station server delivered the meals for what was their second attempt at a first date. "The way you rushed out of here last week, I was sure I'd said or done something to scare you off."

"I told you why I had to go," Mitch reminded her.

"Yeah, but the friend-with-the-sister-in-labor story sounded like one of those fake emergencies to get out of a first date gone wrong."

"She had an eight-pound baby girl. They named her Harper Rose."

"So not a fake emergency," she acknowledged, slicing into her juicy roasted chicken breast on a bed of garlic mashed potatoes with a balsamic reduction. "Wait a minute—is your friend's sister married to Gabe Berkeley?"

"You know Gabe?" Mitch sampled his steak, unable to find fault with the chef's treatment of the Circle G T-bone.

"No, but I saw him play once, at a dive bar in Denver. The band mostly did cover songs, and not too badly, but it was obvious the drummer was the real talent. He nailed the solo in 'Hot for Teacher' so perfectly, Alex Van Halen would have been proud.

"Of course, most of his bandmates from back then are still jamming in dive bars while he's laying down tracks in the studio for chart-topping artists," she noted.

"I honestly didn't know he was that big of a deal," Mitch admitted. "He certainly doesn't flaunt his celebrity."

"He's that big of a deal," Karli assured him. "I follow him on Twitter, which is how I knew about the baby."

"What I want to know is why you thought our first date had gone wrong," he said.

"*I* didn't think it had, but some guys can't run fast enough when they find out I'm an engineer. It's one of the reasons I lead with that," she admitted. "I don't want to waste my time with a guy who's intimidated by smart women."

"Understandable," he said.

Karli studied him over the rim of her wineglass. "So tell me what you look for in a woman."

"I don't know if it's anything specific," he said, poking at an asparagus spear with his fork. "I've dated blondes, brunettes and redheads, women who were tall and short, skinny and curvy."

"So you don't have a physical type," she acknowledged. "But what about personality traits? What appeals to you?"

He shrugged. "I guess I like a woman who knows what she wants—and who's confident in who she is."

She nodded, encouraging him to continue.

"Someone who's loyal to her friends, good with kids and committed to family. Someone slow to anger and quick to laugh." An image of Lindsay laughing as she drank tea and nibbled on arrowroot cookies slipped into his mind, and he felt his lips curve.

"You're describing someone specific, aren't you?" Karli guessed. "I'm thinking...the single mom."

Busted.

"She fits the general description," he acknowledged.

"So why are you here with me?"

"I figured I owed you a meal—at the very least."

"You did," she agreed. "And while I appreciate that you're making an effort, it's obvious that you're not really into me."

He didn't bother to deny it. "I'm sorry."

"Don't be," she said. "I know it's you, not me."

He managed a wry smile. "Proving that you're every bit as smart as that fancy degree says you are."

She scooped up a forkful of mashed potatoes. "So how long have you been in love with her?"

He feigned ignorance. "Who?"

She rolled her eyes. "The single mom."

"We're just friends."

"Uh-huh," she said, clearly not buying it.

"I've known her since we were kids."

"In another word, forever," Karli mused. "So what's the problem? She doesn't feel the same way?"

"It's...complicated."

"It always is."

"She's a widow," he confided. "And her husband was one of my best friends."

"That is complicated," she agreed.

He nodded.

The conversation shifted to more generic topics as they finished their dinner and drinks, then Mitch paid the check and they walked out of the restaurant together.

"I'm sorry tonight was a bust," he said.

"It wasn't a complete bust," she said. "The meal was delicious—so thank you for that."

"It was the least I could do."

"You're right," she agreed. "And now I'm regretting my decision not to have dessert."

He chuckled. "Do you want to go back inside and order something to take home with you?"

She shook her head. "No, but thanks."

"I really did enjoy tonight," he told her.

"The night is still young." She kissed his cheek. "Go be with the one you want."

Lindsay glanced at the clock as she scrolled through the listings on her TV menu. It was nine o'clock on a Saturday night—the beginning of those long, empty hours between when her kids went to bed and she did.

Maybe she should get a pet. Elliott and Avenlea would love a dog or cat, and it would be good company for her. Heck, even watching a goldfish swim around in a bowl would be more interesting than anything on TV.

Or she could simply go to bed early. It had been a busy week, with all the excitement over Harper Rose and her parents' return to Haven to meet their newest granddaughter. But she didn't have Marilyn and Jackson for company, because they'd decided to stay with Kristyne and Gabe this time, to help the new parents with the baby.

Her cell phone chimed and she practically leaped to snatch it up off the table.

Are you up?

She replied:

It's 9 o'clock. What time do you think I go to bed?

As if she hadn't just been considering putting on her pajamas and crawling under the covers.

I try not to think about you in bed.

And though she knew she was treading on dangerous ground, she couldn't resist replying:

You try not to think about me in my bed? Or you try not to think about me when you're in bed?

Both are equally risky.

A statement of fact—and maybe also a warning.

I thought you had a date tonight. Why are you texting me?

I did have a date. And I'm texting because you haven't invited me to come in.

He was *here*?

She went to the windows and peeked through the blinds.

Yep, there was his truck in the driveway.

She hurried to the door and unbolted the lock.

"You're an idiot," she said, shaking her head as he stepped inside.

He grinned. "I've been called a lot worse."

"How long were you planning to sit in my driveway before letting me know that you were here?"

He shrugged. "Probably not much longer. Mrs. Renaldi pushed back her curtains at least three times, as if to let me know that she knew I was there."

"She *is* the unofficial neighborhood watch, you know." She moved back to the family room. "Do you want coffee?"

"No, thanks."

"So…how was your date?"

Considering that it was over before nine o'clock, she was surprised when he said, "Actually, it was great. It turns out that Karli's not just beautiful but smart and witty and fun. We shared a fabulous meal and interesting conversation."

She didn't particularly want to hear all the details, but she'd been the one to insist they remain firmly within the friend zone and, as a friend, it was her duty to listen.

"That is great," she said. *A lie.* "I'm happy for you." *Another lie.* "But I have to wonder, if she's so great…why are you here?"

"Because she's not you," he said simply. "And I don't want anyone but you."

She might have resisted the words, but the intensity and sincerity of his gaze sent them arrowing straight to her heart. Still, she had to be smart. To think about what was at stake.

"I know you're afraid to risk our friendship, and I understand why," he continued. "But there's so much more we could have together. So much more we could be to one another. Don't you think we deserve a chance to try?"

Before Lindsay could respond to either his confession or his question, he was kissing her. His mouth hot and hungry against hers, not asking but demanding a response. And she gave it, not just willingly but eagerly.

Her lips parted to allow him to deepen the kiss, and the sensual flick of his tongue against hers sent heat racing through her veins, making her burn. He kissed her until her mind was completely blank and her knees were weak.

Lucky for her, he had those strong shoulders that she could hold on to. He'd always been her anchor in the storm, but this time he was the cause of the chaos. He was responsible for the desire churning in her veins and clawing at her belly.

And then, just as suddenly as he'd taken her in his arms, he released her again, his breathing as ragged as her own.

"Just promise me that you'll think about it, okay?" he asked.

She nodded, certain it would be a long time before she'd be able to think about anything else.

On Wednesday, Mitch decided that an early-morning trip into town to pick up equine supplements from the feed store justified a quick detour to Sweet Caroline's. He ordered his coffee and, after careful consideration of all the options in the display case, a chocolate glazed—his tried and true favorite.

The popular bakery had limited indoor seating and when he

looked around for a vacant chair, he spotted one at a nearby table where Heather was buckling her daughter into a high chair. She took a wipe out of her diaper bag and used it to clean the tray before she gave the little girl a sippy cup of juice.

Mitchell carried his coffee and doughnut over. "Do you mind if I join you?"

She looked around and seemed chagrined to discover there were no other empty seats available. "Of course not," she said, though her tone was less welcoming than her words.

"I forgot how busy this place can be in the mornings," he said, settling into the chair across from her.

"The Daily Grind is even busier."

"Better coffee there," he acknowledged. "Better doughnuts here."

"Do'," Silver said, stretching her arms to reach for the doughnut in front of her mother.

"Do you want a piece of doughnut?" Heather asked.

The little girl's wispy pigtails bobbed up and down as she nodded.

Mitch bit into his chocolate glazed.

Heather tore off a small piece of her cruller. "Say please."

"P'ease."

She set the doughnut on the tray and wiped her sugary fingers on a paper napkin.

"So where are you guys on your way to this morning?" he asked.

"From," Heather clarified. "We just came from story time at the library."

"Then you probably saw Lindsay. She works there part-time now."

Heather nodded. "I know."

Silver shoved the piece of doughnut into her mouth and reached her hands out to her mom again. "Mo'."

"Chew what's in your mouth first," Heather admonished.

Silver closed her mouth and chewed.

Heather smiled for her daughter, but the smile faded when she turned her attention back to him again. "What do you want, Mitchell?"

"I just thought it'd be nice to have some company while I drink my coffee," he said.

"Why don't I believe you?"

He shrugged. "There's no reason you shouldn't. *I've* never lied to you."

She didn't miss the emphasis. "Obviously you think someone else did."

"I could be wrong—" though his tone was conversational, he dropped his voice to ensure he wouldn't be overheard by anyone at the nearby tables "—but I'm guessing that Nathan at least twisted some truths to get you into bed three years ago."

Despite the color that stained Heather's cheeks, she met his gaze levelly. "There was no bed involved. We did it in the back of his dad's SUV—just like in high school."

Mitch wouldn't have broached the subject if he hadn't felt fairly confident that Nathan was Silver's father, but still, a part of him had hoped that Heather would shoot down his theory once and for all.

"But yes," she continued softly. "I think he twisted a lot of truths." She shifted her attention when Silver held out her open palm, offering a bite of doughnut to her mom this time, and the expression on her face morphed from guilt and regret to fierce and protective maternal love. "But I can't regret being played for a fool, because I ended up with Silver, and she's the best thing that ever happened to me."

She tore off another piece of doughnut for her daughter.

"But how did you know?" she asked Mitch. "She doesn't look like Nathan. Not really."

"But she does look like his son. And a little bit like his daughter. *Other* daughter," he clarified.

"You think so?"

He nodded.

She sighed.

"Did Nathan know?" he asked her now.

"No." She shook her head. "I was going to tell him I was pregnant. I thought he had a right to know—maybe even that he'd *want* to know. But then I found out that he'd gone back to his wife."

"You thought they were separated?"

"Yeah. He always did know how to play me," she acknowledged ruefully. "But when he never reached out to me again, after we...reconnected, I suspected that the time we'd spent together hadn't meant anything more to him than an opportunity to relive high school."

Mitch couldn't defend his friend's actions—nor did he want to. In any event, while Heather might have been taken in by his lies as much as his charm, she clearly understood what Nathan was all about.

"Still, if you'd told him about Silver, he would have acknowledged her," he said, because he believed it was true. His friend might have been a bastard in a lot of ways, but he'd been a terrific dad who doted on his kids, and Mitch had no reason to believe the affection he felt for his children wouldn't extend to one born out of wedlock.

"My daughter deserved more than to be *acknowledged* as the bastard child of a cheating husband," she said tightly. "She deserved a father. A family."

"I guess it's lucky, then, that you were able to give her one."

"We *are* lucky," she agreed. "James is a wonderful husband and father."

"Does *he* know?"

"Of course he knows. I might have lied to my mother, because she couldn't keep a secret if it was handed to her in a locked box, but I wouldn't lie to my husband." She put the last piece of doughnut on the napkin in front of her daughter then looked at Mitch again. "Are you going to tell Lindsay?"

He scrubbed his hands over his face and swore under his

breath. "I guess I'm going to have to," he said. "She needs to know."

"Does she, though?" Heather challenged. "I mean, what purpose would it serve?"

"At the very least, it would ensure she's not blindsided when the truth comes out—because the truth always comes out."

"No one has any reason to suspect that Silver isn't James's daughter," Heather said. "And anyway, he's been offered a big promotion at the company that would mean a move to El Paso."

"Do you really think moving out of state, away from your family, is going to keep your secret safe?"

"James and Silver are my family," she said. "And I'd go to the ends of the earth to protect them."

Mitch waited three days, but he wasn't sure he could wait any longer. He didn't want to tell Lindsay, but he really couldn't see any way around it. If she found out from someone else and then discovered that he knew but had kept the truth from her, she might never forgive him.

And it was inevitable that she would find out, because nothing remained a secret forever in Haven. Truthfully, he was a little surprised that people weren't already speculating about Silver's paternity. Although, the fact that Heather had given birth only five months after the wedding might have been enough of a scandal to appease the gossips—at least for a while.

But Mitch had no doubt that once the little girl was old enough to go to school—the same school that Elliott and Avenlea would be attending—the speculation would be fierce. Of course, Avenlea wasn't yet three, so she wouldn't be starting school for almost two years, and Silver would be a year after that. Or maybe Silver would be going to school in El Paso, if James Dekker decided to take the promotion that Heather had mentioned. So maybe there was no rush to tell Lindsay about her husband's infidelity.

Except that it was always risky to count on the truth remaining a secret. All it would take was one person to remark in passing that Heather Dekker's daughter had a smile just like Nathan Thomas's little girl, and the fact that Nathan had been in Haven nine months prior to Silver's birth would add fuel to the fire.

But before he said anything to Lindsay, he needed more information.

"Mitchell—this is a pleasant surprise," Suzanne Thomas said, greeting him with a smile.

"I apologize for dropping in uninvited," he said.

"Don't be silly." She stepped away from the door, a wordless invitation. "You know we're always happy to see you. In fact, Lindsay and the kids are coming over later for dinner, if you want to stay and eat with us. I've got a Circle G prime rib roast the oven."

He appreciated her loyalty to his family brand, but he had no appetite for dinner and even less for the conversation they needed to have. "Thanks, but I'll make this quick and get out of your way."

"Make what quick? Is there a problem?" she asked, sounding more curious than concerned.

He thought about the little girl with the sweet smile and big blue eyes—an innocent child caught up in a web of lies woven by the adults in her life, and he needed to know who was complicit. He didn't want to tarnish Suzanne and Arthur's memories of their son, but if Mitch's instincts were correct, he wouldn't be telling them anything they didn't already know—or at least suspect.

"I wouldn't say it's a problem so much as a situation," he replied to her question.

"Come into the kitchen," she suggested. "I've got potatoes on the stove."

He took off his boots and followed her across the mosaic ceramic tile floor, down the dark paneled hallway illuminated by crystal sconces. Like all the other houses on Miners' Pass, the Thomases' home was spacious and beautiful, though the decor was a little formal for his taste. It was difficult to imagine sticky fingerprints on the fridge or toys scattered across the Aubusson carpet in the front parlor—and seriously, who had a parlor these days?—but according to Lindsay, Elliott and Avenlea loved spending time at Gramma and Grampa T's. But perhaps Suzanne and Arthur had relaxed their previously strict house rules for their grandchildren, in the hope that they wouldn't someday run off to Alaska, as their only son had done.

Although Nate had been one of his best friends, Mitch hadn't been oblivious to the fact that he was selfish, spoiled and entitled. Not surprising, considering that he was an only child who'd always been given everything he wanted—or taken it, if it wasn't given.

But despite his flaws, Nate had loved Lindsay. If Mitch hadn't been certain of that, he never would have stood up for his friend at the wedding.

"Have a seat." Suzanne gestured to the trio of leather stools lined up at the island. "Can I get you something to drink? A beer, perhaps?"

"No, thank you," he said.

But he took a seat while she poked at the potatoes boiling in a pot on the stove.

"Is Mr. Thomas home?"

"He's in his office, reviewing briefs for a hearing on Monday—did you want me to get him?"

"No," he said, figuring she could fill in the details for her husband later—if he didn't already know. "There's no need to interrupt him."

She set down the fork and turned to face him again. "So what's on your mind?"

"Heather Dekker," he said, getting straight to the point.

Suzanne's perfectly shaped brows drew together. "I don't think I recognize that name," she said. "Should I?"

"She and Nate dated off and on in high school, when she was Heather Foss."

"He dated so many girls in high school." She shook her head a little. "It was hard to keep track of them all—until Lindsay."

Which was undoubtedly true, but her response was so deliberately vague that Mitch suspected she remembered more than she wanted to admit. Especially when he recalled a scene he'd witnessed outside of the funeral home at Nate's visitation.

He'd gotten caught up at the ranch and was late arriving, so he'd been surprised to pull in the parking lot and discover that his friend's mother wasn't inside accepting the condolences of family and friends, but outside with another woman, almost hidden from view behind an enormous stone planter. He'd only caught a glimpse of the other woman from the back as he turned into the drive, and by the time he'd parked and made his way to the entrance, she was gone and Suzanne was heading back inside.

He'd barely given it a second thought in the moment, more focused on being there for his friend's family than what he'd seen—which really wasn't anything at all. But after his conversation with Heather, he'd replayed the memory of that day and realized that the woman he'd seen Suzanne talking to might very well have been Heather.

Of course, *might* was hardly definitive. There were undoubtedly a number of women in Haven who were of a similar height and build with the same hair color as Heather, so maybe he should let it go. Whatever had happened between Nate and his ex-girlfriend, and whether Suzanne and Arthur knew, had nothing to do with him.

But it had a lot to do with Lindsay and Elliott and Avenlea. Nate's widow and children would inevitably be impacted when the truth came out. And that's why Mitch was here: for Lindsay.

"Did you know that Heather has a two-year-old daughter?" he asked now, watching Suzanne closely.

"No." She turned to pick up the fork and poke at the potatoes again. "And I'm not sure why you think that would be of any interest to me."

"Because her little girl has dark curls like Elliott and a smile just like Avenlea's."

"All children look alike to a certain extent," she remarked.

"She also has blue eyes like Nathan."

Suzanne stared at him, her expression darkening. "I don't like what you're implying," she said. "Maybe you should go now."

But Mitch wasn't going anywhere until he had the answers he came for.

"Silver is Nathan's daughter, Mrs. Thomas. Your grand-daughter."

"That's a lie," she snapped, the polite facade gone. "I know my son wasn't perfect, but he's gone now, and I'd appreciate it if you didn't disparage his reputation."

"I'm not trying to disparage his reputation. I just want to know if you knew that he broke his wedding vows," he pressed.

"I don't believe that he did," she said, still firmly in denial.

Or maybe not so firmly, he mused, noting that she kept her gaze averted as she straightened a tea towel hanging on the oven door that didn't need straightening, and adjusted the angle of the knife block.

"But you suspected something," he realized.

Her hand trembled slightly as she repositioned the salt and pepper shakers.

"I know you think you're protecting Nathan's memory," he said. "But what about Lindsay? Have you given any thought to what it will mean to her?"

"If you were really concerned about Lindsay, you'd drop this right now," she said.

He'd told himself the very same thing, but he knew that secrets never remained secret forever. "She's going to find out," he said. "You know she is. I'm just trying to put the pieces together so that I can figure out a way to control the narrative and hopefully lessen her pain."

"Lindsay is the daughter I never had," Suzanne said, obviously wavering. "I couldn't love her any more if she was my own."

"Then tell me what you know, please."

She picked up the tea towel again, deciding to fold it now. "That woman stopped by, about six weeks after Nathan was home for my sixty-fifth birthday party," she finally said.

"Heather?" he asked, needing to be certain.

Suzanne nodded. "She wanted to know how she could get in touch with Nathan, because the number he'd given to her was no longer in service."

"Six weeks," he echoed. "So probably around the time she realized she was pregnant."

"I don't know," his friend's mother said again, her tone more weary than angry now. "She didn't tell me why she wanted to contact Nathan and I didn't ask. But I did tell her that whatever she thought she needed to talk to him about, it couldn't be important enough to bother him when he and his wife were celebrating the birth of their second child, and she agreed."

"And that was it?" he asked incredulously.

"She never came here again," Suzanne said. And in her mind, clearly that was the end of it.

But she'd shown up at the funeral home, Mitch was certain of that now. Of course, a lot of Nathan's friends from high school had been there to express their condolences—though Heather was the only one he'd seen having a tête-à-tête with Suzanne. "You're telling me that you never wondered—not even when, several months later, you must have heard that Heather was pregnant?"

She lifted her chin. "It wasn't any of my business. And she was married by then anyway."

"But you suspected that your son had cheated on his pregnant wife—and you didn't even ask him about it?"

CHAPTER TWELVE

BEFORE SUZANNE COULD respond to his question, a shocked gasp sounded from the kitchen doorway.

Mitch's head swiveled to where Lindsay was standing, her expression stricken, a pie plate trembling in her grasp, and he silently cursed himself for being the cause of the pain he'd wanted only to spare her.

"You're early," Suzanne said to her daughter-in-law. "We weren't expecting you until four."

Lindsay's gaze shifted from her mother-in-law to Mitch and back again. "As soon as Grampa T told them the bunk beds had been delivered, they started pestering me to come over, but we had to wait for the pie to come out of the oven."

"Are they with Grampa now?" Suzanne wondered, rescuing dessert from her daughter-in-law's tenuous grasp. "Did Arthur take them upstairs to see the beds?"

Lindsay nodded, then gave her head a slight shake. "Can we backtrack for just a minute here?"

"Sure," Suzanne said, sounding anything but certain.

"Is it true… Did Nathan…did he have an affair?"

Suzanne looked at Mitch—a wordless plea for help.

But he couldn't help her, not when the truth could only cause Lindsay more pain. He rose from his seat but resisted the urge to go to her, understanding that she needed time to accept the awful truth that she was hearing.

"Nathan loved you," Suzanne said. "You have to know that."

"I didn't ask if he loved me." Lindsay's voice quavered, just a little. "I asked if he had an affair."

Her mother-in-law's eyes filled with tears. "I don't know."

Lindsay turned to Mitch then. "Damn it, Mitchell. Tell me the truth. Did Nathan have an affair?"

She was obviously shocked and shaken, and well on her way to feeling the devastation he'd wanted to spare her. But he couldn't lie; he wouldn't be part of the deception. He nodded slowly.

"With Heather?"

He nodded again.

"And you knew." The anguish in her eyes and the raw tone of her voice gutted him.

She obviously felt betrayed, not just by her husband but by her friend, and he couldn't blame her.

"Why don't you sit down?" Suzanne suggested, the tea towel now twisted in her hands. "Let me put on the kettle to make you a cup of tea and—"

"No!" Lindsay closed her eyes and exhaled a long, slow breath. "No, thank you."

"Please sit down," her mother-in-law urged.

Lindsay shook her head. "I can't. I have to go. I need to think."

Suzanne immediately protested. "But dinner's almost ready and the kids—"

"Ohmygod. Elliott and Avenlea." She pressed her hands to her cheeks, her eyes shiny with unshed tears. "Can they stay here for a while?"

"Of course they can," Suzanne said. "But you should stay, too. Give yourself some time to—"

"I can't," Lindsay said again, her voice raw. "I really just need to be alone right now."

And with that, she turned and fled.

* * *

Lindsay felt hot and trembly and sick to her stomach, and she prayed that she'd make it home before she threw up. Tears burned the backs of her eyes, but she refused to give in to the need to cry. Not yet. She wouldn't fall apart until she was alone—and then she was most definitely going to fall apart.

Relief rushed through her body when she pulled into her driveway. Almost immediately, Mitchell's truck parked behind her vehicle. She pretended she didn't see it as she made her way toward the front door, dropping her keys twice as she attempted to unlock it.

He gently took the keys from her hand to complete the task, making it impossible for her to ignore him any longer.

"Thank you," she said stiffly. "But I really want to be alone right now."

"I don't think you do," he told her.

"Well, you don't always know what's best for me," she argued, blocking the now open doorway.

"Maybe not," he acknowledged. "But I know that you must have questions, and I might be able to fill in some of the blanks for you."

"That's right," she said, nodding. "Because you knew that my husband cheated and didn't tell me."

"I didn't know anything for certain until a few days ago."

"But you obviously suspected something before then," she noted, stepping away from the door to let him enter.

He followed her into the kitchen. "When I saw Heather at The Trading Post early in January," he admitted.

"What happened? Were you in the middle of the canned goods aisle and she just blurted out that she'd slept with my husband?"

"No." Mitch shook his head, cringing inside at the realization that Lindsay had only overheard the last part of his conversation with her mother-in-law, so she knew only part of the story. And not even the biggest part.

Which meant that he was going to have to be the one to tell her the rest. And in that moment, he actually hated his dead friend for what he'd done, leaving him to—if not clean up the mess—at least try to explain it.

He thought back to that day when he'd almost literally run into Heather and Silver and said, "It was the frozen food section."

Lindsay gave him an incredulous look. "Well, that makes a lot more sense."

"I didn't mean to say that out loud," he admitted, scrubbing his hands over his face. "I never wanted to be the one telling you any of this. Honestly, I wish there was nothing to tell."

"Yeah, I'm sure this is hard for you," she said, her voice fairly dripping with sarcasm.

"Can you please just listen to me for two minutes so that I can get this out?" he asked wearily.

She pressed her lips together.

"And maybe you should sit down," he suggested.

She remained where she was standing, facing him with her back to the counter, her fingers wrapped around the edge so tightly her knuckles were white. "Just tell me."

This was not at all how he'd imagined the truth coming out, but he had no one to blame but himself. As soon as Suzanne had said that Lindsay and the kids were going to be there for dinner, he should have given up on the idea of talking to her about Nathan's affair.

But hindsight was always 20/20.

"When I saw Heather, she was shopping for her daughter's second birthday. This was early January—just a week or so after the New Year.

"I knew she had a child," he continued. "I'd even seen her with Silver a couple times before, but I never knew—or realized—that she was born nine months after Nate was home for his mom's birthday."

"No." Lindsay's already pale face turned impossibly whiter.

He nodded grimly.

"It's not true," she said. "It can't be true."

"I'm so sorry, Linds."

She shook her head, refusing to believe what he was telling her. But the stricken look told him that she knew the truth, deep in her heart.

"No. There's no way...it's not possible." She pushed away from the counter and moved across the room. "Why are you doing this? Are you trying to hurt me?"

"No. Never." He started toward her, instinctively wanting to offer comfort. But he knew she wouldn't accept it from him. Not now when she blamed him for her world crashing down around her. So he stopped halfway and shoved his hands into his pockets. "Do you think this is easy for me? Do you think I *want* to be telling you this?"

She turned to face him then, and the sight of the tears on her cheeks was like a knife through his heart.

"You have to know I wouldn't be telling you this if I wasn't one hundred percent sure."

Lindsay did know, and that was why it hurt so much.

Because Mitchell would never lie to her about something like this. But he'd kept the truth from her, and that was almost as bad.

"I didn't want to believe it, either," he told her. "And at first, I tried to convince myself that the timing was nothing more than a coincidence. Then I saw Heather again, just last week at Sweet Caroline's, and she confirmed that Nathan is her daughter's father."

She had to swallow the lump that clogged her throat before she could ask, "How do you know she's not lying?"

"Because she has nothing to gain by lying—and a lot to lose," he said.

"So it happened when he came home for his mom's sixty-fifth birthday," she realized. "When I didn't come, because I was seven months pregnant."

"No one's blaming you," he said gently.

But he was wrong, because she blamed herself.

Because why would Nathan have cheated on her unless he was unhappy in their marriage? Or bored with their sex life?

She'd had a difficult pregnancy with Avenlea. More nausea and fatigue, and almost zero interest in making love with her husband. The doctor had assured her that everything she was feeling was perfectly normal, but Nathan was clearly unhappy about the lack of affection she was showing him. Because he felt neglected, never mind that she was exhausted from caring for a toddler all day—and growing another baby inside her belly. *His* baby!

When he'd talked to her about making the trip to Haven for his mother's milestone birthday, she'd been disappointed that she couldn't be there to celebrate the occasion—and secretly relieved that they would have a few days apart. Just a few days in which she didn't have to feel guilty about not wanting to be intimate or, worse, having to fake interest.

So she'd said goodbye to her husband and son—because even though she couldn't make the trip, she knew it would mean the world to Suzanne to have her grandson there—certain that the time and space would be good for each of them. And she'd actually missed Nathan while he was gone. And she'd believed him when he told her he'd missed her, too.

But the truth was, he'd been too busy hooking up with Heather Foss to spare a thought for the pregnant wife more than twenty-five hundred miles away.

And who had been taking care of Elliott while he'd been screwing his ex-girlfriend?

Suzanne, no doubt. She would have been so thrilled to spend some extra time with her firstborn grandchild that she probably didn't even ask where Nathan was going, never mind what—or who—he was doing.

"Silver...that's a beautiful and unique name."

"It's something of a family name...on her dad's side."

As snippets of that conversation echoed in her mind, Lindsay remembered being struck by the peculiar phrasing of the other woman's remark. Heather hadn't said the name was from her husband's family but from her daughter's father's family.

God, what a fool she'd been, not making the connection between "Silver" and "Sterling"—her mother-in-law's maiden name and, coincidentally, Elliott's middle name.

She shook her head. "So while I was in Moose Creek with Nathan's baby in my belly, he was making a baby with another woman, putting his—"

"Stop," Mitchell said. "Don't do this to yourself, Lindsay. Please."

She swiped at the tears that had spilled onto her cheeks. "I remember when Nathan and Elliott came home from that trip, how excited I was to see them. They'd only been gone five days, but I'd missed them like crazy. Nathan said that he missed me, too. And for the next few weeks after that, he was uncharacteristically attentive, as if to prove how much."

She gave a short laugh. "At least, that's what I thought at the time. Now I realize that his actions were likely motivated by guilt rather than affection."

Guilt because he'd had sex with another woman.

Unprotected sex, obviously, since the act had resulted in a child.

And then he'd come home and had sex with her.

The realization that he'd put her at risk—willfully or not—made her stomach churn again. She knew she was clean, because Dr. Tam had insisted on running a whole gamut of tests when she took Lindsay on as a new patient when she moved back to Haven, so she could at least be grateful for that.

"I'm sorry I didn't tell you as soon I knew," Mitch said. "But I didn't know how. And I didn't want to hurt you."

She nodded and wrapped her arms around her middle, as if that might somehow help her hold it together. But emotions battered at her like waves, and she started to crumble.

"Lindsay?"

She heard Mitchell's voice as if from far away as her knees buckled.

He caught her. Of course he did. Because he was always there for her when she needed him—even when she didn't want to admit how much.

His arms came around her, drawing her close. And then she was sobbing against his chest, soaking his shirt with her tears as emotions raged inside her.

She felt hurt. And angry. Betrayed.

Cheated.

But Nathan hadn't just cheated on her—he'd cheated on his family.

"How could he do this to me?" she asked. "To his children?"

"I don't know, Linds."

She pulled back a little, to swipe her hands over her tear-streaked cheeks. "Maybe I would have grieved less for the husband I'd vowed to love and cherish *till death do us part* if I'd known that he'd already broken those vows."

"I don't think that's true," he said. "Regardless of the mistakes he made, you loved Nathan—and he loved you."

"How could he cheat on me if he loved me?"

"I don't know the answer to that question, either," he said. "The only person who does is Nathan."

"And I lashed out at you, because he isn't here for me to lash out at."

He shrugged those broad shoulders, clearly unconcerned. "You needed a target and I was here."

Because he was always here for her.

The one person she'd always been able to count on.

Strong and steady, just like the heart she could feel beating beneath her cheek pressed against his shirt again.

His hand slid up and down her spine, comforting her as she might comfort Elliott or Avenlea. She snuggled closer to his warmth, his strength, breathing in the familiar scent of his soap, of Mitchell.

She felt a stirring in her blood and was suddenly cognizant that the mood had shifted.

Awareness crackled in the air.

Mitchell held himself perfectly still as she slid her hands up his chest, fascinated by the contrast of hard muscle beneath soft flannel. But she'd always known he was a man of contrasts—strong yet gentle, fierce but kind, passionate and controlled.

Desperate to feel some of that passion now, she lifted herself onto her toes and pressed her mouth to his.

There were rules to the game, Mitch reminded himself, as Lindsay settled her soft, sweet lips against his.

And one of those rules was not to take advantage of an obviously emotional and vulnerable woman—a rule that wasn't easy to remember when every part of her body was pressed against every part of his, causing his own to react in a predictable fashion.

Another rule was not to let himself be taken advantage of—not even by the woman he'd wanted for longer than he was willing to admit. If Lindsay ever decided that she really wanted to be with him, there was no way Mitch would be able to refuse her. Unfortunately, he understood that her actions right now weren't driven by desire for him so much as a desire to get even with Nate.

Devastated by the discovery that her husband had slept with another woman, she was seeking revenge in the arms of another man. And as much as Mitch wanted her, he didn't want to be any part of that twisted scenario.

He took hold of her wrists—capturing the hands that were roaming all over his body—and held them away. "Lindsay, stop."

She blinked at him, confused by his abrupt withdrawal. "What? Why?"

"Because this isn't really what you want," he said gently.

"What are you talking about? Of course it's what I want," she insisted. "And isn't it what you said you wanted—to give us a chance?"

"I *do* want to give us a chance," he assured her.

"Then why are you pushing me away?" she demanded, sounding not just frustrated but hurt.

As if he'd rejected her.

As if he ever could.

"Because what you're trying to do now isn't about us—it's about getting even with Nate."

She took a step back, her expression stricken.

"You don't want *me*," he said, though it pained him to admit it. "You want to be with someone who isn't Nate, because you just found out that he was with someone who wasn't you."

"Ohmygod…you're right." She lifted her hands to cover her face. "I'm a horrible friend. A terrible person."

"Stop it," he admonished gently. "You're not either of those things. You're just trying to deal with a brutal emotional blow."

"You should be furious with me," she said.

"I'll curse you while I'm freezing my balls off in a cold shower at home," he promised.

She managed a smile. "You really are the best man I know."

He kissed her forehead. "And when you decide you really want me and not just revenge on your husband, you know where to find me."

CHAPTER THIRTEEN

SHE WAS LIKELY making a mistake, Lindsay acknowledged as she walked up to the front door of the brick and glass building that housed Haven Mutual Insurance. Two and a half weeks had passed since she'd found out about Nathan's affair, since she'd learned that her husband had fathered a child with another woman.

During that time, she'd told the story more times than she wanted to—to her sister, who'd responded that Nathan was lucky he was already dead because she would happily have killed him for breaking her heart; to her parents, who'd tried to console her long distance while she'd tried not to completely fall apart again; and to Quinn, who'd told her—not unkindly—to stop mourning what was lost and move on with her life.

But Lindsay was still hurt and angry—and frustrated that the only person who could answer her questions was dead. And then she realized that wasn't entirely true, that there was someone else who might be able to provide some of the information she needed. Whether she would cooperate was an entirely different matter, but she had to at least try to have the conversation.

Her sister attempted to talk Lindsay out of it. Kristyne was certain nothing good could come of a confrontation with Heather. But she'd still agreed to let Avenlea hang out with her for a few hours anyway, insisting that the little girl was a big help with her baby cousin. And Lindsay knew that she had to deal with her past before she could move on with her future.

She'd heard that Heather was again working as a receptionist at the insurance company, albeit only part-time, so she'd called first—and then apologized for dialing a wrong number when she recognized her voice on the other end of the line. Just like high school all over again.

Her heart was pounding against her ribs as she walked up the stone steps to the entrance. The sliding glass doors opened automatically, giving her no reason to pause. Lindsay stepped inside the spacious reception area with a wide curved work surface of frosted glass. The waiting room was arranged like a living room, with comfortable chairs and sofas around a frosted glass coffee table that offered an assortment of magazines for browsing. There were two clients waiting, both occupied with their phones, a sign of the times.

Heather glanced up, the ready smile on her face freezing in place when she recognized Lindsay. But she had a role and she played her part. "Can I help you?"

Lindsay shoved her hands in the pockets of her jacket as she stepped closer, so the other woman wouldn't see that they were trembling. "I was hoping we could talk," she said.

"I'm working."

"I know. But maybe we could get together on your lunch hour? Or after work, if that's better for you?"

"I appreciate your willingness to accommodate my schedule, but I can't imagine what you think we have to talk about."

"Can't you?" Lindsay asked.

Heather held up a hand as she answered a call. After a brief exchange, she connected the caller to one of the agents, then shifted her attention to Lindsay again. "I've got the late lunch today. Two o'clock."

"Do you want to meet at Diggers'?" she asked, thinking only

that the proximity of the restaurant just down the street made it a convenient location.

Heather gave a short laugh. "No. I brought a lunch from home. Why don't you pick something up and we'll meet at Prospect Park?"

"You want to eat outside in twenty degree weather?" she asked dubiously.

"Do you have a better idea?"

"How about my place?" she suggested.

The other woman seemed wary of the invitation. "Am I supposed to know where you live?"

"355 Winterberry Drive. The same house I grew up in."

Heather had been there several times when they were in grade school together—for birthday parties and even the occasional sleepover—and a few times in high school, when they were on the yearbook committee together.

"I guess that would work," Heather finally agreed.

Lindsay nodded. "I'll see you around two, then."

This was definitely a mistake, Lindsay decided, as she stirred the soup heating in a pot on the stove.

Did she really expect that Heather was going to tell all just because Lindsay had invited her into her home?

Because she certainly had no intention of baring her soul to "the other woman" in order to get answers to the questions that plagued her thoughts.

Then the doorbell rang, and she realized that it was too late now to stop the events that she'd set in motion. She also realized that, until she opened the door and saw Heather standing there, she'd been more skeptical than optimistic that the other woman would actually show.

"I made soup," Lindsay said, as she ushered Heather into the kitchen. "Actually, I heated up soup, from a can. Garden vegetable."

"I'm good." Heather held up her reusable insulated lunch bag covered with bright pink poppies.

It wasn't really Heather's style—or not the style of the girl Lindsay had known years earlier—but she could imagine it was something her daughter had picked out. Though Lindsay didn't really spend any one-on-one time with the kids at story time, she'd noticed that Silver always wanted to sit on a pink pillow—and that the color was a popular choice for her wardrobe, too.

"Do you want coffee? Or tea?"

"No, thanks."

She stirred the soup simmering on the stove.

"So… I'm guessing that Mitchell told you," Heather said, keeping an eye on her as she unwrapped the cellophane from her sandwich.

Lindsay nodded.

"And you invited me here to tell me that I'm a tramp and a home wrecker and you hope I rot in hell?" the other woman guessed.

"No," she said. Though admittedly those same and other descriptions and sentiments had popped into her head at one time or another over the past two and a half weeks. But in her more rational moments, Lindsay had forced herself to acknowledge that Heather wasn't to blame for what had happened—or not entirely anyway. "I wanted to talk to you because I have questions that I'd really like to ask my husband, but since he's dead and buried, you're my next best hope for answers."

"So this is a lunchtime interrogation." She started to rewrap her sandwich. "No, thanks."

"I know you don't owe me anything," Lindsay said. "But I'd hoped—as a wife and a mom—you'd appreciate my need for some answers."

Heather still seemed wary, but she settled back into the chair. "What do you want me to tell you—that he tried to deflect my advances, but I persisted until he finally stopped saying no?"

"I don't want you to lie to me." Lindsay ladled some soup

into a bowl, though her stomach was in such knots, she knew she wouldn't be able to eat it. "I just want to understand."

"Okay," Heather relented. "The truth is, Nathan told me that you'd split up."

And how ridiculous was it, after everything else she'd learned about her husband in recent weeks, that it hurt anew to hear those words come out of the other woman's mouth?

How was it possible that finding out that he'd lied about the status of their marriage in order to get into another woman's pants was almost as heart-wrenching as the discovery that he'd cheated on her?

Had he removed his wedding ring to perpetuate the illusion that their marriage was over?

She didn't ask.

Because apparently there *were* some things that she didn't want to know.

"And you believed him?" Lindsay challenged, wanting to shift some of the blame for her husband's actions.

"I had no reason not to," Heather said. "He'd come home with his son—"

"Also *my* son," Lindsay interjected.

The other woman nodded. "And I asked how you were doing, and he said he didn't really know…that you'd chosen to stay in Alaska to pack up your stuff, and as soon as he got back, you were taking Elliott and leaving."

"I didn't *choose* to stay in Alaska," Lindsay told her. "I wasn't allowed to fly because I was almost seven months pregnant."

"I didn't know," Heather said quietly. "And maybe I didn't want to know. My second divorce had just been finalized and I was feeling alone and lonely and being with Nate reminded me of simpler times. Happier times. And maybe it was a boost to my self-confidence, too, that he could want me again, after dumping me in high school."

Lindsay swirled her spoon around in her soup for a minute before she finally asked, "Did you…want to get pregnant?"

"No." Heather shook her head. "The possibility never crossed my mind. I went on the pill in high school, so I wouldn't have to think twice about birth control. And I stayed on it right up until me and Leon—husband number two—decided to try to have a baby. Obviously that didn't happen for us and, after the divorce, I didn't imagine that I'd have any need for birth control.

"But I'm not sorry I got pregnant, because I wanted a baby. Not with another woman's husband," she acknowledged ruefully, "but I wanted a baby."

"She's a sweet girl," Lindsay said, because it was true. She might want to hate Nathan and Heather—and maybe she did—but their daughter was an innocent child.

"She's my world," Heather said simply, sincerely.

Lindsay decided to stop pretending she was eating the soup and pushed her bowl aside.

"For what it's worth… I know what it's like to be betrayed by someone you love," the other woman confided.

"Your husband cheated on you?"

Heather nodded. "The first one."

"How did you find out?"

"Explicit text messages on his phone. Of course, he said it was a mistake and promised it would never happen again. And then it happened again."

"Is that why you divorced?" Lindsay asked.

Heather nodded. "And now you're wondering what you would have done if you'd found out, while Nathan was still alive, that he'd been unfaithful," she guessed.

Actually, she'd been wondering that for the past two and a half weeks.

"I never thought that I'd be one of those women who would stay with a man who cheated." Of course, she'd also never thought Nathan was the type of man to cheat. "But when I think about what we had…and that leaving would have meant giving up our family… I'm not sure I would have been strong enough to do it."

"I didn't leave Trey because I was strong," Heather said. "I left because it was easy. Because when that trust was broken, there was nothing holding us together.

"It's different when you have a family," she continued. "A family is something worth fighting for. I mean, obviously everyone's situation is different and there are all kinds of reasons to make the decision to stay or go. I'm just saying you shouldn't judge yourself for whatever decision you might have made."

Maybe she was right. And in the end, it was all just speculation anyway, because Nathan was gone and there was nothing left to fight for.

"Well, this conversation has taken a turn I wasn't expecting," Lindsay confided.

"For what it's worth, I *am* sorry you were hurt," Heather said.

She only nodded.

The other woman glanced at the clock. "I need to head back to work."

"One more question," Lindsay said.

Heather paused, and visibly braced herself.

"Did you change story-time groups at the library so that you wouldn't have to see me there?"

"I thought it would avoid any potential awkwardness—for both of us."

"You should switch Silver back to the Wednesday session."

"Why?" Heather asked warily.

"Because Irene is a great supervisor, but I'm a better storyteller."

Lindsay often thought about writing down words of advice for her daughter in the future. Today's advice would be: if and when you marry, don't bake a cake for your mother-in-law's birthday during your first year of marriage, because it sets a precedent of expectation that will trap you for all the years that follow.

And that precedent was why she was carefully swirling buttercream icing on a triple layer red velvet cake.

As a new daughter-in-law wanting to prove herself in the first year that she and Nathan were married, she'd made an angel food cake with fluffy white frosting and confetti sprinkles for Suzanne's birthday. Her mother-in-law had loved the cake so much that she'd remarked—no less than three times—how it was so much more personal than anything picked out of a display case at the bakery. So for Arthur's birthday, Lindsay got out her baking supplies again and made a chocolate cake with raspberry filling and chocolate ganache frosting.

Of course, she hadn't made birthday cakes for her in-laws during all the years that she and Nathan had lived in Moose Creek, because the logistics of shipping a cake twenty-five hundred miles were simply too daunting. (Because yes, she'd looked into it.) Instead, she'd shifted her focus to card making, sending birthday wishes with a personal touch and a first-class stamp.

Then Nathan died and she moved back to Haven with Elliott and Avenlea, only a few weeks before Arthur's birthday. Despite dealing with her own grief and sadness, she could see that her father-in-law was struggling with the loss of his only son. And though she didn't imagine he felt like celebrating at all, she made a cake in the hope that it might cheer him up a little. And then, a few months later, she'd made another cake for Suzanne's birthday, reestablishing the precedent.

Unfortunately, she wasn't finding the same pleasure she usually did in baking this time. Now that she knew about Nathan's affair, she couldn't help but associate his infidelity with Suzanne's birthday. And was it an affair? A fling? And did it matter? Whatever terminology was used, she didn't want to be reminded of it.

So she'd enlisted Elliott and Avenlea's help. They were both old enough now to follow simple instructions, and she was confident their involvement would make the task more fun. They'd been happy to measure and mix—and they loved the cracking eggs part, but when it was time for the cake to be sliced into layers and frosted, she decided that was a task better tackled by adult hands and set them up in the family room to watch TV.

And finally, it was done, which meant it was time to get the kids ready for a visit to Gramma and Grampa's.

Elliott was precisely where she'd left him—in front of the television, but the spot where Avenlea had been sitting was empty.

"Where's your sister?" she asked.

He didn't glance away from the screen as he shrugged. "Don't know."

Lindsay bit back a sigh, silently acknowledging that a five-year-old shouldn't be responsible for his little sister.

"Avenlea?"

She wasn't concerned about her daughter's whereabouts. Avenlea wasn't the type to venture outside on her own, and even if she'd been so inclined, both the front and back doors were wired so that they'd beep when they were opened. But Lindsay knew there was a whole lot of trouble she could get to inside the house.

"Avenlea?" she called out again.

"Up here, Mommy."

She started up the stairs, following the sound of her daughter's voice. "What are you doing?"

The answer to that question was evident even before Avenlea proudly said, "I p'ay dwess-up."

"I see that." Her little fashionista had decided to pair an ivory silk-and-lace nightgown with her own Minnie Mouse top and purple corduroy pants, adding a strand of fake pearls around her neck, Kate Spade sling backs on her feet and more makeup than a courtesan at Sheri's Ranch.

Avenlea shuffled forward, her child's-size-seven feet struggling to master the art of walking in adult-size-eight shoes with a two-inch heel. Lindsay quickly scooped her up—rescuing her from the shoes before she tipped over and broke something more valuable than the heels.

"What you were supposed to be doing, though, was watching *Paw Patrol* with Elliott," she reminded her daughter.

Of course, it was her own fault for leaving the little girl unsupervised while she'd decorated the birthday cake. Yes, Avenlea had been given strict instructions to sit with her brother, but Lindsay should have known better than to expect she'd actually do so. Or to imagine that Elliott wouldn't be so engrossed in the program that he might actually notice if his sister slipped away.

But seriously, it had been no more than ten minutes.

Fifteen at the most.

How could one little girl manage to do so much damage in such a short period of time?

It wasn't just the clothes spilling out of her dresser drawers or the contents of her jewelry box dumped out on her bed—it was also her makeup. Though Lindsay didn't often bother with more than foundation and mascara, she had some quality stuff for the rare occasions it was warranted. And she was pretty sure that was her favorite Estée Lauder "Potent" lipstick on the floor.

The fancy palette of eyeshadows—boasting thirty-two designer shades—had been a gift from Nathan one year for Christmas. And maybe she was ungrateful, but she felt that a gift of makeup from a husband was similar to that of a blender or a vacuum cleaner. But she'd occasionally lifted the heavy mirrored top and swiped a little "fawn" or "bronze" on her eyelids, so that she could tell him she used it.

It looked as though Avenlea had tried each and every one of the thirty-two shades, with a focus on the brightest colors in the palette. And she'd smeared blue and green and purple not just on her eyelids but all over her face.

"I wook pwe-ty?" she asked hopefully.

Like a rainbow fish, she thought, but knew her daughter would take that as a compliment.

"You look like you've got a lot of stuff all over your face," Lindsay said. "But I know my pretty girl is under there somewhere, so let's wash that stuff off and find her."

Avenlea folded her arms over her chest and shook her head. "No wash," she said stubbornly.

"Yes, wash," Lindsay insisted. "Because if we don't clean the makeup off, you might end up with itchy, bumpy spots."

The prospect of a rash motivated Avenlea to follow her mom into the en suite bath. Lindsay sat her on the counter and opened a blue jar. She applied the NIVEA cream carefully to her daughter's face, then dampened a soft washcloth with warm water to clean it off again.

"How did you even know how to put makeup on?" she asked, as she wiped gently with the cloth.

Avenlea scrunched her face up to protest the rubbing. "Gwamma."

"I can't imagine your gramma has ever worn blue or green or pink eyeshadow—and I guarantee you, she never wore all three colors at the same time."

"Pwe-ty co-wuhs."

Lindsay kissed the tip of her daughter's nose. "Pretty girl."

Avenlea beamed happily and lifted a hand to swipe at a hair that was stuck to her damp cheek.

That's when Lindsay saw what her daughter was wearing on her finger.

It seemed to be the story of his life—or at least the last two and a half years—that Mitch was making up excuses to drive into town and stop by the house on Winterberry Drive. At first, his visits had been motivated by concern for his friend, grieving the loss of her husband and struggling to adapt to her new reality as a single mom of two children. Children who were undoubtedly confused about the sudden changes in their lives and missing their dad. More recently, though, he'd been stopping by because he enjoyed hanging out with Lindsay and Elliott and Avenlea.

Spending family time with another man's family, according to his sister.

Luckily, he had a lot of experience ignoring his sister.

Today's excuse for stopping by?

"I owed you ice cream," he said, when Lindsay opened the door.

Her lips curved as she accepted the pint of rocky road. "And I still owe you babysitting money."

He waved it off, noting that her smile seemed a little strained at the edges. And when he looked at her more closely, he saw that her eyes were red-rimmed and her cheeks a little blotchy. "Have you been crying?"

"Apparently I don't wear enough makeup," she muttered, making her way to the kitchen to put the ice cream in the freezer.

"Huh?"

"Never mind."

The house was uncharacteristically quiet. "Are the kids in bed already?"

She nodded. "We had a busy day, and they both crashed early."

Which meant that the adults could chat without being interrupted—at least until Avenlea woke up, as he knew she did a couple of times each night, and wanted Mommy. So he took Lindsay's hand, led her into the family room and tugged her down onto the sofa beside him.

"Now tell me why you were crying," he said.

"You'll think I'm silly," she warned.

"Probably," he agreed, earning a small smile. "But tell me anyway."

"Avenlea decided to play dress-up today and got into my jewelry box…and she lost something that meant a lot to me."

"Not your wedding rings?" He'd noticed that she'd taken them off a few weeks earlier, after she'd found out about Nathan's infidelity, but of course she'd still be distressed if they went missing.

But Lindsay shook her head. "No. This was something I'd had a lot longer than those."

"The locket from your grandmother?" he guessed.

"No. And seriously, if I tell you, you're going to laugh because the only real value of the item is sentimental."

"It's okay," he said. "I already know you're a softy."

"It was my purple flower ring."

"You say that as if I should know what you're talking about, but I don't…wait a minute—do you mean the plastic ring that *I* gave you when we were kids?"

She nodded.

"I didn't realize you still had it." He was stunned—and absurdly touched—by this revelation.

He'd gotten the ring out of a vending machine at Jo's Pizza. He'd slid his quarter into the slot and hoped for a super bouncy ball as he cranked the knob to dispense his prize. When he opened the plastic clamshell container and saw the ring, he'd been deeply disappointed.

"What the heck am I supposed to do with a stupid ring?" his ten-year-old self had grumbled to his brother.

"Give it to your girlfriend," twelve-year-old MG had sneeringly replied.

"Lindsay?"

"You got another girlfriend?"

"She's just a friend," he said, because the word girlfriend *made him squirm ever since Megan Carmichael said she wanted to be his girlfriend and tried to kiss him by the monkey bars at recess. Thankfully, Mitch could run faster than she could.*

But the thought of kissing Lindsay didn't seem nearly as gross.

"You think she'd want it?" he asked, looking at the ring again.

MG shrugged. "If you wanna marry her someday, you hafta give her a ring."

Mitch was only ten—he wasn't ready to think about getting married.

But he supposed that everyone had to get married eventually, so why shouldn't he marry Lindsay?

Still, he'd carried that ring in his pocket for four days before he got up the nerve to ask her—and she'd said yes!

And then he'd mostly forgotten about it...

"Well, I did still have it," Lindsay confided now, sniffling a little. "And now I don't."

"It'll turn up somewhere," he said confidently. "Like those Mr. Potato Head accessories you find stuck between the cushions in the sofa. Or the little LEGO bricks that you never see until you step on them."

"She was wearing it when we left to go see Gramma T for her birthday today, but it wasn't until I asked her to put it back in my jewelry box before she had her bath that we realized it was gone."

He slid an arm across her shoulders and hugged her close. "I'd get you another one if I could, but I'm pretty sure they've updated the prizes in those vending machines at least once or twice in the past twenty years."

"I don't want another one. I want the one you gave me."

She swiped at a tear that spilled onto her cheek while Mitch tried to think of something he might say or do to make her feel better.

"You do realize it was a twenty-five-cent ring, don't you?" he asked gently.

"Of course I do, but..."

"But what?" he prompted.

"You know how a bride is supposed to have something old, something new, something borrowed and something blue?"

"It sounds vaguely familiar," he agreed.

"Well, that ring was my something old, when I married Nathan."

"You had that plastic ring when you walked down the aisle?"

"It wasn't on my finger, obviously. But it was stitched to the bottom hem, on the inside of my dress. It was my first engagement ring, from the first boy who ever loved me."

And wasn't that an unexpected revelation?

Equally unexpected was the emotion that filled his heart, even if he wasn't able—or maybe not willing—to label it.

"Well, don't give up hope," he said. "I'm sure it will reappear somewhere."

Because now that he knew how much that ring meant to her, he would turn the whole town upside down, if he had to, to get it back for her.

CHAPTER FOURTEEN

LINDSAY SETTLED DEEPER into the leather, almost moaning with pleasure as whatever magical contraption was inside the back of the chair moved up and down and across, massaging her tight muscles.

"It feels good, doesn't it?" Quinn asked, relaxing in a matching chair beside her friend.

"Sooo good," she agreed.

"Now aren't you glad you let me talk you into this?"

"Sooo glad."

Quinn laughed softly. "Obviously you were overdue for some pampering."

"It feels so indulgent to sip wine in the middle of the afternoon," she said, as she looked over the rim of her wineglass at her "Crimson" painted toenails.

"That's the point."

"It's just hard to find the time when the kids are so busy. Elliott has school and even though hockey's over for the season, soccer will be starting soon, and Avenlea has story time and swimming and Tiny Tumblers."

"Your fault," Quinn responded without sympathy. "No one told you to schedule every minute of their every day."

"It's hardly every minute of every day."

"Then you should be able to squeeze out a few minutes for this every now and again," her friend said, cleverly boxing Lindsay in with her own words.

But they'd been at the spa for more than a few minutes—most of the afternoon, in fact. And she really wasn't feeling guilty at all that her daughter was spending the day with Suzanne, who was also going to pick Elliott up from school so that Lindsay didn't have to worry about keeping track of time, and then both the kids were going to spend the night at their grandparents' house.

Since the day Lindsay had overheard Mitch and Suzanne talking about Nathan's affair, her mother-in-law couldn't do enough for her—almost as if she was trying to make up for raising a son who could disregard his wedding vows. Not that she and Suzanne had actually talked about what they'd each learned that day, but the truth seemed to be a constant undercurrent in every conversation. And when Lindsay had finally given in to her friend's nagging and asked Suzanne if she could watch Avenlea for half a day so that she could enjoy some time at the spa with Quinn, Suzanne had encouraged her to take the whole day, insisting that she deserved it.

Which was why, by four o'clock in the afternoon, she'd had a facial, a scalp massage, a manicure—with hot paraffin wax treatment—and a pedicure, and now she and Quinn were relaxing in the massage chairs, sipping wine and waiting for their nail polish to dry.

"This chair is great," Lindsay said now. "But next time, I'm going for a real full body massage."

"It's a good way to release the tension," Quinn said. "Not as good as hot, sweaty sex, but a decent alternative."

Lindsay sighed. "I can't remember the last time I had hot, sweaty sex. Truthfully, that might be why I want a massage—just to have someone touch my body."

"I know your coffee dates with Parker turned out to be a

dead end, but I bet your hunky rancher would oil you up if you just said the word."

"He's not *my* hunky rancher," she denied.

"Only because you haven't admitted how much you want him," Quinn insisted, wiggling her "Mauve On Over" toenails.

"I want us to stay friends."

"Haven't you ever heard of friends with benefits?"

"It was a good movie," Lindsay said. "But the ending actually contradicts the title."

"And that's what you're afraid of, isn't it?" her friend guessed. "Falling in love."

"I'm not afraid of falling in love. I'm afraid of losing my best friend."

"You and Nate were friends first, too," Quinn reminded her. "And that worked out."

"If being widowed after five years of marriage, including at least one confirmed indiscretion, counts as working out," she remarked dryly.

"I wasn't thinking about that," Quinn admitted. "Only about how much you loved one another."

"Which actually proves my point," Lindsay said. "I've already lost Nathan. I don't know what I'd do if I lost Mitchell, too."

"If you don't snap him up, some other woman is going to," Quinn warned. "Then you really will lose him, because no wife in her right mind is going to accept her husband being friends with an attractive widow with whom he has a history."

"A history of *friendship*," she pointed out.

"Dotted with a few steamy kisses."

"Still, a few kisses isn't any reason for a future wife to disapprove of our friendship."

"And she might pretend to be okay with it at first, but it won't take long for her to come up with ways to keep him busy, so that he doesn't have time to hang out with you. But those ploys will only be necessary until they have a child, then he will be too busy with his family to trek into town from the Circle G to check on his old pal."

Lindsay swallowed her last mouthful of wine. "Well, good," she said. "He deserves to fall in love, get married and have a family. And anyway, you seem to be forgetting the part where I tried to seduce him and he wasn't interested."

"I've seen the way he looks at you, and I guarantee he wasn't not interested," Quinn said. "You just picked the wrong time to let him know that you wanted to get naked with him."

"You mean an hour after finding out that your husband cheated isn't the right time?" she asked dryly.

"No man with an ounce of self-respect would have done anything different," her friend said. "It doesn't mean he doesn't want you."

Which was pretty much what he'd said, when she'd apologized for her impulsive and pathetic attempted seduction.

"Go to him now," Quinn urged.

"It's Friday."

"Do you have some moral objection to sex on Fridays?"

"I haven't had sex in more than two and a half years. I think I'm good to go on any day that ends in a *Y*," Lindsay replied. "My concern is that Mitchell might actually have other plans."

"So call him," her friend said, with a wink. "And tell him it's his lucky day."

She wanted to talk.

As if they didn't talk—or at least exchange text messages—almost every single day.

And she didn't want to talk on the phone; she wanted to come out to the ranch, but only after ensuring that his brother wasn't home.

So while Mitch waited for Lindsay to arrive, he busied himself tidying up. Not that the place was untidy (because Angela Gilmore hadn't raised her kids to be lazy or messy), but he needed to keep busy so that he didn't make himself crazy wondering what she wanted to talk about that necessitated a trip out to the Circle G on a Friday night.

He was wiping down the mirror in his bathroom—he and MG each had their own—when a tentative knock sounded.

He opened the door to find Lindsay standing on the wooden porch, a long coat open over a dark green wrap-style dress with a scoop neckline and short skirt. On her feet were knee-high black boots with a sexy two-inch heel.

"Hi," he said.

"Hi," she said back, and then, "I found you."

"You texted to make sure I was home," he reminded her.

She nodded. "I meant… You told me that I'd know where to find you…when I figured out what I wanted."

Now he knew what she was talking about.

And she was at his door—*hallelujah*.

Still, he curled his fingers into his palms so that he didn't reach out and haul her into his arms until he was sure that she was sure. "Have you figured it out now?"

She nodded. "I want you, Mitchell."

There was no hesitation in her words, no flicker in her gaze. She was sure—and so was he.

He hauled her into his arms, dragged her over the threshold, closed and locked the door and kissed her until they were both breathless.

"Just to clarify," he said, when he'd drawn enough air into his lungs to speak, "you didn't actually come here to talk?"

"I didn't come here to talk," she confirmed. "I just didn't want to admit this was a booty call in my text message."

"Is that what you think this is?"

"I came here to have sex with you, so…yes?"

"Maybe, just for tonight, you could let go of your need to put labels on everything," he suggested as he slid his hands up her back, then down again. And realized that she was still wearing her coat.

"And let's get rid of this, too," he said, helping her remove the outer garment and tossing it over the arm of the sofa. Though he was a little reluctant to see them go, her boots followed.

"We're both still wearing too many clothes," she told him.

It was pretty much an invitation to strip her naked and take her right there, and he was admittedly tempted. But he'd wanted her for so long—and denied his own desires for almost as long—and now that she was here, now that the moment he'd been waiting for was finally at hand, he didn't want to rush it. He wanted to savor every second, every kiss, every touch. He wanted to love her like she'd never been loved before, so she'd remember this night—and him—forever.

But before they got too far, he had to know: "Where are Elliott and Avenlea?"

"It's sweet that you'd ask about my children at a time like this," she said. "But I kind of hoped we'd focus on you and me tonight."

"I'm focused," he promised, lazily exploring her curves with his hands.

"They're spending the night at Gramma and Grampa T's."

"Are you spending the night here?"

"I could...if you decide that you want me to."

"I want you to," he said.

"I meant for you to decide...after."

"Do you think I'm going to change my mind...after?" he teased.

"I've only ever been with one man," she confided. "You might be disappointed."

"I'm not going to be disappointed," he said, his tone serious now. "And I promise to do my best to ensure you're not disappointed, either."

"Okay." She exhaled audibly, then smiled as she reached for the tie at the side of her dress.

"Let me," he suggested, capturing her hand and drawing it away.

"I was letting you, but you were taking too long."

"Didn't we just establish that we have all night?"

"Yeah, but I was kind of hoping we might do it more than once in that span of time."

"And we will," he promised. "Just relax."

"More than two years," she reminded him. "How am I supposed to relax when I'm so tightly wound up, I feel as if I'm going to explode?"

And he was definitely looking forward to *that*, but first he asked, "Do you trust me?"

"There's no one I trust more," she assured him.

"Then trust that I'm going to take care of you," he said, leading her to his bedroom.

He closed and locked that door, too. Though he wasn't expecting his brother to return tonight, several other family members also had keys to the bunkhouse, and he didn't trust all of them to respect the boundary of the locked exterior door.

Now he reached for the tie of her dress and tugged to release it—only to discover another tie on the inside. But he made quick work of that one, too, and finally parted the fabric to reveal lots of silky skin and a pale pink bra and panty set.

His hands trembled as they skimmed over her body, eager to touch. He wanted to be gentle, but his palms were hard and callused—an inevitable by-product of the manual labor he did every day. It occurred to him that he should apologize for their roughness, but when she sighed, it was a sound of pure pleasure that assured him she didn't mind.

He took his time exploring every dip and curve, gauging her enjoyment by the soft sounds she made.

"And you wanted to rush through this part," he teased.

"I didn't know about this part," she said, as his lips trailed kisses down her throat.

"Now you know." He whispered the words against her lips—a prelude to another long, slow kiss.

"You're so good at that," she murmured.

"Kissing is like dancing," he told her. "It's all about your partner."

"That's kind of cheesy…and really sweet."

He knew she was worried that making love would change things between them, but everything had already changed. Starting at New Year's Eve with that first kiss, the feelings that he'd kept buried deep for so long had risen to the surface again, demanding to be acknowledged, urging him to take hold with both hands of the chance he'd been waiting for—the woman he'd always wanted.

His mouth skimmed along the lacy edge of her bra; she shivered.

"Are you cold?"

She shook her head.

Her nipples were already peaked. He could see the tips pressing against the delicate lace. He brushed his lips over one tight point, through the thin fabric barrier, and heard her breath catch. He swirled his tongue around the nipple, then over it. She arched her back, wordlessly seeking more.

He unsnapped the clasp between her breasts and gently peeled back the cups, baring her breasts to his hungry gaze and hungrier mouth. She gasped when his lips closed over the bare flesh, and moaned when he began to suckle.

"Mitch…oh…"

He slid a hand between her thighs, dipping a finger beneath the swatch of lace, and found her not just wet but dripping.

Now *he* groaned.

He hooked his fingers in the sides of her panties and drew them over her hips and down her legs. Then he held up a hand, wordlessly asking for silence. "I just need a minute to worship quietly."

The comment surprised a laugh out of her, but he hadn't been joking. Never had he been with a woman who was more perfect to him. Not in a lingerie model sort of way, but in a real woman way, with actual hips and narrow silvery lines on her abdomen—evidence of the babies she'd carried, the lives she'd borne.

"I know I'm not the first woman you've ever seen naked," she said.

"No," he admitted. "But this is the first time I'm seeing *you* naked."

"When do I get to see you naked?" she wanted to know.

"When I'm not worried about losing what little self-control I'm clinging to," he told her.

"Self-control is overrated," Lindsay said, reaching for his belt.

He let her have her way, cooperating with her efforts to rid him of his clothes. Shirt, jeans and socks were quickly tossed aside, but then Mitchell took the reins again.

His lips feathered lightly over her skin, caressing more than kissing, skimming the hollow between her breasts, her belly button and lower. He parted her thighs and settled between them, his unshaven jaw rasping against her tender skin.

She cried out his name as her release came, hard and fast. Her fingers curled in the sheet, grasping for purchase as wave after wave of sensation crashed over her, but he didn't let up.

It was almost more than she could stand, and yet, it wasn't enough. She wanted the fulfillment that she knew would only come when he was buried deep inside her.

"Mitchell...please."

He reached into the drawer of his bedside table then and found a square packet, tearing it open and sheathing himself to ensure their mutual protection. Then, finally, he lowered himself into position and slowly eased into her, inch by inch, giving her body time to accept and accommodate all of him.

Her breath shuddered out of her lungs as he filled her.

"Okay?" he asked.

She nodded.

He started to move, slowly at first, and new waves of sensation began to build, churning like the sea before a storm.

Then faster. Deeper. Harder.

The storm was all around her now, battering at her from all directions. She held on to him, her hands clutching at his shoulders, clinging to her rock.

"I've got you," he promised, just before he captured her mouth again.

They were connected, from head to toe and in between. Two bodies joined in pursuit of one goal—mutual pleasure...and finding it together.

She was cradled in strong arms, wrapped in the warmth of his hard body. She didn't have the energy to move. Or maybe it was the will that she lacked. Yeah, it had taken them a long time to get here, but right now, she was exactly where she wanted to be.

Who knew that Mitchell would prove to be such an attentive and thorough lover? Well, any one of the women who'd found her way to his bed before Lindsay, but she wasn't going to think of them now. She wasn't going to think about anything but the fact that she was up close and personal with a naked man whose hard body was already showing a willingness to go another round.

"Quinn was right," she murmured, as he nuzzled her throat.

"About what?"

"She said that hot, sweaty sex is the best way to release tension."

"You were very tense," he noted.

She laughed softly.

And that was another surprise.

She'd been worried that making love with Mitchell would somehow change their whole relationship, because sex had a way of pulling back the curtain and exposing all of one's intimate secrets. She hadn't considered that Mitchell already knew her more intimately than anyone else ever had—that the only part of herself she hadn't shared was her body. And after even that had been given to him, she actually felt closer and more connected.

And when he rolled her onto her back and rose over her, they connected again.

CHAPTER FIFTEEN

LINDSAY WAS HAPPY when the spring sunshine finally melted the last lingering vestiges of snow from the ground. Or maybe it was her spring romance that was responsible for the lightness in her heart.

She enjoyed all the seasons, but the twice-daily journey to and from Ridgeview Elementary School was a lot easier when she didn't have to push Avenlea's stroller through snow and slush. Today her daughter had insisted on walking, and she wasn't yet sure if that was a bonus or not.

As they made their way along the familiar route, Lindsay found herself pausing in front of a two-story red brick house with white shutters. It had been Abe and Ethel Nicholson's house for as long as she could remember, then Abe died and Ethel moved to Elko to be closer to her son and grandchildren. The house had sold quickly and, according to the sign on the lawn, was for sale now again. But it was the woman cleaning the windows, side by side with a little girl, who caught her attention.

As if sensing her presence—or maybe she could see the sidewalk reflected in the glass—Heather turned around.

"Hey," Lindsay said awkwardly. "I didn't know you lived here."

"For now," the other woman agreed.

"Sto-wee!" Silver shouted, obviously recognizing Lindsay as a storyteller from the library.

"Hello, Silver." She urged Avenlea forward, to introduce the two girls. "This is my daughter, Avenlea. Avenlea, this is Silver."

"Hi," Avenlea said.

Silver responded with a shy smile and a wave.

Lindsay found herself looking from one girl to the other, searching for signs that they shared a father. She wasn't sure if she was relieved or disappointed that there were no glaring similarities, but there were definite hints of the little girl's paternity: the curls in her baby-soft hair were reminiscent of Elliott's curls; the cupid's-bow mouth was shaped just like Avenlea's; and the clear blue color of her eyes was Nathan's.

"I guess your husband decided to take that job in El Paso," Lindsay said.

Heather nodded. "He's there now, house-hunting."

"Are you looking forward to the move?"

"Change is always hard, but yes, I think it will be good for all of us—and undoubtedly a relief to certain other people in this town."

Lindsay frowned, wondering who she could be talking about. Only a handful of people knew the truth about Silver's paternity and she couldn't imagine anyone—

"We crossed paths with Nathan's mom at The Paper Dragon," Heather told her, naming the specialty card and gift shop on Main Street. "Or maybe I should say we *almost* crossed paths with Nathan's mom, because when she saw us, she quickly turned the other way."

"I think she's uncomfortable acknowledging that her son had two daughters with two different women only eight months apart."

"Especially when one of those women was his wife."

Lindsay nodded. "But she'll come around," she said, wanting to believe it was true.

"It doesn't matter," Heather said.

But of course it did matter, because Suzanne wasn't just Nathan's mom—she was Silver's grandmother.

Obviously the toddler had lots of people in her life who loved her, but the apparent rejection of her existence by family would sting. And even though Silver wasn't aware of the connection or the rejection, Heather was, and Lindsay understood the instinctive need of a mother to protect and soothe her child.

"And anyway, the fewer people who know—or acknowledge—the truth, the better. I dealt with enough whispers and snickers when my belly popped out only two months after James and I were married."

"People will talk, if and when the truth of Silver's paternity gets out," Lindsay acknowledged. "And it will be the hottest topic around town for ten minutes, until something newer and hotter comes up, so you shouldn't waste your time worrying about it."

"You're not worried about how that ten minutes of gossip will affect Elliott and Avenlea?"

"Of course I am," she admitted. "But I think they'll accept the truth easier, in the end, if it isn't covered up by a lie."

"That's something to think about," the other woman mused.

"I just want to know that you're not leaving Haven because we came back."

"We're not," Heather said. "We're leaving because this is a great career opportunity for James. They've offered him the position twice before, and if he turns it down this time, it probably won't be offered to him again."

Lindsay nodded. "Then I'll wish you luck in Texas and ask you to keep in touch."

The other woman was obviously surprised by this. "Why would you want me to keep in touch?"

"Because Silver is Elliott and Avenlea's half sister," she said. "And regardless of how you and I might feel about one another, they're family."

Heather nodded slowly as she shifted her gaze to the two little girls, their heads close as they chatted together.

Sisters already on their way to becoming friends.

"There's no need to be nervous," Angela Gilmore said, joining Lindsay at the paddock fence late the following Saturday morning.

"What gave me away?"

"Your white-knuckle grip on the rail."

Lindsay looked down at her hands. Sure enough, the knuckles were white and her fingernails were biting into the wood. She'd hoped to take pictures, to document this milestone moment, but there was no point in taking her phone out of her pocket when she knew she wouldn't be able to hold it steady.

"Mitch won't let her get hurt," Angela assured her.

"I know," she agreed.

And yet, that knowledge did nothing to loosen the knots in her belly.

"But she's a little girl on a big horse," the older woman noted, instinctively understanding the source of Lindsay's apprehension.

Technically Maurice was a pony but, compared to her daughter, he was a beast.

"Mitchell put Elliott on the back of his first pony before he was three, so he insisted that Avenlea should have the same opportunity." Elliott was riding, too, sitting tall in the saddle of Gaston—a second pony that Mitchell had on a lead.

"And look at her," Angela urged. "She has absolutely no fear."

"Sometimes a little fear is healthy," Lindsay noted.

Mitchell's mom chuckled. "I heard about her jumping off the climber at the park."

"She's lucky she didn't need stitches."

And Lindsay was lucky that the amount of blood seemed to have dissuaded her daughter from repeating the action—so far anyway.

"Of course, she'll probably forget all about the park now and want to come out here every day to ride the pony."

"It doesn't seem that many years ago that you were out here almost every day to go riding with Mitchell," Angela noted.

"I know my mom sometimes complained that I spent more time here than at home," Lindsay agreed.

"We were always happy to see you. And while I'm sorry for the circumstances that brought you home again, I'm glad you're home."

"I'm glad to be back," she agreed.

Angela gave her a quick hug.

They watched for several more minutes, Angela chatting away—deliberately distracting Lindsay from worrying about her children.

The "lesson" didn't last long, but both the kids were grinning when Mitchell set them back on solid ground.

Lindsay exhaled a silent sigh of relief as they raced toward her, still wearing their riding helmets.

"Now it's your turn," Angela said to her. "Go saddle up Reba and take a ride with Mitchell."

Lindsay immediately shook her head. "I can't."

"Why not?"

"Because I haven't been on the back of a horse in…years."

"Then you're long overdue. Go on," Mitchell's mom insisted. "I'll keep an eye on Elliott and Avenlea."

But Mitchell was one step ahead, and the mare was already tacked and waiting for her when Elliott and Avenlea skipped off with Angela, happy to embark on new adventures.

He helped her up in the saddle and encouraged her to walk around the paddock, to get accustomed to the feel of the horse beneath her, while he went to tack his own mount. She signaled the mare to switch from a walk to a trot.

"Looks like it's coming back to you," he noted approvingly, as he led Kenny out of the barn.

"Just like riding a bike," she said. "Except it's riding a horse."

He grinned and effortlessly vaulted into the saddle on the back of the chestnut gelding.

Lindsay, feeling a little more confident now, urged the mare to canter, then tested control by bringing her back down to a trot and a walk again.

"But I have to admit, it feels as if you and your mom conspired against me," she grumbled, as he brought Kenny up alongside Reba.

"I'm not forcing you to go anywhere you don't want to go," he said. "We can stay right here in the paddock, if that's where you're more comfortable."

Though his tone was casual enough, she sensed that there was a deeper meaning to his words—almost as if he was asking about their relationship as much as a trail ride.

She lifted her eyes to meet his. "Open the gate."

He grinned again and did as she instructed.

She let him lead the way, and they headed toward the mountains that rose up in the distance, following the path of Crooked Creek. Fed by the recent snowmelt, the creek, for which the neighboring ranch had been named, gurgled and bubbled over the rocks.

"Hold up," Mitchell said.

She held up, thinking that he'd spotted some kind of hazard that might spook her mount into throwing its rider. "What is it—a snake?"

"Nothing like that," he assured her, as he brought his mount close to hers. Then he tipped his hat back, lowered his head and kissed her, long and slow and deep.

"I'll hold up for one of your kisses anytime," she said, when he finally eased his mouth from hers.

"I couldn't resist," he told her. "You just look so pretty, with your cheeks pink from the wind and your eyes shining bright."

"I forgot how much I loved riding," she admitted. "No doubt I'll regret this outing tomorrow, when every muscle in my body aches, but right now it feels good."

"Yeah, it does," he said, brushing his lips over hers again. "I'm glad you let my mom talk you into it."

"Have you ever tried to say no to your mom?"

"I've tried," he said. "I haven't succeeded."

"Because she's a five-foot four-inch bulldozer," Lindsay said.

He chuckled. "That's a pretty good description—and one that she'd own proudly."

"So…how long do you think we can be gone before she starts to worry—or wonder?" she asked curiously.

"Are you kidding? She's so thrilled to have Elliott and Avenlea to dote on, we could be gone for a week and, when we returned, she'd ask why we came back so soon."

"Well, it's not really fair, you know. All of David Gilmore's adult children are married—or at least engaged—and having babies. Is it too much to ask for at least one of her kids to give her a grandbaby or two to spoil?"

"Sounds like you two had quite a chat," he mused wryly.

"I think she was trying to take my mind off the fact that my not yet three-year-old daughter was riding a pony that weighs twenty times more than Avenlea."

"You know I'd never let her be hurt."

"And that's the only reason she was in that saddle."

She felt her cell phone vibrate inside her pocket. "It's a message from Suzanne," she said, when she'd pulled it out to glance at the screen.

"Is there a problem?"

"A partner from Arthur's old firm is in town and wants to take them out for dinner, so she's asking if we can postpone the sleepover until next week." Lindsay was already texting a reply.

"I guess that means you don't have to rush back to town."

"It also means that I won't be able to come back here tonight," she said, genuinely disappointed.

"I could come to your place," he suggested.

She shook her head. "A tempting offer, but you know Avenlea wakes up several times in the night."

"So we'll reschedule for next week," he said.

"Or..."

"I'm listening."

"If I remember correctly, there's a hunting cabin not too far from here."

"On the other side of the creek," he told her.

Which meant it was on Crooked Creek property.

"That's right," she said, nodding. "It was Brielle who had a sleepover there one time." She smiled. "Which is how I know where the key is."

Mother's Day started early for Lindsay, with a video chat with her mom in Phoenix. The glittery sparkle on Marilyn Delgado's cheek confirmed that she'd received the cards that Elliott and Avenlea had made and Lindsay had sent—along with an electronic gift card for her favorite boutique in their retirement village.

The cards had turned out well, and the kids had seemed to enjoy making them, but Lindsay had already decided that next year she'd give her money to Hallmark and save herself finding glitter everywhere more than two weeks after their card-making session.

After breakfast they stopped by to see Aunt Kristyne, who was celebrating her first ever Mother's Day. They didn't stay long, because it was obvious Gabe had plans to completely spoil the new mom—and because they still had more flowers and glittery cards to deliver to Gramma T.

At the Thomases' house on Miners' Pass, they sat out on the back deck, chatting and enjoying the afternoon sunshine. Elliott and Avenlea, never happy sitting for too long unless there was a screen in front of them, were kicking a ball around in the backyard. When they'd worked up a thirst, Arthur took them into the house to get them a drink.

"And maybe some ice cream," he said with a wink.

It was the perfect opening, Lindsay decided, to talk to her mother-in-law without the kids interrupting.

"I thought you might like to know that Silver comes to story time at nine-thirty on Wednesdays."

"Why would that be of any interest to me?"

"Because she's your granddaughter and you should get to know her."

Suzanne's hand trembled slightly as she lifted her cup of tea, then set it down again without drinking. "I don't understand how you can be so accepting of the...situation."

"I'm never going to be happy that Nate cheated on me," Lindsay said. "But he did, and a beautiful little girl came out of it."

Her mother-in-law was quiet for a long minute before she said, "I heard they're moving to Texas."

Lindsay nodded. "At the end of the summer."

"That's probably for the best. Then you won't have to worry about running into that woman and her daughter every time you run an errand."

"I'm not worried."

"You should be." Suzanne pressed her lips together to hide their quivering. "Because if people knew—or even suspected—that Nathan was the father of that child...they'd say horrible things about my son. Your husband."

"Horrible things such as that he cheated on his pregnant wife with his high school girlfriend and got her pregnant?"

"He made a mistake."

"No." Lindsay shook her head. "He broke his vows. It wasn't an accident—it was a choice."

"I wish he'd never come home for my party," her mother-in-law confided now. "If he'd stayed in Alaska, it never would have happened."

Lindsay had thought the same thing when she first learned of her husband's infidelity. But once she'd taken some time to think about it, she wasn't so sure. In any event, the how and why and even the who didn't matter—what mattered was Silver.

"I know how much it means to you to know that a part of Nathan lives on in his children. Well, a part of him lives on in Silver, too. How can you not want to know her? To love her as much as I know you love Elliott and Avenlea?"

"I know she's a part of him," Suzanne finally admitted, her eyes shiny with unshed tears. "But acknowledging her paternity seems disloyal...to you."

Lindsay's throat tightened with unexpected emotion. "The human heart has an amazing capacity to love," she said gently. "Don't close yours off from the possibility of loving Silver— or letting her love you and Arthur. And I know she will, if you give her a chance."

By the time Lindsay got her kids home later that afternoon, she was ready for a nap. Instead, she had to put fresh sheets on the beds she'd stripped earlier that morning—Avenlea's first, because the little girl was overdue for *her* nap—then deal with the laundry that had piled up throughout the week.

Thankfully, Elliott was content to play with his LEGO bricks while she tackled the chores, and she managed to clean both the upstairs and downstairs bathrooms in between loads of washing.

Oh, the glamorous life of a single mom, she thought, as she walked out of the laundry room with a basket of clean clothes on her hip.

"I'm hungry," Elliott said, when she peeked in the family room to check on him.

Avenlea, now up from her nap, echoed the sentiment. "I hun-wee, too."

"Me, three," Lindsay said.

Her son wasn't amused. "What's for supper?"

Which was when she realized that in all the planning she'd done for the day, she hadn't given a single thought to dinner.

"I'll take a look in the freezer to see if we've got any chicken fingers," she decided. Though she preferred to make her own chicken strips, she tried to keep a box of the frozen variety in the freezer for occasions such as this.

"Yay!" Avenlea said, proving that they were indeed a go-to kid-pleaser.

Unfortunately, there were only three chicken fingers—and a whole bunch of crumbs—left in the box.

"How about cheese strings and olives?" she suggested, thinking of the appetizer plate Mitchell had managed to put together on New Year's Eve despite her fridge being mostly empty.

"Olives?" Elliott made a face. "Yuck."

"Yuck," Avenlea echoed, conveniently forgetting that she gobbled them like candy whenever Lindsay put them on the table.

"Okay, let's figure out a Plan C," she said, moving things around in the freezer in the hope that she might find one of her mom's neatly labeled containers hidden at the back.

"Doorbell!" Elliott shouted, in case she hadn't heard it.

"Don't open—"

"It's Uncle Mitch!" he called out.

"Uncamitch!" Avenlea echoed.

"He's got pizza!"

"An' fwo-wuhs!"

Lindsay closed the freezer and went to the door to greet her friend (with some far-too-infrequent but spectacular benefits).

"Happy Mother's Day," he said, offering her a bouquet of orange lilies, yellow gerberas and red carnations with spikes of purple Veronica flowers and pennycress.

"Oh, Mitchell—they're beautiful." She kissed his cheek—the only display of affection she would allow herself in front of her children.

He slid his arm around her, to give her a friendly hug, but let his hand slide over the curve of her butt as she moved away.

She sent him a warning look; he grinned, unrepentant.

"Thank you for the flowers. And the pizza."

"I didn't want you to have to cook today."

An incredibly thoughtful gesture, but it was his company that really made her happy. She hadn't expected to see him today, assuming that he'd be spending the day celebrating his own mother.

While she filled a vase with water for her flowers, Mitchell got out plates and napkins. They moved easily around one another—and Elliott and Avenlea—in the kitchen, almost as if they were a family.

And maybe they could be, someday. But now, she was trying to enjoy the moments they had together and not think too far ahead.

After everyone had their fill of pizza, Lindsay started to push away from the table, but Mitchell asked her to stay put. He whispered first in Elliott's ear, then in Avenlea's, and her children scampered away.

"Are you conspiring again?" she asked suspiciously.

"It's not a conspiracy, it's a surprise," he said, as the kids came back to the table.

He nodded to Avenlea, who brought her hands out from behind her back to give her mom an oversize envelope. Inside was an oversize card, obviously homemade but thankfully not covered in glitter.

The front cover read: "Happy Mother's Day to the best mom..." And when she opened it up, the sentiment finished inside with, "Hands down!"

And around the words were their handprints, labeled and dated for posterity.

"Oh." She blinked away the tears that filled her eyes again and looked at Mitchell questioningly. "Did *you* do this?"

He shook his head. "I wish I could take the credit, but no, it was my mom. The day you brought the kids out to the Circle G. Actually, it was Olivia's idea—something they do as an art project at school."

"Thank you," she said, opening her arms to draw her son and daughter in for a family hug.

"There's something else, too," Elliott said, wriggling free of her grasp to give her a small square box neatly wrapped in silver paper with a tiny gold bow.

She recognized the trademark wrapping of The Gold Mine—a local jewelry store. She turned the box over and slid a fingernail beneath the seam, breaking the tape.

"Just tear the paper," Mitchell urged.

"It's too pretty to tear," she protested.

"Is she this careful on Christmas morning?" he asked Elliott. The little boy nodded, rolling his eyes.

"It takes forever and ever."

"Forever? I think I'd have to see it to believe it."

She wanted to say that maybe this year he would, but she wasn't sure if they were at the stage in their relationship where they should be planning more than seven months into the future. Instead, she focused on unwrapping her present, then opening the hinged lid of the gray velvet box.

Inside was a delicate gold chain with a heart-shaped pendant inscribed with the word "Mommy" in cursive script.

"This is—" she had to pause to clear her throat "—really beautiful."

"Turn it over," Mitchell suggested.

She turned the heart over to see that Elliott and Avenlea's birth dates had been engraved on the reverse.

"You like it?" Elliott asked.

"It is the best Mother's Day present ever," she said, drawing both her kids close for another hug—and kisses this time.

And then, because she couldn't resist, she kissed Mitchell, too.

The next weekend was Avenlea's third birthday.

Lindsay had invited several of her daughter's friends from day care to the party. Of course it was a princess-themed party, with pink and purple streamers and balloons, silver crowns for the guests to decorate, and a pin-the-tiara-on-the-princess game.

Of course, when "Unca Mitch's" surprise bouncy castle was delivered, a few of the neighborhood children excitedly crashed the party, too. (Wanting to prove that she was a big girl now that she was three, Avenlea was trying hard to enunciate her words more clearly.)

There were crown-shaped peanut butter and jelly sandwiches (she'd checked to make sure none of the guests had a nut allergy), fruit wands and sparkling raspberry lemonade, and vanilla cupcakes with pink icing or chocolate cupcakes with purple icing for dessert.

The party was scheduled to last ninety minutes—long enough for the guests to decorate their crowns, play some games, and have something to eat and drink, and short enough that they'd be on their way home before they started getting bored or cranky, as three year olds tended to do. Pickup time was noted on the invitation as two o'clock; it was now almost four and Lindsay had only just sent the last birthday guest home with her princess-themed loot bag.

"I thought you said this was going to be a low-key party," Kristyne commented, as she settled at the kitchen table to nurse her baby.

"That was the plan," Lindsay agreed, ignoring the twinge she felt as she watched Harper suckle at her mother's breast. She began to pack up the leftovers.

She'd still been nursing Avenlea when Nathan was killed, but the upheaval and stress had forced her to switch her infant daughter to a bottle much sooner than she'd intended. Not that Avenlea seemed to have suffered in any way because of it, but Lindsay couldn't help feeling as if they'd both been short-changed as a result of the abrupt weaning. Of course, the loss of the little girl's father was a much bigger struggle, and when Lindsay had said her final goodbye to her husband, she'd been certain she was saying goodbye to any hope of expanding her family.

She and Mitch hadn't talked about what the future might hold for them—they were nowhere near that stage in their relationship. But a tiny hope had begun to resurrect itself within her.

"Do you need me to tell you that a bouncy castle is not low-key?" Kristyne asked her now. "No wonder all the neighborhood kids were here."

"The bouncy castle was Mitchell's doing." She looked out the window over the sink that gave her a prime view of the backyard, where Mitchell and Gabe were jumping inside the inflatable playhouse with Elliott and Avenlea. Just like little kids.

"And the smile on your face... I'm guessing that's Mitchell's doing, too?" her sister said, sounding amused.

Lindsay didn't even try to deny it. "Yeah."

"It's been a long time since I've seen you smile like that," Kristyne noted. "It makes me happy to see you happy."

"I am happy," she said, as she continued to wrap up the leftover food. "Sometimes I worry that I don't have any right to be so happy."

"Why would you say that?" her sister demanded.

"Because Nathan's gone and—"

"Stop right there," Kristyne interjected. "How can you think you owe him any loyalty—more than two years after his death—when he didn't offer you the same while he was alive?"

"It's not about loyalty," Lindsay denied. "At least, I don't think so. It's just that he was my first love...and I really thought it would last forever."

It felt silly to admit it aloud, especially to her sister, who, though two years younger, had a lot more experience with romantic relationships.

"Nathan wasn't your first love," Kristyne said confidently. "He might have been your first lover, but you loved Mitchell first."

"That was nothing more than a childhood crush."

"And now?" her sister prompted.

"And now..." her gaze shifted to the window again "...we're taking things one day at a time."

"So you haven't talked about getting married and having a couple more kids?" Kristyne, always attuned to her sister's thoughts and feelings, pressed.

"No." Lindsay's response was immediate and adamant.

"Why not?" Kristyne eased her nipple from her daughter's mouth and shifted the baby to the other breast to continue feeding. "If I'd had any doubts before today, watching Mitchell with all those kids proved he'd be a great father."

Lindsay had watched him, too. And watching him, her heart had yearned.

"And did you see him with Harper?" her sister asked.

"I saw the panicked look on his face when you shoved your baby into his arms."

"I had to go to the bathroom, Gabe wasn't in the immediate vicinity and my bladder control isn't what it used to be," Kristyne said in her defense. "But by the time I came back, Mitchell had Harper tucked in the crook of his arm and was cooing to her like a pro."

"Yeah, I saw that, too," Lindsay confided.

"You always said you wanted four kids."

"One day at a time," she reminded her sister.

"Hmm," Kristyne said. "Are you worried that the Thomases will disapprove of your relationship with Mitchell?"

"No," she said. Truthfully, she hadn't given any thought to how Nathan's parents might react when they found out that she was in a relationship with someone new—until today, at the party, when Mitchell leaned close to say something to her and she caught Suzanne frowning in their direction.

"Because I noticed that they didn't hang around for very long this afternoon," her sister continued.

"They were on their way to Elko, to meet friends for dinner."

"I guess that would explain why they were overdressed for a backyard party." Kristyne lifted the now-sleeping infant to her shoulder and gently rubbed her back.

"I can do that part," Lindsay said, reaching for the baby.

Her sister relinquished her daughter willingly so that she could more easily refasten the cups of her nursing bra.

As Kristyne was adjusting her top, Lindsay heard her computer ringing in the den.

"Mom and Dad said they were going to Skype at four thirty," she said, suddenly remembering.

"You answer that—I'll get the birthday girl," Kristyne said.

Within minutes, everyone was gathered around the computer to join in the conversation. Of course, Avenlea was front and center, leaning close to the camera to ensure Gramma and Grampa D could see her as she regaled them with details of her party.

"An' we jumped in the bouncy castle an' had cupcakes an' pwesents."

"You had a bouncy castle?" Though Marilyn was talking to her granddaughter, she looked at the birthday girl's mom quizzically.

"Courtesy of Uncle Mitch," Lindsay explained, with a pointed glance at the man in question.

He just shrugged and grinned.

"An' I gots wots an' wots of pwesents," Avenlea announced. "Even Hawpuh bwin'd me a pwesent."

"Brought," Lindsay automatically corrected her daughter.

"A Bitty Baby Doll," Avenlea continued. "And Auntie Kwisty ate Hawpuh's cupcake *an'* hew own cupcake."

"Tattletale," Kristyne muttered from the background.

"She ate mine, too," Gabe piped up.

"They were minicupcakes," his wife muttered. "And the doctor said that I need an extra four to five hundred calories while I'm nursing."

"I don't think she meant four to five hundred cupcake calories," her husband said.

"But don' wo-wy," Avenlea continued talking to her grandparents. "Mommy saved cupcakes for you. She put 'em in the fwee-zuh so Auntie Kwisty couldn't find 'em."

"But now I know where to look," Kristyne said, grinning.

Avenlea clapped a hand over her mouth.

"I think it's a little late for that," Lindsay told her daughter.

Marilyn and Jackson exchanged amused glances. "Well, that was very thoughtful. Thank you, Lindsay. And we're sorry we couldn't be there for your party, Avenlea, but we're happy to know you had a good birthday."

"'S'okay," the birthday girl said. "Weast you sended a pwesent."

"Avenlea," Lindsay admonished, heat rising in her cheeks. "It's about the *thought*, not the *present*."

"Well, I'm gwad Gwamma an' Gwampa *fought* to send a pwesent," Avenlea said, making everyone laugh.

CHAPTER SIXTEEN

"I THINK I'D RATHER wrangle cattle than chase after kids all day," Mitch said. "I'm exhausted."

"It was a busy day," Lindsay acknowledged, dropping onto the sofa beside him and letting her head tip back against his shoulder. "But a really good one."

"All the kids seemed to have fun."

"Mmm-hmm," she agreed. "I just wish Silver had come to the party."

"You invited Heather's daughter?" He didn't know why he was surprised—it was exactly the kind of thing Lindsay would do.

She nodded. "Heather RSVP'd her regrets, but I was hoping she'd change her mind."

"It might have been interesting if she'd shown up when Arthur and Suzanne were here. Avenlea's party would have been the talk of the town—a bouncy castle *and* fireworks."

"Or you would have been disappointed by the lack of fireworks," she said. "Because there weren't any when Arthur came into the library last week while Silver was there for story time."

"I'm guessing the timing of his visit wasn't a coincidence?"

Now she shook her head. "He wanted to meet his youngest granddaughter."

"How did that go?"

"I wasn't privy to their conversation, but I think it went well," she said. "I saw him talking to Heather while Silver played at the train table with a couple other kids, and though they left a short while later, Arthur stopped at the desk first to thank me."

"Suzanne wasn't there?"

"No, but I have no doubt he'll bring her around."

"Whatever Suzanne knew or suspected three years ago, it seems safe to assume that she didn't share it with her husband," he noted.

"I'd agree. As smart as my father-in-law is when it comes to legal matters, he's remarkably oblivious to the world around him."

"It was good to see him today," Mitch said. "And Suzanne."

"It was good of you to give up your Saturday to help with the birthday party."

"I had fun, too," he said.

"You did look like you were having fun," she acknowledged. "Especially when you took off your boots and joined the kids in the bouncy castle."

He grinned. "Yeah, it was worth every penny."

She shook her head, but he could tell that she was fighting against the smile tugging at the corners of her mouth.

"Do you know what I was thinking tonight—when you were helping get Elliott and Avenlea ready for bed?" she asked.

"'Will these kids please go to sleep so that I can get this man naked'?" he guessed.

She lost the battle against the smile. "Aside from that, I was thinking about how easy you are with the kids, how good you are at all the family stuff."

"You have great kids," he said.

"And I was wondering," she continued, determined to finish her thought, "why you never got married and had a bunch of kids of your own."

"I'm only thirty-four years old," he reminded her. "Maybe you shouldn't write me off just yet."

"You're thirty-four years old and you haven't, as far as I know, ever had a relationship that lasted longer than two years. And your most recent only lasted six months."

"Are you worried that our relationship might have an expiration date?" he asked her.

"No. Maybe."

"Well, don't," he told her. "There's one very specific reason that none of those other relationships worked out—because I was already in love with you."

He hadn't meant to tell her just yet. And not when they were casually sprawled on her sofa at the end of a long day. That was his mistake.

And though he'd known they were at different stages in their relationship, he hadn't anticipated that she'd be surprised to learn the truth of his feelings for her. But maybe he should have, because he'd been in love with her for half his life and she was still trying to wrap her head around the fact that she was in an intimate relationship with someone other than the man she'd married.

So he'd asked her not to say anything, inwardly cringing as he imagined the various ways she might respond.

You have to know how much I care about you.

You're one of my best friends in the world—of course I love you, too.

And he really didn't want to hear either of those sentiments.

So he'd kissed her goodbye and left before he pushed her for more than she was ready to give.

For weeks—okay, months—he'd been reminding himself to be patient. To remember that he'd loved her a lot longer than she'd loved him. Because although she hadn't said the words back to him that night, he had to believe that she loved him, too.

But she'd been through a lot in the past few years. Not just the sudden and unexpected death of her husband, but the more recent discovery of his infidelity and the existence of another child. She was smart to be cautious, to take some time, to be sure.

And while she was taking her time, he would be there for her, as he'd always been there for her. Showing her how good they were together—not just him and Lindsay, but Elliott and Avenlea, too. A family.

So the following Saturday, he showed up at her door again, not to put any pressure on her but hopefully persuade her to bring the kids out to the Circle G to go riding again. Then they could barbecue some steaks—he'd cut up steak bites for Elliott and Avenlea to dip in ketchup—and just enjoy a beautiful day together.

His easy smile slipped when Suzanne Thomas answered the door and he realized that he'd been so preoccupied with making plans for the day, he hadn't noticed that the vehicle in the driveway didn't belong to Lindsay but to her mother-in-law.

After his friend's passing, Mitch had occasionally gone into town to check in on Suzanne and Arthur, and he knew they'd appreciated his efforts. But since he'd confronted Suzanne about Nathan's affair, he'd received a much chillier reception whenever their paths crossed. While Arthur seemed to be of the opinion that what was done was done, Suzanne appeared to blame him for forcing her to acknowledge her son's infidelity.

"Hello, Mrs. Thomas," he said.

"Mitchell." She inclined her head slightly. "Lindsay didn't mention that you would be stopping by."

"She didn't know," he said. "I had some things to do in town and thought I'd take a chance that she'd be home."

"Well, she's not," Suzanne said.

Her polite but cool response was almost drowned out by Avenlea shouting: "Unca Mitch! Unca Mitch!"

He scooped her up in his arms; she planted a smacking kiss on his cheek.

"Are you gonna have wunch wif us? Gwamma's makin' mac an' cheese not fwom a box!"

"Mac and cheese not from a box?" he echoed incredulously. "I didn't know there was any such thing."

Which was a great big fib, because his mom had always made it from scratch, too. But there were admittedly a couple of the trademark blue boxes in his pantry at the Circle G.

"Can you stay?" Avenlea asked. "P'ease?"

Suzanne didn't object to the invitation, but she didn't say anything to indicate that he would be welcome to join them, either. But that was okay—he had no desire to prolong this awkward encounter with her.

"Sorry, princess. I've got some errands to run."

"I wun ew-ans wif you?"

"Not today," he said.

"'Mo-wow?" she asked hopefully.

He had to smile. "I'll let you know. Okay?"

"'Kay," she agreed, bending over his arm to indicate that she wanted down.

He set her back on the floor and she raced off again, returning to whatever she'd been doing when she heard him at the door.

Suzanne, who'd watched the interaction with thinly veiled disapproval, seemed eager now to send him on his way. "When Lindsay gets home from Sunset Vista, I'll be sure to tell her that you stopped by."

The mention of Sunset Vista was clearly to make a point—and not at all subtle.

Mitch knew that Lindsay visited the memorial gardens regularly if not frequently—usually on Nathan's birthday, their anniversary and the anniversary of his death. Today wasn't any of those days. But he pushed his questions about the visit aside in the interest of making peace with Suzanne, because he knew it was important for his future with Lindsay that he get along with her in-laws, who would always be part of her life.

"Nate was my friend, too," he reminded her.

"But you didn't let that stop you from taking up with his wife, did you?"

He didn't know how she knew about the change in his relationship with Lindsay—or even if she did. Perhaps she was just fishing for information. Either way, he wasn't going to lie to her.

"His widow," he corrected, meeting her gaze steadily. "Who honored the vows she made to her husband every single day of the five and a half years they were married."

Suzanne looked away first. "Because she loved him."

An undeniable fact that Mitch had accepted long ago. But Nathan was her past, and he wanted to be her future—if Lindsay would let him.

"But he's gone now," he said gently. "And if Lindsay's finally ready to move on with her life with someone else, would that be so bad? Shouldn't she have a chance to be happy again?

"Wouldn't it be nice for Elliott and Avenlea to have someone in their lives? Not to take the place of their dad, but maybe fill a little bit of the hole left by his absence?

"Shouldn't you, as their grandmother, want that for them? Or are you afraid that if Lindsay moves on, she'll cut you out of your grandchildren's lives? And if you are, then you don't know her at all."

"Of course I want what's best for Lindsay and Elliott and Avenlea," she said. "I just don't think she's as committed to you as you are to her."

"I guess that's something for me and her to figure out."

"Has she told you that she loves you?" Suzanne asked.

It was a shot in the dark—there was no way she could know what he and Lindsay had talked about. But something in his expression must have confirmed that the words hit their target, because she took aim again.

"She hasn't, has she? Because she's still in love with Nathan."

Mitch didn't want to believe it, but maybe it was true.

And if it was true, maybe it was time for him to cut his losses and move on—even if it meant cutting his own heart out in the process.

Lindsay took her time strolling through the gardens, basking in the sunshine and breathing in the scents of fresh-cut grass and spring flowers. She looked around, for the first time truly seeing and appreciating the neatly manicured lawns, trees with discreet plaques, benches dedicated in memory of loved ones who'd passed.

She and Nathan had never seriously talked about what arrangements should be made in case of an untimely death. A common oversight on the part of young couples, or so she'd been told after the fact. But she did remember a comment he'd made when they'd attended a funeral together for one of his distant relatives. As they'd stood by the graveside, listening to the minister say a last prayer, he'd told her that he never wanted to be buried in the ground. *"Cremate me and scatter my ashes."*

Her memory of that expressed wish had led to direct conflict with Arthur and Suzanne, who insisted that their son should be immortalized with an ornate marker carved of glossy marble. In the end, they'd compromised on cremation with some of the ashes scattered and the rest interred here, so that Avenlea and Elliott would have a place to go where they might feel connected to their dad. Lindsay had been pretty sure it was Suzanne who wanted to feel connected, but today she was equally glad there was a place to go, to say goodbye.

She hadn't brought flowers, because she knew that Suzanne had made arrangements for regular deliveries. This week it was yellow daffodils. As she looked at Nathan's name and the dates of his life etched in the stone facade of the niche, beside the sunny blossoms, she couldn't help but mourn a life cut so tragically short.

"You might be wondering why I'm here today," she said.

"Or maybe you know. Either way, I've spent a lot of time trying to sort through my feelings about a lot of things lately, and I wanted to share them with you.

"Losing you absolutely devastated me, but I was finally starting to come to terms with the fact that you were gone, finally able to appreciate the memories of our years together and the beautiful children we had together.

"And then, finding out that you'd cheated on me…it was almost like losing you again. Because that discovery took away a part of us, forcing me to accept that what I knew and believed about our relationship wasn't true."

She'd been hurt and angry, not just because of what he'd done, but because her discovery of his actions had taken away the one thing she had left—her memories of *them*. Making her grieve all over again for the loss of what they'd had and leaving her with more questions than answers.

But then, a few days later when she was tucking Elliott and Avenlea into their beds, she realized that the why—and even the how many—didn't really matter. Because it was over and done and nothing in the past could be changed.

So she'd forgiven him, because holding on to her hurt and anger wasn't doing her any good. Because she needed to let go in order to move on.

And she was finally ready to move on.

"One of the strangest parts of all this is that I've gotten to know Heather a lot better than I ever did in high school. And I've gotten to know her daughter—*your daughter*—too. I don't know what would have happened between us if you'd found out that she was pregnant before that last trip, but I do wish you'd had the chance to know Silver. She looks a little bit like each of Elliott and Avenlea, but she's one hundred percent her own person, and I know you would have loved her as much as you loved our children."

Lindsay lifted a hand to brush an errant tear from her lashes. "I won't ever let Elliott and Avenlea forget you, but it's time to let someone else into our lives to complete our family. Maybe you know I'm talking about Mitchell. And maybe you saw that one coming. Apparently I'm the only one who was surprised to learn that he'd had feelings for me for a long time—and even more surprised to discover the depth of my feelings for him.

"I'm not asking for your permission or blessing. I just wanted you to know that I'm moving on. I will always love you and be grateful to you for the two amazing children we had together, but I'm ready to love someone else now, to trust and hope in the future again."

She didn't know what she expected to feel at the end of her monologue, but when she finished saying what she needed to say, she felt better. Not just unburdened but optimistic. Excited about and looking forward to her future with Mitchell—and eager to tell him so.

Except that Mitchell wasn't home when she got to the Circle G. His truck was in the driveway, but when she knocked, it was MG who answered the door.

"You might want to check the barn," he suggested, in response to her query about his brother. "He said something about going for a ride."

So she checked the barn, but he wasn't there, either—and neither was Kenny, confirming MG's suspicion that Mitchell was out on horseback. Which left her with two options: saddle up one of the other horses and try to track him down or wait for him to return.

Waiting obviously made the most sense, but Lindsay felt as if she'd been waiting for this moment long enough and she didn't want to wait any longer.

She was contemplating her next move when Olivia exited a stall at the far end of the barn with Reba.

"He's not here," Mitchell's sister said, dispensing with the usual pleasantries.

Lindsay nodded. "Do you think it would be okay if I saddled up one of your horses and went after him?"

"That depends on what you plan on saying when you find him."

"Isn't that between your brother and me?"

"Not if I'm the one who has to mop up the blood pouring out of his broken heart."

"I would never do anything to hurt Mitchell."

"Then why did he look crushed when he got back from your place?" Olivia challenged, starting to pass.

"Wait." Lindsay stepped in front of her, blocking her path. "When was Mitchell at my place?"

Now his sister frowned. "Earlier today."

"I haven't seen him since Thursday." But if what Olivia was saying was true, if he'd stopped by her place… She winced. "Suzanne's watching the kids for me today."

The other woman studied her for a long moment while she considered this explanation, then finally handed Reba's reins to her. "I've got other things I should be doing anyway."

"Are you going to give me any hint as to which direction he might have headed?" she asked, as Mitchell's sister walked away.

"North."

It was a vague and rather unhelpful response, but after Lindsay had mounted the horse and turned to face north, she realized it was the same direction Mitchell had always taken whenever they went riding together. Nudging the mare into action, she followed the familiar route, silently praying that it was the right one.

Twenty minutes later, she found him by the stand of trees where they used to hang out when they were younger. He was reclined on the ground, his back against the trunk of one of the trees, with a small notebook and a pen in hand. Kenny was nearby, grazing.

He rose to his feet as she drew nearer, tucking the book and pen in his back pocket.

"Hey," he said cautiously.

Lindsay smiled. "Hey."

He helped her dismount—because riding a horse wasn't quite as easy as riding a bike—and then tapped Reba's flank, giving the mare permission to graze with Kenny.

"Did I know you were coming out to the ranch today?" he asked.

"I didn't know until I was on my way here," she said. "But I wanted to tell you that I've been thinking about what you said, last week, and—"

"It's okay," he interrupted. "You don't have to say it. I understand."

She blinked, startled by the abruptness of his tone as much as the interruption. "What do you understand?"

"That you're not ready for a relationship."

She folded her arms over her chest then and huffed out a breath. "You're doing it again."

He frowned. "Doing what?"

"Telling me how I feel, what I want."

"I'm just trying to make this easier on both of us," he told her. "And honestly, it's just as well, because I'm tired of coming in second place to a dead guy."

"Is that really how you feel?"

"It's what it is. And maybe it's partly my own fault, for waiting too long to tell you how I felt. Because I loved you then and I love you now, but I can't do this anymore."

She shook her head. "Well, you're wrong." she said. "About all of it. I *am* ready for a relationship—with *you*."

"Is that what you came out here to say?"

"Actually, what I came out here to say is that I love you, too."

He swallowed. "You do?"

"Why do you sound so surprised?"

"Because you went to the cemetery today."

"You jumped to all kinds of crazy conclusions because I needed to set some things straight with my late husband?" she asked incredulously.

He looked chagrined. "In my defense, I didn't really jump so much as I was pushed."

"Suzanne," she realized.

"I shouldn't have let her get into my head," he admitted. "But everything was always a competition with Nate, and he never let me forget whenever he came first—like he did with you."

"But I did love you first, even if it was only with the innocent heart of a young girl," she said. "More important, I love you now and I'll love you forever."

"I love you, too," he said, drawing her into his arms.

"And yet you were going to let me walk away," she said accusingly.

"Only because I thought it was what you wanted, and because all I've ever wanted is for you to be happy."

"If you really want me to be happy, you'll hold on to me and never let me go," she said.

"I can do that," he promised.

She lifted her arms to link her hands behind his head. "Are you going to kiss me now?"

"Since when do you wait for me to make the first move?" he teased.

"Good point," she said, and pulled his mouth down to hers.

EPILOGUE

Three weeks later

ONCE EVERY FIVE WEEKS, Lindsay had to work a Saturday afternoon shift at the library. Since she was working today, Mitch decided it was the perfect time for him to set his plan in motion. A carefully woven plan that started to unravel as soon as he got back from his shopping excursion with Elliott and Avenlea—and hadn't that been an adventure?—and discovered Lindsay's SUV in the driveway despite the fact that it was only three o'clock and she was scheduled to work until four.

"Where have you guys been?" she asked, when they walked through the door.

"Mommy! Mommy!" The little girl was across the room before he could stop her. "Unca Mitch took us shoppin' an' I got a—"

"Secret," Mitch interjected loudly.

"Whoopsie!" She giggled. "So-wee."

"I told you she can't keep a secret," Elliott said, shaking his head with all the exasperation a big brother could muster.

"But she promised that she would," Mitchell said pointedly to Avenlea.

She nodded solemnly. "I pwomise."

Lindsay watched the exchange with amusement. "What's the secret?"

"We're gonna get—"

"In trouble if you give away the secret," Mitch cut her off again.

She clapped a hand over her mouth.

He sighed, shaking his head. "Two minutes," he said. "We haven't been in the house two minutes."

"I told you," Elliott said again.

Mitch turned to Lindsay then with the look of stern disapproval that he'd been practicing on the kids. "I can't believe you were trying to get your three-year-old daughter to spill a secret."

She shrugged, unapologetic. "It was worth a shot."

"What are you doing home already?" he asked instead.

"The power was out at the community center, so the library closed early."

"Obviously circumstances are conspiring against me," he muttered.

"Do you want me to leave?" she asked, sounding amused.

He shook his head. "No. This isn't quite how I'd envisioned doing this, but since I can't count on Avenlea to keep the secret for another two minutes, we're going to improvise."

"What's *improvise* mean?" Elliott asked.

"It means working with what you've got," Mitch explained. "Which is a little girl bursting at the seams, so go ahead, Avenlea, and tell your mom the secret."

"We wanna get may-weed!" she announced, bouncing up and down with excitement.

It took Lindsay a second to translate her daughter's "may-weed" to "married," and then her heart leaped and lodged in her throat.

"Who wants to get married?" she asked cautiously.

"We do," Elliott said. "All of us. So Uncle Mitch can live here and we can be a real family."

She looked at Mitchell then, and saw that he'd dropped down to one knee and was opening a jeweler's box, inside of which was—

Oh.

She laughed, even as her eyes filled with tears that blurred her view of the purple plastic flower ring nestled against the velvet lining.

"I can't believe it," she said. "Where did you find one exactly the same?"

"It's not exactly the same. It's the actual ring I gave you twenty-three years ago."

"But...how?"

He shrugged. "It was either sheer luck or destiny that I happened to glance down one day as I was leaving and spotted something purple peeking through the snow."

"Avenlea must have dropped it when we left the house that day."

"I so-wee, Mommy," the little girl chimed in now.

Lindsay brushed a hand over her daughter's hair. "It's okay," she said. "Because Uncle Mitch found it."

"I told you it would turn up," he reminded her.

"My first engagement ring," she said, her lips curving. "Given to me by the first boy I ever loved."

"Do you remember what you said when I asked you to marry me that day?" Mitchell asked her.

Her smile widened. "I said that if I had to get married, it might as well be to someone I liked."

"Do you still like me?"

"Yes." She held his gaze for a long moment. "I like you a lot."

"Enough to marry me?" he asked hopefully.

"Yes," she said again, and nodded. "Definitely yes."

He took the ring out of the box now and slid it onto the tip of her third finger—because the band was too small for it to go any farther.

"Obviously I didn't think this through," he said.

"Maybe they could resize it at The Gold Mine," she suggested teasingly.

"Or you could put that one back in your jewelry box for safekeeping and wear this one instead."

This time, the ring he offered was a diamond. Actually, a lot of diamonds, arranged in the shape of a flower.

"It's a little unconventional for an engagement ring," he acknowledged. "I wanted to stick with the flower theme—but the jeweler promised that you could exchange it for something else, if you want."

"It's unconventional," she agreed. "And absolutely perfect."

He brushed a quick kiss over her lips, but she knew there would be more kisses—and more other stuff—to celebrate later.

"I gots a fwo-wuh, too," Avenlea told her mom now, lifting the delicate silver chain that was around her throat to show off a daisy-shaped pendant with a tiny sparkling stone at its center. "Unca Mitch said it's a pwomise that he's gonna be wif us fo-evuh."

"I got a Marc-André Fleury rookie card," Elliott said with a grin.

"His nickname is 'Flower,'" Mitchell explained.

Because of course he'd figured out a way to let both her children know that his proposal was about them, too. That he didn't just want to marry their mom, he wanted them all to be a family.

"So everyone came home from your shopping trip happy," she said to Mitchell. "But what did you get?"

He pulled Lindsay and Elliott and Avenlea in for a family hug. "Everything I've always wanted."

* * * * *

Second Chance With Her Guarded GP

Kate Hardy

MEDICAL
Pulse-racing passion

Kate Hardy has always loved books and could read before she went to school. She discovered Harlequin novels when she was twelve and decided that this was what she wanted to do. When she isn't writing, Kate enjoys reading, cinema, ballroom dancing and the gym. You can contact her via her website, katehardy.com.

Books by Kate Hardy

Harlequin Medical

Twin Docs' Perfect Match
Baby Miracle for the ER Doc

Changing Shifts
Fling with Her Hot-Shot Consultant

Miracles at Muswell Hill Hospital
Christmas with Her Daredevil Doc
Their Pregnancy Gift

Unlocking the Italian Doc's Heart
Carrying the Single Dad's Baby
Heart Surgeon, Prince…Husband!
A Nurse and a Pup to Heal Him
Mistletoe Proposal on the Children's Ward
Forever Family for the Midwife

Visit the Author Profile page
at millsandboon.com.au for more titles.

Dear Reader,

What would you do for someone you love?

When Ollie's twin, Rob, needs a kidney, Ollie immediately offers to be a living donor—but his fiancée can't cope and calls off their wedding. Ollie's hurt and guarded and doesn't plan to get involved again...until he meets Gemma.

Gemma's overcome the worst: losing her little sister to a virus that affected her heart. She does adventurous things to raise money for medical research so other families won't lose someone they love. She doesn't want a relationship, either...until she meets Ollie.

Ollie and Gemma are drawn to each other despite their differences. Can they help heal each other's past hurts and move forward to the future they both want but are too scared to reach for?

I hope you enjoy Ollie and Gemma's journey (and the seals)!

With love,

Kate Hardy

For Vicki Ward Hibbins,
with love and thanks for the seal light bulb!

**Praise for
Kate Hardy**

"Ms. Hardy has definitely penned a fascinating
read in this book... Once the hero confesses to the
heroine his plan for a marriage of convenience, I
was absolutely hooked."

—*Harlequin Junkie* on
Heart Surgeon, Prince...Husband!

CHAPTER ONE

OLIVER LANGLEY TOOK a deep breath.

This was it. His new start. Not the life he'd thought he'd have, six months ago: but that had been before the world had tilted on its axis and mixed everything up. Before his twin brother Rob had gone to work for a humanitarian aid organisation in the aftermath of an earthquake and his appendix had burst. Before Rob had ended up with severe blood poisoning that had wiped out his kidneys. Before Ollie had donated a kidney to his twin.

Before Ollie's fiancée had called off their wedding.

Which had been his own fault for asking her to move the wedding. 'Tab, with Rob being on dialysis, he's not well enough even to be at the wedding, let alone be my best man.' He'd been so sure his fiancée would see things the same way that he did. It made perfect sense to move the wedding until after the transplant, giving both him and Rob time to recover from the operation and meaning that Ollie's entire family would be there to share the day. 'Let's move the wedding back a few months. The transplant's hopefully going to be at the beginning of June, so we'll both be properly recovered by August. We can have a late summer wedding instead.'

'Move the wedding.' It had been a statement, not a question. She'd gone silent, as if considering it, then shaken her head. 'No.'

He'd stared at her. 'Tab, I know it'll be a bit of work, changing all the arrangements, but I'll do as much of it as I can.'

'That's not what I mean, Ollie.'

He'd stared at her, not understanding. 'Then what do you mean?'

'I—I've been thinking for a while. We should call it off.'

'Call it off?' He'd gone cold. 'Why? Have you met someone else?'

'No. It's not you. It's me.'

Which meant the problem *was* him and she was trying to be nice. 'Tab, whatever it is, we can work it out. Whatever I've done to upset you, I'm sorry.' He loved her. He wanted to marry her, to make a family with her. He'd thought she felt the same way and wanted the same things. But it was becoming horribly clear that he'd got it all wrong.

Her eyes had filled with tears. 'It's not you, it's me,' she said again. 'You're giving Rob a kidney—of course you are. He's your brother and you love him. Anyone would do the same, in your shoes.'

'But?' He'd forced himself to say the word she'd left out.

She'd looked him in the eye. 'What if something goes wrong? What if *you* get ill, and your one remaining kidney doesn't work any more, and you have to go on dialysis? What if they can't find a match for you, and you die?'

'That's not going to happen, Tab.' He'd tried to put his arms round her to comfort and reassure her but she'd pulled away.

'You're not listening, Ollie. I can't do this.'

'Why?'

'You know how it's been with my dad.'

'Yes.' Tabby's father had chronic fatigue syndrome. He'd been too ill to do much for years.

'Mum stuck by her wedding vows—in sickness and in health. I didn't realise when I was younger, but she worked herself to the bone, making sure my brother and I were OK, and keeping us financially afloat, and looking after Dad. Obviously when we got older and realised how ill Dad was, Tom and I did as much as we could do to help. But my mum's struggled every single day, Ollie. She's sacrificed her life to look after Dad. And I can't do that for you. I just *can't*.'

He'd frowned. 'But I'm not ill, Tab. OK, I'll need a bit of time to recover from the transplant, but I'll be fine. Rob will get better and everything will be back to normal soon enough.'

'But you can't promise me you'll always be well and I won't have to look after you, Ollie. You can't possibly promise something like that.' Tabby had shaken her head. 'I'm sorry, Ollie. I can't marry you.' She'd fought to hold back the tears. 'I know it's selfish and I know it's unfair, but I just don't love you enough to take that risk. I don't want a life like my mum's. I don't want to marry you.' She'd taken off the engagement ring and given it back to him. 'I'm so sorry, Ollie. But I can't do this.'

'Tab, you've just got an attack of cold feet. We'll get through this,' he said. 'We love each other. It'll be fine.'

'No, Ollie. That's the point. I do love you—but not *enough*. I'm sorry.'

He hadn't been able to change her mind.

She'd got in touch to wish him and Rob luck with the transplant, but she'd made it clear she didn't want him back. He wasn't enough for her. To the point where she hadn't even wanted him to help cancel all the arrangements; Tabby insisted on doing it all herself.

Ollie had spent a couple of weeks brooding after the operation, and he'd realised that he needed some time away from London. So he'd taken a six-month sabbatical from the practice in Camden where he was a salaried GP, lent his flat to a friend, and had gone back to Northumbria to stay with Rob and their parents. The open skies, hills and greenery had given him a breathing space from the bustle of London and time to think about what he wanted to do with his life.

Though the enforced time off after the transplant, once he'd untangled the wedding, had left Ollie with the fidgets. Much as he loved their parents and completely understood why their mum was fussing over her twin boys, Ollie liked having his own space and the smothering was driving him mad. He was pretty sure that doing the job he loved would help him get his equilibrium back and help him move on from the mess of his wedding-that-wasn't.

Then he'd seen the ad for a three-month maternity cover post at Ashermouth Bay Surgery, which would take him nearly up to the end of his sabbatical. He'd applied for the job; once the practice had given him a formal offer, he'd found a three-month let and moved into one of the old fishermen's cottages near the harbour, within walking distance of the practice.

And today was his first day at his new job. He might not have been enough for his fiancée, but he knew he was definitely good enough as a doctor.

The building was single-storey, built of red brick and with a tiled roof. There were window-boxes filled with welcoming bright red geraniums, and a raised brick flower bed in front of the door, filled with lavender. The whole place looked bright and welcoming; and next to the door was a sign listing the practice staff, from the doctors and nurses through to the reception and admin team.

Ollie was slightly surprised to see his own name on the sign, underneath that of Aadya Devi, the GP whose maternity leave he was covering, but it made him feel welcome. Part of the team. He really liked that.

He took a deep breath, pushed the door open and walked in to the reception area.

The receptionist was chatting to a woman in a nurse's uniform, who had her back to him. Clearly neither of them had heard him come in, because they were too busy talking about him.

'Dr Langley's starting this morning,' the receptionist said.

'Our newbie,' the nurse said, sounding pleased.

At thirty, Ollie didn't quite see himself as a 'newbie', but never mind. He was new to the practice, so he supposed it was an accurate description.

'Caroline's asked me to help him settle in, as she's away this week,' the nurse added.

Caroline was the senior partner at the practice: a GP in her late fifties, with a no-nonsense attitude and a ready laugh. Ollie had liked her very much at the interview.

He didn't really need someone to help him settle in, but OK. He got that this place was a welcoming one. That they believed in teamwork.

'And, of course, he's fresh meat,' the nurse said.

The receptionist laughed. 'Oh, Gem. Trust *you* to think of that.'

Ollie, who had just opened his mouth ready to say hello, stood there in silence, gobsmacked.

Fresh meat?

Right now, he was still smarting too much from the fallout from the wedding-that-wasn't to want any kind of relationship. And it rankled that someone was discussing him in that way. Fresh meat. A slab of beefcake. Clearly this 'Gem' woman made a habit of this, given the receptionist's comment.

Well, he'd just have to make sure she realised that she was barking up completely the wrong tree. And he didn't care if his metaphors were mixed.

He gave a loud cough. 'Good morning.'

'Oh! Good morning.' The receptionist smiled at him. 'We're not actually open yet, but can I help you?'

'I'm Oliver Langley,' he said.

The receptionist's cheeks went pink as she clearly realised that he'd overheard the end of their conversation.

Yeah. She might well be embarrassed. Fresh meat, indeed.

'I'm Maddie Jones, the receptionist—well, obviously,' she

said. 'Welcome to the practice. Can I get you a cup of coffee, Dr Langley?'

'Thank you, but I'm fine,' he said coolly. 'I don't expect to be waited on.'

The nurse next to her also turned round to greet him.

'Good morning, Dr Langley. Nice to meet you,' she said with a smile.

Surely she must realise that he'd overheard what she'd just said about him? And yet she was still being all smiley and sparkly-eyed. Brazening it out? That didn't sit well with him at all.

'I'm Gemma Baxter,' she said. 'I'm one of the practice nurse practitioners. Caroline asked me to look after you this week, as she's away on holiday.'

'That's kind of you, Nurse Baxter,' he said, keeping his voice expressionless, 'but quite unnecessary.'

'Call me Gemma. And, if nothing else,' she said, 'I can at least show you where everything is in the surgery.' She disappeared for a moment, then came through to join him in the waiting area. 'It's pretty obvious that this is the waiting area,' she said, gesturing to the chairs. 'The nurses' and HCA's rooms are this side of Reception—' she gestured to the corridor to their left '—the pharmacy's through the double doors to the right, the patient toilets are over there in the corner, and the doctors' rooms are this side.'

She gestured to the other corridor. 'If you'd like to follow me? The staff toilets, the kitchen and rest room are here, behind Reception and the admin team.' She led him into the kitchen. 'Coffee, tea, hot chocolate and fruit tea are in the cupboard above the kettle, along with the mugs. The dishwasher's next to the fridge, and there's a rota for emptying it; and the microwave's self-explanatory. We all put a couple of pounds into the kitty every week and Maddie keeps the supplies topped up. If there's anything you want that isn't here, just let Maddie know.'

She smiled at him. 'I need to start checking the out-of-hours notifications and hospital letters before my triage calls and vaccination clinic this morning, so I'm going to leave you here. Your room's the third on the right, but obviously you'll see your name on the door anyway.'

'Thank you for the tour,' he said. That 'fresh meat' comment had rubbed him up the wrong way, but he was going to have to work with her for the next three months so it'd be sensible to be polite and make the best of it.

'I'll come and find you at lunchtime,' she said. 'As it's your first day, lunch is on me.'

'That's—' But he didn't have time to tell her that it was totally unnecessary and he'd sort out his own lunch, thanks all the same, because she'd already gone through to the other corridor.

Ollie made himself a coffee, then headed for his consulting room. It was a bright, airy space; there was a watercolour on the wall of a castle overlooking the sea, which he vaguely recognised as a local attraction. A desk; a couple of chairs for his patient and a parent or support person; and a computer. Everything neatly ordered and in its place; nothing personal.

He checked his phone for the username and password the practice administrator had sent him last week, logged on to the system and changed the password. Then he put an alarm on his phone to remind him when telephone triage started, and once his emails came up he started to work through the discharge summaries, hospital letters and referrals from over the weekend.

Gemma knew she was making a bit of a snap judgement—the sort of thing she normally disapproved of—but Oliver Langley seemed so closed-off. He hadn't responded to the warmth of her smile or her greeting, and he'd been positively chilly when she'd said she'd show him round. She sincerely hoped he'd be a bit warmer with their patients. When you were worried about your health, the last thing you needed was a doctor being snooty with you. You needed someone who'd listen and who'd reassure you.

Yes, sure, he was gorgeous: tall, with dark floppy hair and

blue eyes, reminding her of a young Hugh Grant. But, when you were a medic, it didn't matter what you looked like; what mattered was how you behaved towards people. So far, from what Gemma had seen, Oliver Langley was very self-contained. If he was the best fit for the practice, as Caroline had claimed, Gemma hated to think what the other interviewees had been like. Robots, perhaps?

Hopefully she could work some kind of charm offensive on him over lunch. She intended to get a genuine smile out of him, even if she had to exhaust her entire stock of terrible jokes.

She took a gulp of the coffee she'd made earlier and checked the out-of-hours log, to see which of their patients had needed urgent treatment over the weekend and needed following up. Then she clicked onto the triage list Maddie had sent through, before starting her hour and a half of phone triage.

The system was one of the things the practice had kept from the Covid days. It was more efficient for dealing with minor illnesses and giving advice about coughs and colds and minor fevers; but in Gemma's view you could often tell a lot from a patient's body language—something that could prompt her to ask questions to unlock what her patient was *really* worrying about. That was something that telephone triage had taken away, since the Covid days. And trying to diagnose a rash or whether a wound had turned septic, from looking at a blurred photograph taken on a phone and sent in low resolution so it would actually reach the surgery email, had been next to impossible.

At least things were a bit easier now. They were all adjusting to the 'new normal'. She worked her way through the triage list until it was time to start her vaccination clinic. Even though the vaccination meant she had to make little ones cry, it also meant she got a chance for baby cuddles. Gemma would never admit to being broody, but if she was honest with herself her biological clock always sat up and took notice when she had this kind of clinic.

It had been twelve years since she'd lost her little sister—

since she'd lost her entire family, because her parents had closed off, too, unable to deal with their loss. Gemma had been so desperate to feel loved and to stop the pain of missing Sarah that she'd chosen completely the wrong way to do it; she'd gone off the rails and slept with way too many boys. Once her best friend's mum had sat her down and talked some sense into her, Gemma had ended up going the other way: so determined not to be needy that she wouldn't let her boyfriends close, and the relationships had fizzled out within weeks. She'd never managed to find anyone she'd really clicked with.

So the chances of her attending this particular clinic rather than running it were looking more and more remote. It was a good six months since she'd last had a casual date, let alone anything more meaningful. The nearest she'd get to having a real family of her own was being godmother to Scarlett, her best friend's daughter. She was grateful for that, but at the same time she wondered why she still hadn't been able to fix her own family. Why she still couldn't get through to her parents.

She shook herself. Ridiculous. Why was she thinking about this now?

Perhaps, she thought, because Oliver Langley was precisely the sort of man she'd gone for, back in her difficult days. Tall, dark-haired, blue-eyed and gorgeous. And his coolness towards her had unsettled her; she was used to people reacting to her warmth and friendliness in kind.

Well, tough. It was his problem, not hers, and she didn't have time to worry about it now. She had a job to do. She went into the corridor and called her first patient for her clinic.

CHAPTER TWO

'I'VE BEEN DREADING this appointment. I really hate needles,' Fenella Nichols confessed as she sat down by Gemma's desk, settling the baby on her lap.

Gemma could've guessed that, because the year-old baby was fussing, having picked up on her mum's stress. 'A lot of people do,' she said with a smile. 'But you're doing absolutely the right thing, bringing Laura here to protect her. Meningitis is nasty stuff, and so are mumps and measles and rubella. And you've dressed her perfectly, so I've got easy access to her thigh and her arm and it won't cause her a lot of worry.' She stroked the baby's cheek. 'Hello, gorgeous. Do I get a smile?'

To her relief, the baby gurgled.

'You've got her red book?' Gemma checked.

'Yes.' Fenella produced it and put it on the desk.

'Great. How's everything going?' This was the point where Gemma knew that if there were any real worries, Fenella would unburden herself and Gemma could start to fix things.

'My husband thinks she's a bit behind. I mean, I know she's a bit on the small side, but I thought she takes after me.'

Fenella was slender and just about five feet tall, a good six inches shorter than Gemma. 'You're probably right. I'll measure her and look at her centile chart,' Gemma promised. 'And I can hear for myself that she's starting to get chatty.'

'Dada, dog and duck are her favourite words,' Fenella said with a smile. 'And she's pulling herself up on the furniture.'

'It won't be long until she's walking, then. You'll be seeing the health visitor about her milestones,' Gemma said, 'but from what you're saying there's nothing to worry about.' Gemma waved at the baby, who waved back. Then she took a picture book from the tray on her desk, opened it and held it in front of the baby. 'Can you see the duck, Laura?'

The baby cooed and pointed at the picture of a duck.

'Can you help Laura find the lamb in the book, Fenella?'

With both mum and baby distracted, it was easy for Gemma to prepare Laura's thigh for the vaccination and administer it. Laura cried for a moment, but was soon distracted by her mum turning the page to another picture. 'Dog!' she said, pointing.

'That's brilliant,' Gemma said. 'You might see a red area come up around the injection site later this morning, Fenella, but that'll go in a couple of days. And sometimes after the meningitis vaccine babies get a bit of a temperature, but I'm going to give Laura some liquid paracetamol now to help stop that happening. Make sure you give her plenty to drink, and if she feels a bit hot take off a layer or two. You can give her more paracetamol if you need to in four hours, and if you're worried give us a call.'

'All right. Thank you, Gemma.'

Gemma weighed and measured the baby, recording the figures as well as the vaccination details in the red book. 'Laura's following the same trend line she's been on since birth, a shade under the middle, so I'm very happy. Is there anything you're concerned about, or anything you'd like to chat over?'

'No.' Fenella smiled. 'But I think I'm going to make my husband bring her for the next injections.'

Gemma laughed. 'That sounds like a good plan.'

Her next patient was a little older, so she distracted him from the 'sharp scratch' by getting him to sing 'Old Macdonald Had a Zoo' with her.

'Zoo?' his mum asked, laughing.

'Absolutely,' Gemma said with a grin. 'It makes a change from a farm with cows and sheep. With a zoo, we can have elephants, tigers, lions, crocodiles...'

'Crocodiles!' the little boy said, his eyes going round with excitement.

'A snap-snap here,' Gemma sang.

In all the excitement of the song, the little boy forgot to be upset about the needle.

This was one of the bits of the job Gemma loved: the interaction with her younger patients. If she hadn't decided to go into general practice, she would definitely have worked in paediatrics.

She dispensed a sticker announcing 'I was THIS brave' at the end of the appointment, did the necessary cleaning in the treatment room, and called in her next patient. As it was the school holidays, she also had a couple of teenagers at the clinic who'd missed their meningitis vaccine and needed to catch up.

'So you're off to uni in a couple of months?' she asked the first one.

'*If* I get my grades.' Millie bit her lip. 'I'm dreading results day.'

'You have my sympathy. I still remember mine.' The second time round had given Gemma the grades she'd needed, but the first time had been a disaster. Her year of going off the rails had meant she'd failed her exams spectacularly and she'd had to repeat the second year of her A levels and resit her exams. 'Just remember that there's always a plan B,' Gemma said. 'Even if you don't get your first choice, you're still going to have a good time because you'll be doing the subject you love.'

'I guess.' Millie grimaced. 'Mum's worrying.'

'That's what mums do,' Gemma said. 'But this is one worry you can tick off her list.' She smiled. 'My mum was the same.'

Well. Almost. After Sarah's death, her mum had seemed to close off. But her best friend Claire's mum Yvonne had worried about her. And Yvonne had been the one to sit down with Gemma and finally make her get her act together after she'd failed her exams. 'She got me to make a list of what I was worrying about. Then we talked about it and made a plan together. My mum—' well, Claire's mum '—worried about me eating properly, so I got her to teach me how to make some meals that were quick, easy and cheap.'

'That's a really good idea. Thank you,' Millie said.

'Good luck, and I hope you have a wonderful time at uni,' Gemma said when Millie left.

Her clinic finished on time; she sorted out her paperwork, checked on the practice app that Oliver's last appointment had finished, then went to knock on his door.

'Time for lunch,' she said, giving him her warmest smile in the hope that it might thaw him out a bit.

He looked up from his desk. 'Really, there's no need.'

He was going to be stubborn about it? Well, maybe he needed to learn that he wasn't the only one who could be stubborn. He might only be here temporarily, but for those three months he was going to be part of the team. Being snooty and refusing to mix with everyone wasn't an option. 'There's every need,' she said. 'You're new to the village and it's your first day at the practice. We're a team and we look after each other. I thought we could have lunch by the cliffs—the local bakery does the best sandwiches ever. And, as it's your first day, it's my shout.'

When he opened his mouth, she guessed he was about to refuse, and added swiftly, 'No protests allowed.' He looked wary, and she sighed. 'Look, it's just a sandwich and some coffee. A welcome-to-the-practice sort of thing. You're not under any obligation to me whatsoever if you accept.'

He looked awkward, then. 'Thank you,' he muttered.

She'd get a proper smile out of him if it killed her. 'I'm glad that's settled. It's a five-minute walk from here to the bakery, and five minutes from there to the cliffs.'

He followed her out of the door. Still silent, she noticed. OK. She'd start the conversation. Something easy. Food was always a safe subject. 'For the purposes of transparency, the bakery happens to be owned by my best friend, but I stand by what I said. Claire makes amazingly good sourdough and her brownies have to be tasted to be believed.'

'Right.'

Oh, for pity's sake. Could he not meet her halfway and at least make an *effort* at small talk? She tried again. 'Are you not a cake person?'

He wrinkled his nose. 'Not really.'

So he wouldn't be buying cake from her on her regular Friday morning bake sale. 'Looks as if we're opposites, then,' she said lightly, 'because I think cake makes the world go round.'

Was she being paranoid, or was he looking at her as if she had two heads? If she hadn't promised Caroline she'd look after him, she would've walked away and left him to his own grouchy company.

At the bakery, once they'd chosen their sandwiches and he'd ordered an espresso, she added a lemon and raspberry cake to their order along with one of Claire's savoury muffins.

Oliver carried the brown paper bag with their lunch, but he didn't make conversation on the steep path up to the cliffs.

Was he shy, perhaps? He might find it easier to be professional with his patients than with his coworkers, but somehow she was going to have to persuade him to thaw a little. They really didn't need any tension at work.

Finally they made it to the clifftop. Gemma took the picnic blanket from her backpack and spread it on the grass with a flourish. 'Have a seat,' she said with a smile.

'Do you always carry a picnic blanket?' he asked, looking surprised.

She nodded. 'If it's not raining, I usually come up here for lunch. The view's amazing.'

'It is,' he agreed, looking out at the sand and the sea.

'It's the best place I know to clear your head and set you up for the rest of the day.'

He sat down next to her, opened the paper bag, checked the labels written on the contents and handed her a coffee and a sandwich. 'Thank you for lunch.'

'You're welcome. How was your first morning?'

'Fine.'

He was still being cool. So much for hoping that lunch might win him round.

'Win me round?' The coolness was verging on arctic, now.

She grimaced. 'I said that aloud, didn't I? I'm sorry.' She took a deep breath. 'We don't seem to be getting on very well. I was trying to be nice and look out for a new colleague. If I've come across as in your face or patronising, I apologise.'

He was still looking at her as if she had two heads. She sighed inwardly. What would it take to get a decent working relationship going with her new colleague?

Then again, she hadn't managed to fix her relationship with her parents. She was the common factor in both situations, so maybe *she* was the problem. Maybe she should just give up— on both counts. 'Now I know you're not a cake person, I won't try to sell you a Friday Fundraiser cake.'

'What's a Friday Fundraiser cake?'

'Before Covid, I used to have a cake stall in the waiting room on Friday mornings to raise money for the local cardiac unit. I'd sell cake and cookies to patients, staff, anyone who happened to be around.' She sighed. 'Caroline's given me the go-ahead to do it again now, but it's on a much smaller scale because we don't have as many face-to-face appointments as we used to.' She shrugged.

'But it's better than nothing. All the little bits add up. I do a big fundraiser every three or four months; my skydive in the spring had to be postponed because of bad weather, so I'm doing it next month. There's no obligation to sponsor me, but if you'd like to then I'd be very grateful, even if it's only a pound.' She gave him a wry smile. 'I've been fundraising for about ten years, so I think everyone else in the practice has got donation fatigue, by now—if I'm honest, probably everyone in the village.'

Donation fatigue?

Ollie thought about it, and then the penny dropped.

'That's why you told Maddie I was fresh meat?'

She looked horrified. 'Oh, no! I mean—yes, I did say that, but the way you just said it makes it sound *terrible*. I'm so sorry. And I'm not...' She shook her head, her eyes widening as a thought clearly struck her. 'Oh, no. Did you think I was some kind of man-eater planning to hit on you?'

It had rather crossed his mind.

And he was pretty sure it showed on his face, because she said quickly, 'That's not who I am.' She bit her lip. 'I barely know you. You could be married with children, or at least involved with someone. Of course I wasn't sizing you up as a potential partner. No wonder you've been so reserved with me, thinking I was about to pounce on you. I'm really sorry.' She grimaced. 'What a horrible way to welcome you to the practice.'

Ollie looked at her. The dismay on her face seemed genuine.

'Look, forget what I just said about asking you to sponsor me,' she said. 'I know they say there's no such thing as a free lunch, but this really *is* one. I just wanted to do what Caroline asked of me and welcome you to the practice. To show you where the best place is to grab a sandwich, even if I am a tiny bit biased, and somewhere nice to sit and eat or even just walk for a bit if you need to clear your head, because when you're new to the area it's always good to have someone showing you these things.'

Even though Ollie didn't quite trust his own judgement any more—not after he'd got it so wrong with Tabby, thinking that she'd loved him as much as he'd loved her—the look in Gemma's eyes seemed genuine. And she seemed to be trying very hard to hold out an olive branch. Maybe he should do the same.

'I think we got off on completely the wrong foot,' he said. 'Let's start again. I'm Oliver Langley and I'm the locum for Aadya Devi, for the next three months.' He held out his hand.

'Gemma Baxter, nurse practitioner,' she said, taking his hand and shaking it. 'Welcome to Ashermouth Bay Surgery, Dr Langley.'

Shaking her hand was a mistake, Ollie realised quickly. His fingers tingled at her touch and adrenalin pumped through him, making his heart start to pound. He couldn't remember the last time he'd been this aware of anyone, even Tabby, and he couldn't quite let himself meet Gemma's eyes. 'Thank you,' he muttered, dropping her hand again.

'Caroline said you were from London. What made you decide to come to Northumberland?'

To escape the fallout of his bad decisions. To hide and lick his wounds. To be a living donor for his twin's kidney transplant. Not that he planned to explain any of that. Even though he knew it wasn't the real reason why, he said, 'My parents moved up here ten years ago. Dad developed angina, and Mum wanted him to retire early and take things a bit easier. So they spend their days pottering around in the garden and going out for lunch.'

'Sounds nice,' she said. 'And they must be so pleased that you'll be closer to them now than you were in London.'

And his twin, but Ollie wasn't quite ready to share that yet. 'What about you?' he asked. 'Are you from round here?'

'Yes. I grew up in Ashermouth Bay. I did my training in Liverpool, but I knew I wanted to work back here,' she said. 'Luckily, when I qualified, one of the nurses at the practice was thinking about retiring, so I had the chance to work here and do my nurse practitioner training part-time.'

'So your family lives here?'

A shadow seemed to pass across her face, or maybe he was imagining it, but then she said, 'Not far from here.'

'And you always wanted to work in general practice rather than at the hospital?'

She nodded. 'I like the idea of really knowing my patients, watching them grow up and looking after their whole families. Being part of a community—in a hospital, you might look after someone for a few days or a few weeks, but it isn't the same.' She looked at him. 'Did you always plan to be a GP?'

'I nearly went into obstetrics,' he said. 'I trained in London. I enjoyed all my rotations, and delivering babies was amazing. But then my dad was diagnosed with angina, and it made me have a rethink.'

'You weren't tempted to specialise in cardiology?'

He shook his head. 'Partly because it was a little bit too close to the bone. But I realised I wanted to be the kind of doctor who'd be able to pick up a problem before his patient really started to suffer from it. Which meant being a GP.'

'Good plan,' she said.

He finished his sandwich. 'You were right. This bread's as good as any I've eaten in a posh café in London.'

'Wait until you try the muffin,' she said. 'I know you're not a cake person, but this is savoury.' She rummaged in the brown paper bag and brought out a wrapped muffin. 'Your challenge, should you accept it, is to tell me what's in the muffin.'

He liked the slightly teasing look in her eyes. And he was shocked to realise that, actually, he liked *her*.

'So what's in it?' she tested.

'Spices and cheese,' he said.

She gave him a mock-sorrowful look. 'That's much too general.'

'Remember what the G in GP stands for,' he retorted.

She laughed, and it made her light up from the inside. Her dark eyes sparkled and there was an almost irresistible curve to her mouth. And Ollie found himself staring at Gemma Baxter, spellbound, for a moment.

He really hadn't expected this.

It was nearly four months since he'd split up with Tabby. Although he knew he had to move on, he hadn't really noticed any other women since then. Until today: and he really wasn't sure he was ready for this right now.

He needed to backtrack, fast, before he said something stupid. He didn't want to let Gemma close; yet, at the same time, he didn't want to freeze her out. He'd thought Gemma was the careless type when he'd first met her, but he was beginning to realise that there was more to her than that. Someone careless wouldn't be doing a skydive for charity.

The best compromise would be to stick to a safe subject. 'So tell me about Ashermouth Bay.'

'What do you want to know?' she asked. 'About the sort of things that are popular with tourists, or a potted history of the town?'

'A bit of both,' he said.

'OK. Ashermouth Bay used to be a fishing village,' she said. 'Obviously times change, and now the town's more reliant on tourism than on fishing. Though you can still take a boat trip out to see the puffins on the islands offshore, and if you're lucky you might see dolphins and porpoises on the way. There's a colony of seals nearby, too, and they tend to come into the bay when the pups are born—which is basically about now. If walking's your thing, you can walk right along the bay at low tide and go up to the castle; and you can see a bit of an old shipwreck along the way.'

'That's just the sort of thing I would've loved as a kid,' he said.

'The local history group does a ghost walk once a month in the village,' she said, 'with tales of smugglers and pirates. If castles are your thing, there are loads of them nearby—though

I'm guessing, as you said your parents live near here, you already know all about them.'

'My mum loves visiting stately homes for the gardens,' he said. 'And I've driven her and Dad to a few when I've come to visit.'

'If you like sport, the village has a cricket team and a football team,' she said. 'And there's an adventure centre based in the harbour if you want to do surfing, paddle-boarding, kite-surfing and the like.'

All things Ollie knew his brother would adore; out of the two of them, Rob was the adrenalin junkie. It was why his twin worked in a fast-paced emergency department in Manchester, was a member of the local mountain rescue team as well as enjoying climbing on his days off, and spent his holidays working for a humanitarian aid organisation. Ollie adored his brother, but he was happy being grounded rather than pushing himself to take extra risks, the way Rob did. The family joke was that Ollie had Rob's share of being sensible and Rob had Ollie's share of being adventurous. 'The cliffs and the beach sound just fine to me,' he said.

She glanced at her watch. 'We need to be heading back.'

'Admin and phone calls before afternoon surgery?' he asked.

'Absolutely.' She smiled at him.

'Thank you for lunch,' he said.

'You're very welcome.'

'Let me help you fold the blanket.' Though when his fingers accidentally brushed against hers, again he felt the prickle of adrenalin down his spine.

Ridiculous.

They were colleagues. He wasn't looking for a relationship. There were a dozen reasons why he shouldn't even think about what it might be like to kiss Gemma Baxter.

But he'd noticed the curve of her mouth, the fullness of her lower lip. And he couldn't help wondering.

He shook himself. They were colleagues, and nothing more.

And he needed to make some kind of small talk on the way back to the practice, to make sure she didn't have a clue about the thoughts running through his head.

Once he'd thawed out a little, Oliver Langley had turned out to be surprisingly nice, Gemma thought. Maybe he was right and they'd just got off on the wrong foot. And Caroline had said she'd thought he'd fit in well with the team.

The one thing that shocked her, though, was when Oliver had finally given her a genuine smile. It had completely transformed his face, turning him from that cool, austere stranger into someone absolutely gorgeous. His smile had made her heart beat a little bit too quickly for her liking.

She couldn't afford to let herself be attracted to their new locum. Quite apart from the fact that he might already be involved with someone else, she didn't have a great track record. Even if you ignored that year of disastrous relationships and the following two years of not dating anyone at all while she concentrated on getting through her exams and putting herself back together, her love life ever since had been hopeless. All her relationships had fizzled out within a few weeks. She'd never met anyone that she'd felt really connected to, someone she really wanted to share her life with.

Claire, her best friend, had a theory that it was because Gemma was so terrified of being needy and clingy, she went too far the other way and wouldn't actually let anyone in.

But it wasn't about being needy or clingy. It was about trust. She'd loved her little sister and her parents. But her parents had shut off from her after Sarah's death, lost in their grief, and Gemma had never been able to connect with them since. And maybe that was what was still holding her back, even after she'd had counselling: if she really loved someone and let them close, what if it all went wrong, the way it had with her parents, and they left her?

So it was easier to keep her relationships short and sweet and avoid that risk completely. Make sure she was the one to leave, not them.

Gemma's afternoon was a busy mixture of triage calls and surgery; after she'd finished writing up the notes from her last patient, she changed out of her uniform and drove to her parents' house for her monthly duty visit. She wasn't giving up on them, the way they'd given up on her. One day, she'd manage to get her family back. She just had to find the right key to unlock their hearts.

'Aadya's locum started at the surgery today,' she said brightly.

'Oh,' her mum said.

'He seems nice.'

'That's good,' her dad said.

The silence stretched out painfully until Gemma couldn't take any more. 'Shall I make us a cup of tea?' she suggested.

'If you like, love,' her mum said.

Putting the kettle on and sorting out mugs gave her five minutes of respite to think up some new topics of conversation. What her parents had been doing in the garden; the puppy Maddie was getting in a couple of weeks; how much sponsorship money she'd raised so far for the skydive. But it was such a struggle, when they gave anodyne responses every time. Her parents were the only people she knew who always gave a closed answer to an open question.

How very different it was when she dropped in to see Claire's mum. There was never any awkwardness or not knowing what to say next. Yvonne always greeted her with a hug, asked her how her day was, and chatted to her about the classes she ran in the craft shop next to Claire's bakery. Gemma had tried to persuade her own mum to go along to a class, thinking that she might enjoy the embroidery class or knitting, but she'd always been gently but firmly rebuffed. Her parents simply couldn't bear to come back to the village they'd lived in when Sarah died; they visited once a month to put flowers on their daughter's grave, but that was as much as they could manage.

And they'd never, ever visited Gemma's flat. She knew it was because they found it hard to face all the might-have-beens, but it still felt like another layer of rejection.

After another hour of struggling to get her parents to talk to her, she did the washing up, kissed both parents' cheeks, and drove home. Feeling too miserable to eat dinner, and knowing that a walk and the sound of the sea swishing against the shore would lift her mood, she headed to the beach to watch the changing colours in the sky.

One day she'd break through to her parents again. And then she'd have the confidence to find someone to share her life with—someone who wouldn't abandon her when things got tough—and it would ease the loneliness.

But for now she'd focus on how lucky she was. She had good friends, a job she loved, and she lived in one of the nicest bits of the world. Maybe wanting more—wanting love—was just too greedy.

Ollie arrived home to find a note through his front door saying that a parcel had been delivered to his neighbour.

When he'd collected it, he didn't need to look at the card that came with it; only one person would send him a mini-hamper with seriously good cheese, olives, oatmeal crackers, and a bottle of good red wine. But he opened the card anyway.

Hope your first day was great. If it wasn't, you have my permission to scoff all the cheese. Otherwise, you'd better save me some for Thursday night or there will be Big Trouble.
R

He rang his twin. 'Thank you for the parcel.'

'My pleasure. It always made my day when I had a parcel

in hospital, and I think a first day anywhere deserves a parcel.' The smile in Rob's voice was obvious. 'So how did it go?'

'OK,' Ollie said.

'Your colleagues are all nice?'

'Yeah. Though I got off on the wrong foot with the nurse practitioner, to start with.' Ollie explained his clash with Gemma.

'Olls, I know Tabby hurt you—but don't let that change the way you respond to anyone with two X chromosomes,' Rob said softly.

'I'm not responding at all. I'm not looking to get involved with anyone. It's only been three and a half months since Tabby cancelled the wedding.'

'I'm not telling you to rush in and sweep the next woman you meet off her feet. Just don't close yourself off from potential happiness, that's all,' Rob advised.

'Mmm,' Ollie said, not wanting to fight with his twin. But thinking about Gemma Baxter unsettled him. That spark of attraction between them on the cliffs, when their hands had touched—he really hadn't expected that. This three-month locum job was meant to give himself the space to get his head straight again. Starting a new relationship really wasn't a good idea.

'Be kind to yourself, Olls,' Rob said. 'And I'll see you on Thursday.'

CHAPTER THREE

THE NEXT MORNING, when Gemma walked into the staff kitchen at the surgery, Oliver was already there.

'Good morning. The kettle's hot,' he said, indicating his mug. 'Can I make you a drink?'

'Thank you. Coffee, with milk and no sugar, please,' she said, smiling back.

He gave her another of those smiles that made her pulse rocket, and she had to remind herself sharply that Oliver was her new colleague and off limits. Yes, he was attractive; but that didn't mean he was available.

After her triage calls that morning, Gemma was booked in for her weekly visit to the nursing home, where she was able to assess any particular resident the manager was concerned about, and carried on with their rolling programme of six-monthly wellbeing reviews to check every resident's care plan and medication needs. Her path didn't cross with Oliver's again that day, and she was cross with herself for being disappointed. 'He's your colleague. No more, no less,' she reminded herself yet again.

At least she had her Tuesday dance aerobics class with Claire to take her mind off it. Or so she'd thought.

'Your lunch date, yesterday,' Claire said. 'He looked nice.'

'He's my colleague—Aadya's locum,' Gemma said. 'And it wasn't a lunch date. Caroline asked me to help him settle in, that's all.'

'You went very pink when he said something to you in the bakery,' Claire said. 'And he looks like your type.'

Gemma gave her a wry smile. 'For all I know, he's already involved with someone. We're just colleagues.'

'Hmm. Talking of colleagues, Andy's got a new colleague. He's single, and our age,' Claire said. 'Maybe you could both come over to dinner at the weekend.'

Gemma hugged her. 'Love you, Claire-bear, but I really don't need you to find me a partner. I'm fine just as I am.'

Though they both knew she wasn't quite telling the truth.

On Wednesday morning, Gemma had an asthma clinic, and her first patient was booked in for a series of spirometry tests. Samantha was forty years old and a smoker, and had persistent breathlessness and a cough. Although at the last appointment Sam had said that she thought her cough was just a smoker's cough, she'd also admitted that she seemed to get more and more chest infections over the winter and had started wheezing when she walked up the hill, so Gemma wanted to check if there was another lung condition such as asthma or COPD that was making Sam's breathlessness worse.

'This is going to help us get to the bottom of your breathlessness and your cough, Sam,' she said, 'so we can get you the right treatment to help you. Just to remind you what I said at the last appointment, I'm going to test your breathing through a spirometer to get a baseline, then give you some asthma medication, get you to sit in the waiting room while the medication takes effect, and run the test again to see if the medication makes a difference.'

'I remembered to wear loose, comfortable clothing, like you said,' Sam said. 'I didn't have even a single glass of wine last night, and I haven't smoked for twenty-four hours. It was murder, last night—I really wanted just a quick cigarette—but Marty wouldn't let me.'

'Good,' Gemma said with a smile. 'How are your headaches?'

'Not great,' Sam admitted. 'Do you think they're something to do with my breathlessness?'

'Very possibly,' Gemma said. 'Now, I just want to run through a checklist to make sure there isn't anything else that might affect the results.' She ran through the list with Sam, and to her relief there was nothing else.

'Great. We're ready to start. Are you sitting comfortably?' Sam nodded.

'This is how I want you to breathe into the spirometer,' Gemma said, and demonstrated. 'I want you to breathe in and completely fill your lungs with air, close your lips tightly round the mouthpiece, and then blow very hard and fast. We'll do that three times, and then a test where I want you to keep blowing until your lungs are completely empty. I'll put a very soft clip on your nose to make sure all the air goes into the mouthpiece when you breathe out. Is that OK?'

Sam nodded, and Gemma encouraged her through the tests.

'Well done, that's brilliant,' she said. 'Now I'm going to get you to take some asthma medication, and I'd like you to sit in the waiting room for about twenty minutes so it has a chance to open up your airways; then we'll repeat the test and compare the results to each other.'

'My mouth's a bit dry,' Sam said.

'It's fine to have a drink of water while you're waiting,' Gemma said.

'Just not a cigarette?' Sam asked wryly.

'Exactly.'

Gemma helped Sam to take the asthma medication, then saw her next patient for an asthma review while Sam's medication took effect.

'How are you feeling?' she asked when Sam came back into the room. 'Has the medication made it easier to breathe?'

'A bit,' Sam said.

'That's good.'

Once Gemma had done the second set of tests, she compared the two sets of graphs. 'I'd just like to run these past one of the doctors first, if you don't mind?' she said.

'Sure. Do you want me to go back to the waiting room?' Sam asked.

'No, it's fine to wait here. He'll be here in a minute.' According to the roster, Oliver was the duty doctor this morning and was doing phone triage right now. Gemma sent him a note over the practice messaging system.

Before your next call, please can we have a quick word about one of my patients? Did spirometry, but patient not responded as well as I hoped to bronchodilator meds—think we're looking at COPD but would appreciate a second opinion.

Within seconds, a message flashed back.

Good timing—just finished call. Coming now.

Gemma opened the door at his knock.

'Sam, this is Dr Langley, who's working here while Dr Devi's on maternity leave,' she said. 'Dr Langley, this is Sam.' She gave him a potted version of Sam's patient history.

'Nice to meet you, Sam,' Oliver said. 'So may I look at the graphs?'

Gemma handed them over, and he checked them swiftly. 'I agree with you,' he said quietly.

'Sam, this is what a normal pattern of breathing looks like for someone of your height, age, sex and ethnic group,' Gemma said, showing Sam the graph on her computer. 'And this is your pattern.'

'So I'm not breathing out enough air,' Sam said.

'Instead of you blowing most of the air out of your lungs in the first second, there's a shallower curve,' Oliver said. 'It's what we call an obstructive pattern, meaning that you've got a lung condition which narrows your airways, so the air is flowing out more slowly than it should.'

'I was hoping that the medication would open up your airways a lot more, so your pattern would match that of someone who doesn't have a lung condition, and that would've meant I'd diagnose you with asthma,' Gemma said, 'but unfortunately it hasn't. There are some other conditions that can cause breathlessness, so I'm going to send you for a chest X-ray and do some blood tests to check if you're anaemic, or if there's a higher than average concentration of red blood cells in your blood.'

'Chest X-ray?' Sam went white. 'Oh, no. Are you telling me you think I've got lung cancer?'

'I'm just being thorough and ruling things out,' Gemma said. 'From the look of this graph, I think you have something called chronic obstructive pulmonary disease—COPD for short.'

'I agree with Nurse Practitioner Baxter. Chronic means it's long-term and won't go away, obstructive means your airways are narrowed so it's harder for you to breathe out quickly and air gets trapped in your chest, and pulmonary means it affects your lungs,' Oliver added.

Sam grimaced. 'And I've got it because I'm a smoker?'

'We're not judging you, but yes. Nine out of ten cases of COPD are caused by smoking,' Gemma said.

'Though COPD can also run in families,' Oliver said. 'And if you work in a place where you're exposed to a lot of dust, fumes or chemicals, that can contribute.'

'Nobody else in my family gets breathless, and I work in a garden centre. So it has to be the smoking,' Sam said with a sigh. 'I know I shouldn't do it. But I started smoking when I was fifteen, because all my friends were doing it and I didn't want to be left out. And then it got to be a habit. It calms me down when things get tough.

'I've tried to give up a couple of times, and I managed it

when I was pregnant because I didn't want it to affect the baby, but Louisa's toddler tantrums sent me right back to having a quick cigarette in the garden to help calm me down, and I never managed to stop again.' She shook her head and grimaced. 'It's just too hard.'

'COPD isn't a condition we can cure, or even reverse,' Gemma said. 'But the best way to stop it getting any worse is for you to stop smoking.'

'We can support you,' Oliver said. 'There are lots of things that can help you—patches and gums and sprays. And you're three times more likely to be able to give up with our support than if you're struggling on your own.'

'We can also refer you for a pulmonary rehabilitation programme,' Gemma said. 'It's a six-week course with other people who have the same condition as you do. Some of the sessions will teach you exercises to help your breathing, but the trainer will also be able to teach you breathing techniques, how to manage stress, and how to manage your condition better.'

'That sounds good,' Sam said.

'We ask all our patients who have asthma or COPD to have a flu jab every year,' Gemma said, 'because when you have a lung condition you're more vulnerable to catching the flu in the first place, and developing complications.'

'And there's a one-off pneumococcal vaccine, which will help protect you against pneumonia,' Oliver added. 'I know it's a lot to take in, and it sounds scary, but we can help you.'

'You'll get a letter so you can book onto the pulmonary rehab course at a time that works for you,' Gemma said, 'and I'll refer you to a counsellor who can help you stop smoking. Plus you'll have regular appointments with me to see how you're doing, and to check that your symptoms are under control and you're not getting any side effects from the medication.'

'Thank you,' Sam said. 'And I'll try really hard to stop smoking. Really, I will.'

'You're not on your own,' Oliver said. 'That's the main thing. We're here to help.'

Once Sam and Oliver had left her consulting room, Gemma took a sip of water. Now she'd seen Oliver Langley with a patient, she could see exactly why the head of the practice had offered him the job. He was kind, supportive and clear without being patronising; he hadn't judged Sam for smoking; and he was a world away from the cold, slightly haughty man she'd first met on Monday morning. The way he'd worked with Gemma, backing her up, had made her feel as if she'd worked with him for years, rather than today being only his third day on the team.

But Oliver was still practically a stranger. And she needed to be sensible instead of noticing how her heart skipped a beat every time he smiled.

She sent him a note across the practice messaging system after she'd written up the notes and before seeing her next patient.

Thanks for your help with Sam's COPD. Appreciated.

You're welcome, he replied.

Gemma liked the fact that he had nice manners. The more she got to know Oliver Langley, the more she liked him.

Strictly as a colleague, she reminded herself, and saw her next patient.

Just when she'd seen her last appointment of morning surgery, her computer pinged with a message.

Are you busy for lunch, or can I buy you a sandwich and we can maybe sit on the cliffs again?

Which sounded as if they were about to start becoming friends.

She messaged back.

A sandwich would be nice. Thank you. Just writing up my last set of notes and I'll be with you.

Crazy.

Ollie knew he shouldn't be looking forward to lunch with Gemma.

But he was. He'd liked the way she'd been with her patient this morning, all calm and kind and reassuring. And the fact that she'd checked with him on a case she wasn't sure about: her patients' welfare came before her professional pride, which was exactly how it should be.

Gemma Baxter was nothing like the man-eater he'd assumed she was when he'd first set foot in the reception area on Monday morning and overheard that comment.

She was *nice*. Genuine.

And if Rob was here right now he'd grin and say that Gemma was just Ollie's type, with those huge eyes and all that fair hair.

He didn't need a type. This was a burgeoning friendship, that was all—and that was fine by him.

Once they'd chosen sandwiches and headed up to the cliffs, he helped her spread out the picnic blanket. Again, his fingers accidentally touched hers and it felt as if lightning zinged through him. His lower lip tingled, and he couldn't help moistening it with the tip of his tongue.

Oh, for pity's sake. He really needed to get a grip. Work, he thought. That was a safe subject. 'How was your morning?' he asked.

'Pretty good. Thanks for your help with Sam—I've only just taken over the practice asthma clinic, so I'm still finding my feet a bit.'

'No problem. That's what I'm here for,' he said.

'How was your morning?' she asked.

'Pretty good.' He smiled at her. 'I've been thinking. I'd like to sponsor you for your skydive. You said it was next month?'

'Two weeks on Friday,' she said. 'I have to admit, I'm feeling a bit nervous about it now. It's a tandem skydive, so I know I'm going to be perfectly safe with an instructor, but even the idea of stepping out of that plane makes my palms go sweaty.'

'You're clearly not scared of heights, though, or you wouldn't be here on the cliff.'

'No, but I wouldn't choose to go rock-climbing.' She looked at him. 'Though, actually, I guess that could be a potential challenge for the future. Maybe next year.'

He frowned. 'So why are you doing the skydive? I know you said it was for charity, but is it because you're challenging yourself to overcome your fears as well?'

'No, but people get bored of sponsoring the same thing. A skydive's good for raising the profile of the cause, too. There's a good chance it'll go on the local newspaper's website, along with my fundraising page details, so maybe people who don't know me but want to support the cause will donate something.'

'You said you were raising funds for the local hospital's cardiac unit. Is that because you did some of your training there?' he asked.

'No.' She took a deep breath, as if psyching herself up to say something. 'My little sister spent a while there. I'm fundraising in her memory.'

In her memory... Gemma's little sister had *died*?

Before he could process that, she said, 'It was a long time ago now. I caught a bug at school, and Sarah caught it from me. I got better, but she didn't—she was still breathless and struggling. The next thing we knew, she was in the cardiac unit, being diagnosed with myocarditis.'

He'd noticed exactly what she'd said. 'It wasn't your fault. If the bug was going round at school, she could've caught it from one of her friends, not just from you.'

'Uh-huh.'

It sounded as if she still blamed herself, even though as a medic she'd know that wasn't fair. 'Was she on the list for a transplant?' he asked.

'Yes, but we were waiting for months. The right donor just didn't come along.' She looked away. 'Sarah died when I was seventeen and she was thirteen.'

He reached over and squeezed her hand. 'I'm sorry. That must have been devastating for you and your family.'

'It was,' she admitted. 'I've had twelve years to get used to it, but I still miss my little sister. And I really didn't cope very well at the time.' She shrugged. 'This is why I do the fundraising. It won't bring my little sister back and it won't do anything for the donor lists, but the hospital is doing research into permanent artificial hearts. And if that works out, it means another family might not have to lose someone they love dearly.'

'I'm sorry I've brought back bad memories for you.'

'I have a lot of good memories of Sarah.' She smiled, though her eyes were suspiciously shiny and he rather thought she was holding back tears. 'Doing her hair and make-up for a school disco, painting her nails, making cakes with her, playing in the garden.'

Obviously her memories were what carried her through the tough times. 'I'll definitely sponsor you,' he said.

She shook her head. 'I don't want you to feel obliged. It's fine.'

He knew the way to persuade her to accept his offer. 'It's not that I feel obliged,' he said. 'I was very nearly in your shoes, earlier this year.'

Apart from the people in the support group she'd gone to—and that hadn't lasted for long—Gemma had never met anyone else who'd had someone close who needed a heart transplant. 'Someone in your family needed a heart transplant?'

'No. My brother needed a kidney transplant.'

She winced. 'That must've been hard for you all.'

He nodded. 'Rob's a bit of a thrill-seeker. He's an A and E doctor in Manchester. He spends all his free time climbing, and he's on the local mountain rescue team. He took a six-month sabbatical to work with a humanitarian aid agency; he'd gone out to help with a region that had just been hit by an earthquake. He had stomach pains when he'd been there for a couple of days, but he just assumed it was an ordinary tummy upset because he wasn't used to the food and water. And then, when he collapsed, they realised he had acute appendicitis.'

'Poor man—that's really tough.'

'It was. He was airlifted to a hospital, but his appendix burst on the way and he ended up with severe blood poisoning.' Oliver looked grim. 'It wiped out his kidneys, and he was on dialysis for a while.'

'But you got a donor?'

Oliver inclined his head. 'That's the main reason why I came back to Northumbria. We've been recuperating at our parents' house since the transplant.'

She blinked. '*We*—you mean, you were a living donor?'

'It was the obvious solution,' Oliver said. 'Rob's my twin.'

She hadn't expected that. 'Identical?'

'Apparently you can look identical but not actually be identical, so we had to do gene sequencing to check,' Oliver said. 'We're not quite identical. But, even so, getting a kidney from me meant his body was much less likely to reject it, and he's on a lower dose of immunosuppressant drugs than he'd need if anyone else had donated the kidney.'

'So that's why you're working up here now?'

'I was getting a bit stir-crazy,' he said. 'Mum's overdoing the cotton wool treatment.'

Gemma's parents had been too hurt to wrap her in cotton wool. Instead, they'd let their grief build a wall between them and never let her back in. She pushed the thought away.

'I'm the sensible one and it's been driving *me* crazy, so poor Rob is really having to learn to be patient.' He grinned. 'Which will probably do him good.'

'You're both so lucky,' she said. 'Your twin, because he has you; and you, because you could actually do something practical to help.'

'Yes. If it had been a different organ that failed, we would've had to wait for one to become available.' He wrinkled his nose. 'You know yourself, it's not very nice, waiting for someone else to die.'

'No. It'd feel horrible, knowing your loved one's only still with you because someone else lost someone they loved,' Gemma said. 'Though Sarah thought about that, even when we knew it was too late and she was too ill for a transplant to work. She said she'd rather help someone else, even though she couldn't be helped, so she made our parents sign to donate everything that she could.'

'Brave kid,' Oliver said.

'She was. I wish...' Her breath hitched, and he could guess what she was thinking. She wished her sister hadn't died. Wished she'd been the one to be ill, to save her sibling. All the thoughts that had scrambled through his own brain in the early hours of the morning, when he couldn't sleep for thinking of what might have been.

'I often wonder what she would've been doing now,' Gemma said. 'She would've been twenty-five. I think she would've done something with art—she was really good.'

Oliver reached over and squeezed her hand. 'I'm sorry. I know how bad I felt when I thought I was going to lose Rob, earlier this year. It must've been so hard for you.'

'It was,' she agreed. 'And my parents have never recovered from it. They moved from the village, the year after Sarah died, because they couldn't handle all the memories.'

'You said you were seventeen at the time, so I assume they waited for you to finish your A levels before they moved?' he asked.

She shook her head. 'I made a complete mess of my exams and ended up having to resit them. But I didn't have to change schools; my best friend's mum let me stay with them and redo the year.' Yvonne had got her back on the straight and narrow. She'd *cared*. Been the stand-in mum Gemma had desperately needed.

'That's an amazing thing to do for someone,' he said.

'It is, and I'll always be grateful to her. Actually, I've been thinking lately that maybe I could offer a place for a teenager needing support—kind of pay forward what Claire's parents did for me. I live alone, but my working hours are regular so I could be there for someone who needed it.'

Gemma lived alone, and it sounded as if she didn't have a partner.

That really shouldn't make Ollie feel as pleased as it did. He wasn't looking for a relationship and, since Tabby had broken their engagement, he wasn't sure he'd be enough for anyone in any case.

But there was something about Gemma Baxter that drew him. A brightness, a warmth.

She'd come through the kind of nightmare that he'd dreaded happening to Rob and had kept him awake at night for months, and she was doing her best to try to stop other people having to go through it.

No partner.

He really needed to stop this. Yes, he liked Gemma and he was drawn to her. But he wasn't ready to move on with his life. He needed to be fair to her; all he could offer her right now was friendship.

'It'd be a good thing to do,' he agreed. 'Rewarding. You'd know you were really making a difference to someone's life.'

'So how's your brother doing now?' she asked.

'He's recovering well, but it's driving him a bit crazy not being at work. He knows there's no way he can go back out to do the humanitarian aid stuff or the mountain rescue—with only one working kidney, he's too much of a risk to be on a team. And he's not fit enough to go climbing again, either. He needs to be patient for a bit longer. And, for Rob, "rest" is most definitely a four-letter word.'

'So when did it all happen?' she asked.

'He collapsed at the beginning of March. We did the transplant at the beginning of June, and I got the green light from the surgical team a couple of weeks ago to go back to work.'

'So you're still healing from donating the kidney, really.'

'I'm fine. It means no heavy lifting,' Ollie said, 'but that's about all. Luckily there weren't any complications for either of us, though Rob's not pleased that they've told him to wait a few more weeks before he goes back.'

'That's such an amazing thing to do, being a live donor and giving your brother a kidney.'

'I'm guessing you would've done the same for your sister.'

'Of course I would,' she said. 'Any live donation—a whole kidney, a piece of liver or a bit of pancreas. If I could've saved her...' Her eyes were suspiciously glittery.

'I know how lucky we were,' he said quietly. 'I had the chance to make a difference. And Rob's doing OK.'

'I'm glad.'

Ollie almost asked her to join them both for dinner, the following evening, but he didn't want his twin getting the wrong idea. 'Me, too.' He glanced at his watch. 'I guess we need to be getting back.'

'We do. I meant to mention this earlier, but are you busy on Friday evening?'

No, but he wasn't going to commit himself to anything until he knew what she had in mind. 'Why?'

'There's a pub quiz at The Anchor,' she explained. 'We normally field a team from the surgery. It starts at eight, but we've got a table booked to eat beforehand, if you'd like to join us.'

He really appreciated the fact she was trying to include him. 'Thank you. I'd love to.' He'd planned to spend Sunday with his family, but on Friday evening and Saturday he hadn't really been sure what to do with himself. It would be good to get to know his team a bit better.

'Great. Our table's booked for half-past six. The menu's small but I'd recommend absolutely everything on it. Everything's sourced as locally as possible.'

'Sounds good,' Ollie said. 'Count me in.' He took his phone from his pocket. 'What's your number? I'll text you so you'll have mine. And then you can text me back with the link to your fundraising page.'

'Thanks.' She recited her number, and he tapped it into his phone and sent her a text; a few seconds later, he heard a 'ping'.

'Got it,' she said.

And funny how her smile made the bright, sunny day feel even more sparkly.

CHAPTER FOUR

On Thursday, Ollie didn't see Gemma at the practice; according to Maddie, Gemma usually had Thursdays off. But he enjoyed showing his twin round the village that evening after dinner.

'What a view,' Rob said from the cliffs. 'I can see why you moved here, Olls. And you said they do kite-surfing in the bay? Fantastic. When can I book a session?'

Ollie cuffed his arm. 'No adventure stuff until your consultant says it's OK.'

'Just one tiny little session?' Rob wheedled. 'Half an hour—thirty teeny, tiny minutes?'

Ollie shook his head. 'Nope. And if you won't listen to me, I might have to casually mention to Mum that Rob the Risk-Taker is back.'

Rob groaned. 'Please don't. You know I love Mum dearly, and I know that she and Dad were worried sick about me when I was ill, but I really can't take much more of the cotton wool treatment. Neither could you,' he pointed out, 'or you wouldn't have escaped here.'

'True,' Ollie admitted.

'I want to escape, too. I've got an interview next week.'

Ollie stared at his twin in surprise. 'You're going back to Manchester already?'

'No. It's local—the hospital down the road. You know I'd taken that six months off to join the humanitarian aid team; as I've spent most of that time stuck in hospital or recovering, my boss has agreed to extend my sabbatical.'

Ollie felt his eyes widen. 'Please tell me you're not going back to an earthquake zone or what have you.'

'No. Apart from the fact that I have a gazillion hospital appointments, even I'm not that stupid,' Rob said. 'I'm hoping to get a part-time post at the hospital here for the next few months, until my consultant's happy with my recovery.'

'And then you'll go back to Manchester?'

'Yes. I'm desperate to go climbing again,' Rob said, 'but I promise I'm not going to do anything that will set my recovery back.'

'I'm glad to hear it,' Ollie said dryly. 'Though I'm not entirely convinced.'

'Seriously, Olls. If I have a setback, I'll be stuck sitting around recovering for even longer. That's not going to help my itchy feet. I don't want to give Mum more excuses to smother me. And, most importantly, I don't want to worry Dad to the point where his angina flares up,' Rob said. 'I couldn't live with myself if he got ill again because of me.'

'Now *that*,' Ollie said, 'convinces me.'

'Good.' Rob smiled. 'So how are you getting on with your nurse practitioner?'

'I'm getting on fine with all my colleagues,' Ollie said.

'Meaning you like her and you don't want to admit it.'

'She's my colleague, Rob. My *temporary* colleague. It's not a great idea. If we get together and it goes wrong, it'll be awkward at work. We're just going to be friends.'

'You wouldn't let it be awkward because you're a total professional and you put your patients first,' Rob said. 'And there's also no reason why it should go wrong. And, as you said, it's temporary—so why not let yourself be happy while you're here?'

'It's too soon.'

'It's nearly four months. To me, you're on the verge of wallowing—and I can be that harsh because you're my brother and I love you too much to let you carry on being miserable.' Rob shook his head. 'Tabby really hurt you, I know, but the best way to get over a break-up is to meet someone else.'

'That's cynical, Rob.'

'It's a fact, little brother,' Rob said lightly. 'Maybe your nurse practitioner would be good for you.'

'I'm not a user, Rob.'

Rob frowned, 'Of course you're not. What I'm trying to say, in my very clumsy way, is that you've had a rough few months. And you're here for the next three months. Spending a little time with someone you like, getting to know each other and having a bit of fun—it might help you move on. Don't let what happened with Tabby put you off dating anyone else.'

'You're not dating anyone, either,' Ollie pointed out.

'Because I'm still recovering from major surgery.'

Ollie just looked at his brother.

'All right. I like the thrill of the chase and I haven't met anyone who's made me want to settle down. Even though we're practically identical, I'm wired differently from you, Ollie. You can settle. I have itchy feet. And I admit, I get bored easily.' Rob sighed. 'Perhaps it's true about there being a good twin and a bad twin. You're the good one.'

'You're not the "bad twin" at all, Rob. We just want different things.'

'I'm sorry that I caused your break-up with Tabby...'

'You didn't cause the break-up,' Ollie said.

'Look at it logically. It was my fault. If my kidneys hadn't failed, you wouldn't have suggested moving your wedding day and it wouldn't have escalated into—well, cancelling it. Though

I still think the reason she gave you for calling it off was seriously weak.'

'She grew up seeing her mum put her life on hold for her dad, and she didn't want that kind of future for herself. I can understand that,' Ollie said, 'even if I don't think I would've given her that kind of future.'

'Maybe you had a lucky escape,' Rob said. 'Because if the going got tough she wouldn't have stuck it out.'

Or maybe he just wasn't *enough* for anyone, Ollie thought.

'You've got your brooding face on. Stop,' Rob said.

'Sorry. I really thought she was the right one. Which makes me pretty hopeless at judging people,' Ollie said.

Rob clapped his shoulder. 'Actually, it makes you human. Everyone makes mistakes. Just don't close yourself off.'

'Be more Rob, and take a risk?' Ollie asked wryly.

'Just as I'm going to try to be more Ollie, and be sensible,' Rob said. 'So, between us, we can be the best we can be. Deal?'

Ollie thought about it. Be more like his twin. Take risks. The idea put him into a cold sweat; over the years, Rob had taken more than enough risks for both of them.

'Olls,' Rob said softly. 'It'll do both of us good.'

Put like that, how could he refuse? 'Deal.'

On Friday morning, Ollie arrived at the surgery to discover a tray of individually wrapped brownies, lemon cake and oatmeal cookies on one of the low tables, with a plastic jar labelled 'Donations' beside them and a folded card announcing 'Gemma's Friday Fundraisers are back!'

Clearly this was what his colleague had spent her day off doing. Baking.

There was another card on the tray, listing the ingredients in each recipe with the potential allergens highlighted in bold.

Smiling, he picked up a cookie and some lemon cake, and dropped some money into her box.

'What's this—buying cake?' Gemma teased, walking into the reception area. 'I thought you weren't a cake person?'

'I'm not. I'm buying this for my next-door neighbours,' he said. 'I thought they might like a Friday treat.'

'That's kind of you.'

'They've kept an eye out for me since I moved in. It's the least I can do,' he said.

'Are you still OK for the quiz team tonight?' she asked.

'Yes.'

'Good. See you there. Triage awaits,' she said with a smile.

Midway through the morning, Ollie was just writing up his notes when Maddie, the receptionist, burst into his room. 'Dr Langley, help! One of our patients has just collapsed in the waiting room.'

'I'm coming,' Ollie said, grabbing his stethoscope. 'Did you see what happened?'

'No. I was helping a patient when someone else in the waiting room screamed and I saw Mrs Henderson on the floor. Apparently she just fell off her chair.'

There were three main causes of collapse: fainting, seizures and heart problems. Given that Maddie hadn't mentioned Mrs Henderson's shaking limbs, it was likely to be fainting or a cardiac issue. 'Get the defibrillator,' he said, 'find out if anyone saw her hit her head, and I might need you to call an ambulance—and manage the patients in the waiting room, please, so we can give her a bit of privacy.'

'Got it,' Maddie said.

The middle-aged woman was still lying on the floor when they went into the reception area.

'Can you hear me, Mrs Henderson?' Ollie asked loudly, shaking her shoulder as he knelt beside her.

There was no response.

He tilted her head back to clear her airway.

'I've got the defib and she didn't hit her head,' Gemma said, joining him. 'The patient next to her said she just collapsed.'

'Do you by any chance know her medical history?'

'Yes. Nicole Henderson has high blood pressure—she's actually due for a check with me, this morning, because the last two medications I've tried with her haven't worked, and she had a bad reaction to beta blockers.'

This was sounding more and more like a cardiac event. 'Her airway's clear but she's not breathing,' he said. 'I'll start CPR. Can you turn the defib—'

'Already done,' she cut in. 'I'll do the sticky pads. Maddie's got everyone outside so we're good to go. I'll call the ambulance, too.'

She placed the pads on each side of Mrs Henderson's chest. He stopped doing CPR so the machine could analyse Mrs Henderson's heart rhythm. The recorded voice on the defibrillator informed them it was administering a shock, then told him, when it had no effect, to continue CPR.

Gemma had got through to the emergency services. 'The ambulance is on its way,' she said.

Between them, they kept going with chest compressions and breathing, stopping only when the defibrillator's recorded voice told them it needed to check the patient's heart rhythm.

By the time the paramedics arrived and loaded her into the ambulance, Nicole Henderson still hadn't regained consciousness.

'This isn't looking great,' Ollie said wearily. 'Poor woman. Hopefully they'll get her heart restarted on the way in to hospital.'

They both knew that the longer it took to restart the heart, the worse the prognosis. And, given that Gemma's sister had died from a heart condition, Ollie knew this must be tough for her. 'Are you OK?' he asked.

She nodded. 'I just feel I've let my patient down.'

'You couldn't have predicted this,' he said. 'And we did our best here. In some ways, this is the best place she could've collapsed, because we have a defib and enough knowledge between us to give her the right help.'

'I know. It's just...' She grimaced.

He reached out and squeezed her hand. 'You had the defib switched on and the pads ready almost before I could ask. Nobody could've done more. And she might be fine.'

Except the hospital called later that afternoon to say that Nicole Henderson hadn't made it.

He typed Got a minute? on the practice messaging system and sent it to Gemma.

Yes.

Ollie made her a mug of coffee and rapped on her door. 'Sorry, it's not good news. She didn't make it.'

Gemma sighed. 'Poor woman. She was the head of the local junior school. She wasn't popular—let's just say her predecessor was very different and everyone was upset when she retired, because she always fought for the kids and she was great with the parents and teachers—but even so I don't think anyone would actually wish her dead.'

'Don't blame yourself,' he said. 'I reviewed her notes when I wrote up what happened, and I would've treated her the way you did.'

'If only she hadn't rescheduled her appointment from last week.'

'It might still have happened, and it might've been somewhere that didn't have a defib.'

'I suppose so. Thank you for being kind.' She took a deep breath. 'I have referrals to write up and I'm guessing you have paperwork, too. So I won't hold you up. But I appreciate the coffee.'

'You're welcome.' He paused. 'I don't mean this to sound as tactless as it does, but will the quiz tonight be cancelled?'

She shook her head. 'I think, if anything, we need a reminder that there's a bright side to life. And that's not meant to sound callous.'

Gemma Baxter wasn't anything remotely approaching callous, he thought. 'OK. I'll see you later.'

The pub where Ollie had arranged to meet Gemma and the team was only a few minutes' walk from his cottage; when he arrived, the rest of his team was already there, and Gemma stood up to wave to him.

He hadn't seen her out of her uniform before; her faded jeans hugged her curves, and her hair was loose rather than tied back as she wore it for work. Yet again, he was struck by how pretty she was, and it almost made him tongue-tied. Which was crazy. He wasn't looking to get involved with anyone. Yet his twin's words echoed in his head.

'Spending a little time with someone you like, getting to know each other and having a bit of fun—it might help you move on.'

He made his way over to their table.

'Time for introductions,' Gemma said. 'Everyone, this is Oliver—he's Aadya's locum for the next three months.' She swiftly introduced him to the people round the table he hadn't yet met.

'Hello, everyone.' He smiled. 'Can I get anyone a drink?'

'No, we're all sorted,' Kyle, one of the other practice doctors, said, smiling back. 'I heard about Nicole Henderson. You've had a bit of a rough start to your time with us.'

'I'm just sorry I couldn't do more,' Ollie said. 'I hope it's not going to worry Aadya Devi's patients, the idea of having to see me when I've already lost a patient.'

'You and Gemma did everything you could,' Kyle said. 'Nobody's going to blame you.'

Ollie nodded his thanks. But the time he'd sorted out a pint and ordered his food, he was chatting with the others as if he'd always known them.

The quiz turned out to be great fun; although he was woefully inadequate on the local history round, he managed to get a couple of the musical intros that the others couldn't remember, as well as a really obscure geography question.

'How on earth did you know that?' Maddie asked.

'My twin's a climber,' Ollie said. 'He's the adventurous one; I'm the one with common sense.'

'There's nothing wrong with having two feet on the ground,' Kyle said. 'As I would dearly love to tell every single holiday-maker here who tries one of the water activities for the first time and tries to keep up with people who do it all the time, and ends up with a sprain or a strains or a fracture,' he added ruefully.

'Rob—my twin—got a bit excited about the idea of kite-surfing,' Oliver said. 'But he's having to be more me at the moment. He's recovering from a kidney transplant.'

'Ouch. That sounds nasty,' Fayola, their midwife, said. 'What happened?'

'Burst appendix followed by blood poisoning, and it wiped out his kidneys. He was helping with the aftermath of an earthquake at the time,' Ollie explained.

'Oh, now that's unfair,' Lakshmi, their pharmacist, said, sounding sympathetic. 'Poor guy.'

'He's doing well now,' Ollie said. 'But that's why I moved up here from London for a while, to support him and our parents.'

He caught Gemma's raised eyebrow; but he wasn't comfortable putting himself in the role of hero. Anyone would've done the same, in his shoes. Nobody else needed to know that he'd been the living kidney donor.

In the end, their team came second.

'And if anyone hasn't sponsored our Gemma for the skydive,' the quizmaster said, 'come and see us at the bar, because we've got a sponsorship form right here. And there's a collecting tin if you've got any spare change.'

Ollie really liked the fact that the whole village seemed to be so supportive of Gemma's efforts. It felt good to be part of a community like this. In London, he'd found that people kept themselves to themselves a lot more.

They stayed on for another drink after the quiz was over, and then the others all had to be back for their babysitters. Ollie looked at Gemma. 'Do you need to be anywhere right now?'

'No. Why?'

'I was going for a walk on the beach, to see the first stars coming out—something I couldn't really do in London. Do you want to join me?'

'That'd be nice,' she said.

They walked down to the beach together. The sea looked almost navy in the late summer evening light, and the first stars were peeking through. The moon was low and shone a silvery path across the sea. The waves were swishing gently across the shore, the rhythm soft and almost hypnotic, and Ollie felt the day's tensions starting to melt.

'That's the thing about living by the sea. If the day's been tough you can go for a walk and let the swoosh of the water wash the misery away,' she said.

'There were good bits to the day, too,' he said. 'But, yeah, losing a patient in my first week here is a bit of a shaky start.'

'It wasn't your fault,' she said. 'If it's anyone's fault, it's mine, but you argued me out of that earlier. We did our best, and that's all anyone can ask.'

'I guess.'

She stopped. 'Oliver.'

He stopped, too, and turned to face her. 'What?'

'Right now,' she said, 'I think you need a hug.' To his surprise, she took a step towards him and wrapped her arms round him.

Being this close to her meant he could smell the floral scent of her perfume. Light, sweet and summery, it made him think of sunshine. Being hugged by her was like being bathed in sunshine, too, and he couldn't resist wrapping his arms round her.

The waves swished onto the shore, and all Ollie was aware of was the beating of her heart, in the same strong, fierce rhythm as his own. The connection was irresistible, and he found his face pressed against hers. And then it was, oh, so easy to tilt his face just a fraction more, so the corner of his mouth was brushing against hers. His mouth tingled, and he couldn't help holding her closer, moving his face just a fraction further so he was really kissing her, and she was kissing him back.

His head was spinning and it felt as if fireworks were going off overhead, bright starbursts. Even though he knew he shouldn't be doing this—it was too soon after Tabby, and Gemma was his new colleague and he didn't want to complicate things—he couldn't help himself. This felt so *right*. Kissing Gemma, the sea singing a lullaby in the background, her arms wrapped as tightly round him as his were round her...

The moment seemed to last for ever, a moment of sweetness that was like balm to his aching heart.

And then it ended, and he found himself taking a step back and staring at Gemma.

'I'm sorry,' he said. 'That wasn't meant to happen.' A momentary—and major—lapse of reason.

'I think we've both had a tough day and we got caught up in the moonlight,' Gemma said. 'Let's pretend it didn't happen.'

The problem was, Ollie knew he'd rather like it to happen again. But she clearly didn't, so he'd have to ignore his feelings. 'OK. Can I at least walk you home? I know you're local and you're perfectly capable of looking after yourself, but it's dark and...well, it's the way I was brought up.'

'Gallant. I like that.'

And there was no edge to her tone, no mockery; Ollie had the strongest feeling that Gemma understood him and appreciated him.

They walked back to her flat in a companionable silence. At the entrance to the flats, she said, 'Would you like to come in for coffee?'

Part of him did; yet, at the same time, he knew it wasn't

a good idea. He could still remember the touch of her mouth against his and the scent of her hair; it would be more sensible to put a little distance between them so he could get his common sense back. 'Maybe another time?'

She nodded. 'Sure. Goodnight, Oliver.'

'Goodnight, Gemma. See you at work on Monday.'

Ollie spent Sunday with his family, as planned; and the influx of summer visitors and extra people needing medical help meant that he didn't actually have a proper lunch break until Wednesday. He'd just stepped into the bakery when he realised that Gemma was there.

'Great minds think alike,' he said with a smile. 'Are you heading up to the cliffs?'

'I certainly am,' she said. 'You're welcome to join me.'

'Thanks. I'd like that.'

Once they were settled on her picnic blanket, he said, 'So do you have much planned for the week?'

'I'm babysitting my goddaughter Scarlett—Claire's three-year-old—on Friday night, so she and Andy can have a proper date night. Which means I get Claire's amazing macaroni cheese for dinner; then Scarlett and I will sing our way through all the songs from *The Little Mermaid* during her bath; and then I get cuddles and tell her stories until she falls asleep.'

She grinned. 'And then I have a hot date with a classic rom-com, a mug of tea, and some of Claire's ginger cake. Friday night doesn't get better than this.'

His idea of a perfect Friday night sounded a lot like Gemma's. Cuddling up on the sofa with a good film, winding down after a busy week…

'How about you?' she asked.

'Nothing in particular,' he said. 'I might go for a walk on the beach on Saturday. Didn't you say something about a shipwreck being visible?'

'There is, at low tide.' She took her phone from her bag and looked something up. 'Low tide is at four o'clock on Saturday afternoon. If you don't mind a friend tagging along, maybe I could join you for that walk and tell you all the touristy stuff about the wreck.'

'I'd like that,' he said. 'And maybe we can grab fish and chips afterwards, and eat it sitting on the harbour wall.'

'Great idea,' she said with a smile. 'I haven't had fish and chips for ages. Which is a terrible admission, given that we live in a seaside village.'

Funny how her smile made him feel so warm inside. 'Fish and chips is mandatory,' he said, smiling back. 'I like mine with lots of salt and vinegar, but shhh, don't tell our patients that because I nag everyone about their salt intake...'

She laughed. 'Me, too. For both!'

Gemma spent most of Thursday cleaning her flat and baking for her charity cake stall; on Friday, she didn't see Oliver more than once in passing, though he did text her at lunchtime to check that she was still available for their walk on Saturday afternoon.

On Friday afternoon, Mrs Brown, the history teacher she remembered from school, came in. 'I'm so sorry, wasting your time coming in with something as minor as a rash,' she said. 'I did go to the pharmacy on Monday, but the hydrocortisone cream they gave me hasn't helped. The rash is spreading.' She grimaced. 'The itchiness is *unbelievable*. And it's keeping me awake at night.'

'Let me have a look, Mrs Brown,' Gemma said.

Mrs Brown rolled up her cotton trousers to her knees, and Gemma examined the rash. There were pinpricks of deep red on the edges, and the middle sections were raised with a flat surface.

'It looks like an allergic reaction, so we'll start with the obvious stuff. Have you made any changes to your detergents or toiletries over the last couple of weeks?'

'No, and it's not a change in formulation because they're the same batch I've used for a couple of weeks. I'm paranoid about ticks since Harvey—my spaniel—got one last year, so I always wear long trousers on dog-walks, and I haven't brushed against any plants or knelt on anything with bare legs.' Mrs Brown shook her head, seeming puzzled. 'I haven't eaten anything out of the usual, and my blood-pressure tablets are the same ones I've been on for years and years.'

'So that rules out all the usual suspects,' Gemma said.

Mrs Brown grimaced. 'I did wonder if it was shingles—I've heard that's horribly itchy.'

'Usually a shingles rash is only on one side of the body and doesn't cross the midline. This is on both shins, so I'm pretty sure it's not that,' Gemma said. 'Have you ever had eczema or psoriasis?'

'No, and the only things I'm allergic to are penicillin and fabric plasters—neither of which I've been in contact with for years.'

'OK. It's possible to develop allergies at any time of life,' Gemma said, 'so what I'm going to prescribe is something generic that should help. Colloidal oats to wash with, an emollient to keep your legs moisturised, a slightly stronger steroid cream to use twice a day to try and calm the rash down, and an antihistamine which should stop the itching. Until that kicks in, cold compresses are your best friend. And obviously you're sensible enough to know not to scratch.'

'So you've no idea what's causing it?'

'There are about three thousand different rashes,' Gemma said with a smile, 'so, at the moment, all I can say is it's a red, itchy rash and we don't currently know the cause. Or, if you want it in medical-speak, it's erythematous idiopathic pruritic macules.'

'Which sounds a bit more impressive,' Mrs Brown said with a wry smile.

'If it doesn't improve in the next three or four days, come back and I'll do a swab test and refer you to the dermatologist.'

Gemma printed out the prescriptions and handed them over. 'Cold compresses will definitely help to stop the itching.'

She changed at work and went straight to Claire's, where she enjoyed a catch-up with her best friend before Claire and Andy went out for the evening.

Spending time with Scarlett was always fun. They drew pictures and played games until dinner, and then it was bath time.

'Just one more, Aunty Gemma!' Scarlett pleaded.

'Nope. We've done *all* the songs,' Gemma said, and lifted her goddaughter from the bath to wrap her in a towel. 'Time to dry off before you get all wrinkly. And then it's a glass of milk, brush your teeth, and a story.'

'Two stories? Please, please, *please*?' Scarlett wheedled.

Gemma laughed. 'All right. Two stories. Let's get you dry and put your PJs on.'

Given the disaster of her love life—since she'd graduated, all her relationships had ended really quickly—Gemma thought that her goddaughter was probably the nearest she'd ever get to having a little one of her own. And she knew she was lucky. Some people didn't even have that.

After she'd settled Scarlett to sleep, she made herself a mug of tea and switched on the film. It was one of her favourites, and she must have seen it a dozen times over the years, but it still made her smile.

Apart from one thing.

The main actor's colouring was exactly the same as Oliver's. And Oliver's smile—rare, but genuine—made her heart beat just as fast as the actor's did.

She really was going to have to be sensible tomorrow. Even though there was something about him that made her want to forget all about caution. Or maybe especially because he tempted her to stop being careful and take a risk, she corrected herself. He was only here temporarily. The most they could offer each other was a summer of fun. Which might be a good thing:

but Gemma was scared that if she let him close then she'd start to want more. And what if he didn't want the same? What if he left after three months and didn't ask her to go with him?

So it would be better to stick to being friends. Forget that kiss and the way his had made her blood feel as if it was fizzing through her veins.

Oliver Langley was her colleague.

Full stop.

CHAPTER FIVE

SATURDAY WAS BRIGHT and sunny, and Gemma met Oliver at the harbour.

'Time for your touristy trip,' she said. 'We'll start with the spooky local legend, see the seals, then see the shipwreck,' she said with a smile.

'Bring it on,' Oliver said, smiling back. 'What's the spooky bit? A grey lady or something?'

'No, it's a barghest.'

'I've never heard of that,' he said.

'It's a huge black dog with massive teeth and claws and fiery eyes, which only comes out at night. Apparently if you see him, it's a portent of doom. It's left up to your imagination what that doom might be.' She laughed. 'It's very similar to the "black dog" story told all over the country, though. My theory is that the legend was started by smugglers, who hung lanterns with red covers round their ponies' necks to make it look like fiery eyes. If people were scared of the legend of the giant black dog, it meant they'd stay away from the cliffs—and that would mean they were less likely to discover the smugglers' tunnels and any contraband.'

'So there were smugglers at Ashermouth Bay?' he asked.

'There were in most places along the coast in the eighteenth century,' she said. 'There are tunnels in the cliff which lead to the Manor House and the rectory. They used to smuggle brandy, gin and tea. I remember doing the *Watch the Wall, My Darling* at school, and our teacher told us all about the tunnels. Most of the older houses in the village have little hiding places.'

'That's fascinating,' he said. 'Can you actually go down the tunnels now?'

'Strictly guided tours only, and it depends on the tide,' she said. 'The teacher who told us about the tunnels also said that she went in them when she was our age, with some friends; they had to be rescued by the lifeboat team, and one of her friends nearly drowned. And then she casually mentioned that there are rats everywhere, and huge spiders.'

'Enough to put you all off the idea of being brave and exploring by yourself?'

'Indeed.'

Gemma enjoyed walking with Oliver along the damp sand. A couple of times, his hand accidentally brushed hers and sent a zing of awareness through her skin; yet again, she remembered the way he'd kissed her on the beach a week ago, and it made her knees weak. Not wanting to be needy, she took refuge in the guided tour she was supposed to be giving him. 'Next, we have the seals,' she said. 'There's a big colony of grey seals, a bit further up the coast, but these ones are common seals. Their pups are born in June and July, and everyone comes to see them in the bay.'

Oliver looked entranced by the seals, the babies with their white fur and their parents undulating their way slowly along the sand, while others ducked and dived in the water.

'That's lovely. I can see why people come here,' he said.

They'd just reached the roped-off area when they saw a small boy running on the sand. A woman ducked under the rope—his mother, Gemma guessed—but before she could reach him he fell over, next to one of the seal pups. An older seal lunged at him, and he screamed.

'Jake!' the woman called, and sped over to grab him.

'Hopefully the seal just scared him, rather than bit him,' Gemma said.

But the little boy appeared to be clutching at his hand and crying.

'Can we help?' Oliver asked as the woman, carrying the child, ducked back under the rope next to them. 'I'm a doctor— my name's Oliver—and Gemma here's a nurse practitioner.'

'The seal bit him,' the woman said. 'I told Jake not to go near them. I *told* him we had to look at them from afar, but he ran off and went into the roped-off area before I could stop him.'

'We saw him fall,' Gemma said.

'I know seals are protective of their pups at this time of year—that's why the ropes are there—but I...' She shook her head, looking anguished.

'Let's get you over to the lifeguards' hut. They'll have a first-aid kit,' Oliver said.

Between them, they ushered Jake and his mother to the lifeguards' hut.

'Hey, Gem. What's happened?' the lifeguard asked.

'Hi, Callum.' Gemma explained swiftly and introduced Oliver.

'Could we have some hot water, some antiseptic and a dressing?' Oliver asked.

'Sure. I'll fetch them,' Callum said.

Gemma crouched down by the little boy, who was still crying. 'Jake, will you let me look at your hand?'

He shook his head, guarding his hand, and her heart sank.

'Jake, do you want to see a magic trick?' Oliver asked.

It was the last thing she'd expected but, to her relief, the distraction worked, and the little boy nodded.

'See how my hands are open?' Oliver asked, waggling his fingers. 'I need you to put your hands exactly like that, making a star shape with your fingers—but I want you to hold them *really* still—and then I want you to guess the magic word.'

Genius, Gemma thought as the little boy opened both his hands, the shock and pain of the bite forgotten.

'Please!' Jake said.

She couldn't help smiling. 'That's a good magic word.'

'But not the one I'm looking for,' Oliver said. 'Try again.'

Gemma examined Jake's hand while Oliver encouraged the little boy to guess more magic words.

To her relief, the bite was shallow, more of a graze than anything else; but she also knew that a seal's mouth could contain bacteria that could cause a very nasty complication, and the little boy would need a course of antibiotics.

'It's going to sting a bit,' Gemma warned when Callum brought the hot water and antiseptic over. 'Unfortunately our surgery's closed until Monday morning or I'd say call in and we'd prescribe antibiotics.'

'Antibiotics?' Jake's mum looked shocked.

'Are you local or on holiday?' Gemma asked.

'On holiday from Birmingham—this is our first day.'

'Then you need to go either to the walk-in centre in the next town, or to the emergency department at the hospital,' Gemma said. 'Take a seal letter with you, and they'll sort out some tetracycline to make sure an infection doesn't start.'

'Seal letter?' Oliver asked.

'Tetracycline's the most effective antibiotic against the Mycoplasma organism in a seal's mouth,' Gemma explained. 'It's why we have a seal letter for people to take to whatever medical department they go to. If a seal bite isn't treated properly, and the wrong antibiotic is given, the person could develop a complication called "seal finger".'

'Abracadabra!' Jake shouted.

'That's the right magic word. And look what I've found behind your ear,' Oliver said, plucking a coin from behind Jake's ear.

The little boy's eyes were round with amazement. 'That's real magic!'

'It certainly is,' Oliver said with a smile.

'Jake, I'm going to need to wash your hands with some very special soap and water.'

Callum had got a bowl of warm water ready, along with antiseptic soap, and Gemma encouraged Jake to wash his hands.

It obviously stung and the little boy pulled his hands out of the water and cried, but then Oliver stepped in again.

'I'll wash my hands with you,' he said. 'And we'll sing a special washing hands song. Do you know "If You're Happy and You Know it?"'

Jake nodded.

'We're going to change the words a bit,' Oliver said, taking his watch off and stuffing it into the pocket of his jeans. 'Instead of "clap your hands", we'll sing "wash your hands". Ready? And we'll get your mummy to sing it, too.'

'Yay!' Jake said, the stinging forgotten.

Oliver got them to sing along. It didn't matter that his voice was flat; he was so good with the little boy that it put a lump in her throat.

When Jake's hands were clean, Oliver gently helped dry them.

The wound was still bleeding a little bit—to Gemma's relief, because it meant she didn't have to hurt Jake by squeezing the wound to make it bleed. She put a pad over it and a dressing.

'Here's the seal letter,' Callum said, handing it to Jake's mum. 'And I've written the phone number and address of the walk-in centre and the hospital's emergency department on the back for you.'

'Thank you. I'll take him now,' Jake's mum said. 'And thank you, both of you, for helping.'

'That's what we're here for,' Oliver said with a smile.

Once Jake and his mum had left, Callum said, 'Thanks for the back-up, guys. Really appreciated.'

'No worries. Give my love to Sadie when you see her next,' Gemma said, and shepherded Oliver out of the lifeguards' hut.

'Sadie's his big sister. She was one of my sister's best friends,' she explained.

'I'm guessing everyone knows everyone in Ashermouth Bay?' Oliver asked.

'Pretty much,' she said with a smile.

'I have to say, I've never heard of "seal finger" before,' he said.

'To be fair, it's probably not that common in London,' she said.

'But it happens a lot here?'

'There have been a few cases, over the years. I didn't like to say, in front of Jake's mum, but it involves inflammation and cellulitis, and it used to mean the finger would have to be amputated.'

'That's pretty major stuff. So how do you know all about seals?'

'I was a seal warden, the summers when I was fifteen and sixteen. It meant I did a two-hour shift on the beach, most days, talking to visitors about the seals, answering their questions, advising them where to get the best views of the seals and also making sure they stayed well clear of the roped-off area where the seals were resting. If you get too close to the pups, you could scare the mum away and there's a risk she'll abandon the baby.'

'A seal warden.' He raised an eyebrow. 'You're full of surprises.'

'I wanted to be a vet, when I was fifteen,' she said. 'Though, after Sarah died, I decided I wanted to help people rather than animals, so I trained to be a nurse instead.'

'You're good with people,' he said. 'So do you have pets?'

'No. I work full-time, it's just me at home and I live in a flat, so it wouldn't be fair to have a dog. But I do walk a couple of dogs down my road, sometimes.' She looked at him. 'I assume you don't have pets, either?'

'No, and for the same reason. It really wouldn't be fair in London.'

Which reminded her. He was here temporarily. 'Do you think you'll go back to London?'

'I'll see how things go with Rob,' he said. 'Probably.'

And it was ridiculous that her stomach swooped in disappointment.

She kept the conversation light, telling him more about the seals and pointing out the shipwreck. They climbed up the path to the castle on the other side of the bay, then walked back along the cliffs and back down to the harbour. Every so often, his hand brushed against hers, and it felt like electricity zinging along her skin.

What if his fingers caught hers?

What if he held her hand?

It made her feel like a teenager again, waiting for the boy she had a crush on to notice her.

But Oliver had clearly had second thoughts since their kiss on the beach, and he was exquisitely polite with her. Gemma was cross with herself for being disappointed; hadn't she learned the hard way not to rely on other people for her happiness? So she pasted a bright, sparkling smile on her face and pretended everything was just fine.

When they reached the harbour and stood in the queue for the fish and chips, Ollie said, 'This is my shout, by the way.'

'We'll go halves,' Gemma countered.

He shook his head. 'You were kind enough to show me round. It's the least I can do.'

She smiled. 'All right. Thank you.'

They sat on the harbour wall, eating their fish and chips from the recyclable boxes, watching the boats and the gentle swish of the sea. How much slower life was here than it was in London, Ollie thought. And he was really beginning to enjoy living by the sea.

After they'd eaten, he walked her home. A couple of times, his hand brushed against hers, and he was so tempted to hold her hand. But that wasn't the deal they'd agreed. They were friends; and he still didn't trust his judgement. He didn't want to rush this.

They came to a halt outside a small block of flats.

'Would you like to come in for coffee?' she asked.

Ollie knew he ought to make an excuse, but he was curious to know what Gemma's inner sanctum was like. 'That'd be nice,' he said.

'I'm on the ground floor,' she said, and let them into the lobby before unlocking her front door. 'The bathroom's here on the left.'

She said nothing about the closed door on the right, which he assumed was her bedroom.

'Living room,' she said as they walked into the next room. 'And my kitchen-diner's through there. You take your coffee without milk, don't you?'

'And no sugar. Yes, please,' he said.

'Take a seat, and I'll bring the coffee through.'

The whole room was neat and tidy. The walls were neutral, as were the comfortable sofa and armchair with a reading lamp, but there was a throw the colour of sunshine across the back of the sofa, and the material of the cushions was covered in sunflowers. On the mantelpiece there was a vase of sunflowers—clearly Gemma's favourite flowers.

There were framed photographs surrounding the vase; one was of Gemma herself, and a younger girl who looked so much like her that Ollie guessed it was Sarah. There was another of Gemma holding a baby, which he guessed would be the goddaughter she'd mentioned earlier in the week, plus one of her with her fellow students at graduation. There was a photo of Gemma in a bridesmaid's dress, laughing with the bride; he vaguely recognised the other woman, and guessed that was Claire.

There were no photos, he noticed, of Gemma with her parents. Given how family-oriented Gemma seemed, that surprised him.

On the wall was a framed pen-and-ink drawing of seals on the beach.

'That's an amazing picture,' he said when she came back in, carrying two mugs of coffee.

'Sarah drew me that for my sixteenth birthday. It still amazes me to think she was only twelve at the time.'

'She was very talented,' Ollie said, meaning it.

Tears shimmered for a moment in Gemma's dark eyes. 'I loved her so much. But I know she'd be furious with me if I moped around—just as I would've been furious with her if I'd been the one who'd died and she'd been left behind to deal with it.'

If Rob had died from that burst appendix, Ollie thought, he wasn't sure he would've coped well with it. And he was thirty, not a teenager.

'I think she'd be really proud of you,' he said. 'You don't mope at all. Look at what you've achieved. You're a nurse practitioner, and you make a difference to people's lives every single working day. Plus you've raised a lot of money for the cardiac centre where she was treated.'

His kindness was nearly Gemma's undoing. 'I hope she'd be proud of me,' she said.

'What's not to be proud of? If you were my sister, I'd be boasting about you,' he said.

Sisterly wasn't quite the way she was feeling about him, but she damped that down. If he'd wanted to take things further between them, he would've taken her hand on the beach or said something.

'Thank you,' she said instead.

'So you're a reader?' He gestured to her bookcase.

'I love historicals,' she said. 'Yvonne—Claire's mum—got me reading historical crime when I was in sixth form, to give me a break from studying. I loved *The Cadfael Chronicles* series. And then I discovered historical romance.' She paused. 'So are you a reader?'

'Not as much as my mum would like,' he said with a smile. 'I tend to read non-fiction. Journals and the like. And I have a bad habit of watching documentaries.'

'Nothing wrong with that,' she said. 'Though I love films. Musicals and comedies, mainly.'

'With a bit of skydiving on the side.' He smiled. 'The sort of thing my twin would do.'

'I'm really not that brave,' she said. 'The skydiving's a one-off. Though I'm doing a sixty-mile cycle ride down the coast, next month.' She gave him a sidelong look. 'Are you a cyclist?'

'No. But I'll sponsor you,' he said.

'I wasn't dropping a hint.'

'I know, but it's important to you. And I'm your friend, so I'll support you.'

Friend.

Oliver had just made it very clear how he saw her.

So she'd just have to stop secretly wishing for more.

It was another busy week; and Mrs Brown called Gemma on Tuesday. 'I've been taking photographs of the rash, just so you can see how it's changed.'

Gemma looked at the photographs. 'It's definitely looking angrier. It's spreading, and the spots are coalescing.'

'And it's so, so *itchy*. It's keeping me awake at night.'

'Can you email the pictures to me, please?' She gave Mrs Brown the surgery's email address. 'I'm going to have a word with one of my colleagues,' she said, 'and I'll call you back.'

When the photographs arrived, she sent over a note through the practice messaging system.

How are you with rashes? Could do with another pair of eyes.

Oliver called her. 'Is your patient with you right now?'

'No. She's just sent me some photographs. I've added them to her notes.' She gave Oliver the details.

'Let's have a look.' He paused, and she guessed he was checking the file on his screen. 'Actually, you've treated it as I would've done. If it's not responding to steroid cream, I'd say ask her to do a swab test, to see if there's bacterial or viral involvement.'

'And if it's not that, then a referral to Dermatology?'

'Good call,' he said.

Gemma rang Mrs Brown and asked her to drop into the surgery later that morning to do a swab test, then called her next patient.

Eileen Townsend was eighty-one, diabetic, and her daughter had brought her in because she was having a lot of falls. Gemma knew that diabetes could cause elderly patients to have more falls than non-diabetics, because hypoglycaemia could cause light-headedness. She always worried about her elderly patients having a fall, with the extra risk of breaking bones; and reduced mobility often went hand in hand with foot care problems, which a diabetic might not notice.

'I help Mum with her medication,' Mrs Townsend's daughter said, 'and she had her six-monthly check with you three months ago.'

Gemma nodded. 'Nothing's changed since then?'

'Not really,' Mrs Townsend said.

Gemma double-checked her notes. There had been no hospital admissions and no suggestion that Mrs Townsend had had a stroke or developed Parkinson's. Maybe postural hypotension? 'Are you feeling light-headed at all before you fall, Mrs Townsend?'

'No. It just happens,' Mrs Townsend said.

'Would you mind me assessing you physically?' she asked.

'No. Just tell me what I need to do.'

'Can you stand up for me, please?'

Mrs Townsend stood up, and Gemma was pleased to see that she didn't sway, raise her arms or move her feet to balance.

'Wonderful. Can you lift one foot off the floor, just a little bit?'

She struggled to balance on her right foot, and Gemma made a note.

'Lovely. Can you walk round the room for me?' Gemma chatted to her as she walked, and was pleased to see that Mrs Townsend didn't stop walking when she answered a question.

'That's great. And, lastly, I'd like to try one more thing. I'd like you to sit down, walk over to the window, turn round, walk back to the chair and sit down again.'

Gemma timed her, and was pleased to note that it took less than twelve seconds.

'That's all really good,' she said. 'The only thing I think you're struggling with is balance. There are some good strength and balance exercises you can do using a chair—I can print some off for you.' She smiled at Mrs Townsend's daughter. 'And if you can help your mum do the exercises, that'd be brilliant. Though I'd like to try and set up some classes locally. I'll run that one by the head of the practice, and if I can make it happen I'll let you know.'

'Of course I can help my mum,' Mrs Townsend's daughter said.

'Brilliant. The other thing I'd like to do is send the occupational health team out to you for a hazards assessment of your home.'

'I've already checked the hazards. There aren't any trailing wires, I make Mum wear slippers with proper soles so she doesn't slip on the floor, and there aren't any rugs she can trip over,' Mrs Townsend's daughter said.

'That's excellent,' Gemma said. 'But it's not just about hazards you can see—it's looking at how you use the space and what they can do to help. So they might suggest putting risers on the bottom of an armchair to make it easier for your mum to stand up, or a grab rail next to a toilet or a bath. Plus they can set you up with an alarm you wear round your neck, Mrs Townsend, so you can get help really quickly if you do have a fall.'

'I don't want to wear something round my neck,' Mrs Townsend said. 'I'm old, not useless.'

'Of course you're not useless,' Gemma said. 'But you've had a few falls, and your daughter's worried about you—just as I'd be worried if my mum had a few falls. I'd be panicking that she'd fall at night and nobody would know—so she'd just have to lie there in the cold, unable to get up again until someone came in the next morning.'

Mrs Townsend's daughter nodded. 'That's my biggest fear. Mum, if you wore something round your neck so I knew you could get help when you needed it, that'd stop me panicking so much.'

'I suppose you're right,' Mrs Townsend said with a sigh. 'I don't want to lose my independence.'

'An alarm would actually give you a bit more independence because it'd stop your daughter worrying so much,' Gemma said gently.

'All right. I'll do it,' Mrs Townsend agreed.

'I'll sort out the referral,' Gemma promised, 'and they'll call you in a few days to organise a visit.' She printed off the exercises. 'These will all help with your balance and core strength, which means you're less likely to fall.'

'Ballet's meant to be good for that,' her daughter said.

'I'm too old to start being a ballerina,' Mrs Townsend said. 'I can't do all that leaping about.'

'Actually, there are special classes for older beginners,' Gemma said. 'My best friend's mum does it. And not only is it good for her balance, it's also meant she's made new friends. She says it's the best thing she's ever done. I can get the details from her, if you like.'

'That would be really good,' her daughter said. She smiled. 'Your social life will be better than mine, at this rate, Mum.'

'All right. I'll give it a go,' Mrs Townsend said.

Once her patient had gone, Gemma sent a note to Oliver over the practice internal email.

Are you busy at lunch, or can I run something for work by you?

The reply came swiftly.

Of course. Let me know when you've seen your last patient this morning.

Thank you, she typed back.

As usual, they bought lunch from Claire's and headed up to the cliffs.

'So what did you want to run by me?' Oliver asked.

'I had an elderly patient this morning—she's diabetic, and she's had a few falls. I'm sending the occupational health team out to her to see if they can tweak a few things and sort out an alarm she can wear round her neck, but I also checked her balance in the surgery, and I've been thinking for a while that maybe we could work with local instructors to set up some balance and light resistance training for our older patients. Say, a six-week course. That way, we're doing some pre-emptive health work instead of waiting for one of them to have a fall and maybe break a hip.'

'That's a good idea. Some of my patients in London went on a course to teach them the basics,' Oliver said, 'and then they could carry on at home.'

'I was thinking chair exercises,' Gemma said. 'A warm-up, some balance work and some resistance training. One of my friends manages the local gym, and she was saying their studio's not used that much during the day—the gym's classes are all just after the morning school run to grab the mums on the way home from school, lunchtime for the office workers, and in the evenings for everyone else. I was thinking, some of those spare spots could be used for a course. Maybe we could join forces with the gym, and between us we could split the cost.'

'And a gym would have light weights and resistance bands available. That's a good idea.' He looked at her. 'If I'm not interfering, would you like me to help you put a proposal together for Caroline, with a cost-benefit analysis?'

'That'd be nice.'

'OK. Are you free this evening?' he asked.

'Sorry. It's Tuesday, so it's my dance aerobics class with Claire.' She paused. 'Though it's actually my friend who manages the gym who instructs the class. I could sound her out after the class and see how practical it'd be.'

'Great idea. Do that, and maybe come over to mine on Thursday evening if you're free. I'll cook,' he offered.

'You'll cook?'

'Don't look so surprised. I've managed to survive my own cooking for the last decade or so,' he said.

'All right. You're on.' It was a combination of business and friendship, she reminded herself, not a date.

'Is there anything you don't eat?'

'I'm not a huge fan of red meat, but other than that I don't have any allergies or major dislikes.'

'Just an addiction to cake,' he teased. 'OK. What time?'

'Seven?' she suggested.

'Seven's fine.'

'How did you get on with the swabs for Mrs Brown?' Oliver asked when he saw Gemma in the staff room, the next day.

'The bacterial one showed just the usual skin flora,' she said, 'but the viral test was positive for HSV1. My poor patient was horrified, even though I explained that it's the Herpes simplex version that causes cold sores, not the sexually transmitted disease,' Gemma said.

'Two-thirds of the population has HSV1,' Oliver said. 'Most

of the time it stays dormant, but she might get a flare-up if it's really sunny, or if she's got a cold, or if she's stressed.'

'I've prescribed her a course of antivirals,' Gemma said.

'It's an interesting presentation,' Oliver said. 'You don't often see it on the shins.'

'But imagine how horrible it's been for her—being so itchy in the sticky heat we've had,' Gemma said. 'I've told her to keep up the cold compresses, and I've referred her to Dermatology. How's your morning been?'

'Sprains, strains and hay fever,' he said. 'And an asthma case I want to keep an eye on.'

Gemma had swapped her usual Thursday off for Friday, that week, so she could do the skydive; she was too busy for a lunch break, but Oliver texted her in the afternoon to check their dinner meeting was still on.

She played safe and took a bottle of white wine and a hunk of local cheese from the deli. 'I thought you'd prefer this to chocolates,' she said. 'It's a local artisan cheese.'

'Perfect. I love cheese,' Oliver said with a smile. 'You didn't have to bring anything, but I'm glad you did. Come through.'

Even though she knew Oliver was only renting the place for a couple of months, his cottage still felt personal rather than being like temporary home; there were photographs on the mantelpiece and a couple of journals on the coffee table.

'Can I be nosey?' she asked, gesturing to the mantelpiece.

'Sure. They're very obviously my twin and my parents,' he said.

He hadn't been kidding about Rob being his identical twin. The only way she could tell them apart in the photographs was that Rob had shorter hair, in an almost military cut. But, weirdly, it was only the photographs of Oliver that caused her heart to skip a beat.

'So did you train together?' she asked, looking at the two graduation photographs.

'No. He went north-west, so he could take advantage of the climbing locally, and I went to London,' Oliver said.

'He looks nice.'

'He is. He's one of the good guys,' Oliver said. 'Anyway. I assume you walked here, as you haven't asked me for a car permit, so can I get you a glass of wine?'

'That'd be lovely, thank you.' She took a last look at the photographs—and oh, how she envied him the graduation photographs with his parents and his brother. They all looked so close, so like the family she longed for. The family she'd once had.

She followed him into the kitchen, where he'd set a little bistro table for two.

'Something smells wonderful,' she said. 'Is there anything I can do to help?'

'Just sit down,' he said with a smile, and took a casserole dish out of the oven. 'It's an oven-baked risotto. Chicken, aubergine and artichoke.'

He'd paired it with a dish of baby plum tomatoes, a green salad and balsamic dressing.

'This is really delicious,' she said after her first taste. 'I might have to beg the recipe.'

'It's a foolproof one from the internet. I'll send you the link,' he said with a smile. 'So how did you get on at the gym?'

'Pretty well. Melanie said that it'd be nice to give something back to the community, and she's got a couple of mornings where we could have a slot for a class. She's prepared to do some training to make sure she's teaching the class properly. She suggested doing it with a nominal charge for the six-week course, and then a discounted rate for anyone who wants to do the follow-up classes.'

'So if the practice paid for the six-week course, our patients would benefit and so would the community,' Oliver said. 'I've put together some figures from my old practice, showing how much strength and balance training reduces the risk of falls, so we can see the cost savings between paying for a course of preventative strength and balance training and treating patients after they've fallen.'

'That,' she said, 'is brilliant. It's Caroline's first week back, this week, so I'll leave it until next week before I talk to her about it—but then perhaps we could see her together and talk her through the project?'

'That works for me,' Oliver said. 'So do you go to the gym a lot?'

'Mainly my dance aerobics class. The rest of the time, I'm training for whatever fundraising I'm doing. The skydive is this month; I'm doing a sixty-mile cycle ride along the coast next month. And then I was thinking about doing a swimming thing. I'll do it in the pool at the gym, but if you add all the lengths together it'll be the equivalent of swimming the English Channel.' She smiled. 'Just without all the grease, choppy seas and having to wait a couple of years to book a slot to do it.'

'And it's a lot safer.'

'There is that.' She took a deep breath. 'I have to admit, I'm a bit scared about tomorrow. I've never jumped from a plane before.'

'You'll be fine,' he said, and his belief in her warmed her all the way through.

CHAPTER SIX

FRIDAY MORNING DAWNED bright and sunny. Gemma, who'd worried about the event being rained off, felt more relaxed; yet, at the same time, adrenalin fizzed through her.

Today she was going to jump from a plane. She was going to jump two miles up from the ground. And, OK, it was a tandem jump and the experienced skydiver would be in control... but it was still a long, long way down.

She showered, then dressed in loose, comfortable clothing and trainers, following the instructions that had come from the skydiving company. Her phone buzzed almost constantly with texts from people wishing her good luck, including one from Oliver. Though there was nothing, she noticed, from her parents. Not that they ever wished her luck when she was doing a fundraising event. Would they ever soften towards her and be close again? she wondered. If she was honest with herself, probably not. But she wouldn't give up on them. She wouldn't stop trying to get through to them. She owed it to Sarah to get their family back together.

Even though her stomach felt twisted with nerves, she made herself eat a bowl of porridge, then headed out to her car.

Except the car didn't look right.

A closer examination told her she had a flat tyre. Oh, no. It would take her ages to fix it. She didn't have time; and it looked as if she was going to miss her slot. If she called a taxi, would she get to the airfield in time? She dragged a hand through her hair. Of all the days to get a flat tyre...

'Is everything OK, Gemma?'

She glanced up to see Oliver in his running gear. 'Flat tyre,' she said. 'And I haven't got time to fix it. I was just about to call a taxi and hope it would get me to the airfield in time for my slot.'

'I'll take you,' he said.

'But—'

'It's my day off,' he cut in gently. 'All I planned to do today was go for a run and clean the house. Both of them can wait. Besides, by the time a taxi gets here, we could be halfway to the airfield.'

She knew that was true. 'Thank you,' she said. 'I really appreciate it.'

'No problem. Come with me.'

It wasn't long until they were at his house. 'Give me thirty seconds to change my shorts for jeans,' he said. 'Luckily I was still warming up when I got to yours, so I'm not disgustingly sweaty and in need of a shower.' The cheeky grin he gave her made her heart feel as if it had done a somersault.

He came downstairs a few moments later, having changed his clothes. 'Let's go,' he said. 'Can you put the airfield's postcode into the satnav?'

'Sure.'

Her nerves must've shown in her voice because he asked gently, 'Are you OK?'

'Yes. Well, no,' she admitted. 'I'm trying not to think about the stats of how many parachutes fail.'

'Very few,' he said. 'According to my twin, fewer than one in three thousand people even sprain an ankle when they jump out of a plane.'

'Does he do a lot of that sort of thing?'

'Yes. He likes the adrenalin rush. You'll be fine. Think of the money you're raising.'

Her palms were sweaty and the back of her neck itched. But she couldn't back out now.

'I really appreciate you giving me a lift,' Gemma said when they arrived at the airfield.

'No problem.' Ollie paused. 'I've been thinking about you. I might as well wait for you. By the time I get back to Ashermouth, it'll be time to turn round and come to collect you, so I might as well sit in the sun with a mug of tea and watch the planes.'

'I can't ask you to give up your day off like this.'

'You're not,' he said. 'And it's fine. You're the one actually doing the skydive. I'm surprised Claire didn't come with you.'

'She was going to, but the girl who was covering for her called in sick this morning, and Friday's a busy day at the bakery.' Gemma shrugged. 'It's fine. I'm a grown-up.'

Gemma was a brave and capable woman, from what Ollie had seen of her so far; but for a moment vulnerability showed in her eyes. 'Hey. You're Gemma Baxter, village superstar, and you can do this. You can do anything,' he said. Even though he knew physical contact with her wasn't a sensible idea, he was pretty sure she needed a hug, so he wrapped his arms round her and held her close for a few moments. 'Go and sign in and do your safety briefing,' he said.

Gemma wasn't sure whether the adrenalin bubbling through her was because of what she was about to do or because Oliver had hugged her, or a confused mixture of the two, but she duly went off for the safety briefing, training and fitting of protective equipment.

Oliver was waiting with the supporters of her fellow skydivers, and gave her an encouraging smile. 'Hey. I imagine Claire would've taken a photo of you in your gear, so give us a grin.'

He lifted his phone and took a snap. 'Nope. That was more like a grimace. Let's do it again.'

'Say cheese?' she asked wryly.

'No. Say yoga and put both thumbs up.'

'What?' But she did it, and he grinned.

'Perfect. Now go earn that sponsor money. I'll be there to applaud as you land.'

Gemma followed the instructor to board the aircraft. It looked impossibly tiny.

'Let's get you attached to me,' her instructor said. Once he'd put the four clips in place, it felt almost as if she was wearing him like a backpack.

During the fifteen minutes it took to get the plane up to ten thousand feet, the instructor did the equipment check and the final brief.

'Here we go,' he said, and the door opened.

A rush of cold wind filled the plane, and Gemma felt goosebumps prickle over her skin. She was going to be the fourth and final jumper from their batch, giving her nerves even more time to sizzle.

Finally it was her turn. She sat on the edge of the doorway, ready to go. The fields below looked like a patchwork of gold and green; puffy bits of white clouds billowed here and there.

'One, two, three—go!' the instructor said.

And then they tipped forward. They were head-down, plummeting down to the ground in free-fall.

Even though Gemma knew they were falling at a hundred and twenty miles an hour, she felt weightless, as if they were floating on air. She'd expected it to feel a bit like a roller coaster, with all the swooping; but because there were no twists and turns or sudden changes of direction, it was fine.

The instructor tapped her on the shoulder, and she uncrossed her arms, bringing them up in front of her as she'd been taught down on the ground.

It was incredibly noisy.

And incredibly exhilarating.

And somehow it was peaceful, all at the same time; in her head, she could hear Tom Petty singing 'Free Fallin''.

The cameraman she'd hired to take a video of the skydive reached out to give her a fist bump, and she grinned.

She was really, really doing this.

She brought her hands in momentarily to make a heart symbol, to remind everyone what she was fundraising for, and yelled, 'Sarah, this is for you!' Even if nobody could hear her on the video, they could at least lip read. Then the instructor opened the parachute. Instead of the jolt she'd expected when the canopy opened, it was a gentle, steady rise.

It took them about five minutes to float all the way down. As she'd been told earlier, she lifted her knees and straightened her legs as she was sitting down. The ground rushed up to meet them; but the landing was smooth, the canopy came down behind them, and the ground crew were there to help them out of the parachute and harness.

All of them gave her a high five. 'Well done! Do you know how much you've raised?'

'Unless anyone's donated since I got on the plane...' She told them the amount, smiling broadly. Everyone had been so generous.

Oliver met her with a broad smile. 'How incredible were you?'

'Thank you.' She grinned. 'Sorry, I'm all over the place right now. I'm still full of adrenalin from the skydive.' Which was only half the reason; Oliver's nearness was definitely making her feel all wobbly.

'You were so brave.'

'My palms were sweating, my heart was thumping and I thought I was going to pass out in the plane. Even though I knew it was safe, it was terrifying. The bit where you sit on the edge of the plane, just before you lean forward and fall out...'

'It sounds horrendous. But you did it.'

'All I did was jump out of a plane, strapped to someone else.'

'You're still amazing,' he countered.

She took off the kit, went to the debriefing, collected the website link for her video so she could share it with everyone who'd supported her, then sent a round-robin text to tell everyone she was down safely and she'd done it.

'So what's the plan now?' he asked.

'Home, please. I need to change that flat tyre.'

'Tell you what. Make me a cheese toastie, and I'll fix it for you.'

'But you've already rescued me once today. It feels as if I'm taking advantage of you.' Taking advantage of him. That could have another meaning. And the vision of Oliver all rumpled and lazy—smiling, after making love with her—made the blood rush straight to her face.

'You're not taking advantage of me,' he said.

Was it her imagination or was there extra colour in his cheeks, too? Was he remembering that kiss on the beach and wondering what it would be like if it happened again? For a moment, she couldn't breathe.

'If anything,' he said, 'you're doing me a favour because I can put off doing the chores.'

'Maybe I can do some chores for you in exchange, then,' she said.

'Five ironed shirts for a flat tyre?'

'Bargain,' she said. 'Let's collect your ironing on the way back.'

'Deal,' he said.

By the time he'd finished changing her tyre, she'd ironed five shirts and had the toasted cheese sandwiches ready to go.

'Thank you for saving me from the tyranny of the ironing board,' he said.

'Thank *you* for putting the spare tyre on for me,' she said. 'I'll call in to the tyre place this afternoon and get it sorted out.'

'You're very welcome.'

Once he'd eaten his sandwich, he smiled at her. 'I'll let you get on with the rest of your day. See you at The Anchor tonight for the skydive celebrations.'

'Thanks, Oliver. For everything.'

And his smile made her feel as if the world was full of sunshine.

That evening, when Gemma went to The Anchor to meet up with her friends and colleagues, people seemed to be congratulating her from the moment she walked through the door. She was greeted with hugs, offers of extra sponsorship, and glasses of Prosecco mixed with raspberry liqueur.

The landlord took the website address and password from Gemma and showed the skydive on the pub's large television screen, and everyone cheered at the moment when she jumped out of the plane.

Although the room was busy, she was very aware that Oliver was with the rest of the practice team.

'Hey. You were incredible,' he said.

Did he really think that? The idea made her feel all warm and glowing.

And why had she not noticed before just how blue his eyes were, and how beautiful his mouth was?

'All I did was jump out of a plane. And people have been so generous. If the money helps with the research and it stops another family having to lose their Sarah...' Her throat felt tight.

As if he guessed what was going through her head, he wrapped his arms round her. 'You're making a difference.'

And now her knees really had turned to jelly.

Being held by Oliver Langley made her all in a spin. She was so aware of him: the warmth of his body, his strength, the citrus scent of his shower gel. She almost—almost—closed her eyes and tipped her head back, inviting a kiss. It was scary how much she wanted him to kiss her.

But then the noise of their surroundings rushed in at her.

They were in the village pub. In front of everyone. And she was in danger of acting very inappropriately.

She took one tiny step back; he released her, but she noticed that he was looking at her mouth. So did he feel this weird pull of attraction, too? She wasn't quite sure how to broach it. Not here, not now; but maybe the next time they spent time together—as friends—she'd be brave and suggest doing something together. A proper date.

Gemma enjoyed the rest of the evening; when she left to go home, as soon as she walked outside she suddenly felt woozy.

'Gemma? Are you all right?' Oliver asked, coming out to join her.

'Just a bit dizzy, that's all.' She winced. 'Probably too much Prosecco. Rookie mistake. People kept refilling my glass, and I didn't even think about it. I don't make a habit of getting drunk.' At that point, she tripped and Oliver caught her.

'Everyone does it at some point,' he said. 'Put your arm round my waist and lean on me. I'll walk you home.'

'Thank you. And sorry for being a burden. I feel like such an idiot.'

'It's fine,' he reassured her.

Just like that moment earlier when he'd hugged her, it felt lovely to have his arm round her. Gemma leaned her head against his shoulder, again noticing that gorgeous citrus scent. 'You're such a sweetie,' she said.

He laughed. 'That's the bubbles talking.'

'No. You were all starchy and grumpy when I first met you. But that's not who you are. You're warm and lovely. And you smell lovely.' She squeezed him gently. 'Oli-lovely-ver.'

'Come on, Skydive Girl. Let's get you home.'

He was laughing. With her, not at her. And he had a really, really lovely laugh, Gemma thought.

When they got to her flat, he asked for her keys, unlocked the door and ushered her inside. 'Let me make you a cup of tea. You need to rehydrate a bit, or you'll feel terrible in the morning.'

'Oli-lovely-ver,' she said again. 'Thank you.'

'Come and sit down.' He guided her to the sofa. 'One mug of tea. Milk, no sugar, right?'

'Perfect.' She beamed at him.

Gemma Baxter was a very sweet drunk, Ollie thought. She'd made him smile, with that 'Oli-lovely-ver' business. He filled the kettle and switched it on, then hunted in the cupboards for mugs and tea. He'd noted earlier that Gemma was neat and tidy, and things were stored in sensible and obvious places, he discovered.

But when he went back into the living room with two mugs of tea, he realised that she was fast asleep on the sofa. It was probably a combination of a reaction to the adrenalin that had been pumping through her system all day and the drinks that people had bought her that evening.

He put the mugs down on the coffee table. What now? There was a throw resting on the back of the sofa; he could tuck it over her and leave her on the sofa to sleep off all the Prosecco. Though then she'd probably wake with a sore neck or shoulder as well as a shocking headache.

Or he could carry her to her bed. She'd still have the hangover headache tomorrow, but at least she'd be comfortable.

He lifted her up, and she didn't wake at all. She just curled into him, all warm and soft. And there was a hint of rose and vanilla in her hair that made him want to hold her closer. Not that he'd ever take advantage like that.

He carried her to her room, pushed the duvet aside and laid her down on the bed.

Not wanting to be intrusive, he left her fully clothed, though he did remove her shoes. Then he tucked the duvet round her, and she snuggled against the pillow. He closed the curtains; the noise didn't wake her, so he pulled the door almost closed and went back into her living room.

He could leave her to sleep it off and write her a note; but he didn't really want to leave her on her own. If she was ill in the night and something happened, he'd never forgive himself.

The sofa was way too short for him to lie down on, but he could sort of sprawl on it and wrap the throw round himself. He'd slept on uncomfortable sofas often enough in his student days. OK, so it was years since he'd been a student, but he'd be fine. The most important thing was that Gemma was safe.

He finished his mug of tea, quietly washed up, then settled himself on the sofa with the throw. He dozed fitfully, and checked on Gemma a couple of times during the night; to his relief, she was fine.

The next morning, he washed his face, borrowed Gemma's toothpaste and used his finger as a makeshift brush to stop his mouth feeling quite so revolting, then went into her kitchen to make coffee. He also poured her a large glass of water, and took it through to her.

'Good morning.'

Gemma kept her eyes firmly closed.

Someone was talking to her. But she lived on her own, so that wasn't possible. Was she hallucinating?

A male voice. Not Andy's Northumbrian accent, so she hadn't stayed over at Claire's—anyway, why would she stay over at Claire's when she only lived a few minutes' walk away?

And she could smell coffee. So she couldn't be at home, because she lived on her own and there was nobody to make coffee for her. Yet this felt like her own bed.

What was going on?

She squinted through one eye.

Someone was standing next to her bed, holding a mug—hence the smell of coffee—and a large glass of water.

Not just someone: Oliver Langley.

Horror swept through her. What was Oliver doing here? She couldn't remember a thing about the end of the evening, yesterday. Oh, no. Had she thrown herself at him? Please don't let her have reverted to the way she'd behaved in that awful year after Sarah died, and made a fool of herself...

Hideously embarrassed and ashamed, she mumbled, 'So sorry.' Her face felt as if it was on fire and she couldn't look at him. Still with her eyes closed, she began, 'I, um, whatever I did or said last night—'

'You fell asleep on your sofa while I was making you a cup of tea,' he cut in. 'I carried you in here, put you in bed, took your shoes off and covered you up. And I slept on your sofa.'

She wasn't sure whether to be relieved, grateful or mortified. He'd clearly stayed to keep an eye on her because she'd been that tipsy last night. How shameful was that? 'Thank you for looking after me.'

'Sit up and drink some water,' he said. 'You'll feel better.'

Still cringing inwardly, she did as he suggested. And he was right; the water helped. 'Thank you.'

'I'm going to make us some toast,' he said. 'I hope you don't mind, but I used some of your toothpaste.'

'Of course I don't mind. Help yourself to anything you need. There are towels in the airing cupboard and a spare toothbrush in the bathroom cabinet.'

'Actually, I used my finger.' He grinned. 'Took me right back to being a student.'

'I'm so sorry,' she said again. 'I don't normally drink more than a glass or two of wine. I don't know what happened last night.'

'People were topping up your glass while you were talking,' he said. 'Plus you were still on a high from the skydive.'

She swallowed hard. 'We...um...didn't...?'

'No. I wouldn't take advantage of anyone like that.'

'Of course you wouldn't. You're one of the good guys.' A hot tide of shame swept through her. 'I'm sorry. I didn't mean to imply you'd...' Oh, help. She was digging herself into a bigger hole here.

'Besides,' he said, a tiny quirk at the corner of his mouth, 'if I had spent the night with you, I rather hope you'd remember it.'

The heat of the shame turned to something else equally hot: a surge of pure desire.

This really wasn't a good idea.

Oliver was in her bedroom. She was in bed. Fully clothed, admittedly, but in bed. And she'd made way too many mistakes of this type before.

'Let's go into the kitchen and have that toast,' she said.

Paracetamol, more water, the mug of coffee and three slices of toast later, Gemma felt human again, and she'd pretty much got her thoughts sorted.

'So let me start again. Thank you for looking after me last night. I apologise if I made a fool of myself. And—' she took a deep breath, cringing inwardly but knowing this had to be done '—I apologise if I threw myself at you.'

'You didn't throw yourself at me,' he said quietly. 'And there's no need to apologise. You were a bit woozy and you fell asleep when I went to make you a mug of tea. I didn't want to leave you on your own. If it had been the other way round, I'm pretty sure you would've looked after me.'

'Of course. That's what friends do.'

'What makes you think you threw yourself at me?'

The question was mild; yet the true answer would shock him, she was sure. She certainly wasn't going to admit that he was absolutely her type and she really liked him. He'd made it clear he only saw her as a friend.

Which meant she'd have to confide in him. Tell him what a mess she'd been.

'It's a bit of a long story. When I was seventeen,' she said, 'I had a bit of a...difficult year.'

The year Gemma's sister had died, Oliver remembered.

'I didn't deal with it very well. I tried lots of ways to escape,' she said. 'I never did drugs or cigarettes, and I've never been a big one for alcohol—but I had sex. Lots of sex. I kind of went through most of the lads in the sixth form and I earned myself a shocking reputation.'

Because she'd been hurting. Because she'd been looking for a way to avoid the pain. Seventeen, and so vulnerable. Ollie's heart went out to her. The boys of her own age wouldn't have thought about why she was throwing herself at them and held back; at that age, the testosterone surge would've taken over and they would've been more than happy to sleep with her. It wouldn't have occurred to any of them that they were taking advantage of someone vulnerable. No wonder this morning Gemma had thought they'd spent the night together: she'd obviously been taken advantage of before.

He reached across the table and took her hand. He squeezed it once, just enough to be sympathetic, but letting her hand go again before the gesture crossed the border into being creepy. 'I'm sorry you had such a rough time.'

She shrugged. 'It was self-inflicted.'

'Didn't your parents…?'

The stricken look on her face stopped him. Clearly, they hadn't. 'I'm sorry,' he said. 'I didn't mean to trample on a sore spot.'

'They were hurting, too. It's pretty difficult to support a teenager who's gone off the rails, and even harder to do that when your heart's broken,' she said softly. 'They just folded in on themselves after Sarah died. I couldn't talk to them about anything. I couldn't tell them how I was feeling, how much I missed my sister, how hard it was to get up in the morning. So I went for the escape route. Or what I thought was one. It was just a mess and I feel bad now because they already had enough to deal with. I just made it worse.'

'What about counselling?' he asked.

'I had counselling in my first year at uni and that really helped me, but when I suggested it to my parents they pretty much blanked me. They're not ones for talking.' She swallowed hard. 'After they moved from Ashermouth Bay, I never lived with them again.'

'You said you stayed with your best friend's family.'

She nodded. 'Claire was worried about me and the way I was behaving. She talked to her mum about it, but even Yvonne couldn't get through to me. Not until results day, when I failed all my exams really badly. Claire dragged me back to her place and made me sit down with her mum. Yvonne said that it was time for plan B, a chance to get my life back into gear. She said she'd been thinking about it and she and Claire's dad had agreed that I could move in with them. I'd resit the second year of my A levels, while Claire would be doing the first year of her catering course at the local college. The deal was, I'd stop the sex.' She shook her head.

'I think the only saving grace of that awful year was that I'd insisted on using condoms, so I didn't get pregnant or catch an STD. But I got called a lot of fairly nasty names. Yvonne said she understood why I was sleeping around, but that behaviour was only hurting me more instead of making things better. She said from that day onward I was going to be one of her girls, part of her family.' She swallowed hard. 'And it was so good to be part of a family again. To feel that I belonged. That I was loved.'

Ollie was seriously unimpressed by Gemma's parents—however tough life was, however miserable it made you, you didn't just give up on your remaining child, the way it sounded as if they had. But he was glad someone had been there to step in and help. 'Claire's mum sounds really special.'

'She is. And what she did for me... I want to pay that forward,' Gemma said earnestly. 'I'd like to offer a troubled teenager a place to stay. A place to get their Plan B sorted. I want to be someone who won't judge because she's been there and knows what it feels like—someone who offers a second chance to get things right, and the support that teenager needs to get through it.'

'I've only known you for a little while, but that's enough for me to know you'd be amazing in a role like that. The authorities will snap you up.'

'You really think so?'

'I really think so.' He reached over to squeeze her hand again. 'Thank you for being so honest with me. I want to reassure you that I'm not going to gossip about you with anyone.'

'Pretty much everyone in the village knows my history. Though thankfully nobody seems to hold it against me nowadays.' She gave him a rueful smile. 'But thank you.'

'It's fine.' Ollie could almost hear his twin's voice in his head. *You like her, so tell her. Take a risk. Be more Rob.* 'Gemma. I like you, and I think you might like me. We're becoming friends, but...' He took a deep breath. *Be more Rob.* 'I want to be more than that.'

'I don't have a good track record,' she warned. 'I've kind of gone the other way from my teens. Claire says I'm so scared of being needy again, I don't let anyone close. So my relationships tend to fizzle out after only a few weeks.'

'I understand that,' he said.

Gemma had trusted him with her past; maybe he should do the same. 'My track record isn't great, either,' he said. 'I was supposed to get married at the beginning of May.'

'When you gave Rob your kidney?'

'A month before the operation. But he wouldn't have been well enough to be at the wedding.'

'Why didn't you just move the wedding?' she asked.

He appreciated the fact she'd thought of the same solution that he had. 'Tabby—my fiancée—called it off. Her dad had ME, so she grew up seeing her mum having to look after him as well as work and look after the kids. And she didn't want that kind of life for herself.'

'But you donated a kidney. Your brother was the one on dialysis, the one who might have problems if his body rejects the new kidney, not you,' Gemma said.

'Her view was what if something happened to me, too?' he

said dryly. 'Though when I look back I'm pretty sure it was an excuse.'

'Do you think she fell for someone else and just didn't want to hurt you by telling you?'

He shook his head. 'I think she was having cold feet. She didn't want to marry me because she didn't love me enough. You're right in that Rob's kidney was an excuse. But the real reason—and I know it's real because she told me—is that I wasn't enough for her.' He wrinkled his nose. 'And that's messed with my head a bit.'

'It would mess with anyone's head,' Gemma said. 'I'm sorry you got hurt. But the problem was with her, not you.'

He wasn't so sure. 'With me not being enough, and you not letting anyone close, we might be setting ourselves up for trouble,' he said. 'Maybe we can just see how things go.'

'I'd like that,' she said.

For the first time since Tabby had broken their engagement, he actually felt positive about the idea of dating someone. Dating *Gemma*.

'I'm going to give you the rest of the day to get over your hangover. And I'm not going to kiss you right now, because neither of us is particularly fragrant.' He held her gaze. 'But, just so you know, I'm planning to kiss you tonight. I'd like to take you out to dinner.'

'Actually,' she said, 'I'd rather like to take *you* out to dinner. And I'll drive. I'll book a table and let you know what time I'll pick you up.'

'That's bossy,' he said, but the fact she was asserting herself appealed to him. 'OK. But I'll meet you here. The walk will do me good. Let me know what time.'

'You're on,' she said, and her smile made his heart skip a beat. He couldn't remember the last time he'd felt this enthused about an evening out.

Maybe, just maybe, he and Gemma could help each other heal from the unhappiness of their pasts. And maybe they could go forward together. Tonight would be that first step.

CHAPTER SEVEN

ONCE OLIVER HAD LEFT, Gemma showered and washed her hair; being clean again made her feel much more human and sorted out most of her hangover.

And it also gave her time to think about what had happened this morning. Now Oliver knew the very worst of her: but it hadn't made a difference to him.

He liked her.

Really liked her.

He'd told her he was planning to kiss her, tonight, and it made her feel like a teenager again—but in a good way, light-hearted and carefree, rather than in an angsty, world-on-her-shoulders kind of way.

He'd suggested going out to dinner. The place where she really wanted to take him tended to be booked up weeks in advance. But it was always worth a try, so she rang them to ask if they could possibly squeeze in a table for two.

'You're in luck,' the manager told her. 'I've just had a cancellation. I can fit you in at eight.'

'That's perfect,' Gemma said. And it was a very good sign. She texted Oliver.

Managed to get table for eight. Pick you up at seven thirty? Dress code smart-casual.

Should she add a kiss at the end, or not? Then again, they were officially dating. She took a risk and added a kiss.

He replied immediately.

Seven-thirty's perfect. I'll walk over to your place. x

Excitement bubbled through Gemma's veins. He'd sent her a kiss back by text. And he was going to kiss her properly tonight…

She caught up with the chores, then took some flowers down to the churchyard. 'Hey, Sarah. I've met someone. You'd like him,' she said, arranging the flowers in the vase on her sister's grave. 'His ex was pretty unfair to him and broke his heart. It's early days, but we're going to see how things go between us.' She finished arranging the flowers. 'I miss you, Sarah. I wish you were here so I could chat to you while I was getting ready tonight.' But her little sister would always be with her in her heart. 'Love you,' she said softly, and headed back home.

Gemma took care with her make-up that evening, and wore her favourite little black dress. At seven thirty precisely, her doorbell buzzed. She pressed the button on the intercom.

'Hi, Gemma. It's Oliver.'

'Right on time,' she said.

'Can I come up?'

'Sure.'

Her heart skipped a beat when she opened her front door. She'd seen him in a suit for work, and wearing jeans outside the surgery, but Oliver Langley dressed up for a night out was something else. Tonight he wore dark trousers, highly polished shoes, and a blue linen shirt that really brought out the colour of his eyes.

'You scrub up very nicely, Dr Langley,' she said, feeling the colour slide into her face.

He looked her up and down. 'Thank you. You look beautiful, Gemma,' he said. 'Your hair is amazing.'

She'd straightened it so it was smooth and shiny and fell to her shoulders. 'Thank you.'

To her surprise, he handed her a bunch of sunflowers. 'For you.'

'Thank you. They're gorgeous. Was that a lucky guess, or did you know they were my favourites?' she asked.

'You had sunflowers in a vase the first time I came round,' he said.

He was that observant? She was impressed. The men she'd dated in the past had never really noticed that sort of thing. The few dates who had actually bought her flowers had chosen red roses or something pink—a safe choice, and she'd appreciated it because she loved flowers, but these ones felt more special.

'Plus,' he added, 'they make me think of you because you're like sunshine.'

'What a lovely thing to say.' The more so because it felt like a genuine compliment. 'Come in while I put them in water.'

'So where are we going tonight?' he asked, following her into the kitchen.

'The Lighthouse. It's a pub in the next village down the coast—it used to be a lighthouse, hence the name, but after it was decommissioned it was turned into a bar and restaurant.' She smiled at him. 'It's foodie heaven, so I think you'll enjoy it. Plus the views are pretty amazing.'

'Sounds lovely,' he said.

She put the sunflowers in a vase. 'You're OK about me driving you?'

He laughed. 'I might be starchy sometimes, but I'm not sexist. I'm absolutely fine with you driving.'

Gemma was a careful, competent driver. Not that Ollie had expected anything less. She drove them to the next village and parked outside what looked at first like a lighthouse, and then when they walked through the front door he realised that the whole of the wall overlooking the sea was made of glass.

'Does this mean we get to see the sunset while we eat?'

'Sort of. We're on the east coast, so we get more of the sunrise than the sunset,' she said, 'but the sky and the sea will still look very pretty.'

Once they were seated, he asked, 'What do you recommend?'

She glanced up at the chalk board and smiled. 'Crab cakes are on the specials today. Definitely them for a starter,' she said. 'For the mains, just about anything; everything's as local as possible, so the fish is particularly good.' She paused. 'Is it just cake you're not a fan of, or sweet stuff in general?'

'I'm not really a pudding or cake person,' he said. 'Which is another difference between me and my twin. Rob will do almost anything for chocolate.'

'That's a pity, because the salted caramel cheesecake here is amazing. But, since you don't like puddings, I'd recommend the cheese plate,' she said. 'They're all local artisan cheeses, and the team here makes their own oatcakes. Actually, it's really hard to choose between pudding and cheese. I might have to toss a coin.'

He ordered the same starter, main and sides as Gemma. The portions were generous and the food was excellent, but the company was even better. He felt more relaxed with Gemma than he'd felt in years. How weird was that? He hadn't been looking to start dating anyone. And yet here he was, on a first date with a woman he liked very much. A woman he wanted to kiss. A woman who made him feel as if the sun was shining through the middle of a rainstorm.

And now was his chance to get to know her better.

'So when you're not chucking yourself out of a plane or whatever for fundraising,' he said, 'what do you do for fun?'

'Play with my goddaughter,' she said promptly. 'I have my dance aerobics class on Tuesday nights; if Yvonne is hosting a crafting workshop on an evening or a Saturday afternoon, I go to support her and I'm in charge of making coffee. Sometimes I have a girly night in with my friends; that usually involves cake, watching a film, a glass of wine and a mug of hot chocolate. Oh, and a big bowl of home-made sweet popcorn.' She smiled. 'What about you?'

'I run in the morning before work. In London, I used to run along the Regent's Canal, and here I get to run along the harbour and the beach.' That was something Ollie still found a sheer delight; the sound of the sea really calmed him and pushed any worries away. 'When Rob was in Manchester and I was in London, we used to play virtual chess, though as we live nearer each other right now we can do that in person. None of my close friends in London have children yet, so most weekends I'd go with a group of them to watch the rugby or cricket.'

'I get the running, but cricket?' she teased. 'A game that takes days to play rather than a few minutes. Not my thing at all.'

'Rugby?'

She wrinkled her nose. 'Sorry. I'm not into watching any contact sports. I keep thinking of all the medical complications—the torn rotator cuffs, the sprains, the fractures and the cases of herpes gladiatorum. I'll stick to my dance aerobics.'

He loved the teasing glint in her eyes. 'OK. So we've established that you like sweet and I like savoury; I like cricket and rugby and you don't. How about music?'

'Anything I can sing and dance to,' she said promptly, 'and I reserve the right to sing off key. You?'

'Rock,' he said. 'Rob dabbled with the idea of being a rock star. He thought we could be the next Kaiser Chiefs. We started a band when we were thirteen. He was the singer and lead guitarist, one of our friends was the drummer, and he made me learn the bass guitar and do the harmonies. I can't hold a tune, so I was absolutely pants.' He grinned. 'And so was he.'

'Oh, that's cruel,' she said.

'No, it's honest,' he said, laughing. 'Our drummer was out

of time, too. It was fun, but we were awful. Our parents were so relieved when we gave it up. Then Rob discovered a climbing wall and found out that not only did he love climbing, he was really good at it.'

'What about you? Are you a climber?'

'Slogging your way up a sheer rock face, when it's chucking it down with rain and there's only a tiny little rope between you and disaster? Nope. That's really not my idea of fun,' he said. 'I'd much rather sit in the dry, watching rugby. Or playing chess.'

'I don't play chess,' she said. 'But Claire's family is really into board games. We used to have game nights every Friday—anything from board games to charades or cards. We'd have build-your-own fajitas for dinner first, which was Yvonne's way of sneaking extra veg into our diet without us noticing. It was a lot of fun.'

'It sounds it,' he said.

'So where did you learn to do that magic trick, making a coin appear behind that little boy's ear?'

'My rotation in paediatrics. The consultant taught me that a magic trick is the best way to distract a child and get them to relax. There's the coin one, and for the older ones there's the one with the magic envelope.'

'Magic envelope?' Gemma asked. 'Tell me more.'

He ran through the rules. 'You write a number on a piece of paper, and put it in a sealed envelope. Then you ask them the year they were born, the year they started school, how many years it's been since they started school, and how old they'll be at the end of this year. Get them to add the four numbers together and tell you what it is. Then you ask them to open the envelope. They'll discover that it contains the number they just told you—which is basically double whatever this year is.'

'That's clever,' she said.

'It's a simple maths tricks but it's handy for distracting an older child when you need to get a blood sample, or you're going to do something that's going to be a bit uncomfortable.'

'I'll remember that one,' she said. 'So today the G in GP stands for "genius".'

He laughed. 'I can't take the credit. It was my consultant who taught me.'

'Ah, but *you've* just taught *me*,' she pointed out.

Once they'd finished their meal; Gemma excused herself to go to the toilet and paid the bill on the way so Oliver wouldn't have the chance to argue.

'Thank you for dinner,' he said as they left the restaurant. 'Next time we do something together, it's my treat.'

So there was definitely going to be a next time? Maybe this time her relationship wouldn't all be over almost as soon as it had begun; the hope made her feel warm all over. 'That'd be nice,' she said with a smile. 'Shall we go and have a last look at the sky and the sea?'

They walked over to the edge of the cliffs, hand in hand. Such a tiny contact, but so sweet. She could really get used to holding hands with Oliver Langley. And she wanted more. A lot more.

The bright colours of the sunset had faded to a rosy after-glow, and the moon was a tiny sliver of a crescent in the darken-ing sky. 'There's Jupiter,' Gemma said, pointing out the bright planet, 'and Mars. If you look out to the east in the early morn-ing, you'll see Venus.'

'In London, I never really got to see the sky properly,' he said. 'Out here, it's magical.' He turned her to face him. 'You make me feel magical, too, Gemma,' he said softly. 'And, right now, I really want to kiss you.'

'I want to kiss you, too,' she said.

He dipped his head and brushed his mouth against hers, and her lips tingled at the touch.

'Sweet, sweet Gemma,' he said softly, and kissed her again.

It felt as if fireworks were going off in her head. She'd never experienced anything like this before, and she wasn't sure if it made her feel more amazed or terrified.

When Oliver broke the kiss and pulled away slightly, she held his gaze. His pupils were huge, making his eyes seem almost black in the twilight.

She reached up to touch his mouth, and ran her forefinger along his bottom lip,

He nipped gently at her finger.

Suddenly, Gemma found breathing difficult.

'Gemma,' he said, his voice husky. 'I wasn't expecting this to happen.'

'Me neither,' she whispered. And this was crazy. She knew he was only here temporarily, and he'd probably go back to his life in London once his locum job here had finished and his twin had recovered from the transplant. Was she dating him purely because being a temporary colleague made him safe— she wouldn't be reckless enough to lose her heart to someone who wouldn't stick around? Or would it be like the misery of all those years ago when her parents had moved and left her behind?

'We ought to be heading back,' she said. Even though both of them knew there was no reason why they couldn't stand on the cliffs all evening, just kissing, the unexpected intensity of her feelings scared her.

'Uh-huh,' he said—but he held her hand all the way back to the car. And he kissed her again before she unlocked the door.

Gemma drove them back to Ashermouth Bay and parked outside his cottage.

'Would you like to come in for a cup of coffee?' Ollie asked.

Was he being polite, or did he really want to spend more time with her? Or did he mean something other than coffee? It was hard to judge. She wanted to spend more time with him, yet at the same time she thought it would be a mistake. What was the point of getting closer to him if he wasn't going to stick around?

Should she stay or should she go?

'Gemma? I'm asking you in for coffee,' he said quietly. 'I'm not going to rip your clothes off the second you walk in the front door.'

She felt the colour fizz through her face. 'Like the boyfriends in my past, you mean.'

'I wasn't being snippy. Back then, you were seventeen and hurting and maybe not in the place to make the right choices for you. It's different now. I just wanted to let you know that I appreciate you've been honest with me about your past and I'm not going to make assumptions or pressure you to do anything you're not comfortable with.'

So coffee meant just coffee. It meant spending a bit more time with her. Funny how that made her heart feel as if it had just flipped over and eased the tightness in her chest.

'Then thank you. Coffee would be nice.'

'Good.' He took her hand, lifted it to his mouth, pressed a kiss against her palm and folded her fingers over it.

The gesture was unexpectedly sweet, and melted away the last vestiges of her misgivings.

Inside the house, he connected his phone to a speaker. 'Would you like to choose some music while I make you a cappuccino?'

'Cappuccino? As in a *proper* cappuccino?' she checked.

He nodded.

'So are you telling me you have a proper coffee maker in your kitchen? A bean-to-cup one?'

'With a frothing arm. Yup.' He grinned. 'Busted. I didn't tell you that gadgets are my bad habit. Rob gives me quite a hard time about it.'

She groaned. 'And to think I've been giving you instant coffee, when you make the posh stuff.'

He smiled. 'It's OK. I didn't judge you.'

'Didn't you?' She raised an eyebrow at him.

'Only a little bit.' He gave her a little-boy-lost look. 'So I guess I owe you a kiss for being judgmental, then.'

'Yes,' she said. 'I rather think you do. Because there's nothing wrong with instant coffee.'

'Would you choose instant coffee over a proper cappuccino?' he asked.

'No,' she admitted. 'But bean-to-cup machines are a bit—well, fancy.'

'They're a brilliant invention,' he said, laughing. 'As I'll prove to you.' He closed the curtains, put the table lamp on and switched off the overhead light; then he came back over to her. 'One apology kiss coming right up.'

His mouth was soft and warm and sweet, teasing her lips until she opened her mouth and let him deepen the kiss.

'Hold that thought,' he said, 'and choose some music.' He unlocked his phone and went into the streaming app. 'Pick something you like, then come and supervise, if you like.'

'My expertise is in drinking cappuccinos, not making them,' she said. But she picked a mellow playlist, then followed him into the kitchen.

His movements were deft and sure, and the cappuccino was perfect.

'If you ever get bored with being a doctor, you could make a decent barista,' she teased.

He inclined his head. 'Thank you.'

She enjoyed sitting with him on his sofa, his arm around her while she rested her head on his shoulder, just listening to music. Every so often, Oliver kissed her, and each kiss made her head spin.

'Much as I've enjoyed this evening,' Gemma said, 'I'm not going to overstay my welcome. Thank you for the coffee. I'll wash up before I go.'

'No need. Everything will go in the dishwasher,' he said. 'So what are your plans for the rest of the weekend?'

'Tomorrow morning, I'm training for the sponsored cycle ride—seeing how far I can get in two and a half hours,' she said. 'But I'm free in the afternoon, if you'd like to do something.'

'Maybe we can go for a walk,' he suggested.

'That'd be nice. Round the next bay, there's a ruined castle. It's really pretty on the beach there.'

'Great. What time works for you?' he asked.

'About three?' she suggested.

'I'll pick you up,' he said. He kissed her again, his mouth teasing hers. 'Thank you for this evening. I've really enjoyed it.'

'Me, too,' she said, feeling suddenly shy.

'Sweet dreams. See you tomorrow,' he said, and stole a last kiss.

On Sunday morning, Gemma did a long cycle ride, setting an alarm on her watch so she knew when to turn round at the halfway point. Back home, she was pleased to discover that she'd managed thirty-five miles, which meant she was more than halfway to her goal. If she kept doing the short rides during the week and the longer rides at the weekend, she should be fine for the sixty-mile sponsored ride.

In the afternoon, Oliver picked her up at three and drove her to the next bay. It was a pretty walk by the ruined castle and down the cliff path to the sands.

'This is perfect,' he said. 'A proper sandy beach.'

The beach was quiet; there were a couple of families sitting on picnic blankets with small children painstakingly building sandcastles next to them with the aid of a bucket and spade. There were three or four dogs running along the wet sand further down, retrieving tennis balls to drop at their owners' feet; and some couples walking along the edge of the shore, ankle-deep as the waves swooshed in.

Gemma slipped off her shoes and dropped them in her tote bag. 'There's enough room in my bag for your shoes, too,' she told Oliver. 'Let's go for a paddle. There's nothing nicer than walking on flat, wet sand.'

'Agreed—but I'll carry the bag,' he said, and put his shoes in her bag.

They both rolled their jeans up to the knee, then strolled along the shoreline. The sea was deliciously cool against their skin in the heat of the afternoon.

'This is my idea of the perfect afternoon,' he said.

She smiled at him. 'Mine, too.'

They didn't need to chatter; just walking together, hand in hand, was enough. Oliver felt so familiar that it was as if she'd known him for years, not just a few short weeks. Gemma couldn't remember ever feeling so relaxed with someone she was dating. It took her a while to work out just what it was about Oliver: but then she realised.

She trusted him.

He'd seen her at her worst, and he hadn't rejected her. He hadn't taken advantage of her, either; instead, he'd looked after her. Cherished her. Made her feel special.

But then Gemma glanced out to sea and noticed something. 'Oliver, do you see those two boys swimming a bit further out? They look as if they're in trouble.'

He followed her gaze. 'I agree. Do you get rip tides here?'

'Thankfully, not in this bay,' she said. 'But there aren't any lifeguards on this beach, just the public rescue equipment. Do you mind hanging onto my bag and I'll go and see what I can do?' When she could see him about to protest, she reminded him gently, 'It's not that long since the transplant. If you over-exert yourself or get an infection, you'll regret it.'

'I know you have a point,' he said, 'but I feel useless.'

'You won't be useless at all,' she said. 'You can call the ambulance, because it's pretty obvious at least one of them is going to need treatment. Don't worry, I'm not going to do anything stupid and I won't put myself in danger—because that just means another person will need rescuing.'

'You two out there! If you're OK,' she yelled to the boys, 'wave to me!'

One of the boys was clearly struggling to stay afloat, submerging completely from time to time; the other looked panicky, and neither of them waved back at her.

'I'm going in,' she said to Oliver. 'Call the ambulance.'

She ran up to the bright orange housing containing the lifebuoy ring, then went back to the sea. Although she and Oliver been walking at the edge of the sea, with the waves swishing round their ankles, the water felt colder than she'd expected. She swam out to them, knowing that Oliver was calling for back-up medical help. But, in the short time it took her to reach them, the struggling boy had gone under again, and this time he hadn't bobbed back up.

She dived under the waves and managed to find him and get him to the surface.

'I'm not sure whether you can hear me or not,' she said, 'but you're safe. Don't struggle. I'm taking you back to shore.' She trod water for a moment, holding him up, and turned to the other boy. 'I know you're scared and tired, but grab this ring and try to follow me back to shore. Don't worry about being fast. Just keep going and focus on one stroke at a time. I'll come back for you and help you, but I need to get your friend to shore first.'

'My brother,' the other boy said, his voice quavery and full of fear. 'His name's Gary.'

'OK. I've got him and I'll get him back to shore,' she reassured him. 'You're not on your own. Try and get to a place where you can get both feet on the ground and your head's above water, and I'll come back for you.'

She focused on getting Gary back to the shore. Ollie was there to meet her, and a couple of other people had clearly noticed what was going on and had gathered beside him.

'The ambulance is on its way here,' he said.

'Good. This is Gary. His brother's still out there, trying to make his way in,' she said. 'He's got a lifebuoy but I said I'd go back to help him.'

'I'll go,' one of the men said. 'I'm a strong swimmer. Oliver said you were both medics, so you'll be needed more here.'

'Thanks,' she said.

'People are bringing towels and blankets,' Oliver said, and helped her to carry Gary to a towel that someone had spread out.

'Brilliant,' she said gratefully. 'He went under a few times, and I'm not sure whether he's still breathing. I just wanted to get him back here so we could do something.'

Oliver knelt next to the boy and gently shook his shoulder. 'Gary? Can you hear me? Open your eyes for me.'

The boy didn't respond.

He and Gemma exchanged a glance. This wasn't a good sign.

'Checking his airway,' Oliver said, tilting the boy's head back and lifting his chin. 'Clear,' he said. But he frowned as he checked the boy's breathing. 'I can't feel any breath on my cheek, I can't hear breathing sounds, and his chest isn't moving, so I'm going to start CPR. Is the other boy OK?'

Gemma looked over to the sea. 'Looks it. The guy who went in to help him—they're close enough to be walking in, now,' she said.

'Good.' Oliver started giving chest compressions, keeping to the beat of the song 'Stayin' Alive'.

Gemma knew that chest compressions were their best chance of keeping him alive. But she also knew that giving chest compressions meant a lot of exertion, and it really hadn't been that long since Oliver had donated a kidney to his brother.

'Come on, Gary, you're not going to die on me,' Oliver said.

'Let me take over for a couple of minutes,' Gemma said. 'We'll split it between us so neither of us gets too tired.'

The other boy ran over and threw himself down next to them. 'Is my brother all right? He's not going to die, is he?'

'Not on our watch, I hope,' Oliver said. 'Can you tell us what happened?'

'We were swimming. Not far out, because we're not that stupid. And we haven't been drinking or anything. We just wanted to have a bit of fun. But then Gary went under. He said he was getting cramp in his foot and he couldn't swim any more. I tried to get him but I couldn't.' The boy's face was pale with fear. 'He can't die. He can't. Our parents will never forgive me.'

Gemma knew how that felt. 'We're not going to let him die,' she said, and kept doing the compressions.

The man who'd helped with the rescue came over, carrying the lifebuoy. 'I'll put this back,' he said.

At that point, to Gemma's relief, Gary started to cough. Oliver helped her roll the boy onto his side. As she'd expected, his stomach contents gushed out of his mouth; there seemed to be a huge amount of salty water. But at least he was breathing,

'What's your name?' Oliver asked the older boy.

'Ethan.'

'Ethan, we've got an ambulance on the way. You might want to find your parents and grab your stuff.'

'There's just me and Gary here. Our parents wanted to go and see some garden or other. We said we wanted to stay here, because gardens are boring. We just wanted to have a sw—' Ethan broke off, almost sobbing.

'It's OK,' Oliver said. 'Gary's going to be OK. Go and find your stuff and come back to us.'

Other people had brought towels and blankets, and between them Gemma and Oliver put Gary into the recovery position and covered him with towels to keep him warm.

By the time Ethan got back with their things, the paramedics had arrived. They took over sorting out Gary's breathing and Ollie helped them get Gary onto a scoop so they could take him back to the ambulance.

'Looks as if you could do with checking over, too, lad,' one of the paramedics said to Ethan. 'Come on. We'll get you sorted out.'

'Can we call your mum and dad for you?' Gemma asked.

'No, I'll call my mum.' Ethan swallowed hard. 'Thank you, everyone. But especially you,' he said to Gemma. 'You saved my brother's life.'

'Next time you swim in the sea, make sure you warm up

your muscles properly before you go in, because then you're less likely to get cramp,' she said, clapping his shoulder. 'Take care.'

'He has a point,' Ollie said when the paramedics had gone. 'Without you bringing Gary in he'd have drowned, and Ethan was struggling as well—if you hadn't given him that lifebuoy, he could've drowned, too.'

She shrugged. 'Anyone else would've done the same as me.'

Why wouldn't she accept a genuine compliment? Why did she do herself down? he wondered. 'Impressive swimming, Nurse Practitioner Baxter.'

'Not really.' She shrugged again. 'Growing up in a seaside town means you do all your swimming safety training actually in the sea, with the coastguard trainers.'

'I did mine in the pool round the corner from school,' he said. 'The whole thing with the pyjamas as a float.'

'A pool's good. But I'm glad I did my training in the sea. Open water's a bit different—if nothing else, it's colder and there's the tide to think about. Are you OK?' she asked.

'Doing CPR didn't overexert me, if that's what you were worrying about. But right now I think I need to get you home so you can get out of those wet clothes. Sorry, I don't have a towel or spare clothes in the car I can offer you.'

'That's not a problem, but I don't want to ruin your car seat. Do you have a plastic bag I can sit on?' she asked.

'No, but I have a foil blanket.'

She blinked. 'Seriously?'

'Seriously.' When they got back to the car, Ollie fished the foil blanket out of the glove compartment.

'So how come you keep a foil blanket in your car?' she asked.

'It's a mix of my mum and my brother. Because Rob does the mountain rescue stuff, he always has a foil blanket with him. When our parents moved here, he made them keep one in the car in case they ever get stuck somewhere; and then Mum made me put one in my car.'

'It feels a bit of a waste, using it to sit on, but I guess at least it'll keep your seat dry. I'll buy you a replacement,' she said.

Ollie smiled at her. 'It's fine—you look like a mermaid with wet hair.'

'It's going to be impossible by the time I get home.' She plaited it roughly.

'Let's get you home,' he said, and drove them back to her flat.

'You're welcome to come in for a cup of horrible instant coffee, given that I don't have a posh coffee machine like you do,' she said with a smile.

He laughed. 'I might go for tea, in that case, but only if you're sure.'

'I'm sure. Put the kettle on and make yourself whatever you want to drink. Everything's in a logical place. I'll be as quick as I can.'

By the time she'd showered and washed her hair, dressed in dry clothes again and put her wet things in the washing machine, Ollie had made himself a mug of tea and her a mug of coffee.

'Thank you,' she said gratefully. 'I could do with this.'

He raised his mug to her. 'To you. Without you, there could be a family in mourning right now.'

'To us,' she corrected. 'Without you giving him CPR, Gary wouldn't have stood a chance.'

He grimaced. 'It still feels weird, the post-Covid "don't give rescue breaths" protocol.'

'Circulation's the really important thing, though,' Gemma pointed out. 'If your heart stops, you die; if you collapse, you need chest compressions getting your circulation going more than you need breaths inflating your lungs.'

'I know, but it still feels a bit off,' he said.

'I'm going to ring the hospital and see how Gary is,' she said. When she put the phone down, she looked relieved. 'They said he's comfortable—but, then, that's the usual hospital comment to anyone who isn't family—and his parents are with him. I've given them my number if Gary and Ethan's parents want to get in touch.'

'This wasn't quite what I had in mind for a romantic afternoon stroll,' he said ruefully.

'No, but we've made a difference to someone, and that's a good thing,' she said.

He kissed her. 'Yes. It's a very good thing.'

CHAPTER EIGHT

Over the next couple of weeks, Gemma and Oliver grew closer. It was fast becoming the happiest summer she could ever remember. On the evenings and weekends when she wasn't at a gym class or helping Yvonne with an event or already had arrangements with friends, she spent her time with Oliver—everything from dinner to walking on the beach, to watching the sunset on the cliffs and watching the stars come out over the sea. No pressure, no regrets or baggage: just enjoying each other's company.

Walking hand in hand in the famous rose garden at Alnwick with Oliver was the most romantic Saturday afternoon Gemma had ever spent. The sun was bright but not fiercely hot; the scent of the flowers was incredibly strong and made her feel as if they were strolling through an enchanted storybook garden. And when Oliver pulled her into a secluded arbour and stole a kiss, it made her feel as if the air around them was sparkling with happiness.

Even the monthly visit to her parents, the next day, was bearable this time.

'I went to the rose garden at Alnwick yesterday,' she said. 'It's really amazing. I've never seen so many roses in one place before.'

'That's nice,' her mum said. The usual shutdown. Except this time it didn't hurt as much. Being with Oliver had taught Gemma to look at things a little differently. He appreciated her for who she was—and maybe she didn't need to change her parents. Maybe it was time for her to face the fact that this was the best she was going to get. So instead of feeling miserable that they wouldn't—or couldn't—respond, she should see not having a fight with them as a win.

'I took some photos to show you,' she said brightly, and opened up the app in her phone. 'I nearly bought you a rose bush in the shop, but then I thought it might be nice to choose one together.'

'We'll see,' her father said.

Meaning no.

'OK. We'll put a date in the diary, have a nice afternoon together—with tea and scones—and then I'll buy you a rose bush. Or another plant, if you don't want to be bothered with roses,' she said.

Even though she didn't manage to pin them down to an actual date, they hadn't rejected her out of hand. This was progress, of sorts.

Better still, she had Oliver to go back to at the end of the day. Instead of feeling lonely and hopeless, the way she usually did after seeing her parents, she'd be spending the evening with someone who *did* want to spend time with her.

'How was your visit?' he asked.

'They actually looked at the photographs of Alnwick,' she said. 'And I got a smile.'

Ollie's heart ached for her. If he'd been in her shoes, he knew his parents would've wanted to spend as much time as they could with him, rather than push him away. 'A smile is good,' he said. But he rather thought she needed a hug, and held her close.

Taking her out for dinner would be the easy option; he wanted to make her feel special and cherished. So he'd do something for her instead of paying someone else to do it. 'How about I make us dinner? We could sit in the garden in the sun, with a glass of wine, and just chill.'

'That would be lovely. Can I help make dinner?'

He was about to say no, he wanted to spoil her, but then he realised: she'd said before that her parents stonewalled her. Right now, she needed to feel included. 'Sure. But I'll fine you a kiss for every time you get under my feet in my little galley kitchen,' he said, keeping it light.

'Challenge accepted. And I'll fine you two kisses for getting under my feet.' Her smile reached her eyes, this time, and he knew he'd said the right thing.

On Monday, they had a meeting with Caroline, the head of the practice, about the strength and balance classes for the elderly.

'It was Gemma's idea,' Oliver said. 'But I have friends whose practices have trialled something like this and they shared their stats with me. The cost-benefit analysis shows it'd be a good investment; the amount spent on the classes will be more than offset by the amount saved by not having to treat so many falls.'

'Plus there's the soft side of things: the effect it'll have on the community. I've spoken to Melanie at the gym,' Gemma said. 'She thinks it's a great idea and she's prepared to do the training to make sure she gets the right balance of exercises—um, I didn't actually intend that pun,' she said, when Oliver pulled a face at her. 'She has morning weekday slots available. She suggested a nominal fee for the first six weeks; and then reduced-price classes for people who wanted to continue.'

'You've really worked it out between you, haven't you?' Caroline asked. 'Much as I'd like to go with my heart rather than my head, we do need to look at it in the context of all our patients, because we have to allocate costs fairly. Let me read what you've put together, and I'll come back to you by Friday.'

On Friday, Caroline agreed to the plan.

Celebratory dinner tonight? Oliver suggested by text.

Gemma had been going to Claire's. She texted her best friend, asking if she could invite Oliver.

So I get to meet him properly? YES!

That was the immediate reply.

She texted Oliver.

I'm at Claire's for dinner. Come with me?

Would he think this was taking things too fast, meeting her best friend so soon?

Fortunately she had work to distract her—including a call with Mrs Brown, whose itchy rash had disappeared before the dermatology department could do a biopsy.

And then Oliver texted her back.

I'd love to. What are C's favourite flowers?

She almost sagged in relief.

You really don't have to take flowers, but gerberas.

Good. Let me know what time.

Meeting Gemma's best friend. That was a sign she was letting him a lot closer, Ollie thought. Which was a good thing.

At the same time, he felt faintly intimidated. He knew that Claire would assess him—just as Rob would assess Gemma, if Ollie let them meet each other. And he was pretty sure that the uppermost question in Claire's mind would be whether he'd be good for Gemma or if he'd hurt her.

He hoped he knew the answer, but all he could do was be himself.

After work, he bought a large bunch of zingy orange gerberas and a bottle of good red wine. He didn't have a clue what kind of gift to take a three-year-old, but Gemma had mentioned reading stories to her goddaughter, so he asked for a recommendation in the village bookshop and came out with a book he hoped Scarlett didn't already have.

From what Gemma had said, they'd arrive at just about bedtime for Scarlett, so she'd get a cuddle and a story.

Claire greeted them both with a hug. 'Nice to meet you properly, Oliver,' she said.

'And you,' he replied. 'Thank you for inviting me.' He handed over the gifts he'd brought.

'That's so sweet of you.' She beamed at him. 'And to think of Scarlett, too? Thank you so much. Come through and I'll get you a drink.'

In the living room, Gemma scooped up her goddaughter, who flung her arms round Gemma's neck, squealing, 'Aunty Gemma!'

'Oliver, this is Andy and Scarlett,' Gemma introduced him quickly. 'This is my friend Oliver.'

Andy nodded and smiled.

'Hello,' Scarlett said shyly.

'Oliver brought you something nice,' Claire said, and gave Scarlett the book.

'It's a story about a mermaid!' Scarlett said with a gasp of delight, looking at the front cover. 'Can we read it now, Aunty Gemma?'

Claire coughed. 'Words missing, Scarlett. What do you say to Oliver?'

'Thank you, Oliver,' the little girl said solemnly.

'My pleasure,' Oliver said.

'Come and read it with us,' Gemma said.

And somehow he found himself doing the voice of the shark, who became best friends with the mermaid.

It gave Ollie a jolt.

Sitting here with Gemma, a little girl cuddled between them, reading a story... It was lovely. Sweet, domesticated, and exactly what he'd hoped for when he'd been engaged to Tabby. He wanted to settle down. Have a family. Read stories, build sandcastles, maybe have a cat or dog.

Except he didn't know what Gemma wanted. Did she want to settle down and have a family? She'd spoken about offering a home for a troubled teen; what about babies?

It was too soon to discuss that. He'd known Gemma for a few weeks, and they'd barely started dating. What did she want from a partner? Would he be enough for her? He'd always thought of himself as grounded and sensible, but since Tabby had told him he wasn't enough for her it had made him doubt himself, wonder if instead he was staid and boring. And Gemma herself had said that her relationships tended to fizzle out. They'd agreed to see how things went between them. He really should stop thinking about the future and concentrate on the here and now.

But Ollie still felt as if he fitted here. Once Scarlett was in bed, asleep, and Claire had served the best lasagne he'd ever eaten, he found it easy to chat to Gemma's best friend and her husband, as if he'd known them for years.

Even when he insisted on helping clear up in the kitchen and Claire grilled him, he still felt comfortable.

'Just be careful with her,' Claire said quietly. 'She's not had a great time, the last few years.'

'You and your family made a difference, though,' he said, equally quietly.

'She told you?' Claire looked surprised.

He nodded. 'About Sarah, about her difficult year and about moving in with your family. I'm glad she had you all looking out for her.'

'I don't want to see her hurt again,' Claire said.

'I won't hurt her,' Ollie promised. 'I know she's special.'

Claire gave him a long, assessing gaze. 'I believe you. The question is, will she?'

It gave Ollie pause for thought, but he still found himself becoming closer to Gemma as the next week ticked past. And closer to Ashermouth Bay, too; in London, neighbours could pass you in the street without having a clue that you lived next door. Here, everyone knew everyone. When he went for his morning run, people would wave or call a greeting across the street. If he popped out to the shops, he'd bump into patients who'd stop for a chat, and not just about their health.

Ollie really liked being part of the community here. Being on the surgery's pub quiz team, joining in with all the jokes and good-natured teasing, being right in the middle of things. He was beginning to think that this was exactly where he belonged. And maybe he should think about staying here instead of going back to London.

On Tuesday morning, Ollie had a nervous patient. 'How can I help, Mrs Parker?' he asked.

'It's my little boy,' she said. 'Yesterday, nursery said James was a bit grumpy. This morning, he's covered in spots. I think he's got chickenpox.'

'I had heard there was an outbreak,' Oliver said. 'How old is James?'

'Three.'

'Chickenpox is usually pretty mild, at that age,' Oliver said, clearly trying to reassure her. 'Were they red spots, practically coming out as you looked at him?'

'Yes,' Penny said.

'In a day or so, they might start to blister and be itchy. He'll have a bit of a temperature, he might tell you he has a tummy ache, and he might be off his food,' Oliver said. 'Keep him at home until five days after the last spots have crusted over. Give him some paracetamol to bring his temperature down, try not to let him scratch the spots, and use calamine lotion to stop the itching.'

Penny bit her lip. 'It's not just James, though.' She smoothed a hand over her bump. 'It's this little one.'

'Would I be right in guessing that you didn't have chickenpox when you were young?' Oliver asked.

'When I was in primary school, there was an outbreak and Mum sent me to play with every single kid who had it,' Penny said. 'But I never got it. And the baby's due in a month. And I read...' Her voice sounded choked. 'If I get it, and the baby's early...'

'First of all, don't panic,' Oliver said. 'We can check your booking-in bloods and see if you've got any antibodies for chickenpox. If you have, panic over; if not, then we can give you some antiviral medicine. It might not stop you getting chickenpox, but it'll be much less severe and it will help to protect the baby as well.'

'Thank you.' Penny's smile was less wobbly now. 'I was so worried.'

'Of course you were,' Oliver said. 'But we can do a lot to help. Try not to look on the scary side. And definitely don't search things on the Internet, because that's where people like to outdo each other on the horror stories.'

'It's a bit late for that,' Penny said wryly. 'But thank you.'

When she'd gone, he rang the hospital and got them to run a test on Penny's booking-in bloods, explaining the situation and that he had a very anxious mum waiting for the results.

'You're looking twitchy,' Gemma said later that afternoon in the staff rest room. 'Too much coffee?' she teased.

'No. Waiting for test results. I had a worried mum in this morning; her baby's due in a month and her little one has gone down with chickenpox—which she hasn't had.'

'Penny Parker?' Gemma asked.

'Do you know her?'

'We were at school together. She's an absolute sweetheart,'

Gemma said. 'So James has chickenpox? Scarlett is in his nursery class, so no doubt she'll be bringing a letter home to warn parents to look out for spots and a temperature.'

Thankfully, the results came in half an hour later, and Ollie was able to ring Penny and tell her that she was immune and didn't need to worry.

On Wednesday evening, Ollie was playing a board game with Gemma when his doorbell rang.

'Are you expecting visitors?' Gemma asked.

'No,' Ollie said, and frowned. 'I hope next door are OK. Jim was saying his knee was giving him a lot of trouble. I've been trying to persuade him to come in so I can examine him properly and maybe refer him for an X-ray.'

When he opened the door, he was surprised to see his twin on the doorstep. 'Rob! I didn't know you were coming over this evening.'

'I'm bored,' Rob said. 'Bored, bored, bored. And, just in case you didn't get the message, first time round, I'm—'

'Bored,' Ollie finished, smiling. 'Got it. Come in.'

'If Mum wraps any more cotton wool round me, I'm going to start looking like a very out-of-season snowm— Oh. Hello.' Rob looked at Gemma, then at his twin. 'Sorry, Olls. I didn't realise you had company.'

'Rob, this is Gemma. My girlfriend.'

Gemma's eyes widened for a moment; but then she smiled, and it felt as if the world was full of sunshine.

'Gemma, this is my—'

'Older, and infinitely more charming twin brother,' Rob said with a smile. 'Robert Langley—Rob, to my friends. Lovely to meet you, Gemma.' He shook her hand, then glanced at the table. 'So who's winning?'

'Gemma is,' Ollie said. 'Go and make coffee, Rob.'

'I've got a better idea. *You* make the coffee, and I'll take your turn for you on the game,' Rob said.

* * *

Which clearly signalled his intention to grill her, Gemma thought. No doubt this was how Oliver had felt at Claire's. Well, all she could do was be herself and hope that Rob would like her.

'Olls showed me your skydive video,' Rob said when Oliver had gone into the kitchen. 'I'm impressed.'

'Coming from someone who does stuff for humanitarian organisations and is on a mountain rescue team, you shouldn't be,' Gemma said. 'What I did was only for a few minutes. You do it all the time.'

'Sadly, I won't be able to do the aid stuff in future, because of the kidney—I'm too much of a risk,' Rob said. 'So do you do a lot of this sort of thing for fundraising?'

'I'm sure Oliver's already told you—my little sister had myocarditis and she didn't get a transplant in time. I've been fundraising for the local hospital ever since I qualified and came back here to work. They're doing research into permanent artificial hearts.'

'Which would be a huge game-changer,' Rob said. 'Is it too late to sponsor you for your skydive?'

'Yes, but I do a cake stall at the surgery on Fridays.'

'Cake? Excellent. Make Olls buy some for me. He hates cake, but I don't,' Rob said.

She smiled. 'I will. Let me know your favourite sort, and I'll make it for this Friday.'

'Anything with chocolate,' Rob said. 'So what else are you planning?'

'I do two big events a year. The skydive had to be postponed so the next one's a bit close—I'm doing a sixty-mile cycle ride down the coast next month,' she said, 'and then after that I'm considering doing a swimming challenge, though I'm planning to swim in the pool at the gym rather than the actual English Channel.'

'Good idea, because then you don't have to wait a couple of

years for a slot and then hope that the weather conditions will work out,' Rob said. 'Given the cliffs I've seen along here, I assume you've done climbing or abseiling?'

She shook her head. 'Not for me. Too scary. I'd rather walk along the top of the cliffs and enjoy the view in safety.'

'Or along the beach and rescue a drowning teenager,' Rob said.

Oliver had told his brother about that? She flapped a dismissive hand. 'Everyone around here does their school lifesaving stuff in the sea. Anyone else would've done the same thing.'

'But you're the one who actually went in to get him,' Rob said softly.

'Oliver wanted to, but I didn't want him overexerting himself. I know technically he's allowed to swim in the sea again, but there's a big difference between casual swimming and towing someone in. Plus we needed someone to get in touch with the emergency services. It was a team effort.'

'Uh-huh.' But Rob's smile held approval. 'Olls says there are all kinds of things here. Kite-surfing—'

'No, no and no. Be more me,' Oliver said, coming back into the room. 'Your consultant would have kittens if he could hear you.'

'I know,' Rob said mildly. 'He's given me the green light to go back to work part time. Mum's panicking. But I'm going to be sensible. I told her about that bargain we made: I'm going to be more Ollie and you're going to be more Rob.'

'Me being the sensible one, and Rob being the—'

'Almost sensible one,' Rob cut in with a grin.

The bickering, Gemma could see, was purely for show; the way Oliver and Rob looked at each other told her how much they loved each other.

She thoroughly enjoyed playing the board game with Oliver and his brother; despite the physical distance between them over the last few years, they were clearly very close and talked to each other a lot. The same kind of relationship she would've had with Sarah, she thought wistfully. Love and acceptance of each other, flaws and all.

'I like her, Olls,' Rob said when Gemma left at the end of the evening. 'A lot. She's the complete opposite of Tabby. And she's perfect for you.'

'It's early days,' Ollie said. 'And I'm only here temporarily.'

'Don't overthink things,' Rob advised. 'You still haven't decided whether you're going back to London or somewhere else. Stick around for a bit. See how it goes.'

Ollie wanted to. But he still couldn't quite shake himself of the fear. Would he be enough for Gemma, the way he hadn't been for Tabby? Or was he setting himself up for heartache again?

Two days later, Penny rang Gemma. 'Gem, I'm so sorry to do this—Mum's away or I'd call her. I don't know what else to do. It's Gran.'

Gemma knew that Penny's grandmother was staying for a few days while her bathroom was being refitted. 'What's happened?'

'She's got a really high temperature.' Penny dragged in a breath. 'I don't know if it's flu, or something else.'

The spectre of Covid, Gemma thought, which could be deadly in older patients.

'I'm so sorry. I just don't know what to do. I can't leave James, and—'

'I'm on my way,' Gemma said. 'I'm your friend. And friends help each other. See you in a minute.'

She filled Oliver in.

'The pizza's not coming to any harm in the fridge,' Oliver said. 'I'll turn the oven off now. Let's go. We'll take my bag with us. And my car,' he added.

Penny greeted them with relief at her front door.

'Run us through your gran's symptoms,' Oliver said.

'Her temperature's thirty-nine, she's got a headache, she's been coughing and says it's hard to breathe, and she's tired and she doesn't want to eat.' Penny bit her lip.

'There are plenty of viruses that do exactly the same thing, including summer flu,' Oliver said. 'Try not to worry.'

'Has she mentioned any loss of smell or taste?' Gemma asked.

Penny shook her head.

'That's a good thing,' Oliver said. 'Let's go and see her.'

Penny introduced Oliver and Gemma to her grandmother, and Oliver listened to the elderly woman's chest while Gemma checked her pulse. Mrs Bailey was coughing, and admitted that it hurt more when she breathed in.

'Crackles,' Oliver said to Gemma quietly. 'How's her pulse?'

'Fast. I'm thinking pneumonia,' Gemma said.

'I agree,' Oliver said. 'Mrs Bailey, we think you have pneumonia. You need antibiotics, but the surgery isn't open at this time of night so I can't prescribe them. We need to get you to hospital.'

'But how did Gran get pneumonia?' Penny asked, looking distraught.

'Lots of things cause pneumonia. Have you ever had chickenpox, Mrs Bailey?' Oliver asked gently.

'Not that I remember. Anyway, I don't have any spots.'

'Chickenpox doesn't always cover you completely with spots; sometimes there might only be one or two little ones,' Gemma said.

'And James has chickenpox. I'll drive you to hospital, Gran,' Penny said.

'You're eight months pregnant and you're worried sick. I'll drive,' Oliver said. 'I'll call the emergency department to let them know we're coming.'

Penny shook her head. 'I can't ask you to do that—and, if Gran's got chickenpox, what if you get it from her?'

'I won't. My brother and I both had it when we were six,' Oliver said. 'And I remember because it was Christmas and it snowed, and we couldn't go out to make a snowman.'

'If you want to go with Oliver and your gran, Penny,' Gemma said, 'I'll stay here and keep an eye on James.'

Penny's bottom lip wobbled. 'Gem. I don't know how to thank you.'

'Hey. You were there for me when I needed a friend. James will be fine with me,' Gemma said, giving her a hug.

'He's asleep right now,' Penny said.

'If he wakes up, I'll give him a cuddle and read him a story until he goes back to sleep,' Gemma promised.

'You're one of the best,' Penny said. 'Both of you are.'

'Let's get your gran comfortable in my car,' Oliver said.

At the hospital, Florence Jacobs, the registrar on duty, examined Penny's gran and admitted her to a ward. 'It's a precaution,' she said to Penny. 'Pneumonia can be a bit nasty. I'd rather have your gran here so we can monitor her for a couple of days and make sure the antibiotics are working. You can come back in and see her tomorrow, and bring anything you want to make her a bit more comfortable.'

'But—what about her nightie, and her things?'

'Call Gemma and ask her to pack a bag,' Oliver said. 'I'll bring it back here when I drop you home.'

'I can't ask—'

'You're not asking. I'm offering,' he said gently.

'I've ruined your evening with Gemma.'

'It's fine,' he said with a smile. 'Everyone needs a friend to lean on from time to time. Call Gemma.'

'You're so lovely,' she said.

Oli-lovely-ver. He could hear Gemma's voice in his head, and it made him smile. 'My pleasure.' It was good to feel part of a community. Part of Gemma's community. And Oliver found himself wondering what the chances were of Aadya deciding to take a little more maternity leave so he could stay a bit longer. He liked working in Ashermouth Bay, and he liked being with Gemma. More than liked.

And, even though Ollie still didn't trust his own judgement, after Tabby, Rob liked her.

Maybe he and Gemma could be good for each other.

Maybe she was the one he ought to let close.

And maybe, just maybe, he'd be the one that she finally let close, too…

CHAPTER NINE

THE FOLLOWING SATURDAY AFTERNOON, Yvonne was running a workshop and Gemma was helping out. But Ollie had managed to get tickets to see a band he really liked and had talked Gemma into going with him. They grabbed some burritos before the show, and were in the queue early enough to be at the front.

'Are you sure about this?' she asked. 'What if someone knocks into you?'

He could guess what she was worried about: his scar. 'I'm fine,' he said. 'Really.' He stole a kiss. 'But I appreciate the concern.'

During the show, he stood behind Gemma with his arms wrapped round her. It was good to hold her close. And on an evening like this: it was perfect, with the buzz of the crowd and the sheer joy of being there seeing a band he'd liked for years. Gemma knew some of their hits and sang along with everyone else, and Ollie didn't care that neither of them was singing in tune. This was just great. Especially as she was leaning back against him to be even closer.

'That was fantastic,' she said, as they walked back to his car with their arms wrapped round each other.

'It's been a while since I've been to a show,' he said.

'I guess in London you have a lot more choice,' she said.

'There's a lot of good music here, too,' he said.

When he'd driven her home, she asked him in for coffee.

And he spent so long kissing her in her kitchen that they completely forgot about the kettle.

'Um. Sorry,' he said, when he finally broke the kiss.

'I'm not.' She stroked his face. 'Stay tonight?'

His heart skipped a beat. 'Are you asking…?'

She blushed, making her look even prettier. 'Yes.'

He stole another kiss. 'Then yes. Please.'

'Mind you, I've got to be up early to do the cycling training,' she warned.

'I would offer to do it with you,' he said, 'except I don't have a bike and, even if I borrowed one, I'm not used to cycling long-distance so I'd hold you back.'

'Fair comment,' she said.

'But is there something else I could do to support you?'

'We could do with another race medic,' she said. 'But that's a bit of an ask.'

'The event's important to you,' he said, 'so I'll support you. Sign me up and let me know the details.'

'Really?'

'Really.' He held her gaze. 'And tomorrow maybe I could meet you at the end of your ride and take you for lunch.'

'I'm going to be hideously sweaty,' she said. 'Not fit to go out.'

'In that case, how about I cook you a late Sunday lunch here, with proper crispy roast potatoes?' he suggested.

'That,' she said, 'would be perfect.' She kissed him. Then she took his hand. 'It's been a while since I've done this.'

'Me, too,' he said.

'There's a bit of me that's…well, scared,' she admitted.

He stroked her face. 'I won't hurt you,' he promised. 'We don't have to do anything. I can just sleep with you in my arms, if you want. Or I can go home on my own, if you decide you're not ready for this.'

'Oli-lovely-ver,' she said. 'I trust you. And I—I want to make love with you.'

'Good,' he said.

'Do you—' she blushed even harder '—have any condoms?'

'Yes,' he said.

'Then come to bed with me, Oliver,' she said.

He kissed her, and let her lead him to her bedroom.

Gemma woke in the middle of the night, her head cradled on Oliver's shoulder and her arm wrapped round his waist. Closing her eyes, she listened to his deep, regular breathing.

Oliver had been a generous lover. Even though the first time they'd made love should've been awkward and a bit rubbish, it hadn't been. It had felt like—like coming home, she thought. The first time it had ever felt this good, this right.

Maybe this time she'd made the right choice. Maybe this time she'd found someone worth being close to.

Finally, she drifted off to sleep.

When her alarm shrilled the next morning, she leaned over to the bedside table to switch it off. Oliver nuzzled the back of her neck. 'Good morning.'

She turned back to face him and smiled. 'Good morning.' The morning after the night before, she'd half expected to feel shy with him; but instead she just felt happy. As if everything was in its right place.

'I'll get up and head for home so you can get ready for your training,' he said. 'See you for lunch.'

'I look forward to it,' she said. 'What can I bring?'

'Just yourself.' He kissed her again. 'Enjoy your training. Come over whenever you're ready. I plan to do lunch for two o'clock, but let me know if you need it to be later.'

'It sounds perfect. Thank you.'

Once he was back home, Ollie downed a protein shake, changed into his running gear, and went for a run along the sea.

The sun was shining, the sky was the perfect shimmery blue of summer, and life felt good. He couldn't remember the last time he'd felt this happy; and he knew it was all because of Gemma.

He'd finished setting the bistro table in the garden when his phone pinged.

See you in ten minutes.

She was as good as her word, too, not keeping him waiting; and when he opened the door she greeted him with a kiss and handed him a brown paper bag.

'What's this?'

'Host gift. I did consider flowers,' she said, 'but I don't get gardener vibes from you. So I thought you might like these.'

He looked in the bag to discover locally roasted coffee—beans, rather than ground, in deference to his coffee machine—and locally made chutney. 'Thank you. That's lovely. Lunch will be another twenty minutes, so shall I make us coffee and we can sit in the garden?'

She kissed him again. 'That'd be lovely. And something smells gorgeous.'

Gemma, he thought, appreciated him. She paid attention and she'd noticed what he liked.

So maybe this time he'd got it right. And it filled him with joy.

It was a busy week at the practice; Penny's grandmother recovered from her pneumonia, quite a few more of the children in the village came down with chickenpox, and Ollie found himself treating sprains and strains from tourists who'd overdone sporting activities on holiday as well as gardeners who'd wanted to make the most of the good weather. Every day he felt that he was getting to know the people in the village a little more, and really making a difference at the practice. And every night, he and Gemma made love, and it made him feel as if the barriers he'd put round his heart were melting away.

Until Thursday evening, when Gemma was doing something with Claire and he was catching up with some journals, and his phone rang.

He glanced at the screen and felt a flush of guilt as he saw the name of one of his colleagues at the practice in London. 'Hey, Mandy,' he said. 'Sorry, I've been a bit hopeless about staying in touch.'

'It's fine. We know you've had a lot on your plate, with Rob and the transplant.'

'So what can I do for you? Did you and Tristan fancy coming up for a weekend? You'd love the beaches here. You can walk for miles.'

'It's not that,' she said. She took a deep breath. 'I just thought it might be better if you heard the news from someone you know, rather than come across it on social media and what have you.'

Ollie had pretty much ignored social media since he'd been in Northumbria. 'What news?'

'Tabby. She's, um, engaged.'

Tabby. Engaged. To someone else.

He blew out a breath. 'Right.'

'I'm sorry, Ollie. I know you loved her.'

But she hadn't loved him. At least, not enough to marry him. And it had hurt so much when she'd told him. It had taken him months to get over the misery of knowing that he wasn't what she wanted: that he'd got it so wrong. 'I hope she's found someone who can make her happy,' he said, meaning it.

'Are you OK, Ollie?' Mandy asked.

'I'm fine,' he reassured her, even though he was still processing the news. 'And Rob's doing well. He's got a part-time post in the Emergency Department at the hospital near here, to keep him out of mischief for a while.'

'That's good.'

He managed to keep the conversation going for a bit, and extracted a promise that she and Tristan would try to find a spare weekend to come up and visit.

But when he put the phone down, he had time to think about it. Time to brood.

Tabby was engaged to someone else.

It was a good thing that she'd moved on; but the news brought back all his insecurities. Engaged. To be engaged again this soon, Tabby must've started dating the guy within days of calling off the wedding. Which just went to prove that he really, really hadn't been enough for her.

So was he kidding himself that he was enough for Gemma?

Yes, she'd let Ollie close to her; but was he setting himself up for another failure?

The more he thought about it, the more he convinced himself that he was making a huge mistake. His job here was temporary and his contract ended in a couple of weeks' time—as did his sabbatical from his practice in London. He was perfectly fit again after donating a kidney. Which meant that he really ought to think about going back to London.

But that wasn't fair to Gemma, either. He knew how much she loved it here. He couldn't expect her to leave the place where she'd grown up and go back to London with him.

So he was going to have to find a way of letting her down gently.

The question was—how?

Something was wrong, Gemma was sure.

Oliver had suddenly gone distant on her. Too busy for lunch on Friday, she could accept, because she knew how busy they were at work. Suggesting that she have a girly night with Claire and little Scarlett on Friday evening was Oliver being nice. But when he was too busy to see her on Saturday, and went to see his family on Sunday—without asking her to join him and meet his parents as well as seeing his brother again—she started to wonder if she was missing something.

Had Oliver changed his mind about being with her?

His contract at the surgery was due to end in a couple of weeks, when Aadya was coming back from maternity leave. What then? Would he go back to London? Move elsewhere?

She had no idea. But the one thing she was pretty sure about was that, whatever Oliver decided to do, he wouldn't ask her to go with him.

She texted him on Sunday evening.

Everything OK?

It took a while for him to text her back, but it was cool and polite and told her nothing.

Yes, thanks.

What now?

She could be pathetic and wait for him to dump her, the way she'd been at seventeen.

Or she could take control. Be the one who ended it.

When Oliver made excuses not to see her on Monday, that decided her.

She texted him.

Can I call in for a quick word on the way back from the gym tomorrow?

He took so long replying that she thought he was going to say no. But finally she got the answer she wanted.

Sure.

No suggestion of dinner or a drink.

OK. She'd take the hint. And no way was she going to let him do the 'it's not you, it's me' line. She'd been there and done that way too often.

She showered and changed at the gym after her class, then cycled over to Oliver's cottage and rang the bell.

When he opened the door, he didn't smile or kiss her, the way he had last week.

It was as if they'd stepped into some parallel universe. One where they'd never made love, never kissed, weren't even friends.

And this really felt like the rejections from her teens. The boys who'd ghosted her or who'd ignored her, once they'd got what they wanted.

Clearly she hadn't learned from her mistakes.

And how stupid she'd been to think that they were getting closer. Obviously for Oliver it had been just sex.

'Would you like some coffee?' he asked.

But she could see from his face that he was being polite.

She wasn't going to let herself be needy enough to accept. 'No, thanks,' she said. 'This won't take long. I've been thinking...we took things a bit too fast.'

His expression was completely inscrutable. He merely inclined his head.

And this was excruciating, making her realise how stupid she'd been.

'I think,' she said carefully, 'we should go back to being just colleagues.' She couldn't quite stretch it to friendship. Not when he was going to be leaving anyway.

'You're right,' he said.

'Good.' Though there was one last little thing. 'I understand if you've changed your mind about helping at the cycle race.'

He shook his head. 'I promised I'd help. It isn't fair to let you down at the last minute.'

It wasn't fair to let her down, full stop. To let her close and then freeze her out. Then again, she was as much to blame.

She'd obviously tried so hard not to freeze him out that she'd been too needy. No wonder he'd backed away. 'As you wish,' she said. 'Though I think we should travel separately.'

'Of course,' he said.

'Right. Well, see you at the surgery,' she said brightly, and wheeled her bicycle round so he wouldn't see even the tiniest trace of hurt in her face.

We should go back to being just colleagues.

Not even friends. Just two people who worked together.

The words echoed in Ollie's head. Although part of him knew he was being unfair—he'd pushed her away ever since he'd heard the news about Tabby's engagement—part of him felt as if she'd stomped on a bruise. He hadn't been enough for Tabby, and he clearly hadn't been enough for Gemma, either, otherwise she would've fought for him. Or maybe it was his fault for messing it up in the first place. Backing away from her instead of telling her what was going on in his head. No wonder she'd dumped him.

But he was only here for another couple of weeks, so it shouldn't matter. He could keep up the facade until his contract ended.

Though lunch without her felt lonely; and he was really aware now of how echoey the little cottage was. How quiet, without Gemma chattering and laughing and teasing him.

Somehow he got through the weekend.

And then, the following Wednesday, Caroline asked to see him.

Was she going to ask him to leave the practice early, to get rid of any tension in the staff room?

To his shock, it was the opposite. 'Aadya wants to come back part-time,' she said. 'And I think we have enough work to justify another full-time GP. You've fitted into the practice really well.'

If only she knew.

'So I'd like to give you first refusal of the new post,' Caroline said.

The answer was obvious. For Gemma's sake, he'd have to say no.

As if she'd anticipated his refusal, Caroline said, 'I know you'd need to sort things out with your practice in London, and I'd be happy to accommodate that. So don't give me an answer now. Think it over for a week.'

'Thank you. I will,' he said, giving her his best and brightest smile.

Stay at Ashermouth Bay.

If Caroline had asked him this a week or so ago, Ollie knew he would've jumped at the chance.

But that was before he'd learned that Tabby was engaged again. Before he'd realised that he was fooling himself if he thought he'd be enough for anyone. Before he'd pushed Gemma away.

The answer would be no. It couldn't be anything else. But he'd be courteous about it and do what Caroline asked, waiting until next week to give her an answer.

And then he'd leave.

Go back to London.

And pretend he'd never met Gemma Baxter.

CHAPTER TEN

THE DAY BEFORE Gemma was due to do the sponsored cycle ride, Ollie had just bought a pint of milk from the village shop when he bumped into her.

'Oliver,' she said, and gave him a cool nod.

But her face was blotchy and he thought she'd been crying. Even though he knew it was none of his business and he should leave it, he couldn't help asking, 'Are you all right?'

'Fine, thank you.'

Cool, calm—and a complete fib. 'You're not all right,' he said softly. 'What's happened?'

She swallowed hard. 'It's Sarah's birthday. I'm trying to celebrate the day. But...'

'It's hard,' he finished. And, even though he knew he wasn't enough for her, he couldn't just leave her like this, clearly heartbroken and trying to be brave. 'Do you want me to come with you to the churchyard, for company?'

She shook her head. 'I can't go today.'

He frowned. 'Why not?'

'Because... Never mind.'

That didn't sound good. At all. 'In that case, I'm making you coffee. No arguments. It's what any—' he chose his words carefully '—colleague would do for another.'

He shepherded her back to his cottage; she sat at the kitchen table in total silence while he made coffee. This really wasn't like Gemma; she was usually bright and bubbly and chatty.

'So why can't you visit your sister today?' he asked.

'Because our parents are visiting her.'

What? 'Surely they'd want to be with you, too?'

Gemma wouldn't meet his eyes. 'It's difficult. Her birthday, her anniversary—those days seem to bring all the misery of her dying back to them, and they can't handle seeing me as well. It kind of feels as if they still blame me for having the virus in the first place, though I'm probably being paranoid. And then they remember how I went off the rails and made everything worse for them, and...' She shook her head. 'It's just easier to give them space today.'

Oliver went to put his arms round her, but she leaned away. 'Don't. I can't... Not now.'

He wasn't entirely sure whether she was rejecting him or rejecting everyone. Hadn't she said to him that she was hopeless at relationships? And he'd frozen her out because his self-doubts had got in the way.

'Sorry. I'm not good company. I'd rather be on my own right now. Thanks for trying. Sorry to waste your coffee.'

And she left before he could find the right words to stop her.

Oliver thought about it for the rest of the morning.

He might not be able to offer Gemma a future, but he could do something to make her life a bit better. Maybe.

He headed for the bakery to see Claire.

'I'm a bit busy,' she said coolly, and he knew he deserved the brush-off.

'It's about Gemma,' he said. 'It's Sarah's birthday today.'

'Yes. She's coming over tonight for fajitas and board games, to take her mind off it.' Claire frowned. 'Is that why you're here? You want to come, too? But I thought you and Gemma had...'

'Split up? Yes. It's my fault. You can yell at me some other time, but right now is all about Gemma and her parents.'

Claire rolled her eyes. 'Don't talk to me about *them*. I mean, I'm a mum myself now, so I kind of get how hard it must've been for them when Sarah died, but I hate the way...' She stopped. 'Never mind.'

'You hate the way they just abandoned Gemma after Sarah died. And you don't get why they're not wrapping her in cotton wool because she's the only child they have left,' he guessed.

'She told you?' Claire looked shocked. 'Well, that's a good thing. I'm glad she's talking about it. But you're right. I wish her parents...' She grimaced. 'Mum's tried. I've tried. They're just cocooned in their grief and they can't see what they still have.'

'Maybe they need someone who didn't know Sarah to make them see things differently,' Ollie said. 'Like me.'

Claire frowned. 'Why would you do that?'

'Because I care about Gemma.'

'Even though you broke up with her?'

'Claire, as I said, you can yell at me about this another time,' he said, 'but I really need to know where Gemma's parents live.'

Her eyes widened. 'You're going to tackle them *today*?'

'It's probably too much, on Sarah's birthday. I was thinking tomorrow morning,' he said.

'But you can't. It's the race tomorrow. You promised Gem you'd be a race medic.'

'Exactly.' Oliver enlightened Claire about his plan.

'If this goes wrong,' Claire warned, 'Gemma's going to get hurt.'

'She's already hurt. If her parents refuse to listen to me and continue to stay away, what's changed?'

'I guess.' She sighed. 'I have huge reservations about this, and I really don't think you're going to get anywhere with them. But I suppose at least you're trying, for Gemma's sake.' She gave him the address.

'Thank you,' he said.

For the next part of his plan, Ollie rang Rob. 'I need to call in a favour for tomorrow,' he said.

'What kind of favour?' Rob asked.

'I need you to pretend to be me, and be a medic for a sixty-mile sponsored cycle race.'

Rob sounded puzzled. 'Why aren't you going to be there?'

'There's something that needs fixing,' Ollie said. 'I need to do it tomorrow, but I also need to be a race medic. The only way you can be in two places at the same time—or at least seem to be—is if you have an identical twin. Which is why I need your help.'

'Does Gemma know about this?'

'No.'

'Olls, I can't pretend to be her partner.'

'You don't have to. I'm not her partner any more.'

'What? But she's *lovely*, Olls. Why? What happened?'

'I'm not enough for her, just as I wasn't enough for Tabby.' Though Ollie knew he had to be honest. 'I pushed her away. Yes, I'm an idiot and I regret it, but it's too late.'

'Olls—'

'No, it's OK,' he said. 'This isn't about me. It's about her.'

'So what's this fixing you have to do?' Rob asked.

Ollie explained.

'And you're doing this why, exactly?'

'Because it's something I think I can fix for Gemma.'

'You're in love with her, aren't you?'

'I'm not answering that.'

'You don't have to. I *know*,' Rob said. 'All right. I'll help you. But only on condition you actually talk to her and tell her how you really feel about her.'

'There's no point. I'm not enough for her.'

'Did she actually say that?' Rob asked. 'You said yourself, you pushed her away. Stop being an idiot and talk to her. She can't guess what's in your head.'

'I need your help, Rob.'

'Of course I'm going to help you. I owe you everything,' Rob said softly. 'Without you I'd still be on dialysis, waiting for a kidney that might not come in time. But it's precisely because I owe you that I don't want you to mess this up. Promise me you'll talk to her.'

Ollie sighed. 'All right. I promise.'

CHAPTER ELEVEN

ON THE MORNING of the cycle ride, Gemma felt drained, but she'd be letting people down if she didn't do the race. She drove to the village where the starting point was and got her bike out of the back. She couldn't see Oliver's car anywhere, but when she went to register she saw him by the race marshals' tent.

Except it wasn't Oliver.

Even though Rob had let his hair grow out so they really did look identical, Gemma could tell the difference between them. Seeing him didn't feel the same as when she saw Oliver.

So it seemed as if Oliver had sent his twin to be here in his place.

Which just proved he didn't want to be with her and he was going back to London. Why had he even bothered talking to her and being sympathetic yesterday?

It wasn't Rob's fault, so she wasn't going to take it out on him. She went over to him and smiled. 'Thank you for the support, Rob,' she said.

His eyes widened. 'But I'm Oliver.'

She just looked at him, and he sighed. 'We're identical. I even did my hair like Olls does, and I'm wearing his clothes, not mine. How did you know?'

'I just do. Thank you for—well, doing what he clearly didn't want to do.'

'Gemma, we need to—'

'No, we don't need to talk,' she cut in softly. 'But I appreciate you turning up. And I have a race to cycle.'

'Good luck,' he said.

Ollie's doubts grew as he drove to the village where Gemma's parents lived.

What if they weren't there?

What if they were, but refused to talk to him?

Well, he'd just have to persuade them to listen.

When he rang the doorbell, her mum answered. 'Sorry, I don't buy things at the door.'

'I'm not selling anything, Mrs Baxter.'

She frowned. 'How do you know my name? I've never seen you before in my life.'

'My name's Oliver Langley. I work with Gemma,' he said. 'May I come in? Please? All I'm asking is for ten minutes of your time.'

'Ten minutes?' She looked confused.

'For Sarah's sake,' he said softly.

She flinched, but then she nodded. 'Come in.'

She didn't offer him a drink, but she did at least invite him to sit down.

'Firstly,' he said, 'I'd like to say how sorry I am about Sarah. I didn't know her—but my brother had a burst appendix and severe blood poisoning earlier this year, which wiped out his kidneys. So I know how it feels to worry about my brother being on dialysis, and whether my kidney would be suitable for him. Whether it might go wrong and we'd lose him.'

'Twelve years.' A tear trickled down Mrs Baxter's cheek. 'Twelve birthdays we haven't spent with our little girl.'

'And that's hard,' Ollie said. 'I know how desperately I would've missed Rob.' And now was his chance to tell them.

'I'm a doctor. I work with Gemma at Ashermouth Bay surgery. I know how much she misses her sister. How much she misses *you.*'

Neither of Gemma's parents responded.

'I know it's difficult,' he said gently. 'Every time you look at Gemma, you see Sarah in her. Of course you do. They're sisters. If we'd lost Rob, my parents would've found it really hard seeing me, because Rob's my identical twin.'

That made her parents look at him.

'I would've found it hard to see them, too, because I'd see him in their smiles and little mannerisms. But,' he said, 'it would've been a lot harder *not* to see them. Cutting myself off from them might've worked in the short term, but in the long term we'd all have missed out on so much.' He paused. 'You're missing out on Gemma.'

'I don't think there's anything more to say, Dr Langley,' Mr Baxter said.

'You said you'd give me ten minutes,' Oliver reminded them.

'Gemma doesn't need us,' Mrs Baxter said.

'Oh, but she does,' he said. 'She might look as if she's moved on with her life and she's completely together, but she's not. She went off the rails, the year Sarah died.'

Both her parents flinched.

'I'm not judging you,' he said. 'We nearly lost Rob, and I know how bad that felt. How much worse it must have been to lose your thirteen-year-old daughter—way, way too young. But Gemma still needs you. Both of you. She's a qualified nurse practitioner and she looks as if she's totally together and getting on with her life. But she's not. She spends nearly all her spare time raising money for the local cardiac ward, the one that treated Sarah. She pushes herself outside her comfort zone, trying to help so another family won't have to go through what you all went through. And she's amazing. She did a skydive last month. Next month, she's going to start swimming the equivalent of the English Channel.

'Right now, she's doing a sixty-mile cycle ride.' He paused. 'And you know what would make the difference to her? If you were there to meet her at the end of the race.'

'We can't,' Gemma's mother said. 'It's too late. We don't...' She shook her head.

'She's never going to give up on you,' he said. 'I know she comes to see you once a month and she'll keep doing that. Even though you reject her over and over and over again, she'll still keep trying. You lost Sarah, but you still have one daughter left. She's not giving up on you. Don't give up on her.'

'She was—difficult, after Sarah died. We couldn't cope with her behaviour,' Mrs Baxter said.

'She told me. But she's past that, now. She's a daughter you can be proud of,' Oliver said. 'She works so hard. And she's amazing.'

'Why are you here?' Mr Baxter asked.

'Because I care about Gemma. I can't bring Sarah back, but I can at least try to help Gemma mend the rift with you.'

'Does she know you're here?' Mrs Baxter asked.

'No,' Oliver said. 'I'm actually supposed to be supporting the race, being one of the medics.'

'Then why are you here?' Mrs Baxter asked.

'Because I wanted to talk to you. My twin brother agreed to pretend to be me,' Oliver said. 'So I haven't totally let her down. She's still got a race medic. Though I am going to have to apologise later for not telling her the entire truth.'

'What do you want from us?' Mr Baxter asked.

Had he really not been clear enough? 'I want,' Oliver said, 'you to see Gemma as she really is. I want you to be there when she cycles past the finish line. I want her to see you clapping.'

'You want us to go there for the end of the race,' Mrs Baxter said.

'I know it won't be easy for you,' he said. 'That it'll take time to mend things properly. But, if you take this first step, she'll come to meet you with open arms. And I'm happy to drive you there myself.'

'I don't know if we can. It's too hard,' Mr Baxter said.

Oliver wanted to bang their heads together and yell at them to stop being so selfish, but he knew it would be pointless. And now he really understood why Gemma had spent that year desperately searching for love—and why she hadn't let people close since, not wanting to be let down again.

And he was just as bad, he realised with a flush of guilt. He'd hurt her as much as her parents had, doing exactly the same thing: pushing her away.

'OK. Thank you for your time,' he said. 'If you change your mind, I think she'll be over the line at about two o'clock.' He took a notepad from his jacket pocket and scribbled down the address. 'This is where the finish line is. This is my phone number, if you want to talk to me. And this—if you want to go on the internet and see her jumping out of a plane for Sarah.

'Your brave, brilliant daughter. The one who's still here and needs her family. The whole village is proud of her—but that's not enough. She needs *you*.' He checked his phone and copied down the link to the video of her skydive, then handed over the paper to Mrs Baxter. 'I'll see myself out,' he said quietly.

He didn't think they'd turn up today. But maybe, just maybe, they'd think about what he'd said. And maybe they'd thaw towards Gemma in the future.

He could only hope.

A mile before the end of the race, Gemma saw the cyclist in front of her wobble precariously, and then almost as if it was in slow motion the bike lurched to the side and the rider hit the ground.

Gemma stopped immediately.

The cyclist was still on the ground.

Another cyclist stopped, too.

'Are you all right?' Gemma asked.

'I can't get up,' the woman said. 'My arm hurts.'

Between them, Gemma and the other cyclist who'd stopped to help lifted the bike off her.

Gemma really wished Oliver was there with her; but he'd sent his brother in his stead, because he didn't even want to be with her today.

She pushed the thought away. Right now, this wasn't about her; it was about helping this poor woman.

They helped her get to her feet; her left shoulder looked slumped and slightly forward, sending up a red flag for Gemma.

'I'm a nurse practitioner,' Gemma said. 'Can I have a look at your shoulder while we call the race medic?'

'I don't want the race medics. If they come, they won't let me finish and I have to do this.' There were tears in the woman's eyes. 'I lost my husband to leukaemia six months ago. I need to finish this for him. I have loads of sponsorship.'

'OK,' Gemma said. 'But at least let me make you comfortable. You look in pain.'

'It hurts,' the woman admitted, 'but I'm not giving in.'

'Shall I call...?' the other cyclist asked.

'No. Because if I'm right and she's broken her collarbone, we'll walk this last mile and I'll wheel both cycles,' Gemma said.

'I can't ask you to do that,' the woman said.

'You're not asking, I'm offering,' Gemma said, 'because it's important to you to finish and this is the only way it's going to happen. I'm Gemma, by the way.'

'I'm Heather.'

They both looked at the cyclist who'd stopped.

'I'm Paul,' he said.

'Paul, thank you for stopping to help,' Gemma said. 'Can I get you to tell the medics we're on our way, when you've finished the race? But make it clear that Heather's going nowhere in an ambulance until she's gone over the finishing line.'

'Of course I'll tell them. But I'm not leaving you both to

walk in on your own—you're too vulnerable. I'll walk behind you with my rear light flashing,' he said, 'to make sure nobody crashes into you. And I'll call the race organisers to tell them what we're doing.'

'That's so kind,' Heather said, tears filming her eyes.

'You're one in a million,' Gemma said. 'Let's have a look at you, Heather.' She gently lowered the neck of Heather's cycling top and examined her clavicle, noting that swelling had already started. 'Is it tender here?'

'Yes,' Heather said through gritted teeth.

'I've got a bandage and some painkillers in my bag,' Gemma said. 'I think you've broken your collarbone. It's going to get more painful—and you definitely need to go to hospital for an X-ray to check how bad the break is and whether you're going to need pins—but for now I can make you a sling to support your arm and give you some painkillers. Are you on any medication, or is there any reason why you can't have paracetamol?'

'No and no,' Heather said.

'Good. Paul, can you let them know we'll need an ambulance? Tell them it's a fractured left clavicle and she'll need an X-ray,' Gemma said.

Paul quickly phoned the race organisers to let them know what was happening, and Gemma took the medicine kit from her bike, gave Heather painkillers and strapped up Heather's arm to stabilise it. 'Now, you need to move that arm as little as possible or you could risk doing serious damage,' she warned. 'The deal is, you walk beside me and I'll wheel our bikes. It's only about another mile. Fifteen to twenty minutes and we'll be there.'

'Thank you both so much,' Heather said.

The three of them started to walk along the road, with other cyclists sailing past them.

'So why are you doing the cycle ride, Gemma?' Heather asked.

'For my little sister. She needed a heart transplant but a suitable heart couldn't be found in time,' Gemma said.

'That's hard,' Heather said. 'Was she very young?'

'Thirteen, and I was seventeen,' Gemma said. 'I'm nearly thirty now; but I still miss her.' She swallowed hard. 'It was her birthday yesterday.'

'She'll know. Just as Mike knows I'm doing this. I'm such a klutz. Trust me to fall off and break my collarbone. If anyone had said I would be able to even stay upright on a bike, let alone ride one for sixty miles...' Heather gave a rueful smile. 'Mike was the one for sport, not me.' She swallowed hard. 'I turned him down so many times when he asked me out. I didn't think it could work between us because we're so different.'

Like Gemma and Oliver.

'But I'm glad I gave in,' Heather continued. 'Because those three years we had together were the best of my life. Even the bad bits, when we got the diagnosis and when he had chemo—at least we had each other. And I know he's up there right now, looking down, proud of me doing this.' She looked at Gemma. 'What about your partner? Is he here?'

'No. He was meant to be the race medic, but his brother's doing it instead.' She shrugged. 'It wouldn't have worked out between us anyway. He's going back to London.'

'You sound like me,' Heather said. 'Don't make the same mistakes I did. I'm glad of the time Mike and I had together—but it could've been so much more if I hadn't been so stubborn. We might've had time to have kids.'

'I have no idea if Oliver wants kids,' Gemma admitted. And she found herself telling Heather the whole story, how she'd accidentally fallen in love with her new colleague but she was pretty sure he was going to leave her and go back to London. She wasn't good at letting people close; she was so terrified she was going to be needy and clingy and stupid again, like she'd been after her little sister's death, that she went too far the other way and backed off when they were getting too close.

'And then he went distant on me, too—and it just escalated. I didn't want to be the one who was left behind, so I suggested being just colleagues. And he didn't try to argue me out of it.'

'Do you know for definite he's going back to London?'

'What is there to make him stay here?'

'You?' Heather suggested. 'Talk to him. Be honest about how you really feel.'

'He's not even here today,' Gemma said. 'He sent his brother.'

'But he didn't have to send anyone at all,' Heather pointed out. 'Maybe he thought you didn't want him there—but he hasn't let you down, has he? He sent someone else to take his place.'

'I guess.'

'What have you got to lose? If you let him go without telling him how you feel, he might be being just as stubborn as you and you're both missing out.'

'And if he doesn't want me?'

'Then at least you'll know the truth. You won't spend your time full of regrets and wondering if things would've been different if you'd been brave enough to talk to him.'

Ollie brooded all the way to village where the race was due to finish. He was pretty sure Gemma's parents wouldn't turn up; he just hoped he hadn't made things worse for her. Maybe Claire and Rob had been right and he shouldn't have interfered.

He went over to the marshals' tent to see his brother.

'How's it going?' he asked.

'Fine—I've treated two cases of dehydration, one of saddle sores and one poor guy who skidded across some tarmac and made a bit of a mess of his arm. Apparently we've got someone coming in shortly with a broken collarbone.' Rob looked at him. 'How did it go?'

'Awful.' Ollie grimaced. 'Have you seen Gemma?'

'Yes, and you're in trouble. She knew I wasn't you before I even opened my mouth.'

'What did she say?'

'She didn't give me a chance to explain. She said she had a race to ride.'

'I'll face the music later,' Ollie said. 'Thanks for helping. I'll take over from you now.'

'I'm fine. Actually, I'm enjoying having something to do. Go and wait for Gemma by the finish line. And make sure you've got a seriously, seriously good apology ready, because you're going to need it,' Rob warned.

Oliver made his way through to the finish line, knowing he'd messed things up. He felt as if the world was sitting on his shoulders. He had no idea where to start fixing this.

Why hadn't he just left things alone?

And then his phone rang.

It was a number he didn't recognise. He thought about ignoring it; but right now he had nothing better to do and it would waste some time while he waited.

'Dr Langley?' a voice he didn't recognise said on the other end.

'Yes?'

'It's Stephanie Baxter. Um, we thought about what you said. We've been talking. We…um…wondered if we could wait with you.'

Hope bloomed in his heart. Gemma's parents were coming to watch her finish the race? 'Of course you can.' He told her exactly where he was. 'See you soon. And thank you.'

'No. Thank *you*,' she said. 'Because you've just given us a second chance with our daughter.'

Ollie really, really hoped she was right.

People were lining the streets of the village where the race ended, cheering and clapping.

Gemma forced herself to smile, even though she felt like crying. Everything had gone so wrong with Oliver. Was Heather right? Should she be brave and tell him how she felt? But what if he still went back to London without her? She didn't want to face rejection yet again.

She plodded on, one foot in front of the other, and kept Heather going with words of encouragement that weirdly kept her going, too.

'I think,' Paul said, 'Heather needs to ride over that finish line.'

'She can't ride with a broken clavicle,' Gemma said.

'She won't be holding the handlebars,' Paul said. 'If I lift her onto the bike, we can be either side of her to keep the bike stable and we'll steady it while she pedals for the last ten metres.'

So Heather would get to fulfil her dream. 'You're on,' Gemma said.

Between them, they got Heather onto the bike. They co-opted a couple of people lining the route to hold their bikes for them while they helped Heather, who was smiling and crying at the same time as they supported her over the finish line.

The medics were there, waiting to help Heather to the ambulance; for a moment, Gemma thought Oliver was standing there, but her heart didn't have that funny little skip and she realised that it was Rob.

Stupid.

Of course Oliver wouldn't be there.

'Well done,' Rob said, clapping her shoulder. 'That was an amazing thing to do.'

'It wasn't my time that mattered,' she said. 'It was Heather finishing that was important.' She couldn't bring herself to ask where Oliver was. 'I'd better collect my bike and finish officially.'

Paul was waiting for her, and they rode over the finish line together, with people cheering and clapping all around them.

She dismounted and hugged him. 'Thank you. What you did...'

'The same as you did,' he said, 'for a complete stranger. Because we're all in this together. And we want to make a difference.'

'Yeah.'

'I'll look after Heather's bike,' Paul said, 'because I think you've got some people wanting to see you.'

Gemma looked up and saw Oliver standing there. But what really shocked her was that her parents were next to him. Her mum and dad had tears running down their faces, and they held out their arms to her.

She couldn't quite process this.

Why were her parents here? She hadn't even told them where the race was, just that she was doing it.

Oliver took her bike. 'Go to them,' he said softly. 'I'll be waiting when you've talked.'

She stared at him—'But…' She couldn't even begin to frame the questions buzzing through her head.

'I interfered,' he said. 'I'll apologise later, but I think you and your parents need to talk. Don't worry about your bike. I'll go and put it in my car. Give me your race number and I'll sort out any paperwork for you.'

'I…'

'Swap you the paperwork for a recovery drink and a recovery bar,' he said, pushing them into her hands. 'I'll feed you properly later, but you need to replenish your glycogen stores.'

'Spoken like a doctor,' she said wryly, and handed over her race number.

'And like the brother of someone who does this sort of thing himself, so I kind of know the drill. Go with your parents,' he said. 'When you're ready, I'll be in the marshals' tent, where I was supposed to be.'

'Mum. Dad.'

'Our girl. Sixty miles you cycled. And you helped that lass who'd fallen off her bike—you didn't just leave it to the medics to sort her out,' her dad said.

'Well—you *are* a medic. Nurse practitioner,' her mum said.

'How...? Why...?' Gemma cleared her throat and tried again. 'I didn't expect to see you here.'

'Your young man came to see us,' her mum explained.

Gemma frowned. Oliver wasn't hers any more.

'He told us about his brother. How he nearly died.' There was a catch in her dad's voice. 'And he said how much you missed our Sarah. How much you missed *us*.'

'We haven't been proper parents to you,' her mum said. 'Not since Sarah died. We just couldn't get past losing her. And then, when it wasn't quite so raw any more, you...'

Gemma looked at them. She could let them off lightly, brush it under the carpet. Or she could be honest: and that might be a better way. Because at least then any relationship they managed to build would be on a solid foundation, with no areas where they were scared to tread. 'I was difficult to handle,' she said. 'I went off the rails. Because I couldn't cope with losing my little sister *and* losing my parents. Sleeping with all those boys—it made me feel loved again, just for a little while.'

Her dad flinched. 'It wouldn't have happened if we'd been there for you.'

'I'm not blaming you—either of you,' Gemma said. 'What happened, happened. I'm acknowledging it and I've moved past it.'

'Yvonne was the one who saved you. She was the mum I should've been to you. And I was grateful to her for stepping in, because I couldn't do it.' Colour flooded Stephanie's cheeks. 'At the same time, I was so jealous of her. You moved in with her and it felt as if you preferred someone else's family to your own. As if I'd lost both my girls.'

'You never lost me, Mum,' Gemma said. 'I needed to live with Claire's family to get through my exams. You weren't in a place where you could help me—and I couldn't deal with all that extra travelling to get to school. Things were hard enough. And I never gave up on you. I come and see you every month—

even though you never come to see me, and getting either of you to talk to me is like pulling teeth. But I promised Sarah I'd never give up, and I've always hoped that one day I'd get some of my family back.'

'He's right about you, your young man,' her dad said. 'He said you'd never give up on us. And you're a daughter we can be proud of. All that money you raise for charity.'

'For the ward where Sarah died. Where they're doing research into permanent artificial hearts,' Gemma said. 'So maybe one day soon no other family will have to wait for a donor heart and risk losing their Sarah.'

'He showed us your video. You, jumping out of a plane,' her mum said. 'And he told us where we could find you today. We watched you help that woman. And we're—' her voice cracked '—we're so proud of you. Can you ever forgive us?'

Gemma had no words. She just opened her arms.

And, for the first time in too many years, her parents wrapped her in a hug. A real, proper hug. The hug she'd been so desperate to have.

'We love you so much, Gemma,' her dad said.

'It probably doesn't feel like it,' her mum said. 'But we do. And we're so sorry we let you down.'

'It's hard for us, going back to Ashermouth. But if that's where you want to be, then we'll come there to see you,' her dad said. 'Your young man's right—it's time we remembered we had another daughter. We want you in our lives. Properly. The way it should've been all along. It's been so…' His mouth moved but no words came out.

She wasn't going to push them into talking more. Not right now. 'I know,' she said softly. 'I want that, too. And I know it's not going to be magically fixed overnight. We've got a lot of talking to do. But, now we've started, it'll get easier. And if we work at it, we'll make it. Together.'

'We do love you, Gem,' her mum said.

Words she'd wanted to hear for far too long. And both her parents had said it now. 'I love you, too,' she said shakily.

'You'd better go and see your young man,' her dad said. 'But we'll call you tomorrow.'

'And we're so proud of you.' Gemma's mum hugged her again.

'I'll talk to you tomorrow,' Gemma said. Tears blurred her vision as she made her way to the marshals' tent. Oliver had seen the chasm between her and her parents, and he'd laid a huge foundation plank across it.

Your young man.

Did she dare to hope that what he'd done—taught her parents to see her for who she was—meant he really cared about her? Was this his way of saying that maybe they had a future together? Or was this a goodbye present, a way of telling her that he couldn't be there for her but he hoped her parents would be?

Heather had advised her to talk to him. Tell him how she really felt.

And there was only one way to find out the answers to her questions...

Ollie sorted out the race admin for Gemma, then went back to the marshals' tent to help Rob. Various cyclists had come to the medics for help as they'd finished, with sprains, strains and saddle sores.

To his relief, his twin didn't ask him any awkward questions, just let him help treat their patients.

Finally Rob nudged him. 'I'll finish up here. You have a visitor.'

Ollie looked up; when he saw Gemma standing by the table, his heart skipped a beat.

'Hi,' she said.

He couldn't tell if everything was all right or not, but he wanted to let her set the pace. 'Hi.'

'Is Heather all right?' she asked Rob.

'The ambulance took her to hospital. Paul's looking after her bike and he's going to take it back to his place for now, then drop it over to hers,' Rob said. 'Obviously I didn't have your number, but I've taken theirs and texted them to Olls so you can get in touch with them.'

'Thank you,' she said. She looked at Ollie. 'Can we go somewhere quiet and talk?'

'Sure.' Ollie nodded to his twin, then followed Gemma out of the tent. They headed towards the sea, and found a quiet spot away from the crowds.

'That was a really kind thing you did, helping Heather over the finish line like that.'

'It wasn't just me. Paul helped, too. She had a broken clavicle. No way could she have wheeled that bike herself without jolting her arm.' Gemma shrugged.

'You could've waited with her until the marshals came.'

'No, I couldn't. It was important to Heather to finish the race and they would've stopped her. She was doing it in memory of her husband, who died from leukaemia, and we were so close to the end. It's just what anyone else would've done in an event like this when they saw someone was struggling.'

Ollie wasn't quite so sure, but Gemma clearly didn't believe she was special. 'I sorted out the race admin stuff for you,' he said.

'Thank you.' She took a deep breath. 'I didn't expect to see you today. When I saw Rob and realised you'd sent him in your place, I assumed...' Her voice tailed off.

'The worst? That I'd abandoned you?' The way her parents had when she was seventeen, and the way they'd stonewalled her over the last few years?

'Yes,' she admitted.

'I saw how upset you were yesterday and I wanted to do something about it. I know I was interfering. But I didn't want to let you down with this, either—which is why I talked Rob into taking my place,' Ollie explained.

'How did you even find my parents?'

'I asked— Never mind,' he said, not wanting to make things awkward between Gemma and her best friend. 'And I was warned not to interfere.'

'But you went to see them anyway.' Her eyes were red, as if she'd been crying.

He'd been so hopeful when her parents had called him and asked to stand with him at the end—so sure that he'd helped them start to reconnect with Gemma. Maybe he'd got it wrong. Maybe this had been the last straw, and instead they'd told Gemma never to see them again. Guilt flooded through him. 'I'm sorry if I've made things worse.'

'No, you made them...' She swallowed hard. 'Today was the first time in more than a decade that my parents told me they loved me.'

Ollie didn't know what to say. It was a good thing; yet, at the same time, his heart broke a little for her. She'd tried so hard for all those years, had refused to give up: yet all that time she'd been hurting. Lonely. Wanting to be loved.

'They told me they were proud of me.'

'Good. And so they should be,' he said. 'You're an amazing woman.'

'But not,' she said, 'amazing enough for you.'

'Oh, you are,' he said.

'Then I don't get why you backed away from me. I don't understand you, Oliver. Not at all.'

Because he'd panicked. 'I just wanted to help.'

'You did. You've built a massive bridge between me and my parents—it's early days and there's still a lot to work through, but we're finally starting to see things the same way.' She looked at him. 'What I don't understand is why you did that. You and I...we agreed just to be colleagues.'

'Yes.' He knew he should tell her that wasn't what he wanted—but what if she rejected him?

When he didn't explain further, Gemma said, 'Heather told me she thought her husband was her complete opposite and it'd

never work out between them. She held out for a long time before she agreed to date him—and then he was diagnosed with
leukaemia. He died last year. And she said she'll always regret
she wasn't brave enough to let them have more time together.'

His heart skipped a beat. Was Gemma saying that was how
she saw their situation, too? Was this her way of telling him
she wanted to try to make a go of things?

'She said it's important to be honest, to tell someone how
you feel about them and not waste time.' Gemma took a deep
breath. 'It scares me to death, saying this—but at the same time
I know I'll always regret it if I don't. So I'm going to say it. I
know you want to go back to London, and I'm not going to trap
you or ask you to stay; but I also don't want you to go without
knowing the truth. That I love you.'

She loved him.

The words echoed through his head.

She loved him.

But then his insecurities snapped back in. 'How can I be
enough for you?'

It was the last thing Gemma had expected him to say.

But then she remembered what he'd told her. How his ex
had called off the wedding. 'Is this about Tabby? Are you still
in love with her?'

'It's sort of about her,' Oliver said. 'But, no, I'm not still in
love with her. One of my old colleagues told me that Tabby
had got engaged again. And it made me think. I wasn't enough
to make her love me, so why should I think I'd be enough for
someone else?'

'Oliver Langley, do you really have no idea how amazing
you are?' she asked. 'Look at the way you work with us in the
practice. You fitted right in. You're part of the team. You've
helped me make some innovations that will make our older patients' lives better. And you've just managed to do something
that my best friend's family has tried and failed for do for over a

decade—you talked to my parents, you got them to listen to you, and you changed their view of me. You've done what I thought was impossible: you've actually got us talking and starting to heal that rift.

'And, apart from all that, I love you. You make me feel like a teenager again—not full of angst and worry, but seeing all the possibilities in life.' She bit her lip. 'I thought you might have feelings for me, too. Until you backed away.'

'I do have feelings for you. I love you,' he said, 'and I know it's the real thing, because I feel different when I'm with you. The world feels a better place, full of sunshine and hope.' He paused. 'But how do I know I'm not fooling myself? How do I know I'll be enough for you?'

'Do you trust me?' she asked.

He was silent for so long that she thought he was going to tell her he didn't. But then he nodded. 'I trust you.'

'Then believe me. I think you're enough for me. You're the first man I've let close in years and years. You're everything I want in a partner. You're kind, you're funny, you notice the little details, and you make my heart feel as if it's doing cart-wheels when you smile at me.' She took a deep breath. 'I know you're meant to be leaving in a few days, but—'

'Actually,' he cut in, 'I don't have to leave. Caroline says that Aadya wants to come back part-time, and the practice has expanded enough that she could do with another full-time doctor. She's given me first choice of the post.'

'So you could stay here?'

'Yes.'

'And is that what you want?'

'I want,' he said, 'to be with you. I've learned that I like being part of a small community—*this* community. I like living in a village where I know everyone and everyone knows me. Where people support each other. I want to live and work in a community where people really connect with each other.' He looked at her. 'But most of all I want to live with you. I want to make a family with you—whether we have children of our own, whether we support a teen in trouble, or whether it's a mixture of the two.'

So he'd remembered what she'd said to him about paying it forward.

'I saw you with your goddaughter,' he said, 'cuddling her and reading a story. When we read that story to her together. And it made me realise that was what I wanted. You, and our family.' His blue eyes were full of warmth and love. 'This probably isn't the right time to say this, when you've just done a sixty-mile bike ride.'

'Strictly speaking, that's fifty-nine miles cycling and about a mile's walk,' she pointed out.

'A mile's walk pushing two bikes and supporting someone with a broken collarbone,' he said. 'Which is a lot more effort than cycling. Gemma, when I came to Ashermouth Bay, I was miserable and lonely and in a lot of denial. And then I met you. And I found out how the world really ought to be—full of love and sunshine. You make the day sparkle. And I want to spend the rest of my life with you.' He dropped to one knee. 'I probably ought to wait and do this somewhere really romantic. But I can virtually hear my twin yelling in my ear, "Be more Rob!"— and your friend Heather was right. It's important to be honest, to tell someone how you feel about them and not waste time. So I'm going to take the risk and tell you. I've learned that it's not the showy stuff that matters: it's what's in your heart. And I love you, Gemma Baxter. I really, really love you. Will you marry me and make a family with me?'

Marry him.

Make a family with him.

He was offering her everything she wanted. More than that: he'd actually got her parents to make the first move, to start to heal the rift between them.

She leaned down and kissed him. 'Yes.'

* * * * *

Keep reading for an excerpt of
Second Chance With The Bridesmaid
by Jennifer Faye.
Find it in the
Greek Paradise Escape anthology,
out now!

PROLOGUE

July, Paris, France

PITTER-PATTER. PITTER-PATTER.

Adara Galinis's heartbeat accelerated as the elevator slowly rose in one of the poshest hotels in Paris. That wasn't what was making her nervous. As the concierge of an elite island resort that hosted celebrities and millionaires, she was used to the finest surroundings.

Her racing heart had to do with the fact that she had traveled from Greece to Paris on the spur of the moment. She wasn't normally spontaneous. She liked things neat and orderly. Her job provided all the spontaneity she needed in life.

But she had a long weekend off, and in order to spend time with Krystof, she needed to come to him. Ever since they'd met at Valentine's on Ludus Island, they'd been casually seeing each other.

Krystof was best friends with the island's owner, Atlas Othonos. Earlier that year, when Atlas had briefly considered selling the island, he'd contacted Krystof in hopes that he'd want to buy the place. The sale didn't work out, but Adara had caught Krystof's attention. He'd pursued her in a charming sort of way—requesting concierge service and explaining that he wanted to dance with the most beautiful woman at the resort that evening. She was all prepared to extend an invitation on his behalf to whichever woman he'd chosen when he'd announced that the woman he was interested in was her.

She'd hesitated at first. After all, she made it a rule not to fraternize with the guests, but his warm smile and his enchanting way with words had won her over. They'd danced the night away at the Valentine's ball. It had been a magical evening that didn't end until the sun came up the next morning.

Now whenever Krystof stayed at the Ludus Resort, they made sure to spend as much time together as possible. At the end of each visit, he always asked her to fly away with him to some far-flung country. And though the idea tempted her, she'd always turned him down. She just couldn't imagine picking up and leaving without any planning. How was her assistant supposed to know what needed to be done? What if one of her regular clients arrived and she wasn't there? Part of her success was knowing the regulars and anticipating their wants before they had to ask her. She kept extensive files on their regular guests, from their favorite foods and colors to the names of their children and pets.

However, this weekend Hermione, her boss and best friend, had insisted she use some of her accumulated vacation time. Adara had been so focused on her job recently that she'd let her social life slide, and as for hobbies, well, she didn't have any unless you counted shopping.

So when she heard Krystof would be visiting Paris, the shopping mecca of the world, she took it as a sign. She couldn't wait to see him again. Their visits were so infrequent that it was always a rush to be with him. At least that's what she told herself was the reason for her heart racing every time she laid eyes on him.

She ran her hand down over the short, snug black dress. Her effort was a waste, because there was nowhere for the dress to go. It clung to her body like a second skin. It was a far more daring dress than she was accustomed to wearing. She'd bought it specifically for Krystof. She hoped he'd like her surprise.

As the elevator rose, her gaze focused on the increasing numbers. With each floor she passed, her heart beat faster. All too quickly, the elevator quietly came to a stop on the ninth floor. The door whooshed open.

Adara drew in a deep breath and then exhaled. With her fingers wrapped around the handle of her weekender bag, she stepped out. The door closed behind her.

This plush hotel felt so far away from the privately owned island of Ludus. Of course, it wasn't a fair comparison, as the Ludus Resort had been founded by a former king—King Georgios, an amazing man who'd abdicated the throne of Rydiania. She didn't know all the details of why he'd stepped away from the crown, but once he had, his family had promptly disowned him. He'd moved to Greece and bought Ludus Island, where he would live out his days. It was both a sad and an amazing tale.

As she looked around the spacious foyer, she realized her initial assessment had been misguided. Though the wine-colored carpet was plush, and the fixtures were brass on cream-colored walls, that was where it ended. There was no precious artwork on the walls or greenery throughout the hallway. Whereas the Ludus was always looking to make the resort stand out in both big and small ways, it appeared this hotel excelled at a minimalist approach. Interesting.

There was no one about in the foyer. The only sound as she walked was the soft rumble from the wheels of her case. She couldn't wait to see Krystof. She was so excited. She hoped he'd be just as thrilled to see her.

The gold plaque on the wall showed that his room was to the right. She turned that way. Her footsteps were muffled by the thick carpeting. What would he think about her spontaneity? This presumed he was even in his hotel room. What if he was out at a card game or some other such thing?

She would have to phone him, then, to tell him she was here, and the surprise would be ruined, but she was jumping too far ahead. She lifted her head and noticed a stylishly dressed woman at the end of the hallway. The woman knocked on a door. Was the young woman doing the same as her and being spontaneous? She hoped the woman had as good a weekend as she was about to have with Krystof.

Just then, the door in front of the woman swung open. The woman stood off to the side, giving Adara full view of the person inside the hotel room. She stopped walking. The breath caught in Adara's lungs. Krystof stood there. *Oh, my!* Her heart lodged in her throat at the sight of him.

His dark hair was spiky and going every which way, as though he'd just stepped out of the shower. His broad shoulders led to his bare chest. She was too far away to see if there were beads of water on his tanned skin. As her gaze lowered, her mouth grew dry. No man had a right to look as good as him.

He wore nothing more than a white towel draped around his trim waist. She swallowed hard. The only thing wrong with this picture was that she was supposed to be the one standing at his doorway.

His gaze lingered on the other woman. A smile lit up his face. The woman practically threw herself at him. They hugged as though they knew each other very well.

Adara blinked, willing away the image. But when she focused again, he was still holding the woman. So this was what he did when they were apart. Her heart plummeted down to her new black heels.

She turned away before she was spotted. The only thing that could have made this moment worse was if Krystof were to spot her. Her utter humiliation would then be complete.

Her steps were rapid as she retreated to the elevator. She wanted to disappear as quickly as possible. And lucky for her, one of the two sets of elevator doors swung open immediately. An older couple stepped off.

"Could you hold that for me?" Adara asked.

The gentleman held the door for her until she stepped inside. She thanked him. As the door closed, she recalled the image of a smiling, practically naked Krystof drawing that woman into his arms. Tears stung the backs of her eyes. She blinked them away. She wasn't going to fall apart in the elevator. All the while fury churned within her. Why had she let herself believe they shared something special?

It was quite obvious she was just someone to warm his bed whenever one of his other girlfriends wasn't available. How could she have been so blind? Sure, they had said this arrangement was casual, but that was in the beginning—months ago, on Valentine's. She'd thought they were getting closer—starting something more serious. Obviously she was the only one to think this.

She had been so wrong—about him, about herself, about them. She was done with him. Because his idea of casual and hers were two different things. In the end, she wasn't cut out to do casual—not if it meant him seeing other women while he was still involved with her. But it didn't matter now, because they were over.

Don't miss this brand new series by
New York Times bestselling author Lauren Dane!

THE CHASE BROTHERS

Ridiculously hot and notoriously single

One small town.
Four hot brothers.
And enough heat to burn up
anyone who dares to get close.

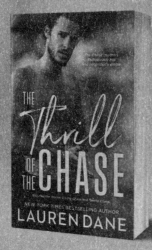 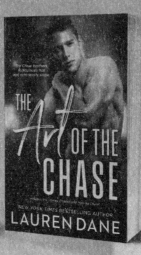

Includes the first two stories
Giving Chase and *Taking Chase*.

Available September 2024.

Includes the next stories
Chased and *Making Chase*.

Available December 2024.

MILLS & BOON

millsandboon.com.au